DEC 0 6 2018

kid
BEOWULF

the song of roland

story & art by
alexis e. fajardo

color by
jose mari flores

prologue color by
brian kolm

Andrews McMeel
Publishing ®
a division of Andrews McMeel Universal

fOR my fatheR

contents

PROLOGUE

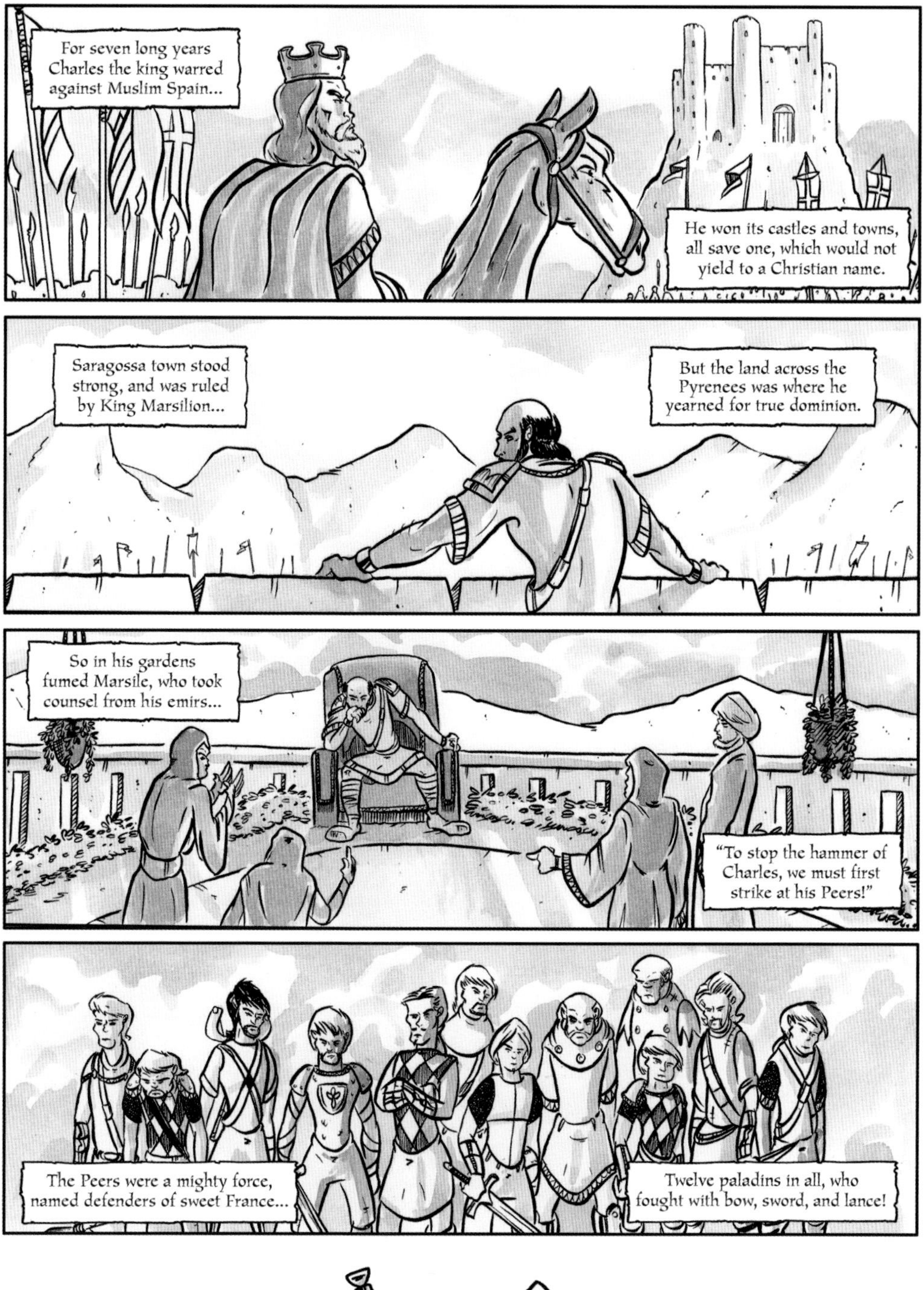
For seven long years Charles the king warred against Muslim Spain...
He won its castles and towns, all save one, which would not yield to a Christian name.
Saragossa town stood strong, and was ruled by King Marsilion...
But the land across the Pyrenees was where he yearned for true dominion.
So in his gardens fumed Marsile, who took counsel from his emirs...
"To stop the hammer of Charles, we must first strike at his Peers!"
The Peers were a mighty force, named defenders of sweet France...
Twelve paladins in all, who fought with bow, sword, and lance!

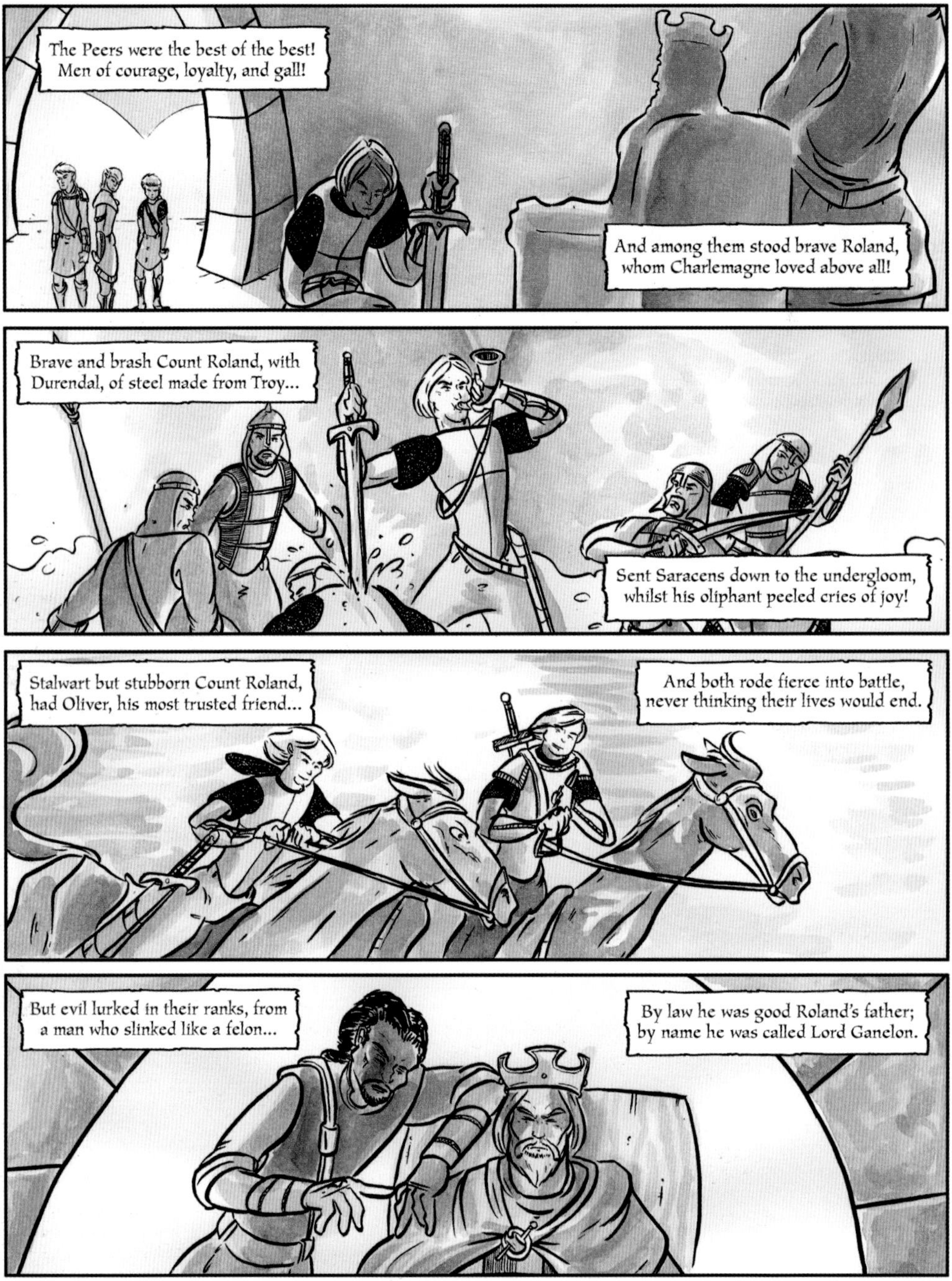
The Peers were the best of the best! Men of courage, loyalty, and gall!
And among them stood brave Roland, whom Charlemagne loved above all!
Brave and brash Count Roland, with Durendal, of steel made from Troy...
Sent Saracens down to the undergloom, whilst his oliphant peeled cries of joy!
Stalwart but stubborn Count Roland, had Oliver, his most trusted friend...
And both rode fierce into battle, never thinking their lives would end.
But evil lurked in their ranks, from a man who slinked like a felon...
By law he was good Roland's father; by name he was called Lord Ganelon.

Rage stoked Ganelon's heart, when he looked upon his stepson...

The boy had strength, talent, and skill, where he, himself, had none.

So when Roland named his father for a task to the Saracen lands...

Ganelon spat: "Treachery!" He saw no honor dispatching demands.

The seeds of hate took root as Ganelon swore his redress...

He would end France and her Peers; he would be merciless!

Marsilion and Ganelon conspired; they planned, plotted, and schemed...

At last they saw the way to put France under a Saracen regime!

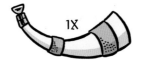

1X

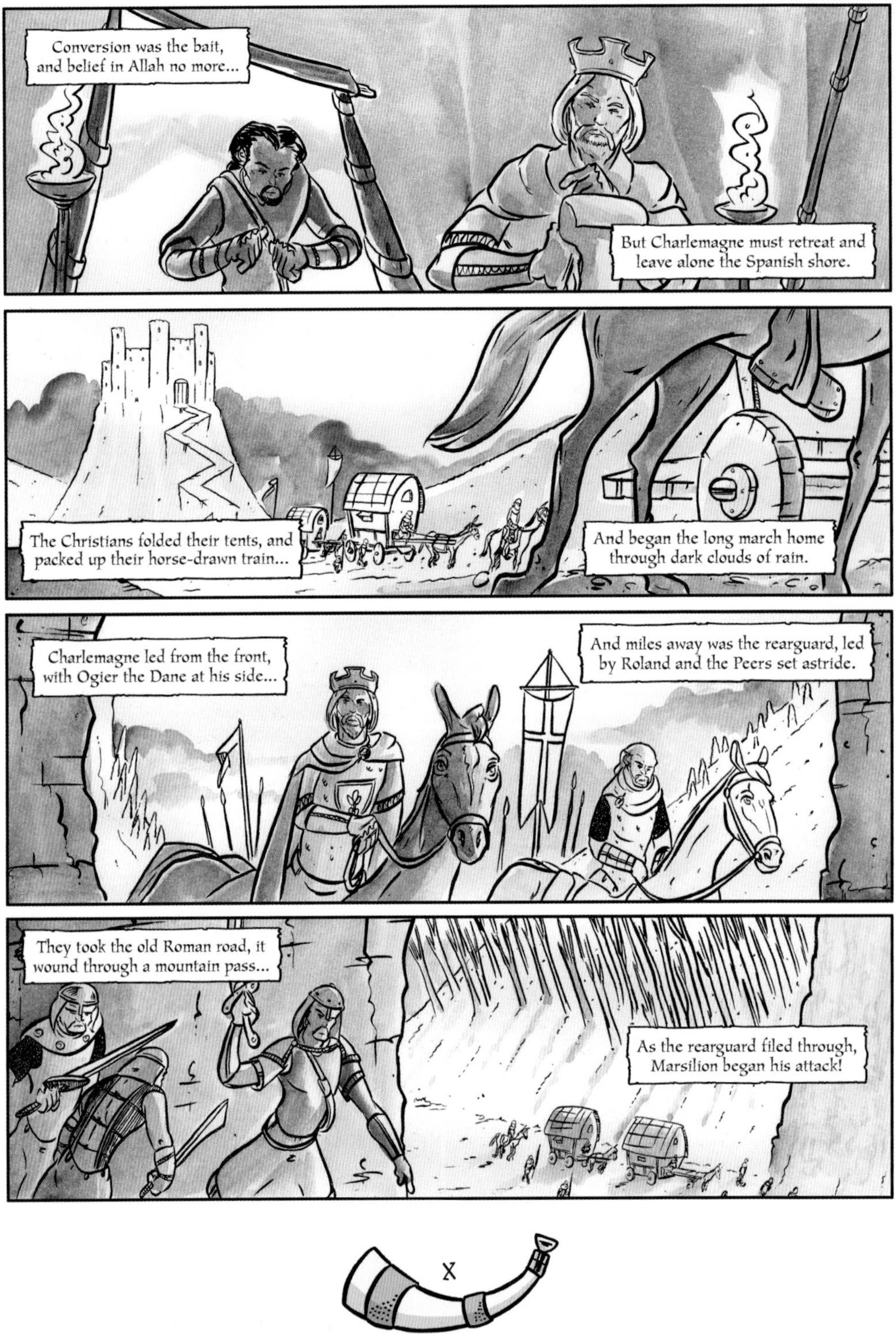
Conversion was the bait, and belief in Allah no more...
But Charlemagne must retreat and leave alone the Spanish shore.
The Christians folded their tents, and packed up their horse-drawn train...
And began the long march home through dark clouds of rain.
Charlemagne led from the front, with Ogier the Dane at his side...
And miles away was the rearguard, led by Roland and the Peers set astride.
They took the old Roman road, it wound through a mountain pass...
As the rearguard filed through, Marsilion began his attack!

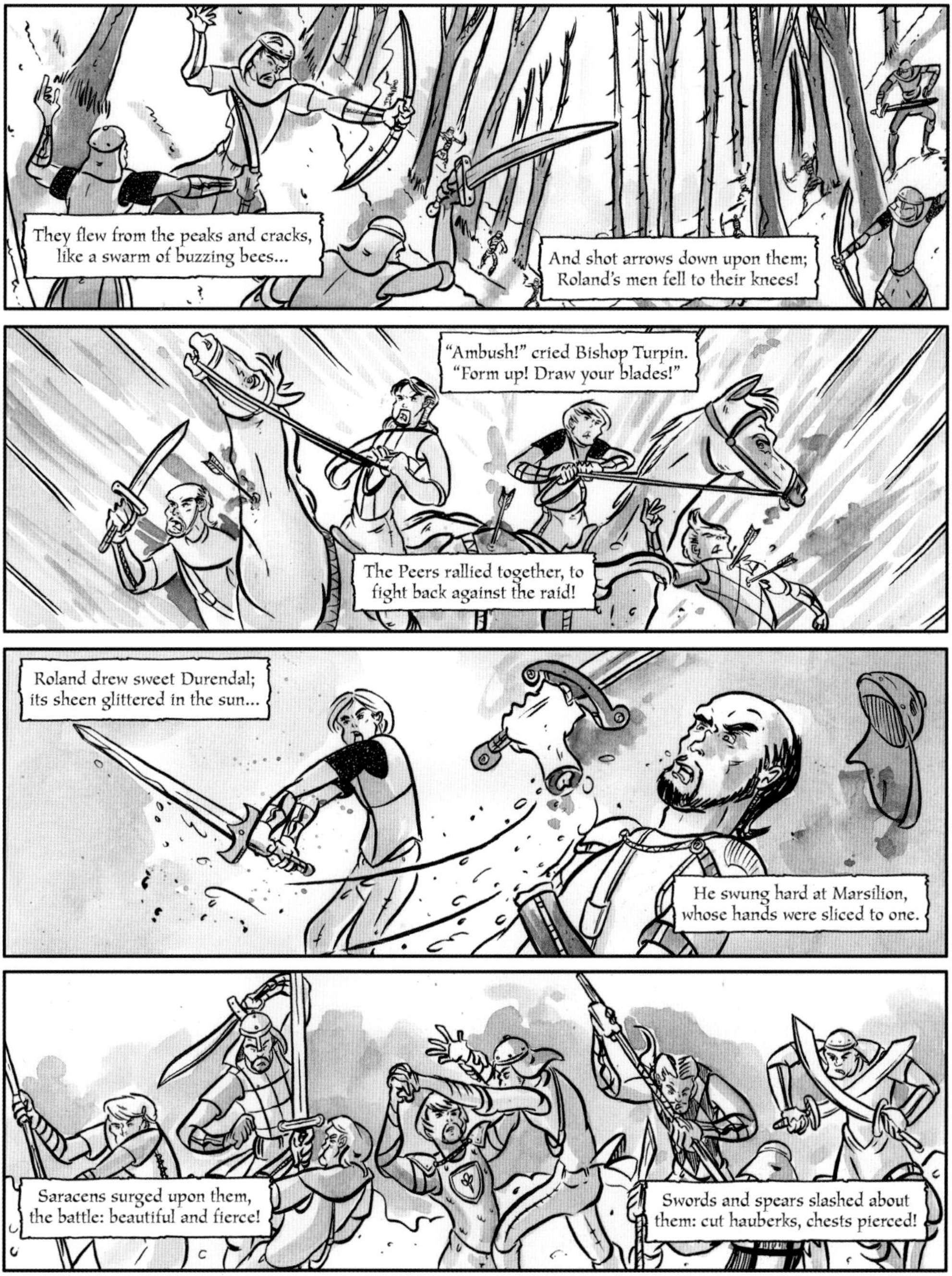
They flew from the peaks and cracks, like a swarm of buzzing bees...
And shot arrows down upon them; Roland's men fell to their knees!
"Ambush!" cried Bishop Turpin. "Form up! Draw your blades!"
The Peers rallied together, to fight back against the raid!
Roland drew sweet Durendal; its sheen glittered in the sun...
He swung hard at Marsilion, whose hands were sliced to one.
Saracens surged upon them, the battle: beautiful and fierce!
Swords and spears slashed about them: cut hauberks, chests pierced!

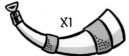

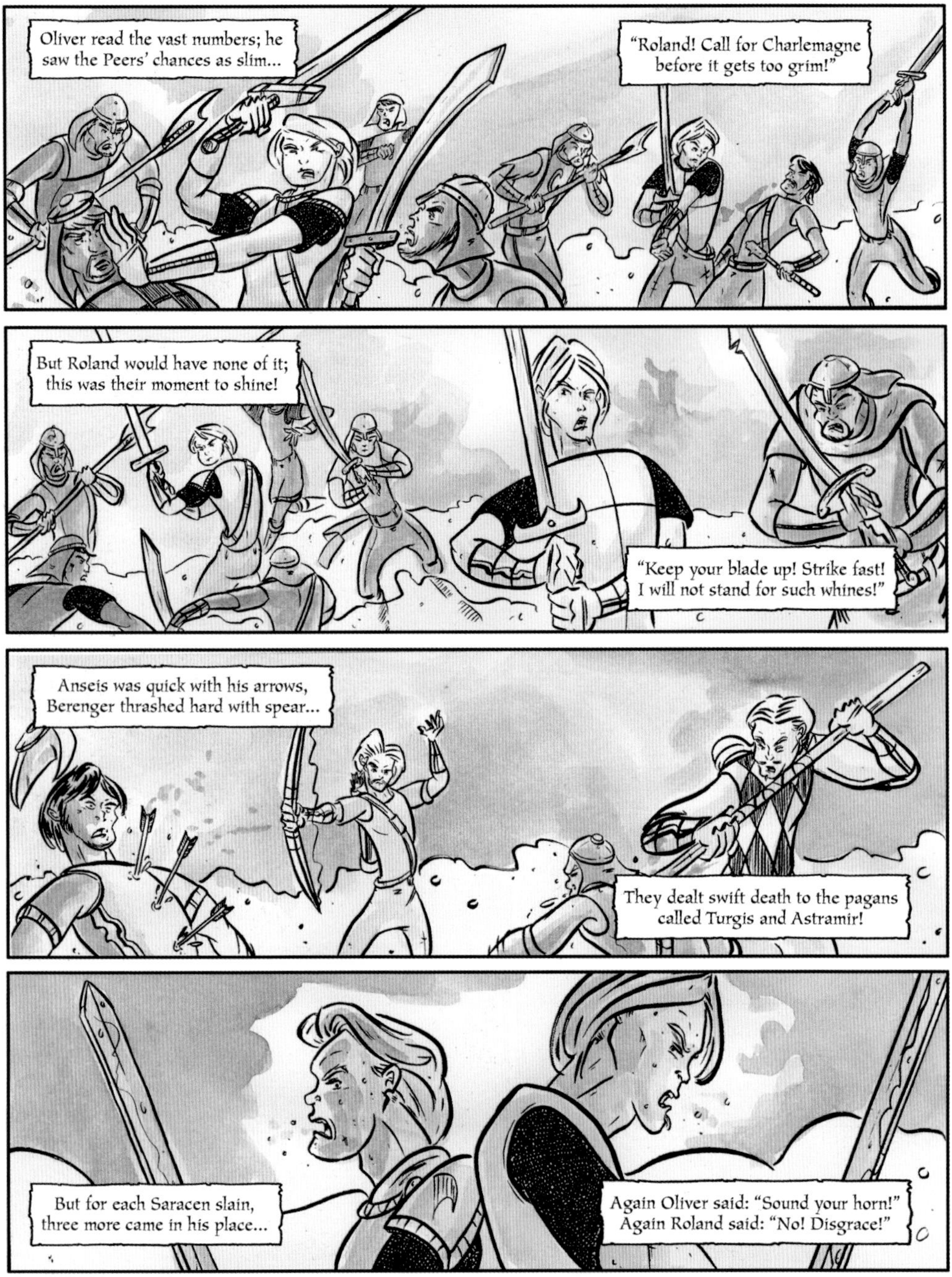
Oliver read the vast numbers; he saw the Peers' chances as slim...
"Roland! Call for Charlemagne before it gets too grim!"
But Roland would have none of it; this was their moment to shine!
"Keep your blade up! Strike fast! I will not stand for such whines!"
Anseis was quick with his arrows, Berenger thrashed hard with spear...
They dealt swift death to the pagans called Turgis and Astramir!
But for each Saracen slain, three more came in his place...
Again Oliver said: "Sound your horn!" Again Roland said: "No! Disgrace!"

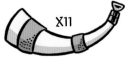

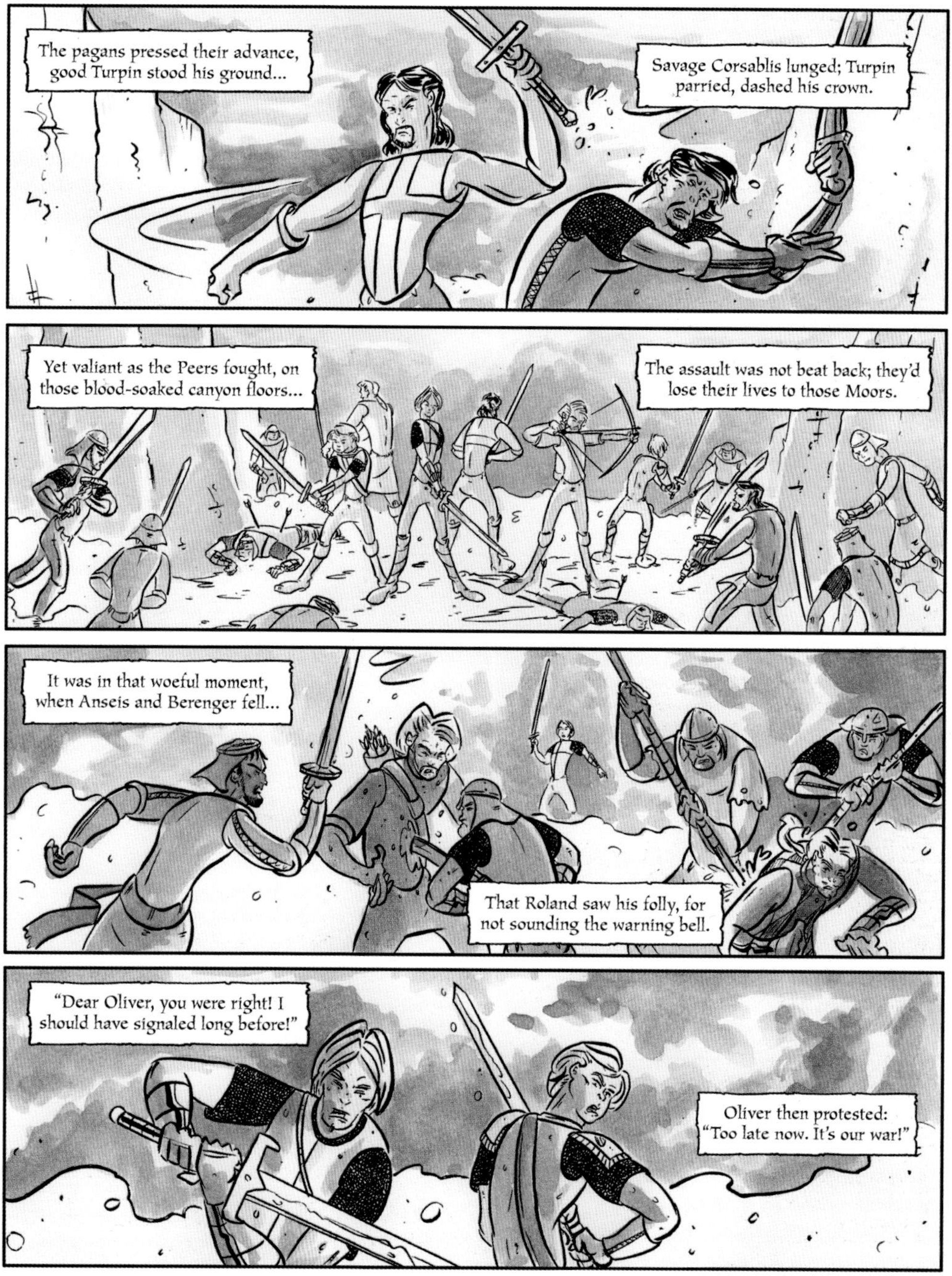
The pagans pressed their advance, good Turpin stood his ground...
Savage Corsablis lunged; Turpin parried, dashed his crown.
Yet valiant as the Peers fought, on those blood-soaked canyon floors...
The assault was not beat back; they'd lose their lives to those Moors.
It was in that woeful moment, when Anseis and Berenger fell...
That Roland saw his folly, for not sounding the warning bell.
"Dear Oliver, you were right! I should have signaled long before!"
Oliver then protested: "Too late now. It's our war!"

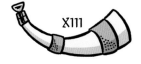

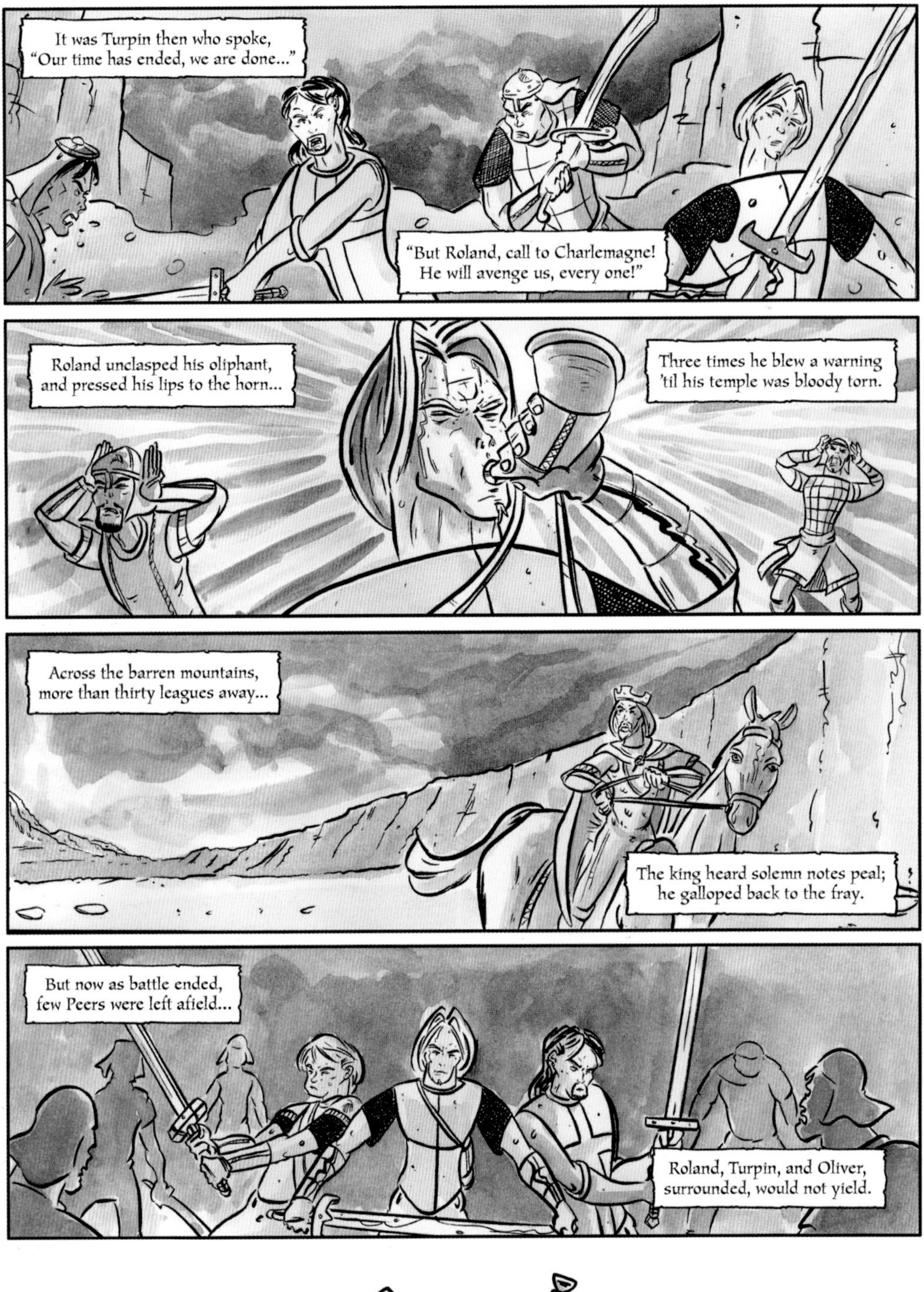
It was Turpin then who spoke,
"Our time has ended, we are done..."
"But Roland, call to Charlemagne!
He will avenge us, every one!"
Roland unclasped his oliphant,
and pressed his lips to the horn...
Three times he blew a warning
'til his temple was bloody torn.
Across the barren mountains,
more than thirty leagues away...
The king heard solemn notes peal;
he galloped back to the fray.
But now as battle ended,
few Peers were left afield...
Roland, Turpin, and Oliver,
surrounded, would not yield.

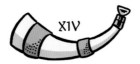

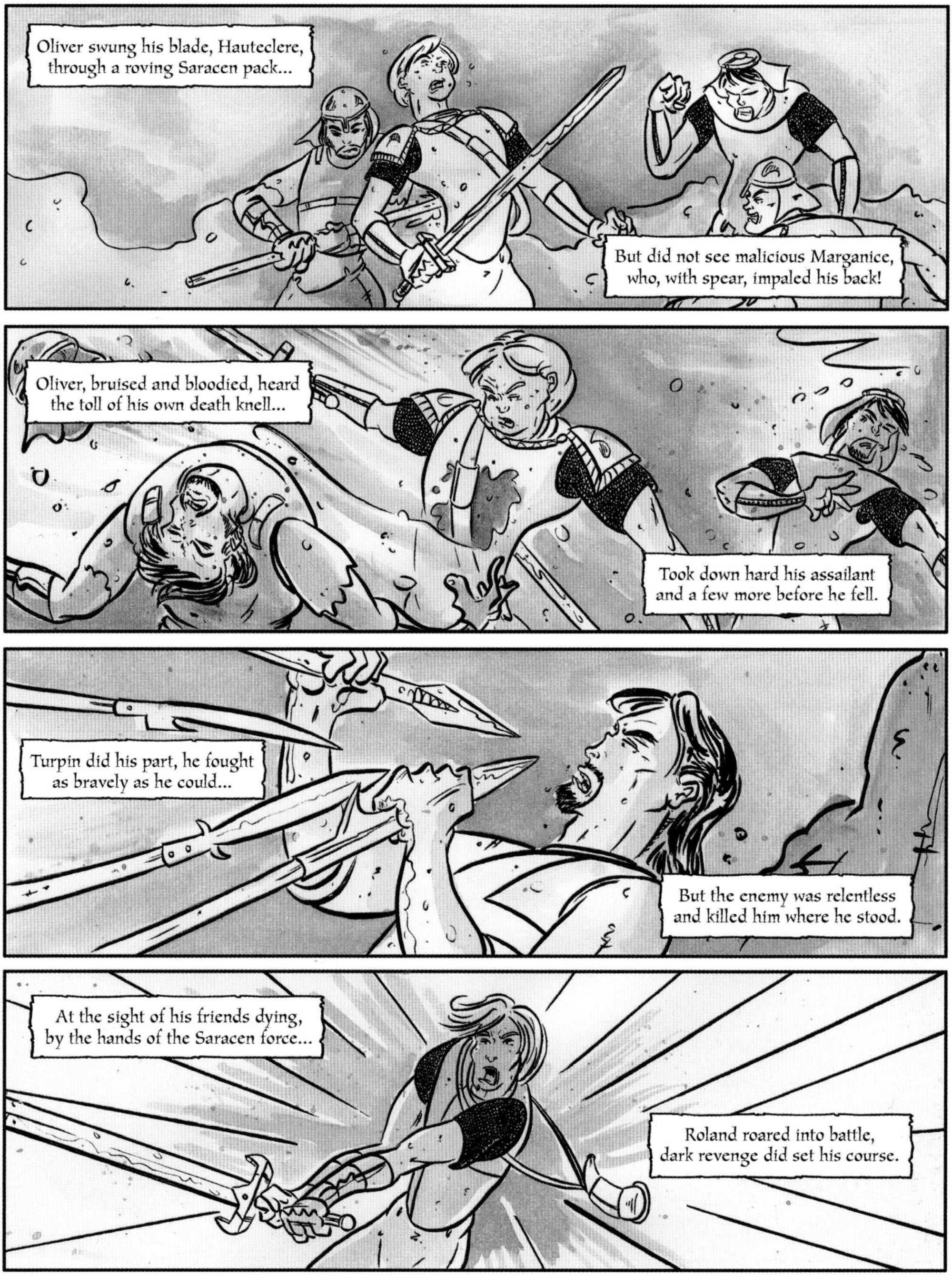
Oliver swung his blade, Hauteclere, through a roving Saracen pack...
But did not see malicious Marganice, who, with spear, impaled his back!
Oliver, bruised and bloodied, heard the toll of his own death knell...
Took down hard his assailant and a few more before he fell.
Turpin did his part, he fought as bravely as he could...
But the enemy was relentless and killed him where he stood.
At the sight of his friends dying, by the hands of the Saracen force...
Roland roared into battle, dark revenge did set his course.

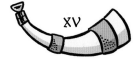

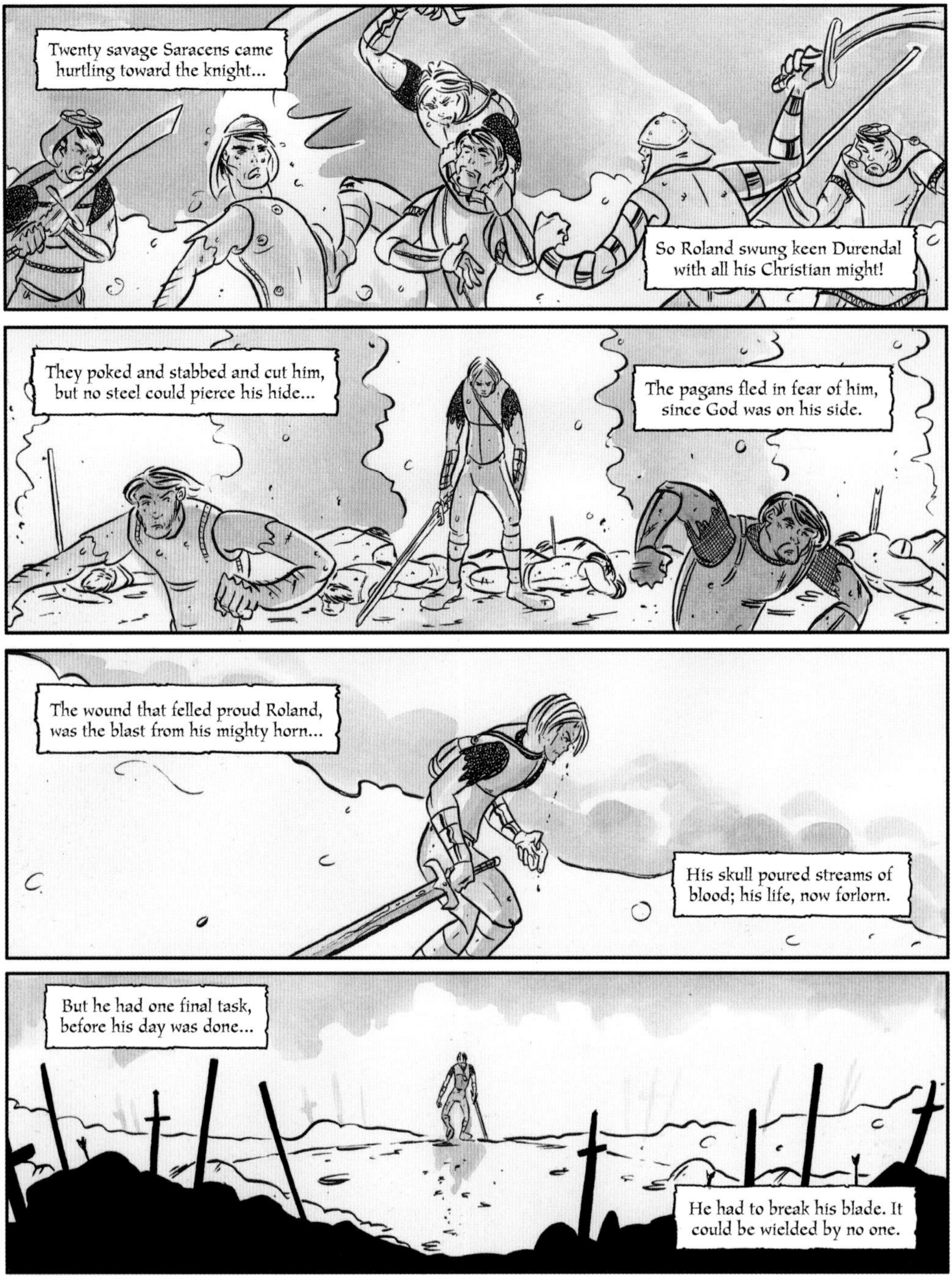
Twenty savage Saracens came hurtling toward the knight...
So Roland swung keen Durendal with all his Christian might!
They poked and stabbed and cut him, but no steel could pierce his hide...
The pagans fled in fear of him, since God was on his side.
The wound that felled proud Roland, was the blast from his mighty horn...
His skull poured streams of blood; his life, now forlorn.
But he had one final task, before his day was done...
He had to break his blade. It could be wielded by no one.

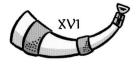

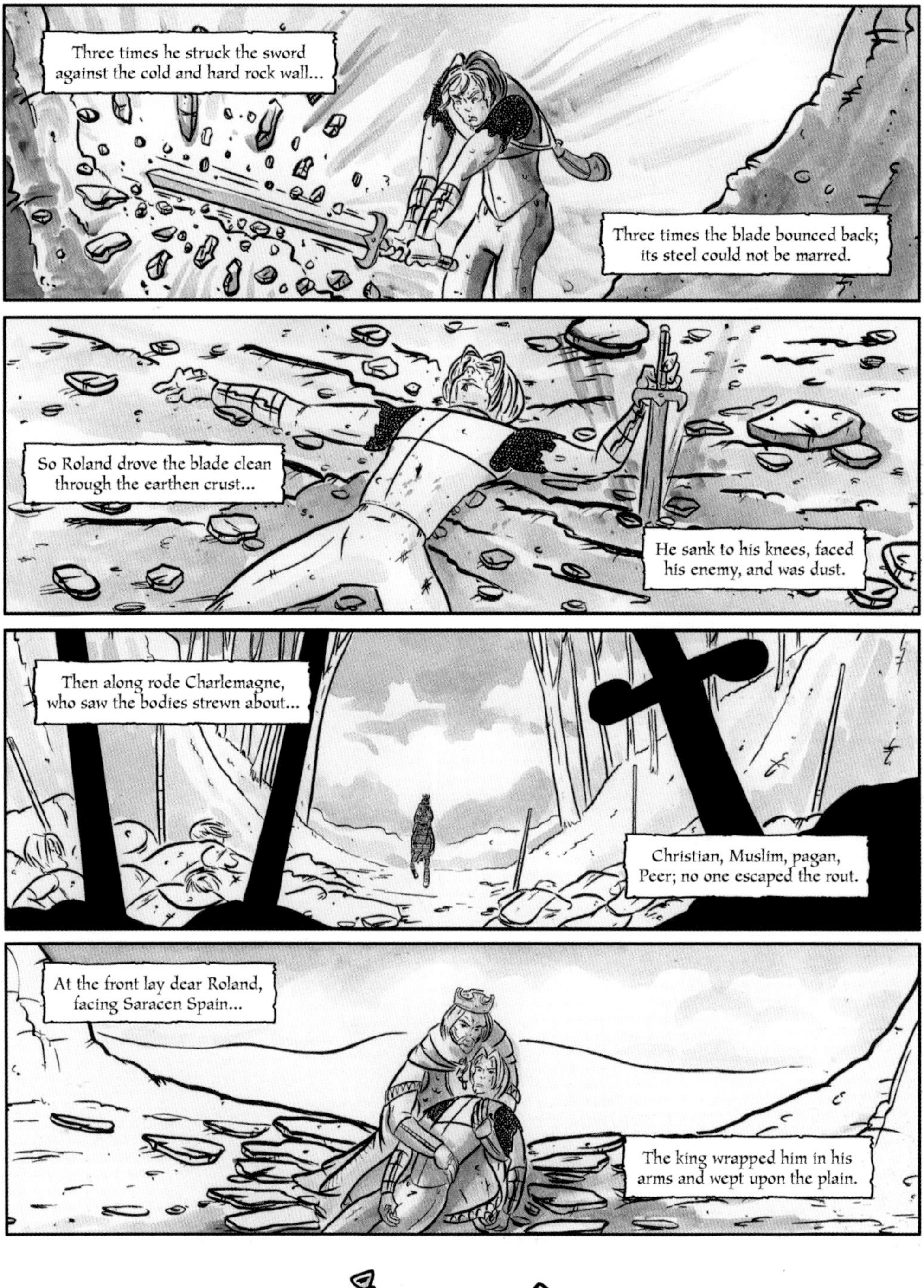
Three times he struck the sword against the cold and hard rock wall...
Three times the blade bounced back; its steel could not be marred.
So Roland drove the blade clean through the earthen crust...
He sank to his knees, faced his enemy, and was dust.
Then along rode Charlemagne, who saw the bodies strewn about...
Christian, Muslim, pagan, Peer; no one escaped the rout.
At the front lay dear Roland, facing Saracen Spain...
The king wrapped him in his arms and wept upon the plain.

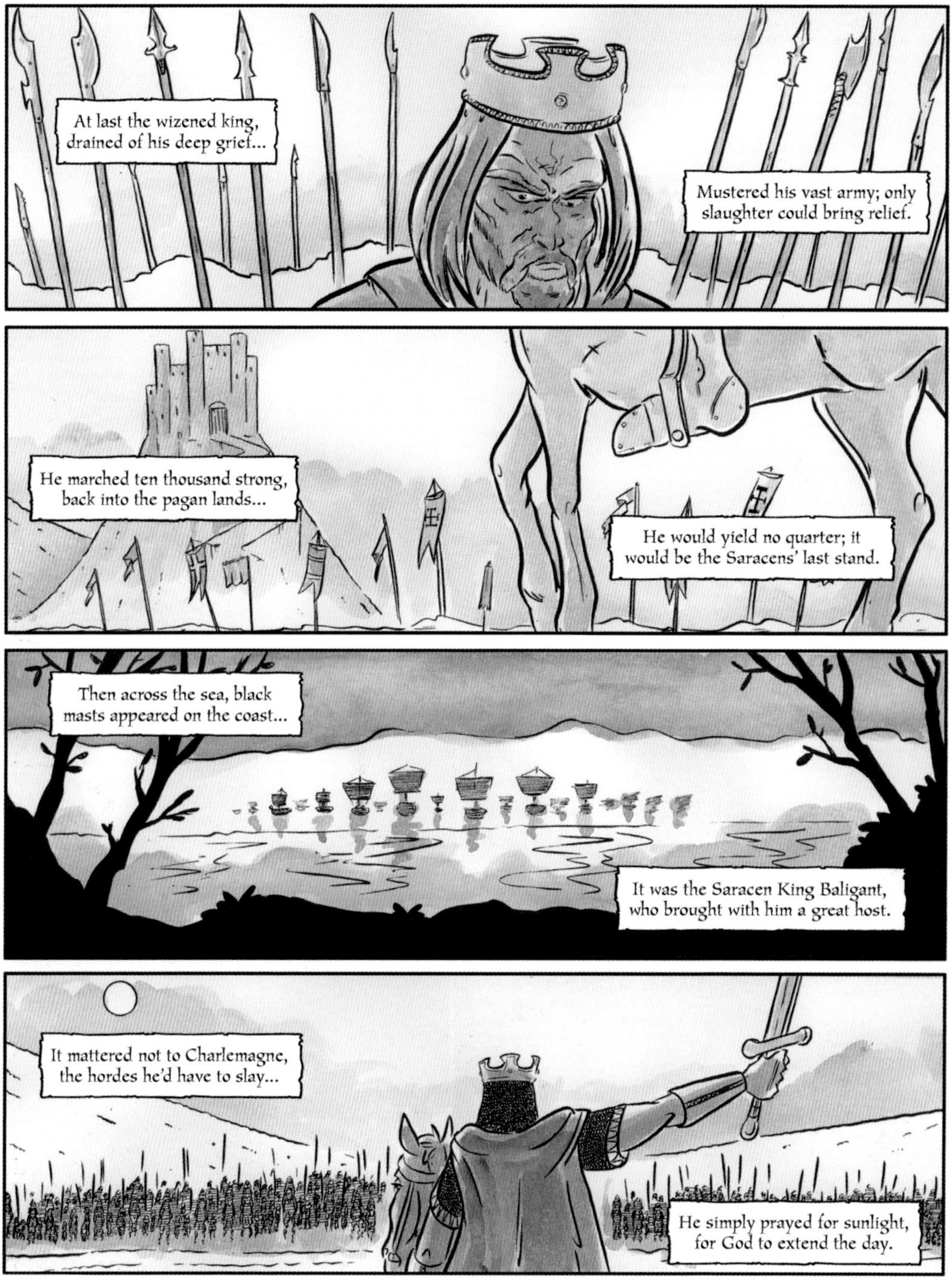
At last the wizened king, drained of his deep grief...
Mustered his vast army; only slaughter could bring relief.
He marched ten thousand strong, back into the pagan lands...
He would yield no quarter; it would be the Saracens' last stand.
Then across the sea, black masts appeared on the coast...
It was the Saracen King Baligant, who brought with him a great host.
It mattered not to Charlemagne, the hordes he'd have to slay...
He simply prayed for sunlight, for God to extend the day.

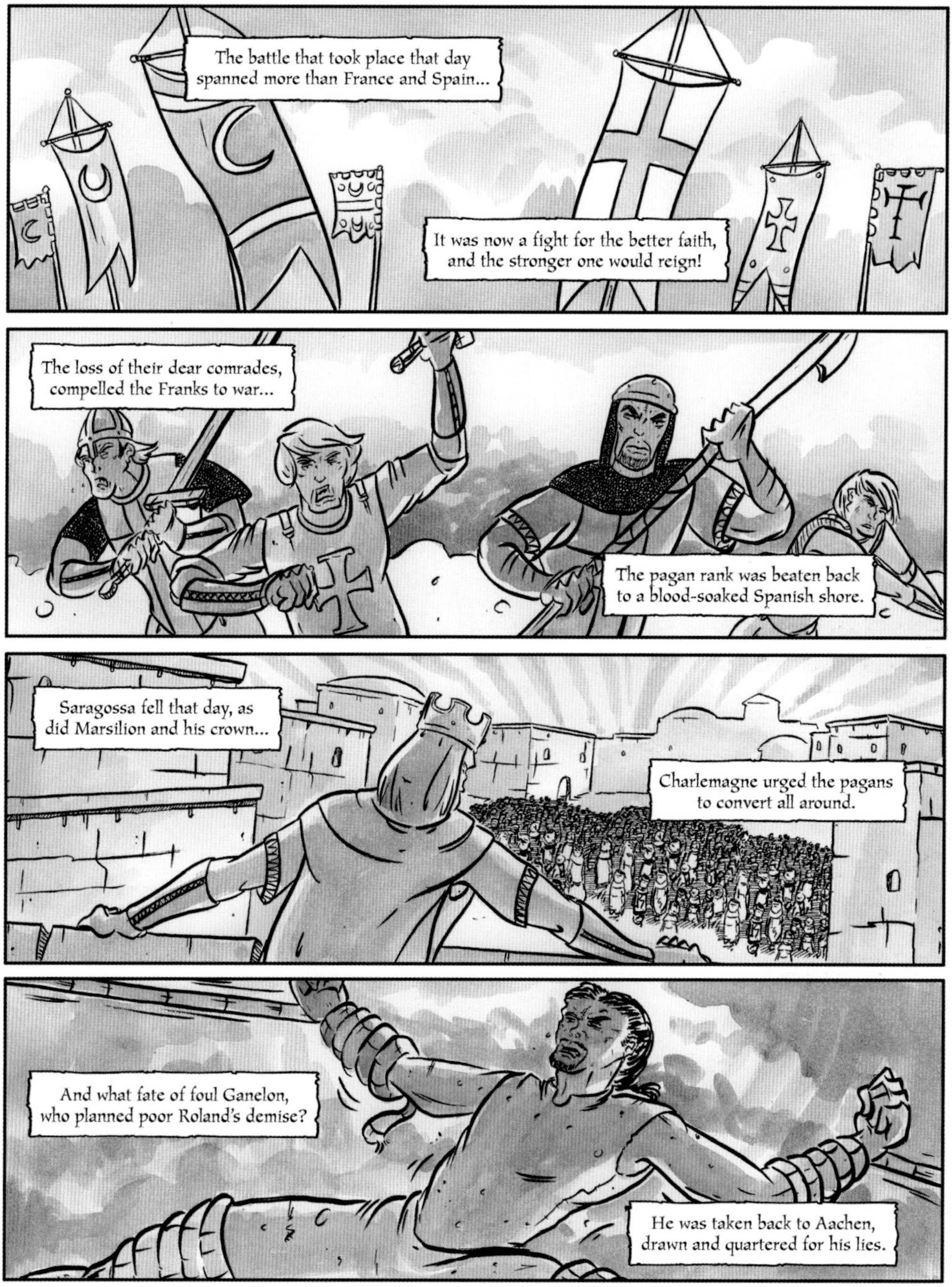
The battle that took place that day spanned more than France and Spain...
It was now a fight for the better faith, and the stronger one would reign!
The loss of their dear comrades, compelled the Franks to war...
The pagan rank was beaten back to a blood-soaked Spanish shore.
Saragossa fell that day, as did Marsilion and his crown...
Charlemagne urged the pagans to convert all around.
And what fate of foul Ganelon, who planned poor Roland's demise?
He was taken back to Aachen, drawn and quartered for his lies.

God brought peace to Roland and the rest of his steadfast Peers...

But for His vassal Charlemagne, God's mission would last for years.

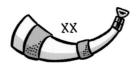

part one

a host of villains

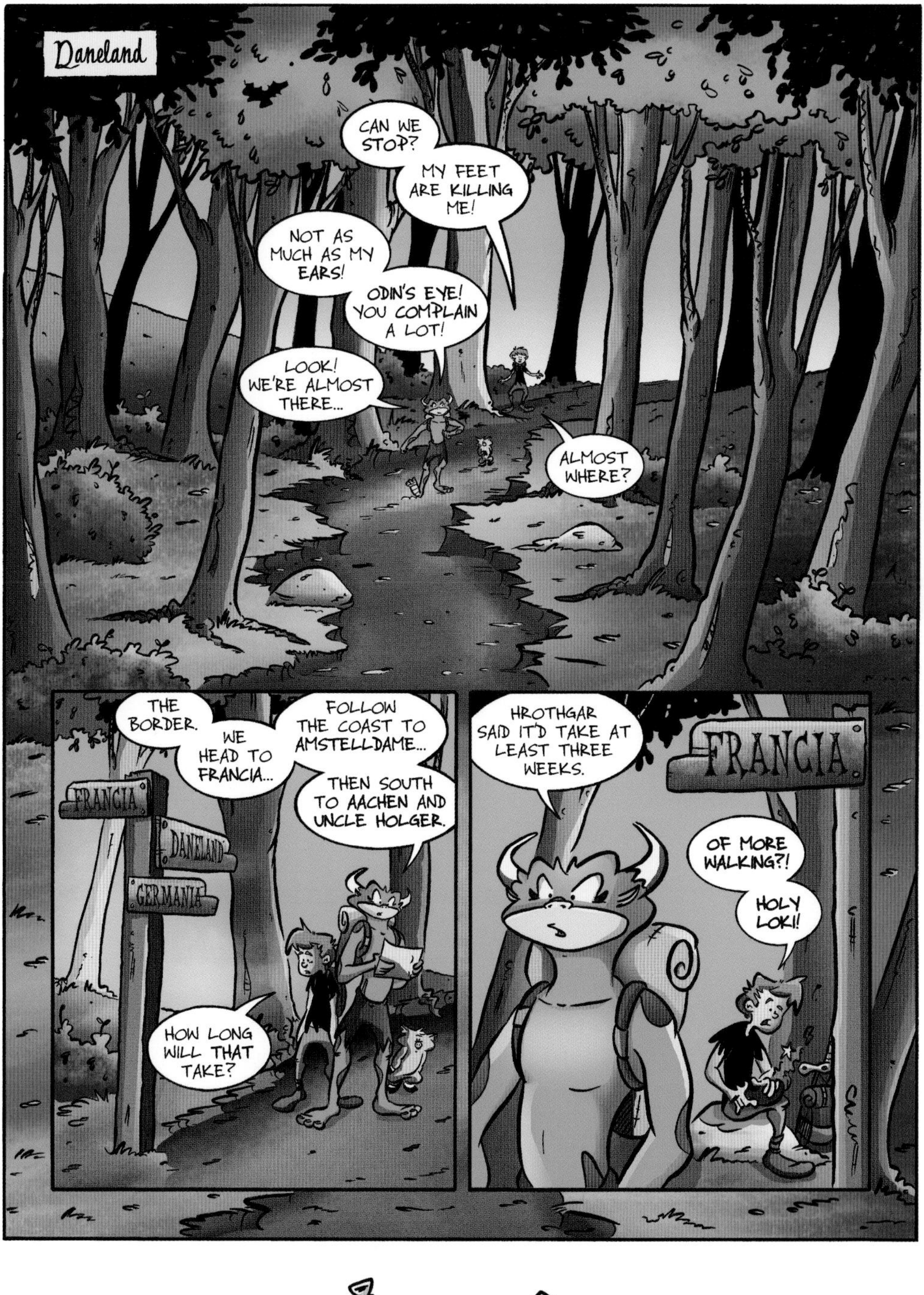
Daneland
CAN WE STOP?
MY FEET ARE KILLING ME!
NOT AS MUCH AS MY EARS!
ODIN'S EYE! YOU COMPLAIN A LOT!
LOOK! WE'RE ALMOST THERE...
ALMOST WHERE?
THE BORDER.
WE HEAD TO FRANCIA...
FOLLOW THE COAST TO AMSTELLDAME...
THEN SOUTH TO AACHEN AND UNCLE HOLGER.
FRANCIA
DANELAND
GERMANIA
HOW LONG WILL THAT TAKE?
HROTHGAR SAID IT'D TAKE AT LEAST THREE WEEKS.
FRANCIA
OF MORE WALKING?!
HOLY LOKI!

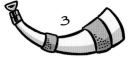

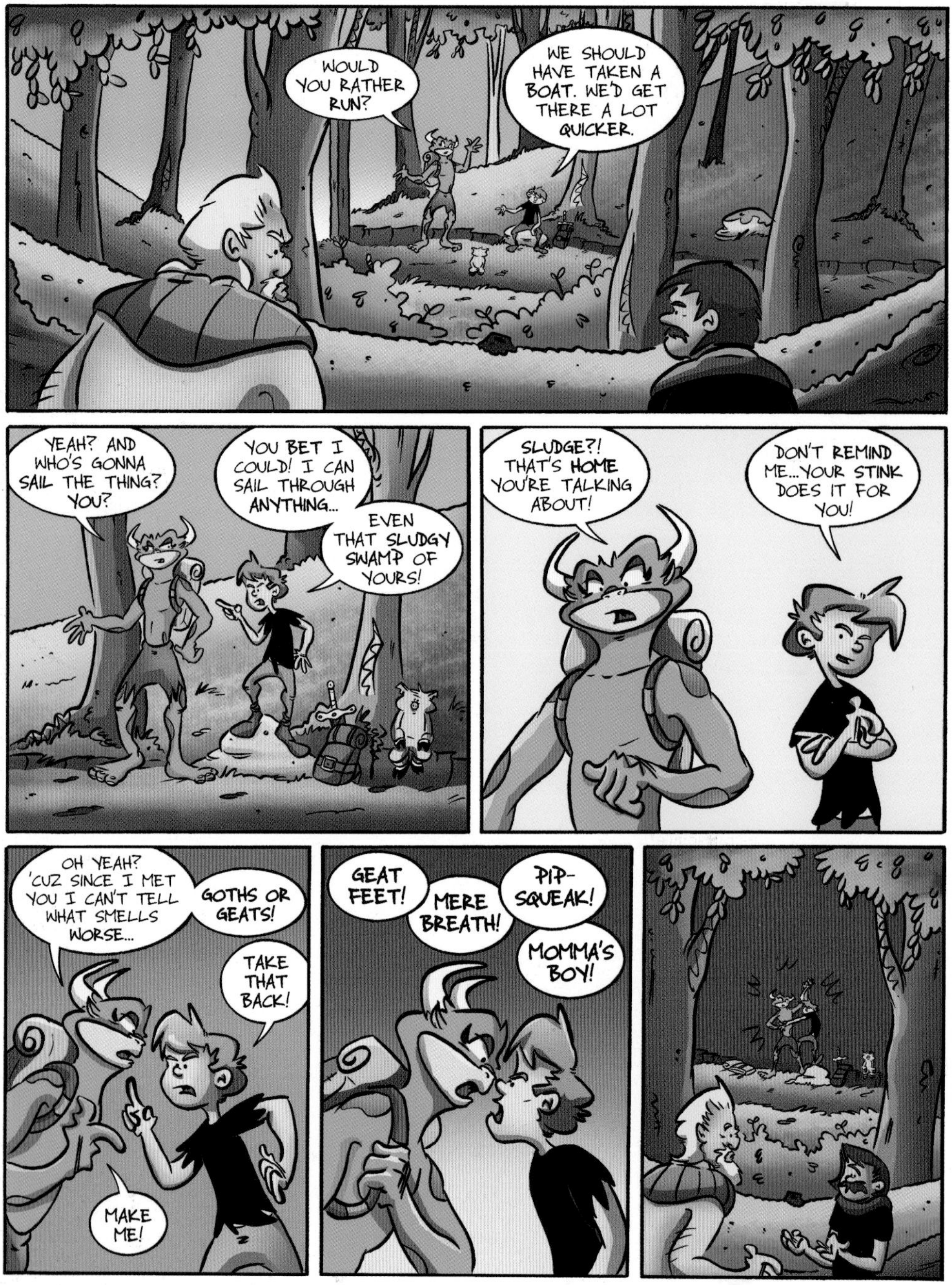
WOULD YOU RATHER RUN?
WE SHOULD HAVE TAKEN A BOAT. WE'D GET THERE A LOT QUICKER.
YEAH? AND WHO'S GONNA SAIL THE THING? YOU?
YOU BET I COULD! I CAN SAIL THROUGH ANYTHING...
EVEN THAT SLUDGY SWAMP OF YOURS!
SLUDGE?! THAT'S HOME YOU'RE TALKING ABOUT!
DON'T REMIND ME...YOUR STINK DOES IT FOR YOU!
OH YEAH? 'CUZ SINCE I MET YOU I CAN'T TELL WHAT SMELLS WORSE...
GOTHS OR GEATS!
TAKE THAT BACK!
MAKE ME!
GEAT FEET!
MERE BREATH!
PIP-SQUEAK!
MOMMA'S BOY!

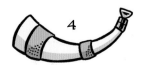

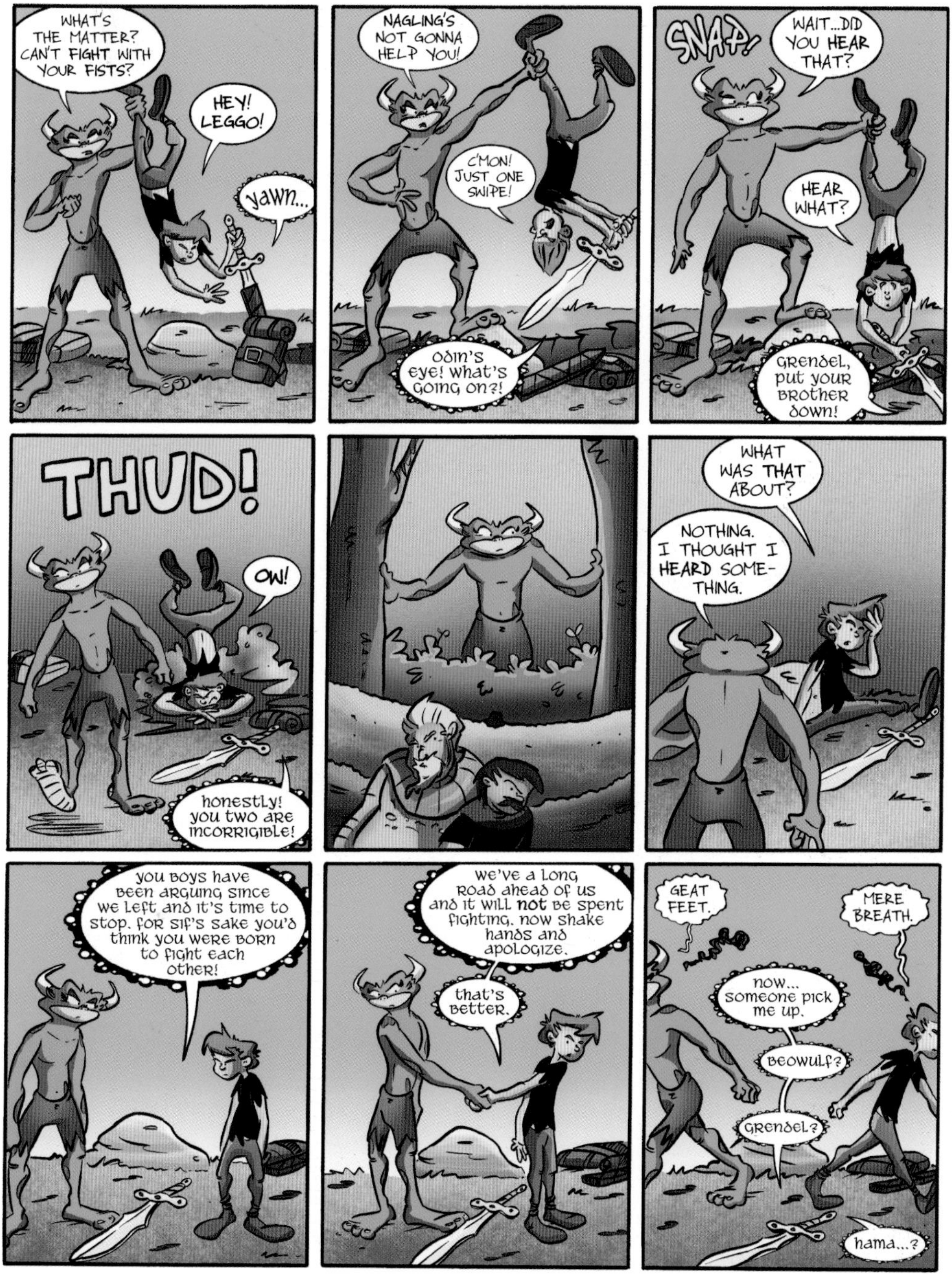
WHAT'S THE MATTER? CAN'T FIGHT WITH YOUR FISTS?
HEY! LEGGO!
yawn...
NAGLING'S NOT GONNA HELP YOU!
C'MON! JUST ONE SWIPE!
odin's eye! what's going on?!
SNAP!
WAIT...DID YOU HEAR THAT?
HEAR WHAT?
grendel, put your brother down!
THUD!
OW!
honestly! you two are incorrigible!
WHAT WAS THAT ABOUT?
NOTHING. I THOUGHT I HEARD SOME-THING.
you boys have been arguing since we left and it's time to stop. for sif's sake you'd think you were born to fight each other!
we've a long road ahead of us and it will not be spent fighting. now shake hands and apologize.
that's better.
GEAT FEET.
MERE BREATH.
now... someone pick me up.
BEOWULF?
GRENDEL?
hama...?

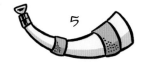

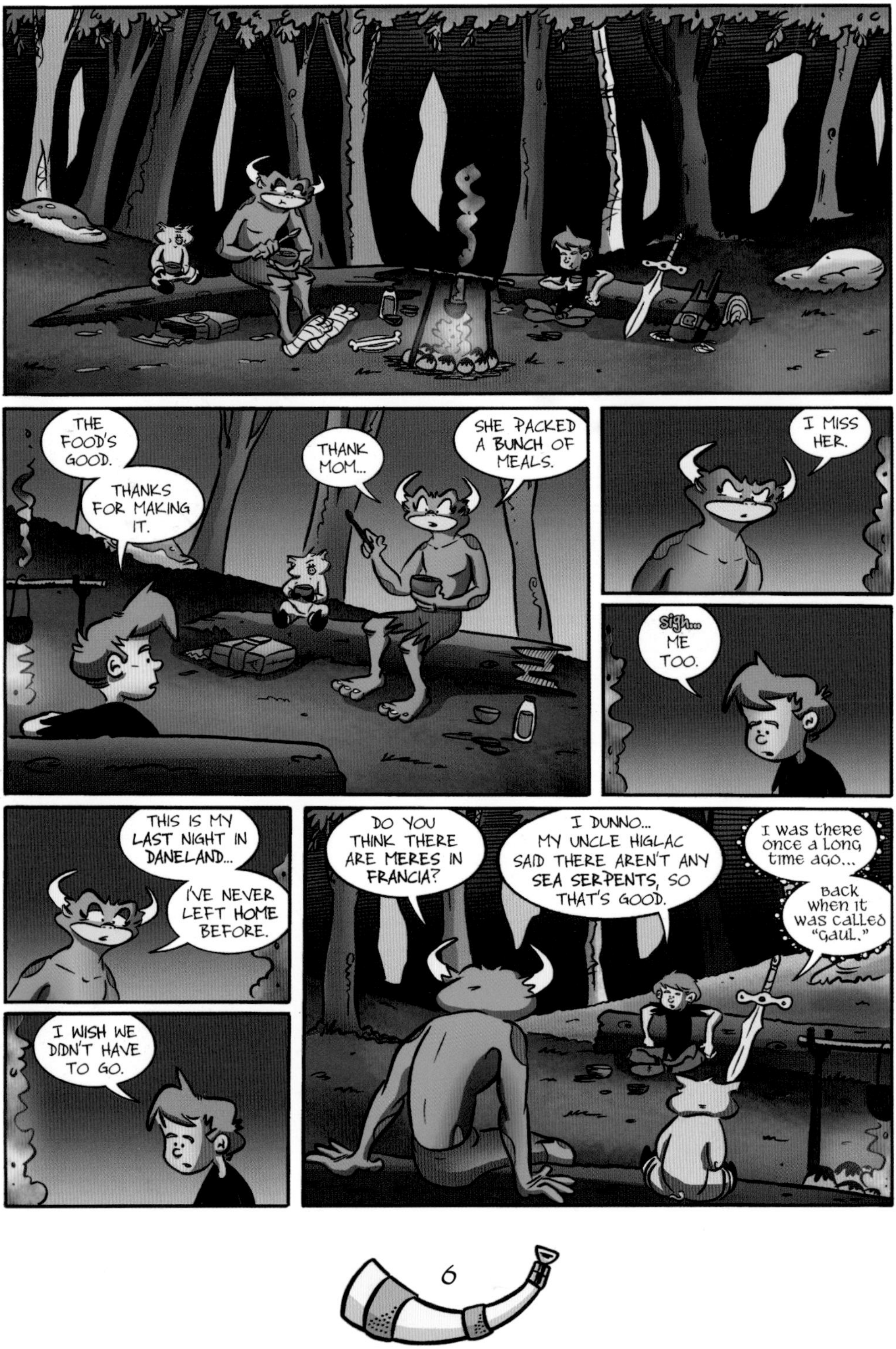
THE FOOD'S GOOD.
THANKS FOR MAKING IT.
THANK MOM...
SHE PACKED A BUNCH OF MEALS.
I MISS HER.
Sigh... ME TOO.
THIS IS MY LAST NIGHT IN DANELAND...
I'VE NEVER LEFT HOME BEFORE.
I WISH WE DIDN'T HAVE TO GO.
DO YOU THINK THERE ARE MERES IN FRANCIA?
I DUNNO... MY UNCLE HIGLAC SAID THERE AREN'T ANY SEA SERPENTS, SO THAT'S GOOD.
I was there once a long time ago...
Back when it was called "Gaul."

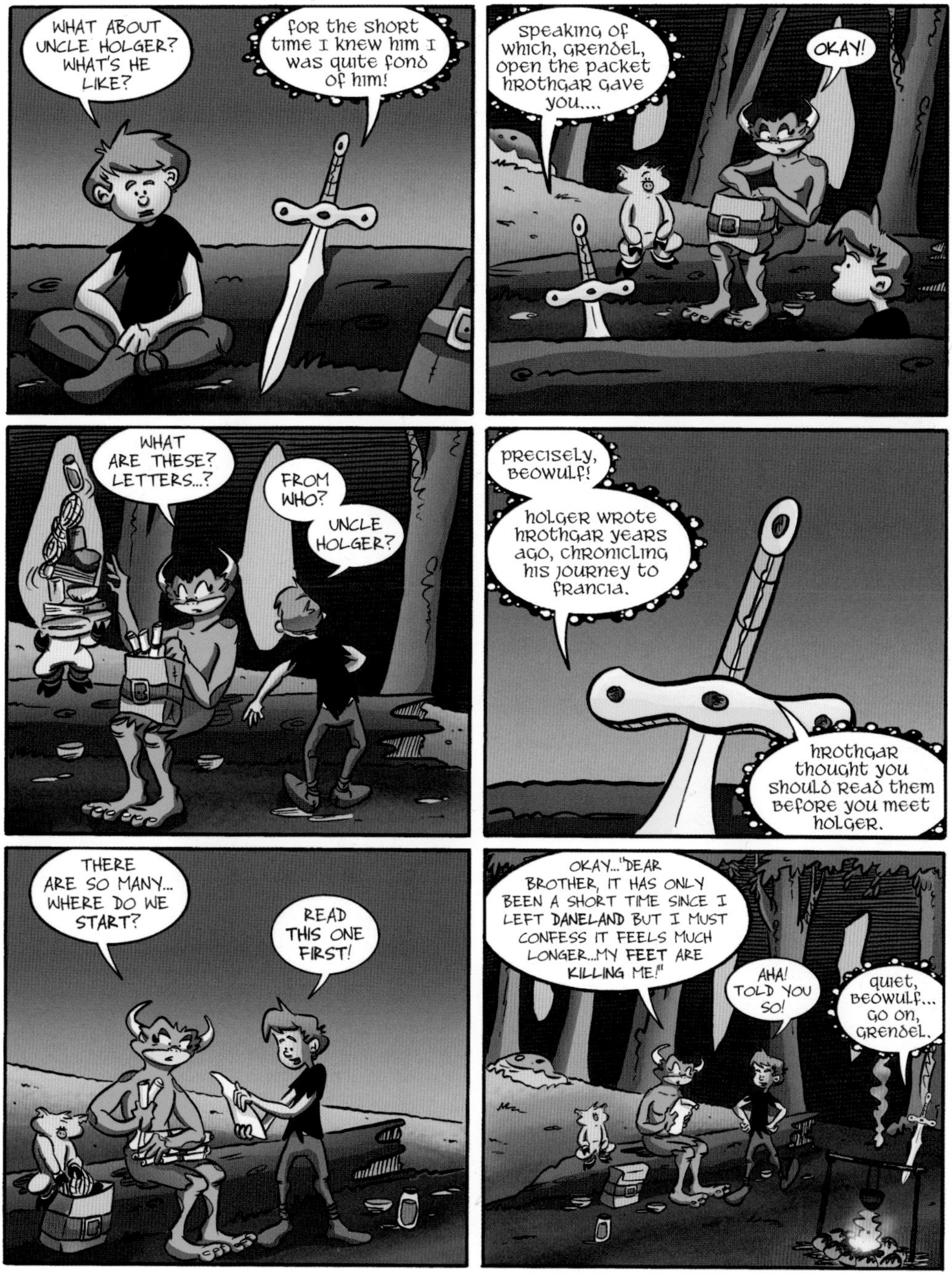
WHAT ABOUT UNCLE HOLGER? WHAT'S HE LIKE?
for the short time I knew him I was quite fond of him!
speaking of which, grendel, open the packet hrothgar gave you....
OKAY!
WHAT ARE THESE? LETTERS...?
FROM WHO?
UNCLE HOLGER?
precisely, beowulf!
holger wrote hrothgar years ago, chronicling his journey to francia.
hrothgar thought you should read them before you meet holger.
THERE ARE SO MANY... WHERE DO WE START?
READ THIS ONE FIRST!
OKAY..."DEAR BROTHER, IT HAS ONLY BEEN A SHORT TIME SINCE I LEFT DANELAND BUT I MUST CONFESS IT FEELS MUCH LONGER...MY FEET ARE KILLING ME!"
AHA! TOLD YOU SO!
quiet, beowulf... go on, grendel.

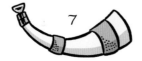

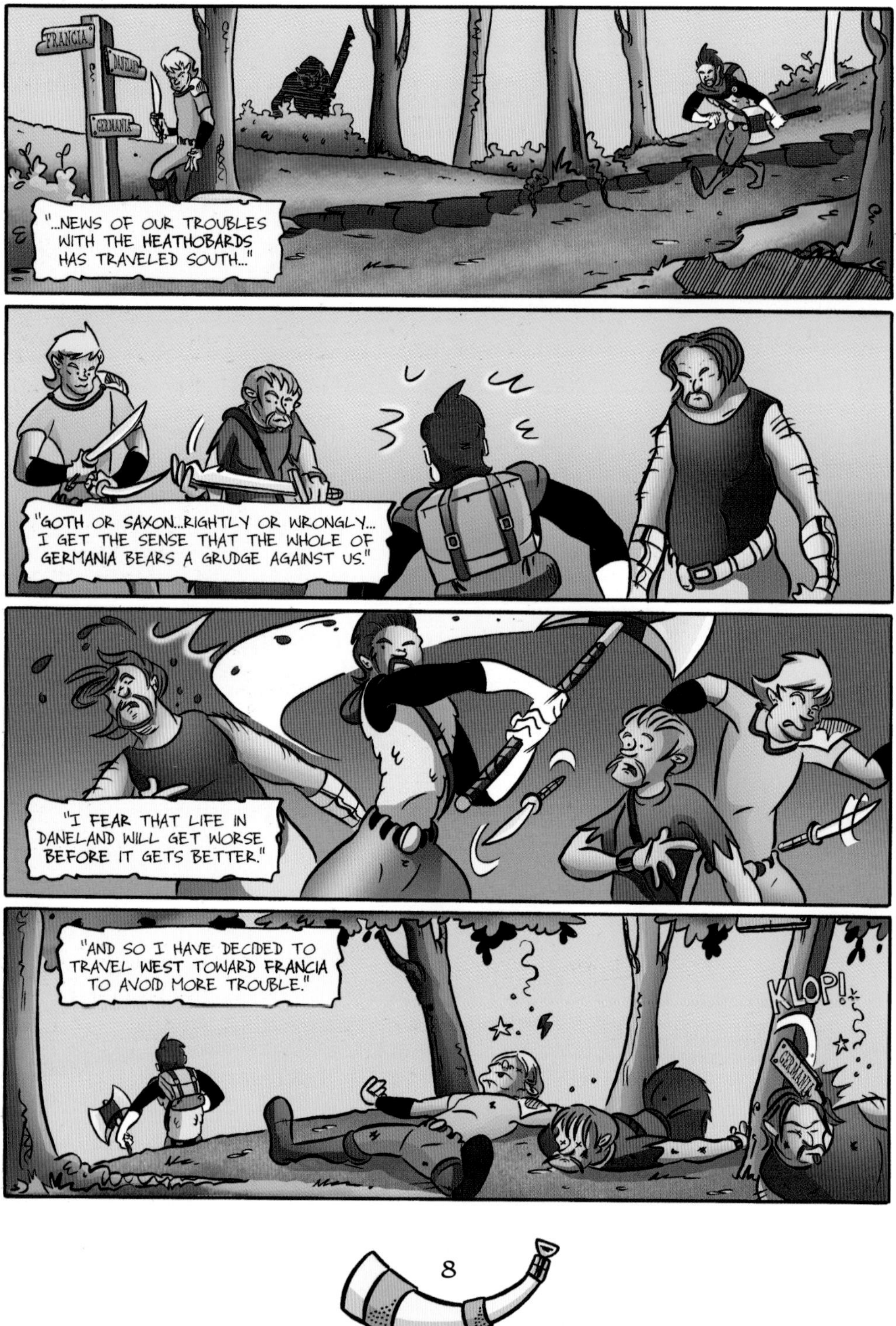
FRANCIA
DANELAND
GERMANIA
"...NEWS OF OUR TROUBLES WITH THE HEATHOBARDS HAS TRAVELED SOUTH..."
"GOTH OR SAXON...RIGHTLY OR WRONGLY... I GET THE SENSE THAT THE WHOLE OF GERMANIA BEARS A GRUDGE AGAINST US."
"I FEAR THAT LIFE IN DANELAND WILL GET WORSE BEFORE IT GETS BETTER."
"AND SO I HAVE DECIDED TO TRAVEL WEST TOWARD FRANCIA TO AVOID MORE TROUBLE."
KLOP!
GERMANIA

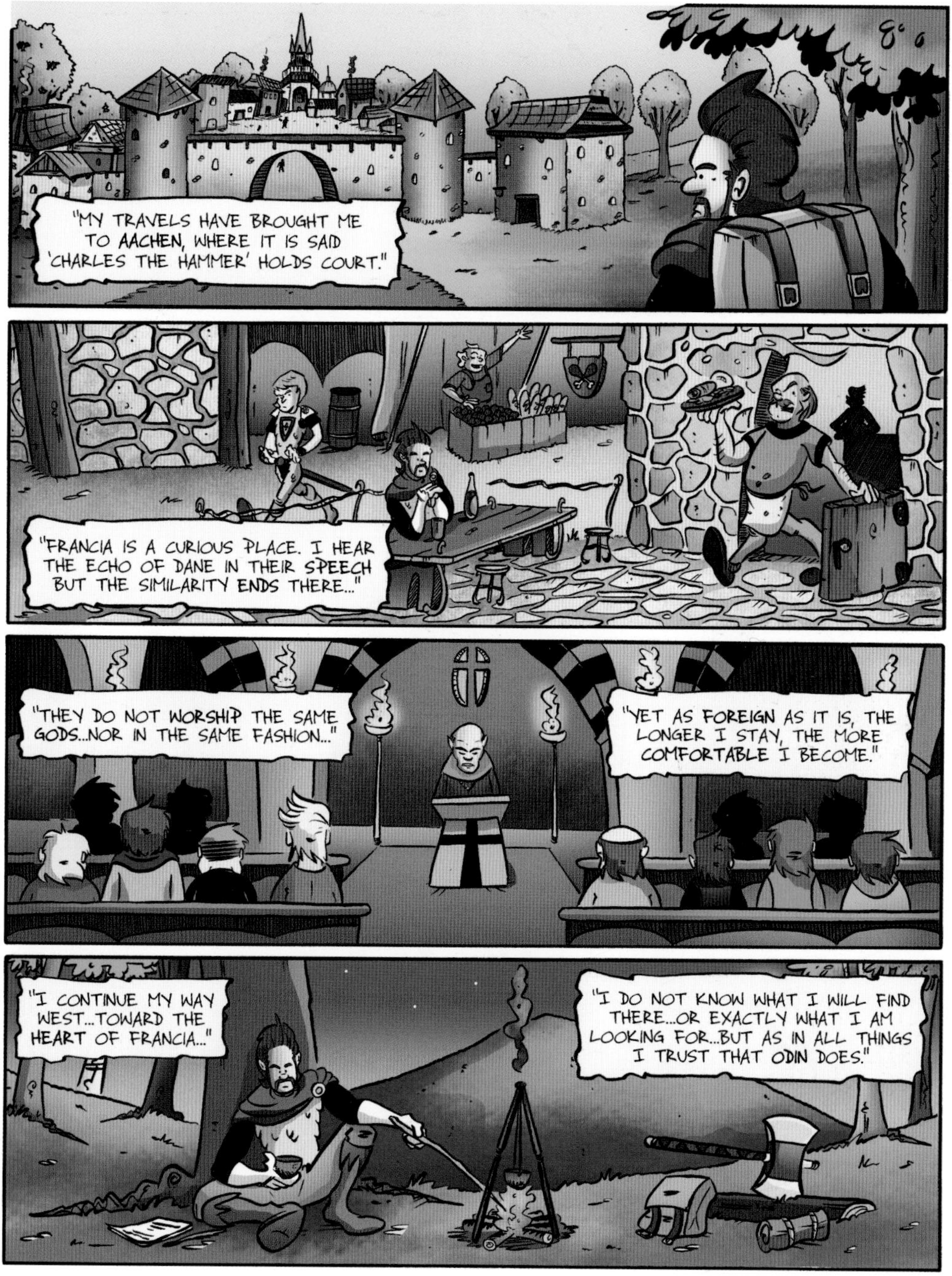
"MY TRAVELS HAVE BROUGHT ME TO AACHEN, WHERE IT IS SAID 'CHARLES THE HAMMER' HOLDS COURT."
"FRANCIA IS A CURIOUS PLACE. I HEAR THE ECHO OF DANE IN THEIR SPEECH BUT THE SIMILARITY ENDS THERE..."
"THEY DO NOT WORSHIP THE SAME GODS...NOR IN THE SAME FASHION..."
"YET AS FOREIGN AS IT IS, THE LONGER I STAY, THE MORE COMFORTABLE I BECOME."
"I CONTINUE MY WAY WEST...TOWARD THE HEART OF FRANCIA..."
"I DO NOT KNOW WHAT I WILL FIND THERE...OR EXACTLY WHAT I AM LOOKING FOR...BUT AS IN ALL THINGS I TRUST THAT ODIN DOES."

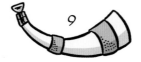

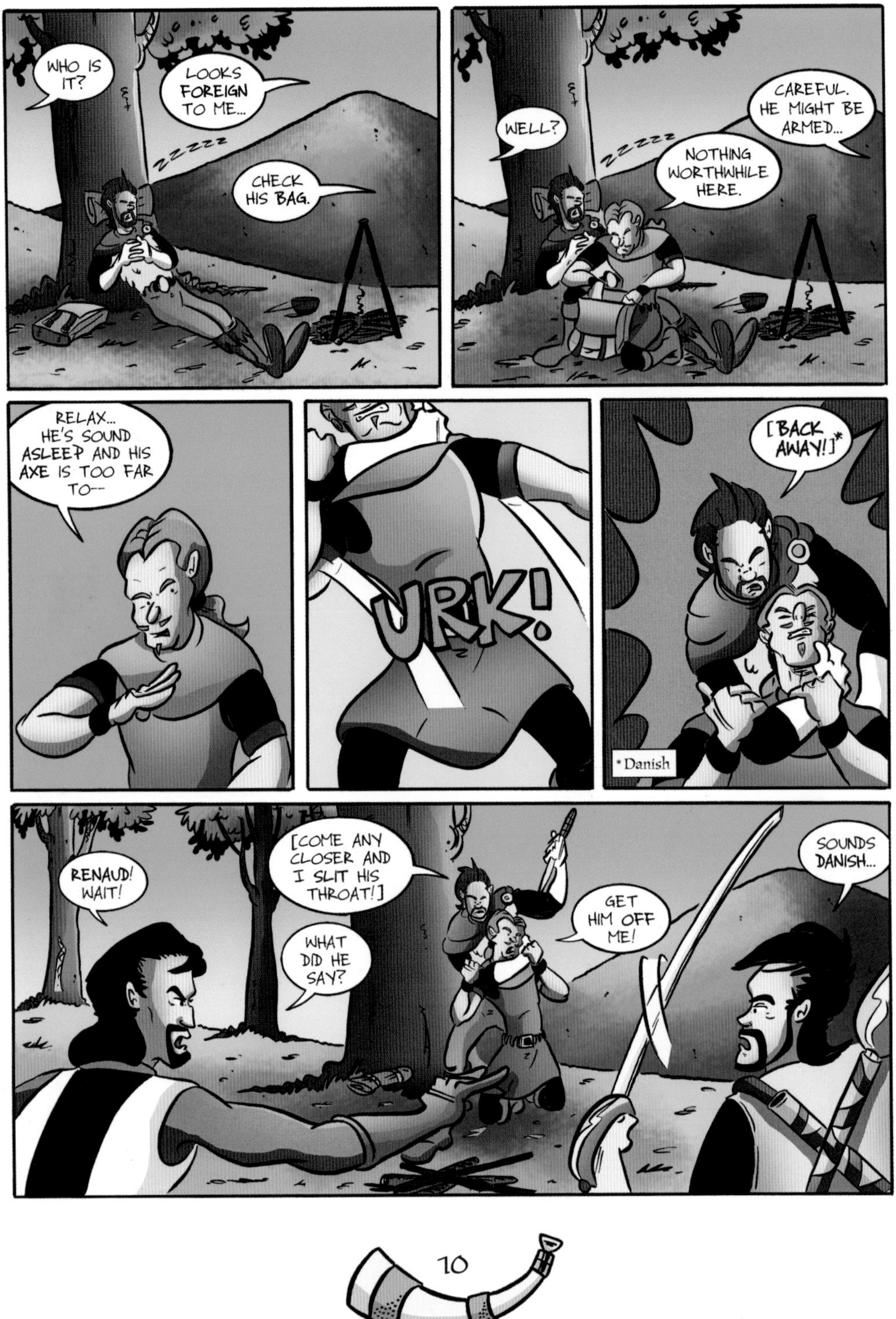
WHO IS IT?
LOOKS FOREIGN TO ME...
ZZZZZ
CHECK HIS BAG.
WELL?
CAREFUL. HE MIGHT BE ARMED...
ZZZZZ
NOTHING WORTHWHILE HERE.
RELAX... HE'S SOUND ASLEEP AND HIS AXE IS TOO FAR TO--
URK!
[BACK AWAY!]*
*Danish
RENAUD! WAIT!
[COME ANY CLOSER AND I SLIT HIS THROAT!]
WHAT DID HE SAY?
GET HIM OFF ME!
SOUNDS DANISH...

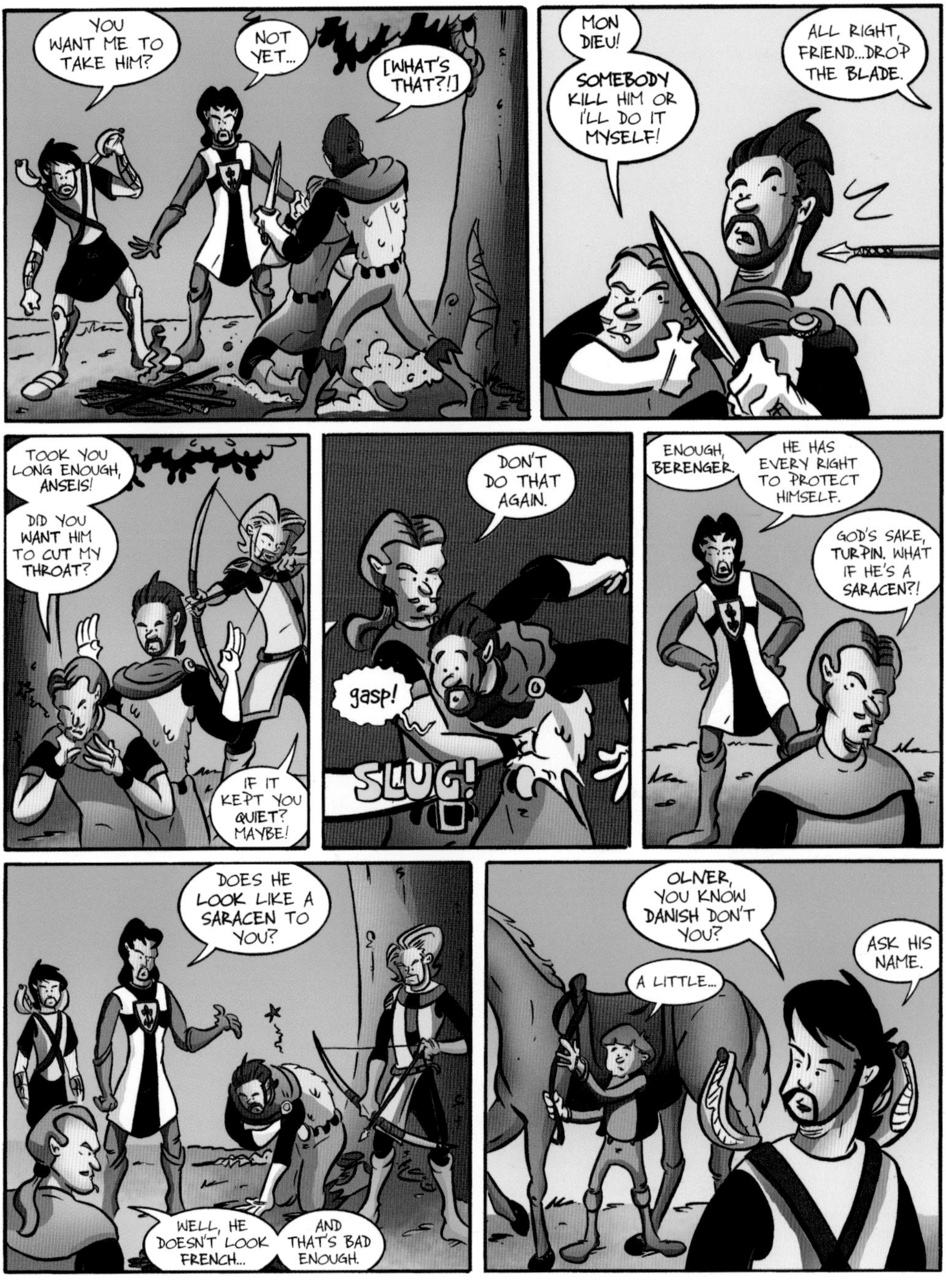
YOU WANT ME TO TAKE HIM?
NOT YET...
[WHAT'S THAT?!]
MON DIEU!
SOMEBODY KILL HIM OR I'LL DO IT MYSELF!
ALL RIGHT, FRIEND...DROP THE BLADE.
TOOK YOU LONG ENOUGH, ANSEIS!
DID YOU WANT HIM TO CUT MY THROAT?
IF IT KEPT YOU QUIET? MAYBE!
DON'T DO THAT AGAIN.
gasp!
SLUG!
ENOUGH, BERENGER.
HE HAS EVERY RIGHT TO PROTECT HIMSELF.
GOD'S SAKE, TURPIN. WHAT IF HE'S A SARACEN?!
DOES HE LOOK LIKE A SARACEN TO YOU?
WELL, HE DOESN'T LOOK FRENCH...
AND THAT'S BAD ENOUGH.
OLIVER, YOU KNOW DANISH DON'T YOU?
A LITTLE...
ASK HIS NAME.

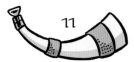

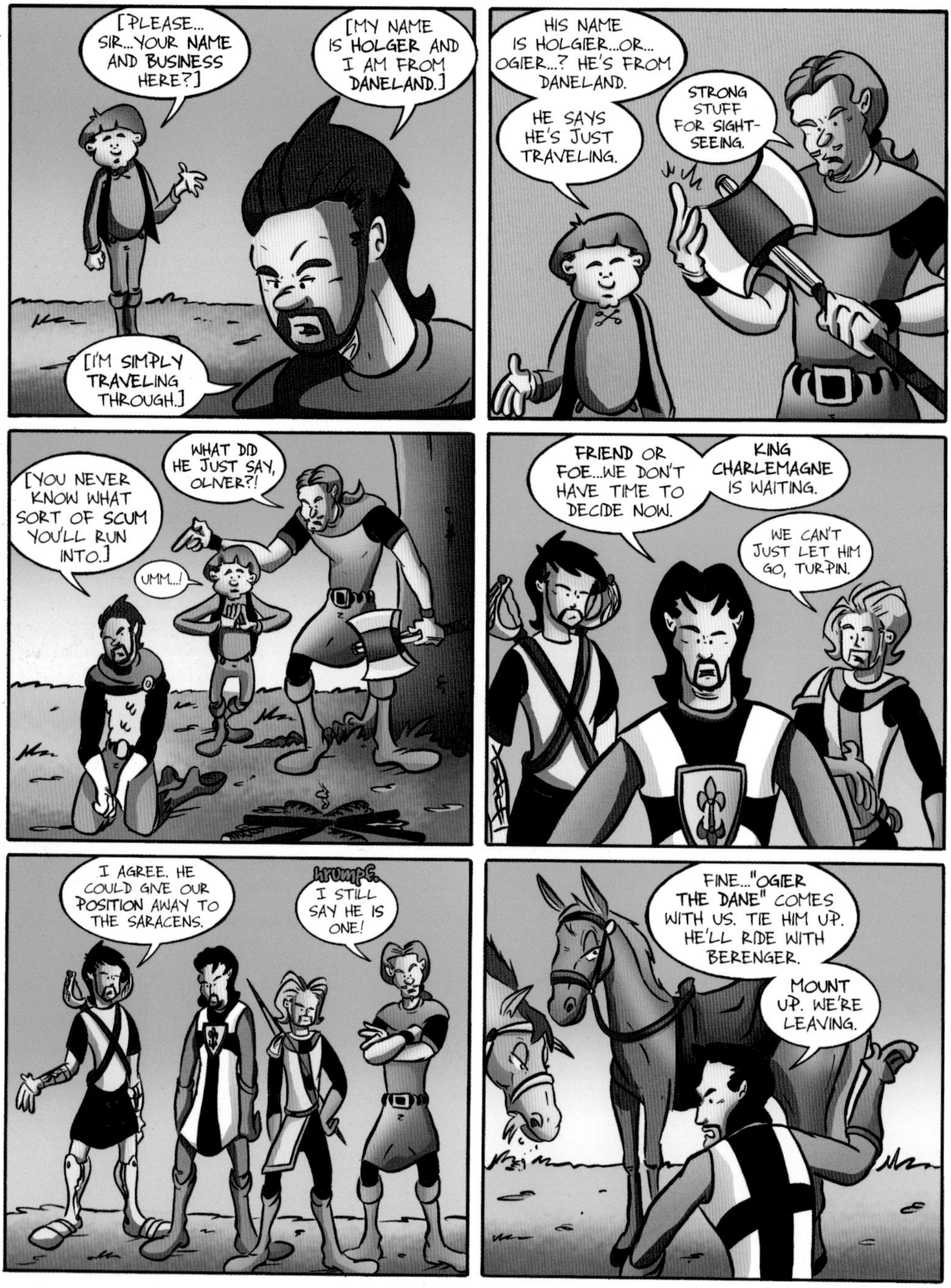
[PLEASE... SIR...YOUR NAME AND BUSINESS HERE?]
[MY NAME IS HOLGER AND I AM FROM DANELAND.]
[I'M SIMPLY TRAVELING THROUGH.]
HIS NAME IS HOLGIER...OR... OGIER...? HE'S FROM DANELAND.
HE SAYS HE'S JUST TRAVELING.
STRONG STUFF FOR SIGHT-SEEING.
[YOU NEVER KNOW WHAT SORT OF SCUM YOU'LL RUN INTO.]
WHAT DID HE JUST SAY, OLIVER?!
UMM...!
FRIEND OR FOE...WE DON'T HAVE TIME TO DECIDE NOW.
KING CHARLEMAGNE IS WAITING.
WE CAN'T JUST LET HIM GO, TURPIN.
I AGREE. HE COULD GIVE OUR POSITION AWAY TO THE SARACENS.
krumpf.
I STILL SAY HE IS ONE!
FINE..."OGIER THE DANE" COMES WITH US. TIE HIM UP. HE'LL RIDE WITH BERENGER.
MOUNT UP. WE'RE LEAVING.

Later...

WELL, THIS IS THE SPOT...

NO SIGN OF CHARLEMAGNE, THOUGH.

HE LEFT FROM PARIS?

TWO DAYS AGO...MORE THAN ENOUGH TIME TO SET UP CAMP.

PERHAPS HE LEFT FOR RENNES WITHOUT US?

IT WOULDN'T BE THE FIRST TIME HE GOT TIRED OF WAITING.

I'LL SCOUT THE AREA AND SEE IF I CAN FIND ANY SIGN OF THEM.

TAKE BERENGER. WE'LL WAIT HERE.

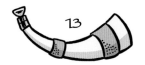

13

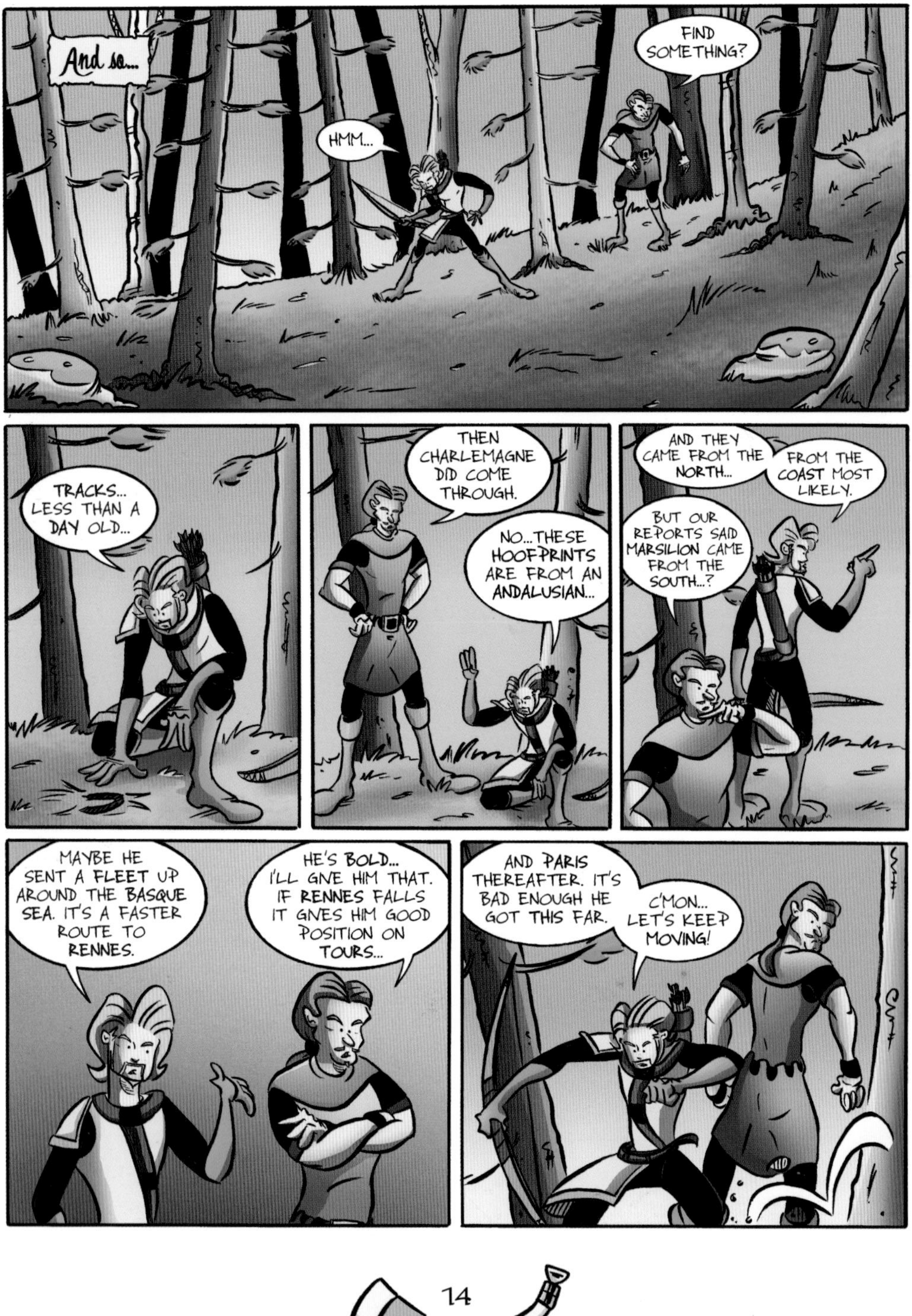
And so...
HMM...
FIND SOMETHING?
TRACKS... LESS THAN A DAY OLD...
THEN CHARLEMAGNE DID COME THROUGH.
NO...THESE HOOFPRINTS ARE FROM AN ANDALUSIAN...
AND THEY CAME FROM THE NORTH...
FROM THE COAST MOST LIKELY.
BUT OUR REPORTS SAID MARSILION CAME FROM THE SOUTH...?
MAYBE HE SENT A FLEET UP AROUND THE BASQUE SEA. IT'S A FASTER ROUTE TO RENNES.
HE'S BOLD... I'LL GIVE HIM THAT. IF RENNES FALLS IT GIVES HIM GOOD POSITION ON TOURS...
AND PARIS THEREAFTER. IT'S BAD ENOUGH HE GOT THIS FAR.
C'MON... LET'S KEEP MOVING!

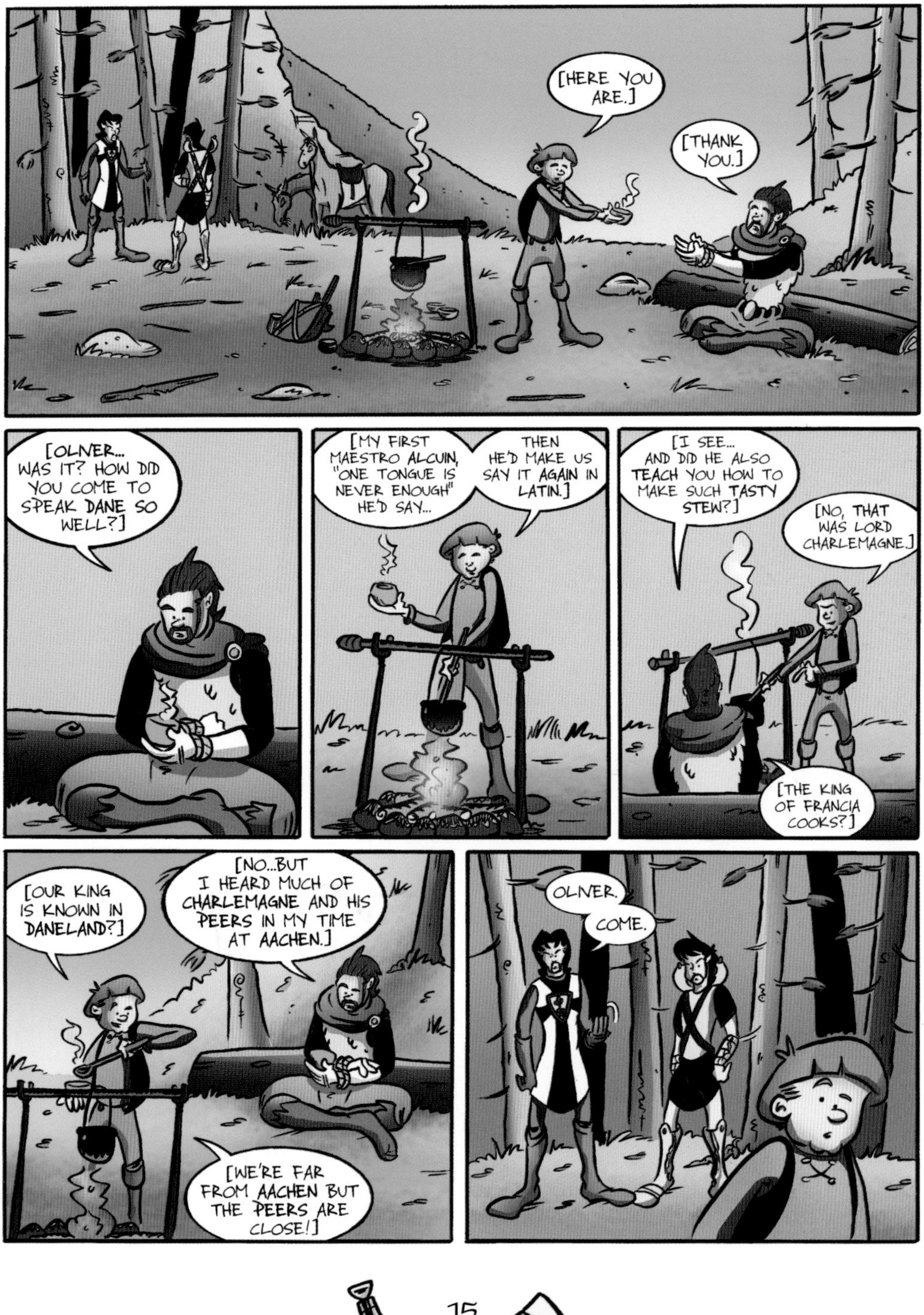
[HERE YOU ARE.]
[THANK YOU.]
[OLIVER... WAS IT? HOW DID YOU COME TO SPEAK DANE SO WELL?]
[MY FIRST MAESTRO ALCUIN, "ONE TONGUE IS NEVER ENOUGH" HE'D SAY...
THEN HE'D MAKE US SAY IT AGAIN IN LATIN.]
[I SEE... AND DID HE ALSO TEACH YOU HOW TO MAKE SUCH TASTY STEW?]
[NO, THAT WAS LORD CHARLEMAGNE.]
[THE KING OF FRANCIA COOKS?]
[OUR KING IS KNOWN IN DANELAND?]
[NO...BUT I HEARD MUCH OF CHARLEMAGNE AND HIS PEERS IN MY TIME AT AACHEN.]
[WE'RE FAR FROM AACHEN BUT THE PEERS ARE CLOSE!]
OLIVER.
COME.

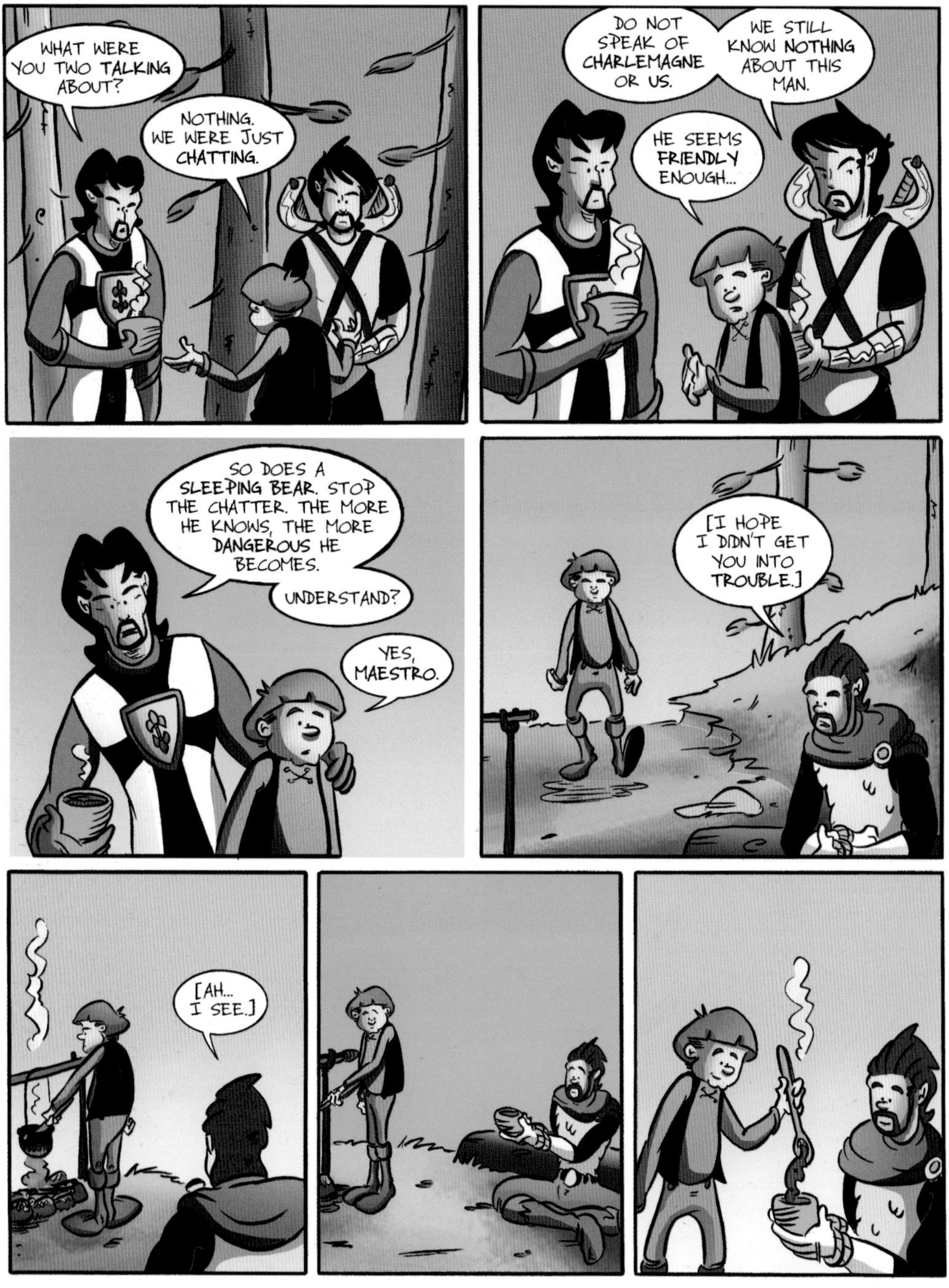
WHAT WERE YOU TWO TALKING ABOUT?
NOTHING. WE WERE JUST CHATTING.
DO NOT SPEAK OF CHARLEMAGNE OR US.
WE STILL KNOW NOTHING ABOUT THIS MAN.
HE SEEMS FRIENDLY ENOUGH...
SO DOES A SLEEPING BEAR. STOP THE CHATTER. THE MORE HE KNOWS, THE MORE DANGEROUS HE BECOMES.
UNDERSTAND?
YES, MAESTRO.
[I HOPE I DIDN'T GET YOU INTO TROUBLE.]
[AH... I SEE.]

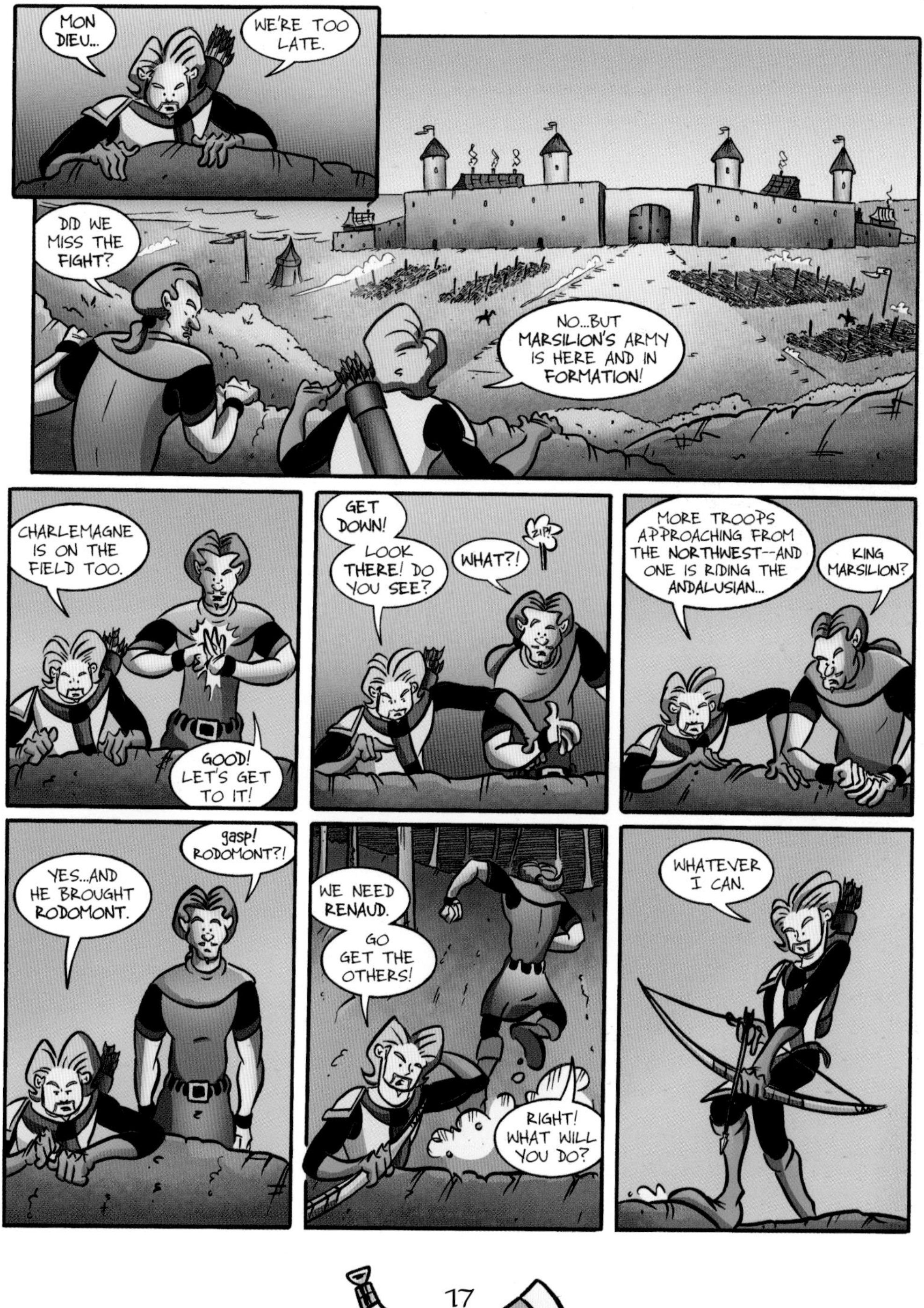
MON DIEU...
WE'RE TOO LATE.
DID WE MISS THE FIGHT?
NO...BUT MARSILION'S ARMY IS HERE AND IN FORMATION!
CHARLEMAGNE IS ON THE FIELD TOO.
GOOD! LET'S GET TO IT!
GET DOWN!
LOOK THERE! DO YOU SEE?
ZIP!
WHAT?!
MORE TROOPS APPROACHING FROM THE NORTHWEST--AND ONE IS RIDING THE ANDALUSIAN...
KING MARSILION?
YES...AND HE BROUGHT RODOMONT.
gasp! RODOMONT?!
WE NEED RENAUD.
GO GET THE OTHERS!
RIGHT! WHAT WILL YOU DO?
WHATEVER I CAN.

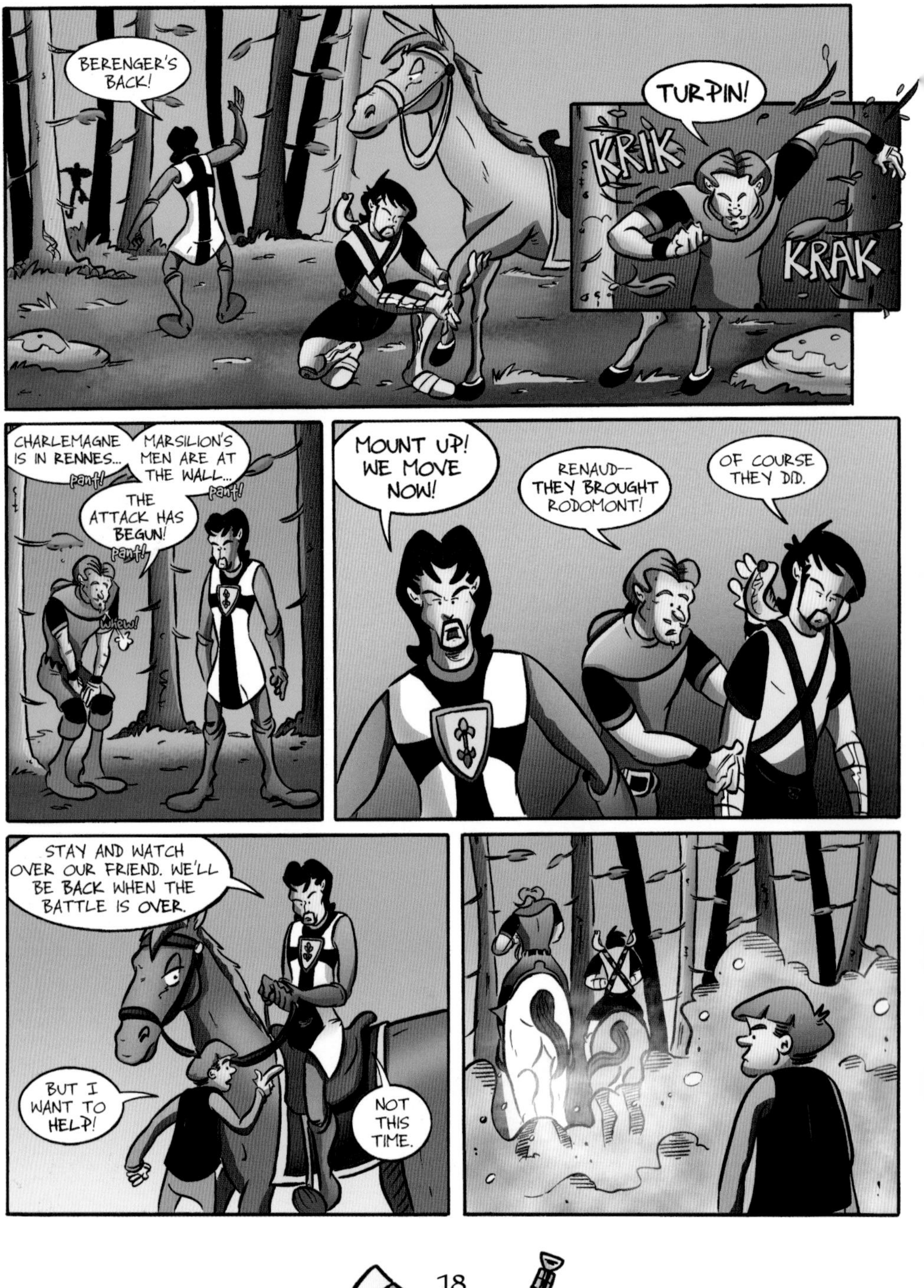
BERENGER'S BACK!
TURPIN!
KRIK
KRAK
CHARLEMAGNE IS IN RENNES... pant!
MARSILION'S MEN ARE AT THE WALL... pant!
THE ATTACK HAS BEGUN! pant!
whew!
MOUNT UP! WE MOVE NOW!
RENAUD-- THEY BROUGHT RODOMONT!
OF COURSE THEY DID.
STAY AND WATCH OVER OUR FRIEND. WE'LL BE BACK WHEN THE BATTLE IS OVER.
BUT I WANT TO HELP!
NOT THIS TIME.

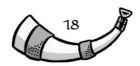

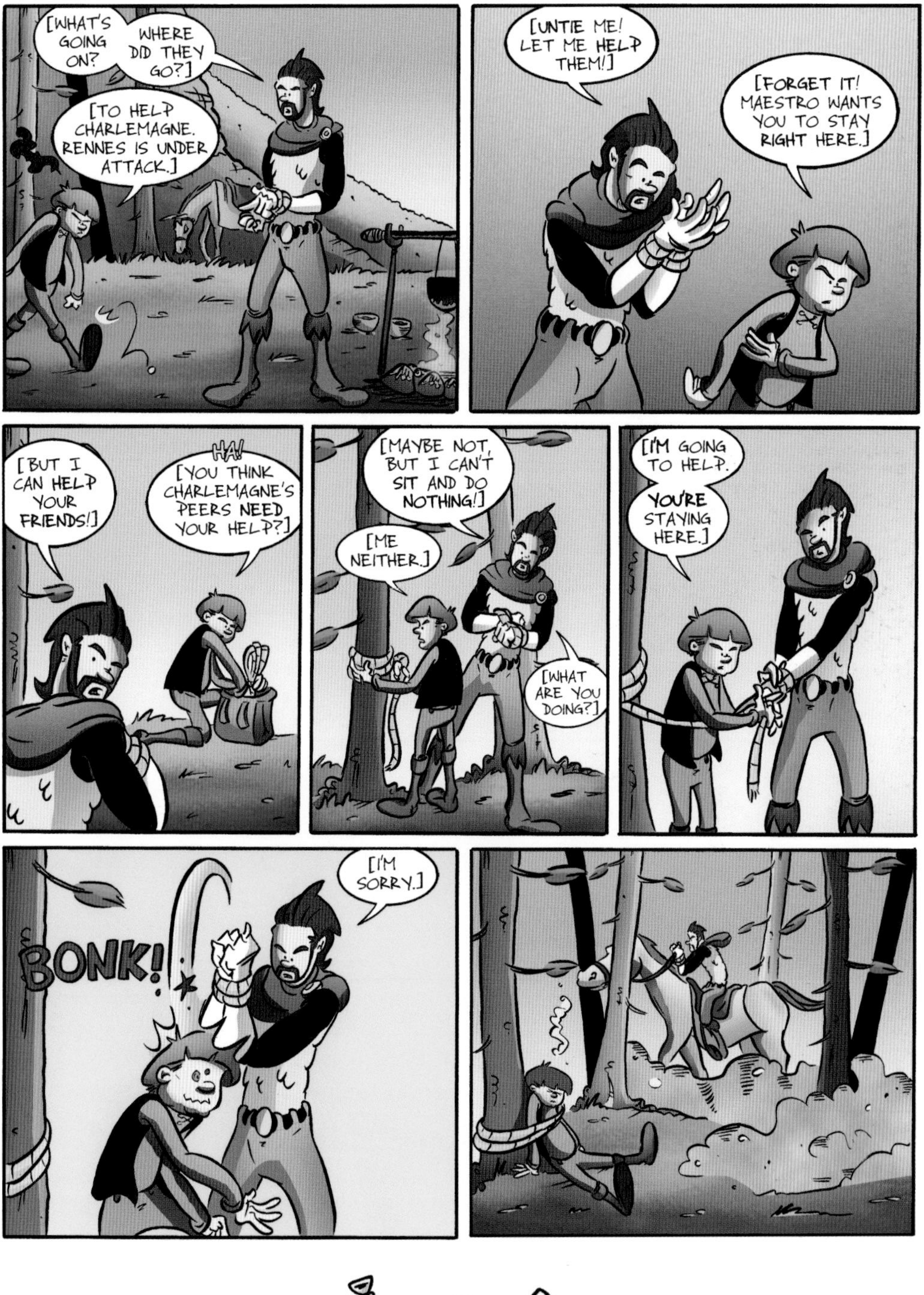
[WHAT'S GOING ON?
WHERE DID THEY GO?]
[TO HELP CHARLEMAGNE. RENNES IS UNDER ATTACK.]
[UNTIE ME! LET ME HELP THEM!]
[FORGET IT! MAESTRO WANTS YOU TO STAY RIGHT HERE.]
[BUT I CAN HELP YOUR FRIENDS!]
HA!
[YOU THINK CHARLEMAGNE'S PEERS NEED YOUR HELP?]
[MAYBE NOT, BUT I CAN'T SIT AND DO NOTHING!]
[ME NEITHER.]
[WHAT ARE YOU DOING?]
[I'M GOING TO HELP.
YOU'RE STAYING HERE.]
[I'M SORRY.]
BONK!

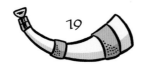

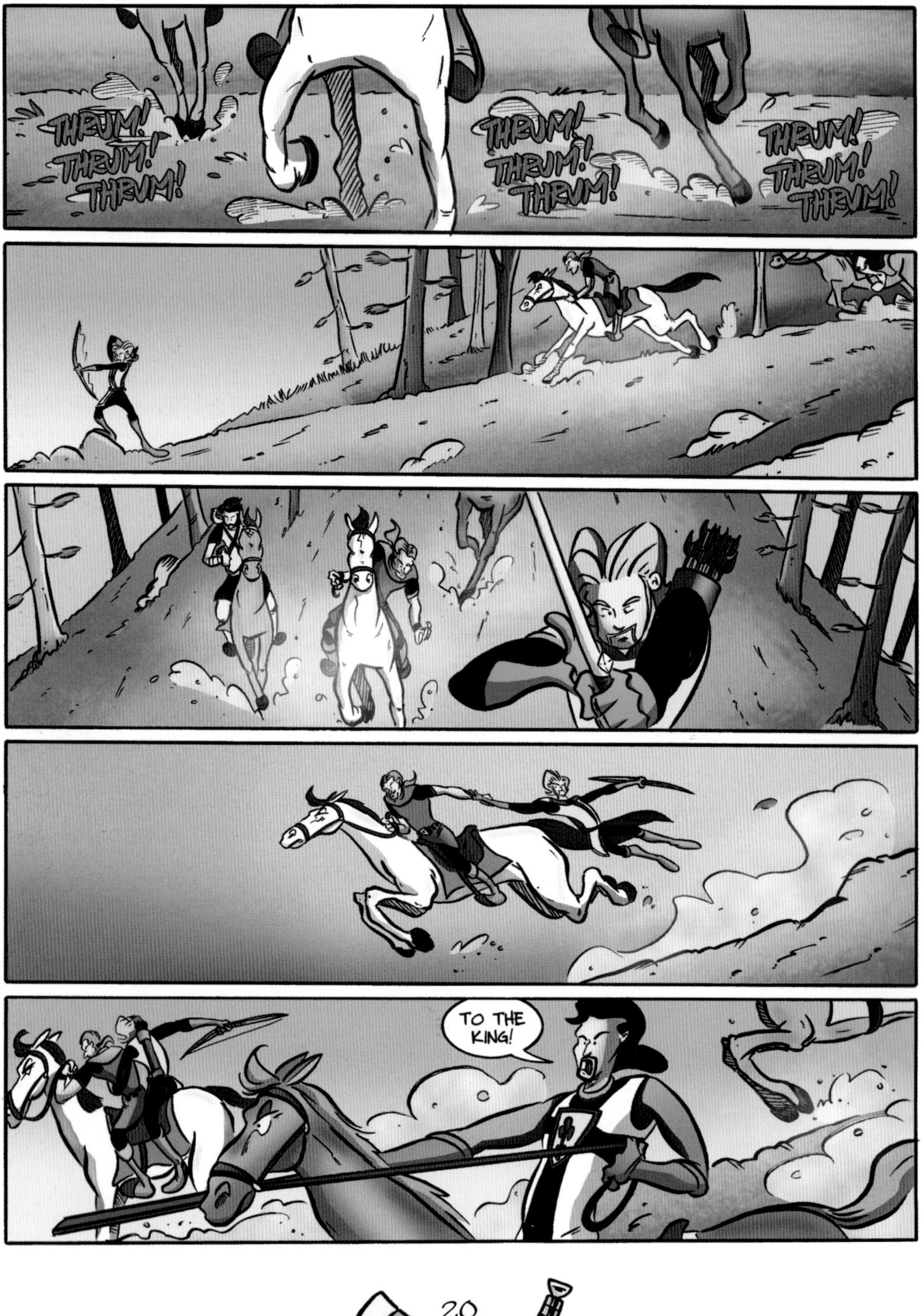
THRUM! THRUM! THRUM!
THRUM! THRUM! THRUM!
THRUM! THRUM! THRUM!
TO THE KING!

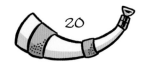

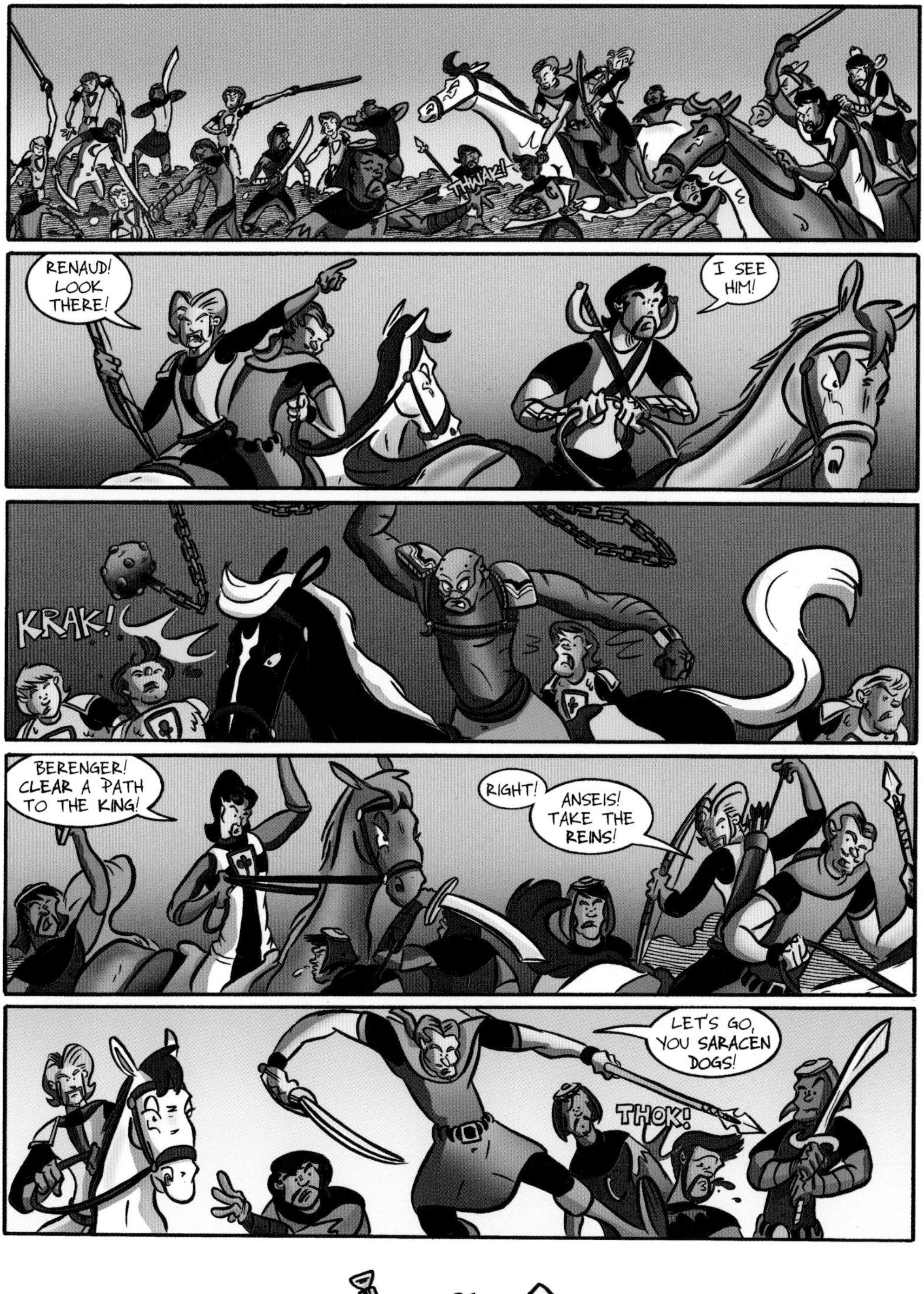
THWAK!
RENAUD! LOOK THERE!
I SEE HIM!
KRAK!
BERENGER! CLEAR A PATH TO THE KING!
RIGHT!
ANSEIS! TAKE THE REINS!
LET'S GO, YOU SARACEN DOGS!
THOK!

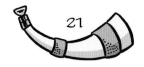

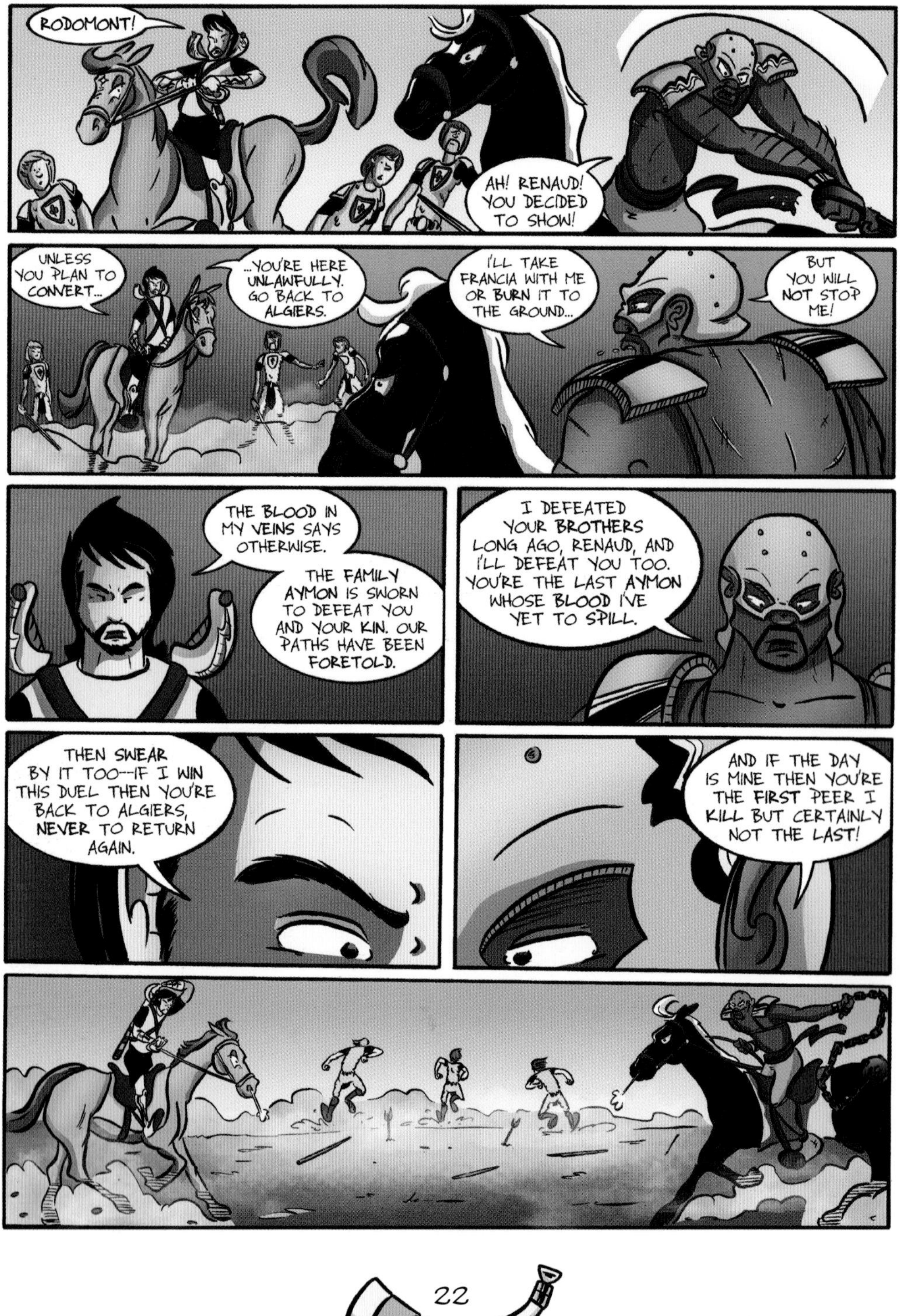
RODOMONT!
AH! RENAUD! YOU DECIDED TO SHOW!
UNLESS YOU PLAN TO CONVERT...
...YOU'RE HERE UNLAWFULLY. GO BACK TO ALGIERS.
I'LL TAKE FRANCIA WITH ME OR BURN IT TO THE GROUND...
BUT YOU WILL NOT STOP ME!
THE BLOOD IN MY VEINS SAYS OTHERWISE.
THE FAMILY AYMON IS SWORN TO DEFEAT YOU AND YOUR KIN. OUR PATHS HAVE BEEN FORETOLD.
I DEFEATED YOUR BROTHERS LONG AGO, RENAUD, AND I'LL DEFEAT YOU TOO. YOU'RE THE LAST AYMON WHOSE BLOOD I'VE YET TO SPILL.
THEN SWEAR BY IT TOO--IF I WIN THIS DUEL THEN YOU'RE BACK TO ALGIERS, NEVER TO RETURN AGAIN.
AND IF THE DAY IS MINE THEN YOU'RE THE FIRST PEER I KILL BUT CERTAINLY NOT THE LAST!

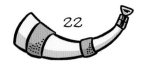

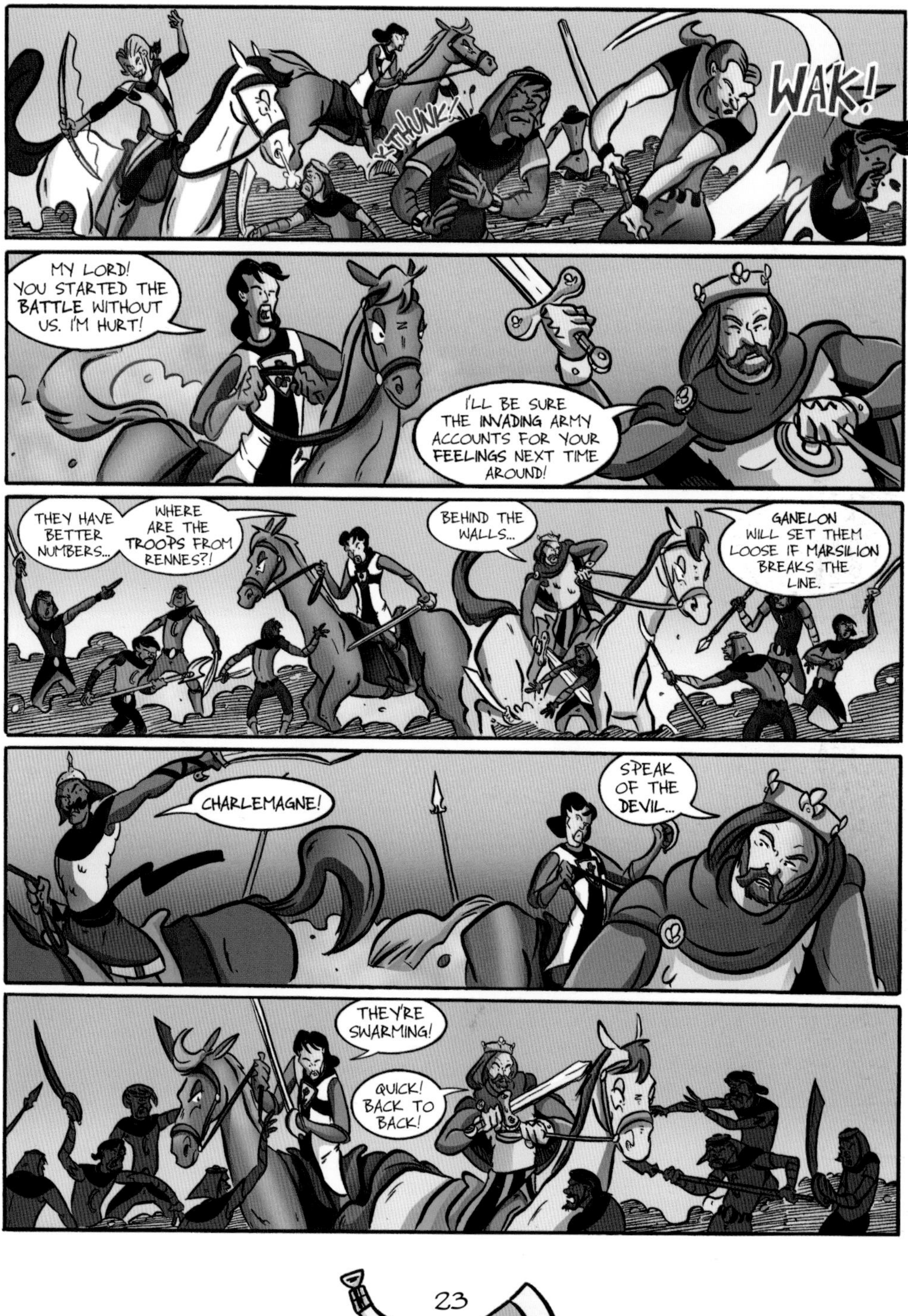
THUNK!
WAK!
MY LORD! YOU STARTED THE BATTLE WITHOUT US. I'M HURT!
I'LL BE SURE THE INVADING ARMY ACCOUNTS FOR YOUR FEELINGS NEXT TIME AROUND!
THEY HAVE BETTER NUMBERS...
WHERE ARE THE TROOPS FROM RENNES?!
BEHIND THE WALLS...
GANELON WILL SET THEM LOOSE IF MARSILION BREAKS THE LINE.
CHARLEMAGNE!
SPEAK OF THE DEVIL...
THEY'RE SWARMING!
QUICK! BACK TO BACK!

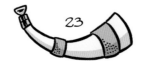

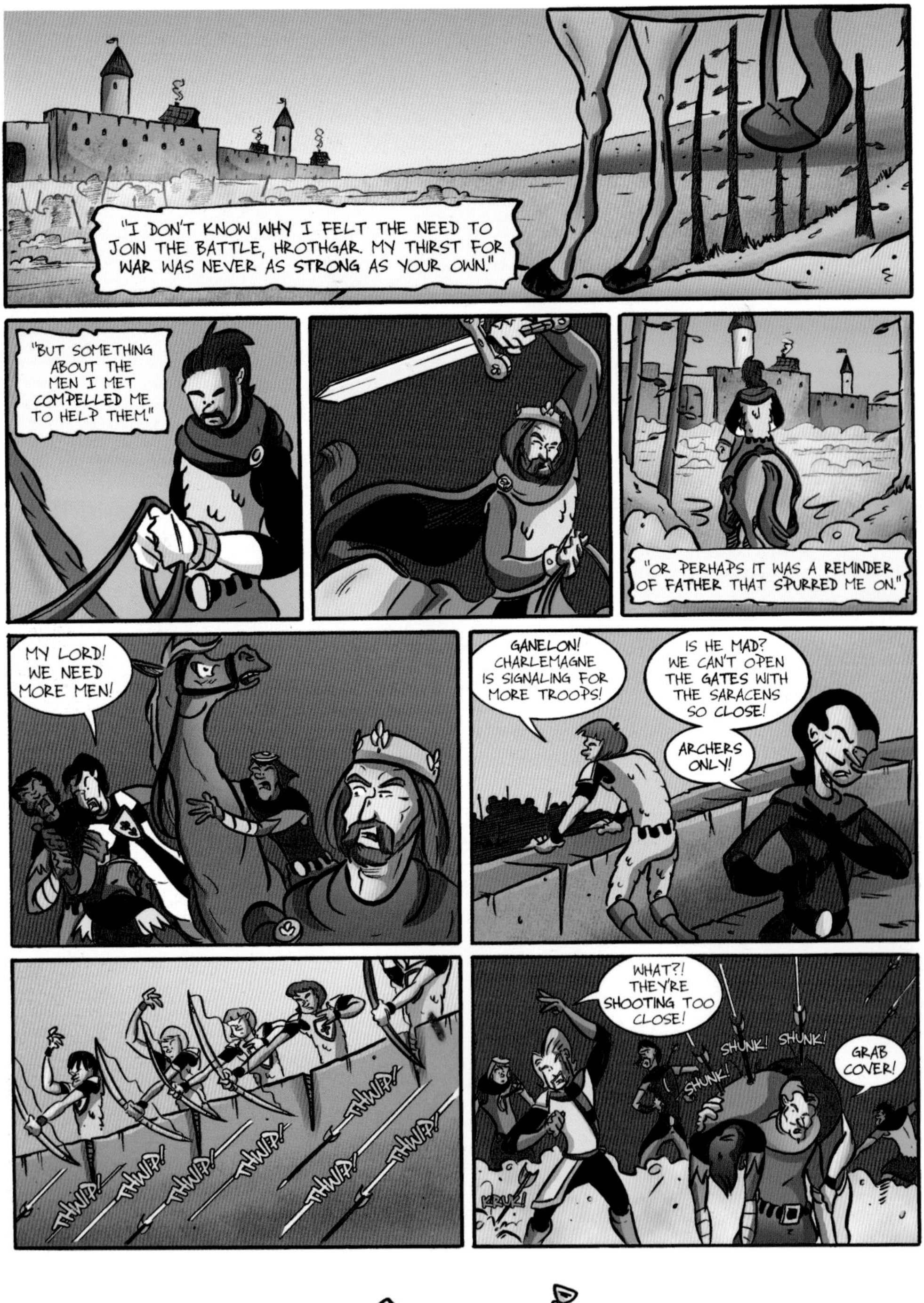
"I DON'T KNOW WHY I FELT THE NEED TO JOIN THE BATTLE, HROTHGAR. MY THIRST FOR WAR WAS NEVER AS STRONG AS YOUR OWN."
"BUT SOMETHING ABOUT THE MEN I MET COMPELLED ME TO HELP THEM."
"OR PERHAPS IT WAS A REMINDER OF FATHER THAT SPURRED ME ON."
MY LORD! WE NEED MORE MEN!
GANELON! CHARLEMAGNE IS SIGNALING FOR MORE TROOPS!
IS HE MAD? WE CAN'T OPEN THE GATES WITH THE SARACENS SO CLOSE!
ARCHERS ONLY!
THWIP!
THWIP!
THWIP!
THWIP!
THWIP!
THWIP!
WHAT?! THEY'RE SHOOTING TOO CLOSE!
SHUNK! SHUNK!
SHUNK!
GRAB COVER!
KRUK!

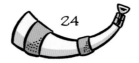

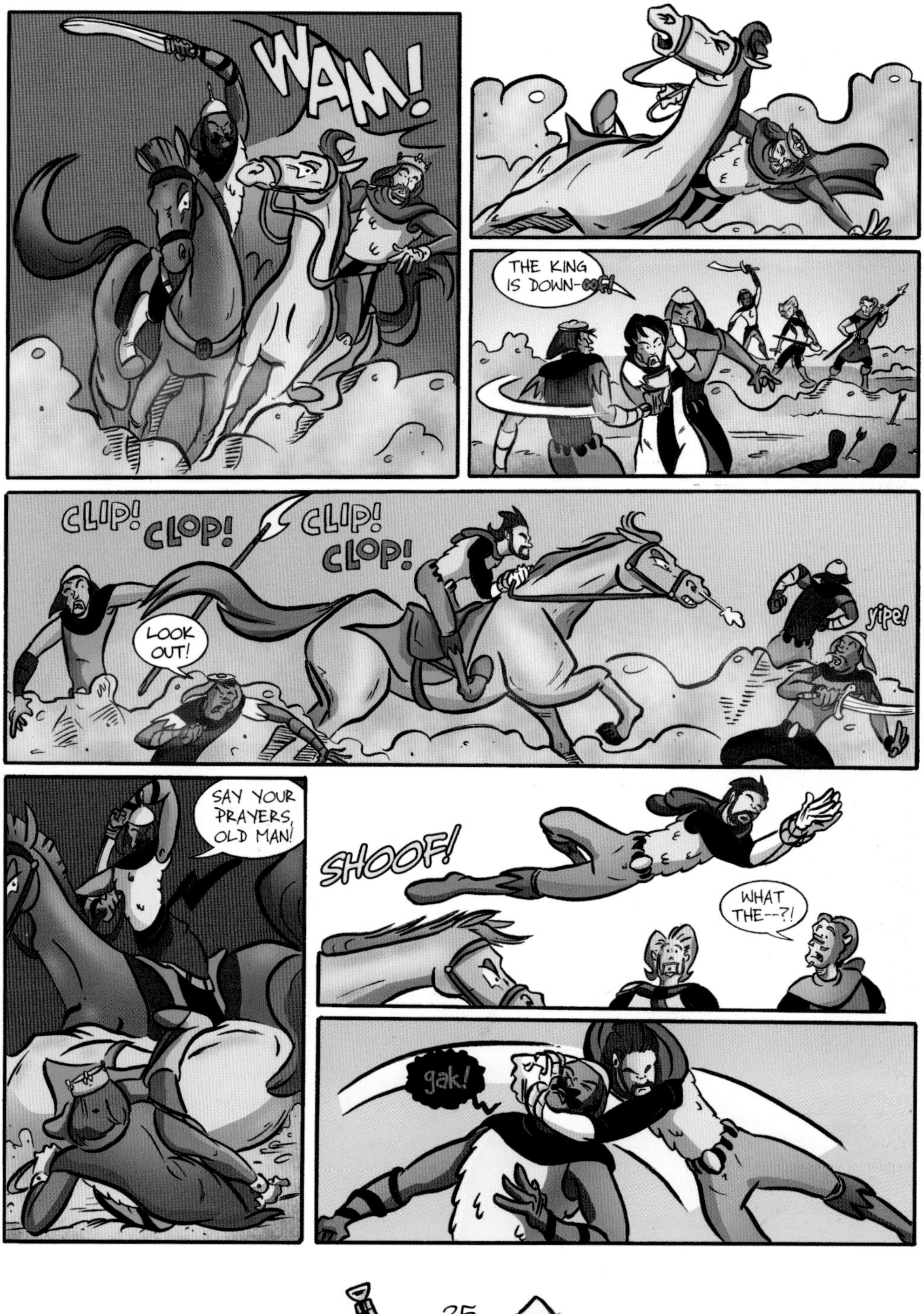
WAM!
THE KING IS DOWN--OOF!
CLIP! CLOP! CLIP! CLOP!
LOOK OUT!
yipe!
SAY YOUR PRAYERS, OLD MAN!
SHOOF!
WHAT THE--?!
gak!

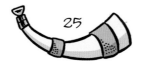

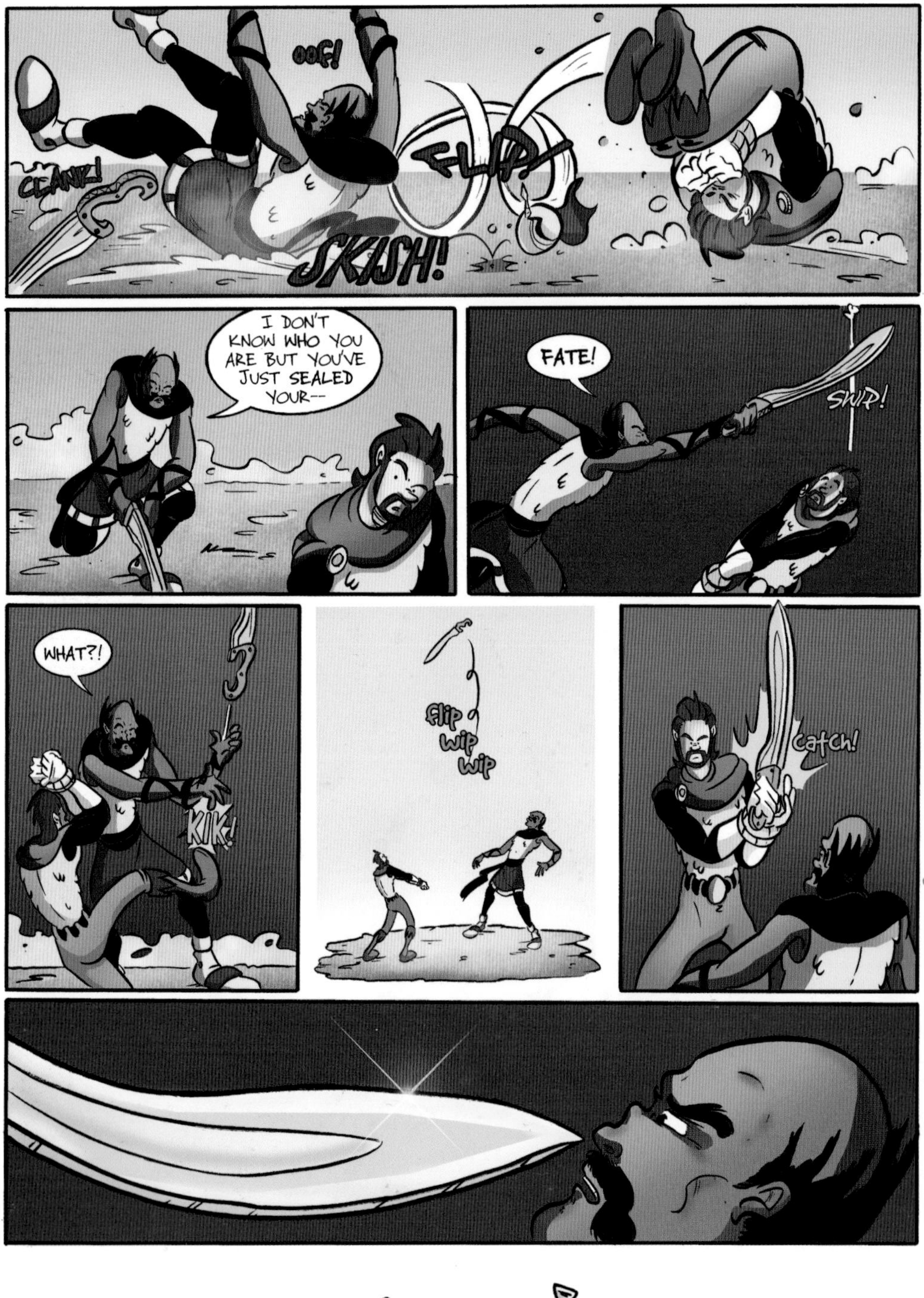
OOF!
CLANK!
FLIP!
SKISH!
I DON'T KNOW WHO YOU ARE BUT YOU'VE JUST SEALED YOUR--
FATE!
SWIR!
WHAT?!
KIK!
flip
wip
wip
catch!

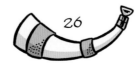

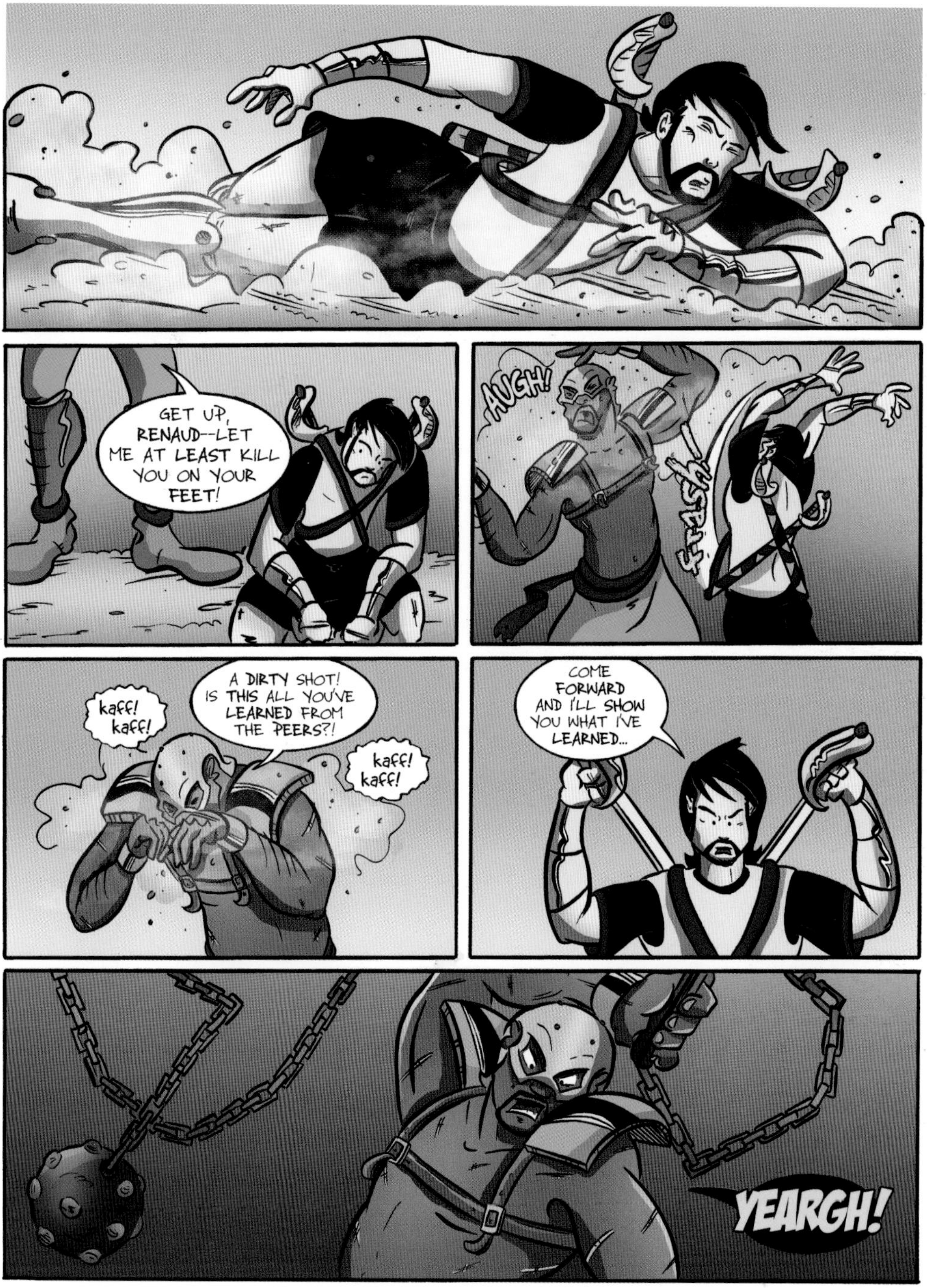
GET UP, RENAUD--LET ME AT LEAST KILL YOU ON YOUR FEET!
AUGH!
FFASH
kaff! kaff!
A DIRTY SHOT! IS THIS ALL YOU'VE LEARNED FROM THE PEERS?!
kaff! kaff!
COME FORWARD AND I'LL SHOW YOU WHAT I'VE LEARNED...
YEARGH!

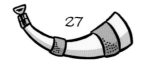

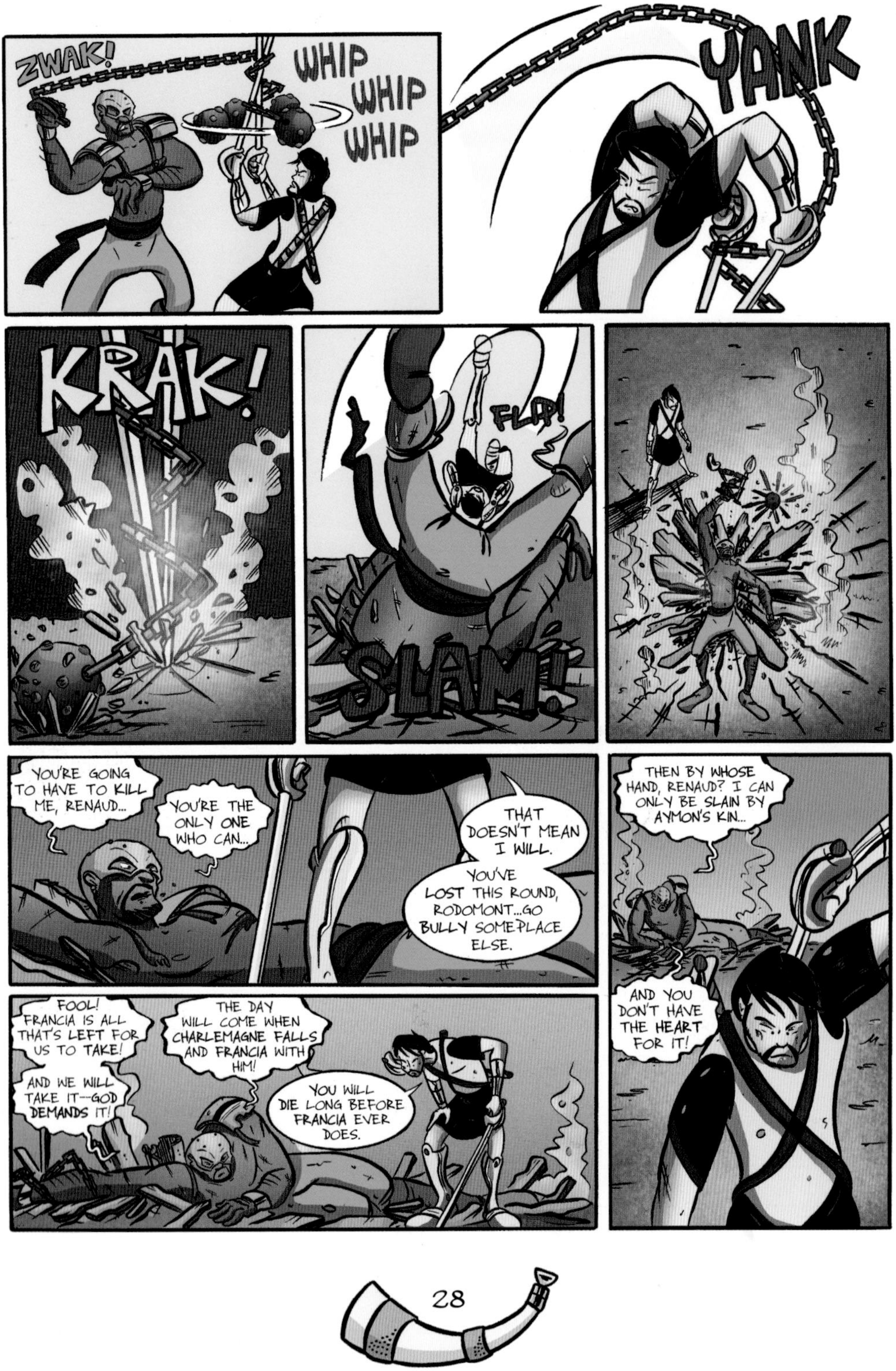
ZWAK!
WHIP WHIP WHIP
YANK
KRAK!
FLIP!
SLAM!
YOU'RE GOING TO HAVE TO KILL ME, RENAUD...
YOU'RE THE ONLY ONE WHO CAN...
THAT DOESN'T MEAN I WILL.
YOU'VE LOST THIS ROUND, RODOMONT...GO BULLY SOMEPLACE ELSE.
THEN BY WHOSE HAND, RENAUD? I CAN ONLY BE SLAIN BY AYMON'S KIN...
AND YOU DON'T HAVE THE HEART FOR IT!
FOOL! FRANCIA IS ALL THAT'S LEFT FOR US TO TAKE!
AND WE WILL TAKE IT--GOD DEMANDS IT!
THE DAY WILL COME WHEN CHARLEMAGNE FALLS AND FRANCIA WITH HIM!
YOU WILL DIE LONG BEFORE FRANCIA EVER DOES.

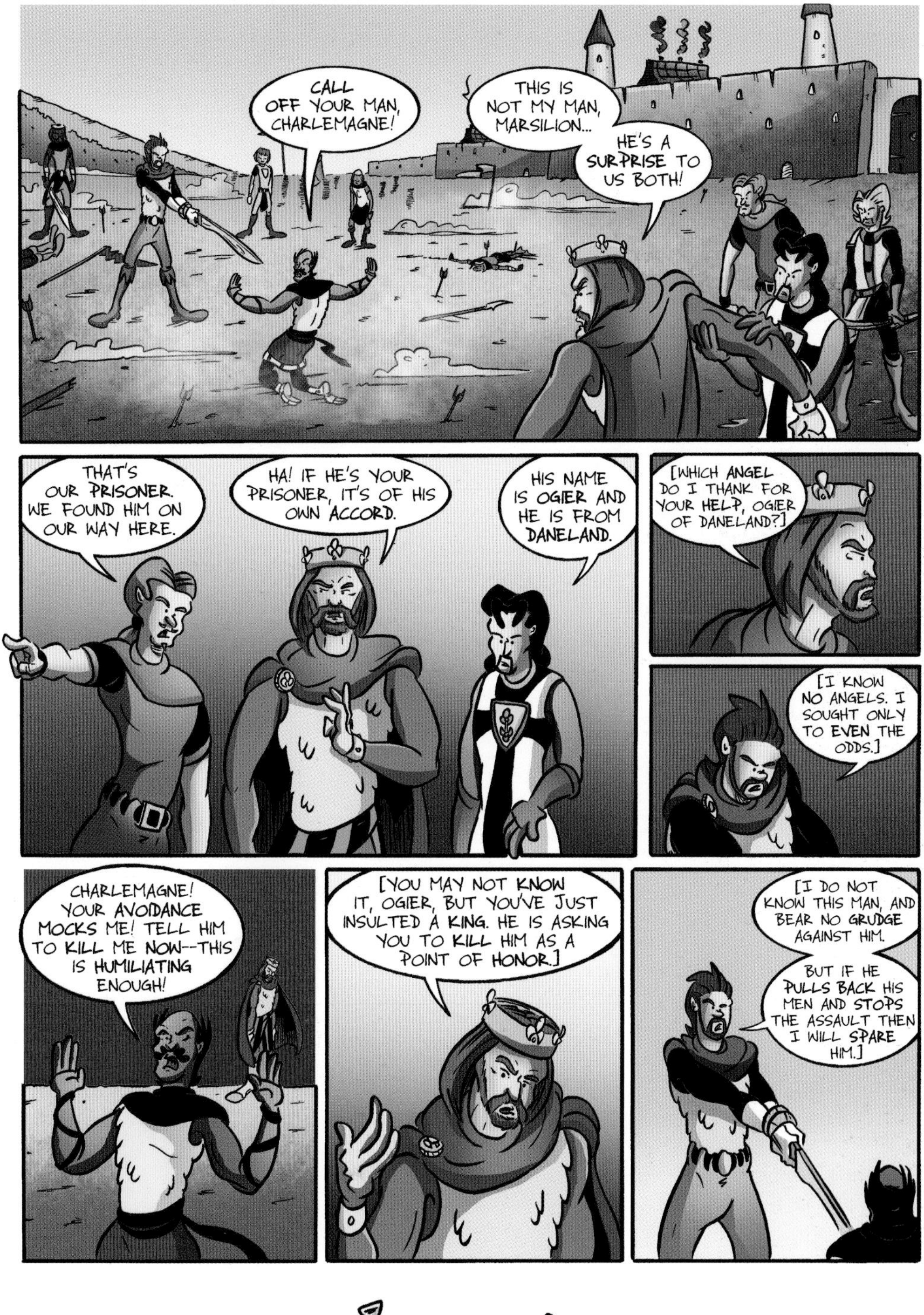
CALL OFF YOUR MAN, CHARLEMAGNE!
THIS IS NOT MY MAN, MARSILION...
HE'S A SURPRISE TO US BOTH!
THAT'S OUR PRISONER. WE FOUND HIM ON OUR WAY HERE.
HA! IF HE'S YOUR PRISONER, IT'S OF HIS OWN ACCORD.
HIS NAME IS OGIER AND HE IS FROM DANELAND.
[WHICH ANGEL DO I THANK FOR YOUR HELP, OGIER OF DANELAND?]
[I KNOW NO ANGELS. I SOUGHT ONLY TO EVEN THE ODDS.]
CHARLEMAGNE! YOUR AVOIDANCE MOCKS ME! TELL HIM TO KILL ME NOW--THIS IS HUMILIATING ENOUGH!
[YOU MAY NOT KNOW IT, OGIER, BUT YOU'VE JUST INSULTED A KING. HE IS ASKING YOU TO KILL HIM AS A POINT OF HONOR.]
[I DO NOT KNOW THIS MAN, AND BEAR NO GRUDGE AGAINST HIM.
BUT IF HE PULLS BACK HIS MEN AND STOPS THE ASSAULT THEN I WILL SPARE HIM.]

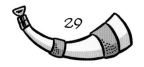

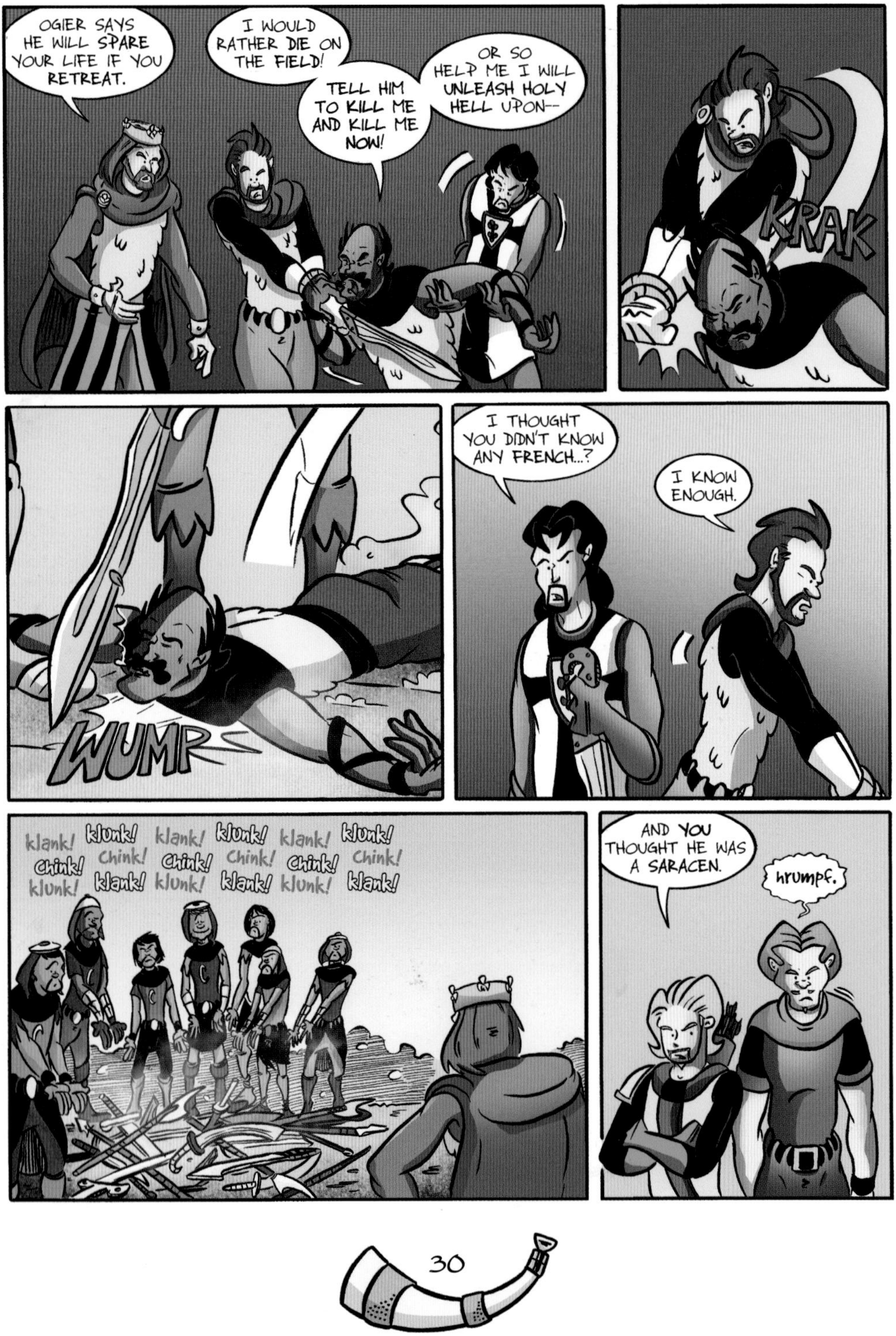
OGIER SAYS HE WILL SPARE YOUR LIFE IF YOU RETREAT.
I WOULD RATHER DIE ON THE FIELD!
TELL HIM TO KILL ME AND KILL ME NOW!
OR SO HELP ME I WILL UNLEASH HOLY HELL UPON--
KRAK
WUMP
I THOUGHT YOU DIDN'T KNOW ANY FRENCH...?
I KNOW ENOUGH.
klank! klunk! klank! klunk! klank! klunk!
Chink! Chink! Chink! Chink! Chink! Chink!
klunk! klank! klunk! klank! klunk! klank!
AND YOU THOUGHT HE WAS A SARACEN.
hrumpf.

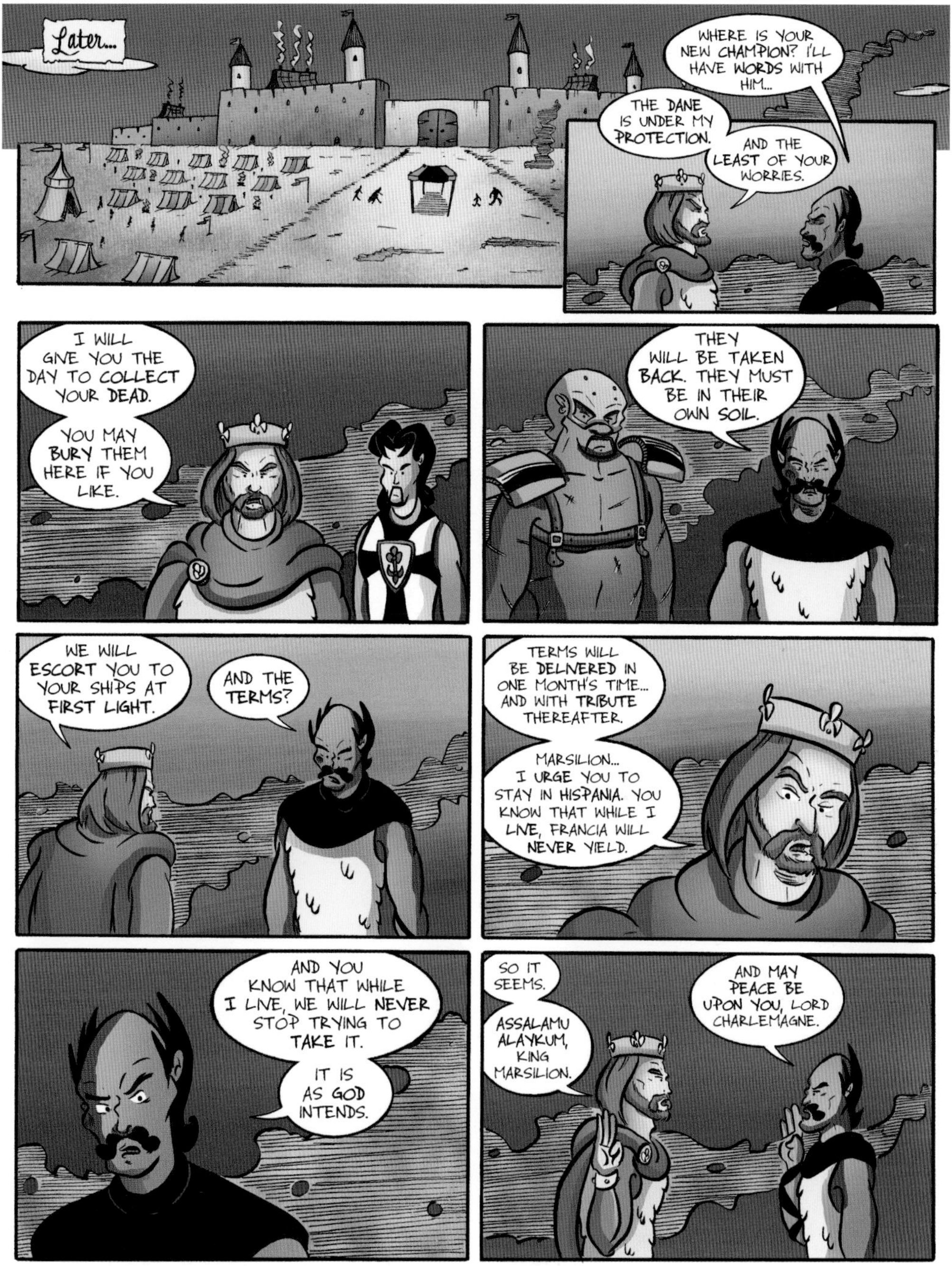
Later...
WHERE IS YOUR NEW CHAMPION? I'LL HAVE WORDS WITH HIM...
THE DANE IS UNDER MY PROTECTION.
AND THE LEAST OF YOUR WORRIES.
I WILL GIVE YOU THE DAY TO COLLECT YOUR DEAD.
YOU MAY BURY THEM HERE IF YOU LIKE.
THEY WILL BE TAKEN BACK. THEY MUST BE IN THEIR OWN SOIL.
WE WILL ESCORT YOU TO YOUR SHIPS AT FIRST LIGHT.
AND THE TERMS?
TERMS WILL BE DELIVERED IN ONE MONTH'S TIME... AND WITH TRIBUTE THEREAFTER.
MARSILION... I URGE YOU TO STAY IN HISPANIA. YOU KNOW THAT WHILE I LIVE, FRANCIA WILL NEVER YIELD.
AND YOU KNOW THAT WHILE I LIVE, WE WILL NEVER STOP TRYING TO TAKE IT.
IT IS AS GOD INTENDS.
SO IT SEEMS.
ASSALAMU ALAYKUM, KING MARSILION.
AND MAY PEACE BE UPON YOU, LORD CHARLEMAGNE.

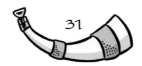

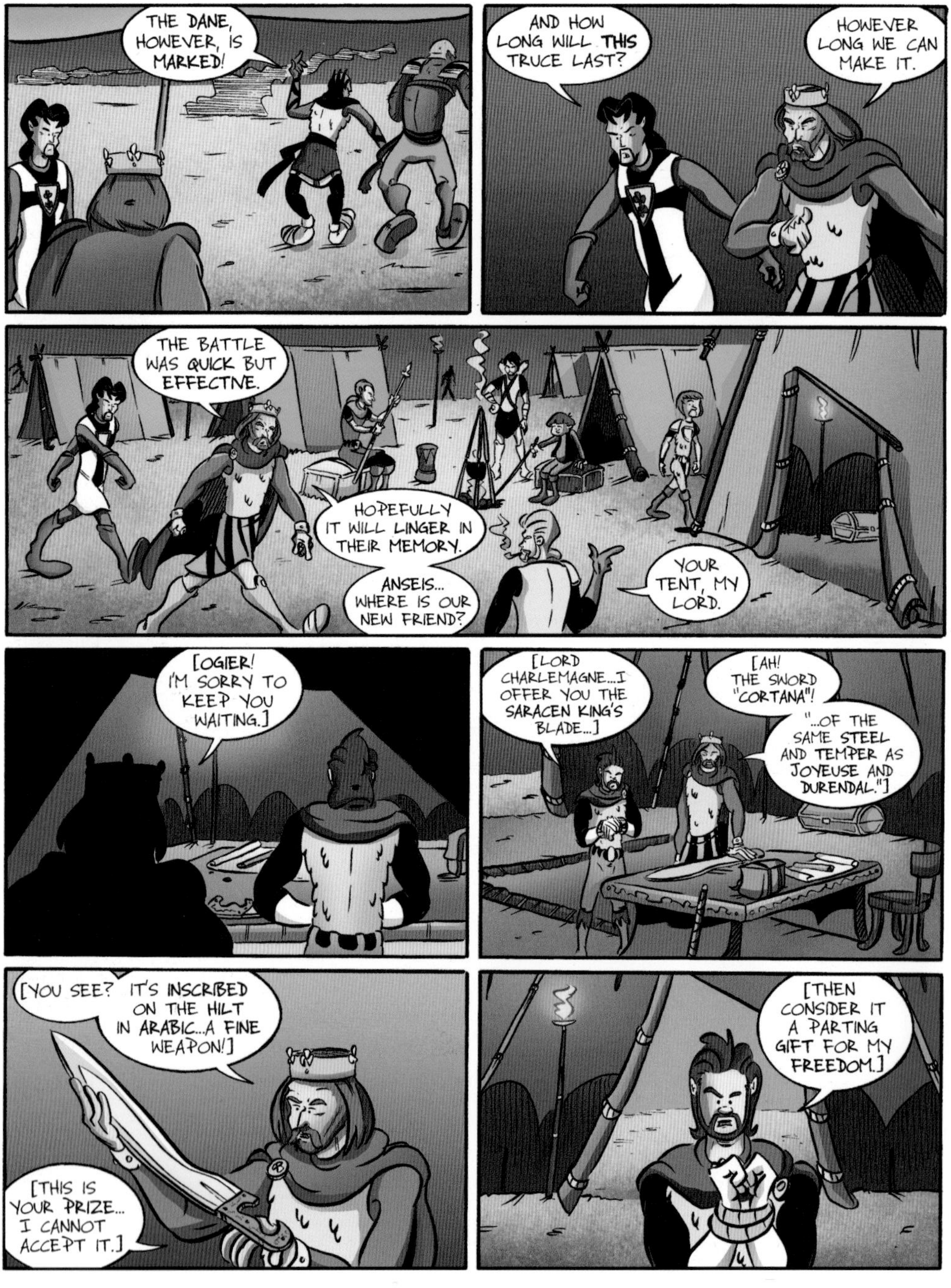
THE DANE, HOWEVER, IS MARKED!
AND HOW LONG WILL THIS TRUCE LAST?
HOWEVER LONG WE CAN MAKE IT.
THE BATTLE WAS QUICK BUT EFFECTIVE.
HOPEFULLY IT WILL LINGER IN THEIR MEMORY.
ANSEIS... WHERE IS OUR NEW FRIEND?
YOUR TENT, MY LORD.
[OGIER! I'M SORRY TO KEEP YOU WAITING.]
[LORD CHARLEMAGNE...I OFFER YOU THE SARACEN KING'S BLADE...]
[AH! THE SWORD "CORTANA"!
"...OF THE SAME STEEL AND TEMPER AS JOYEUSE AND DURENDAL."]
[YOU SEE? IT'S INSCRIBED ON THE HILT IN ARABIC...A FINE WEAPON!]
[THIS IS YOUR PRIZE... I CANNOT ACCEPT IT.]
[THEN CONSIDER IT A PARTING GIFT FOR MY FREEDOM.]

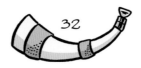

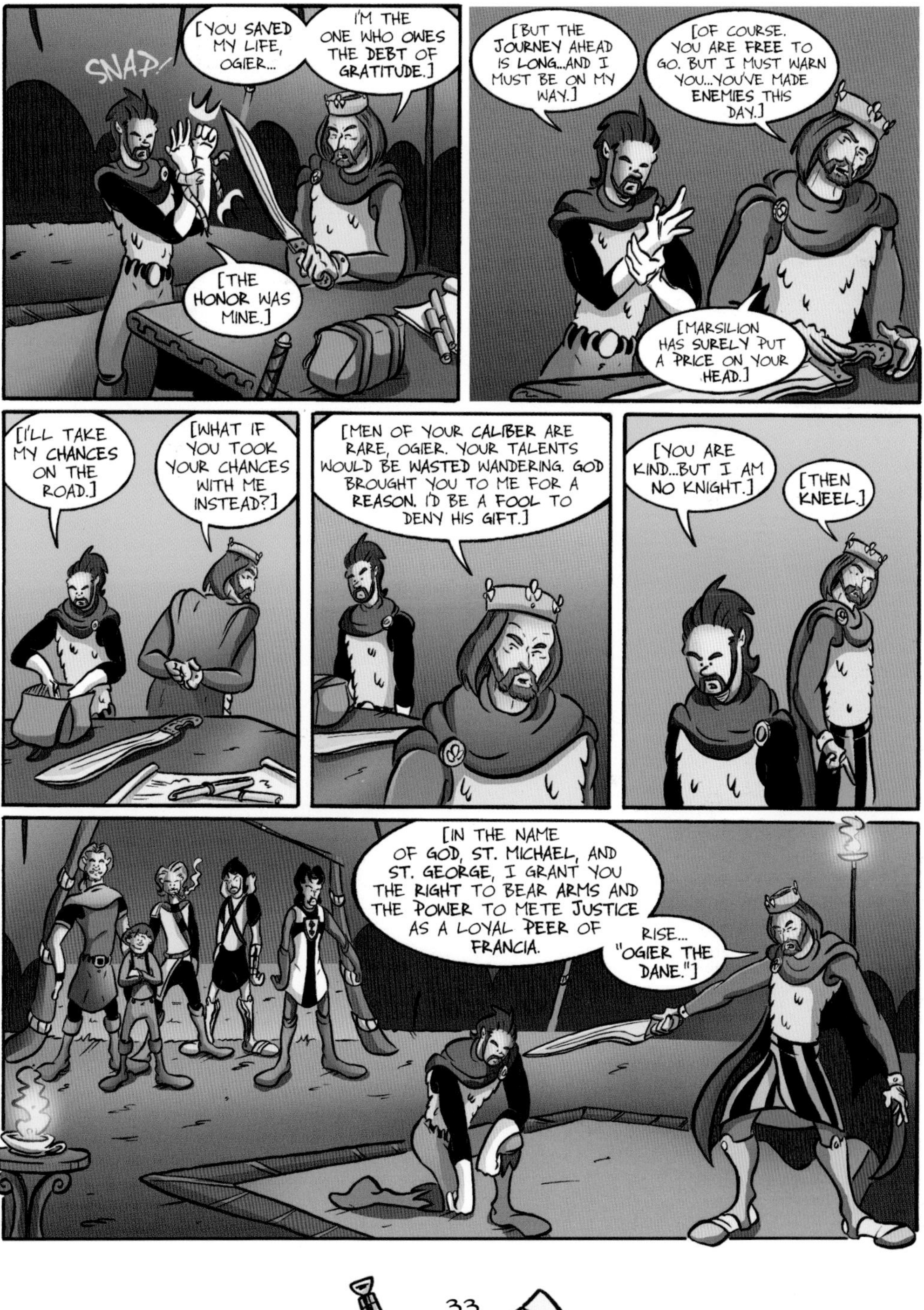
SNAP!
[YOU SAVED MY LIFE, OGIER...
I'M THE ONE WHO OWES THE DEBT OF GRATITUDE.]
[THE HONOR WAS MINE.]
[BUT THE JOURNEY AHEAD IS LONG...AND I MUST BE ON MY WAY.]
[OF COURSE. YOU ARE FREE TO GO. BUT I MUST WARN YOU...YOU'VE MADE ENEMIES THIS DAY.]
[MARSILION HAS SURELY PUT A PRICE ON YOUR HEAD.]
[I'LL TAKE MY CHANCES ON THE ROAD.]
[WHAT IF YOU TOOK YOUR CHANCES WITH ME INSTEAD?]
[MEN OF YOUR CALIBER ARE RARE, OGIER. YOUR TALENTS WOULD BE WASTED WANDERING. GOD BROUGHT YOU TO ME FOR A REASON. I'D BE A FOOL TO DENY HIS GIFT.]
[YOU ARE KIND...BUT I AM NO KNIGHT.]
[THEN KNEEL.]
[IN THE NAME OF GOD, ST. MICHAEL, AND ST. GEORGE, I GRANT YOU THE RIGHT TO BEAR ARMS AND THE POWER TO METE JUSTICE AS A LOYAL PEER OF FRANCIA.
RISE... "OGIER THE DANE."]

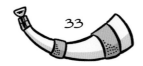

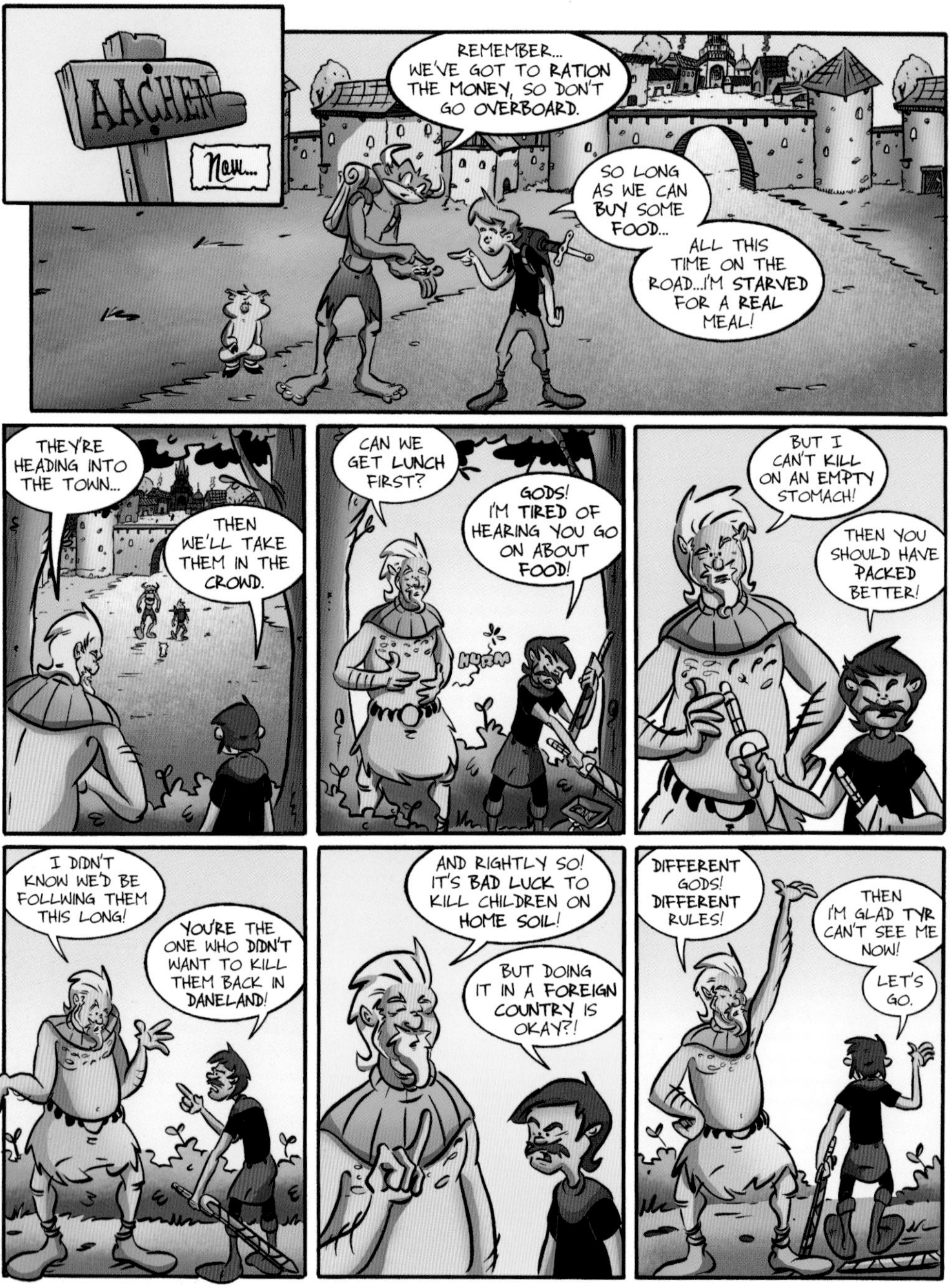
AACHEN
Now...
REMEMBER... WE'VE GOT TO RATION THE MONEY, SO DON'T GO OVERBOARD.
SO LONG AS WE CAN BUY SOME FOOD...
ALL THIS TIME ON THE ROAD...I'M STARVED FOR A REAL MEAL!
THEY'RE HEADING INTO THE TOWN...
THEN WE'LL TAKE THEM IN THE CROWD.
CAN WE GET LUNCH FIRST?
GODS! I'M TIRED OF HEARING YOU GO ON ABOUT FOOD!
HURM
BUT I CAN'T KILL ON AN EMPTY STOMACH!
THEN YOU SHOULD HAVE PACKED BETTER!
I DIDN'T KNOW WE'D BE FOLLWING THEM THIS LONG!
YOU'RE THE ONE WHO DIDN'T WANT TO KILL THEM BACK IN DANELAND!
AND RIGHTLY SO! IT'S BAD LUCK TO KILL CHILDREN ON HOME SOIL!
BUT DOING IT IN A FOREIGN COUNTRY IS OKAY?!
DIFFERENT GODS! DIFFERENT RULES!
THEN I'M GLAD TYR CAN'T SEE ME NOW!
LET'S GO.

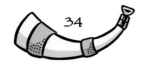

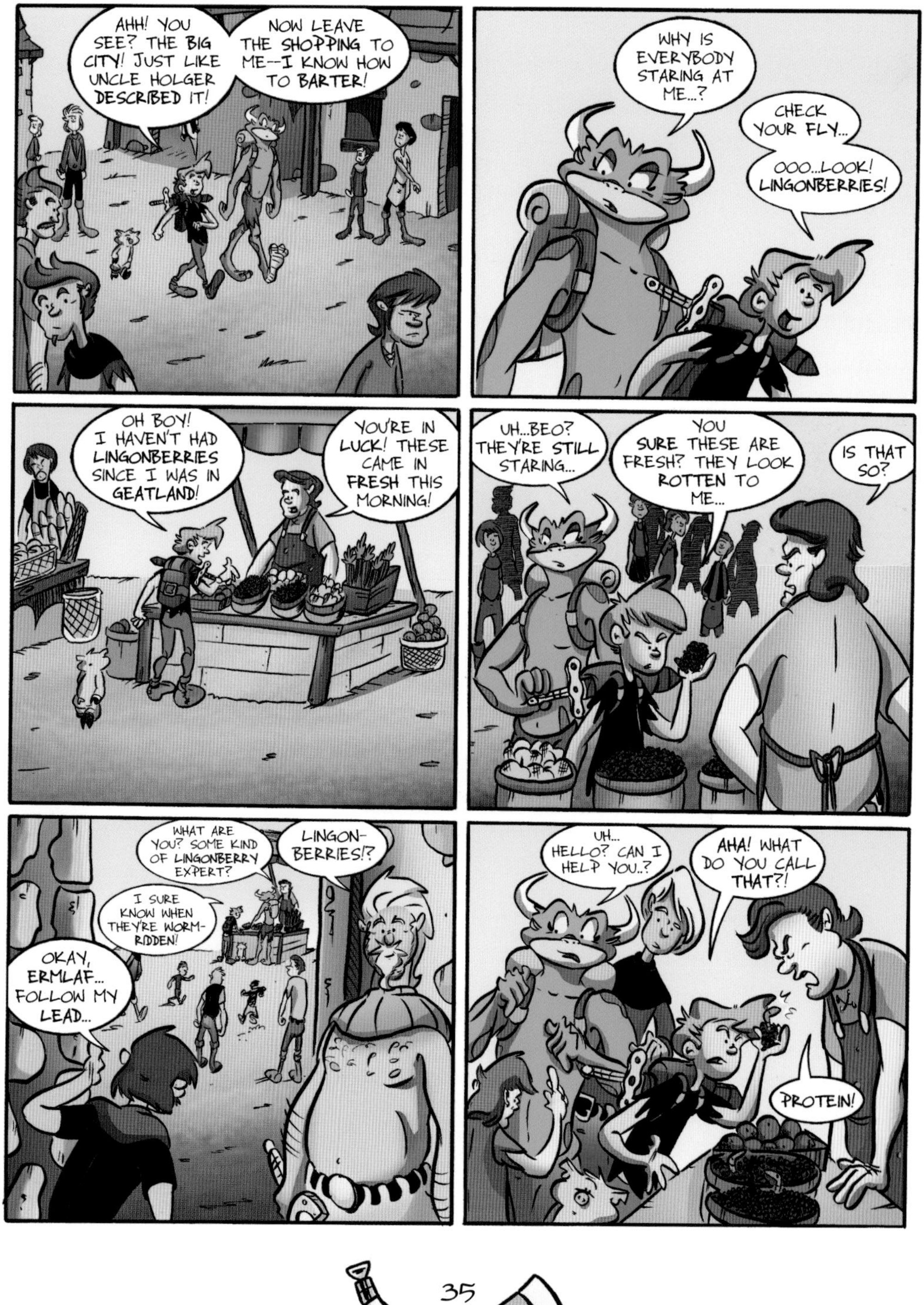
AHH! YOU SEE? THE BIG CITY! JUST LIKE UNCLE HOLGER DESCRIBED IT!
NOW LEAVE THE SHOPPING TO ME--I KNOW HOW TO BARTER!
WHY IS EVERYBODY STARING AT ME...?
CHECK YOUR FLY...
OOO...LOOK! LINGONBERRIES!
OH BOY! I HAVEN'T HAD LINGONBERRIES SINCE I WAS IN GEATLAND!
YOU'RE IN LUCK! THESE CAME IN FRESH THIS MORNING!
UH...BEO? THEY'RE STILL STARING...
YOU SURE THESE ARE FRESH? THEY LOOK ROTTEN TO ME...
IS THAT SO?
WHAT ARE YOU? SOME KIND OF LINGONBERRY EXPERT?
LINGON-BERRIES!?
I SURE KNOW WHEN THEY'RE WORM-RIDDEN!
OKAY, ERMLAF... FOLLOW MY LEAD...
UH... HELLO? CAN I HELP YOU..?
AHA! WHAT DO YOU CALL THAT?!
PROTEIN!

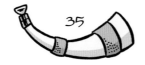

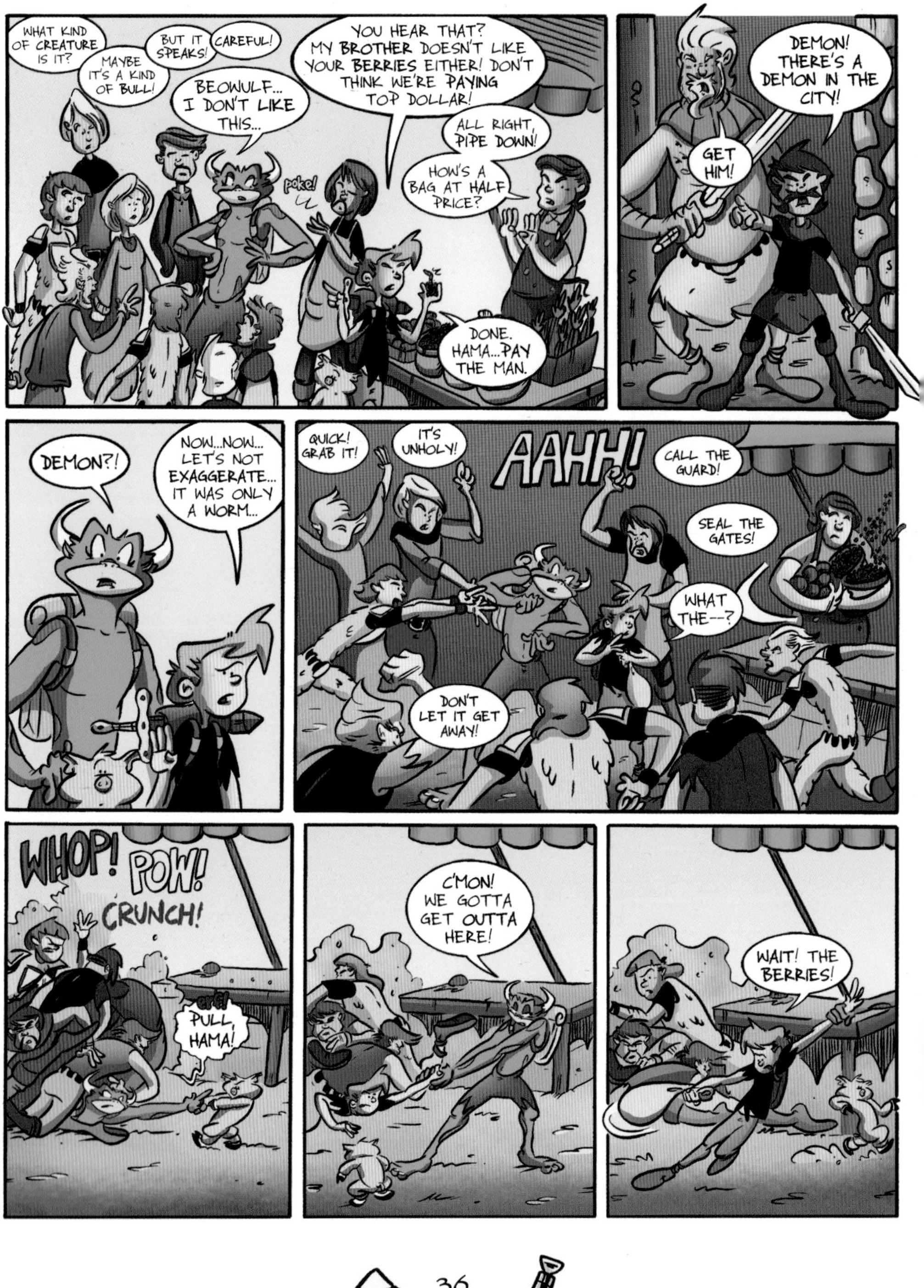

WHAT KIND OF CREATURE IS IT?
MAYBE IT'S A KIND OF BULL!
BUT IT SPEAKS!
CAREFUL!
BEOWULF... I DON'T LIKE THIS...
YOU HEAR THAT? MY BROTHER DOESN'T LIKE YOUR BERRIES EITHER! DON'T THINK WE'RE PAYING TOP DOLLAR!
poke!
ALL RIGHT, PIPE DOWN!
HOW'S A BAG AT HALF PRICE?
DONE. HAMA...PAY THE MAN.
DEMON! THERE'S A DEMON IN THE CITY!
GET HIM!
DEMON?!
NOW...NOW... LET'S NOT EXAGGERATE... IT WAS ONLY A WORM...
QUICK! GRAB IT!
IT'S UNHOLY!
AAHH!
CALL THE GUARD!
SEAL THE GATES!
WHAT THE--?
DON'T LET IT GET AWAY!
WHOP!
POW!
CRUNCH!
PULL, HAMA!
C'MON! WE GOTTA GET OUTTA HERE!
WAIT! THE BERRIES!

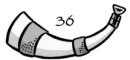

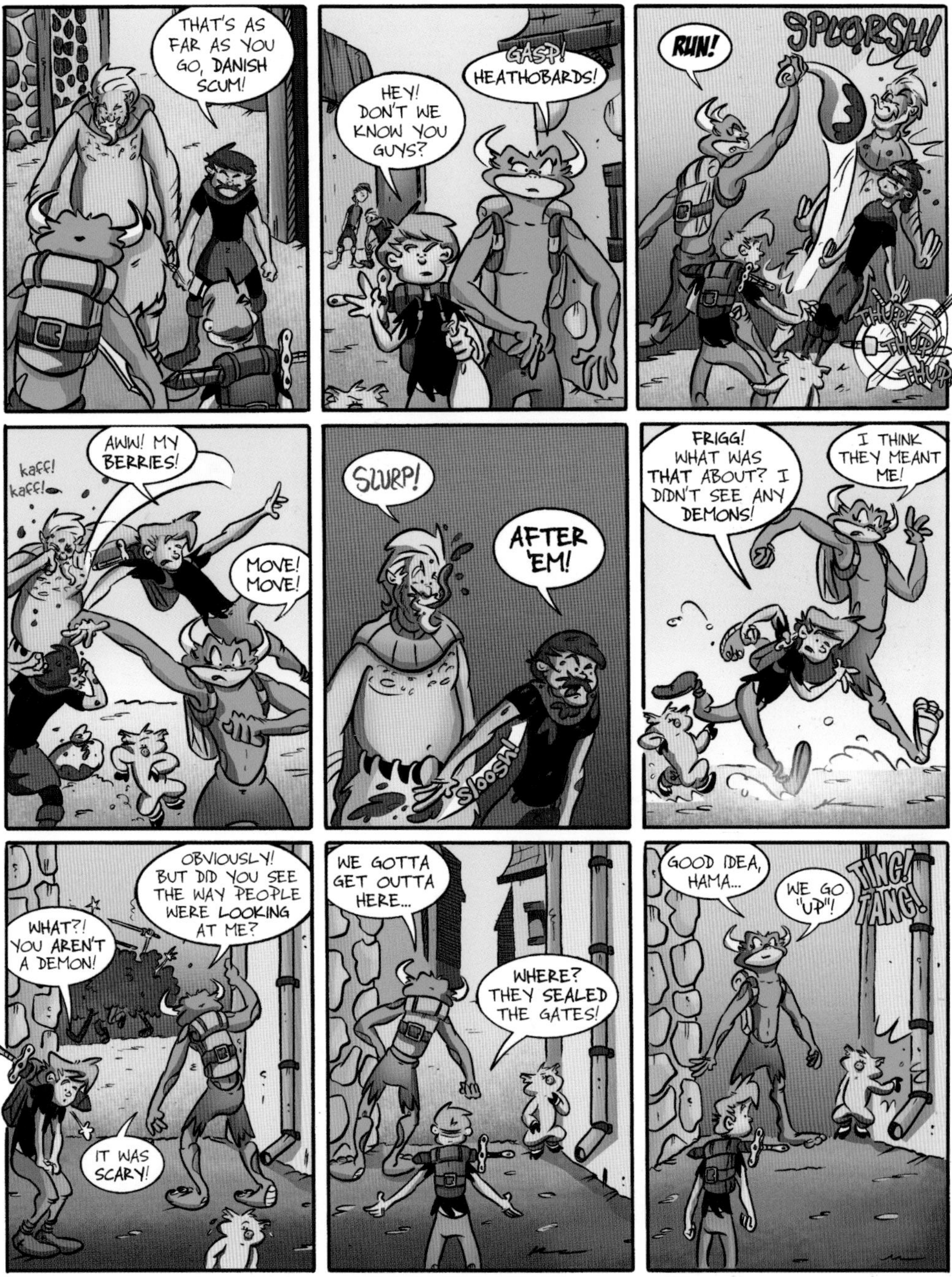
THAT'S AS FAR AS YOU GO, DANISH SCUM!
HEY! DON'T WE KNOW YOU GUYS?
GASP! HEATHOBARDS!
RUN!
SPLORSH!
THUP! THUP! THUP!
kaff! kaff!
AWW! MY BERRIES!
MOVE! MOVE!
SLURP!
AFTER 'EM!
sloosh!
FRIGG! WHAT WAS THAT ABOUT? I DIDN'T SEE ANY DEMONS!
I THINK THEY MEANT ME!
WHAT?! YOU AREN'T A DEMON!
OBVIOUSLY! BUT DID YOU SEE THE WAY PEOPLE WERE LOOKING AT ME?
IT WAS SCARY!
WE GOTTA GET OUTTA HERE...
WHERE? THEY SEALED THE GATES!
GOOD IDEA, HAMA...
WE GO "UP"!
TING! TANG!

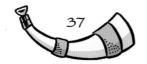

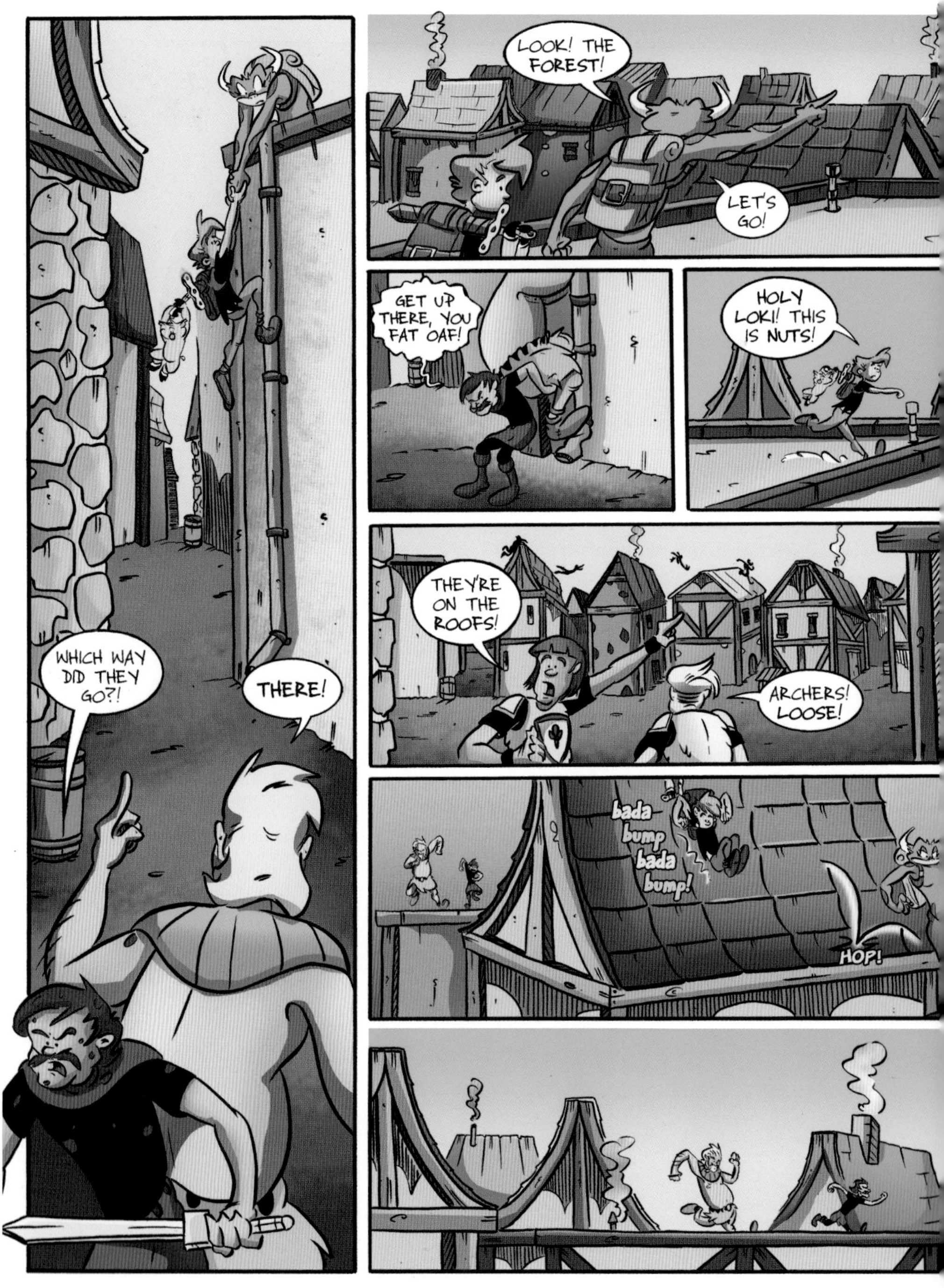
WHICH WAY DID THEY GO?!
THERE!
LOOK! THE FOREST!
LET'S GO!
GET UP THERE, YOU FAT OAF!
HOLY LOKI! THIS IS NUTS!
THEY'RE ON THE ROOFS!
ARCHERS! LOOSE!
bada-bump bada bump!
HOP!

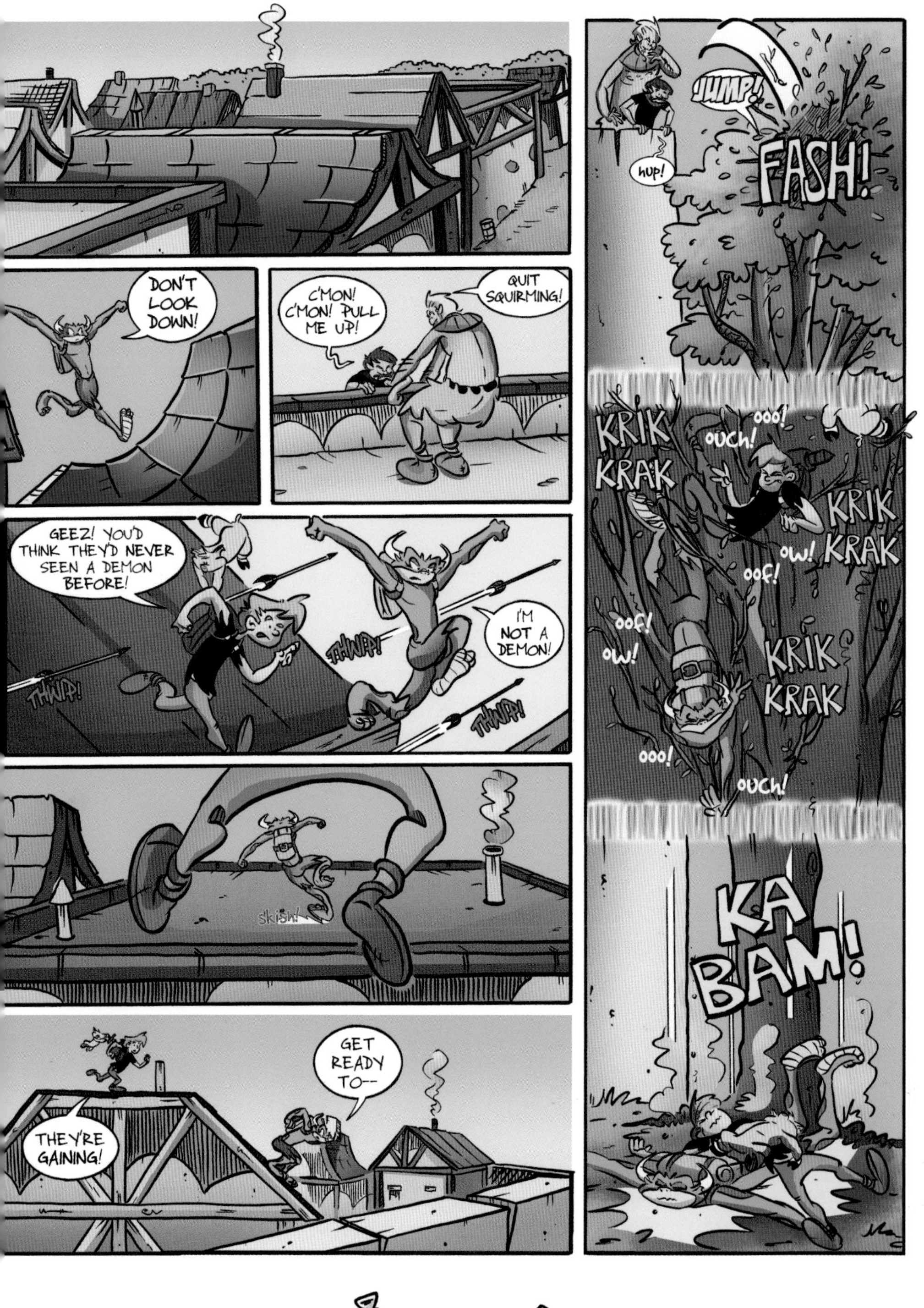
DON'T LOOK DOWN!
C'MON! C'MON! PULL ME UP!
QUIT SQUIRMING!
GEEZ! YOU'D THINK THEY'D NEVER SEEN A DEMON BEFORE!
I'M NOT A DEMON!
THWIP!
THWIP!
THWIP!
SKISH!
THEY'RE GAINING!
GET READY TO--
JUMP!
hup!
FASH!
KRIK KRAK
OUCH!
OOO!
KRIK KRAK
OW!
OOF!
OOF!
OW!
KRIK KRAK
OOO!
OUCH!
KA BAM!

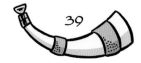

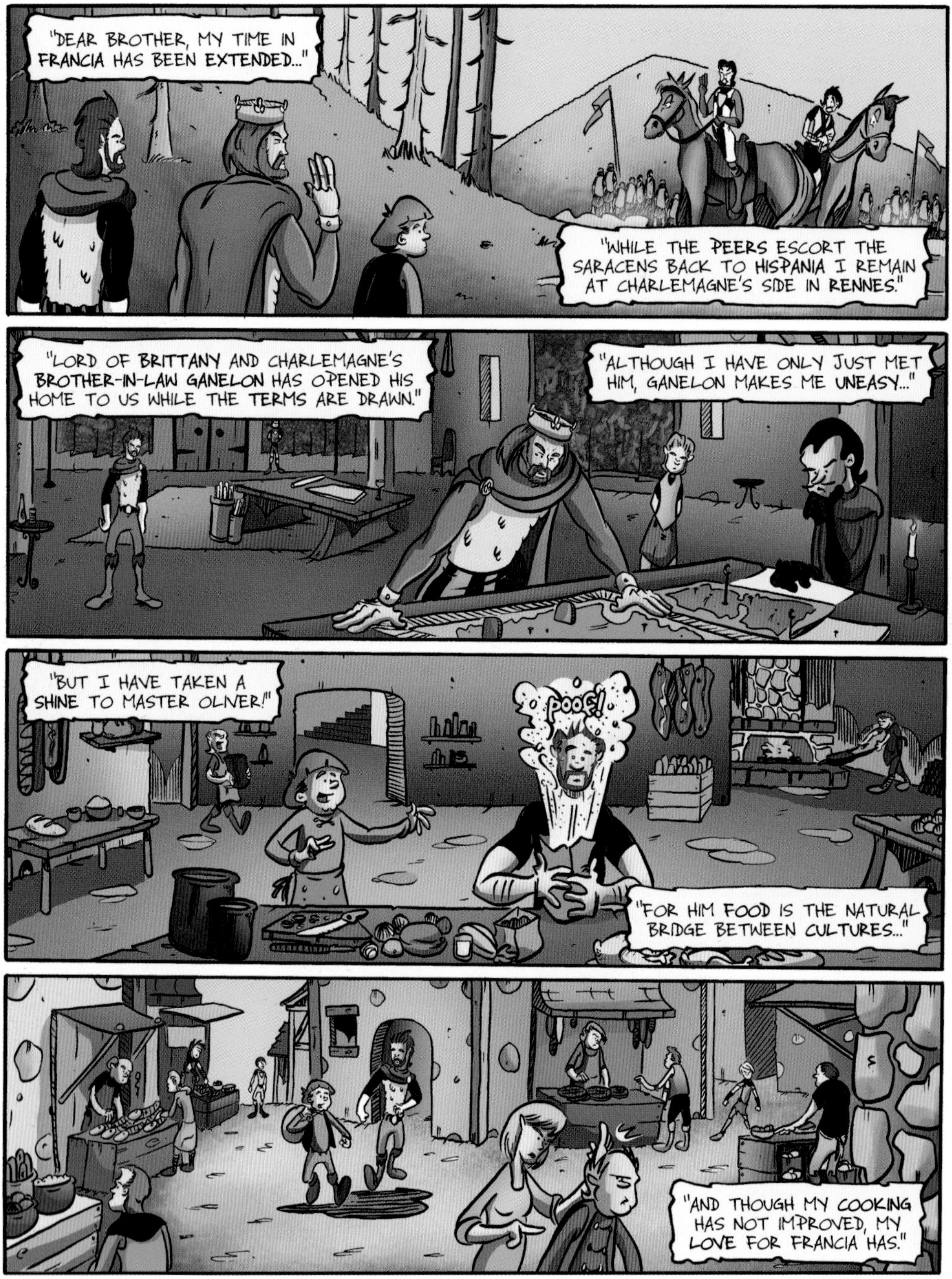
"DEAR BROTHER, MY TIME IN FRANCIA HAS BEEN EXTENDED..."
"WHILE THE PEERS ESCORT THE SARACENS BACK TO HISPANIA I REMAIN AT CHARLEMAGNE'S SIDE IN RENNES."
"LORD OF BRITTANY AND CHARLEMAGNE'S BROTHER-IN-LAW GANELON HAS OPENED HIS HOME TO US WHILE THE TERMS ARE DRAWN."
"ALTHOUGH I HAVE ONLY JUST MET HIM, GANELON MAKES ME UNEASY..."
"BUT I HAVE TAKEN A SHINE TO MASTER OLIVER!"
POOF!
"FOR HIM FOOD IS THE NATURAL BRIDGE BETWEEN CULTURES..."
"AND THOUGH MY COOKING HAS NOT IMPROVED, MY LOVE FOR FRANCIA HAS."

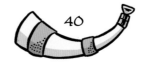

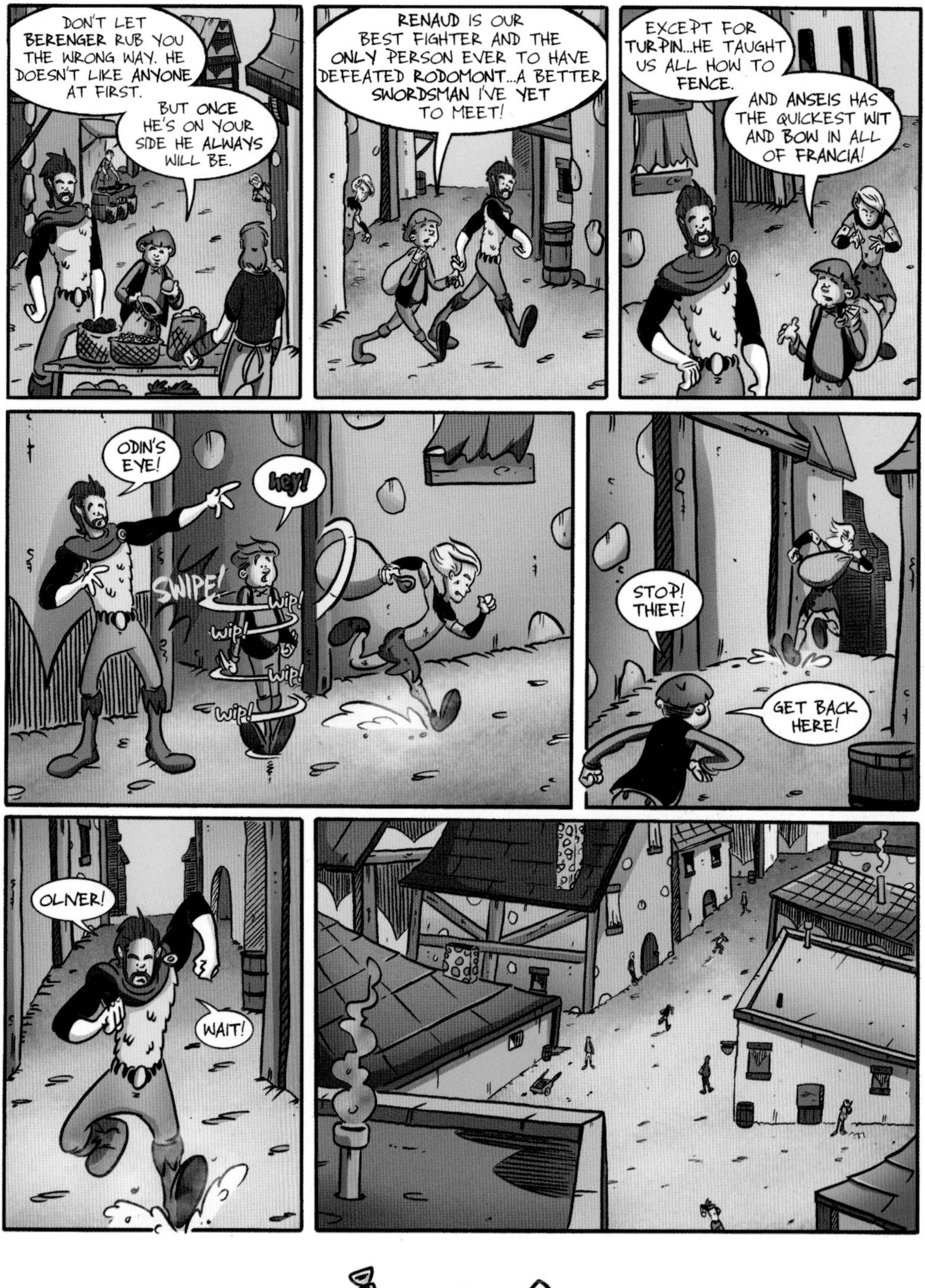
DON'T LET BERENGER RUB YOU THE WRONG WAY. HE DOESN'T LIKE ANYONE AT FIRST.
BUT ONCE HE'S ON YOUR SIDE HE ALWAYS WILL BE.
RENAUD IS OUR BEST FIGHTER AND THE ONLY PERSON EVER TO HAVE DEFEATED RODOMONT...A BETTER SWORDSMAN I'VE YET TO MEET!
EXCEPT FOR TURPIN...HE TAUGHT US ALL HOW TO FENCE.
AND ANSEIS HAS THE QUICKEST WIT AND BOW IN ALL OF FRANCIA!
ODIN'S EYE!
hey!
SWIPE!
wip!
wip!
wip!
wip!
STOP! THIEF!
GET BACK HERE!
OLIVER!
WAIT!

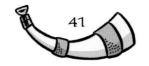

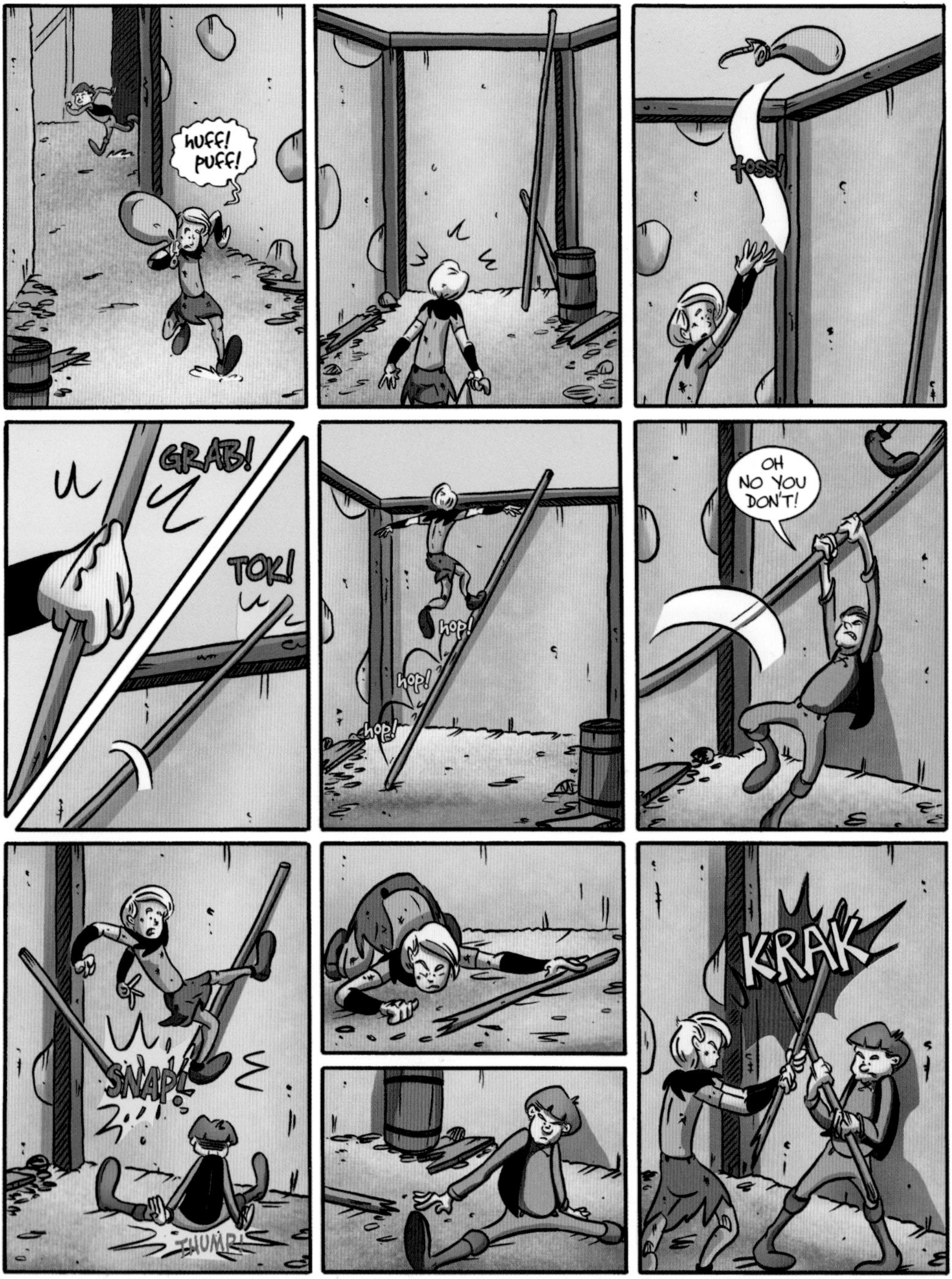
HUFF! PUFF!
TOSS!
GRAB!
TOK!
HOP!
HOP!
HOP!
OH NO YOU DON'T!
SNAP!
THUMP!
KRAK

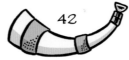

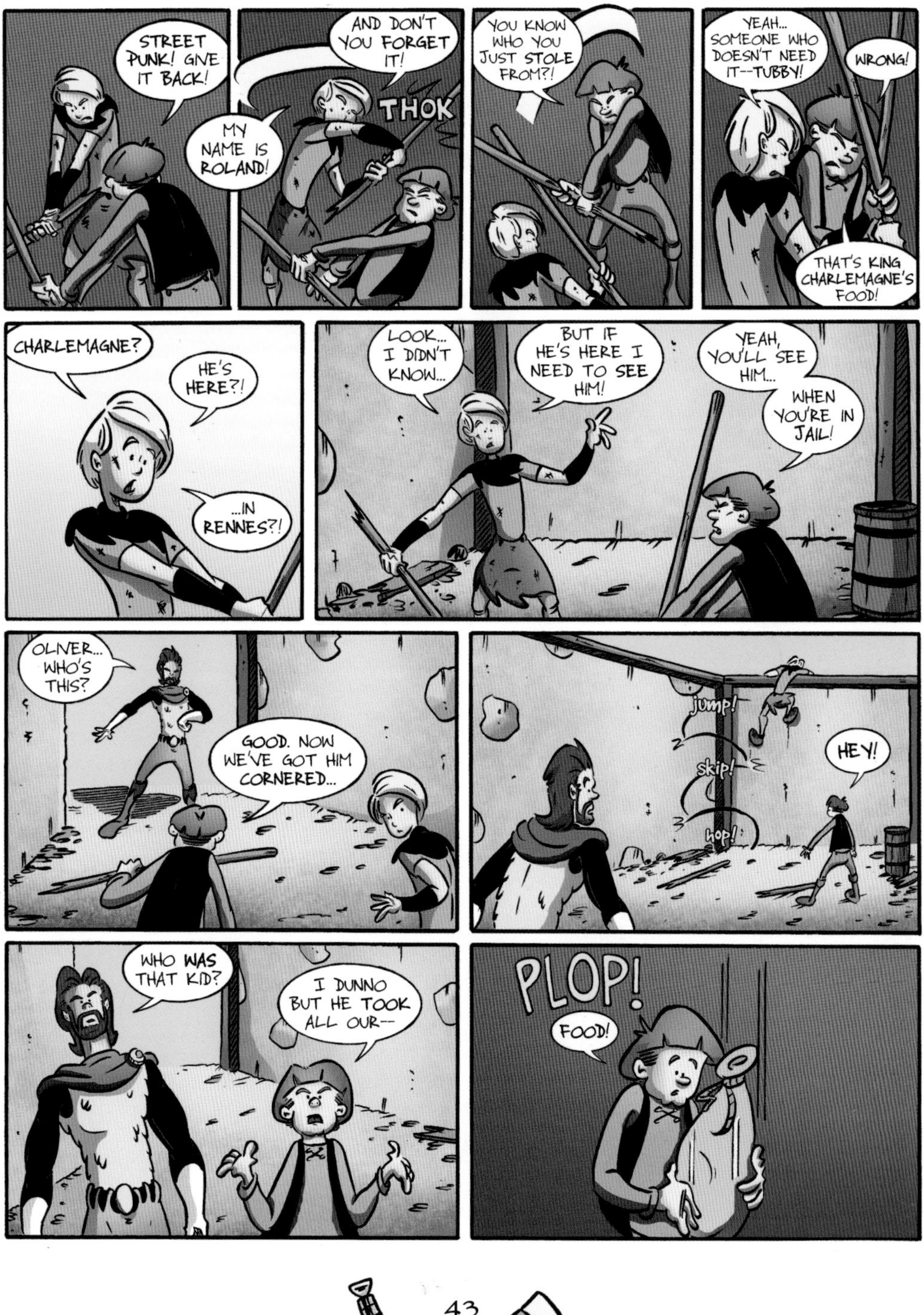
STREET PUNK! GIVE IT BACK!
MY NAME IS ROLAND!
AND DON'T YOU FORGET IT!
THOK
YOU KNOW WHO YOU JUST STOLE FROM?!
YEAH... SOMEONE WHO DOESN'T NEED IT--TUBBY!
WRONG!
THAT'S KING CHARLEMAGNE'S FOOD!
CHARLEMAGNE?
HE'S HERE?!
...IN RENNES?!
LOOK... I DIDN'T KNOW...
BUT IF HE'S HERE I NEED TO SEE HIM!
YEAH, YOU'LL SEE HIM...
WHEN YOU'RE IN JAIL!
OLIVER... WHO'S THIS?
GOOD. NOW WE'VE GOT HIM CORNERED...
jump!
skip!
hop!
HEY!
WHO WAS THAT KID?
I DUNNO BUT HE TOOK ALL OUR--
PLOP!
FOOD!

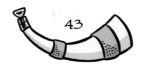

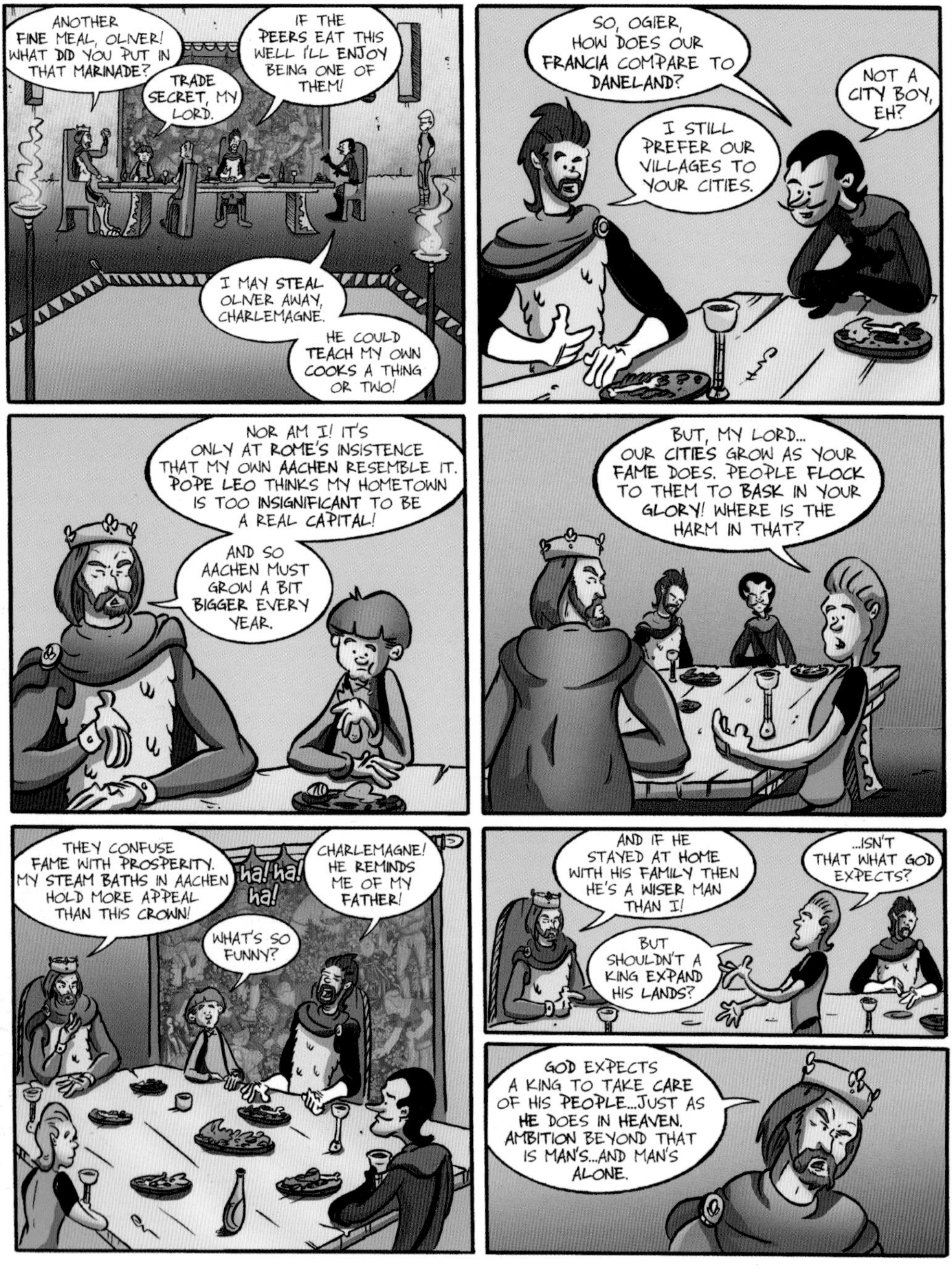
ANOTHER FINE MEAL, OLIVER! WHAT DID YOU PUT IN THAT MARINADE?
TRADE SECRET, MY LORD.
IF THE PEERS EAT THIS WELL I'LL ENJOY BEING ONE OF THEM!
I MAY STEAL OLIVER AWAY, CHARLEMAGNE.
HE COULD TEACH MY OWN COOKS A THING OR TWO!
SO, OGIER, HOW DOES OUR FRANCIA COMPARE TO DANELAND?
I STILL PREFER OUR VILLAGES TO YOUR CITIES.
NOT A CITY BOY, EH?
NOR AM I! IT'S ONLY AT ROME'S INSISTENCE THAT MY OWN AACHEN RESEMBLE IT. POPE LEO THINKS MY HOMETOWN IS TOO INSIGNIFICANT TO BE A REAL CAPITAL!
AND SO AACHEN MUST GROW A BIT BIGGER EVERY YEAR.
BUT, MY LORD... OUR CITIES GROW AS YOUR FAME DOES. PEOPLE FLOCK TO THEM TO BASK IN YOUR GLORY! WHERE IS THE HARM IN THAT?
THEY CONFUSE FAME WITH PROSPERITY. MY STEAM BATHS IN AACHEN HOLD MORE APPEAL THAN THIS CROWN!
ha! ha! ha!
CHARLEMAGNE! HE REMINDS ME OF MY FATHER!
WHAT'S SO FUNNY?
AND IF HE STAYED AT HOME WITH HIS FAMILY THEN HE'S A WISER MAN THAN I!
BUT SHOULDN'T A KING EXPAND HIS LANDS?
...ISN'T THAT WHAT GOD EXPECTS?
GOD EXPECTS A KING TO TAKE CARE OF HIS PEOPLE...JUST AS HE DOES IN HEAVEN. AMBITION BEYOND THAT IS MAN'S...AND MAN'S ALONE.

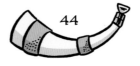

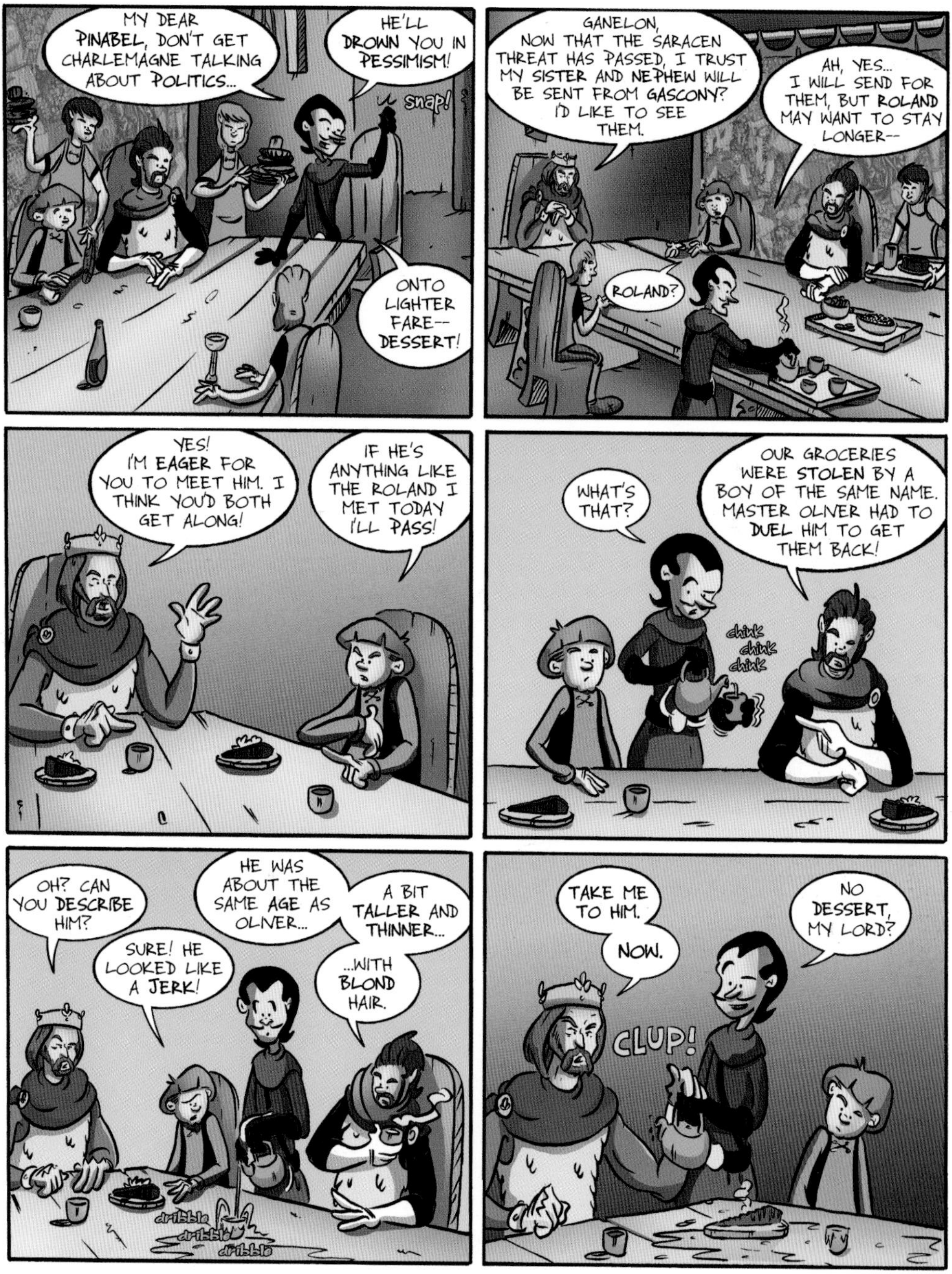

MY DEAR PINABEL, DON'T GET CHARLEMAGNE TALKING ABOUT POLITICS...
HE'LL DROWN YOU IN PESSIMISM!
snap!
ONTO LIGHTER FARE-- DESSERT!
GANELON, NOW THAT THE SARACEN THREAT HAS PASSED, I TRUST MY SISTER AND NEPHEW WILL BE SENT FROM GASCONY? I'D LIKE TO SEE THEM.
AH, YES... I WILL SEND FOR THEM, BUT ROLAND MAY WANT TO STAY LONGER--
ROLAND?
YES! I'M EAGER FOR YOU TO MEET HIM. I THINK YOU'D BOTH GET ALONG!
IF HE'S ANYTHING LIKE THE ROLAND I MET TODAY I'LL PASS!
WHAT'S THAT?
OUR GROCERIES WERE STOLEN BY A BOY OF THE SAME NAME. MASTER OLIVER HAD TO DUEL HIM TO GET THEM BACK!
chink chink chink
OH? CAN YOU DESCRIBE HIM?
SURE! HE LOOKED LIKE A JERK!
HE WAS ABOUT THE SAME AGE AS OLIVER...
A BIT TALLER AND THINNER...
...WITH BLOND HAIR.
dribble dribble dribble
TAKE ME TO HIM.
NOW.
NO DESSERT, MY LORD?
CLUP!

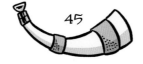

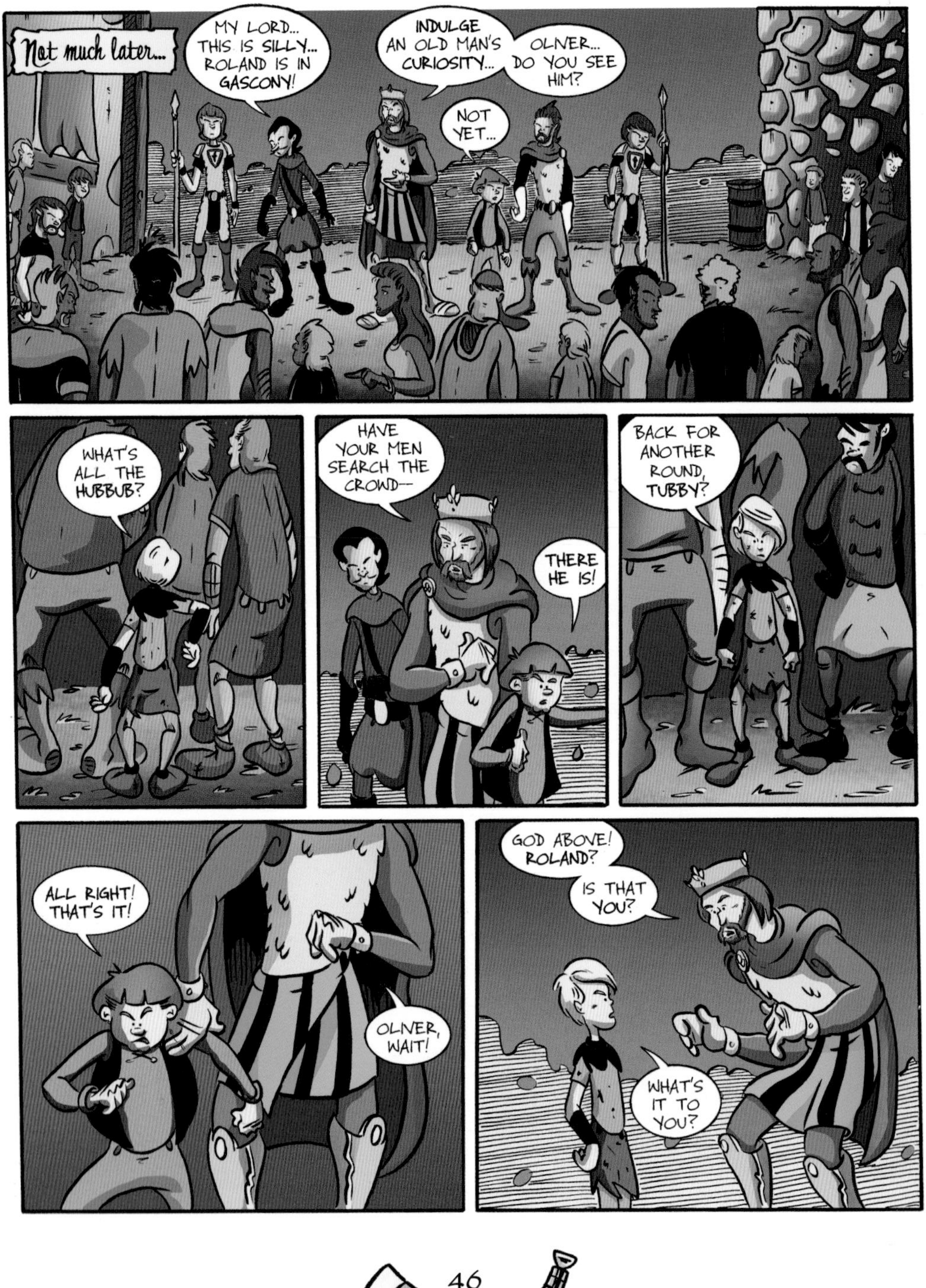
Not much later...
MY LORD... THIS IS SILLY... ROLAND IS IN GASCONY!
INDULGE AN OLD MAN'S CURIOSITY...
OLIVER... DO YOU SEE HIM?
NOT YET...
WHAT'S ALL THE HUBBUB?
HAVE YOUR MEN SEARCH THE CROWD--
THERE HE IS!
BACK FOR ANOTHER ROUND, TUBBY?
ALL RIGHT! THAT'S IT!
OLIVER, WAIT!
GOD ABOVE! ROLAND?
IS THAT YOU?
WHAT'S IT TO YOU?

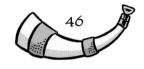

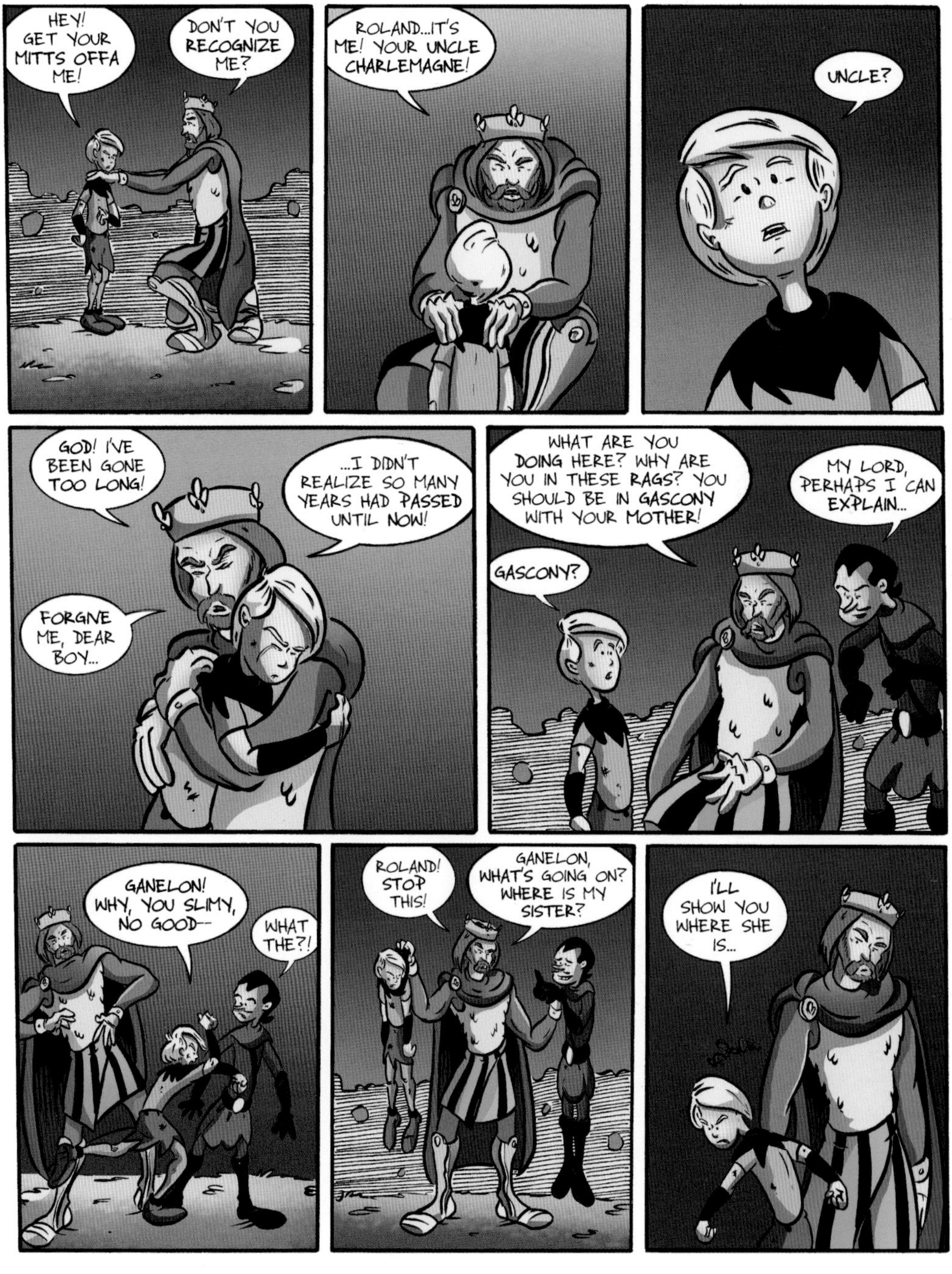
HEY! GET YOUR MITTS OFFA ME!
DON'T YOU RECOGNIZE ME?
ROLAND...IT'S ME! YOUR UNCLE CHARLEMAGNE!
UNCLE?
GOD! I'VE BEEN GONE TOO LONG!
...I DIDN'T REALIZE SO MANY YEARS HAD PASSED UNTIL NOW!
FORGIVE ME, DEAR BOY...
WHAT ARE YOU DOING HERE? WHY ARE YOU IN THESE RAGS? YOU SHOULD BE IN GASCONY WITH YOUR MOTHER!
MY LORD, PERHAPS I CAN EXPLAIN...
GASCONY?
GANELON! WHY, YOU SLIMY, NO GOOD--
WHAT THE?!
ROLAND! STOP THIS!
GANELON, WHAT'S GOING ON? WHERE IS MY SISTER?
I'LL SHOW YOU WHERE SHE IS...

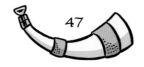

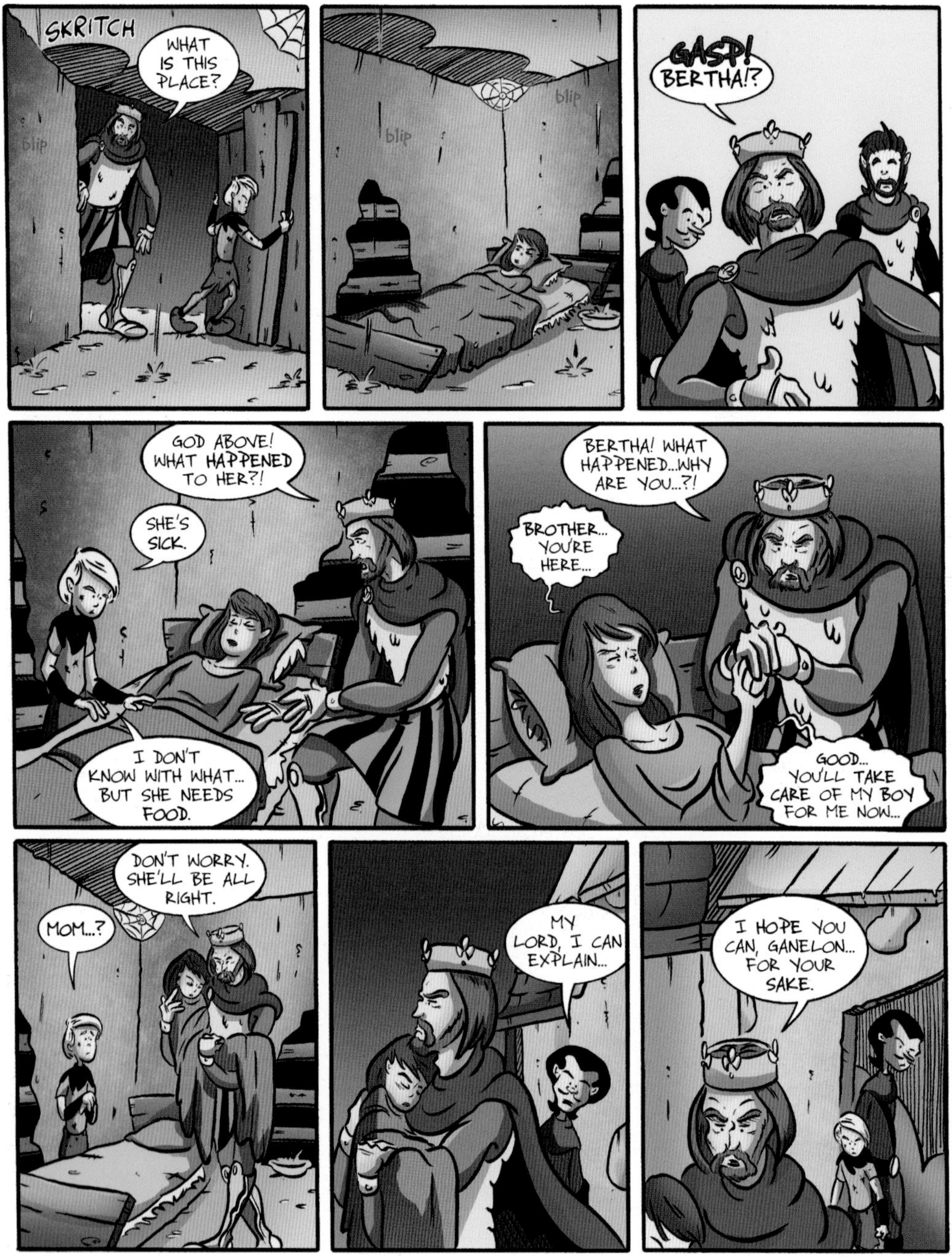
SKRITCH
WHAT IS THIS PLACE?
blip
blip
blip
GASP! BERTHA!?
GOD ABOVE! WHAT HAPPENED TO HER?!
SHE'S SICK.
I DON'T KNOW WITH WHAT... BUT SHE NEEDS FOOD.
BERTHA! WHAT HAPPENED...WHY ARE YOU...?!
BROTHER... YOU'RE HERE...
GOOD... YOU'LL TAKE CARE OF MY BOY FOR ME NOW...
DON'T WORRY. SHE'LL BE ALL RIGHT.
MOM...?
MY LORD, I CAN EXPLAIN...
I HOPE YOU CAN, GANELON... FOR YOUR SAKE.

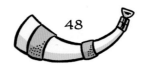

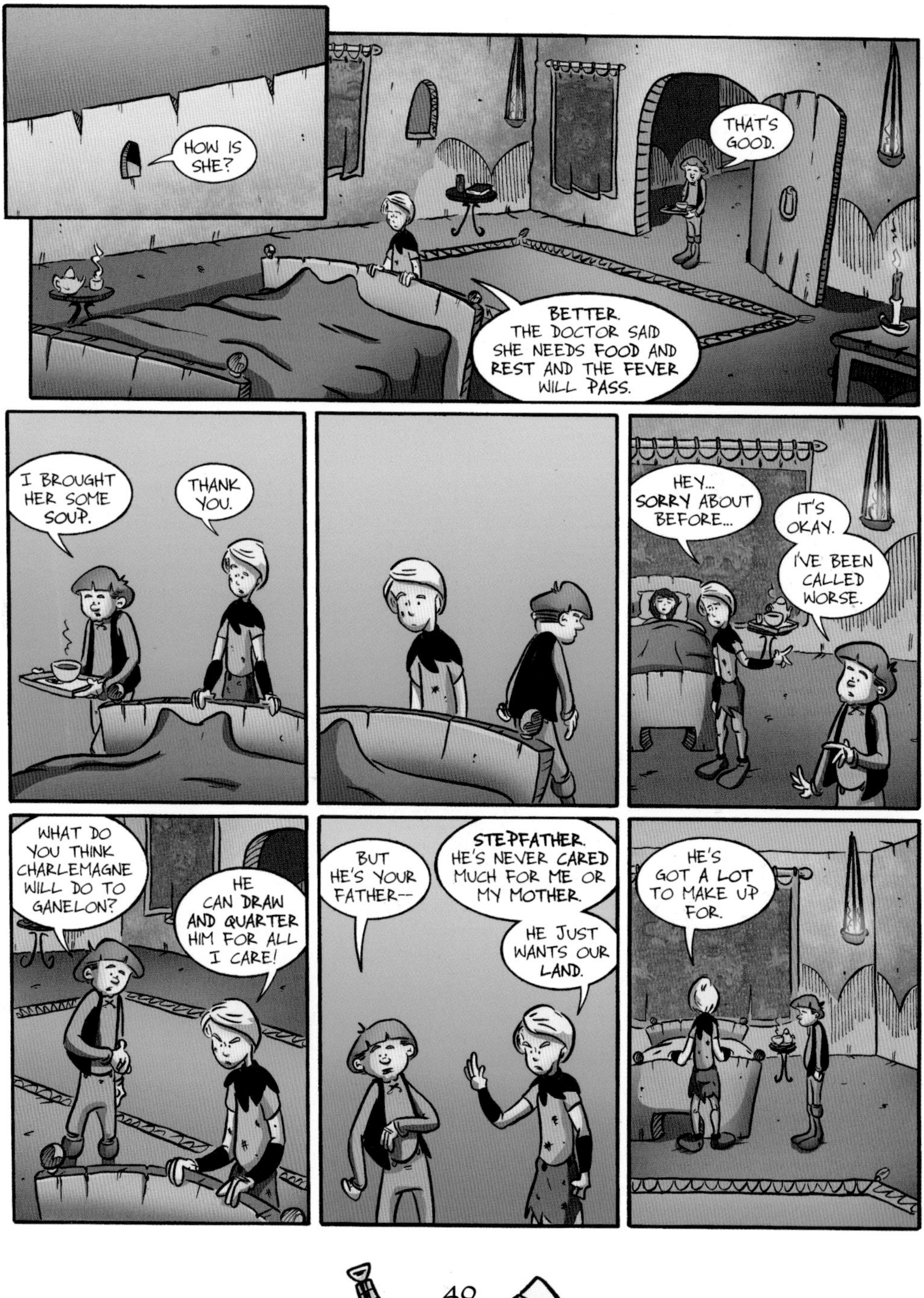
HOW IS SHE?
THAT'S GOOD.
BETTER. THE DOCTOR SAID SHE NEEDS FOOD AND REST AND THE FEVER WILL PASS.
I BROUGHT HER SOME SOUP.
THANK YOU.
HEY... SORRY ABOUT BEFORE...
IT'S OKAY.
I'VE BEEN CALLED WORSE.
WHAT DO YOU THINK CHARLEMAGNE WILL DO TO GANELON?
HE CAN DRAW AND QUARTER HIM FOR ALL I CARE!
BUT HE'S YOUR FATHER--
STEPFATHER. HE'S NEVER CARED MUCH FOR ME OR MY MOTHER.
HE JUST WANTS OUR LAND.
HE'S GOT A LOT TO MAKE UP FOR.

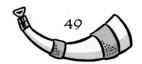

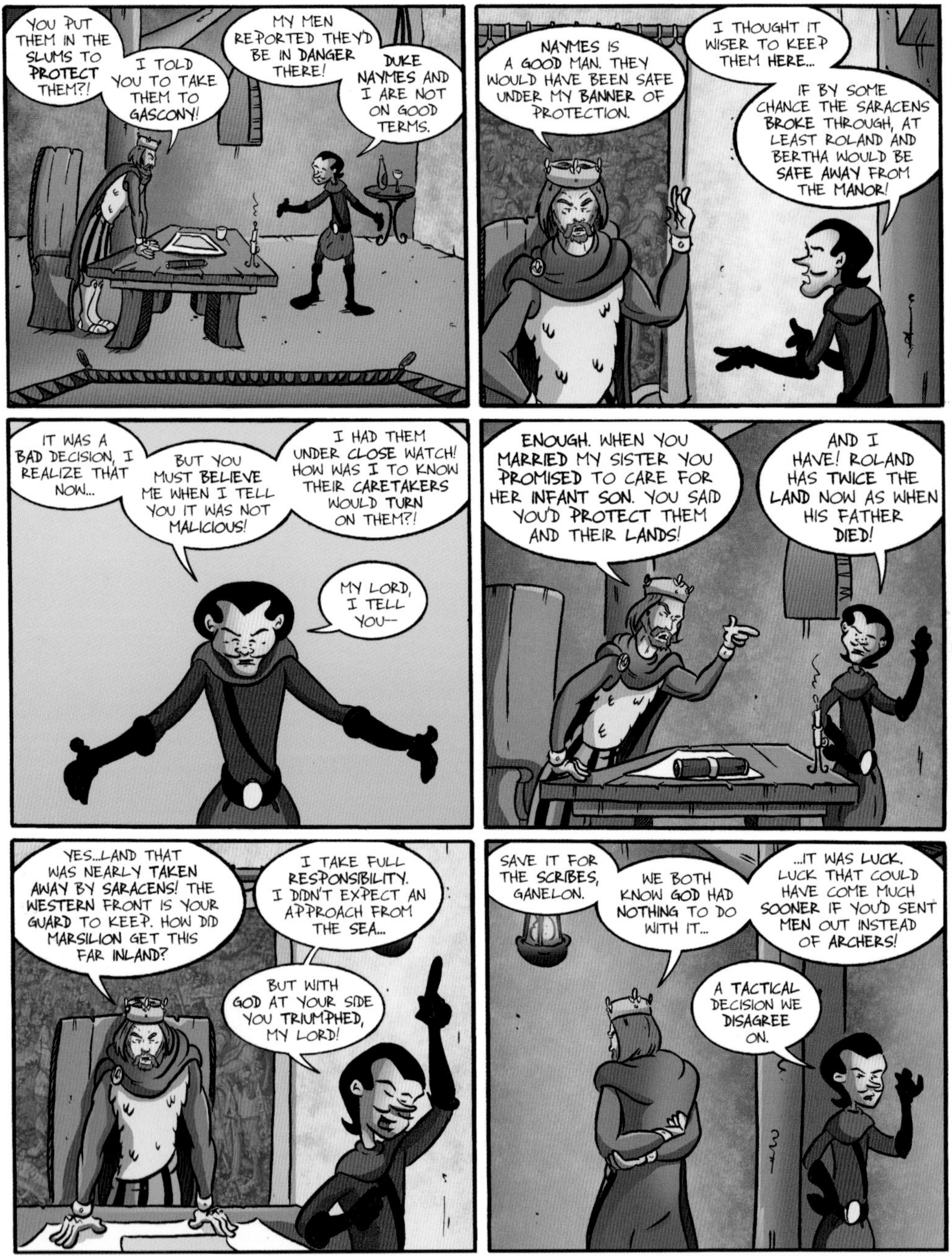
YOU PUT THEM IN THE SLUMS TO PROTECT THEM?!
I TOLD YOU TO TAKE THEM TO GASCONY!
MY MEN REPORTED THEY'D BE IN DANGER THERE!
DUKE NAYMES AND I ARE NOT ON GOOD TERMS.
NAYMES IS A GOOD MAN. THEY WOULD HAVE BEEN SAFE UNDER MY BANNER OF PROTECTION.
I THOUGHT IT WISER TO KEEP THEM HERE...
IF BY SOME CHANCE THE SARACENS BROKE THROUGH, AT LEAST ROLAND AND BERTHA WOULD BE SAFE AWAY FROM THE MANOR!
IT WAS A BAD DECISION, I REALIZE THAT NOW...
BUT YOU MUST BELIEVE ME WHEN I TELL YOU IT WAS NOT MALICIOUS!
I HAD THEM UNDER CLOSE WATCH! HOW WAS I TO KNOW THEIR CARETAKERS WOULD TURN ON THEM?!
MY LORD, I TELL YOU--
ENOUGH. WHEN YOU MARRIED MY SISTER YOU PROMISED TO CARE FOR HER INFANT SON. YOU SAID YOU'D PROTECT THEM AND THEIR LANDS!
AND I HAVE! ROLAND HAS TWICE THE LAND NOW AS WHEN HIS FATHER DIED!
YES...LAND THAT WAS NEARLY TAKEN AWAY BY SARACENS! THE WESTERN FRONT IS YOUR GUARD TO KEEP. HOW DID MARSILION GET THIS FAR INLAND?
I TAKE FULL RESPONSIBILITY. I DIDN'T EXPECT AN APPROACH FROM THE SEA...
BUT WITH GOD AT YOUR SIDE YOU TRIUMPHED, MY LORD!
SAVE IT FOR THE SCRIBES, GANELON.
WE BOTH KNOW GOD HAD NOTHING TO DO WITH IT...
...IT WAS LUCK. LUCK THAT COULD HAVE COME MUCH SOONER IF YOU'D SENT MEN OUT INSTEAD OF ARCHERS!
A TACTICAL DECISION WE DISAGREE ON.

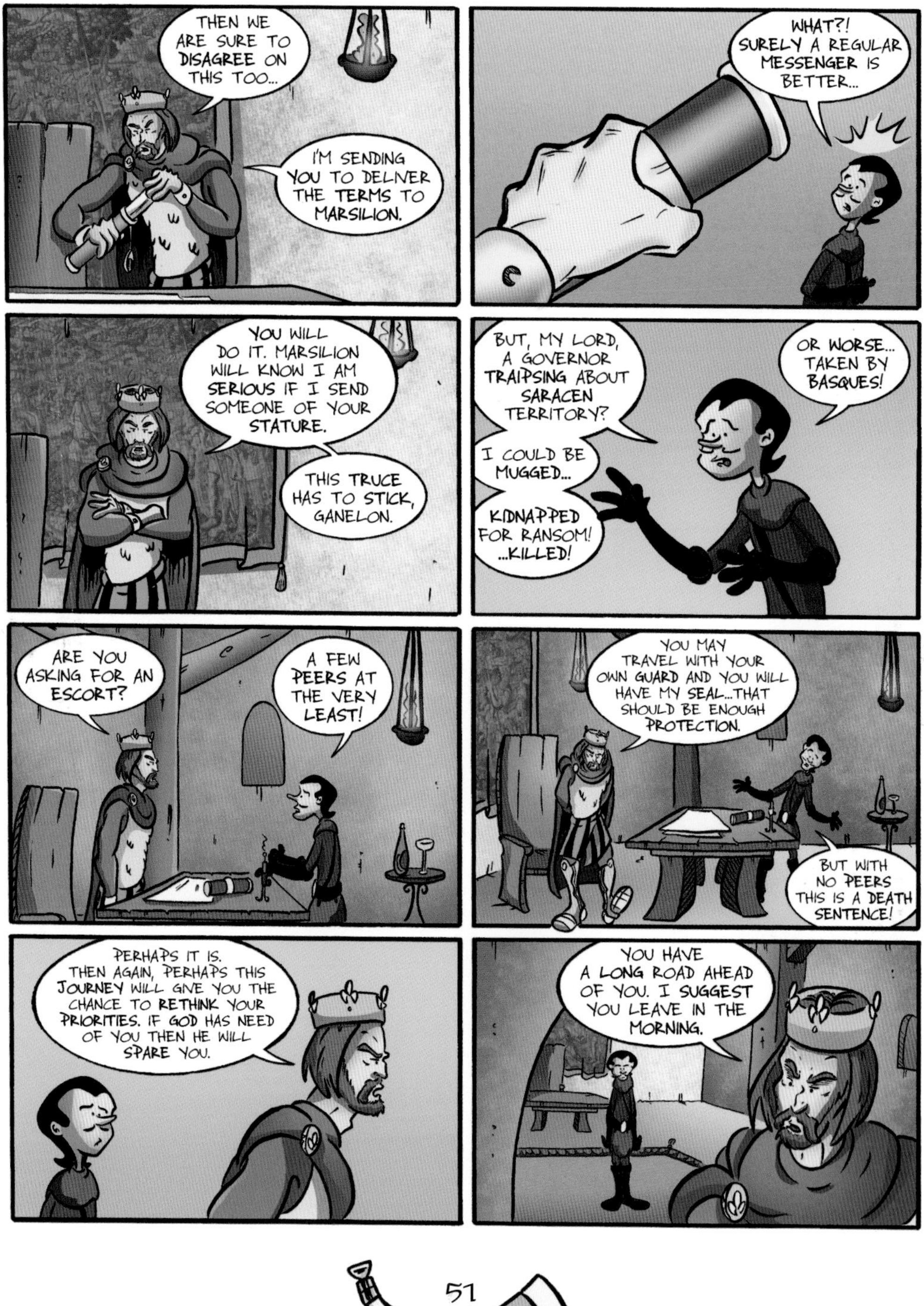
THEN WE ARE SURE TO DISAGREE ON THIS TOO...
I'M SENDING YOU TO DELIVER THE TERMS TO MARSILION.
WHAT?! SURELY A REGULAR MESSENGER IS BETTER...
YOU WILL DO IT. MARSILION WILL KNOW I AM SERIOUS IF I SEND SOMEONE OF YOUR STATURE.
THIS TRUCE HAS TO STICK, GANELON.
BUT, MY LORD, A GOVERNOR TRAIPSING ABOUT SARACEN TERRITORY?
I COULD BE MUGGED...
KIDNAPPED FOR RANSOM! ...KILLED!
OR WORSE... TAKEN BY BASQUES!
ARE YOU ASKING FOR AN ESCORT?
A FEW PEERS AT THE VERY LEAST!
YOU MAY TRAVEL WITH YOUR OWN GUARD AND YOU WILL HAVE MY SEAL...THAT SHOULD BE ENOUGH PROTECTION.
BUT WITH NO PEERS THIS IS A DEATH SENTENCE!
PERHAPS IT IS. THEN AGAIN, PERHAPS THIS JOURNEY WILL GIVE YOU THE CHANCE TO RETHINK YOUR PRIORITIES. IF GOD HAS NEED OF YOU THEN HE WILL SPARE YOU.
YOU HAVE A LONG ROAD AHEAD OF YOU. I SUGGEST YOU LEAVE IN THE MORNING.

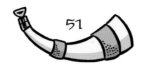

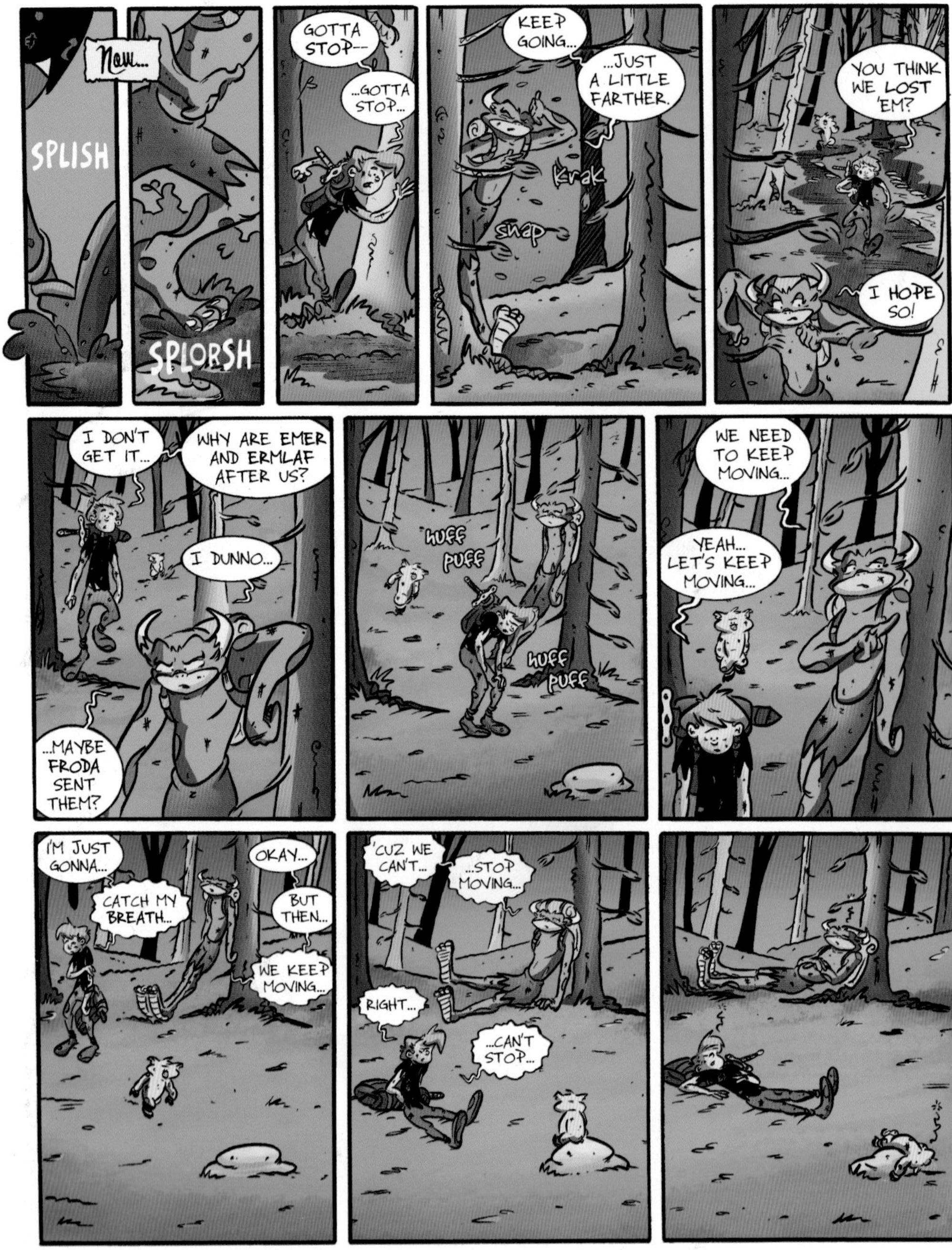
Now...
SPLISH
SPLORSH
GOTTA STOP--
...GOTTA STOP...
KEEP GOING...
...JUST A LITTLE FARTHER.
krak
snap
YOU THINK WE LOST 'EM?
I HOPE SO!
I DON'T GET IT...
WHY ARE EMER AND ERMLAF AFTER US?
I DUNNO...
...MAYBE FRODA SENT THEM?
huff
puff
huff
puff
WE NEED TO KEEP MOVING...
YEAH... LET'S KEEP MOVING...
I'M JUST GONNA...
CATCH MY BREATH...
OKAY...
BUT THEN...
WE KEEP MOVING...
'CUZ WE CAN'T...
...STOP MOVING...
RIGHT...
...CAN'T STOP...

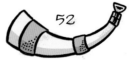

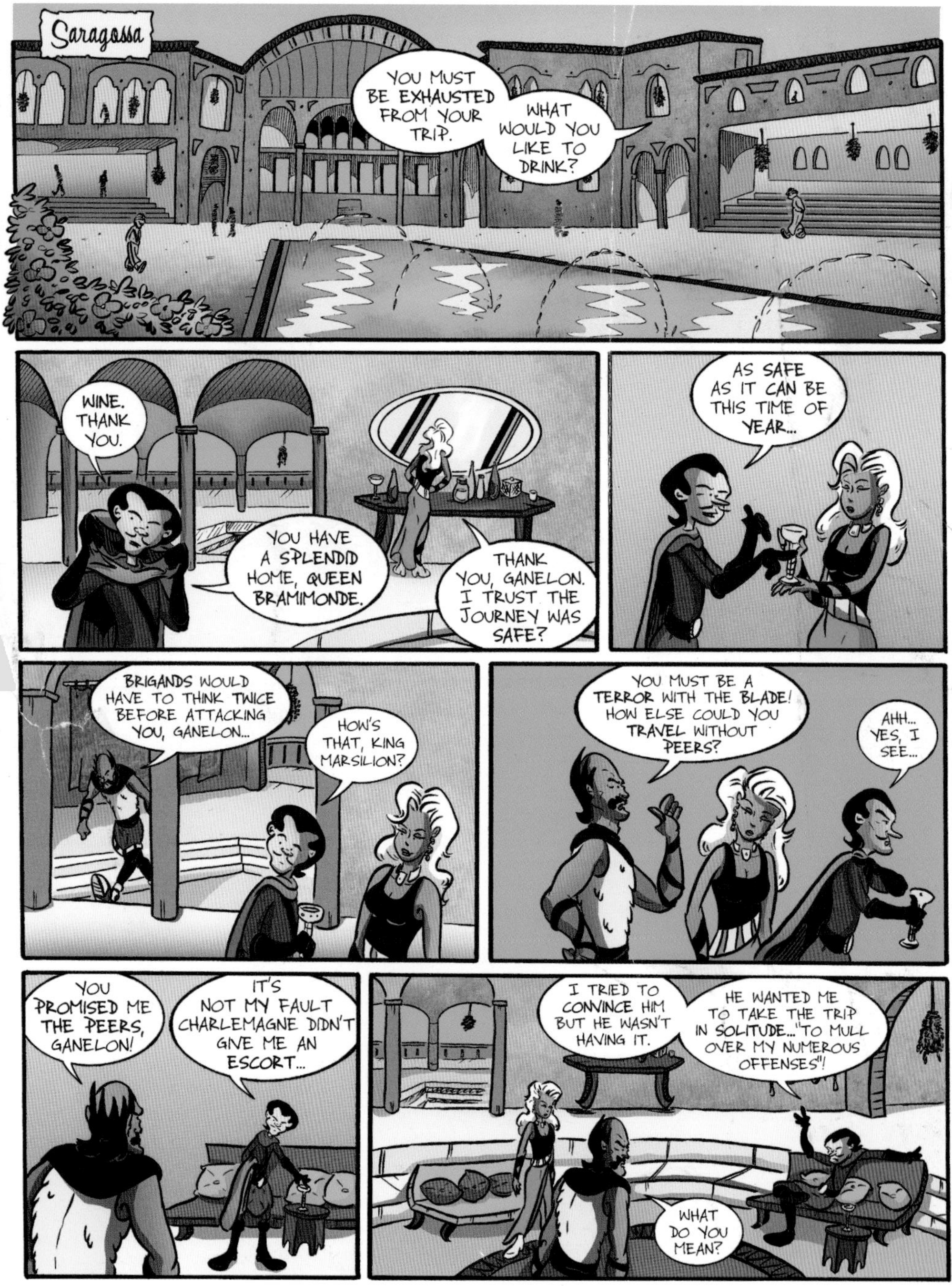
Saragossa
YOU MUST BE EXHAUSTED FROM YOUR TRIP.
WHAT WOULD YOU LIKE TO DRINK?
WINE. THANK YOU.
YOU HAVE A SPLENDID HOME, QUEEN BRAMIMONDE.
THANK YOU, GANELON. I TRUST THE JOURNEY WAS SAFE?
AS SAFE AS IT CAN BE THIS TIME OF YEAR...
BRIGANDS WOULD HAVE TO THINK TWICE BEFORE ATTACKING YOU, GANELON...
HOW'S THAT, KING MARSILION?
YOU MUST BE A TERROR WITH THE BLADE! HOW ELSE COULD YOU TRAVEL WITHOUT PEERS?
AHH... YES, I SEE...
YOU PROMISED ME THE PEERS, GANELON!
IT'S NOT MY FAULT CHARLEMAGNE DIDN'T GIVE ME AN ESCORT...
I TRIED TO CONVINCE HIM BUT HE WASN'T HAVING IT.
HE WANTED ME TO TAKE THE TRIP IN SOLITUDE..."TO MULL OVER MY NUMEROUS OFFENSES"!
WHAT DO YOU MEAN?

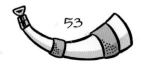

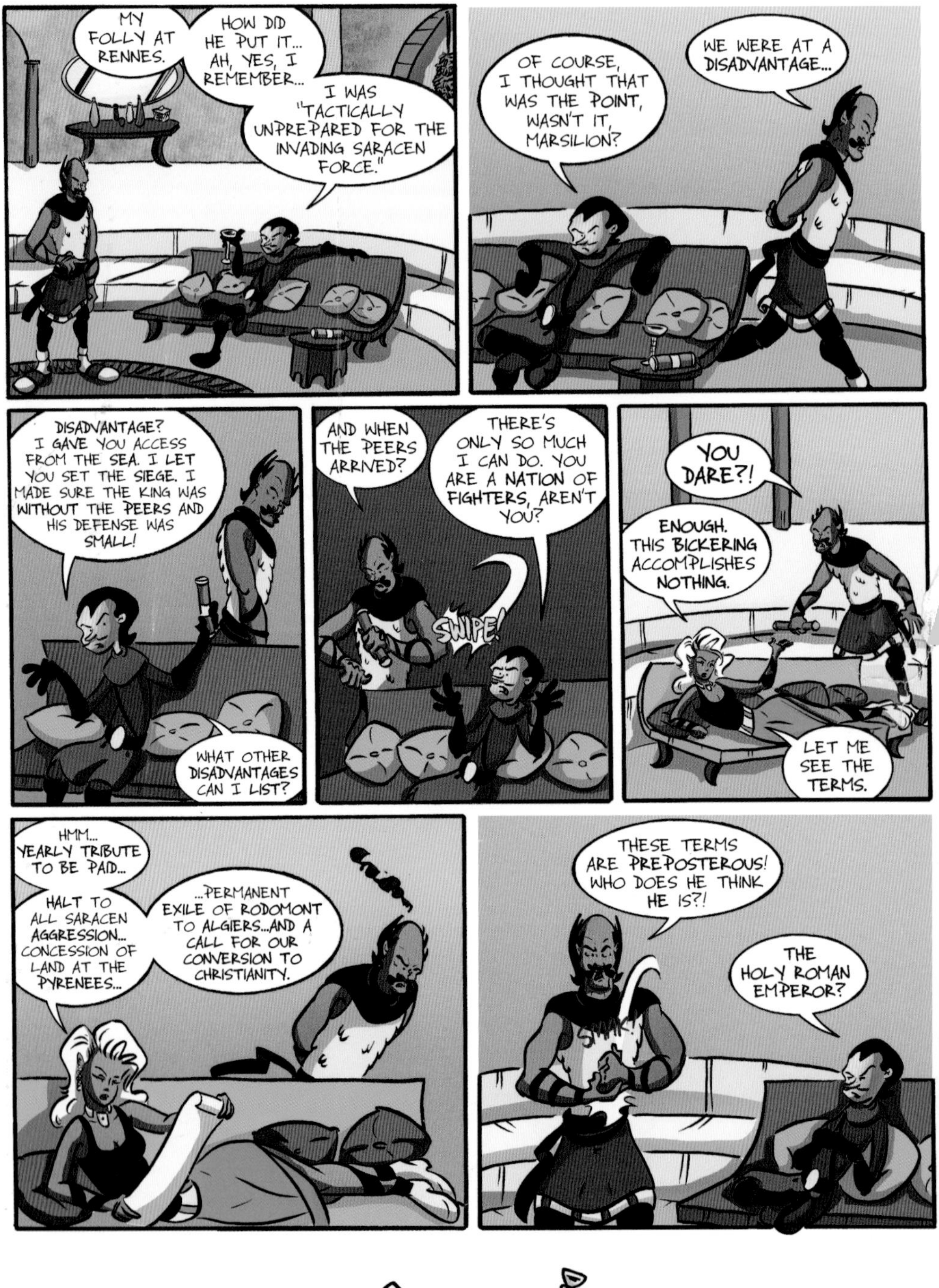
MY FOLLY AT RENNES.
HOW DID HE PUT IT... AH, YES, I REMEMBER...
I WAS "TACTICALLY UNPREPARED FOR THE INVADING SARACEN FORCE."
WE WERE AT A DISADVANTAGE...
OF COURSE, I THOUGHT THAT WAS THE POINT, WASN'T IT, MARSILION?
DISADVANTAGE? I GAVE YOU ACCESS FROM THE SEA. I LET YOU SET THE SIEGE. I MADE SURE THE KING WAS WITHOUT THE PEERS AND HIS DEFENSE WAS SMALL!
WHAT OTHER DISADVANTAGES CAN I LIST?
AND WHEN THE PEERS ARRIVED?
THERE'S ONLY SO MUCH I CAN DO. YOU ARE A NATION OF FIGHTERS, AREN'T YOU?
SWIPE!
YOU DARE?!
ENOUGH. THIS BICKERING ACCOMPLISHES NOTHING.
LET ME SEE THE TERMS.
HMM... YEARLY TRIBUTE TO BE PAID...
HALT TO ALL SARACEN AGGRESSION... CONCESSION OF LAND AT THE PYRENEES...
...PERMANENT EXILE OF RODOMONT TO ALGIERS...AND A CALL FOR OUR CONVERSION TO CHRISTIANITY.
THESE TERMS ARE PREPOSTEROUS! WHO DOES HE THINK HE IS?!
THE HOLY ROMAN EMPEROR?

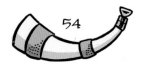

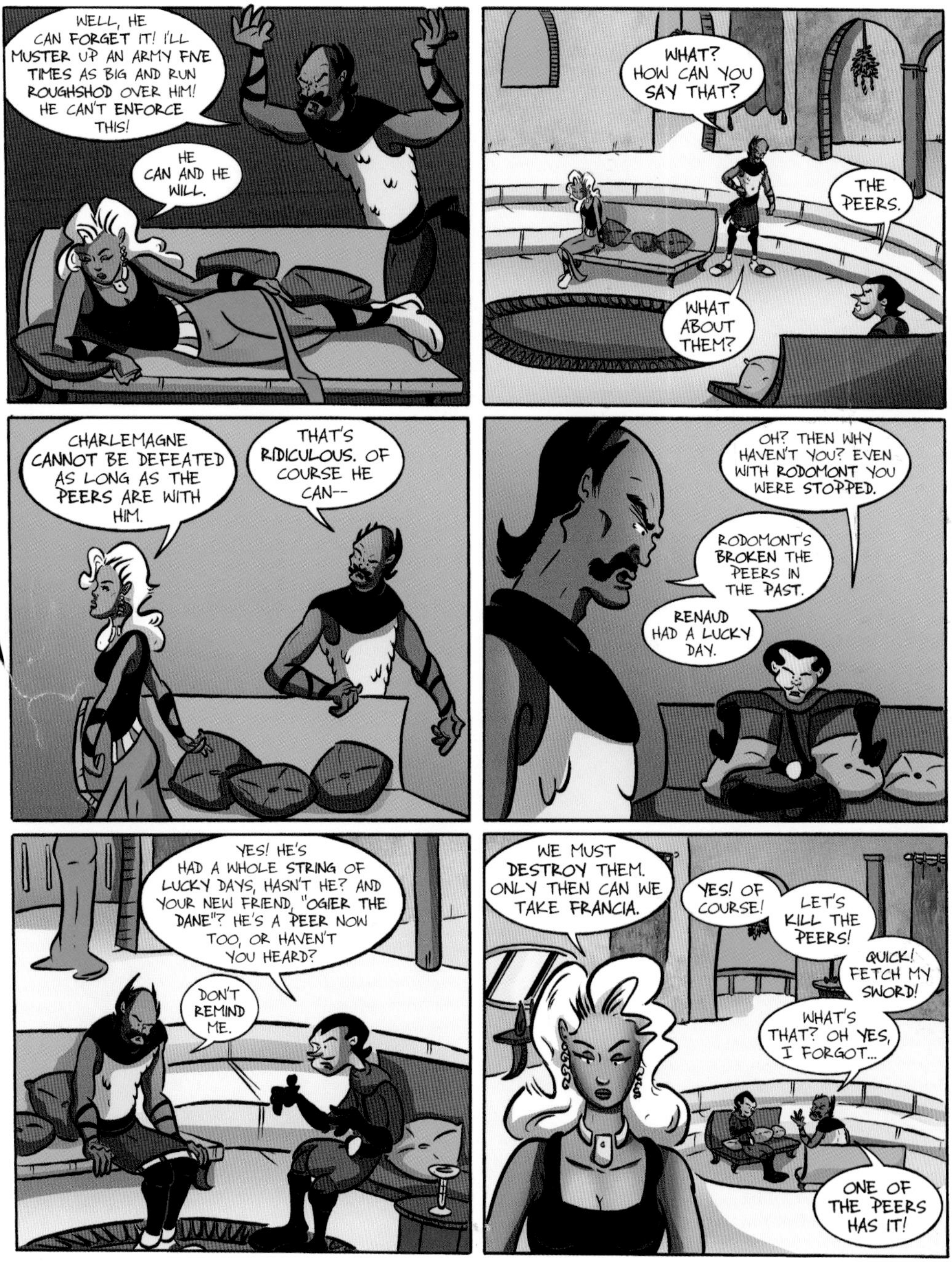
WELL, HE CAN FORGET IT! I'LL MUSTER UP AN ARMY FIVE TIMES AS BIG AND RUN ROUGHSHOD OVER HIM! HE CAN'T ENFORCE THIS!
HE CAN AND HE WILL.
WHAT? HOW CAN YOU SAY THAT?
THE PEERS.
WHAT ABOUT THEM?
CHARLEMAGNE CANNOT BE DEFEATED AS LONG AS THE PEERS ARE WITH HIM.
THAT'S RIDICULOUS. OF COURSE HE CAN--
OH? THEN WHY HAVEN'T YOU? EVEN WITH RODOMONT YOU WERE STOPPED.
RODOMONT'S BROKEN THE PEERS IN THE PAST.
RENAUD HAD A LUCKY DAY.
YES! HE'S HAD A WHOLE STRING OF LUCKY DAYS, HASN'T HE? AND YOUR NEW FRIEND, "OGIER THE DANE"? HE'S A PEER NOW TOO, OR HAVEN'T YOU HEARD?
DON'T REMIND ME.
WE MUST DESTROY THEM. ONLY THEN CAN WE TAKE FRANCIA.
YES! OF COURSE!
LET'S KILL THE PEERS!
QUICK! FETCH MY SWORD!
WHAT'S THAT? OH YES, I FORGOT...
ONE OF THE PEERS HAS IT!

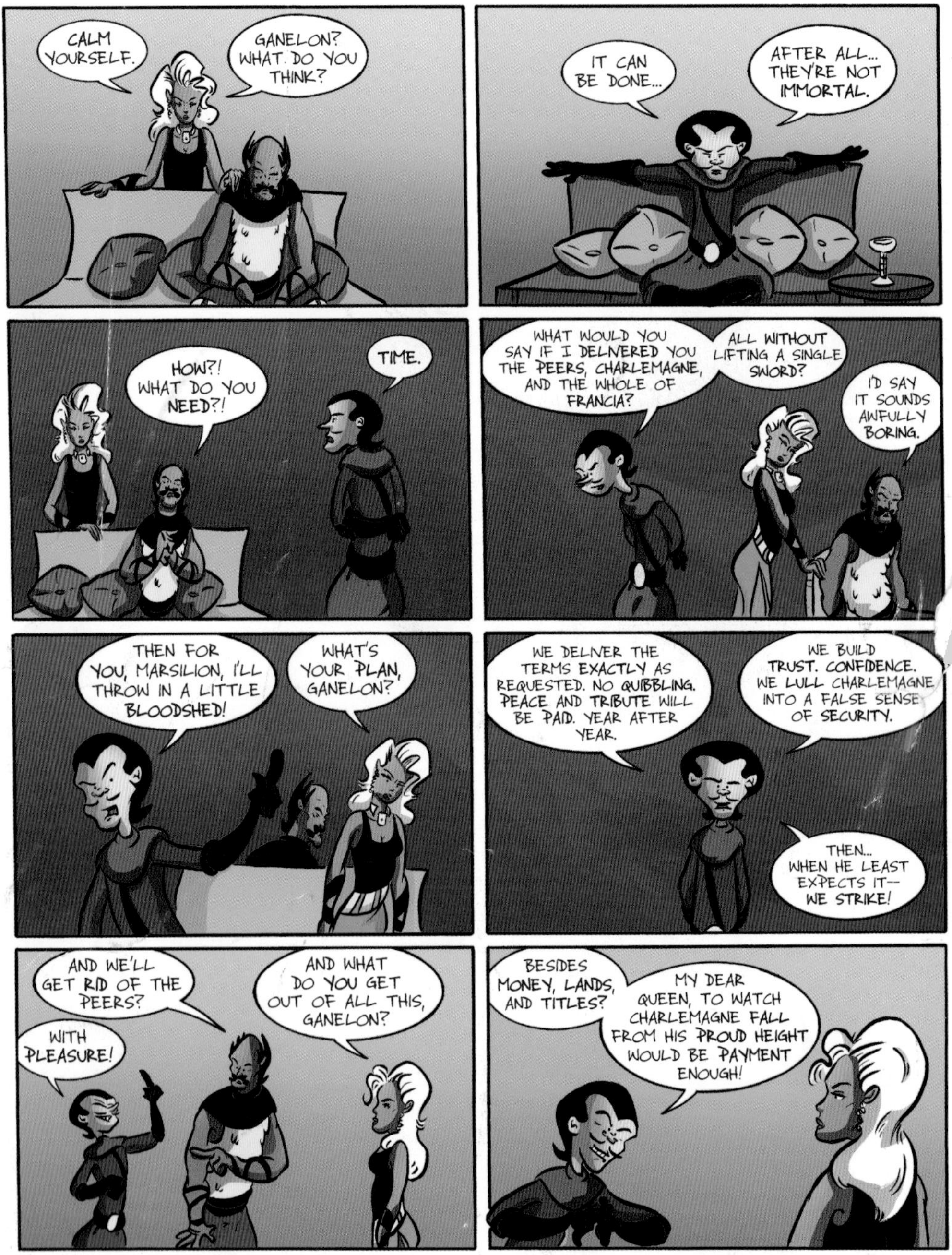
CALM YOURSELF.
GANELON? WHAT DO YOU THINK?
IT CAN BE DONE...
AFTER ALL... THEY'RE NOT IMMORTAL.
HOW?! WHAT DO YOU NEED?!
TIME.
WHAT WOULD YOU SAY IF I DELIVERED YOU THE PEERS, CHARLEMAGNE, AND THE WHOLE OF FRANCIA?
ALL WITHOUT LIFTING A SINGLE SWORD?
I'D SAY IT SOUNDS AWFULLY BORING.
THEN FOR YOU, MARSILION, I'LL THROW IN A LITTLE BLOODSHED!
WHAT'S YOUR PLAN, GANELON?
WE DELIVER THE TERMS EXACTLY AS REQUESTED. NO QUIBBLING. PEACE AND TRIBUTE WILL BE PAID. YEAR AFTER YEAR.
WE BUILD TRUST. CONFIDENCE. WE LULL CHARLEMAGNE INTO A FALSE SENSE OF SECURITY.
THEN... WHEN HE LEAST EXPECTS IT-- WE STRIKE!
AND WE'LL GET RID OF THE PEERS?
WITH PLEASURE!
AND WHAT DO YOU GET OUT OF ALL THIS, GANELON?
BESIDES MONEY, LANDS, AND TITLES?
MY DEAR QUEEN, TO WATCH CHARLEMAGNE FALL FROM HIS PROUD HEIGHT WOULD BE PAYMENT ENOUGH!

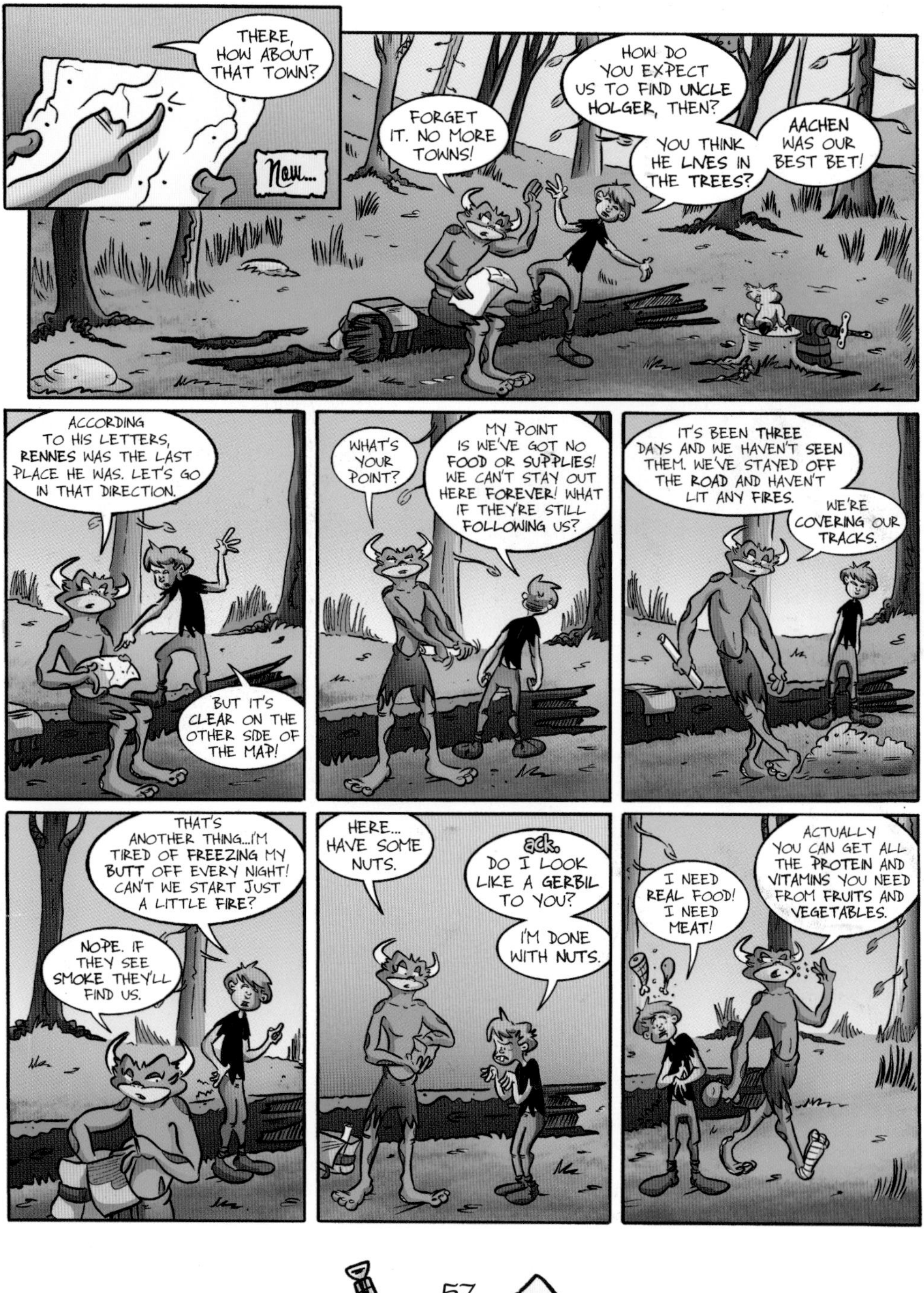
THERE, HOW ABOUT THAT TOWN?
Now...
FORGET IT. NO MORE TOWNS!
HOW DO YOU EXPECT US TO FIND UNCLE HOLGER, THEN?
YOU THINK HE LIVES IN THE TREES?
AACHEN WAS OUR BEST BET!
ACCORDING TO HIS LETTERS, RENNES WAS THE LAST PLACE HE WAS. LET'S GO IN THAT DIRECTION.
BUT IT'S CLEAR ON THE OTHER SIDE OF THE MAP!
WHAT'S YOUR POINT?
MY POINT IS WE'VE GOT NO FOOD OR SUPPLIES! WE CAN'T STAY OUT HERE FOREVER! WHAT IF THEY'RE STILL FOLLOWING US?
IT'S BEEN THREE DAYS AND WE HAVEN'T SEEN THEM. WE'VE STAYED OFF THE ROAD AND HAVEN'T LIT ANY FIRES.
WE'RE COVERING OUR TRACKS.
THAT'S ANOTHER THING...I'M TIRED OF FREEZING MY BUTT OFF EVERY NIGHT! CAN'T WE START JUST A LITTLE FIRE?
NOPE. IF THEY SEE SMOKE THEY'LL FIND US.
HERE... HAVE SOME NUTS.
ack.
DO I LOOK LIKE A GERBIL TO YOU?
I'M DONE WITH NUTS.
I NEED REAL FOOD! I NEED MEAT!
ACTUALLY YOU CAN GET ALL THE PROTEIN AND VITAMINS YOU NEED FROM FRUITS AND VEGETABLES.

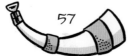

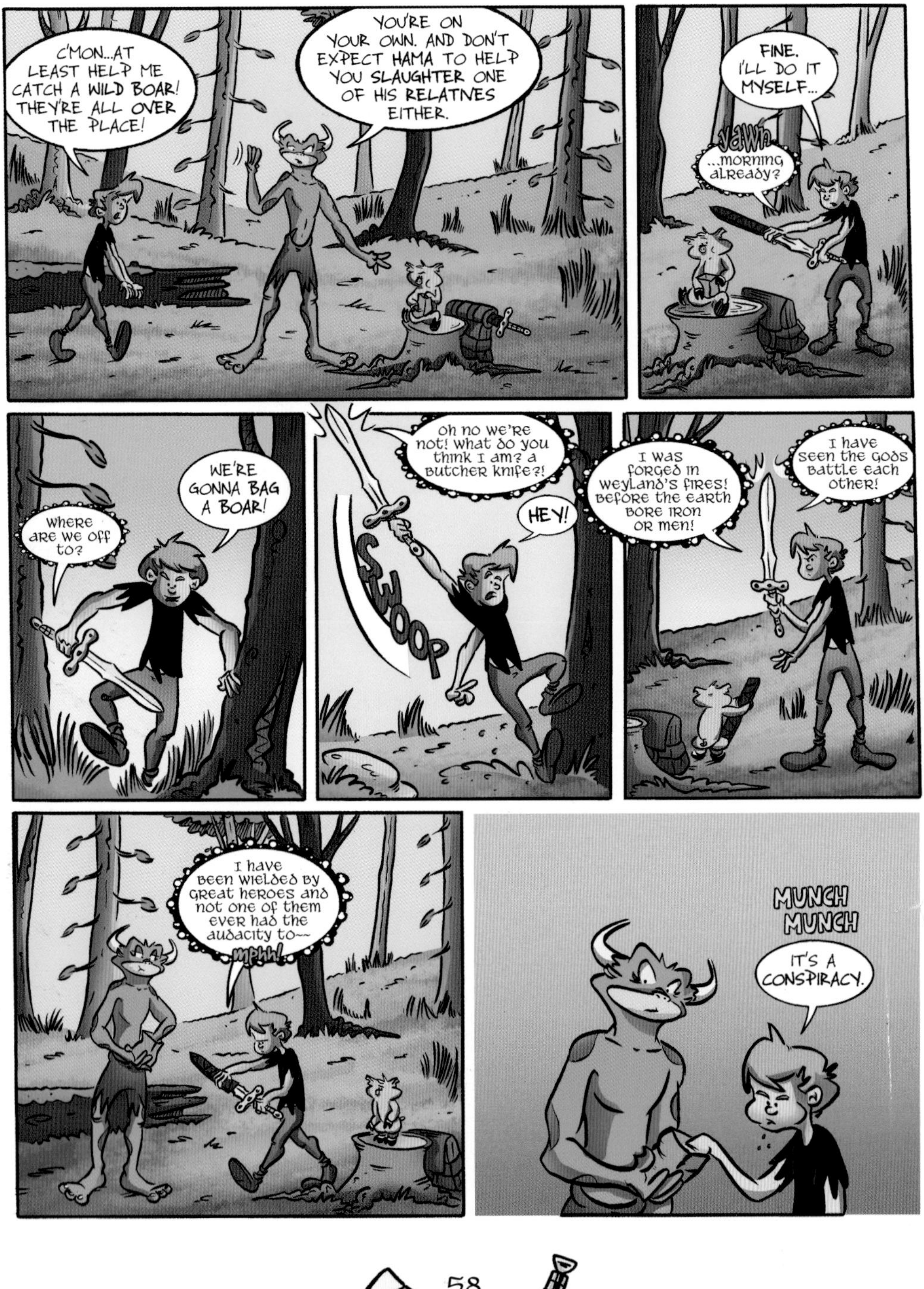
C'MON...AT LEAST HELP ME CATCH A WILD BOAR! THEY'RE ALL OVER THE PLACE!
YOU'RE ON YOUR OWN. AND DON'T EXPECT HAMA TO HELP YOU SLAUGHTER ONE OF HIS RELATIVES EITHER.
FINE. I'LL DO IT MYSELF...
yawn
...morning already?
Where are we off to?
WE'RE GONNA BAG A BOAR!
SWOOP
HEY!
Oh no we're not! what do you think I am? a butcher knife?!
I was forged in Weyland's fires! Before the earth bore iron or men!
I have seen the gods battle each other!
I have been wielded by great heroes and not one of them ever had the audacity to~~
mphh!
MUNCH MUNCH
IT'S A CONSPIRACY.

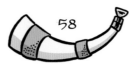

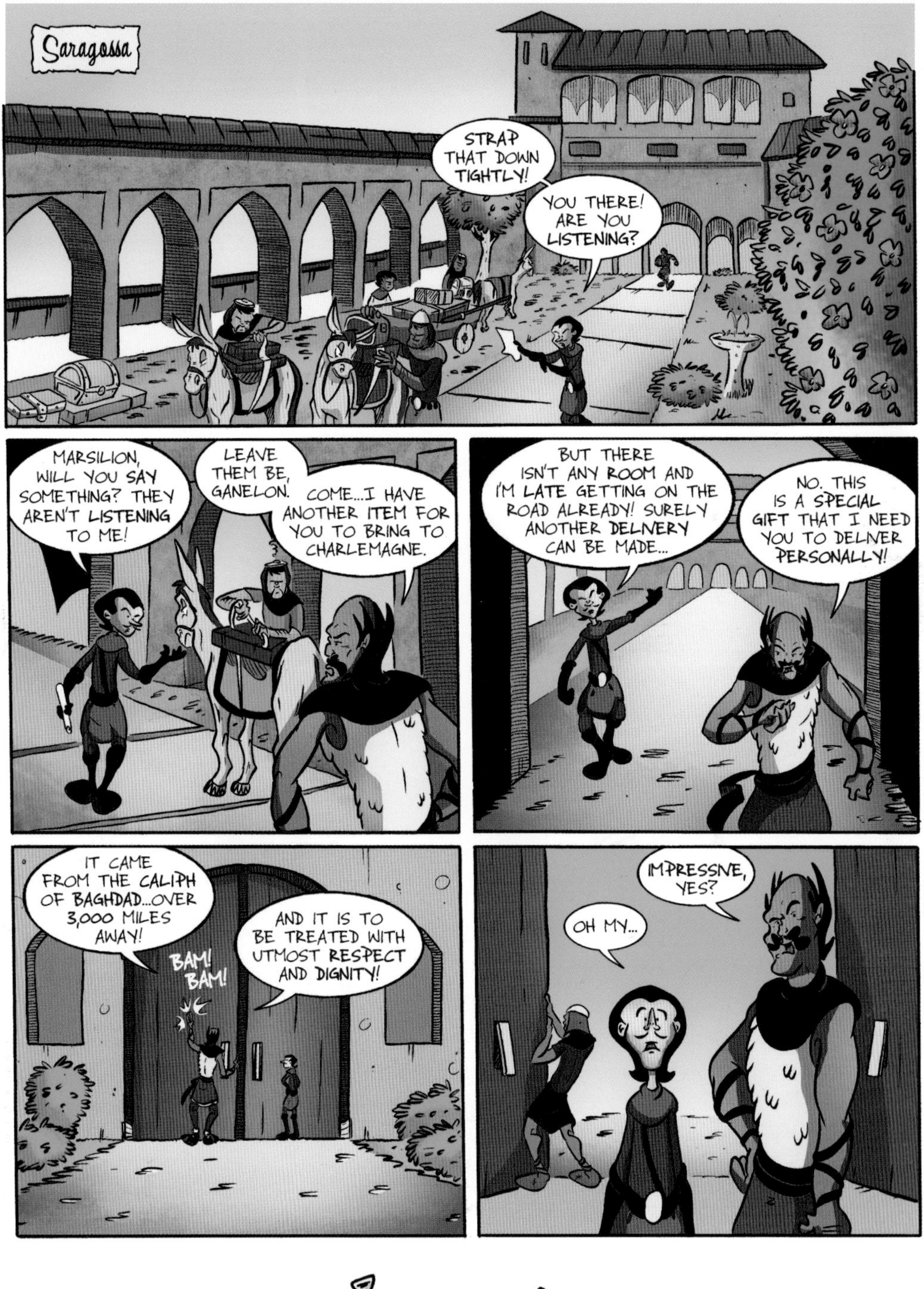
Saragossa
STRAP THAT DOWN TIGHTLY!
YOU THERE! ARE YOU LISTENING?
MARSILION, WILL YOU SAY SOMETHING? THEY AREN'T LISTENING TO ME!
LEAVE THEM BE, GANELON.
COME...I HAVE ANOTHER ITEM FOR YOU TO BRING TO CHARLEMAGNE.
BUT THERE ISN'T ANY ROOM AND I'M LATE GETTING ON THE ROAD ALREADY! SURELY ANOTHER DELIVERY CAN BE MADE...
NO. THIS IS A SPECIAL GIFT THAT I NEED YOU TO DELIVER PERSONALLY!
IT CAME FROM THE CALIPH OF BAGHDAD...OVER 3,000 MILES AWAY!
BAM! BAM!
AND IT IS TO BE TREATED WITH UTMOST RESPECT AND DIGNITY!
IMPRESSIVE, YES?
OH MY...

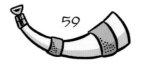

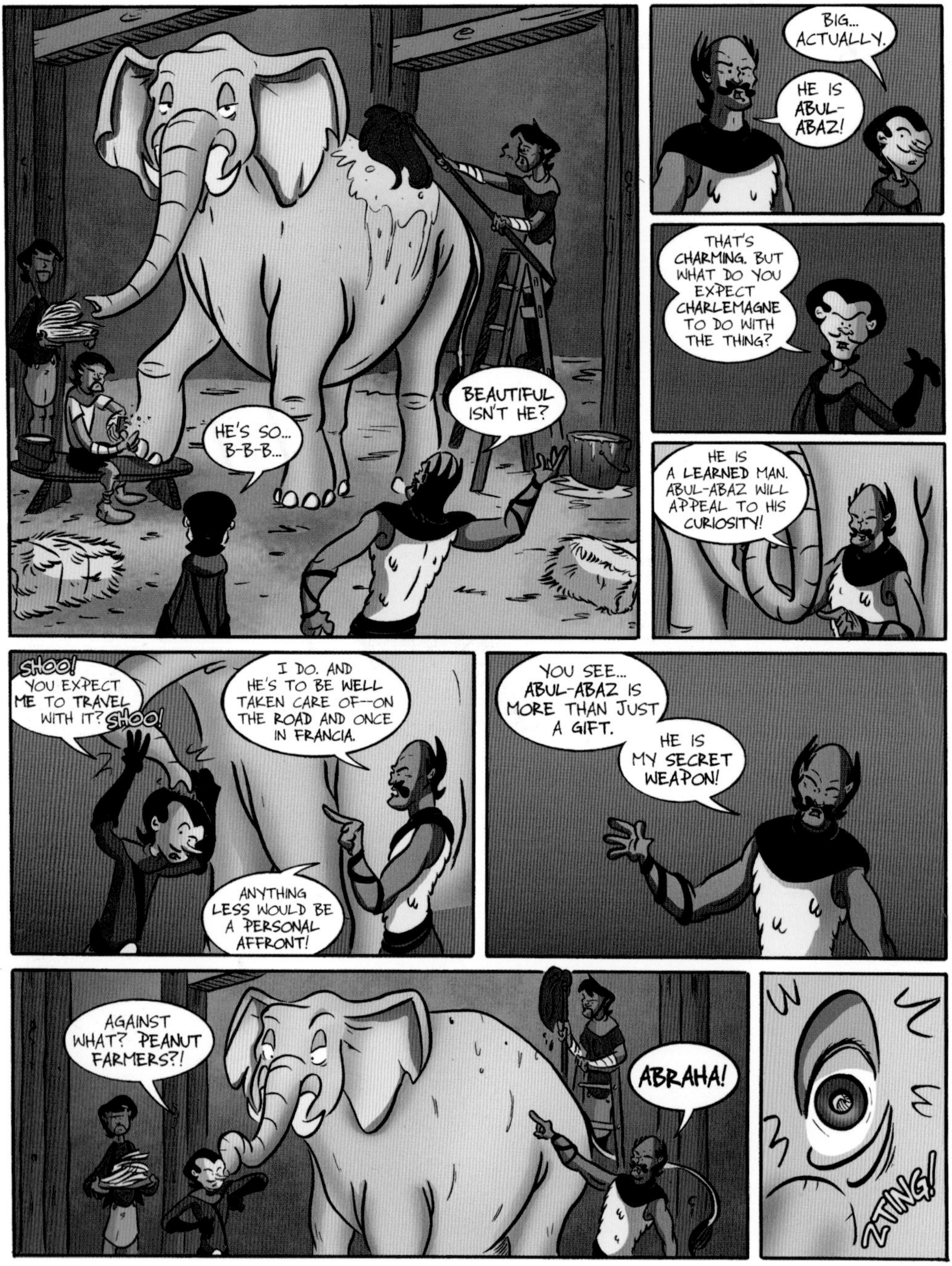
BEAUTIFUL ISN'T HE?
HE'S SO... B-B-B...
BIG... ACTUALLY.
HE IS ABUL-ABAZ!
THAT'S CHARMING. BUT WHAT DO YOU EXPECT CHARLEMAGNE TO DO WITH THE THING?
HE IS A LEARNED MAN. ABUL-ABAZ WILL APPEAL TO HIS CURIOSITY!
SHOO!
YOU EXPECT ME TO TRAVEL WITH IT?
SHOO!
I DO. AND HE'S TO BE WELL TAKEN CARE OF--ON THE ROAD AND ONCE IN FRANCIA.
ANYTHING LESS WOULD BE A PERSONAL AFFRONT!
YOU SEE... ABUL-ABAZ IS MORE THAN JUST A GIFT.
HE IS MY SECRET WEAPON!
AGAINST WHAT? PEANUT FARMERS?!
ABRAHA!
ZTING!

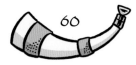

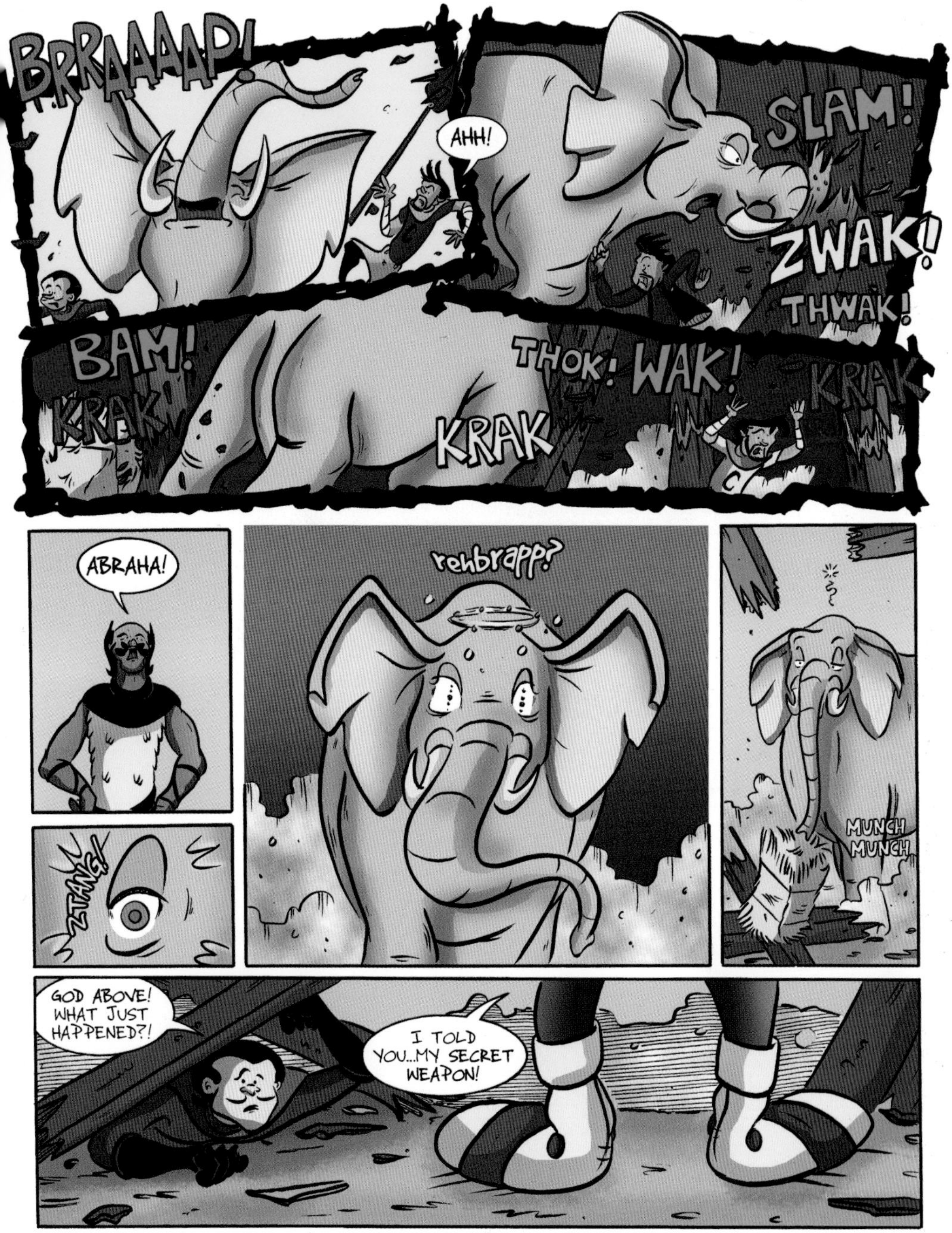
BRRAAAAP!
AHH!
SLAM!
ZWAK!
THWAK!
BAM!
KRAK
THOK! WAK!
KRAK
KRAK
ABRAHA!
ZTANG!
rehbrapp?
MUNCH MUNCH
GOD ABOVE! WHAT JUST HAPPENED?!
I TOLD YOU...MY SECRET WEAPON!

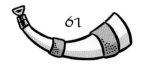

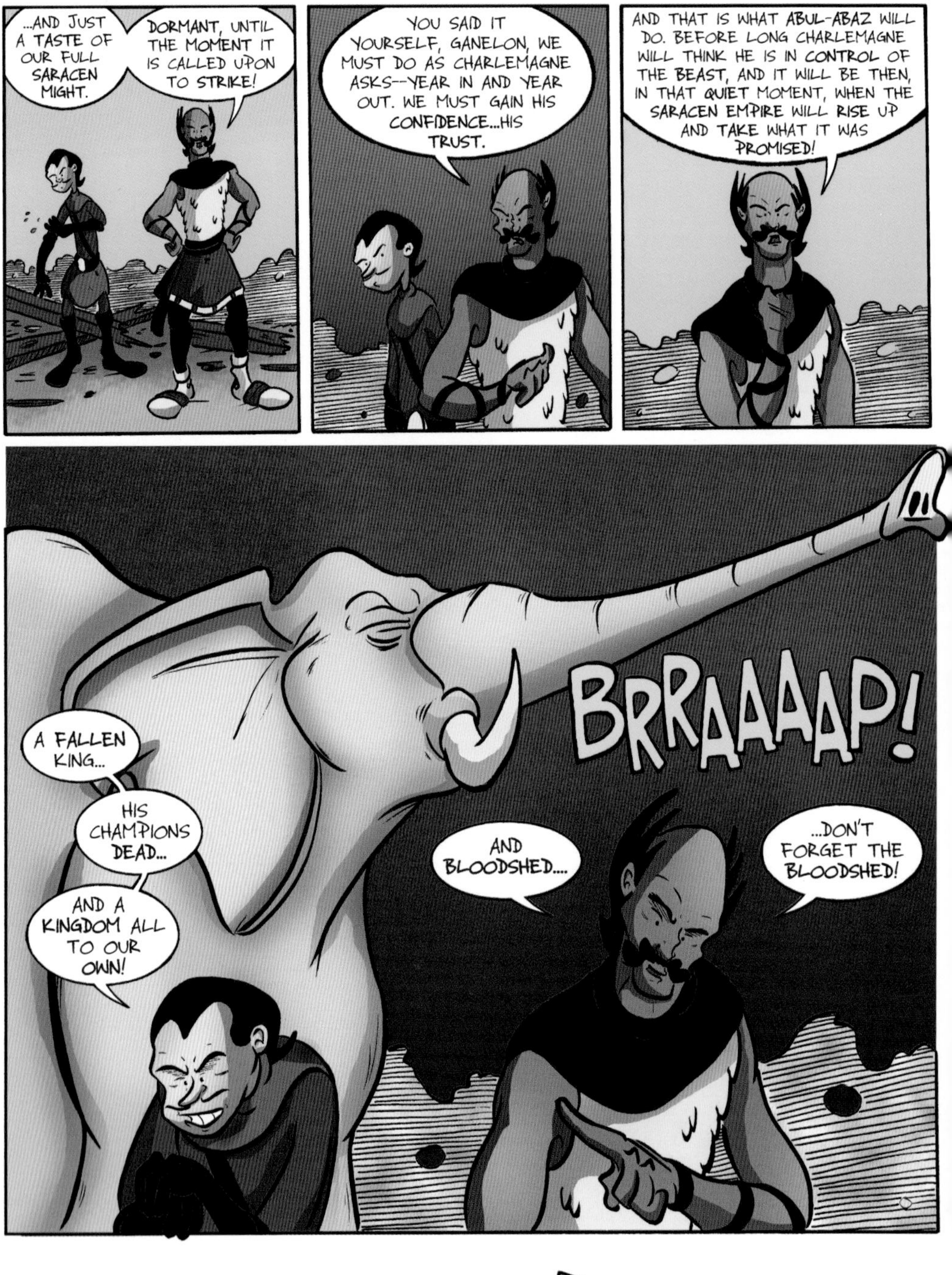
...AND JUST A TASTE OF OUR FULL SARACEN MIGHT.
DORMANT, UNTIL THE MOMENT IT IS CALLED UPON TO STRIKE!
YOU SAID IT YOURSELF, GANELON, WE MUST DO AS CHARLEMAGNE ASKS--YEAR IN AND YEAR OUT. WE MUST GAIN HIS CONFIDENCE...HIS TRUST.
AND THAT IS WHAT ABUL-ABAZ WILL DO. BEFORE LONG CHARLEMAGNE WILL THINK HE IS IN CONTROL OF THE BEAST, AND IT WILL BE THEN, IN THAT QUIET MOMENT, WHEN THE SARACEN EMPIRE WILL RISE UP AND TAKE WHAT IT WAS PROMISED!
BRRAAAAP!
A FALLEN KING...
HIS CHAMPIONS DEAD...
AND A KINGDOM ALL TO OUR OWN!
AND BLOODSHED....
...DON'T FORGET THE BLOODSHED!

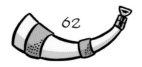

part two

the WRONG OF RONCEVAUX

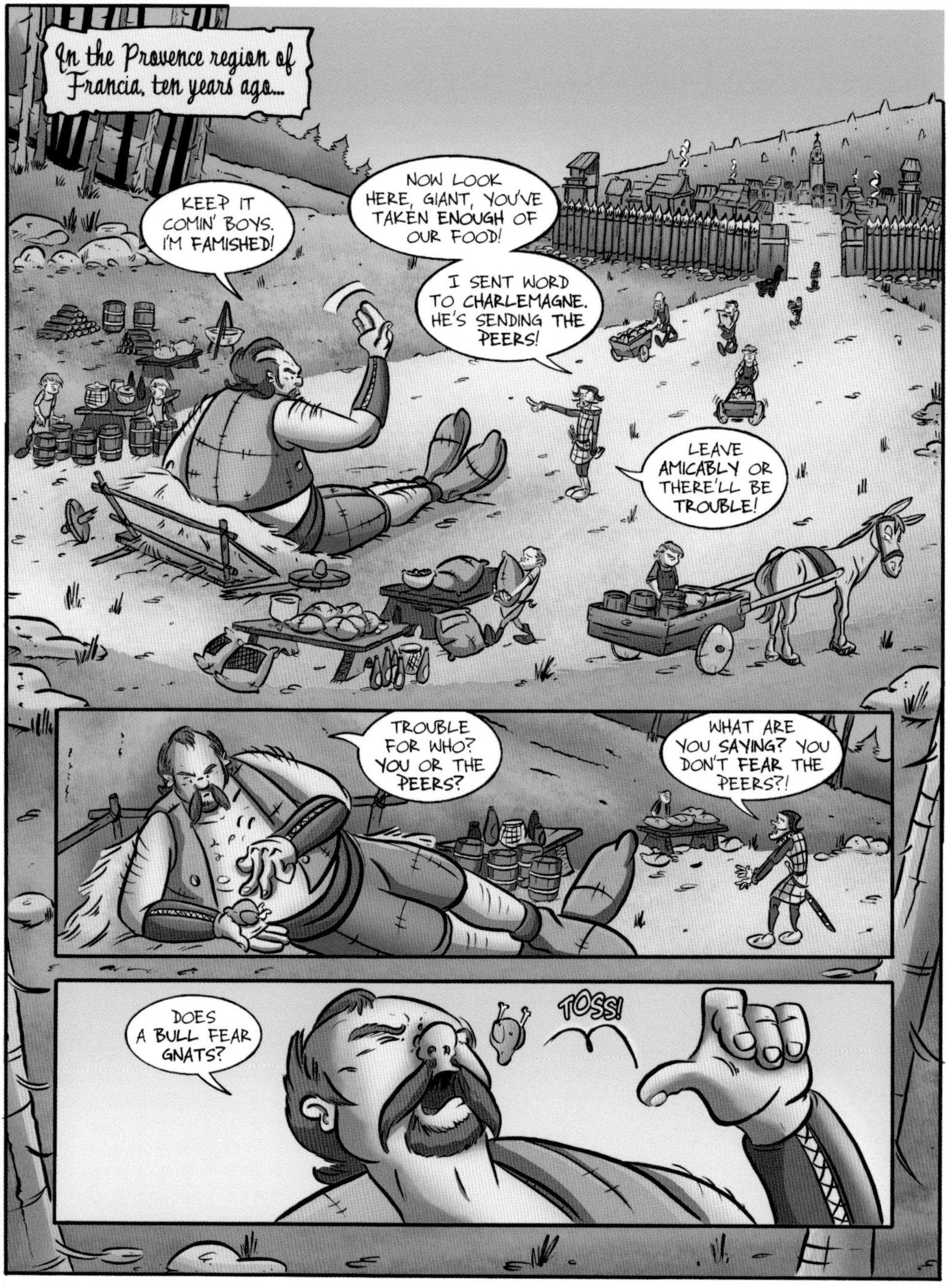
In the Provence region of Francia, ten years ago...
KEEP IT COMIN' BOYS. I'M FAMISHED!
NOW LOOK HERE, GIANT, YOU'VE TAKEN ENOUGH OF OUR FOOD!
I SENT WORD TO CHARLEMAGNE. HE'S SENDING THE PEERS!
LEAVE AMICABLY OR THERE'LL BE TROUBLE!
TROUBLE FOR WHO? YOU OR THE PEERS?
WHAT ARE YOU SAYING? YOU DON'T FEAR THE PEERS?!
DOES A BULL FEAR GNATS?
TOSS!

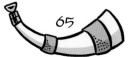

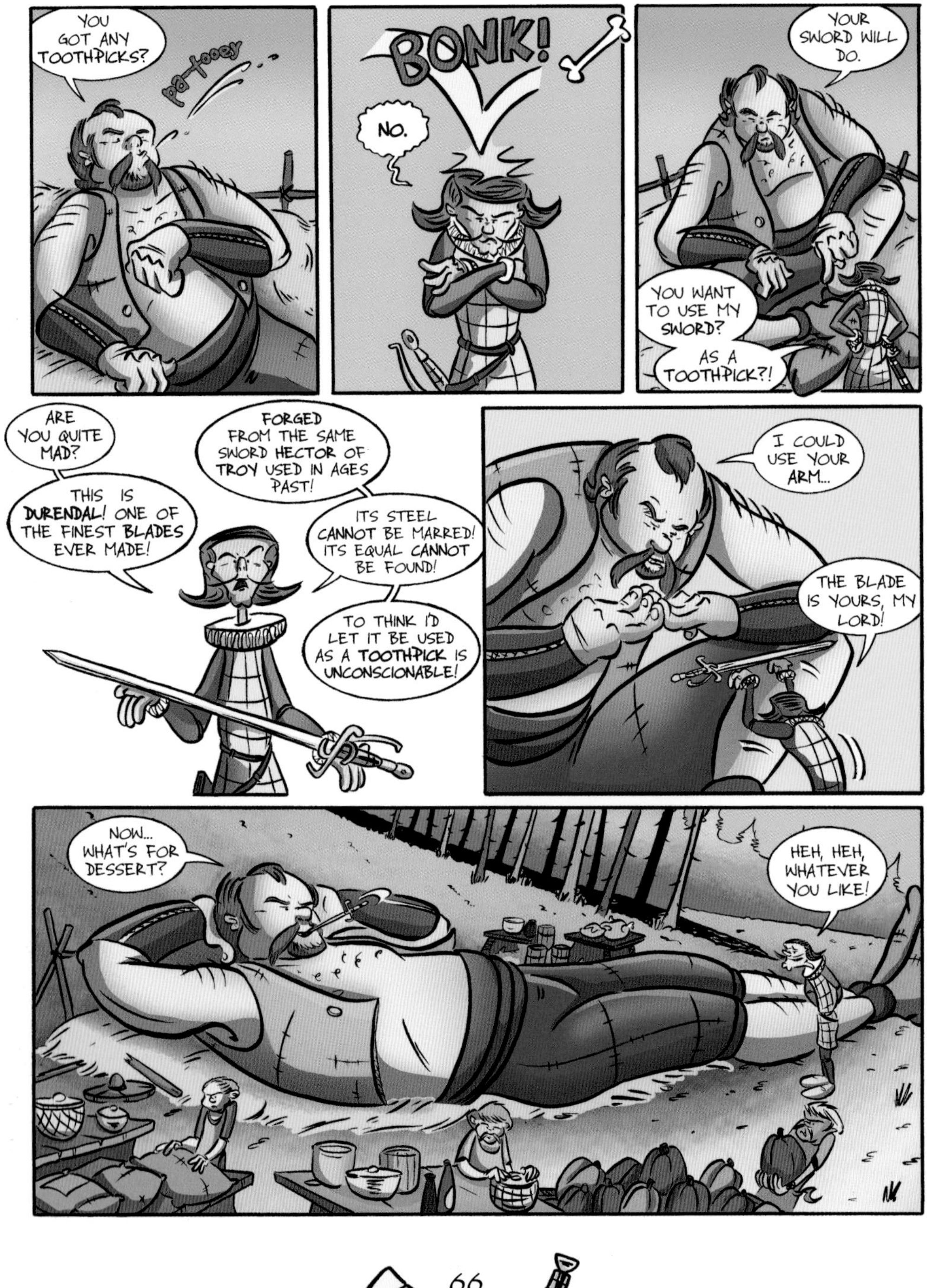
YOU GOT ANY TOOTHPICKS?
pa-tooey
BONK!
NO.
YOUR SWORD WILL DO.
YOU WANT TO USE MY SWORD?
AS A TOOTHPICK?!
ARE YOU QUITE MAD?
THIS IS DURENDAL! ONE OF THE FINEST BLADES EVER MADE!
FORGED FROM THE SAME SWORD HECTOR OF TROY USED IN AGES PAST!
ITS STEEL CANNOT BE MARRED! ITS EQUAL CANNOT BE FOUND!
TO THINK I'D LET IT BE USED AS A TOOTHPICK IS UNCONSCIONABLE!
I COULD USE YOUR ARM...
THE BLADE IS YOURS, MY LORD!
NOW... WHAT'S FOR DESSERT?
HEH, HEH, WHATEVER YOU LIKE!

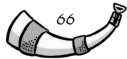

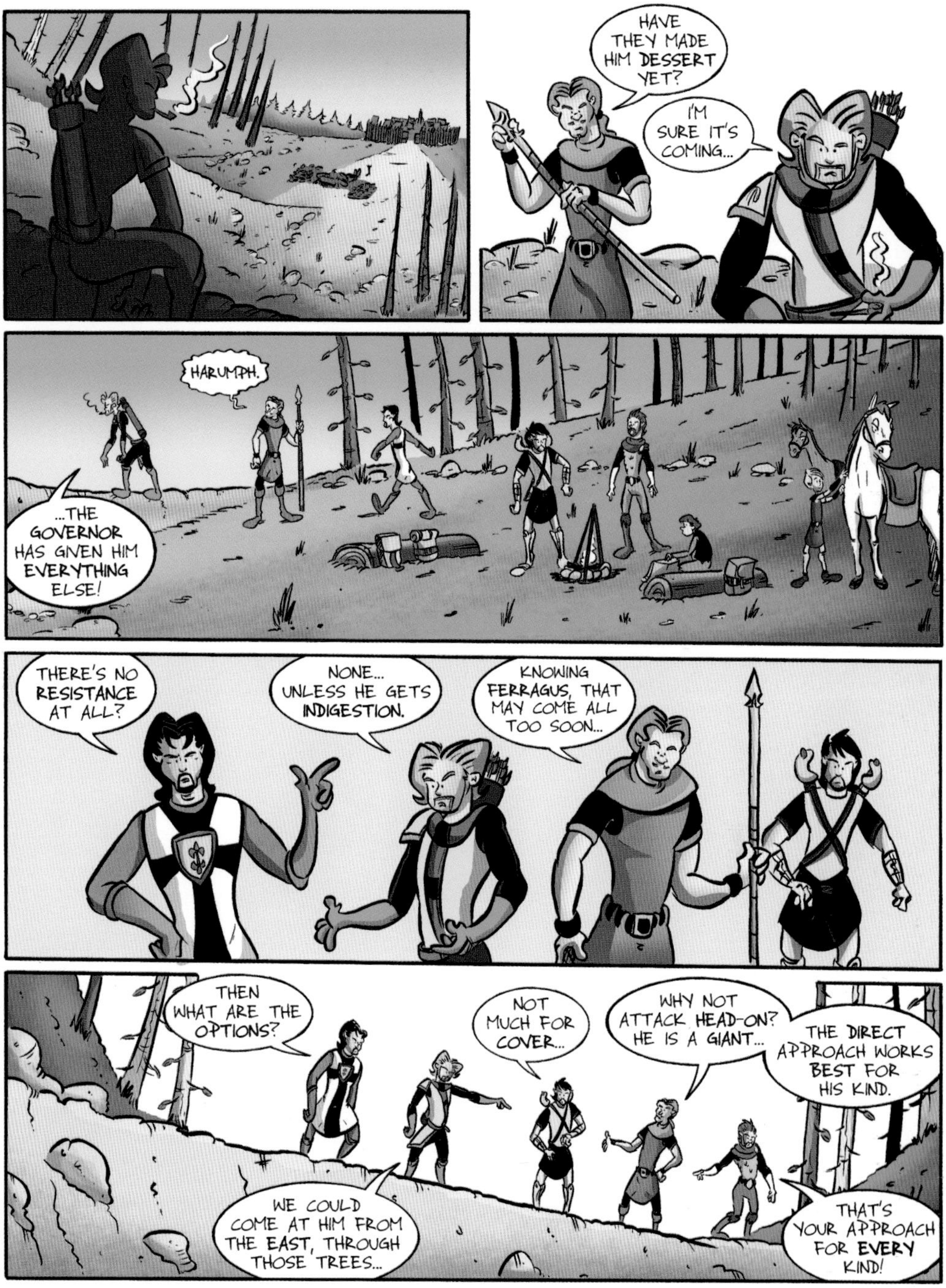
HAVE THEY MADE HIM DESSERT YET?
I'M SURE IT'S COMING...
HARUMPH.
...THE GOVERNOR HAS GIVEN HIM EVERYTHING ELSE!
THERE'S NO RESISTANCE AT ALL?
NONE... UNLESS HE GETS INDIGESTION.
KNOWING FERRAGUS, THAT MAY COME ALL TOO SOON...
THEN WHAT ARE THE OPTIONS?
WE COULD COME AT HIM FROM THE EAST, THROUGH THOSE TREES...
NOT MUCH FOR COVER...
WHY NOT ATTACK HEAD-ON? HE IS A GIANT...
THE DIRECT APPROACH WORKS BEST FOR HIS KIND.
THAT'S YOUR APPROACH FOR EVERY KIND!

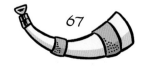

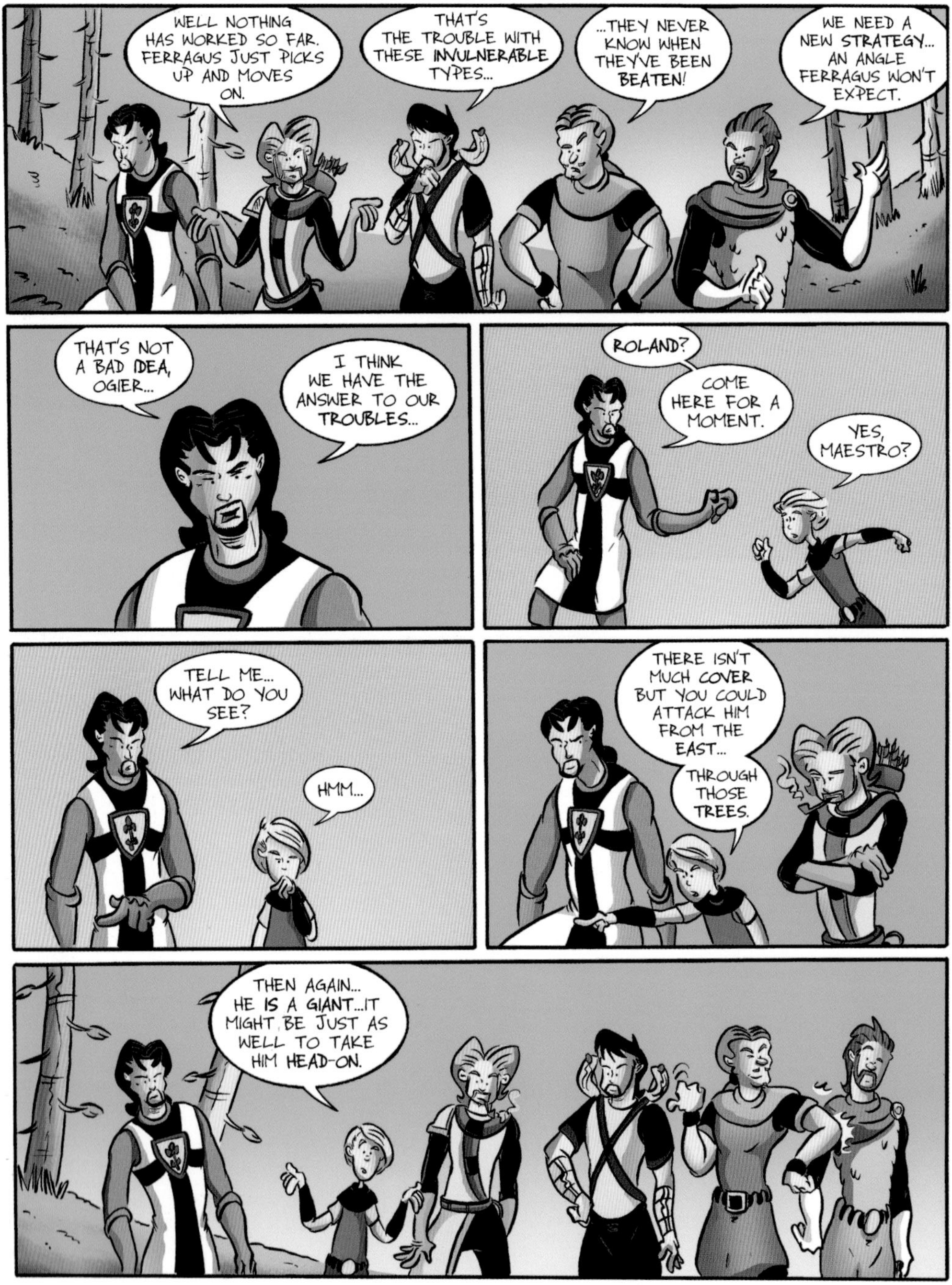
WELL NOTHING HAS WORKED SO FAR. FERRAGUS JUST PICKS UP AND MOVES ON.
THAT'S THE TROUBLE WITH THESE INVULNERABLE TYPES...
...THEY NEVER KNOW WHEN THEY'VE BEEN BEATEN!
WE NEED A NEW STRATEGY... AN ANGLE FERRAGUS WON'T EXPECT.
THAT'S NOT A BAD IDEA, OGIER...
I THINK WE HAVE THE ANSWER TO OUR TROUBLES...
ROLAND?
COME HERE FOR A MOMENT.
YES, MAESTRO?
TELL ME... WHAT DO YOU SEE?
HMM...
THERE ISN'T MUCH COVER BUT YOU COULD ATTACK HIM FROM THE EAST...
THROUGH THOSE TREES.
THEN AGAIN... HE IS A GIANT...IT MIGHT BE JUST AS WELL TO TAKE HIM HEAD-ON.

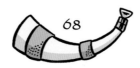

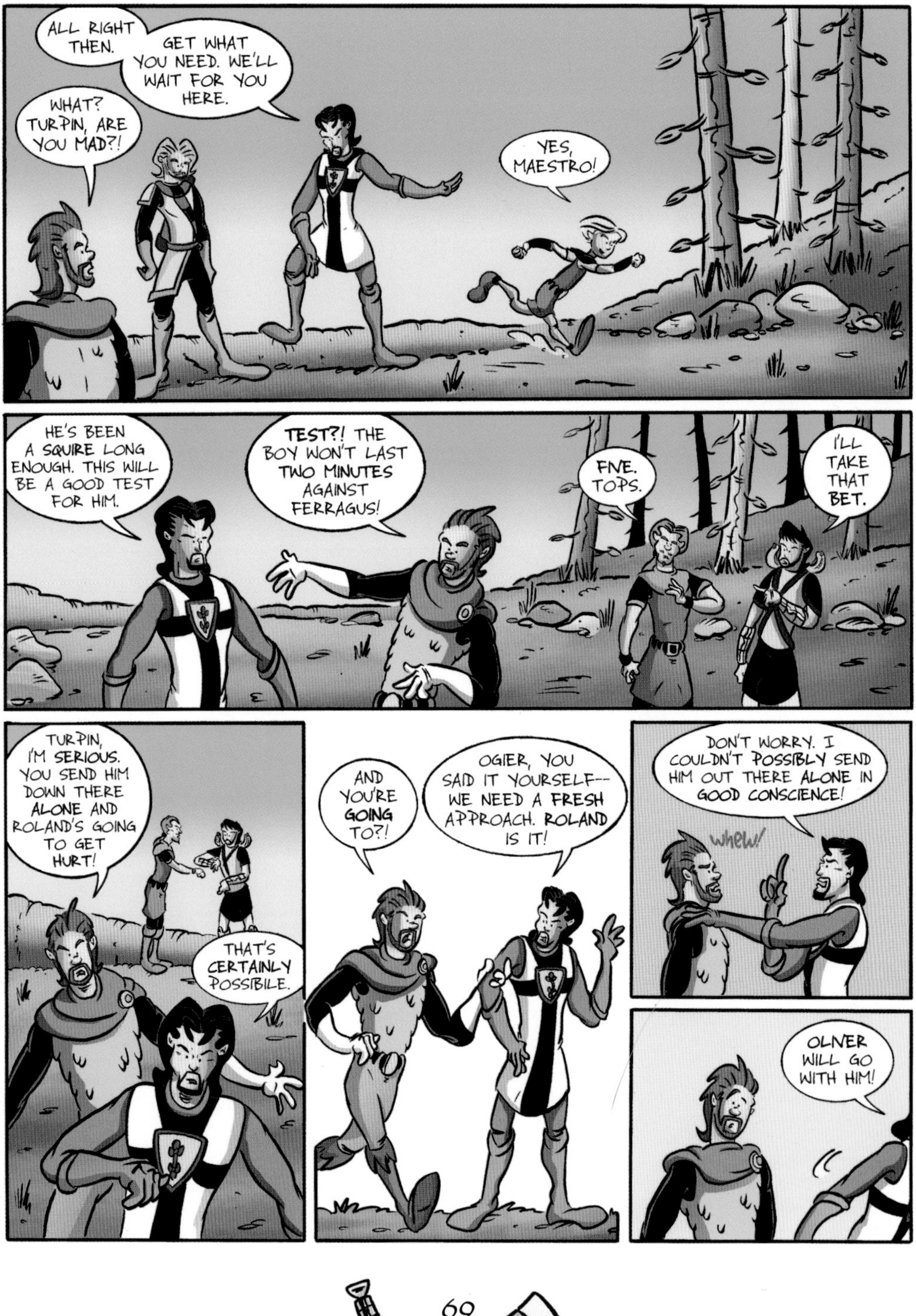
ALL RIGHT THEN.
GET WHAT YOU NEED. WE'LL WAIT FOR YOU HERE.
WHAT? TURPIN, ARE YOU MAD?!
YES, MAESTRO!
HE'S BEEN A SQUIRE LONG ENOUGH. THIS WILL BE A GOOD TEST FOR HIM.
TEST?! THE BOY WON'T LAST TWO MINUTES AGAINST FERRAGUS!
FIVE. TOPS.
I'LL TAKE THAT BET.
TURPIN, I'M SERIOUS. YOU SEND HIM DOWN THERE ALONE AND ROLAND'S GOING TO GET HURT!
THAT'S CERTAINLY POSSIBILE.
AND YOU'RE GOING TO?!
OGIER, YOU SAID IT YOURSELF-- WE NEED A FRESH APPROACH. ROLAND IS IT!
DON'T WORRY. I COULDN'T POSSIBLY SEND HIM OUT THERE ALONE IN GOOD CONSCIENCE!
WHEW!
OLIVER WILL GO WITH HIM!

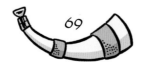

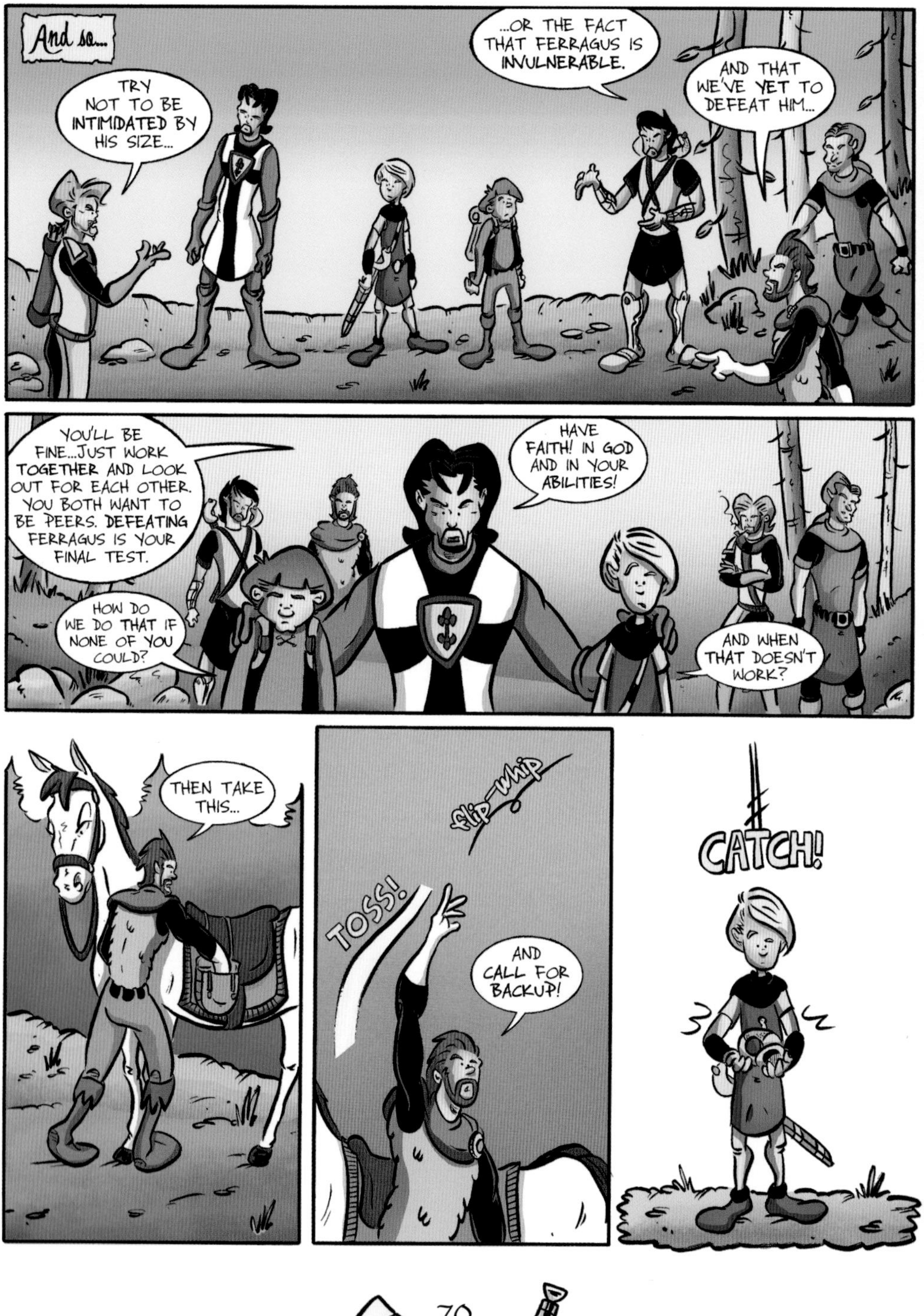
And so...
TRY NOT TO BE INTIMIDATED BY HIS SIZE...
...OR THE FACT THAT FERRAGUS IS INVULNERABLE.
AND THAT WE'VE YET TO DEFEAT HIM...
YOU'LL BE FINE...JUST WORK TOGETHER AND LOOK OUT FOR EACH OTHER. YOU BOTH WANT TO BE PEERS. DEFEATING FERRAGUS IS YOUR FINAL TEST.
HAVE FAITH! IN GOD AND IN YOUR ABILITIES!
HOW DO WE DO THAT IF NONE OF YOU COULD?
AND WHEN THAT DOESN'T WORK?
THEN TAKE THIS...
flip-whip
TOSS!
AND CALL FOR BACKUP!
CATCH!

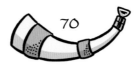

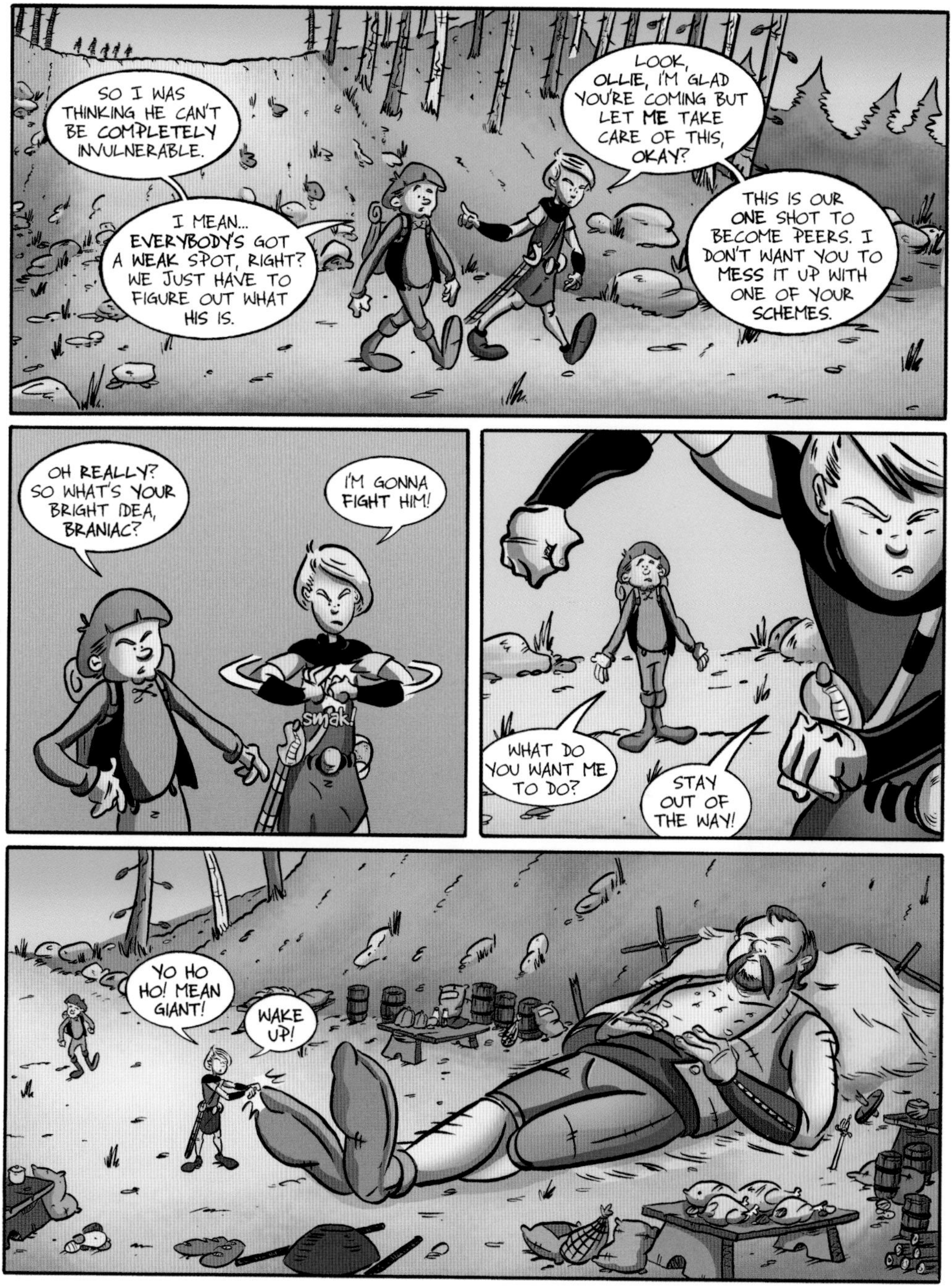
SO I WAS THINKING HE CAN'T BE COMPLETELY INVULNERABLE.
I MEAN... EVERYBODY'S GOT A WEAK SPOT, RIGHT? WE JUST HAVE TO FIGURE OUT WHAT HIS IS.
LOOK, OLLIE, I'M GLAD YOU'RE COMING BUT LET ME TAKE CARE OF THIS, OKAY?
THIS IS OUR ONE SHOT TO BECOME PEERS. I DON'T WANT YOU TO MESS IT UP WITH ONE OF YOUR SCHEMES.
OH REALLY? SO WHAT'S YOUR BRIGHT IDEA, BRANIAC?
I'M GONNA FIGHT HIM!
SMAK!
WHAT DO YOU WANT ME TO DO?
STAY OUT OF THE WAY!
YO HO HO! MEAN GIANT!
WAKE UP!

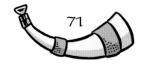

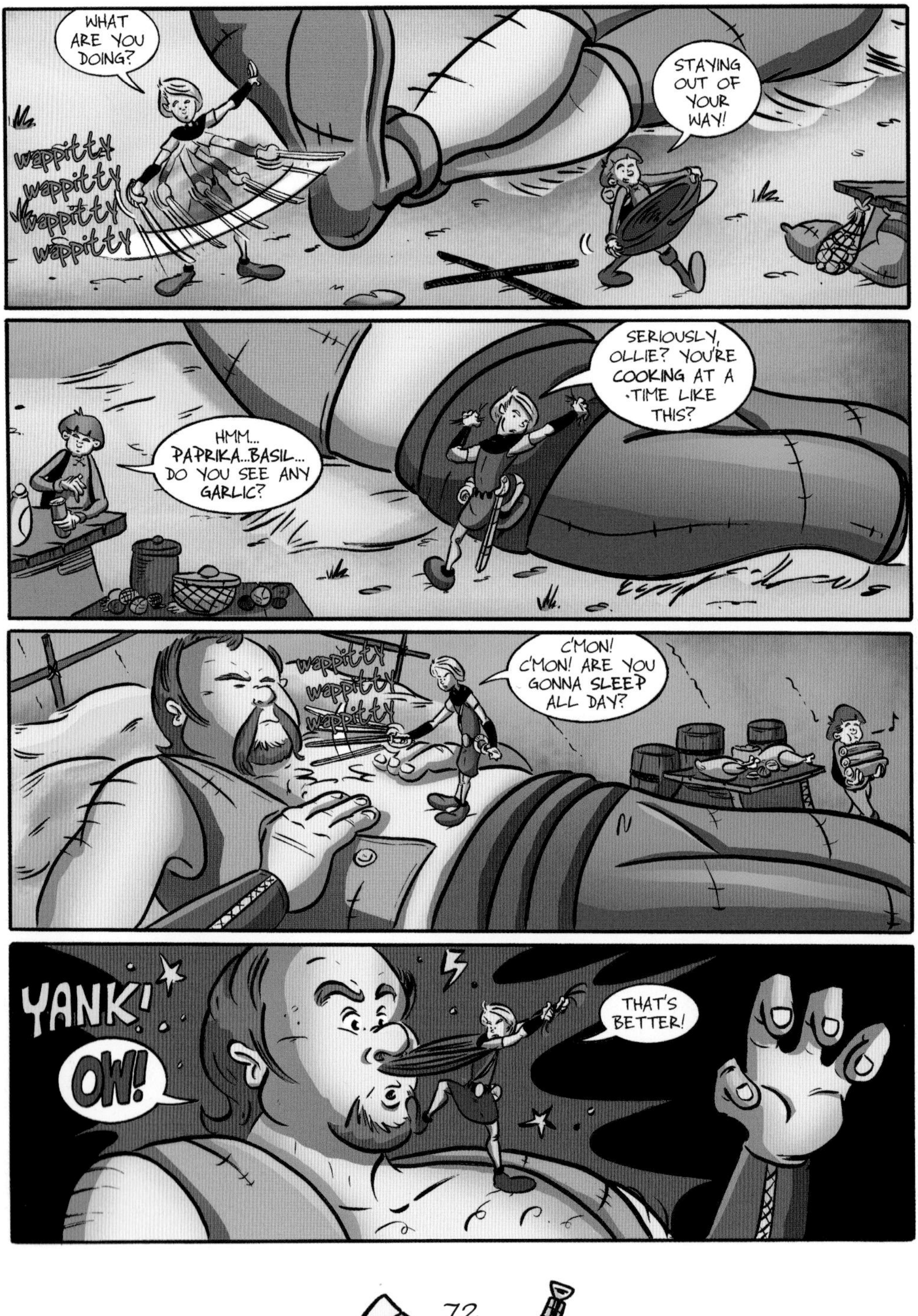
WHAT ARE YOU DOING?
wappitty wappitty wappitty wappitty
STAYING OUT OF YOUR WAY!
SERIOUSLY, OLLIE? YOU'RE COOKING AT A TIME LIKE THIS?
HMM... PAPRIKA...BASIL... DO YOU SEE ANY GARLIC?
wappitty wappitty wappitty
C'MON! C'MON! ARE YOU GONNA SLEEP ALL DAY?
YANK!
OW!
THAT'S BETTER!

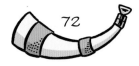

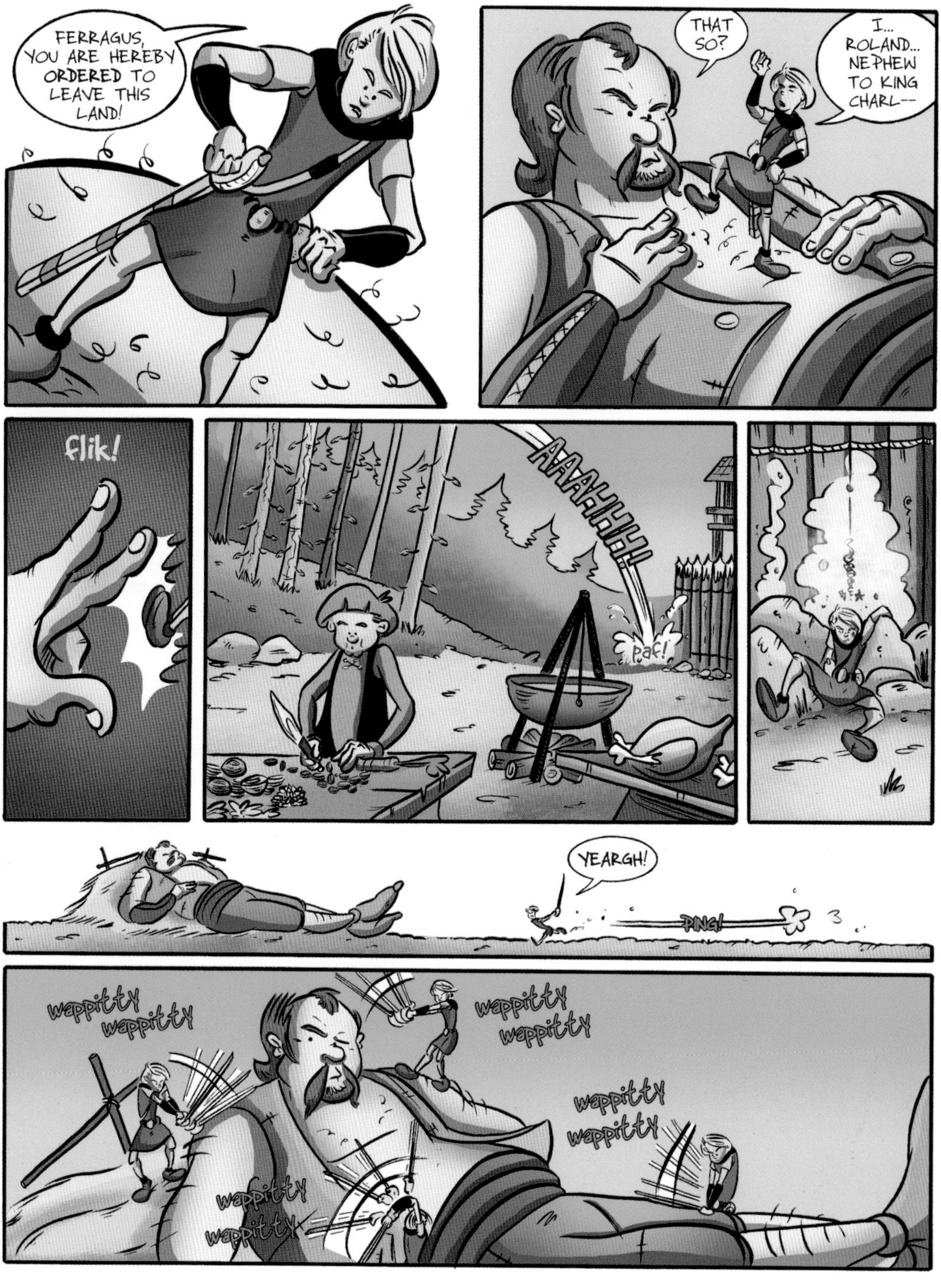
FERRAGUS, YOU ARE HEREBY ORDERED TO LEAVE THIS LAND!
THAT SO?
I... ROLAND... NEPHEW TO KING CHARL--
flik!
AAAAHHHH!
PAF!
YEARGH!
PING!
wappitty wappitty
wappitty wappitty
wappitty wappitty
wappitty wappitty

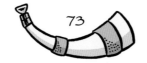

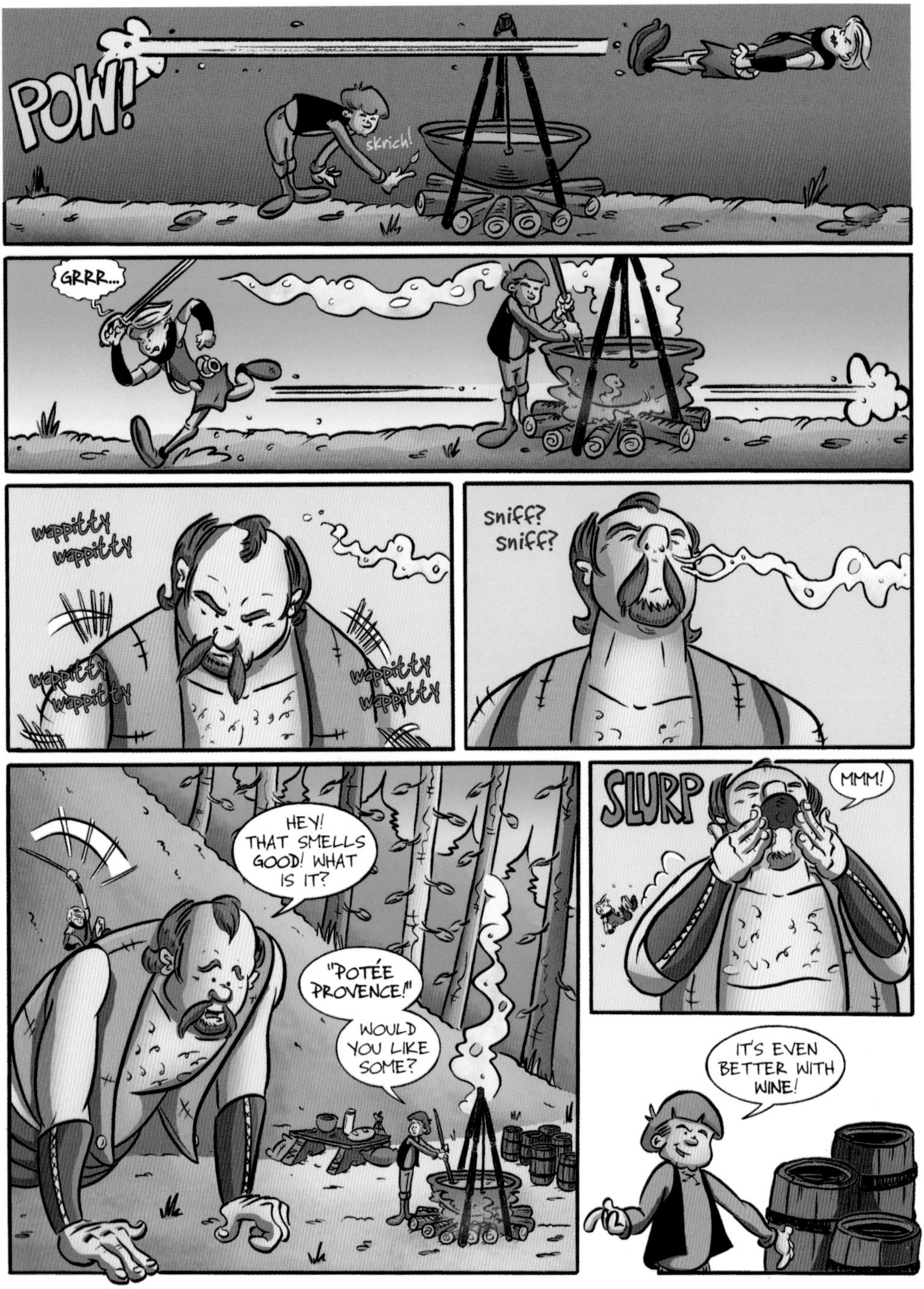
POW!
skrich!
GRRR...
wappitty wappitty
wappitty wappitty
wappitty wappitty
sniff? sniff?
HEY! THAT SMELLS GOOD! WHAT IS IT?
"POTÉE PROVENCE!"
WOULD YOU LIKE SOME?
SLURP
MMM!
IT'S EVEN BETTER WITH WINE!

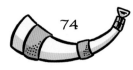

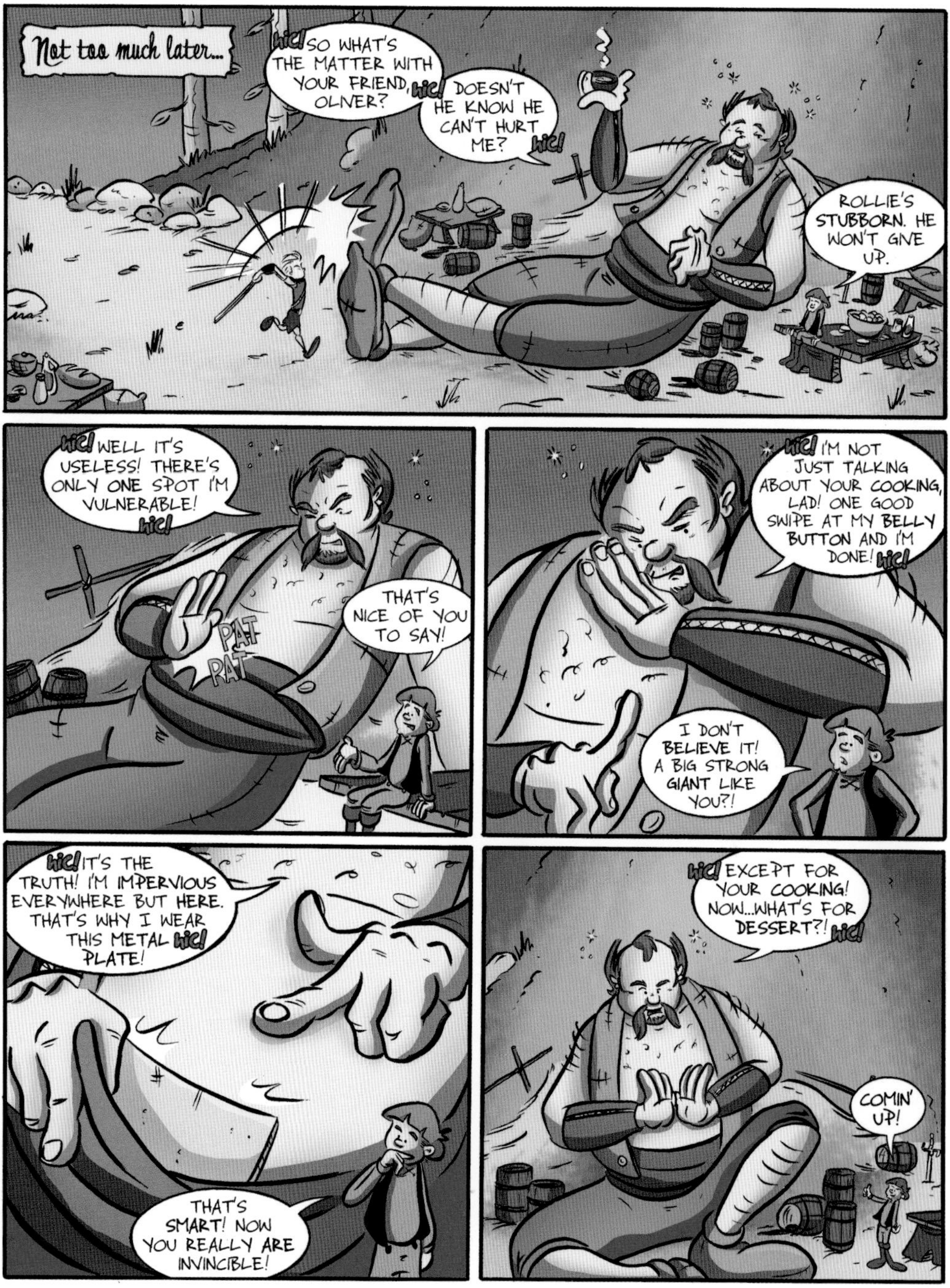
Not too much later...
hic! SO WHAT'S THE MATTER WITH YOUR FRIEND, hic! OLIVER?
DOESN'T HE KNOW HE CAN'T HURT ME? hic!
ROLLIE'S STUBBORN. HE WON'T GIVE UP.
hic! WELL IT'S USELESS! THERE'S ONLY ONE SPOT I'M VULNERABLE! hic!
PAT PAT
THAT'S NICE OF YOU TO SAY!
hic! I'M NOT JUST TALKING ABOUT YOUR COOKING, LAD! ONE GOOD SWIPE AT MY BELLY BUTTON AND I'M DONE! hic!
I DON'T BELIEVE IT! A BIG STRONG GIANT LIKE YOU?!
hic! IT'S THE TRUTH! I'M IMPERVIOUS EVERYWHERE BUT HERE. THAT'S WHY I WEAR THIS METAL hic! PLATE!
THAT'S SMART! NOW YOU REALLY ARE INVINCIBLE!
hic! EXCEPT FOR YOUR COOKING! NOW...WHAT'S FOR DESSERT?! hic!
COMIN' UP!

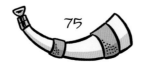

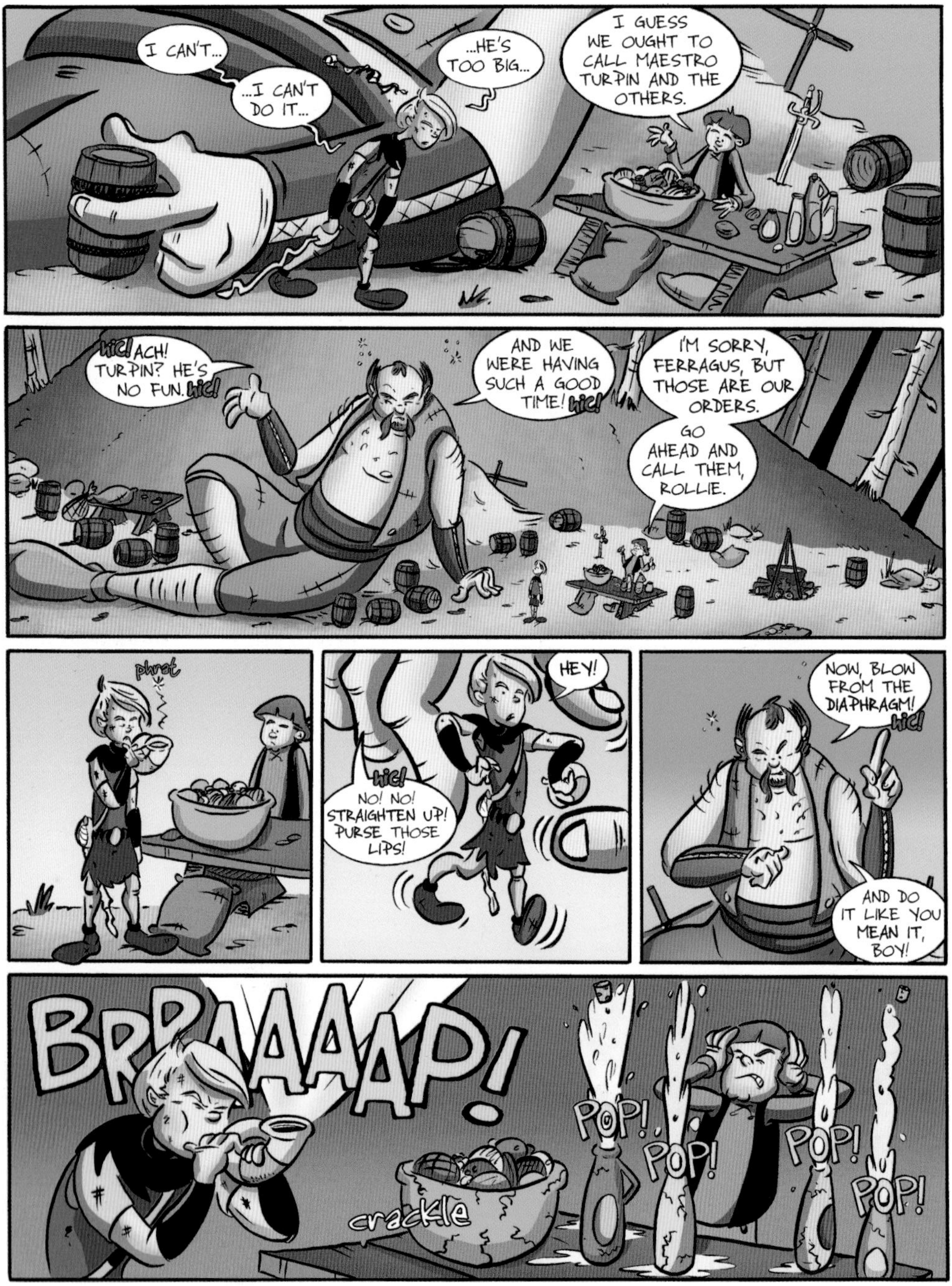
I CAN'T...
...I CAN'T DO IT...
...HE'S TOO BIG...
I GUESS WE OUGHT TO CALL MAESTRO TURPIN AND THE OTHERS.
hic! ACH! TURPIN? HE'S NO FUN. hic!
AND WE WERE HAVING SUCH A GOOD TIME! hic!
I'M SORRY, FERRAGUS, BUT THOSE ARE OUR ORDERS.
GO AHEAD AND CALL THEM, ROLLIE.
phrat
HEY!
hic! NO! NO! STRAIGHTEN UP! PURSE THOSE LIPS!
NOW, BLOW FROM THE DIAPHRAGM! hic!
AND DO IT LIKE YOU MEAN IT, BOY!
BRAAAAP!
POP! POP! POP! POP!
crackle

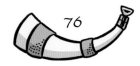

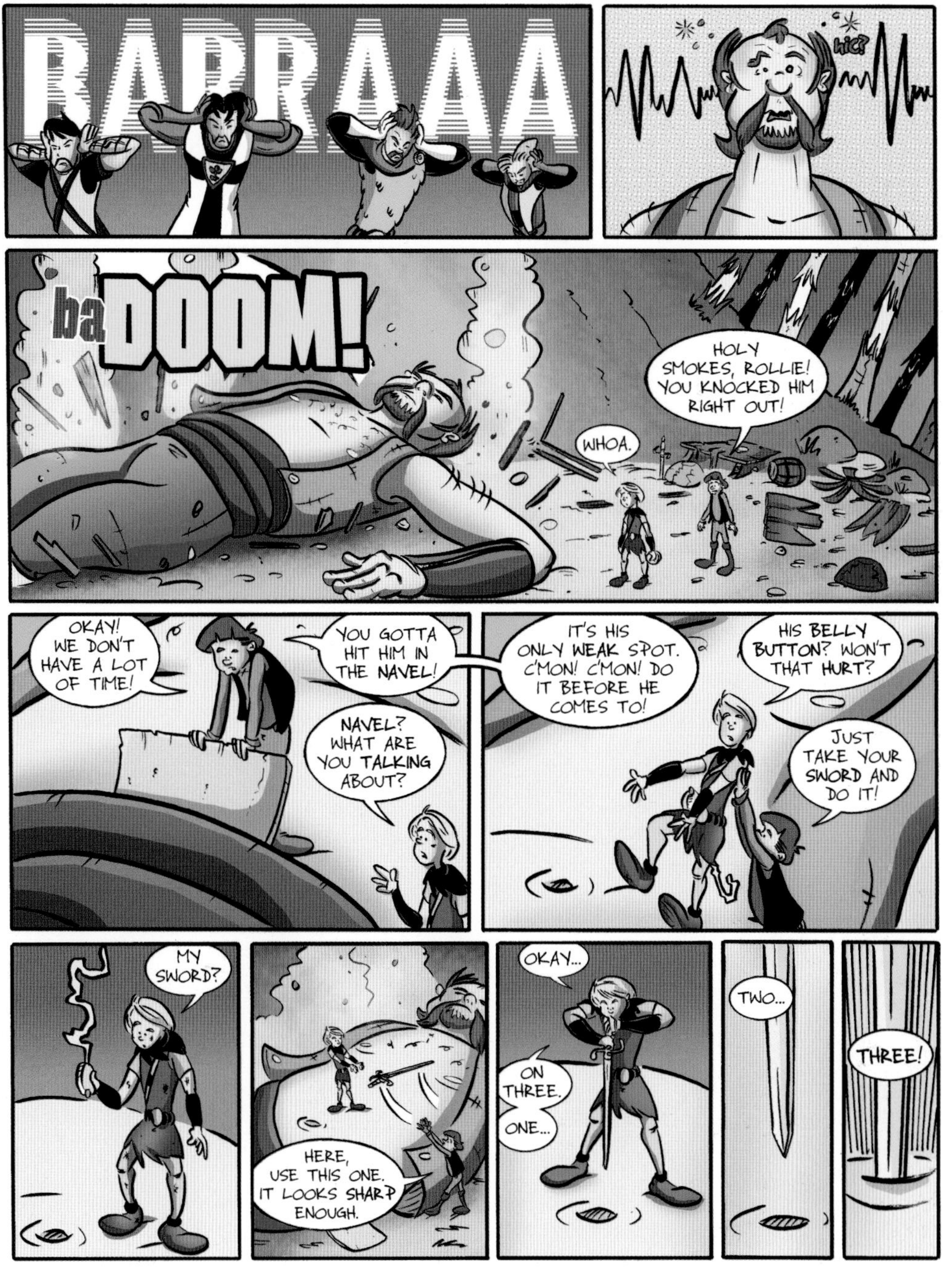
BARRAAA
hic?
baDOOM!
WHOA.
HOLY SMOKES, ROLLIE! YOU KNOCKED HIM RIGHT OUT!
OKAY! WE DON'T HAVE A LOT OF TIME!
YOU GOTTA HIT HIM IN THE NAVEL!
NAVEL? WHAT ARE YOU TALKING ABOUT?
IT'S HIS ONLY WEAK SPOT. C'MON! C'MON! DO IT BEFORE HE COMES TO!
HIS BELLY BUTTON? WON'T THAT HURT?
JUST TAKE YOUR SWORD AND DO IT!
MY SWORD?
HERE, USE THIS ONE. IT LOOKS SHARP ENOUGH.
OKAY...
ON THREE.
ONE...
TWO...
THREE!

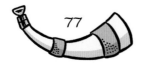

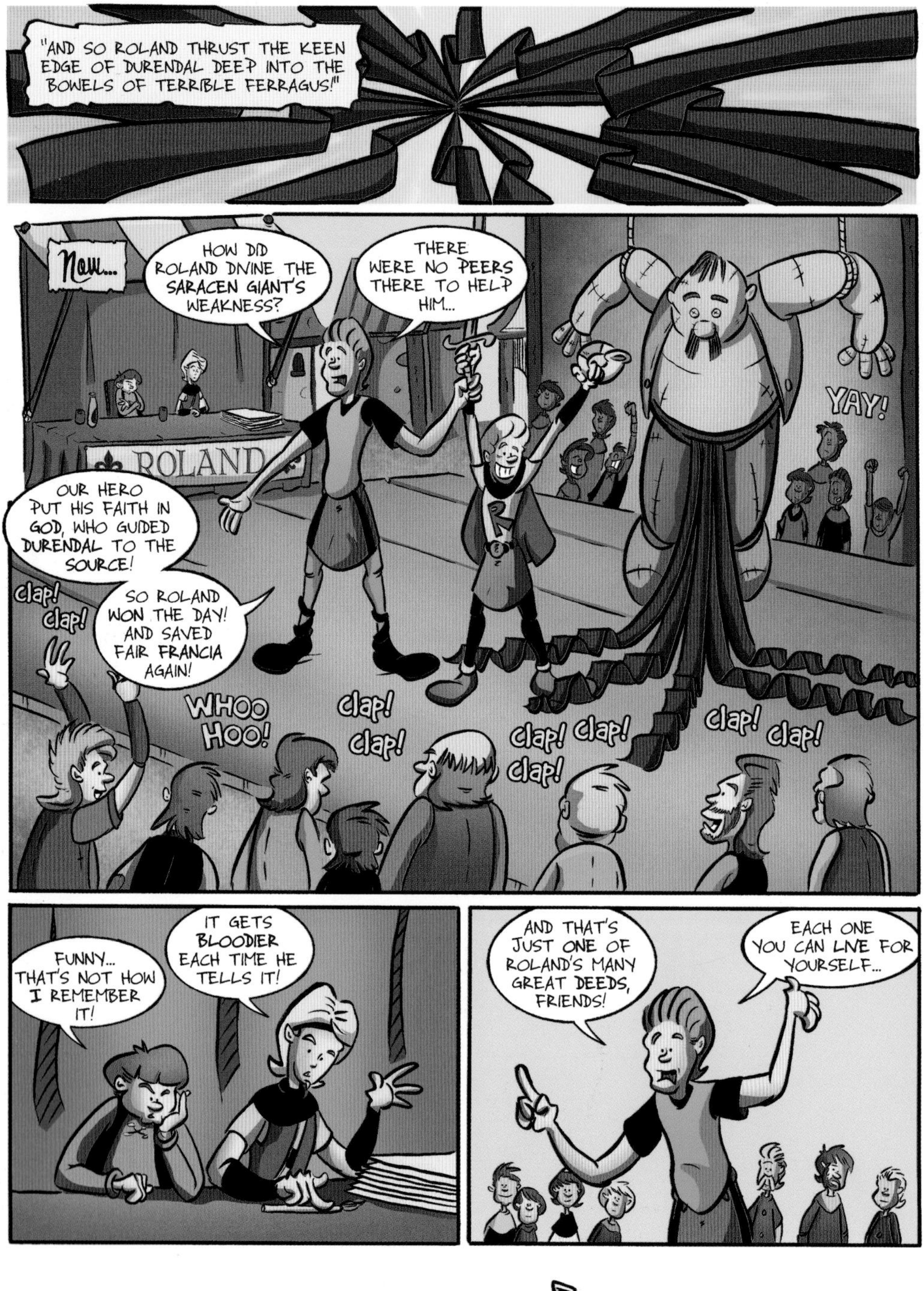
"AND SO ROLAND THRUST THE KEEN EDGE OF DURENDAL DEEP INTO THE BOWELS OF TERRIBLE FERRAGUS!"
Now...
HOW DID ROLAND DIVINE THE SARACEN GIANT'S WEAKNESS?
THERE WERE NO PEERS THERE TO HELP HIM...
ROLAND
YAY!
OUR HERO PUT HIS FAITH IN GOD, WHO GUIDED DURENDAL TO THE SOURCE!
SO ROLAND WON THE DAY! AND SAVED FAIR FRANCIA AGAIN!
clap! clap!
WHOO HOO!
clap! clap!
clap! clap! clap!
clap! clap!
FUNNY... THAT'S NOT HOW I REMEMBER IT!
IT GETS BLOODIER EACH TIME HE TELLS IT!
AND THAT'S JUST ONE OF ROLAND'S MANY GREAT DEEDS, FRIENDS!
EACH ONE YOU CAN LIVE FOR YOURSELF...

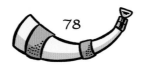

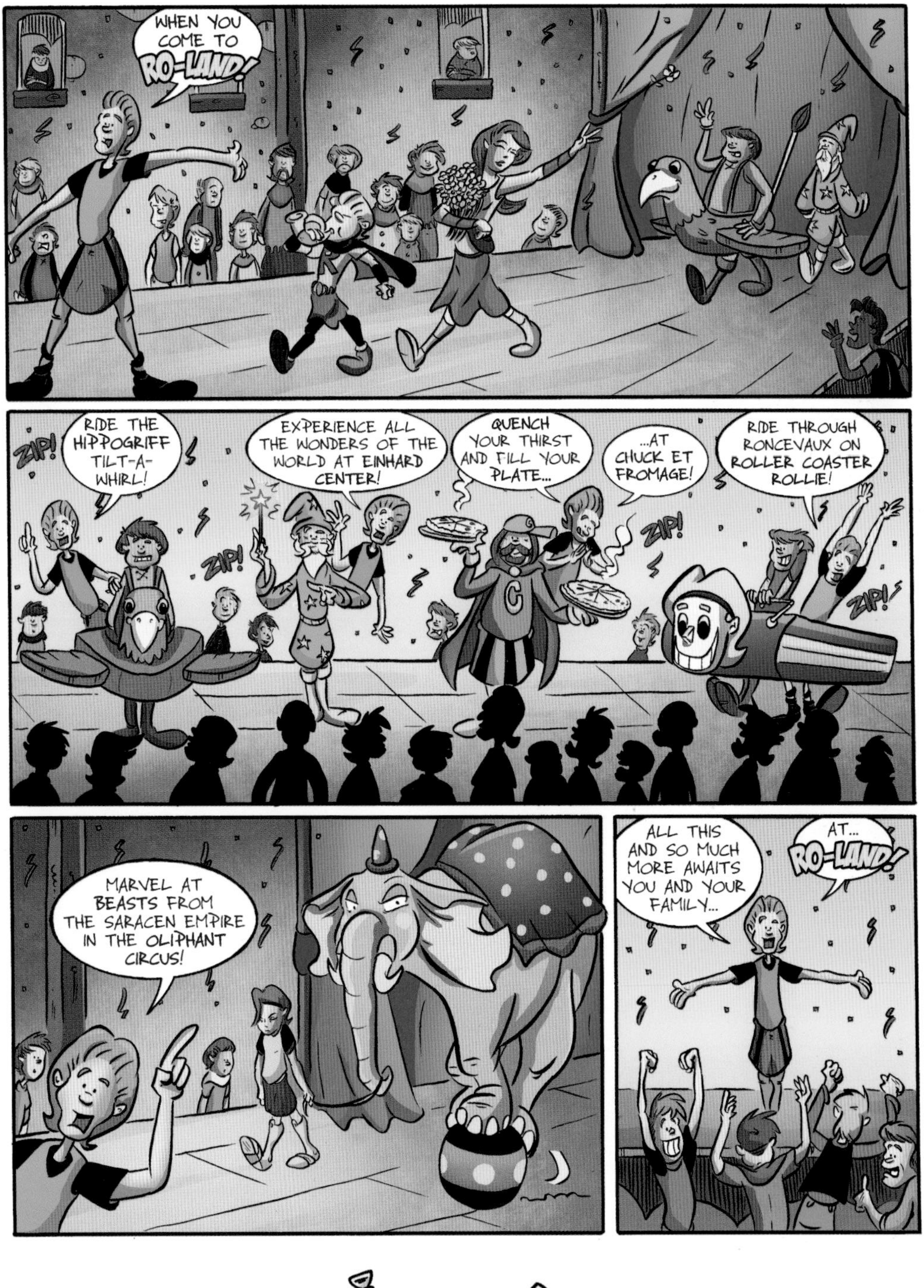
WHEN YOU COME TO RO-LAND!
ZIP!
RIDE THE HIPPOGRIFF TILT-A-WHIRL!
EXPERIENCE ALL THE WONDERS OF THE WORLD AT EINHARD CENTER!
QUENCH YOUR THIRST AND FILL YOUR PLATE...
...AT CHUCK ET FROMAGE!
RIDE THROUGH RONCEVAUX ON ROLLER COASTER ROLLIE!
ZIP!
ZIP!
ZIP!
MARVEL AT BEASTS FROM THE SARACEN EMPIRE IN THE OLIPHANT CIRCUS!
ALL THIS AND SO MUCH MORE AWAITS YOU AND YOUR FAMILY...
AT... RO-LAND!

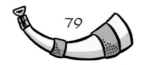

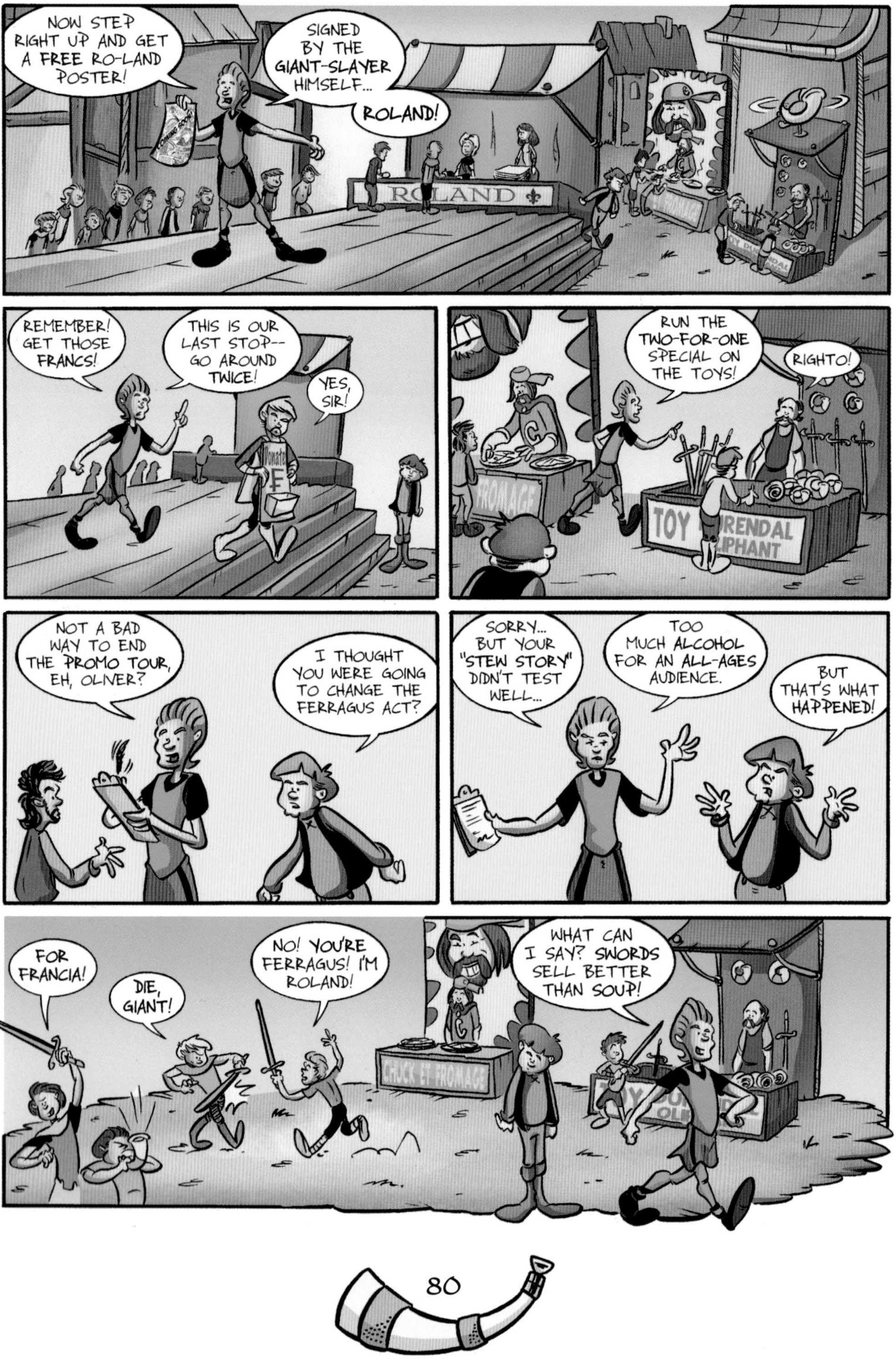
NOW STEP RIGHT UP AND GET A FREE RO-LAND POSTER!
SIGNED BY THE GIANT-SLAYER HIMSELF...
ROLAND!
ROLAND
FROMAGE
REMEMBER! GET THOSE FRANCS!
THIS IS OUR LAST STOP-- GO AROUND TWICE!
YES, SIR!
Donate
RUN THE TWO-FOR-ONE SPECIAL ON THE TOYS!
RIGHTO!
FROMAGE
NOT A BAD WAY TO END THE PROMO TOUR, EH, OLIVER?
I THOUGHT YOU WERE GOING TO CHANGE THE FERRAGUS ACT?
SORRY... BUT YOUR "STEW STORY" DIDN'T TEST WELL...
TOO MUCH ALCOHOL FOR AN ALL-AGES AUDIENCE.
BUT THAT'S WHAT HAPPENED!
FOR FRANCIA!
DIE, GIANT!
NO! YOU'RE FERRAGUS! I'M ROLAND!
WHAT CAN I SAY? SWORDS SELL BETTER THAN SOUP!
CHUCK ET FROMAGE

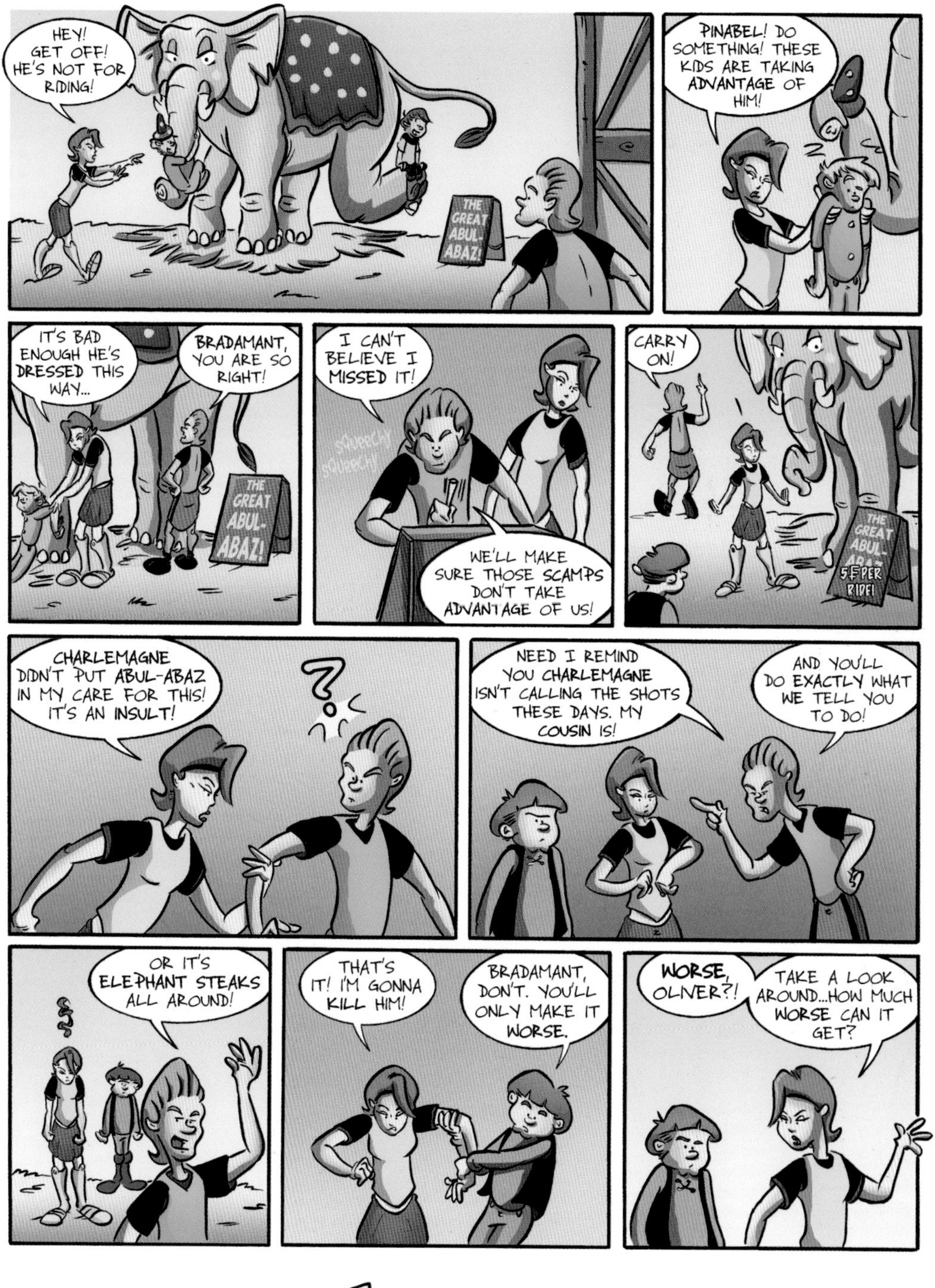
HEY! GET OFF! HE'S NOT FOR RIDING!
THE GREAT ABUL-ABAZ!
PINABEL! DO SOMETHING! THESE KIDS ARE TAKING ADVANTAGE OF HIM!
IT'S BAD ENOUGH HE'S DRESSED THIS WAY...
BRADAMANT, YOU ARE SO RIGHT!
THE GREAT ABUL-ABAZ!
I CAN'T BELIEVE I MISSED IT!
SQUEECH! SQUEECH!
WE'LL MAKE SURE THOSE SCAMPS DON'T TAKE ADVANTAGE OF US!
CARRY ON!
THE GREAT ABUL-
5 F PER RIDE!
CHARLEMAGNE DIDN'T PUT ABUL-ABAZ IN MY CARE FOR THIS! IT'S AN INSULT!
?
NEED I REMIND YOU CHARLEMAGNE ISN'T CALLING THE SHOTS THESE DAYS. MY COUSIN IS!
AND YOU'LL DO EXACTLY WHAT WE TELL YOU TO DO!
OR IT'S ELEPHANT STEAKS ALL AROUND!
THAT'S IT! I'M GONNA KILL HIM!
BRADAMANT, DON'T. YOU'LL ONLY MAKE IT WORSE.
WORSE, OLIVER?!
TAKE A LOOK AROUND...HOW MUCH WORSE CAN IT GET?

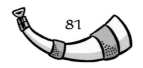

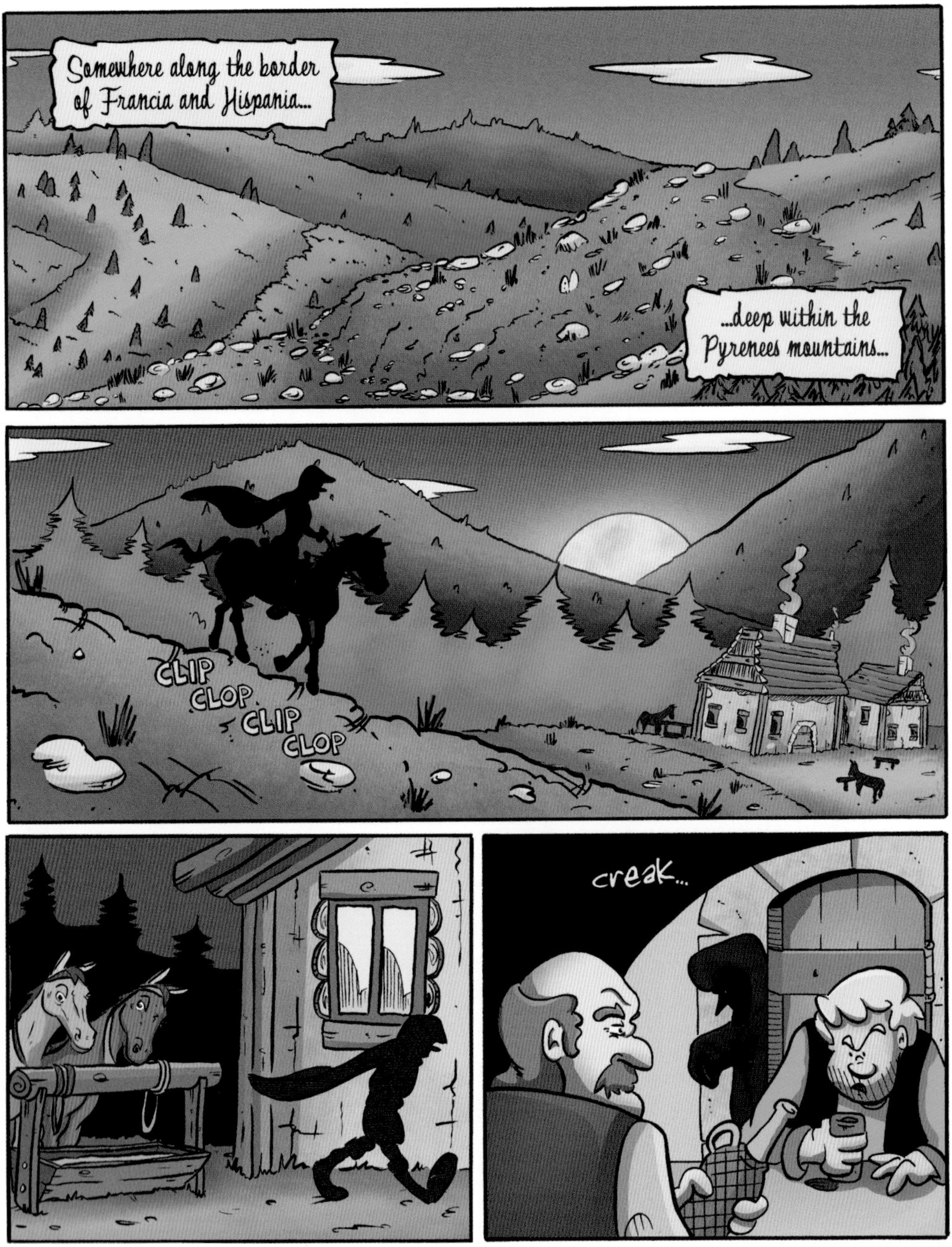
Somewhere along the border of Francia and Hispania...
...deep within the Pyrenees mountains...
CLIP
CLOP
CLIP
CLOP
creak...

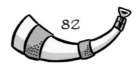

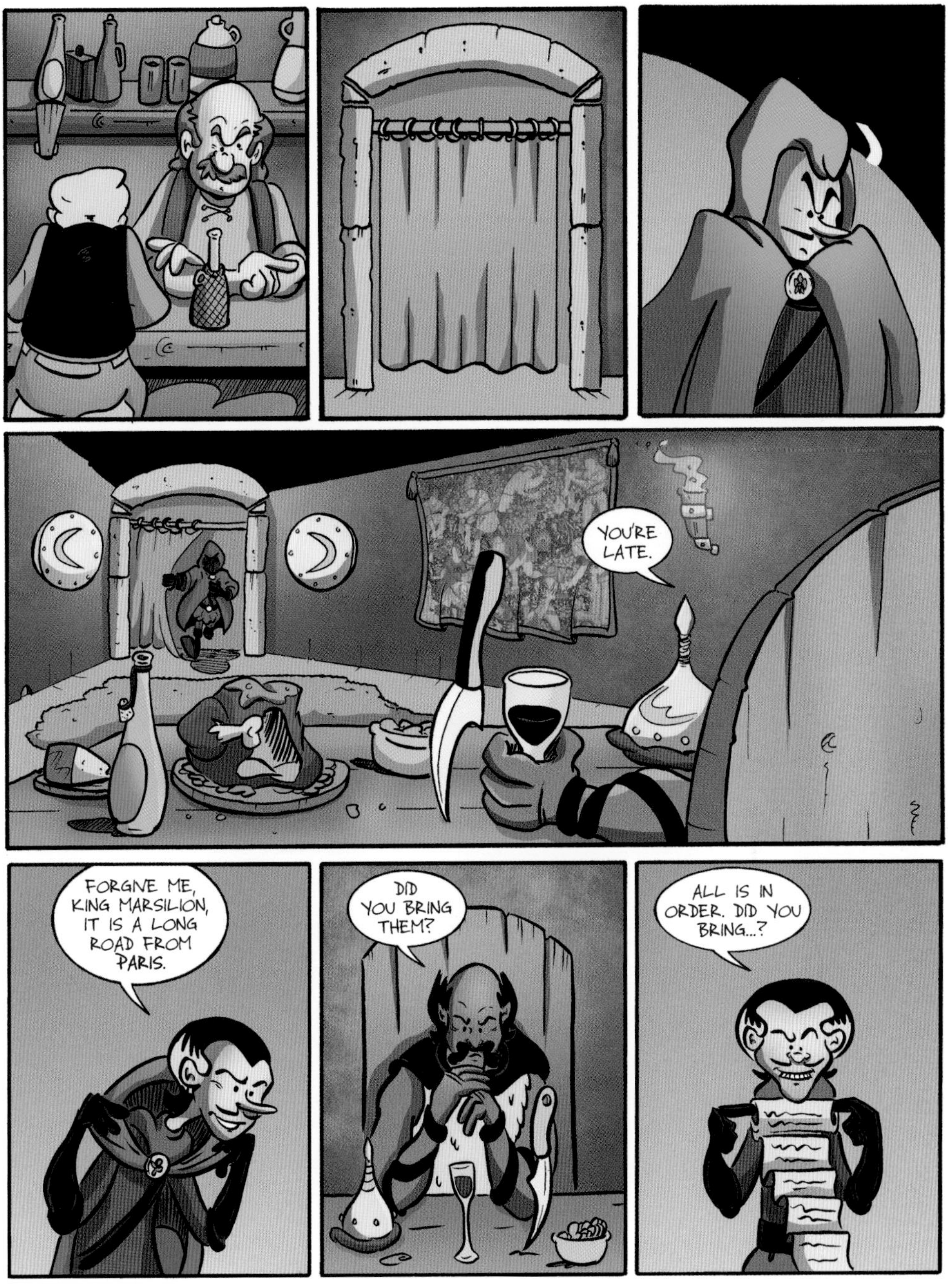
YOU'RE LATE.
FORGIVE ME, KING MARSILION, IT IS A LONG ROAD FROM PARIS.
DID YOU BRING THEM?
ALL IS IN ORDER. DID YOU BRING...?

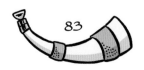

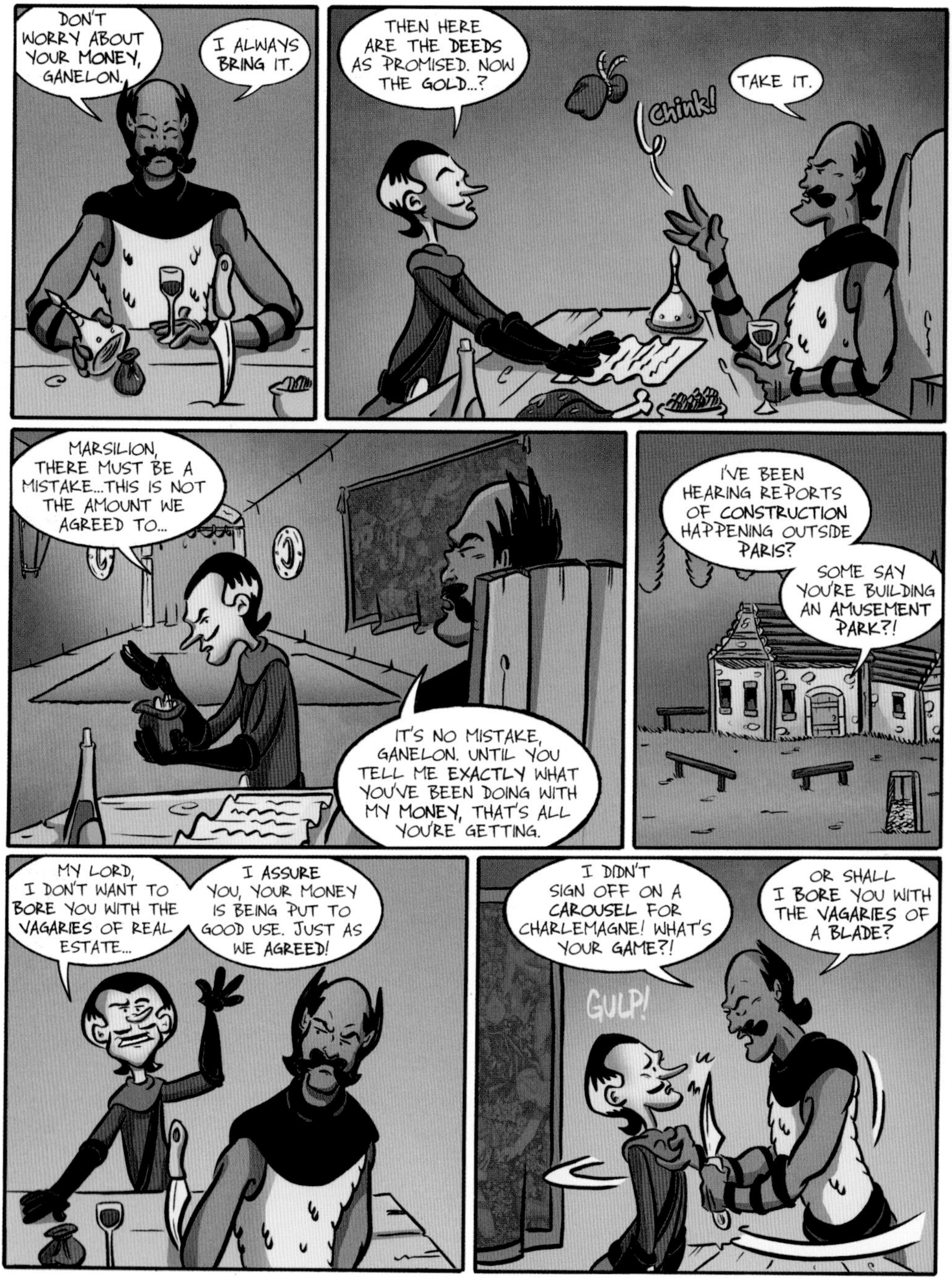
DON'T WORRY ABOUT YOUR MONEY, GANELON.
I ALWAYS BRING IT.
THEN HERE ARE THE DEEDS AS PROMISED. NOW THE GOLD...?
Chink!
TAKE IT.
MARSILION, THERE MUST BE A MISTAKE...THIS IS NOT THE AMOUNT WE AGREED TO...
IT'S NO MISTAKE, GANELON. UNTIL YOU TELL ME EXACTLY WHAT YOU'VE BEEN DOING WITH MY MONEY, THAT'S ALL YOU'RE GETTING.
I'VE BEEN HEARING REPORTS OF CONSTRUCTION HAPPENING OUTSIDE PARIS?
SOME SAY YOU'RE BUILDING AN AMUSEMENT PARK?!
MY LORD, I DON'T WANT TO BORE YOU WITH THE VAGARIES OF REAL ESTATE...
I ASSURE YOU, YOUR MONEY IS BEING PUT TO GOOD USE. JUST AS WE AGREED!
I DIDN'T SIGN OFF ON A CAROUSEL FOR CHARLEMAGNE! WHAT'S YOUR GAME?!
OR SHALL I BORE YOU WITH THE VAGARIES OF A BLADE?
GULP!

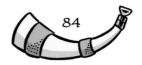

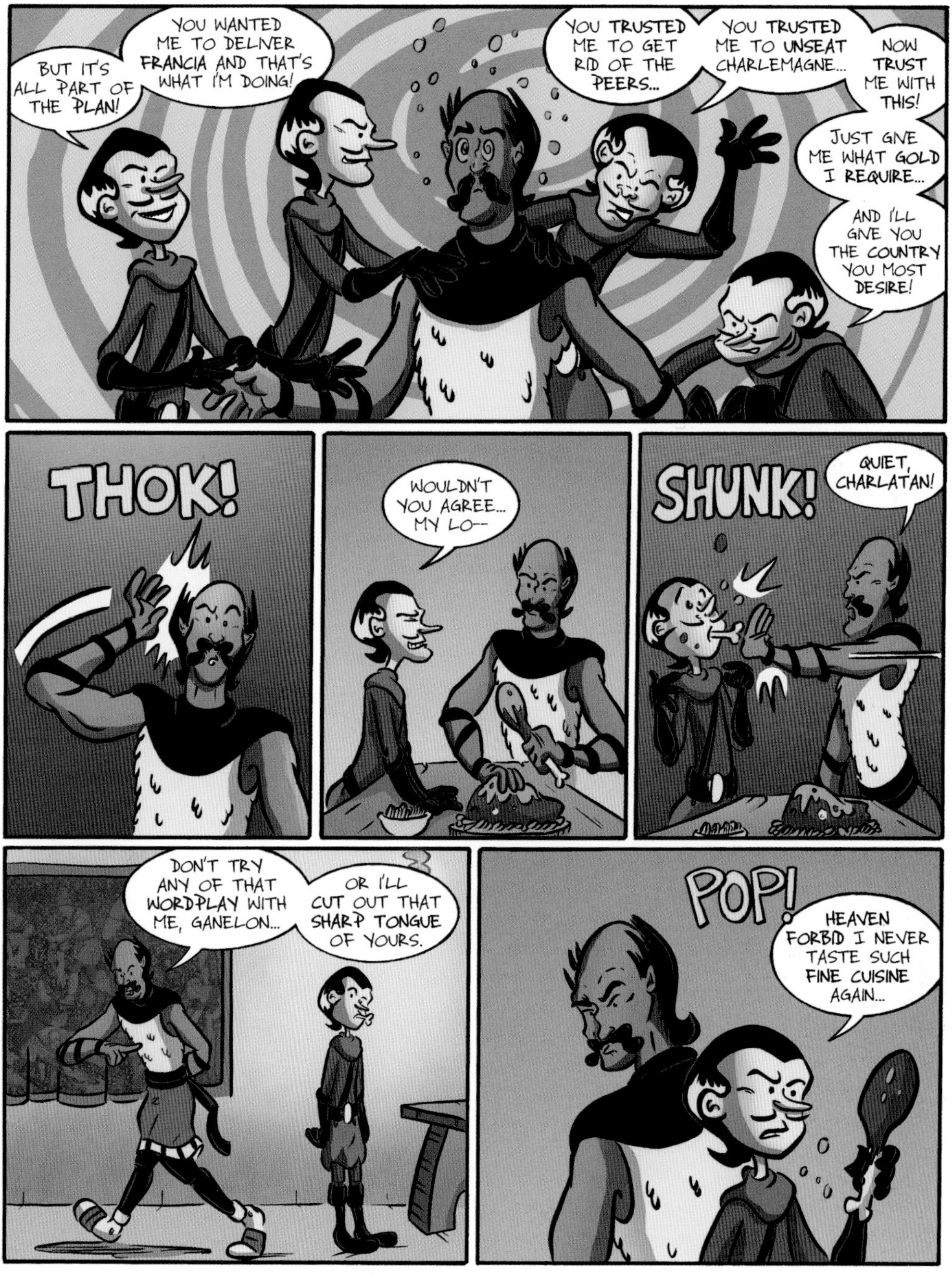
BUT IT'S ALL PART OF THE PLAN!
YOU WANTED ME TO DELIVER FRANCIA AND THAT'S WHAT I'M DOING!
YOU TRUSTED ME TO GET RID OF THE PEERS...
YOU TRUSTED ME TO UNSEAT CHARLEMAGNE...
NOW TRUST ME WITH THIS!
JUST GIVE ME WHAT GOLD I REQUIRE...
AND I'LL GIVE YOU THE COUNTRY YOU MOST DESIRE!
THOK!
WOULDN'T YOU AGREE... MY LO--
SHUNK!
QUIET, CHARLATAN!
DON'T TRY ANY OF THAT WORDPLAY WITH ME, GANELON...
OR I'LL CUT OUT THAT SHARP TONGUE OF YOURS.
POP!
HEAVEN FORBID I NEVER TASTE SUCH FINE CUISINE AGAIN...

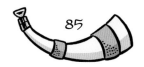

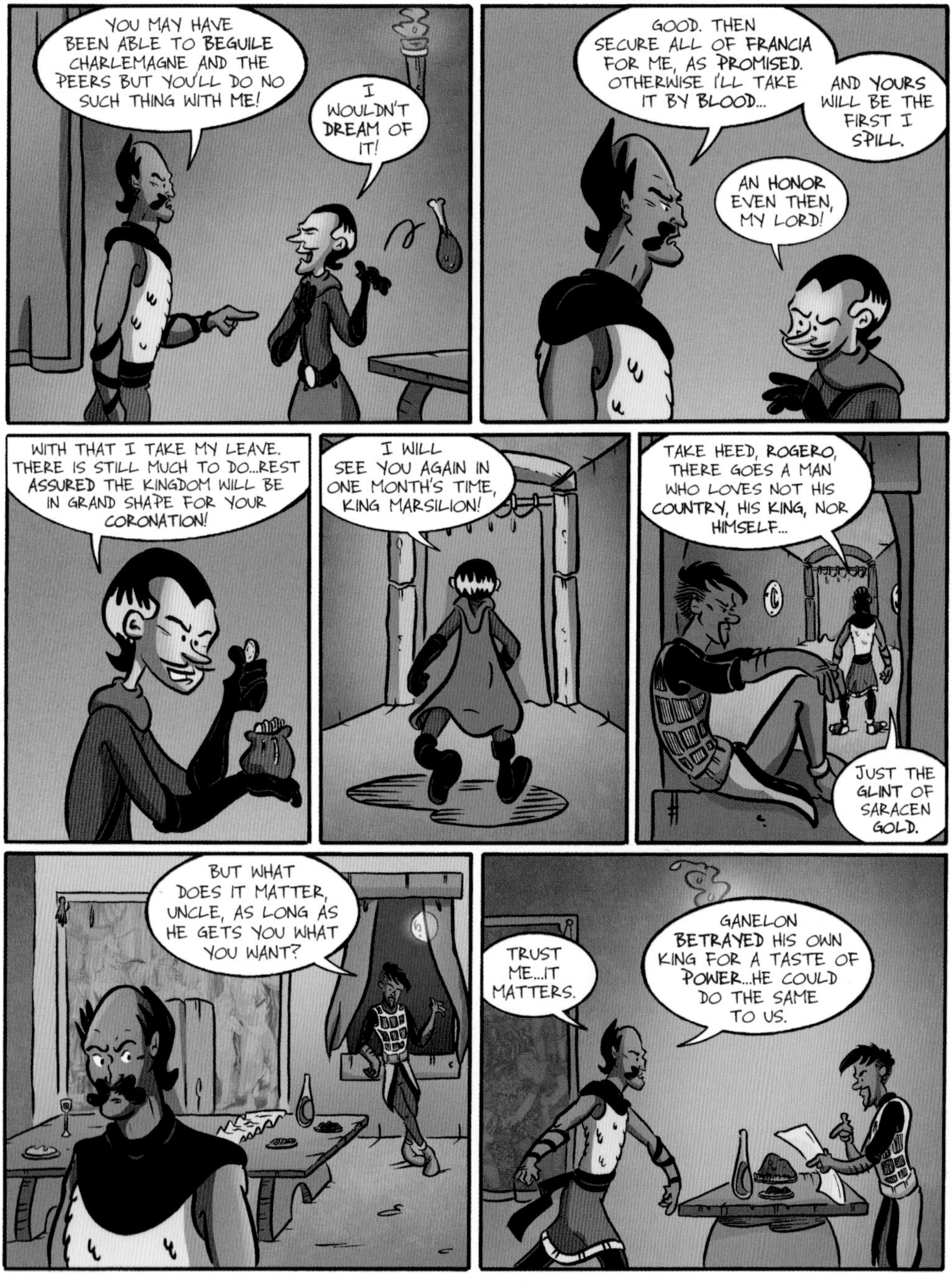
YOU MAY HAVE BEEN ABLE TO BEGUILE CHARLEMAGNE AND THE PEERS BUT YOU'LL DO NO SUCH THING WITH ME!
I WOULDN'T DREAM OF IT!
GOOD. THEN SECURE ALL OF FRANCIA FOR ME, AS PROMISED. OTHERWISE I'LL TAKE IT BY BLOOD...
AND YOURS WILL BE THE FIRST I SPILL.
AN HONOR EVEN THEN, MY LORD!
WITH THAT I TAKE MY LEAVE. THERE IS STILL MUCH TO DO...REST ASSURED THE KINGDOM WILL BE IN GRAND SHAPE FOR YOUR CORONATION!
I WILL SEE YOU AGAIN IN ONE MONTH'S TIME, KING MARSILION!
TAKE HEED, ROGERO, THERE GOES A MAN WHO LOVES NOT HIS COUNTRY, HIS KING, NOR HIMSELF...
JUST THE GLINT OF SARACEN GOLD.
BUT WHAT DOES IT MATTER, UNCLE, AS LONG AS HE GETS YOU WHAT YOU WANT?
TRUST ME...IT MATTERS.
GANELON BETRAYED HIS OWN KING FOR A TASTE OF POWER...HE COULD DO THE SAME TO US.

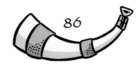

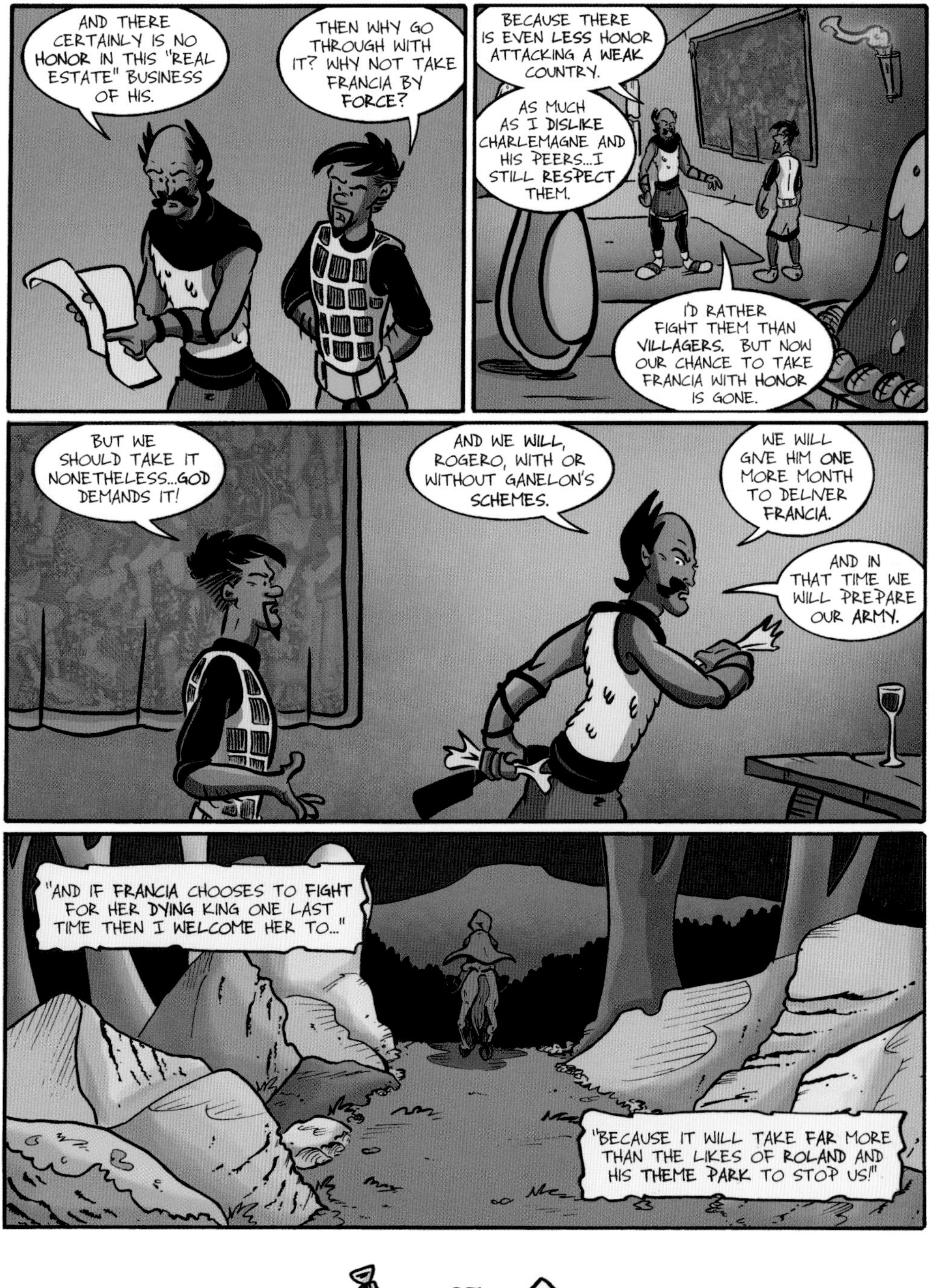
AND THERE CERTAINLY IS NO HONOR IN THIS "REAL ESTATE" BUSINESS OF HIS.
THEN WHY GO THROUGH WITH IT? WHY NOT TAKE FRANCIA BY FORCE?
BECAUSE THERE IS EVEN LESS HONOR ATTACKING A WEAK COUNTRY.
AS MUCH AS I DISLIKE CHARLEMAGNE AND HIS PEERS...I STILL RESPECT THEM.
I'D RATHER FIGHT THEM THAN VILLAGERS. BUT NOW OUR CHANCE TO TAKE FRANCIA WITH HONOR IS GONE.
BUT WE SHOULD TAKE IT NONETHELESS...GOD DEMANDS IT!
AND WE WILL, ROGERO, WITH OR WITHOUT GANELON'S SCHEMES.
WE WILL GIVE HIM ONE MORE MONTH TO DELIVER FRANCIA.
AND IN THAT TIME WE WILL PREPARE OUR ARMY.
"AND IF FRANCIA CHOOSES TO FIGHT FOR HER DYING KING ONE LAST TIME THEN I WELCOME HER TO..."
"BECAUSE IT WILL TAKE FAR MORE THAN THE LIKES OF ROLAND AND HIS THEME PARK TO STOP US!"

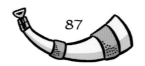

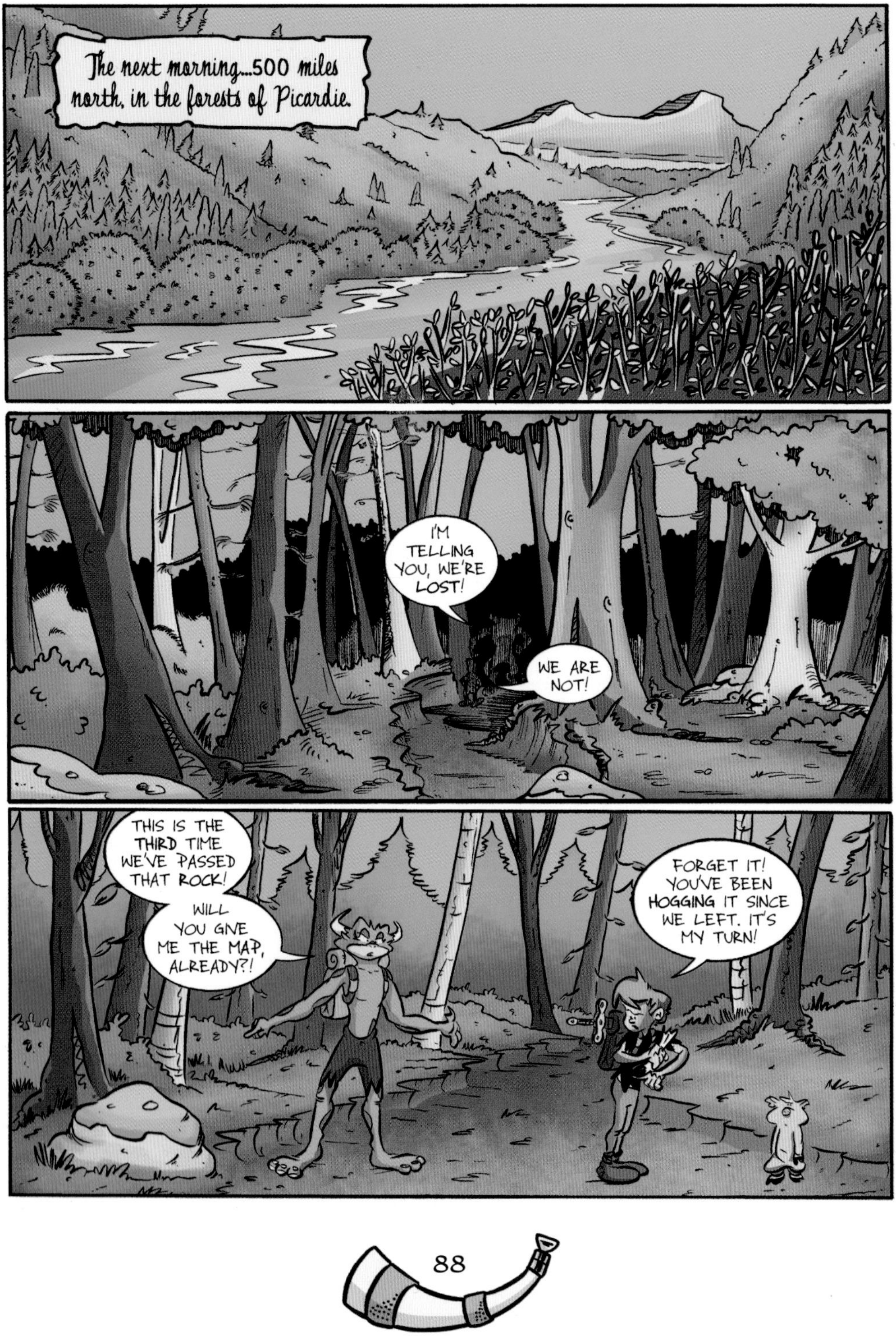
The next morning...500 miles north, in the forests of Picardie.
I'M TELLING YOU, WE'RE LOST!
WE ARE NOT!
THIS IS THE THIRD TIME WE'VE PASSED THAT ROCK!
WILL YOU GIVE ME THE MAP, ALREADY?!
FORGET IT! YOU'VE BEEN HOGGING IT SINCE WE LEFT. IT'S MY TURN!

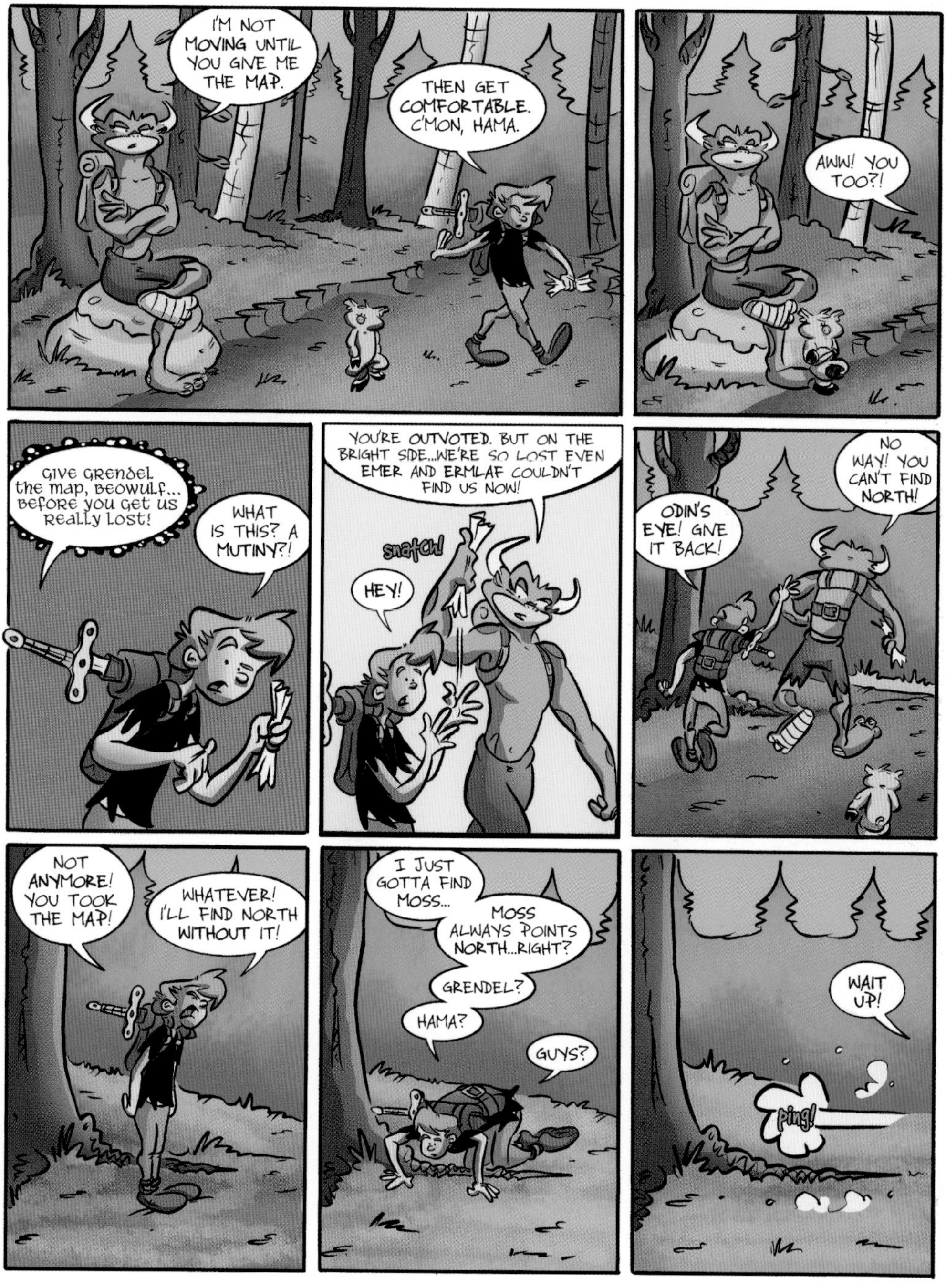
I'M NOT MOVING UNTIL YOU GIVE ME THE MAP.
THEN GET COMFORTABLE. C'MON, HAMA.
AWW! YOU TOO?!
GIVE GRENDEL the map, BEOWULF... BEFORE YOU GET US REALLY LOST!
WHAT IS THIS? A MUTINY?!
YOU'RE OUTVOTED. BUT ON THE BRIGHT SIDE...WE'RE SO LOST EVEN EMER AND ERMLAF COULDN'T FIND US NOW!
snatch!
HEY!
ODIN'S EYE! GIVE IT BACK!
NO WAY! YOU CAN'T FIND NORTH!
NOT ANYMORE! YOU TOOK THE MAP!
WHATEVER! I'LL FIND NORTH WITHOUT IT!
I JUST GOTTA FIND MOSS...
MOSS ALWAYS POINTS NORTH...RIGHT?
GRENDEL?
HAMA?
GUYS?
WAIT UP!
ping!

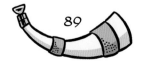

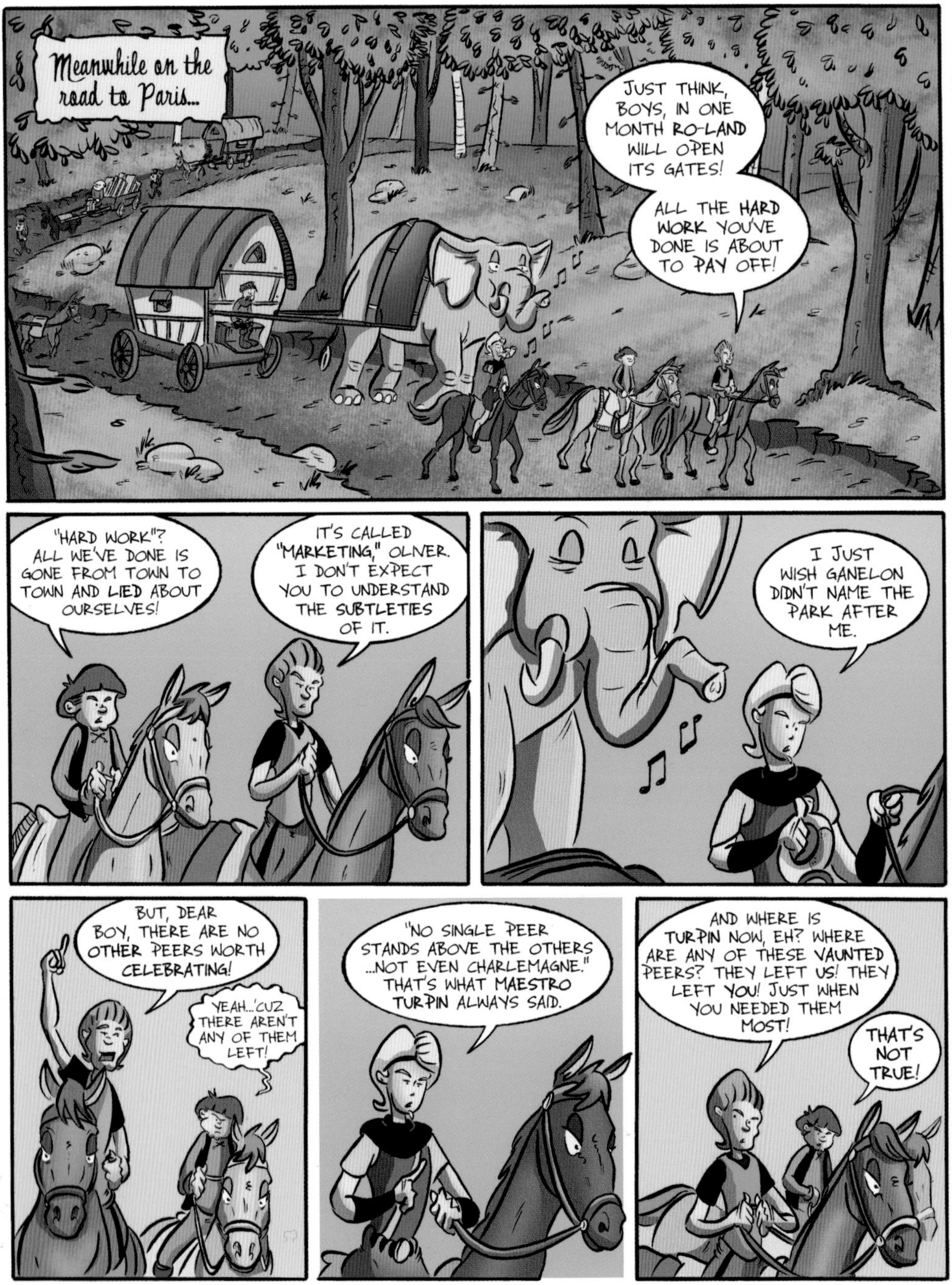
Meanwhile on the road to Paris...
JUST THINK, BOYS, IN ONE MONTH RO-LAND WILL OPEN ITS GATES!
ALL THE HARD WORK YOU'VE DONE IS ABOUT TO PAY OFF!
"HARD WORK"? ALL WE'VE DONE IS GONE FROM TOWN TO TOWN AND LIED ABOUT OURSELVES!
IT'S CALLED "MARKETING," OLIVER. I DON'T EXPECT YOU TO UNDERSTAND THE SUBTLETIES OF IT.
I JUST WISH GANELON DIDN'T NAME THE PARK AFTER ME.
BUT, DEAR BOY, THERE ARE NO OTHER PEERS WORTH CELEBRATING!
YEAH...'CUZ THERE AREN'T ANY OF THEM LEFT!
"NO SINGLE PEER STANDS ABOVE THE OTHERS ...NOT EVEN CHARLEMAGNE." THAT'S WHAT MAESTRO TURPIN ALWAYS SAID.
AND WHERE IS TURPIN NOW, EH? WHERE ARE ANY OF THESE VAUNTED PEERS? THEY LEFT US! THEY LEFT YOU! JUST WHEN YOU NEEDED THEM MOST!
THAT'S NOT TRUE!

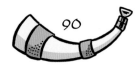

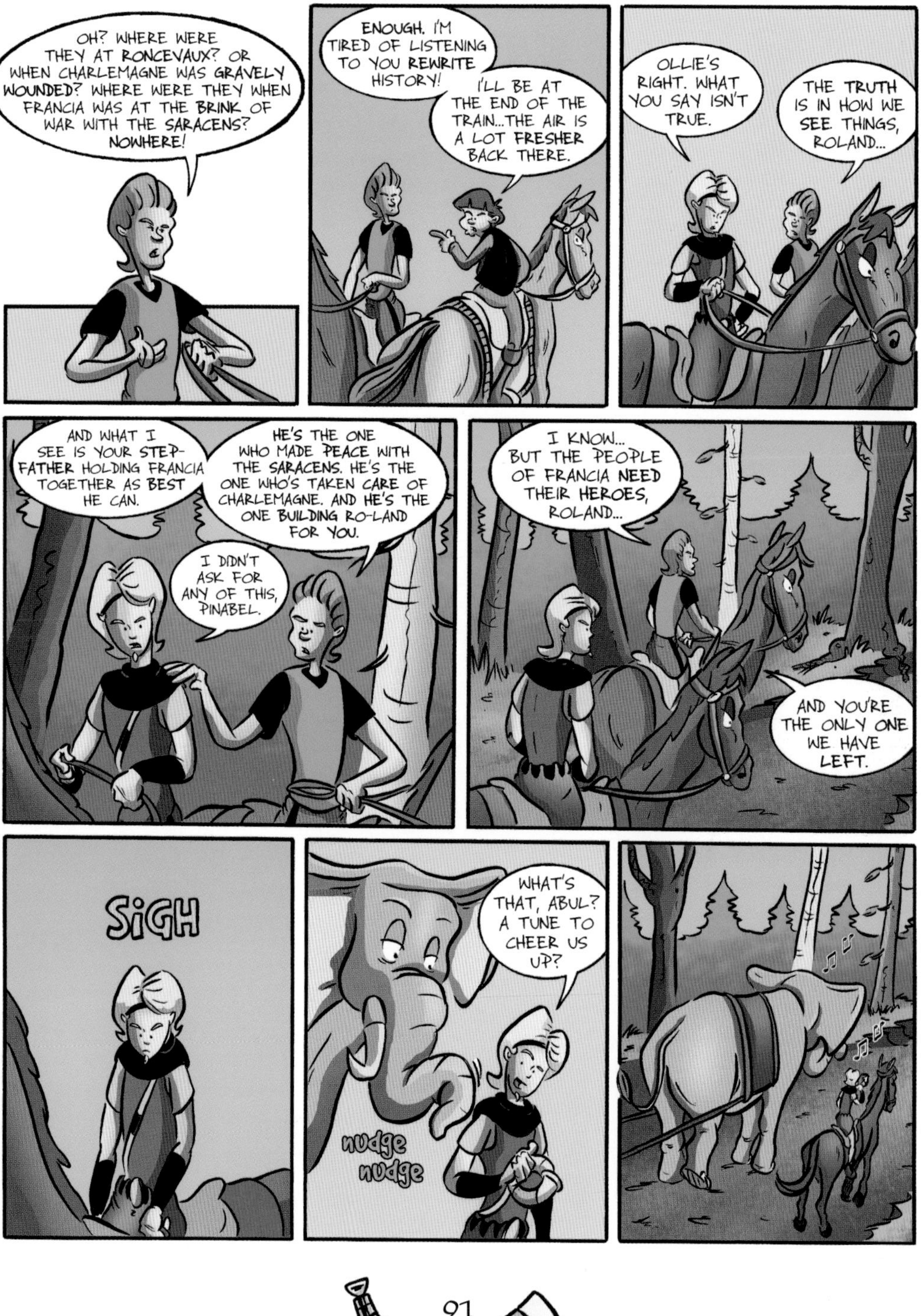
OH? WHERE WERE THEY AT RONCEVAUX? OR WHEN CHARLEMAGNE WAS GRAVELY WOUNDED? WHERE WERE THEY WHEN FRANCIA WAS AT THE BRINK OF WAR WITH THE SARACENS? NOWHERE!
ENOUGH. I'M TIRED OF LISTENING TO YOU REWRITE HISTORY!
I'LL BE AT THE END OF THE TRAIN...THE AIR IS A LOT FRESHER BACK THERE.
OLLIE'S RIGHT. WHAT YOU SAY ISN'T TRUE.
THE TRUTH IS IN HOW WE SEE THINGS, ROLAND...
AND WHAT I SEE IS YOUR STEP-FATHER HOLDING FRANCIA TOGETHER AS BEST HE CAN.
HE'S THE ONE WHO MADE PEACE WITH THE SARACENS. HE'S THE ONE WHO'S TAKEN CARE OF CHARLEMAGNE. AND HE'S THE ONE BUILDING RO-LAND FOR YOU.
I DIDN'T ASK FOR ANY OF THIS, PINABEL.
I KNOW... BUT THE PEOPLE OF FRANCIA NEED THEIR HEROES, ROLAND...
AND YOU'RE THE ONLY ONE WE HAVE LEFT.
SIGH
WHAT'S THAT, ABUL? A TUNE TO CHEER US UP?
nudge nudge

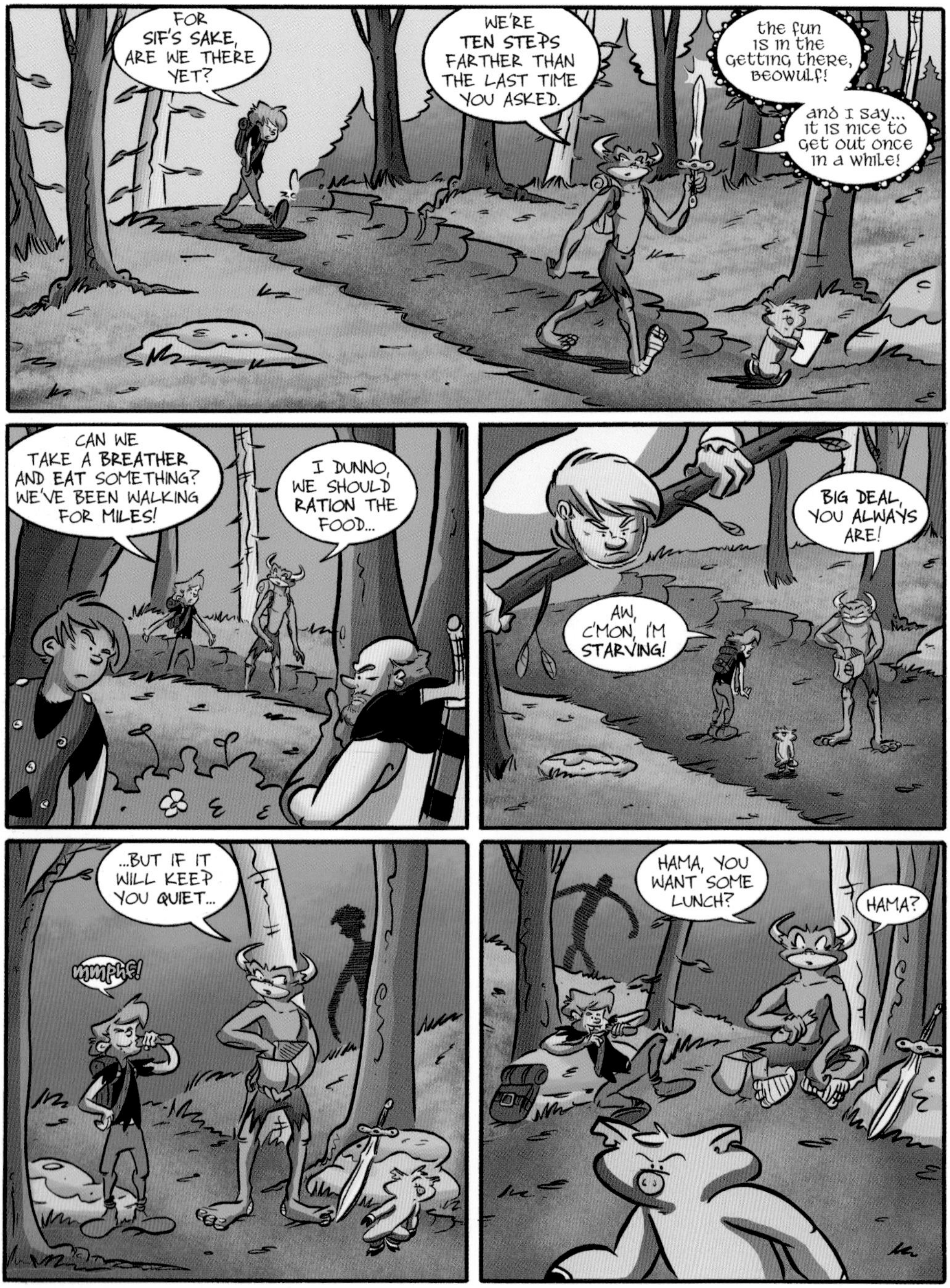
FOR SIF'S SAKE, ARE WE THERE YET?
WE'RE TEN STEPS FARTHER THAN THE LAST TIME YOU ASKED.
the fun is in the getting there, BEOWULF!
and I say... it is nice to get out once in a while!
CAN WE TAKE A BREATHER AND EAT SOMETHING? WE'VE BEEN WALKING FOR MILES!
I DUNNO, WE SHOULD RATION THE FOOD...
BIG DEAL, YOU ALWAYS ARE!
AW, C'MON, I'M STARVING!
...BUT IF IT WILL KEEP YOU QUIET...
mmphf!
HAMA, YOU WANT SOME LUNCH?
HAMA?

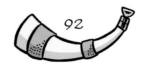

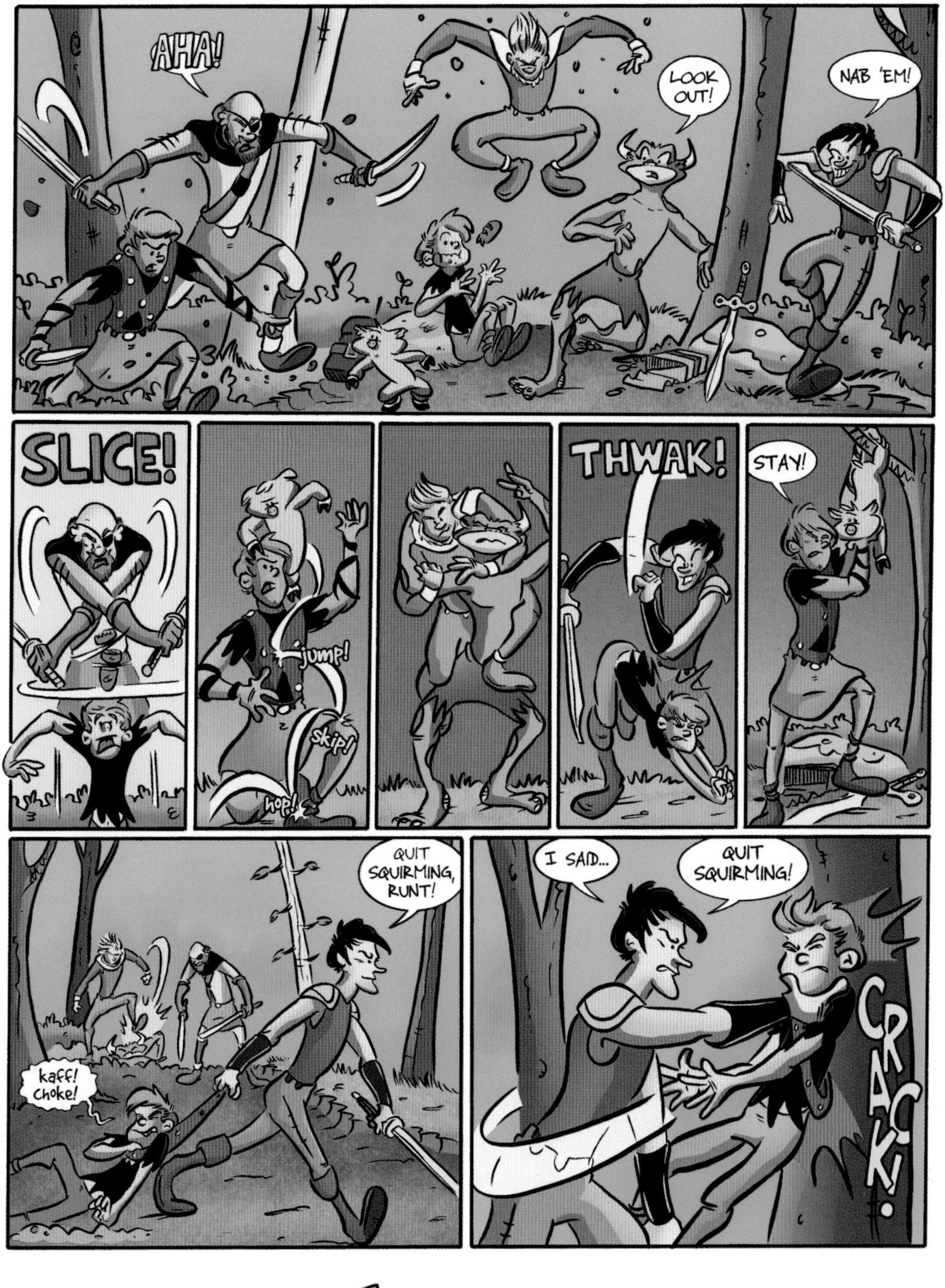
AHA!
LOOK OUT!
NAB 'EM!
SLICE!
jump!
skip!
hop!
THWAK!
STAY!
QUIT SQUIRMING, RUNT!
kaff! choke!
I SAID...
QUIT SQUIRMING!
CRACK!

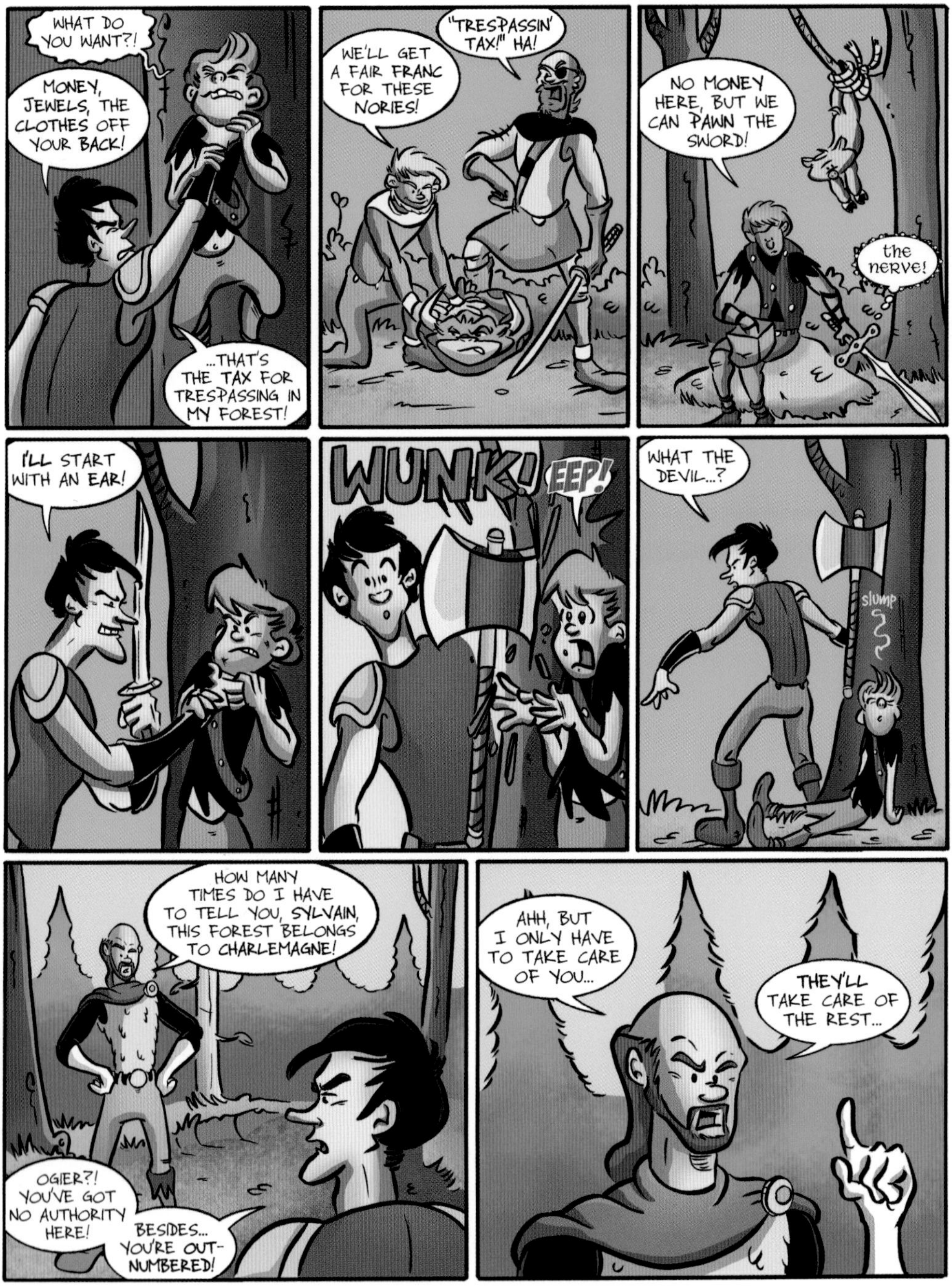
WHAT DO YOU WANT?!
MONEY, JEWELS, THE CLOTHES OFF YOUR BACK!
...THAT'S THE TAX FOR TRESPASSING IN MY FOREST!
WE'LL GET A FAIR FRANC FOR THESE NORIES!
"TRESPASSIN' TAX!" HA!
NO MONEY HERE, BUT WE CAN PAWN THE SWORD!
the nerve!
I'LL START WITH AN EAR!
WUNK!
EEP!
WHAT THE DEVIL...?
slump
HOW MANY TIMES DO I HAVE TO TELL YOU, SYLVAIN, THIS FOREST BELONGS TO CHARLEMAGNE!
OGIER?! YOU'VE GOT NO AUTHORITY HERE!
BESIDES... YOU'RE OUT-NUMBERED!
AHH, BUT I ONLY HAVE TO TAKE CARE OF YOU...
THEY'LL TAKE CARE OF THE REST...

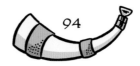

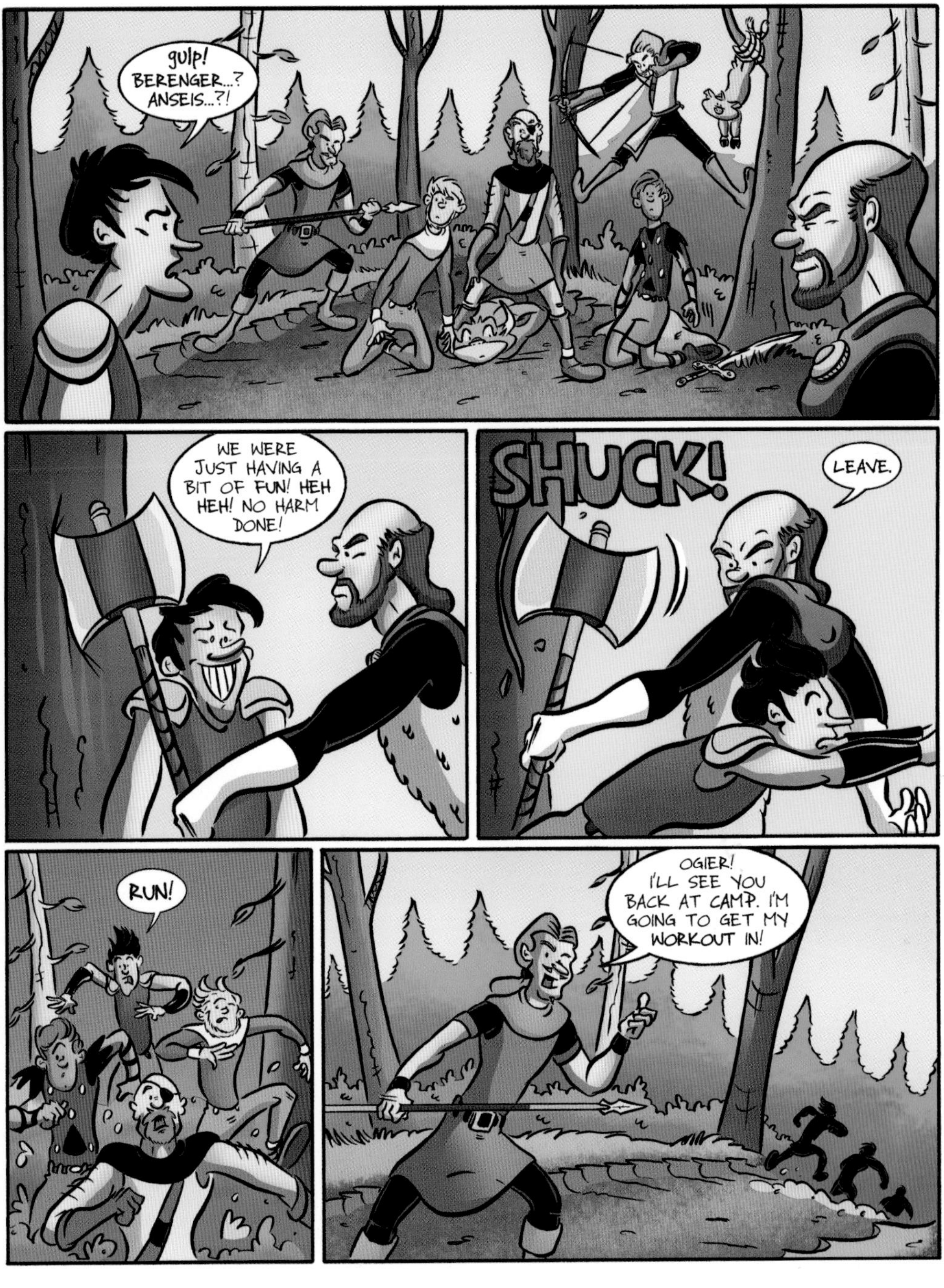
gulp! BERENGER...? ANSEIS...?!
WE WERE JUST HAVING A BIT OF FUN! HEH HEH! NO HARM DONE!
SHUCK!
LEAVE.
RUN!
OGIER! I'LL SEE YOU BACK AT CAMP. I'M GOING TO GET MY WORKOUT IN!

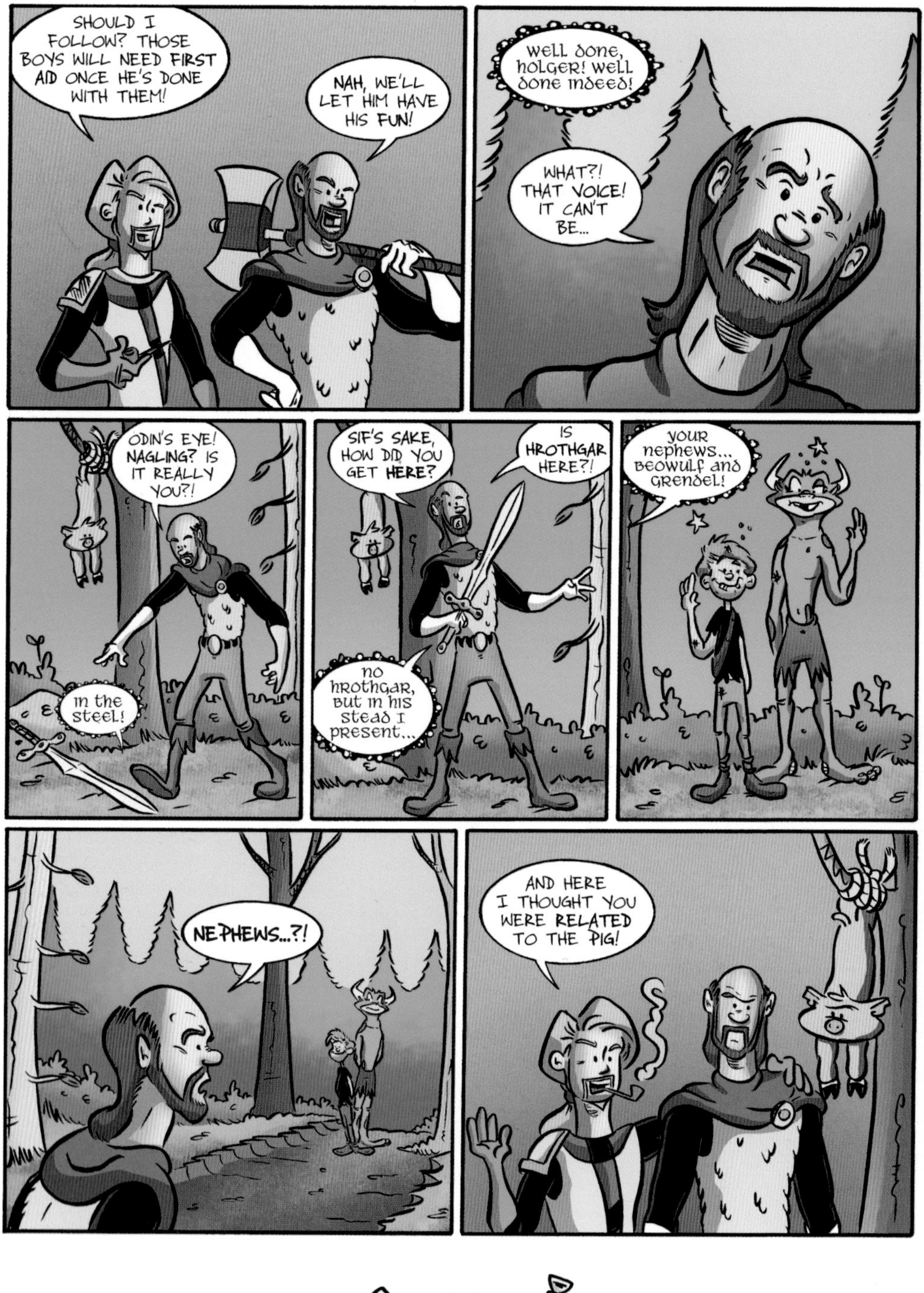
SHOULD I FOLLOW? THOSE BOYS WILL NEED FIRST AID ONCE HE'S DONE WITH THEM!
NAH, WE'LL LET HIM HAVE HIS FUN!
well done, holger! well done indeed!
WHAT?! THAT VOICE! IT CAN'T BE...
ODIN'S EYE! NAGLING? IS IT REALLY YOU?!
in the steel!
SIF'S SAKE, HOW DID YOU GET HERE?
IS HROTHGAR HERE?!
no hrothgar, but in his stead I present...
your nephews... Beowulf and Grendel!
NEPHEWS...?!
AND HERE I THOUGHT YOU WERE RELATED TO THE PIG!

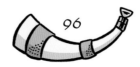

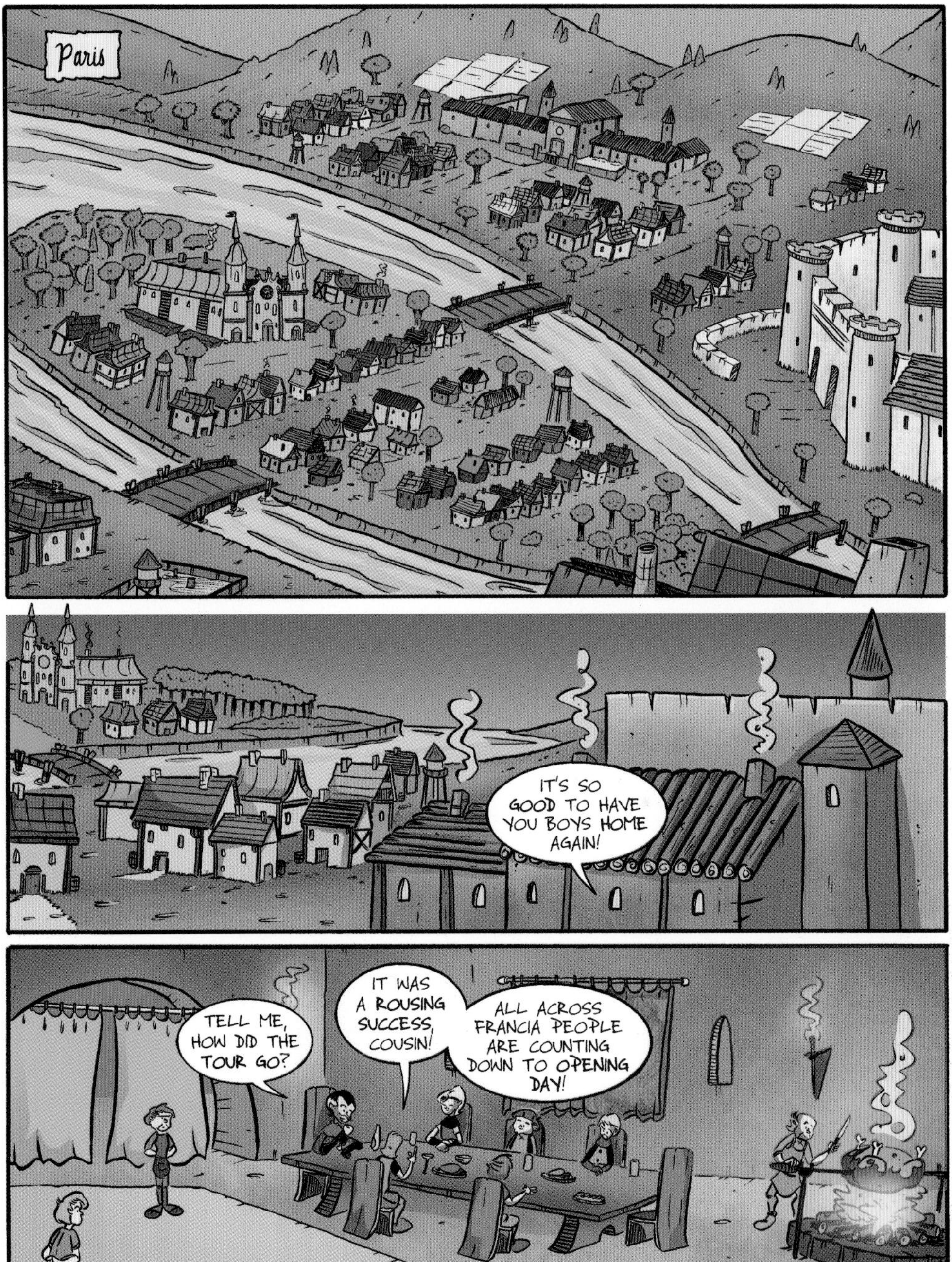
Paris
IT'S SO GOOD TO HAVE YOU BOYS HOME AGAIN!
TELL ME, HOW DID THE TOUR GO?
IT WAS A ROUSING SUCCESS, COUSIN!
ALL ACROSS FRANCIA PEOPLE ARE COUNTING DOWN TO OPENING DAY!

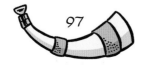

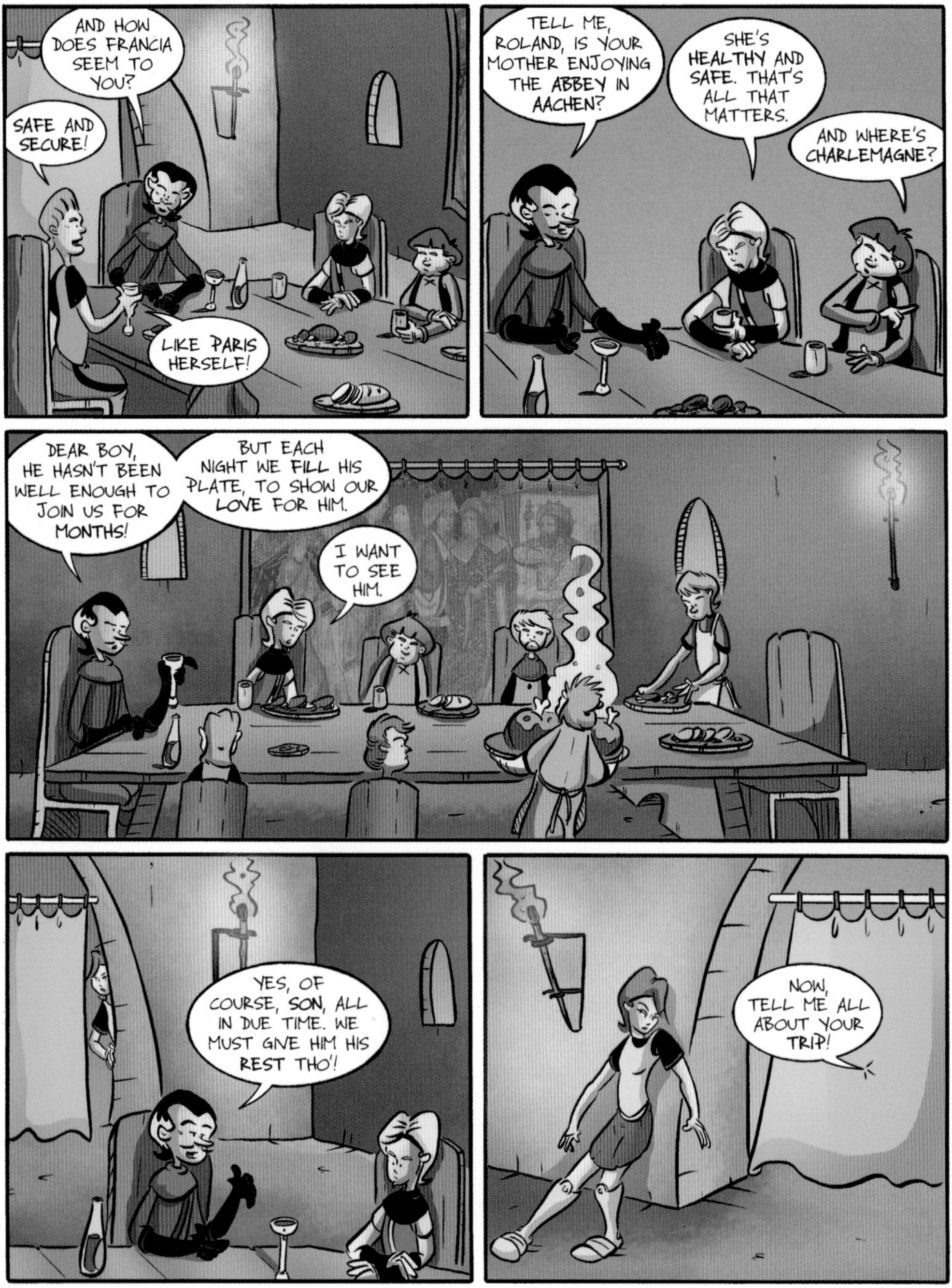
AND HOW DOES FRANCIA SEEM TO YOU?
SAFE AND SECURE!
LIKE PARIS HERSELF!
TELL ME, ROLAND, IS YOUR MOTHER ENJOYING THE ABBEY IN AACHEN?
SHE'S HEALTHY AND SAFE. THAT'S ALL THAT MATTERS.
AND WHERE'S CHARLEMAGNE?
DEAR BOY, HE HASN'T BEEN WELL ENOUGH TO JOIN US FOR MONTHS!
BUT EACH NIGHT WE FILL HIS PLATE, TO SHOW OUR LOVE FOR HIM.
I WANT TO SEE HIM.
YES, OF COURSE, SON, ALL IN DUE TIME. WE MUST GIVE HIM HIS REST THO'!
NOW, TELL ME ALL ABOUT YOUR TRIP!

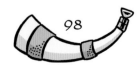

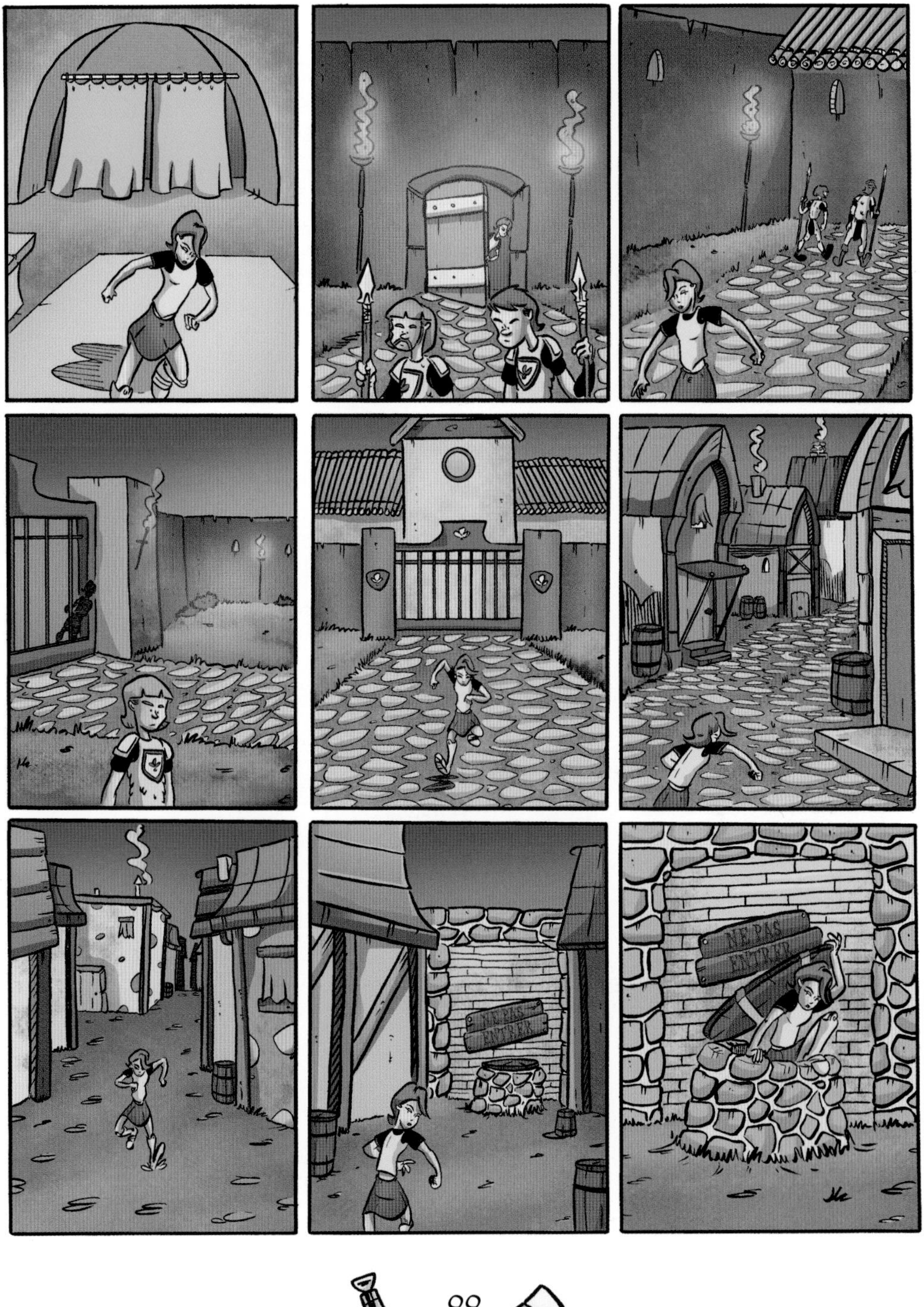
NE PAS
ENTRER
NE PAS
ENTRER

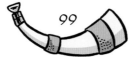

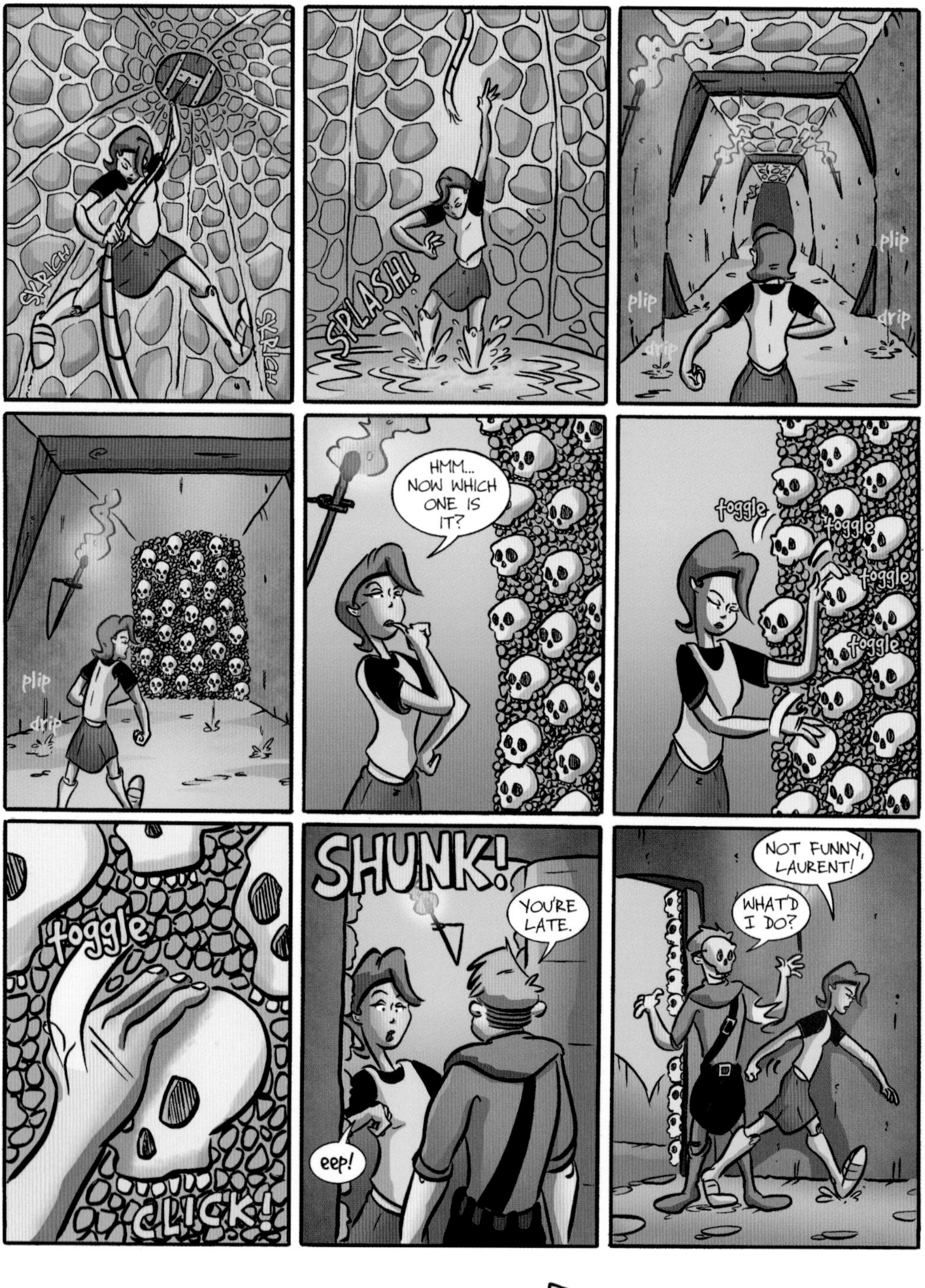
SKRICH
SKRICH
SPLASH!
plip
plip
drip
drip
plip
drip
HMM... NOW WHICH ONE IS IT?
toggle
toggle
toggle
toggle
toggle
CLICK!
SHUNK!
YOU'RE LATE.
eep!
NOT FUNNY, LAURENT!
WHAT'D I DO?

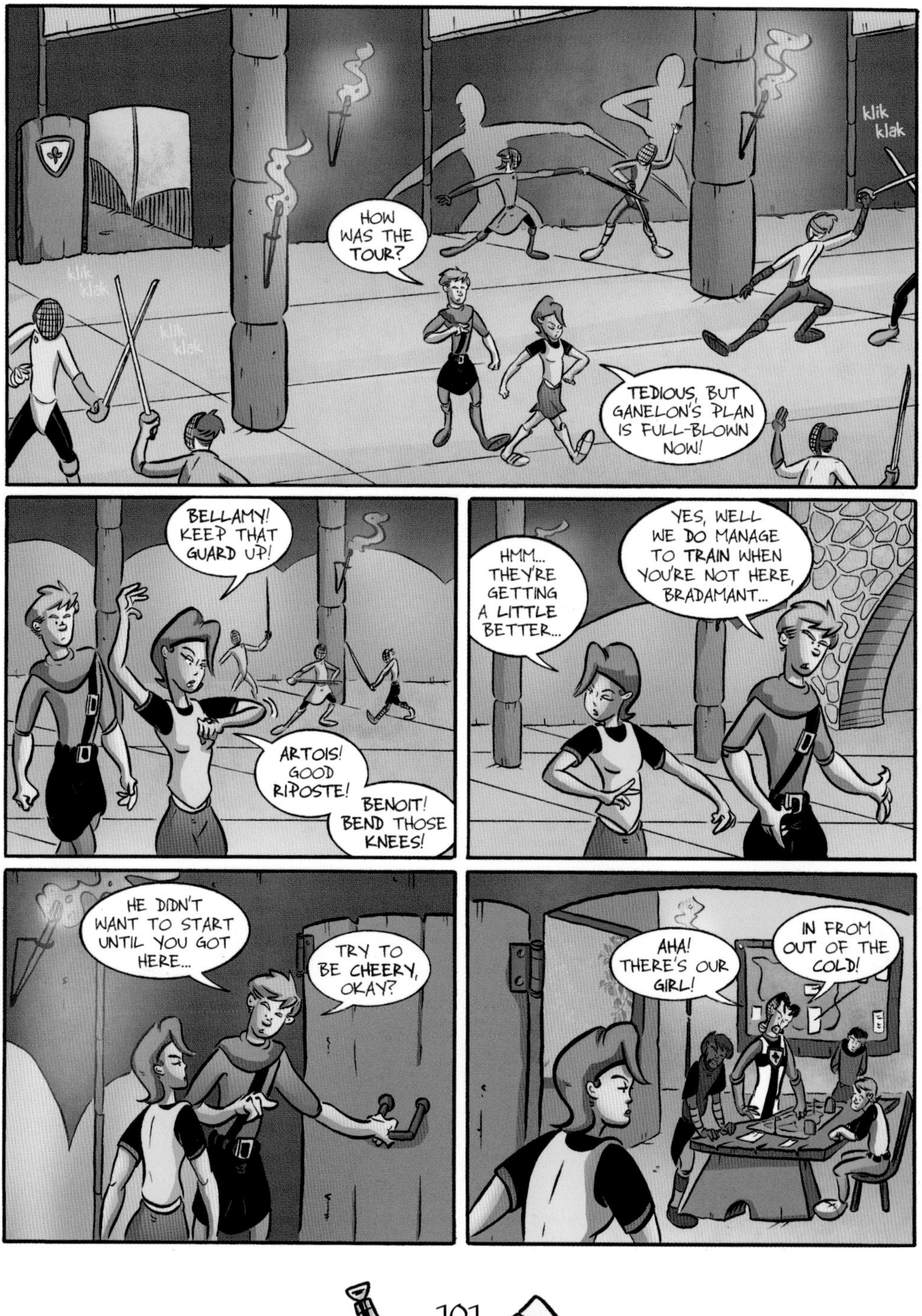
HOW WAS THE TOUR?
klik klak
klik klak
klik klak
TEDIOUS, BUT GANELON'S PLAN IS FULL-BLOWN NOW!
BELLAMY! KEEP THAT GUARD UP!
ARTOIS! GOOD RIPOSTE!
BENOIT! BEND THOSE KNEES!
HMM... THEY'RE GETTING A LITTLE BETTER...
YES, WELL WE DO MANAGE TO TRAIN WHEN YOU'RE NOT HERE, BRADAMANT...
HE DIDN'T WANT TO START UNTIL YOU GOT HERE...
TRY TO BE CHEERY, OKAY?
AHA! THERE'S OUR GIRL!
IN FROM OUT OF THE COLD!

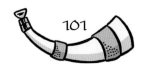

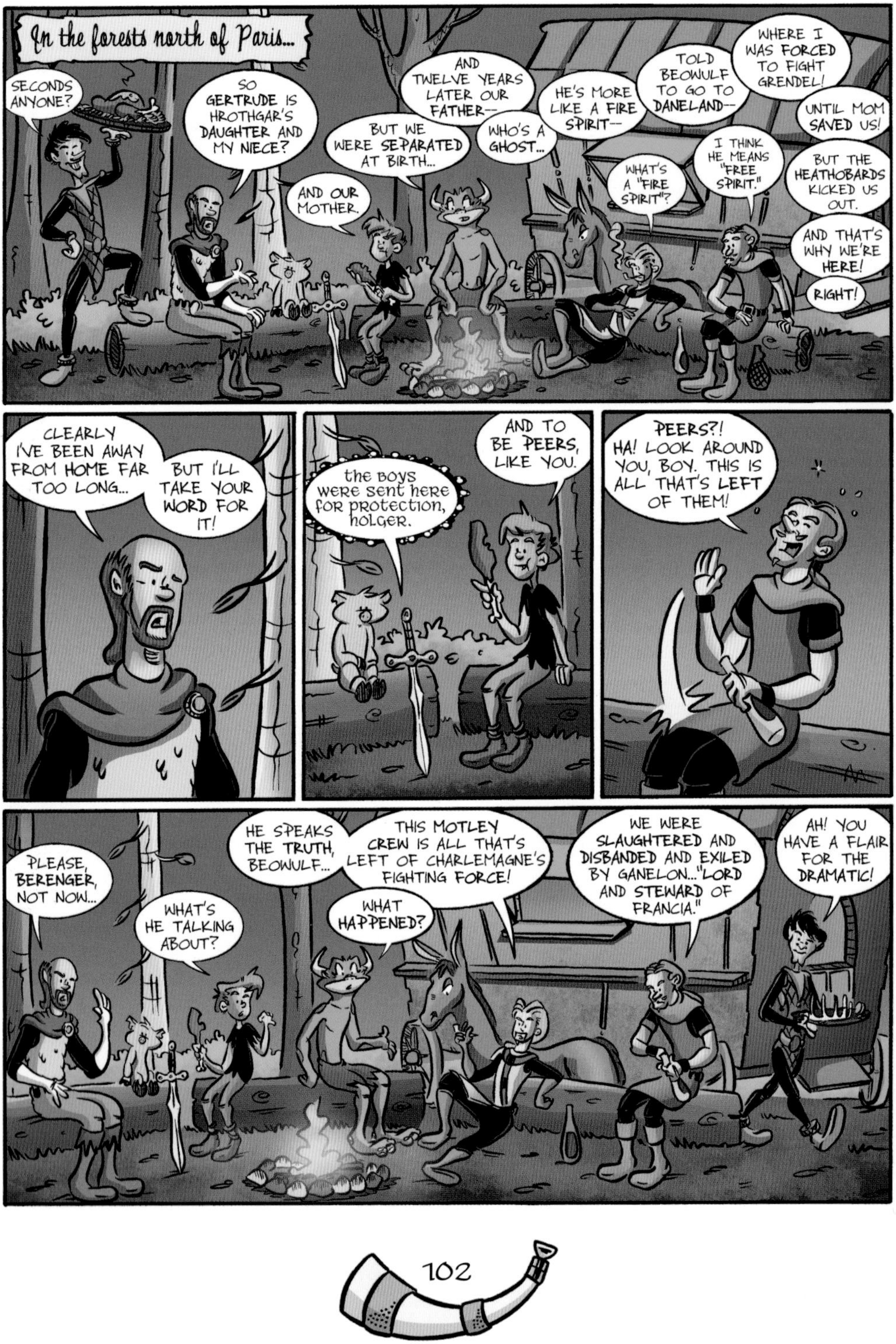
In the forests north of Paris...
SECONDS ANYONE?
SO GERTRUDE IS HROTHGAR'S DAUGHTER AND MY NIECE?
AND OUR MOTHER.
BUT WE WERE SEPARATED AT BIRTH...
AND TWELVE YEARS LATER OUR FATHER--
WHO'S A GHOST...
HE'S MORE LIKE A FIRE SPIRIT--
WHAT'S A "FIRE SPIRIT"?
TOLD BEOWULF TO GO TO DANELAND--
I THINK HE MEANS "FREE SPIRIT."
WHERE I WAS FORCED TO FIGHT GRENDEL!
UNTIL MOM SAVED US!
BUT THE HEATHOBARDS KICKED US OUT.
AND THAT'S WHY WE'RE HERE!
RIGHT!
CLEARLY I'VE BEEN AWAY FROM HOME FAR TOO LONG...
BUT I'LL TAKE YOUR WORD FOR IT!
the boys were sent here for protection, holger.
AND TO BE PEERS, LIKE YOU.
PEERS?! HA! LOOK AROUND YOU, BOY. THIS IS ALL THAT'S LEFT OF THEM!
PLEASE, BERENGER, NOT NOW...
WHAT'S HE TALKING ABOUT?
HE SPEAKS THE TRUTH, BEOWULF...
WHAT HAPPENED?
THIS MOTLEY CREW IS ALL THAT'S LEFT OF CHARLEMAGNE'S FIGHTING FORCE!
WE WERE SLAUGHTERED AND DISBANDED AND EXILED BY GANELON..."LORD AND STEWARD OF FRANCIA."
AH! YOU HAVE A FLAIR FOR THE DRAMATIC!

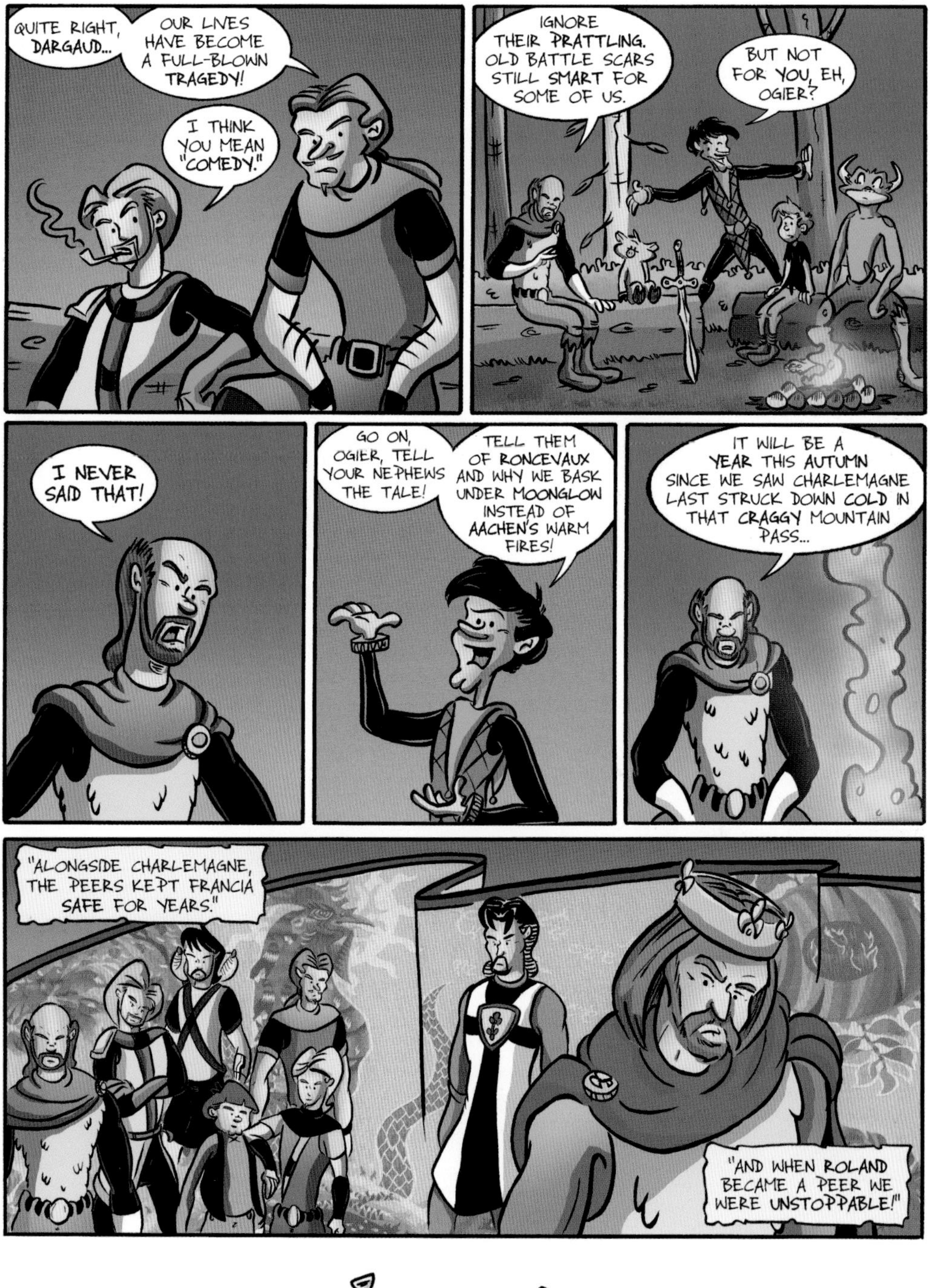
QUITE RIGHT, DARGAUD...
OUR LIVES HAVE BECOME A FULL-BLOWN TRAGEDY!
I THINK YOU MEAN "COMEDY."
IGNORE THEIR PRATTLING. OLD BATTLE SCARS STILL SMART FOR SOME OF US.
BUT NOT FOR YOU, EH, OGIER?
I NEVER SAID THAT!
GO ON, OGIER, TELL YOUR NEPHEWS THE TALE!
TELL THEM OF RONCEVAUX AND WHY WE BASK UNDER MOONGLOW INSTEAD OF AACHEN'S WARM FIRES!
IT WILL BE A YEAR THIS AUTUMN SINCE WE SAW CHARLEMAGNE LAST STRUCK DOWN COLD IN THAT CRAGGY MOUNTAIN PASS...
"ALONGSIDE CHARLEMAGNE, THE PEERS KEPT FRANCIA SAFE FOR YEARS."
"AND WHEN ROLAND BECAME A PEER WE WERE UNSTOPPABLE!"

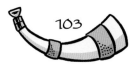

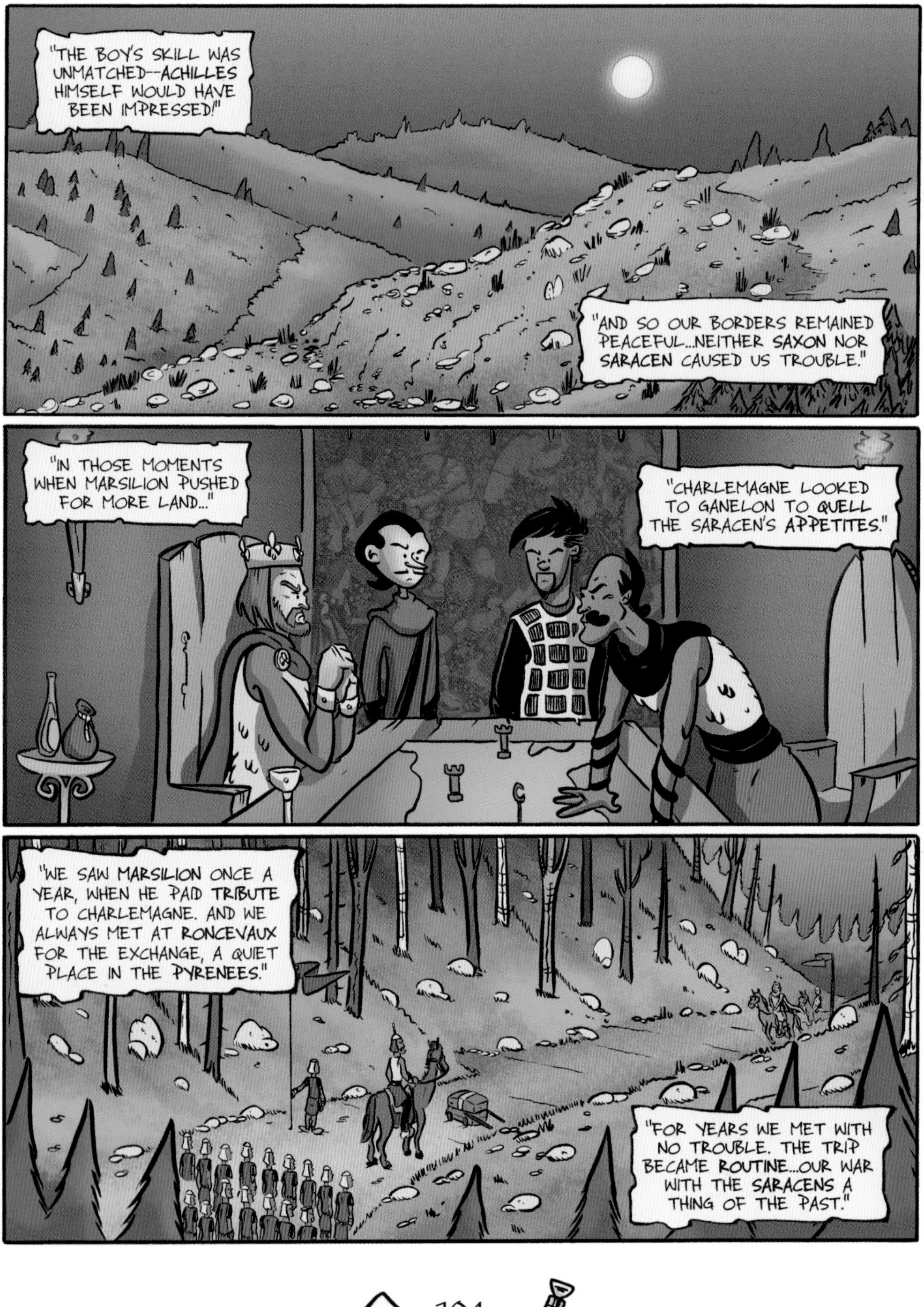
"THE BOY'S SKILL WAS UNMATCHED--ACHILLES HIMSELF WOULD HAVE BEEN IMPRESSED!"
"AND SO OUR BORDERS REMAINED PEACEFUL...NEITHER SAXON NOR SARACEN CAUSED US TROUBLE."
"IN THOSE MOMENTS WHEN MARSILION PUSHED FOR MORE LAND..."
"CHARLEMAGNE LOOKED TO GANELON TO QUELL THE SARACEN'S APPETITES."
"WE SAW MARSILION ONCE A YEAR, WHEN HE PAID TRIBUTE TO CHARLEMAGNE. AND WE ALWAYS MET AT RONCEVAUX FOR THE EXCHANGE, A QUIET PLACE IN THE PYRENEES."
"FOR YEARS WE MET WITH NO TROUBLE. THE TRIP BECAME ROUTINE...OUR WAR WITH THE SARACENS A THING OF THE PAST."

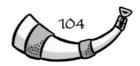

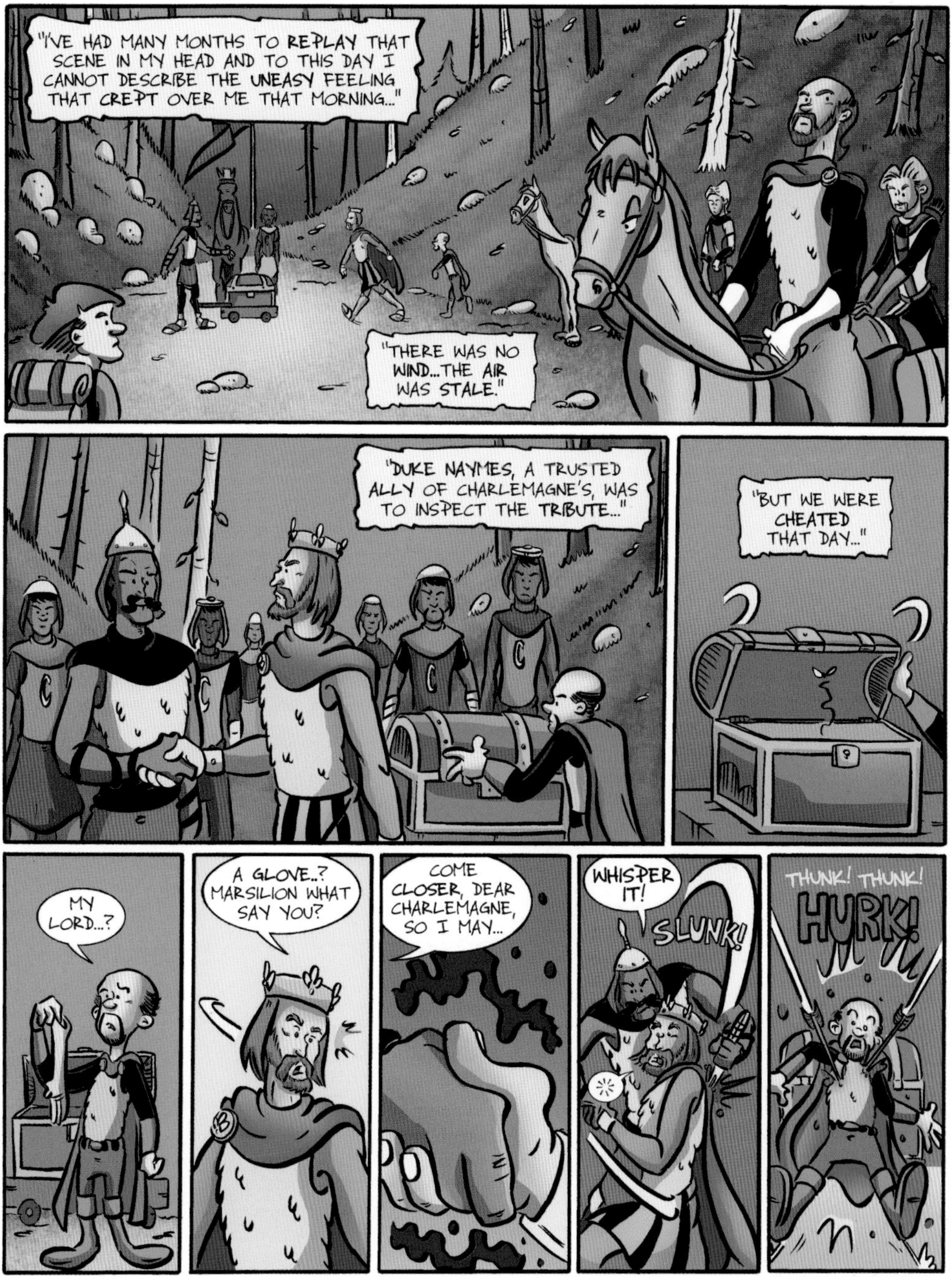
"I'VE HAD MANY MONTHS TO REPLAY THAT SCENE IN MY HEAD AND TO THIS DAY I CANNOT DESCRIBE THE UNEASY FEELING THAT CREPT OVER ME THAT MORNING..."
"THERE WAS NO WIND...THE AIR WAS STALE."
"DUKE NAYMES, A TRUSTED ALLY OF CHARLEMAGNE'S, WAS TO INSPECT THE TRIBUTE..."
"BUT WE WERE CHEATED THAT DAY..."
MY LORD...?
A GLOVE..? MARSILION WHAT SAY YOU?
COME CLOSER, DEAR CHARLEMAGNE, SO I MAY...
WHISPER IT!
SLUNK!
THUNK! THUNK!
HURK!

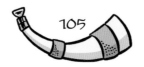

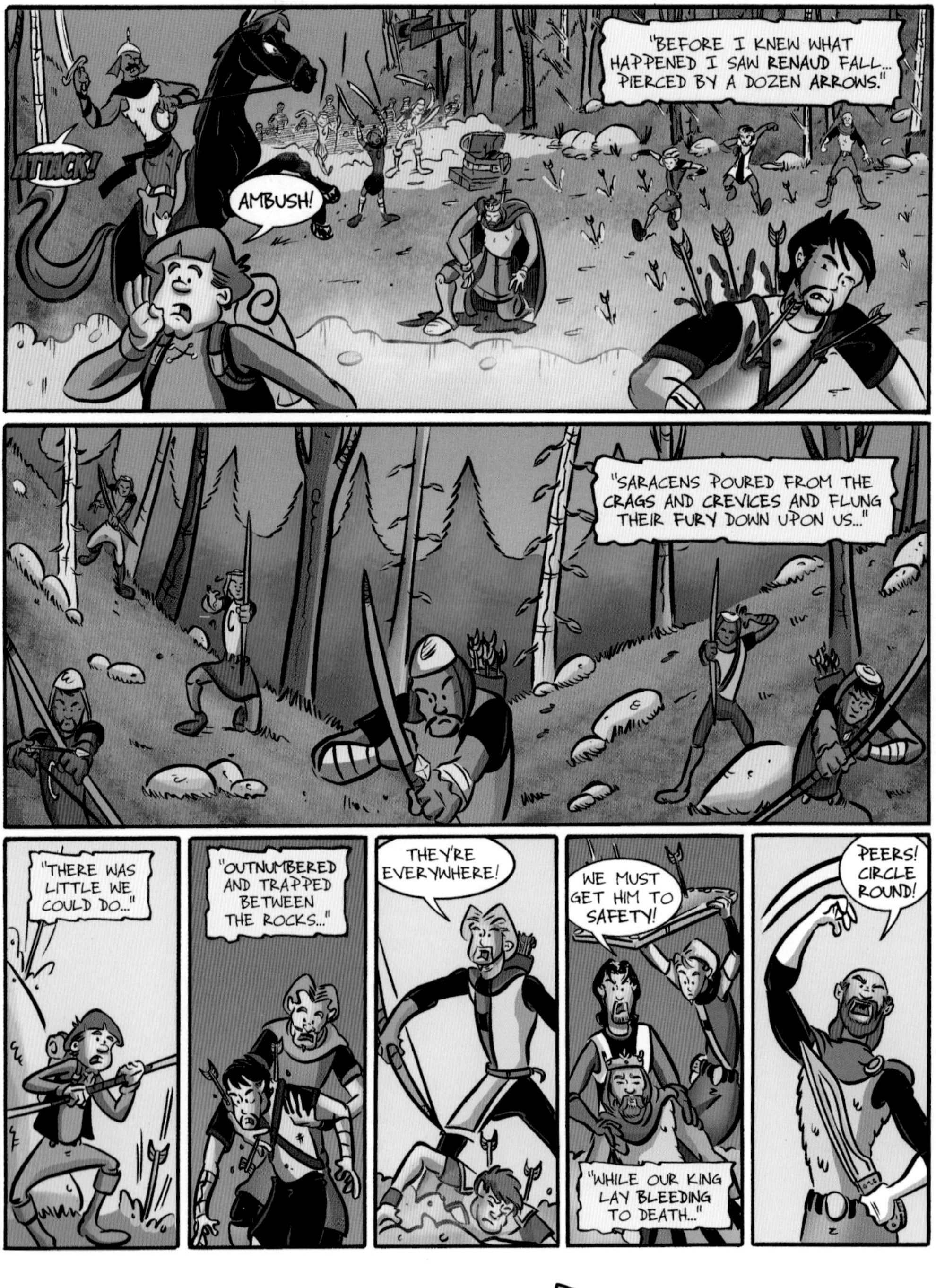
"BEFORE I KNEW WHAT HAPPENED I SAW RENAUD FALL... PIERCED BY A DOZEN ARROWS."
ATTACK!
AMBUSH!
"SARACENS POURED FROM THE CRAGS AND CREVICES AND FLUNG THEIR FURY DOWN UPON US..."
"THERE WAS LITTLE WE COULD DO..."
"OUTNUMBERED AND TRAPPED BETWEEN THE ROCKS..."
THEY'RE EVERYWHERE!
WE MUST GET HIM TO SAFETY!
"WHILE OUR KING LAY BLEEDING TO DEATH..."
PEERS! CIRCLE ROUND!

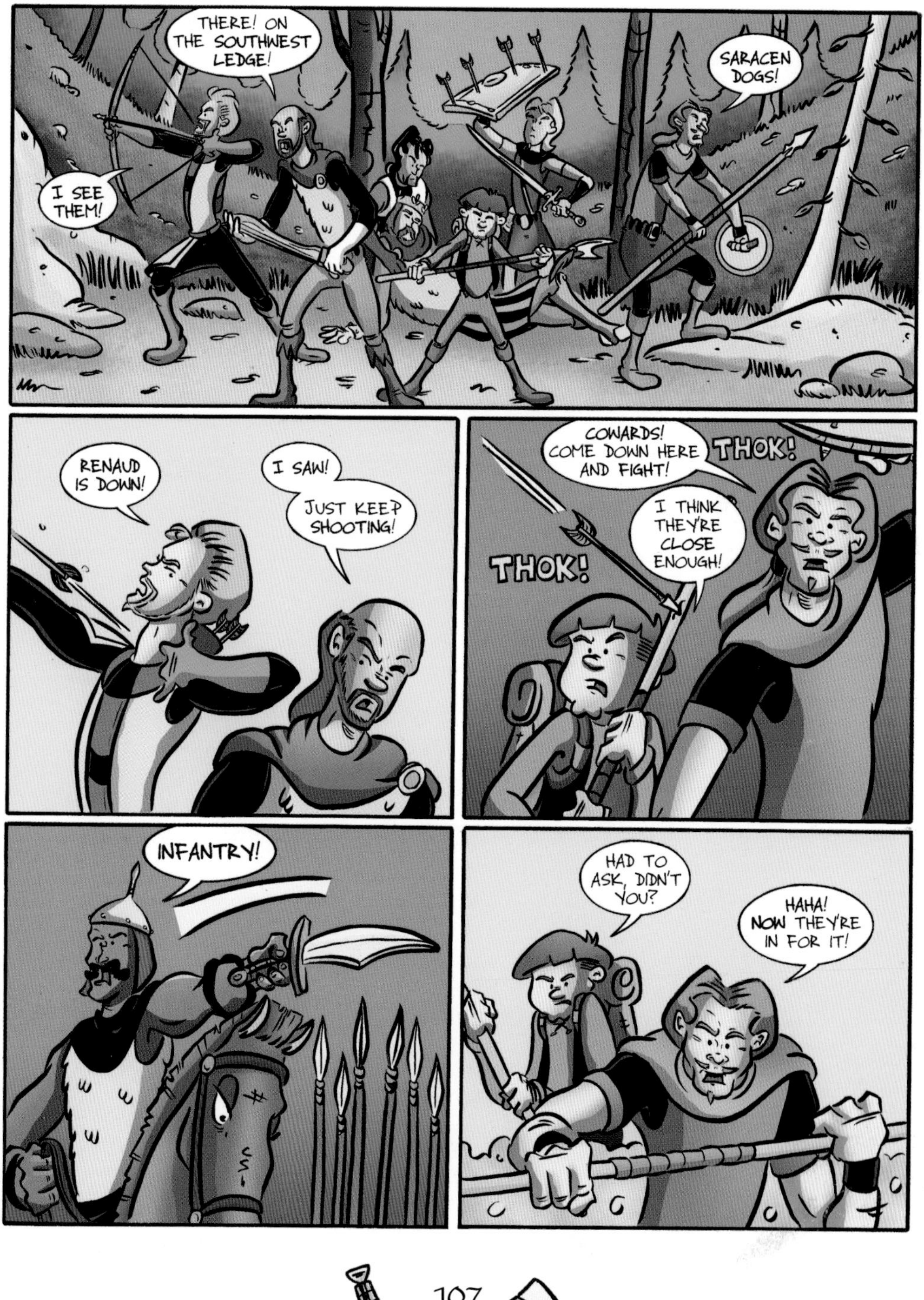
THERE! ON THE SOUTHWEST LEDGE!
SARACEN DOGS!
I SEE THEM!
RENAUD IS DOWN!
I SAW!
JUST KEEP SHOOTING!
COWARDS! COME DOWN HERE AND FIGHT!
THOK!
I THINK THEY'RE CLOSE ENOUGH!
THOK!
INFANTRY!
HAD TO ASK, DIDN'T YOU?
HAHA! NOW THEY'RE IN FOR IT!

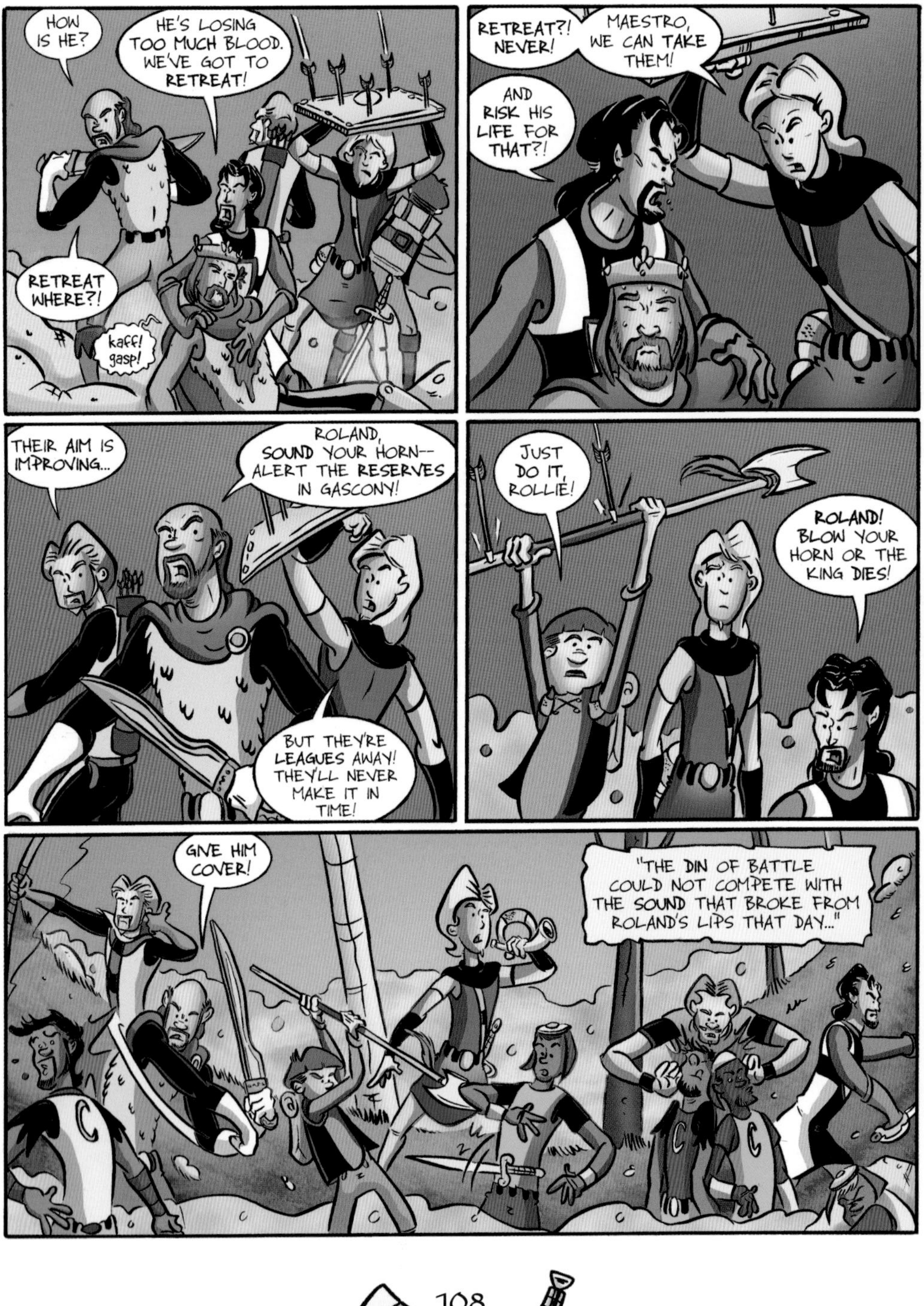
HOW IS HE?
HE'S LOSING TOO MUCH BLOOD. WE'VE GOT TO RETREAT!
RETREAT WHERE?!
kaff! gasp!
RETREAT?! NEVER!
MAESTRO, WE CAN TAKE THEM!
AND RISK HIS LIFE FOR THAT?!
THEIR AIM IS IMPROVING...
ROLAND, SOUND YOUR HORN-- ALERT THE RESERVES IN GASCONY!
BUT THEY'RE LEAGUES AWAY! THEY'LL NEVER MAKE IT IN TIME!
JUST DO IT, ROLLIE!
ROLAND! BLOW YOUR HORN OR THE KING DIES!
GIVE HIM COVER!
"THE DIN OF BATTLE COULD NOT COMPETE WITH THE SOUND THAT BROKE FROM ROLAND'S LIPS THAT DAY..."

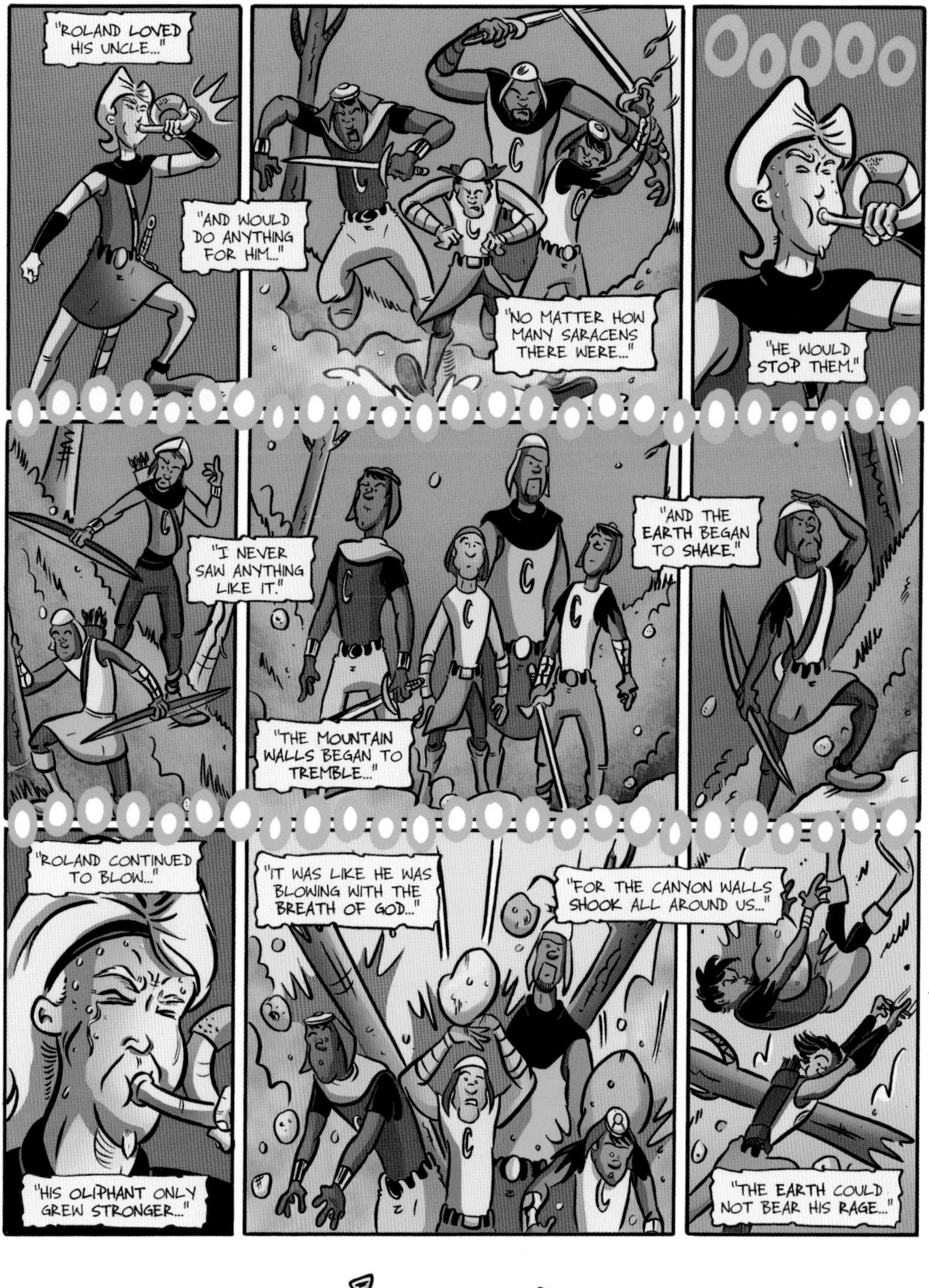
"ROLAND LOVED HIS UNCLE..."
"AND WOULD DO ANYTHING FOR HIM..."
"NO MATTER HOW MANY SARACENS THERE WERE..."
OOOOO
"HE WOULD STOP THEM."
"I NEVER SAW ANYTHING LIKE IT."
"THE MOUNTAIN WALLS BEGAN TO TREMBLE..."
"AND THE EARTH BEGAN TO SHAKE."
"ROLAND CONTINUED TO BLOW..."
"HIS OLIPHANT ONLY GREW STRONGER..."
"IT WAS LIKE HE WAS BLOWING WITH THE BREATH OF GOD..."
"FOR THE CANYON WALLS SHOOK ALL AROUND US..."
"THE EARTH COULD NOT BEAR HIS RAGE..."

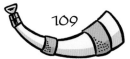

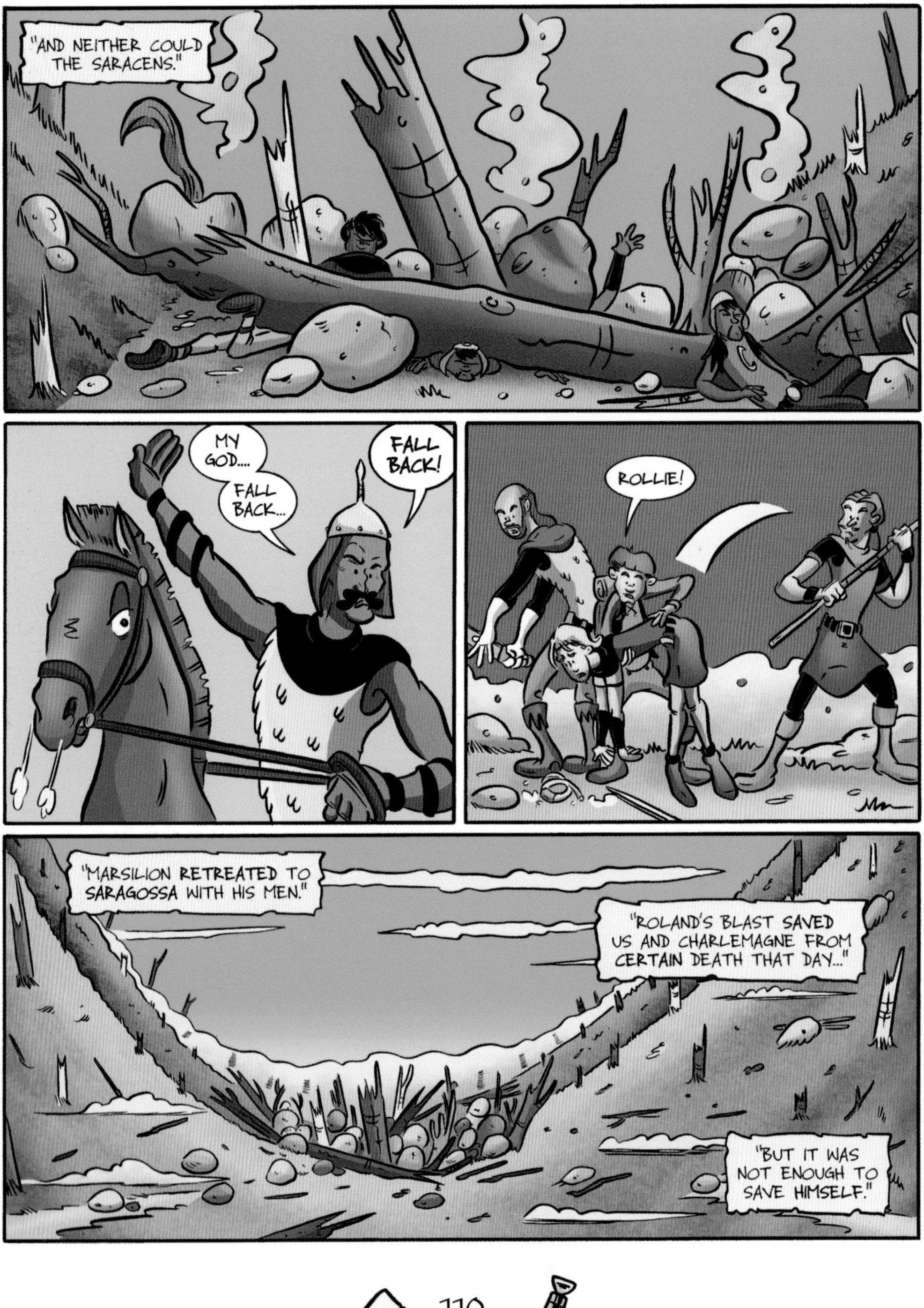
"AND NEITHER COULD THE SARACENS."
MY GOD....
FALL BACK...
FALL BACK!
ROLLIE!
"MARSILION RETREATED TO SARAGOSSA WITH HIS MEN."
"ROLAND'S BLAST SAVED US AND CHARLEMAGNE FROM CERTAIN DEATH THAT DAY..."
"BUT IT WAS NOT ENOUGH TO SAVE HIMSELF."

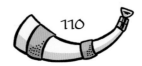

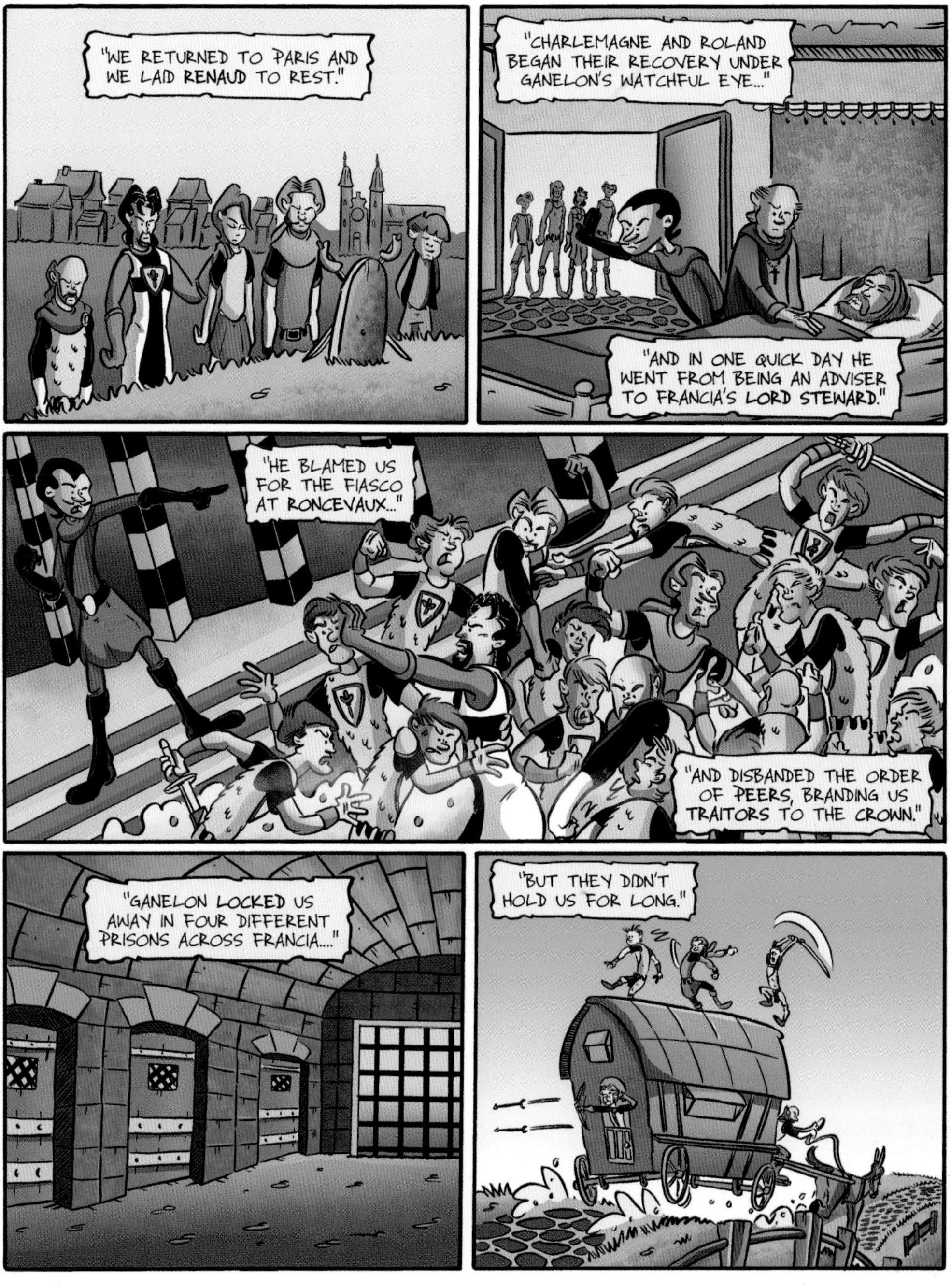
"WE RETURNED TO PARIS AND WE LAID RENAUD TO REST."
"CHARLEMAGNE AND ROLAND BEGAN THEIR RECOVERY UNDER GANELON'S WATCHFUL EYE..."
"AND IN ONE QUICK DAY HE WENT FROM BEING AN ADVISER TO FRANCIA'S LORD STEWARD."
"HE BLAMED US FOR THE FIASCO AT RONCEVAUX..."
"AND DISBANDED THE ORDER OF PEERS, BRANDING US TRAITORS TO THE CROWN."
"GANELON LOCKED US AWAY IN FOUR DIFFERENT PRISONS ACROSS FRANCIA...."
"BUT THEY DIDN'T HOLD US FOR LONG."

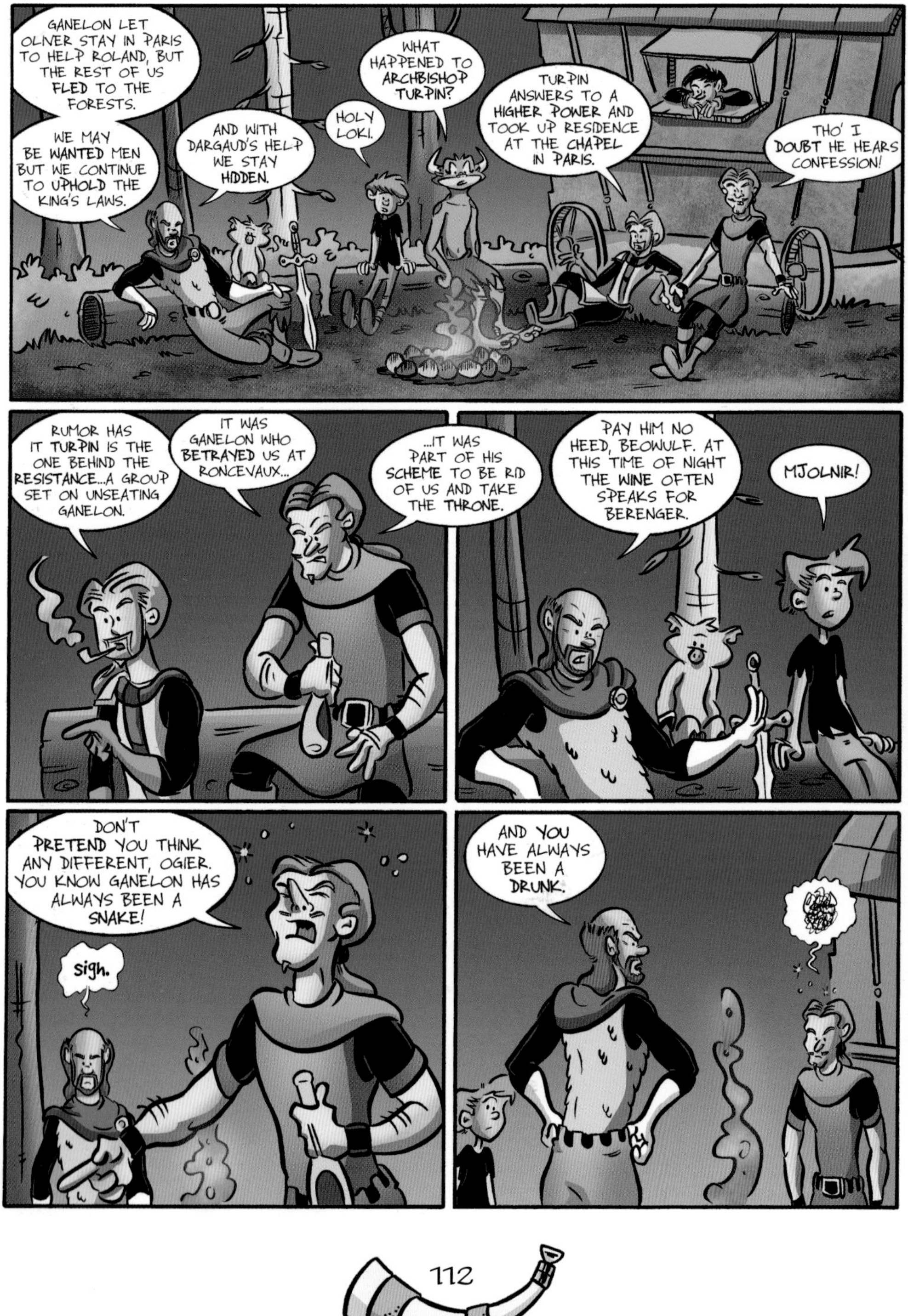
GANELON LET OLIVER STAY IN PARIS TO HELP ROLAND, BUT THE REST OF US FLED TO THE FORESTS.
WE MAY BE WANTED MEN BUT WE CONTINUE TO UPHOLD THE KING'S LAWS.
AND WITH DARGAUD'S HELP WE STAY HIDDEN.
HOLY LOKI.
WHAT HAPPENED TO ARCHBISHOP TURPIN?
TURPIN ANSWERS TO A HIGHER POWER AND TOOK UP RESIDENCE AT THE CHAPEL IN PARIS.
THO' I DOUBT HE HEARS CONFESSION!
RUMOR HAS IT TURPIN IS THE ONE BEHIND THE RESISTANCE...A GROUP SET ON UNSEATING GANELON.
IT WAS GANELON WHO BETRAYED US AT RONCEVAUX...
...IT WAS PART OF HIS SCHEME TO BE RID OF US AND TAKE THE THRONE.
PAY HIM NO HEED, BEOWULF. AT THIS TIME OF NIGHT THE WINE OFTEN SPEAKS FOR BERENGER.
MJOLNIR!
DON'T PRETEND YOU THINK ANY DIFFERENT, OGIER. YOU KNOW GANELON HAS ALWAYS BEEN A SNAKE!
sigh.
AND YOU HAVE ALWAYS BEEN A DRUNK.

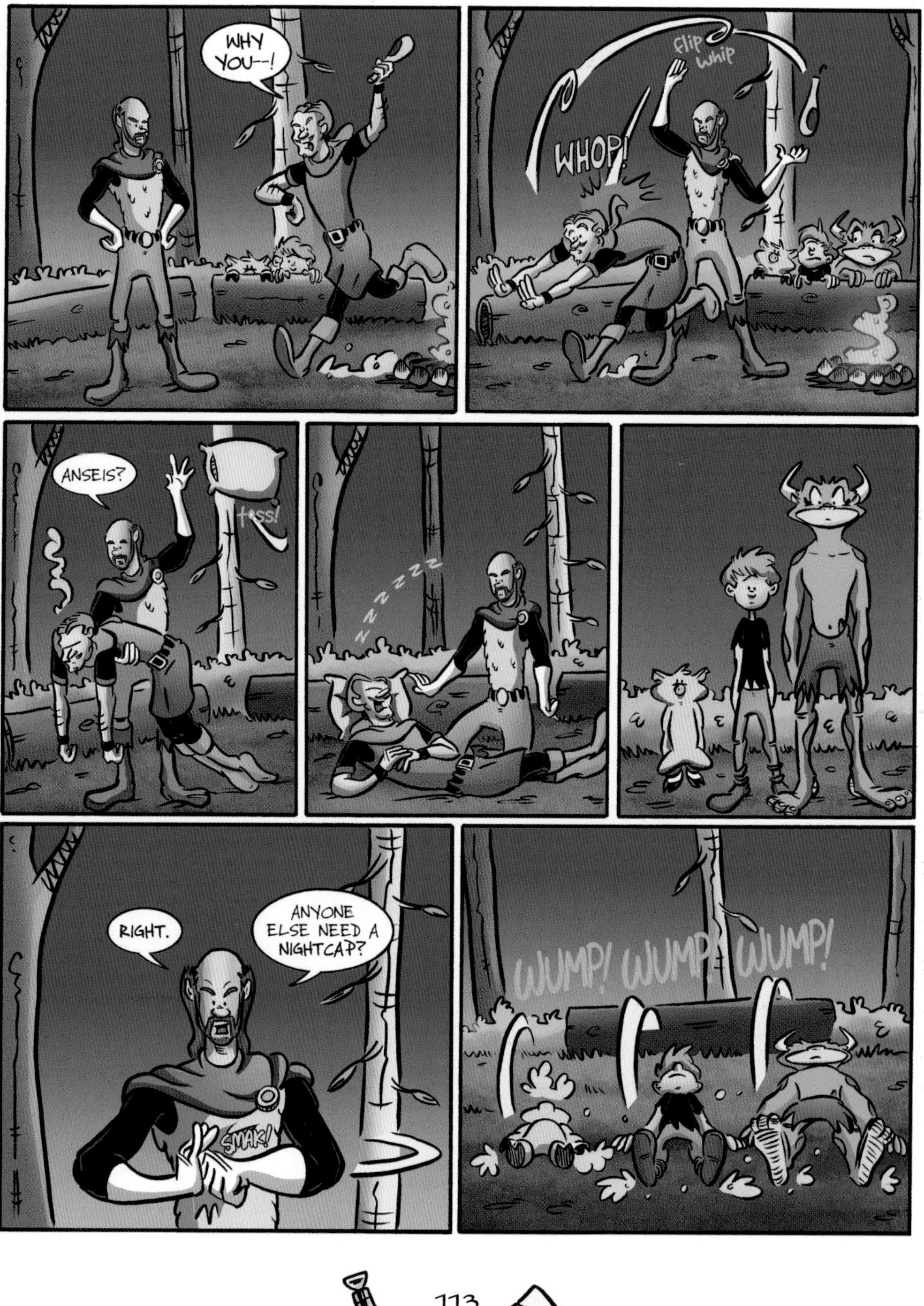
WHY YOU--!
flip
whip
WHOP!
ANSEIS?
toss!
ZZZZZZZ
RIGHT.
ANYONE ELSE NEED A NIGHTCAP?
SMAK!
WUMP! WUMP! WUMP!

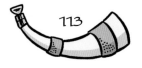

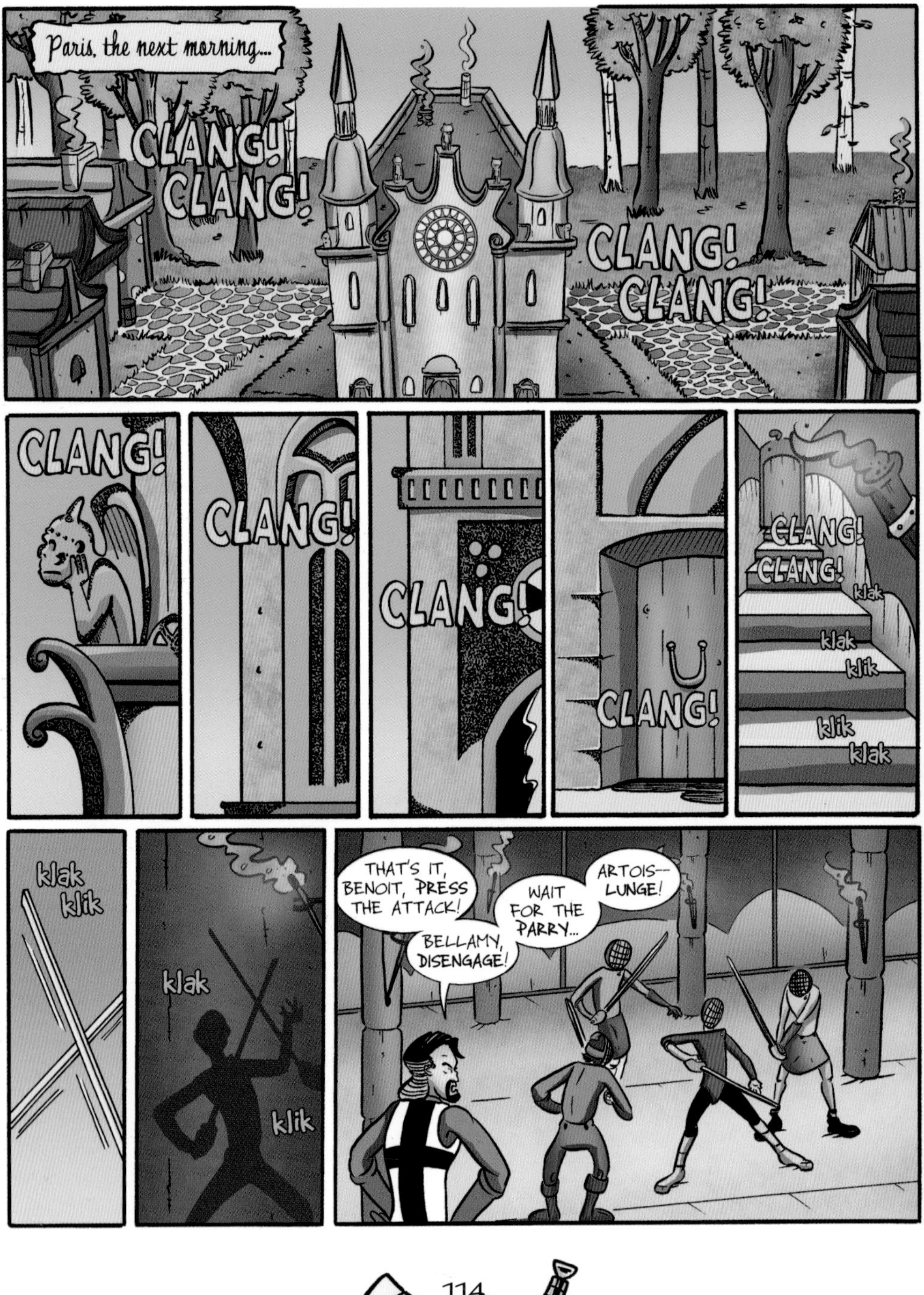
Paris, the next morning...
CLANG! CLANG!
CLANG! CLANG!
CLANG!
CLANG!
CLANG!
CLANG!
CLANG! CLANG!
klak
klak
klik
klik
klak
klak
klik
klak
klik
THAT'S IT, BENOIT, PRESS THE ATTACK!
BELLAMY, DISENGAGE!
WAIT FOR THE PARRY...
ARTOIS--LUNGE!

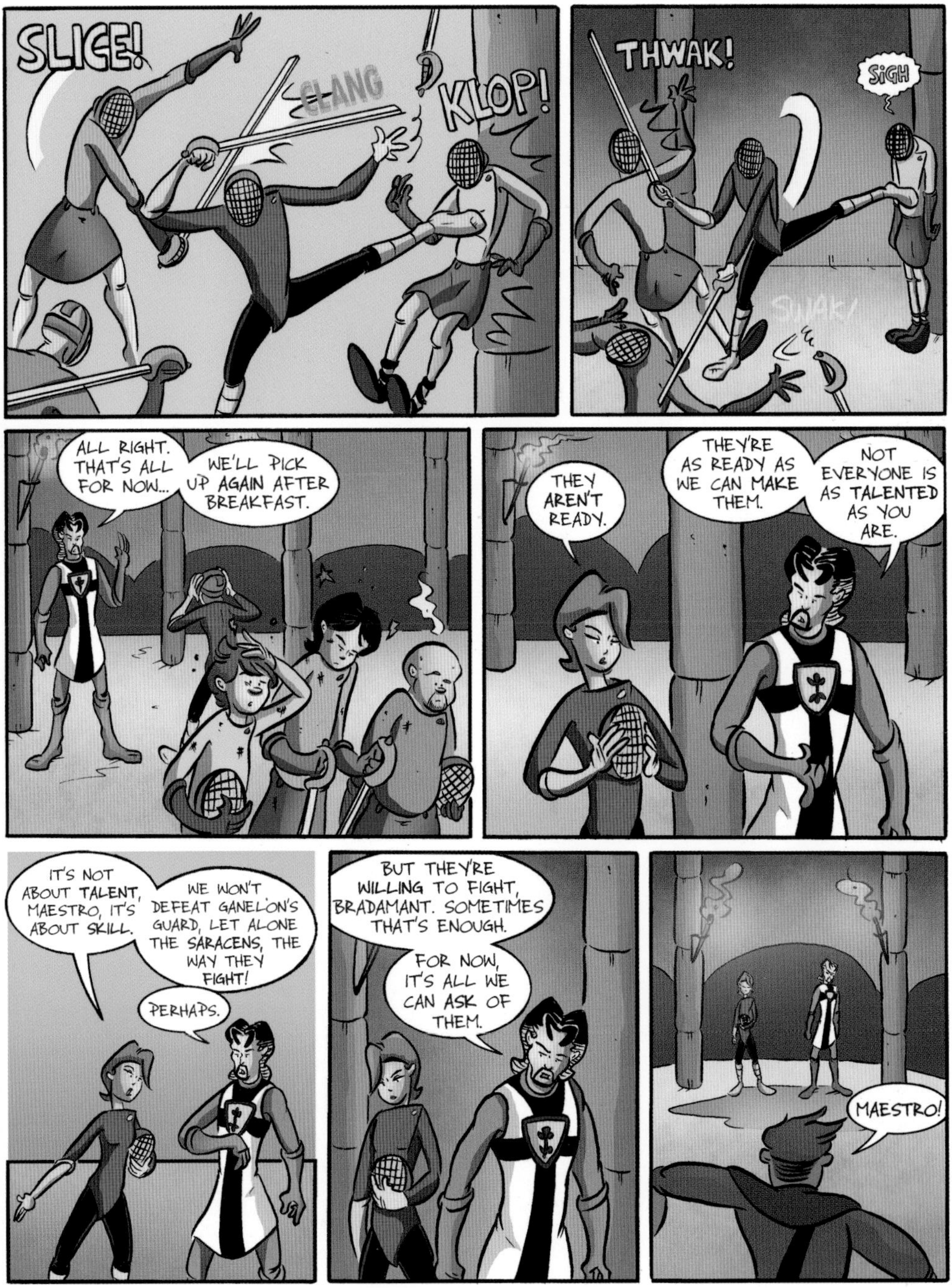
SLICE!
CLANG
KLOP!
THWAK!
SIGH
SWAK!
ALL RIGHT. THAT'S ALL FOR NOW...
WE'LL PICK UP AGAIN AFTER BREAKFAST.
THEY AREN'T READY.
THEY'RE AS READY AS WE CAN MAKE THEM.
NOT EVERYONE IS AS TALENTED AS YOU ARE.
IT'S NOT ABOUT TALENT, MAESTRO, IT'S ABOUT SKILL.
WE WON'T DEFEAT GANELON'S GUARD, LET ALONE THE SARACENS, THE WAY THEY FIGHT!
PERHAPS.
BUT THEY'RE WILLING TO FIGHT, BRADAMANT. SOMETIMES THAT'S ENOUGH.
FOR NOW, IT'S ALL WE CAN ASK OF THEM.
MAESTRO!

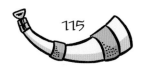

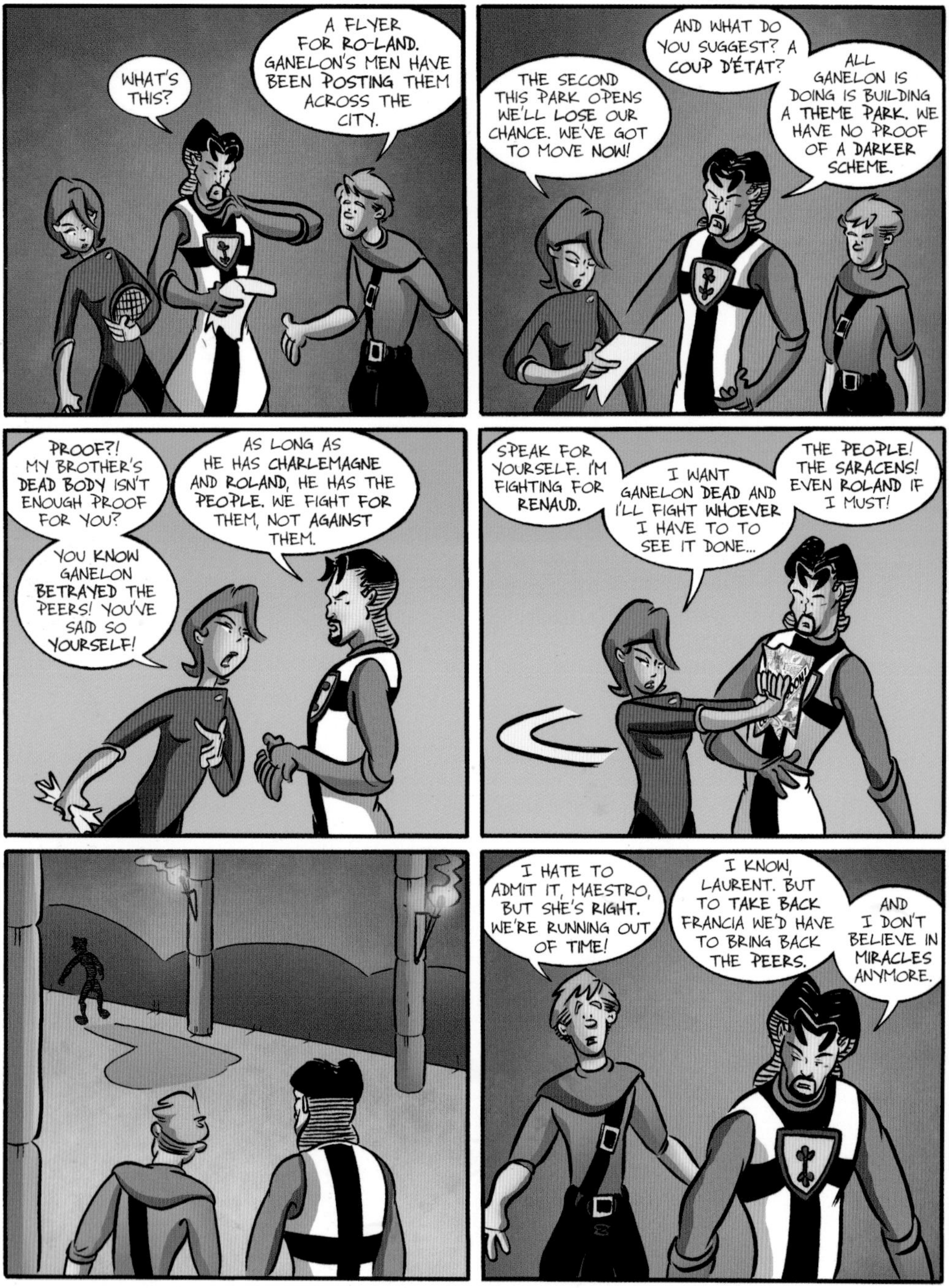
WHAT'S THIS?
A FLYER FOR RO-LAND. GANELON'S MEN HAVE BEEN POSTING THEM ACROSS THE CITY.
THE SECOND THIS PARK OPENS WE'LL LOSE OUR CHANCE. WE'VE GOT TO MOVE NOW!
AND WHAT DO YOU SUGGEST? A COUP D'ÉTAT?
ALL GANELON IS DOING IS BUILDING A THEME PARK. WE HAVE NO PROOF OF A DARKER SCHEME.
PROOF?! MY BROTHER'S DEAD BODY ISN'T ENOUGH PROOF FOR YOU?
YOU KNOW GANELON BETRAYED THE PEERS! YOU'VE SAID SO YOURSELF!
AS LONG AS HE HAS CHARLEMAGNE AND ROLAND, HE HAS THE PEOPLE. WE FIGHT FOR THEM, NOT AGAINST THEM.
SPEAK FOR YOURSELF. I'M FIGHTING FOR RENAUD.
I WANT GANELON DEAD AND I'LL FIGHT WHOEVER I HAVE TO TO SEE IT DONE...
THE PEOPLE! THE SARACENS! EVEN ROLAND IF I MUST!
I HATE TO ADMIT IT, MAESTRO, BUT SHE'S RIGHT. WE'RE RUNNING OUT OF TIME!
I KNOW, LAURENT. BUT TO TAKE BACK FRANCIA WE'D HAVE TO BRING BACK THE PEERS.
AND I DON'T BELIEVE IN MIRACLES ANYMORE.

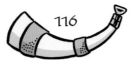

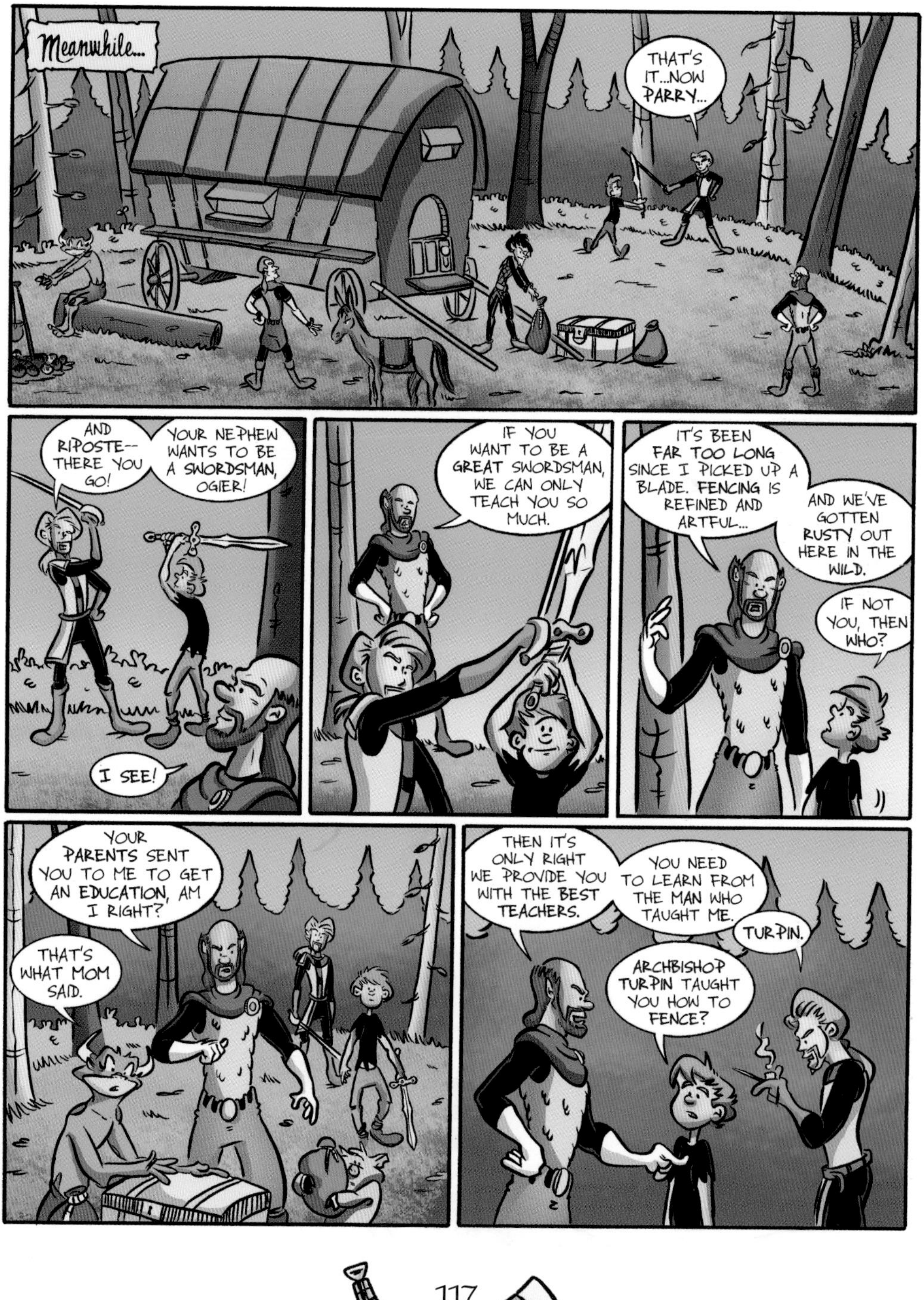
Meanwhile...
THAT'S IT...NOW PARRY...
AND RIPOSTE-- THERE YOU GO!
YOUR NEPHEW WANTS TO BE A SWORDSMAN, OGIER!
I SEE!
IF YOU WANT TO BE A GREAT SWORDSMAN, WE CAN ONLY TEACH YOU SO MUCH.
IT'S BEEN FAR TOO LONG SINCE I PICKED UP A BLADE. FENCING IS REFINED AND ARTFUL...
AND WE'VE GOTTEN RUSTY OUT HERE IN THE WILD.
IF NOT YOU, THEN WHO?
YOUR PARENTS SENT YOU TO ME TO GET AN EDUCATION, AM I RIGHT?
THAT'S WHAT MOM SAID.
THEN IT'S ONLY RIGHT WE PROVIDE YOU WITH THE BEST TEACHERS.
YOU NEED TO LEARN FROM THE MAN WHO TAUGHT ME.
TURPIN.
ARCHBISHOP TURPIN TAUGHT YOU HOW TO FENCE?

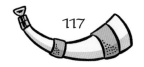

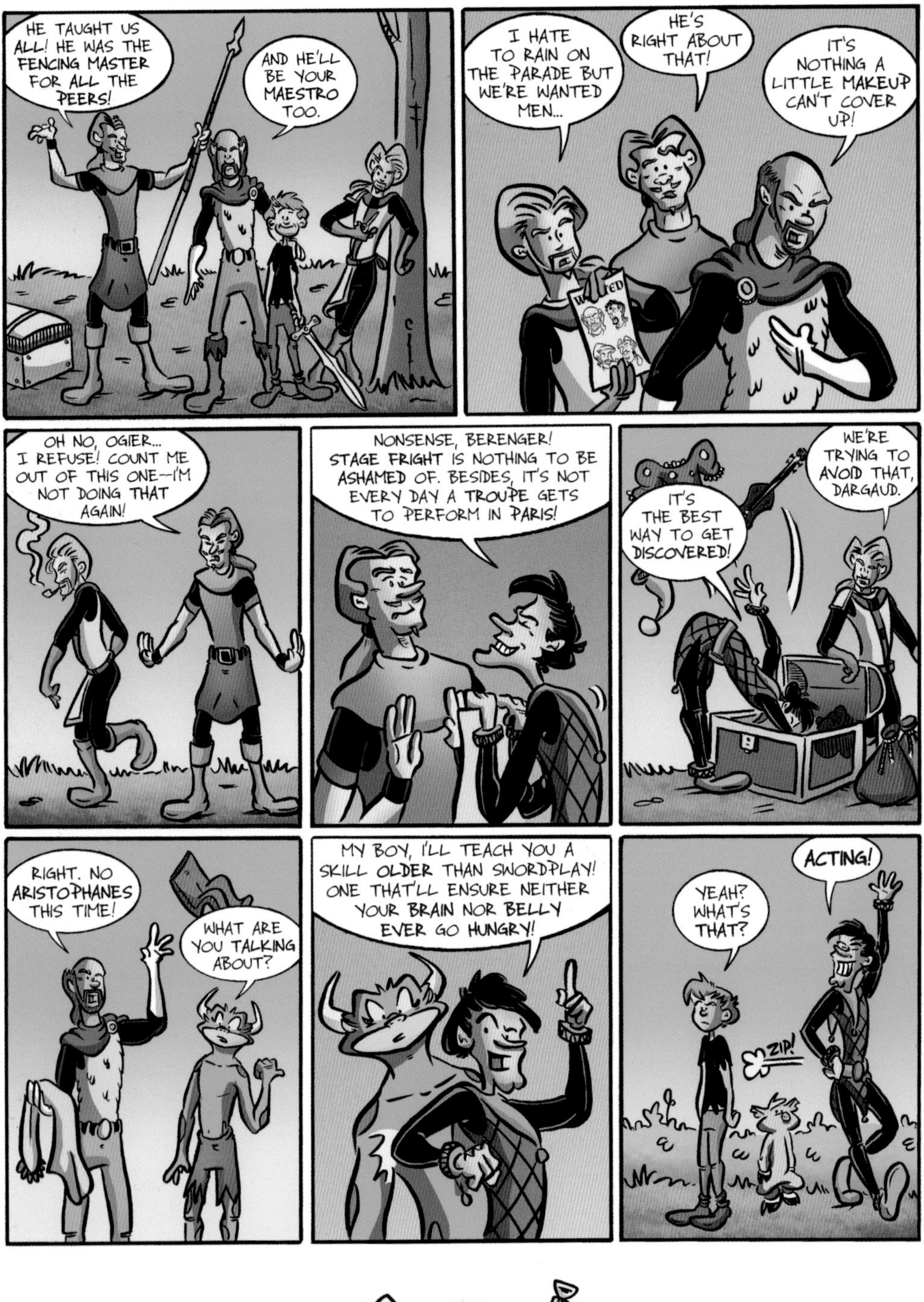
HE TAUGHT US ALL! HE WAS THE FENCING MASTER FOR ALL THE PEERS!
AND HE'LL BE YOUR MAESTRO TOO.
I HATE TO RAIN ON THE PARADE BUT WE'RE WANTED MEN...
HE'S RIGHT ABOUT THAT!
IT'S NOTHING A LITTLE MAKEUP CAN'T COVER UP!
OH NO, OGIER... I REFUSE! COUNT ME OUT OF THIS ONE--I'M NOT DOING THAT AGAIN!
NONSENSE, BERENGER! STAGE FRIGHT IS NOTHING TO BE ASHAMED OF. BESIDES, IT'S NOT EVERY DAY A TROUPE GETS TO PERFORM IN PARIS!
IT'S THE BEST WAY TO GET DISCOVERED!
WE'RE TRYING TO AVOID THAT, DARGAUD.
RIGHT. NO ARISTOPHANES THIS TIME!
WHAT ARE YOU TALKING ABOUT?
MY BOY, I'LL TEACH YOU A SKILL OLDER THAN SWORDPLAY! ONE THAT'LL ENSURE NEITHER YOUR BRAIN NOR BELLY EVER GO HUNGRY!
YEAH? WHAT'S THAT?
ACTING!
ZIP!

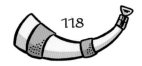

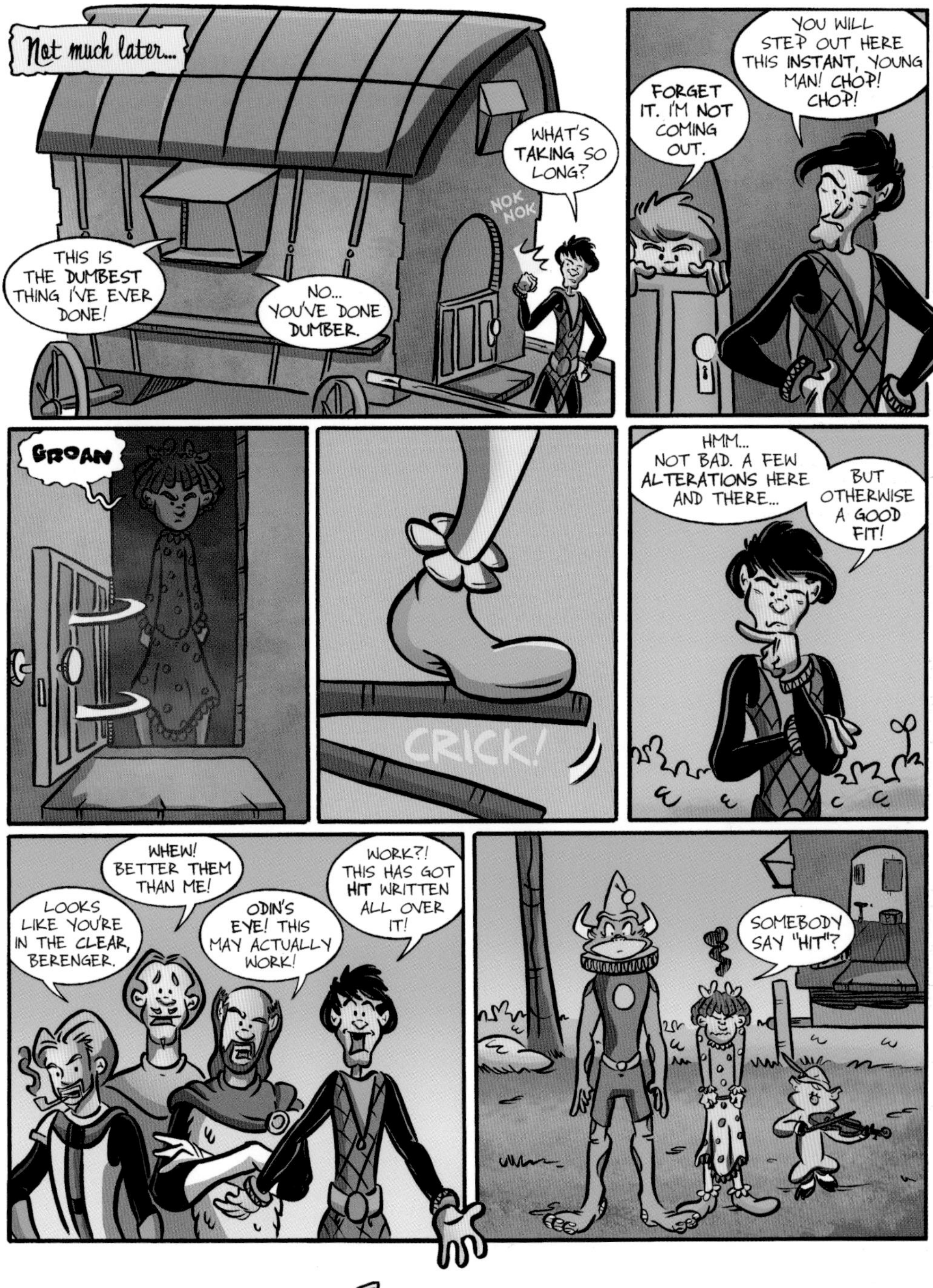
Not much later...
THIS IS THE DUMBEST THING I'VE EVER DONE!
NO... YOU'VE DONE DUMBER.
NOK NOK
WHAT'S TAKING SO LONG?
YOU WILL STEP OUT HERE THIS INSTANT, YOUNG MAN! CHOP! CHOP!
FORGET IT. I'M NOT COMING OUT.
GROAN
CRICK!
HMM... NOT BAD. A FEW ALTERATIONS HERE AND THERE...
BUT OTHERWISE A GOOD FIT!
LOOKS LIKE YOU'RE IN THE CLEAR, BERENGER.
WHEW! BETTER THEM THAN ME!
ODIN'S EYE! THIS MAY ACTUALLY WORK!
WORK?! THIS HAS GOT HIT WRITTEN ALL OVER IT!
SOMEBODY SAY "HIT"?

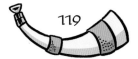

part three

roland makes a stand

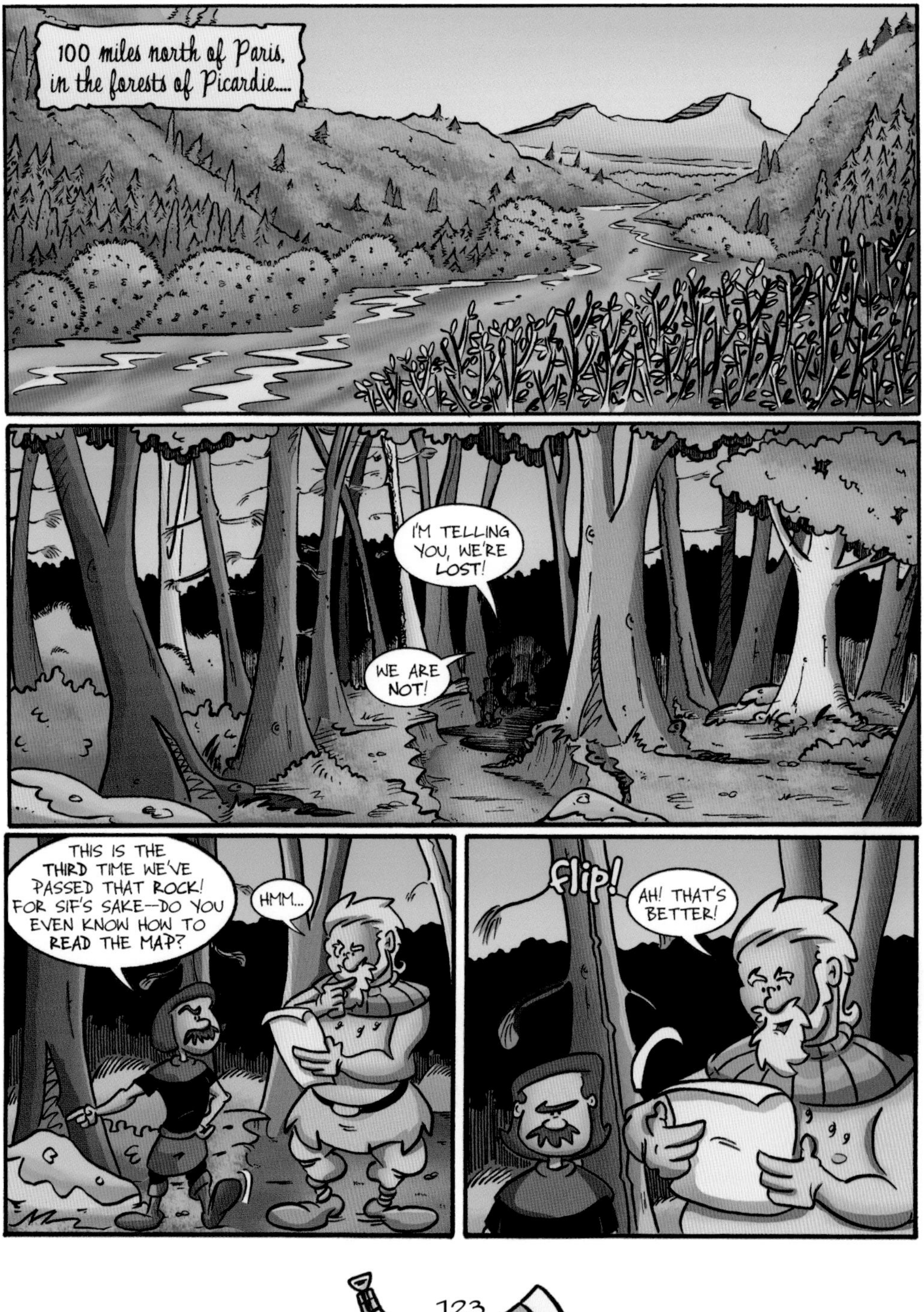
100 miles north of Paris, in the forests of Picardie....
I'M TELLING YOU, WE'RE LOST!
WE ARE NOT!
THIS IS THE THIRD TIME WE'VE PASSED THAT ROCK! FOR SIF'S SAKE--DO YOU EVEN KNOW HOW TO READ THE MAP?
HMM...
Flip!
AH! THAT'S BETTER!

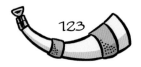

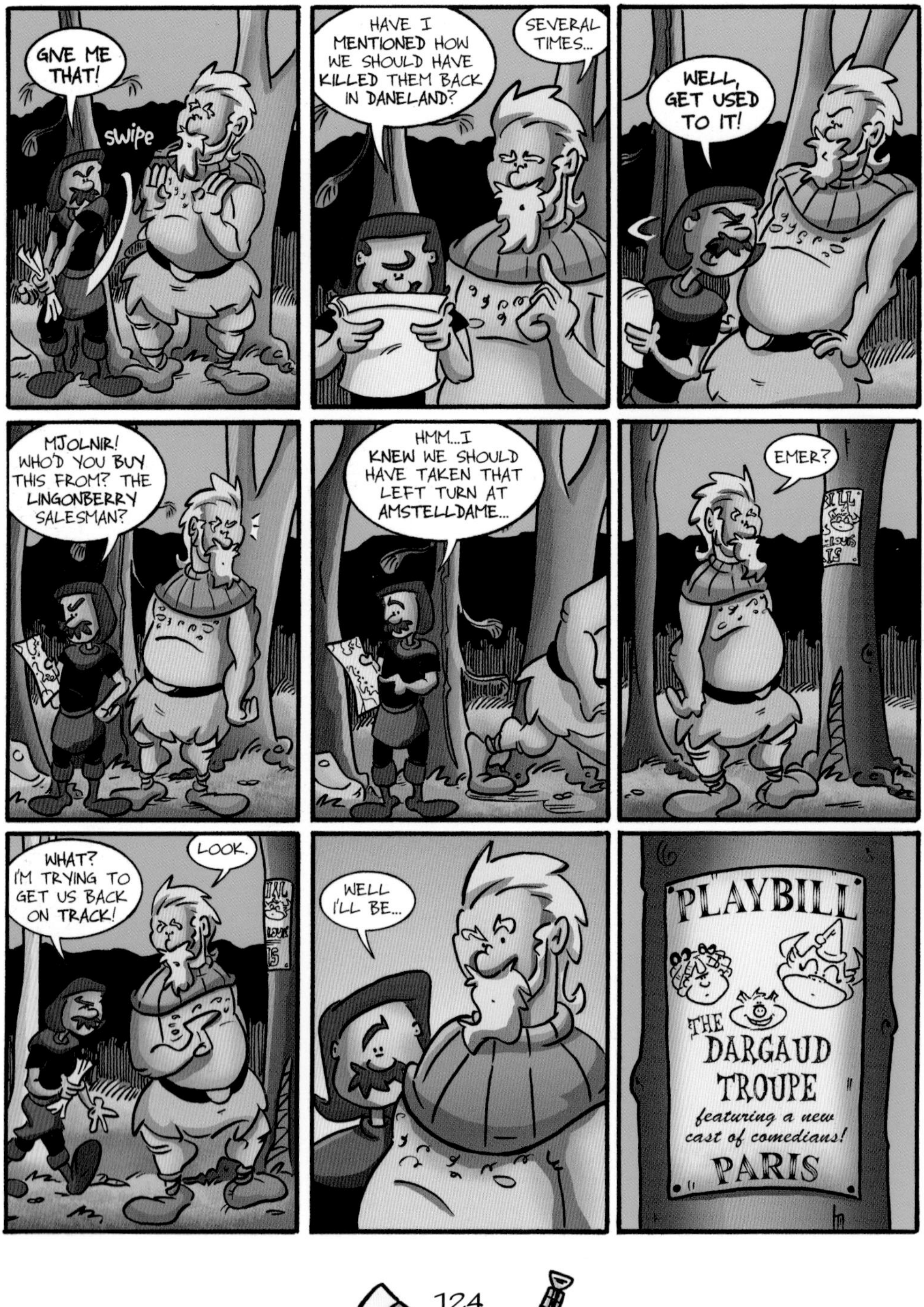
GIVE ME THAT!
swipe
HAVE I MENTIONED HOW WE SHOULD HAVE KILLED THEM BACK IN DANELAND?
SEVERAL TIMES...
WELL, GET USED TO IT!
MJOLNIR! WHO'D YOU BUY THIS FROM? THE LINGONBERRY SALESMAN?
HMM...I KNEW WE SHOULD HAVE TAKEN THAT LEFT TURN AT AMSTELLDAME...
EMER?
WHAT? I'M TRYING TO GET US BACK ON TRACK!
LOOK.
WELL I'LL BE...
PLAYBILL
THE DARGAUD TROUPE
featuring a new cast of comedians!
PARIS

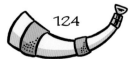

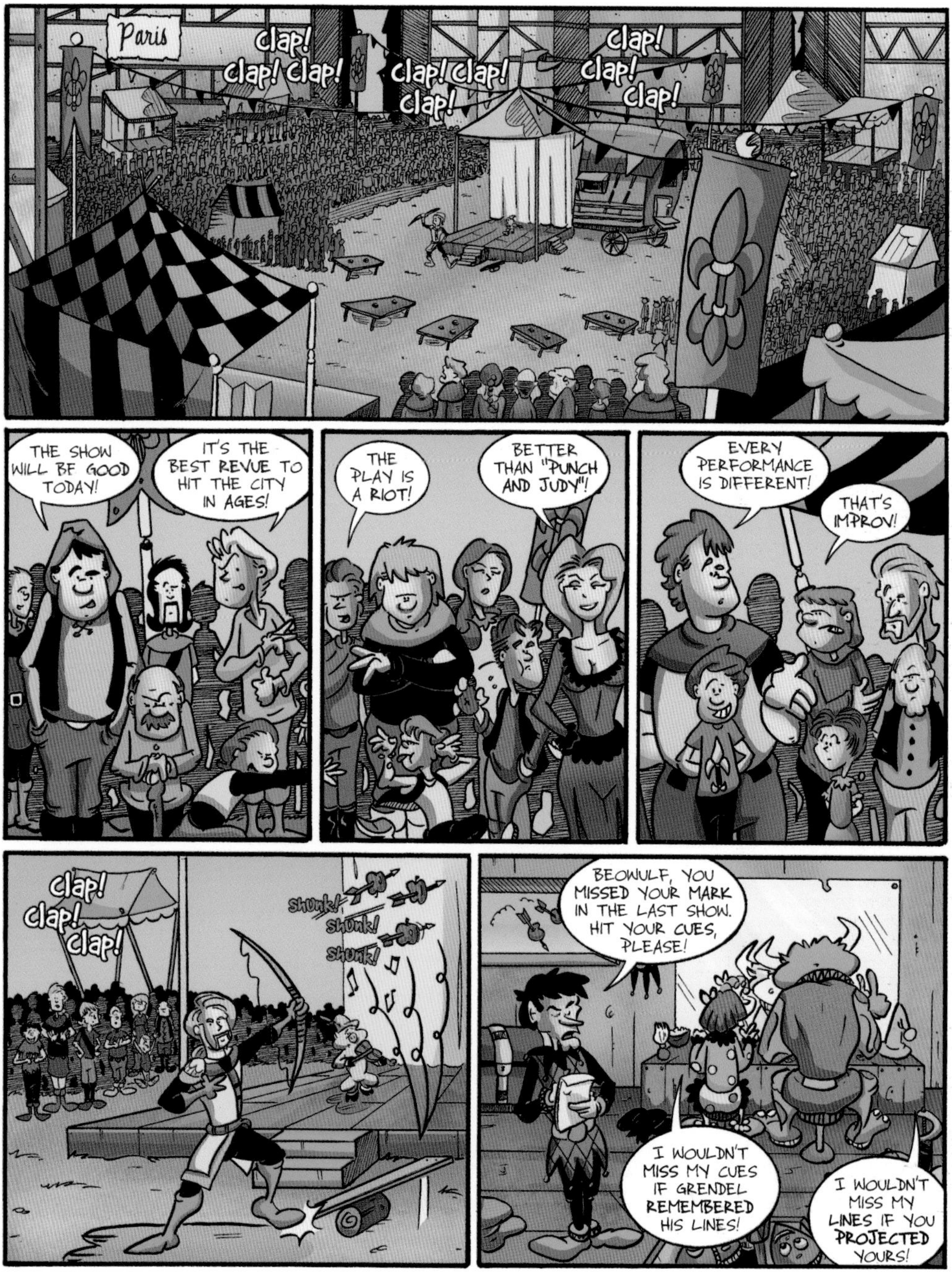
Paris
Clap! Clap! Clap!
Clap! Clap! Clap!
Clap! Clap! Clap!
THE SHOW WILL BE GOOD TODAY!
IT'S THE BEST REVUE TO HIT THE CITY IN AGES!
THE PLAY IS A RIOT!
BETTER THAN "PUNCH AND JUDY"!
EVERY PERFORMANCE IS DIFFERENT!
THAT'S IMPROV!
Clap! Clap! Clap!
Shunk! Shunk! Shunk!
BEOWULF, YOU MISSED YOUR MARK IN THE LAST SHOW. HIT YOUR CUES, PLEASE!
I WOULDN'T MISS MY CUES IF GRENDEL REMEMBERED HIS LINES!
I WOULDN'T MISS MY LINES IF YOU PROJECTED YOURS!

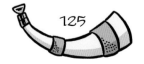

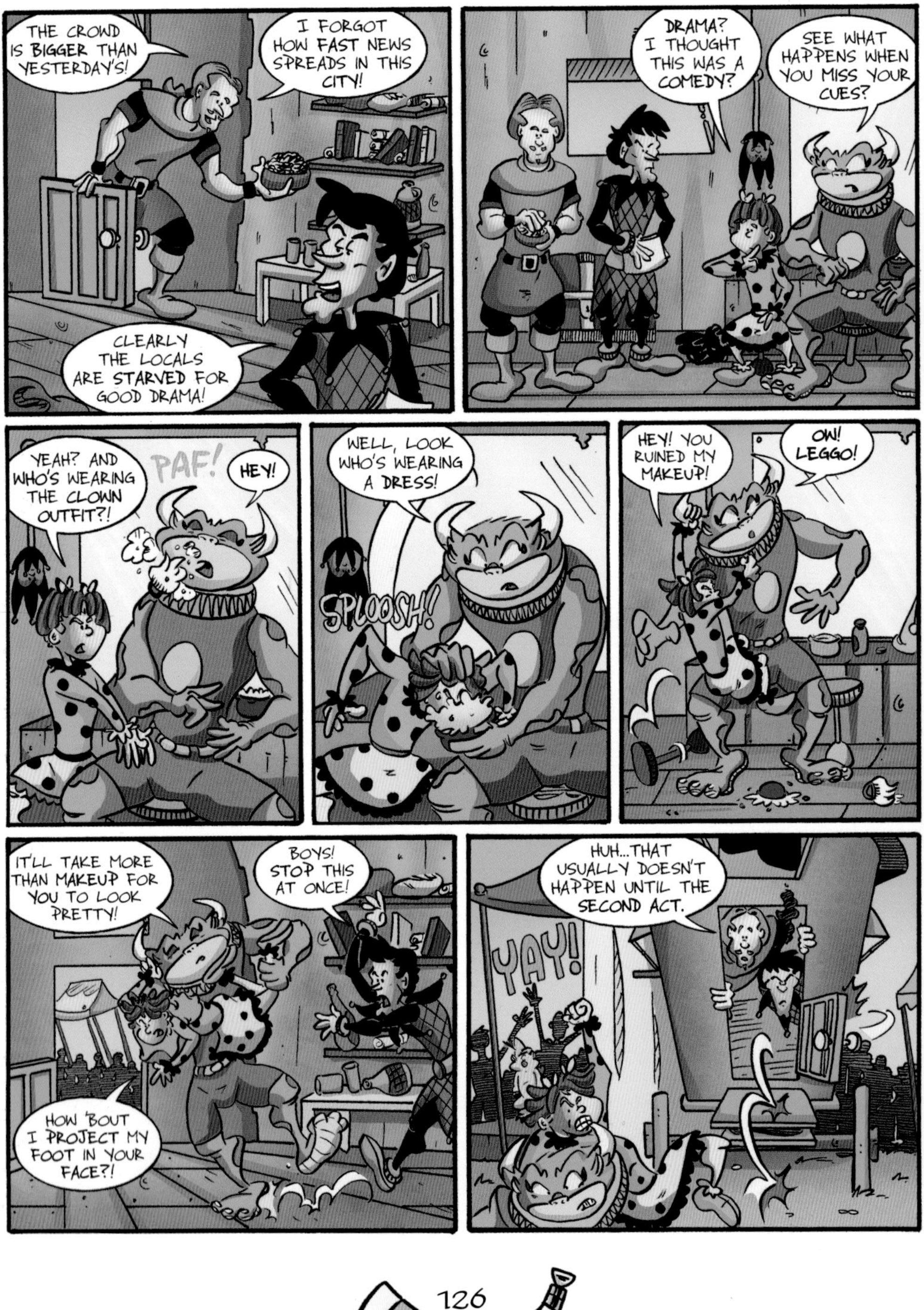
THE CROWD IS BIGGER THAN YESTERDAY'S!
I FORGOT HOW FAST NEWS SPREADS IN THIS CITY!
CLEARLY THE LOCALS ARE STARVED FOR GOOD DRAMA!
DRAMA? I THOUGHT THIS WAS A COMEDY?
SEE WHAT HAPPENS WHEN YOU MISS YOUR CUES?
YEAH? AND WHO'S WEARING THE CLOWN OUTFIT?!
PAF!
HEY!
WELL, LOOK WHO'S WEARING A DRESS!
SPLOOSH!
HEY! YOU RUINED MY MAKEUP!
OW! LEGGO!
IT'LL TAKE MORE THAN MAKEUP FOR YOU TO LOOK PRETTY!
BOYS! STOP THIS AT ONCE!
HOW 'BOUT I PROJECT MY FOOT IN YOUR FACE?!
HUH...THAT USUALLY DOESN'T HAPPEN UNTIL THE SECOND ACT.
YAY!

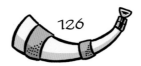

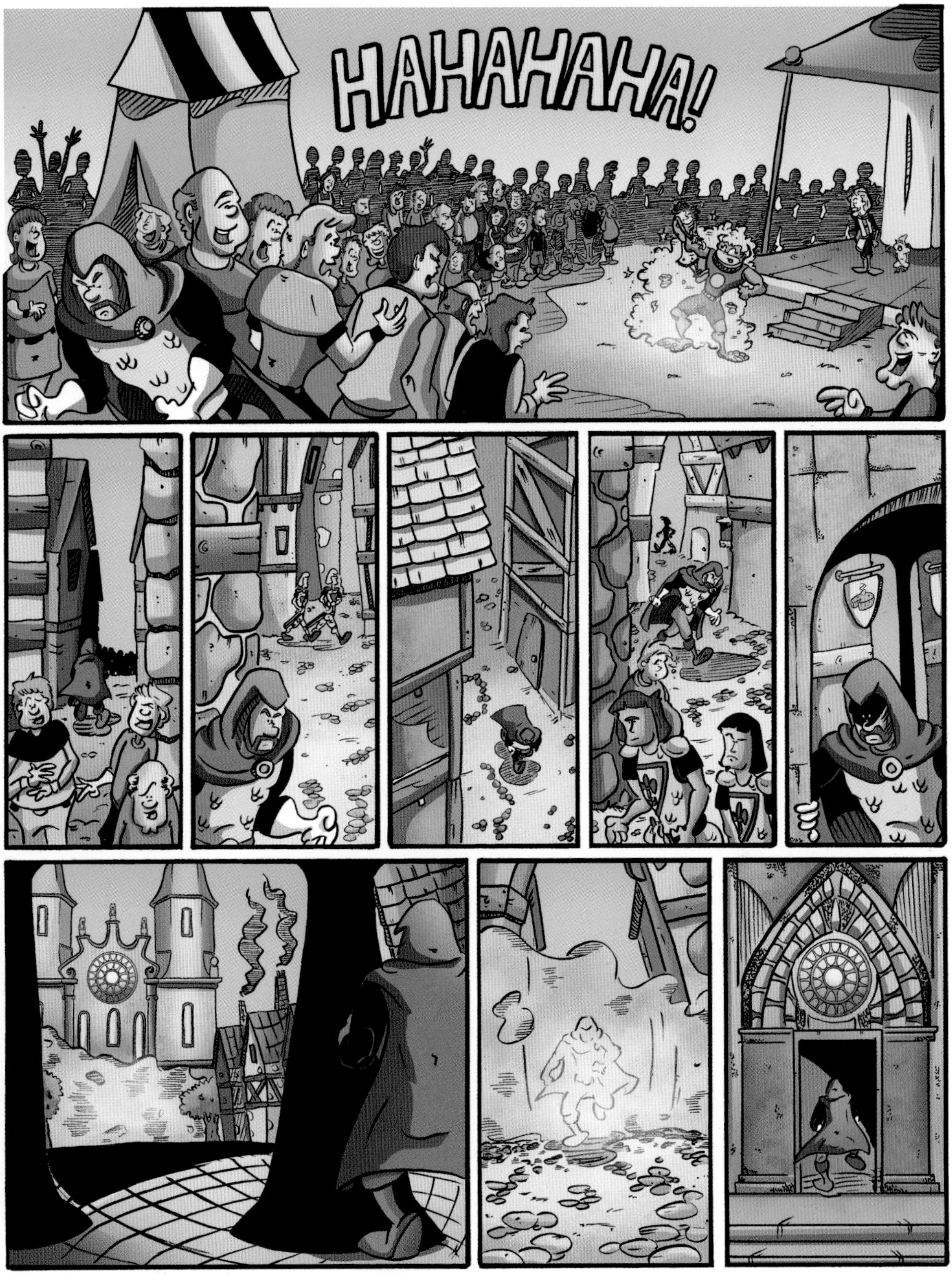
HAHAHAHA!

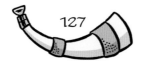

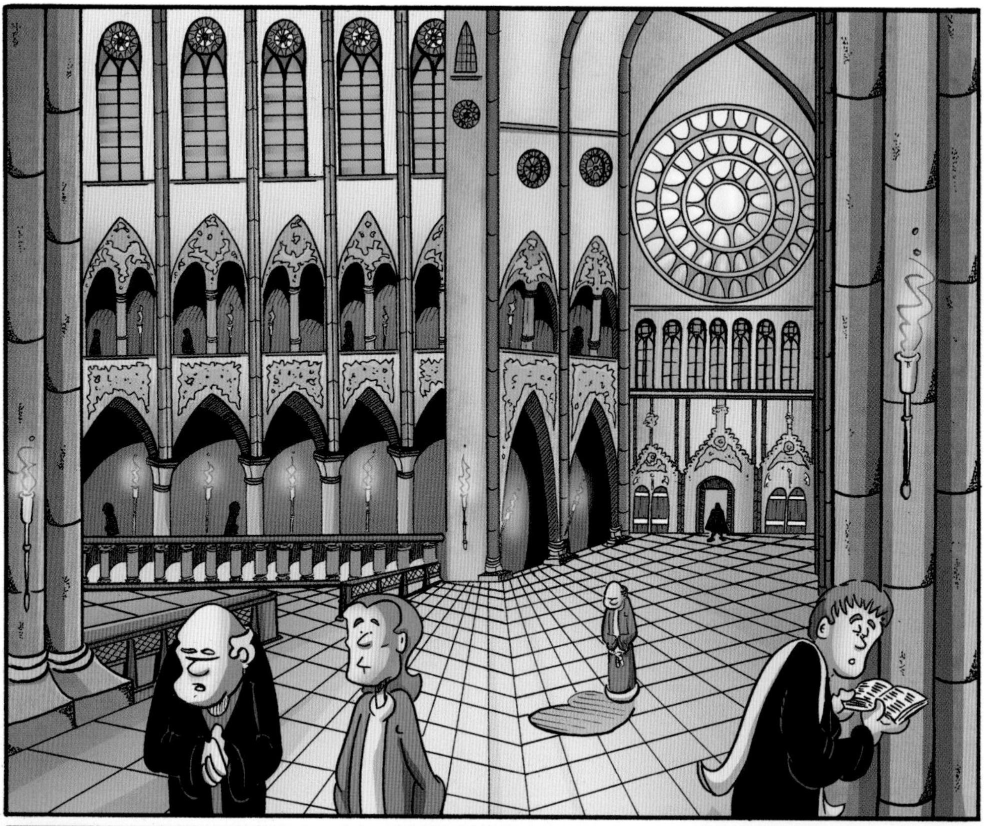

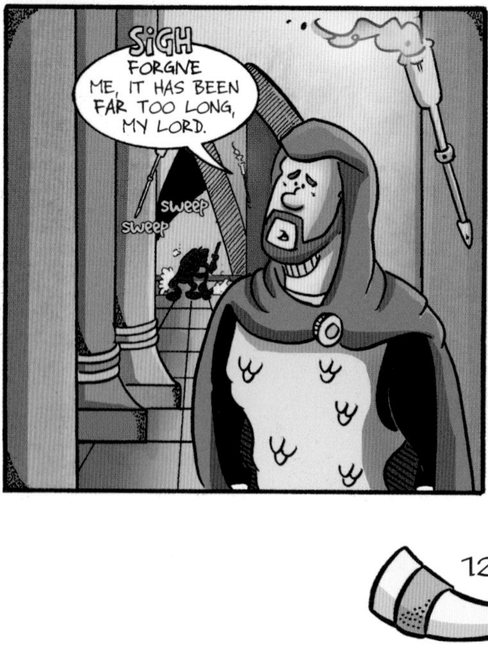
SIGH
FORGIVE ME, IT HAS BEEN FAR TOO LONG, MY LORD.
SWEEP
SWEEP

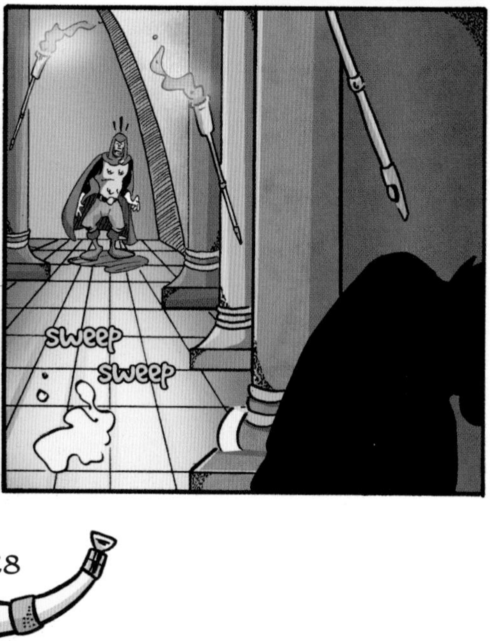
SWEEP
SWEEP

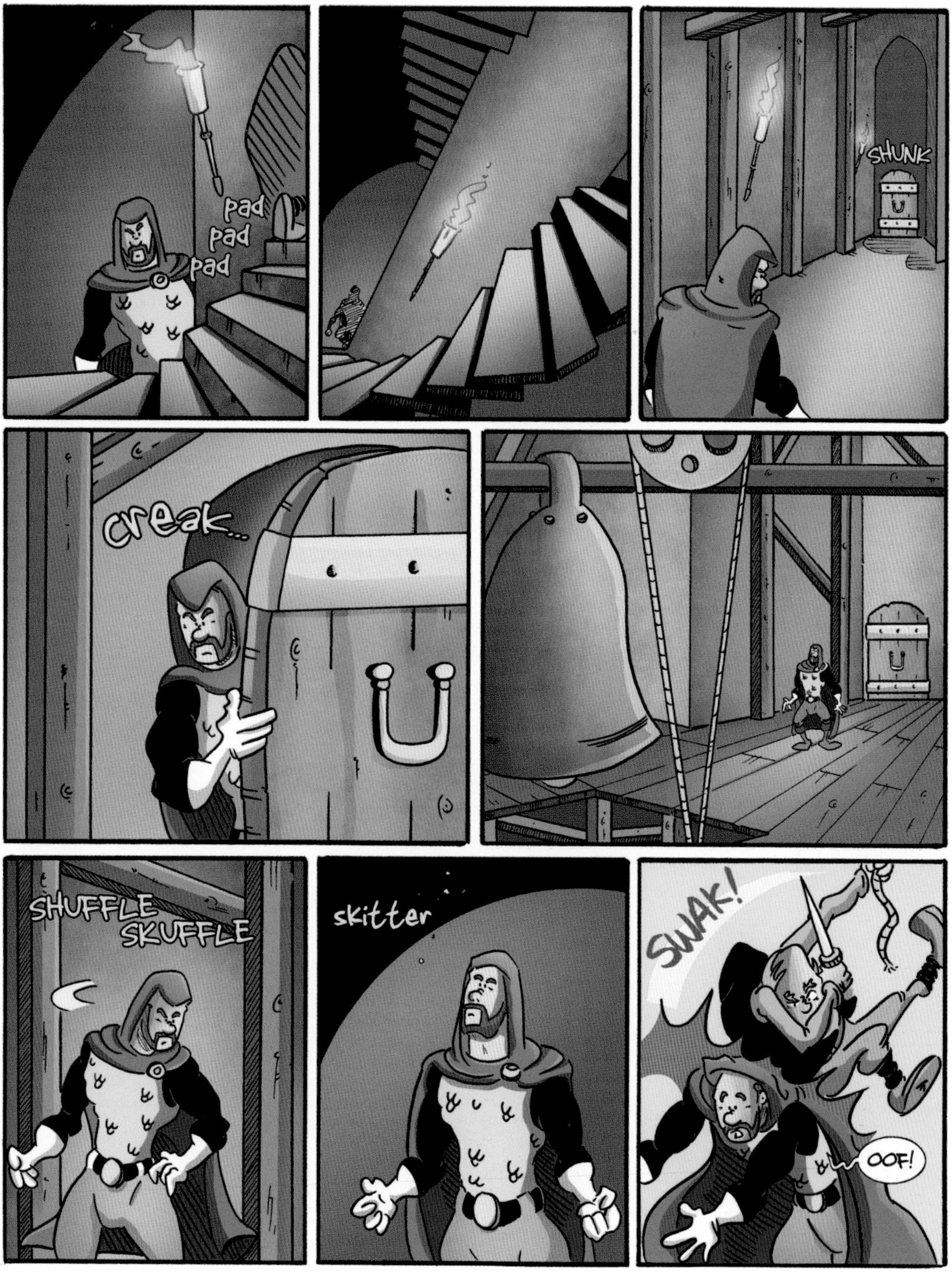
pad
pad
pad
SHUNK
creak...
SHUFFLE
SKUFFLE
skitter
SWAK!
OOF!

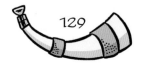

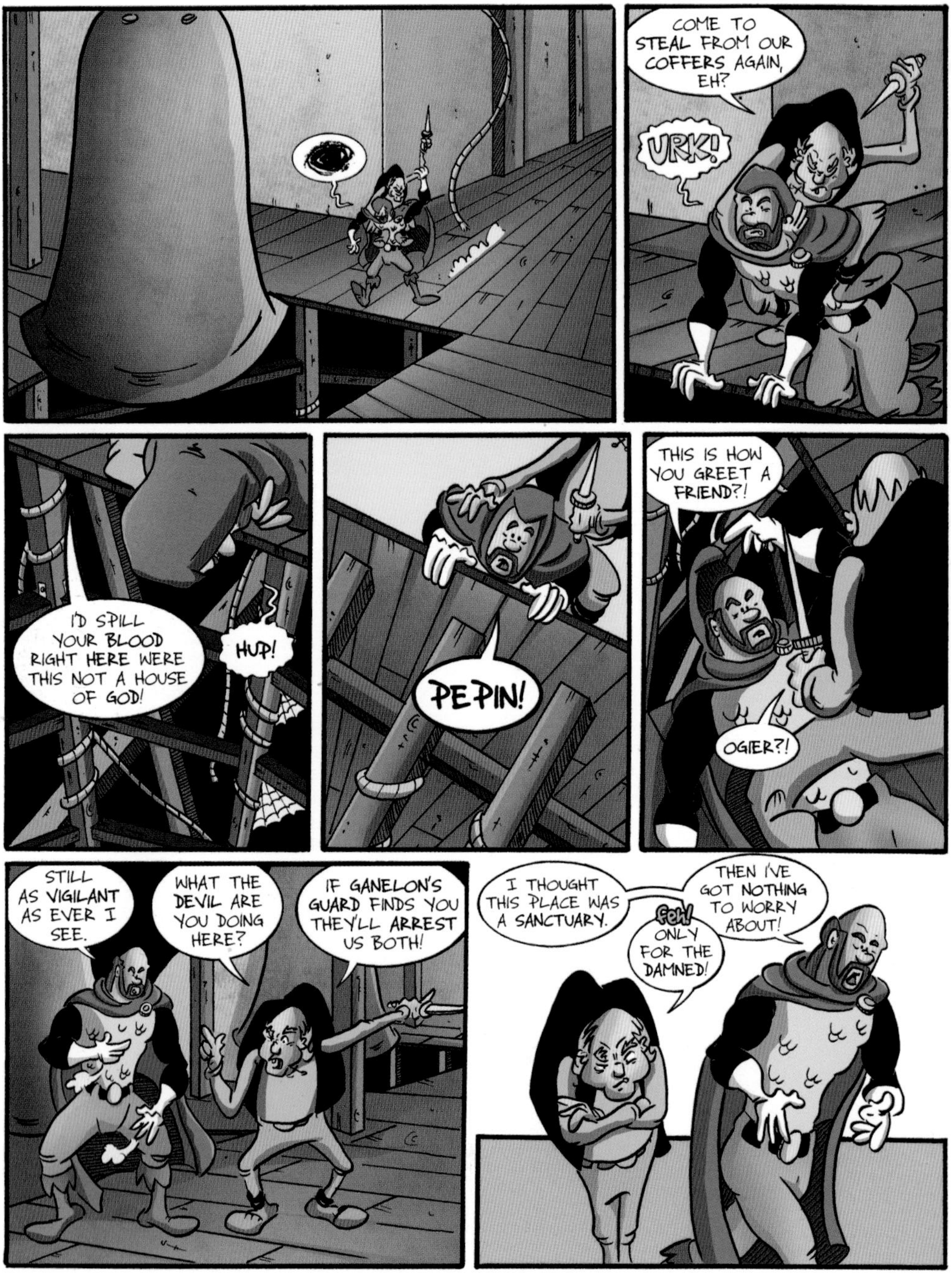
COME TO STEAL FROM OUR COFFERS AGAIN, EH?
URK!
I'D SPILL YOUR BLOOD RIGHT HERE WERE THIS NOT A HOUSE OF GOD!
HUP!
PEPIN!
THIS IS HOW YOU GREET A FRIEND?!
OGIER?!
STILL AS VIGILANT AS EVER I SEE.
WHAT THE DEVIL ARE YOU DOING HERE?
IF GANELON'S GUARD FINDS YOU THEY'LL ARREST US BOTH!
I THOUGHT THIS PLACE WAS A SANCTUARY.
THEN I'VE GOT NOTHING TO WORRY ABOUT!
FEH! ONLY FOR THE DAMNED!

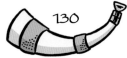

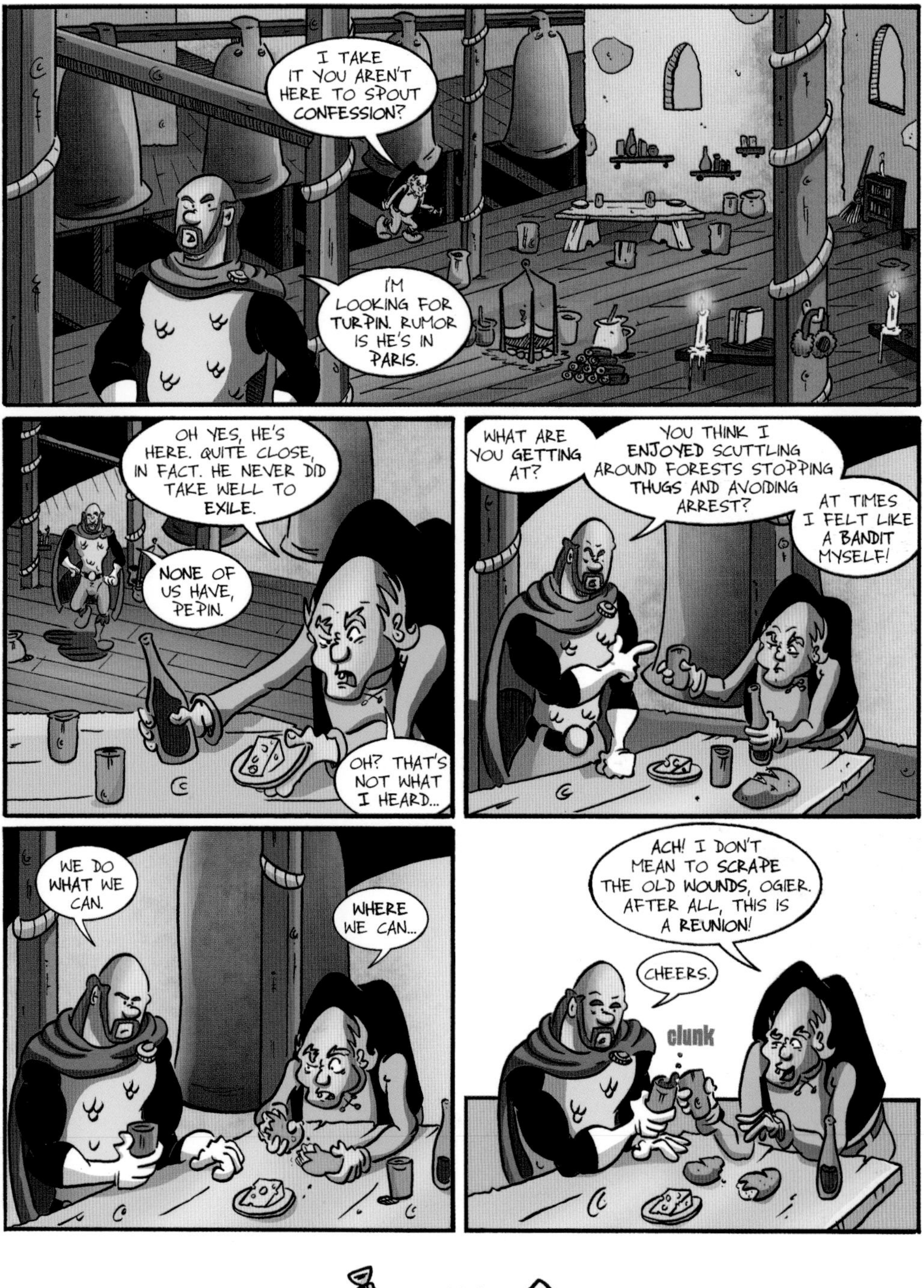
I TAKE IT YOU AREN'T HERE TO SPOUT CONFESSION?
I'M LOOKING FOR TURPIN. RUMOR IS HE'S IN PARIS.
OH YES, HE'S HERE. QUITE CLOSE, IN FACT. HE NEVER DID TAKE WELL TO EXILE.
NONE OF US HAVE, PEPIN.
OH? THAT'S NOT WHAT I HEARD...
WHAT ARE YOU GETTING AT?
YOU THINK I ENJOYED SCUTTLING AROUND FORESTS STOPPING THUGS AND AVOIDING ARREST?
AT TIMES I FELT LIKE A BANDIT MYSELF!
WE DO WHAT WE CAN.
WHERE WE CAN...
ACH! I DON'T MEAN TO SCRAPE THE OLD WOUNDS, OGIER. AFTER ALL, THIS IS A REUNION!
CHEERS.
clunk

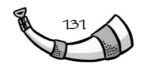

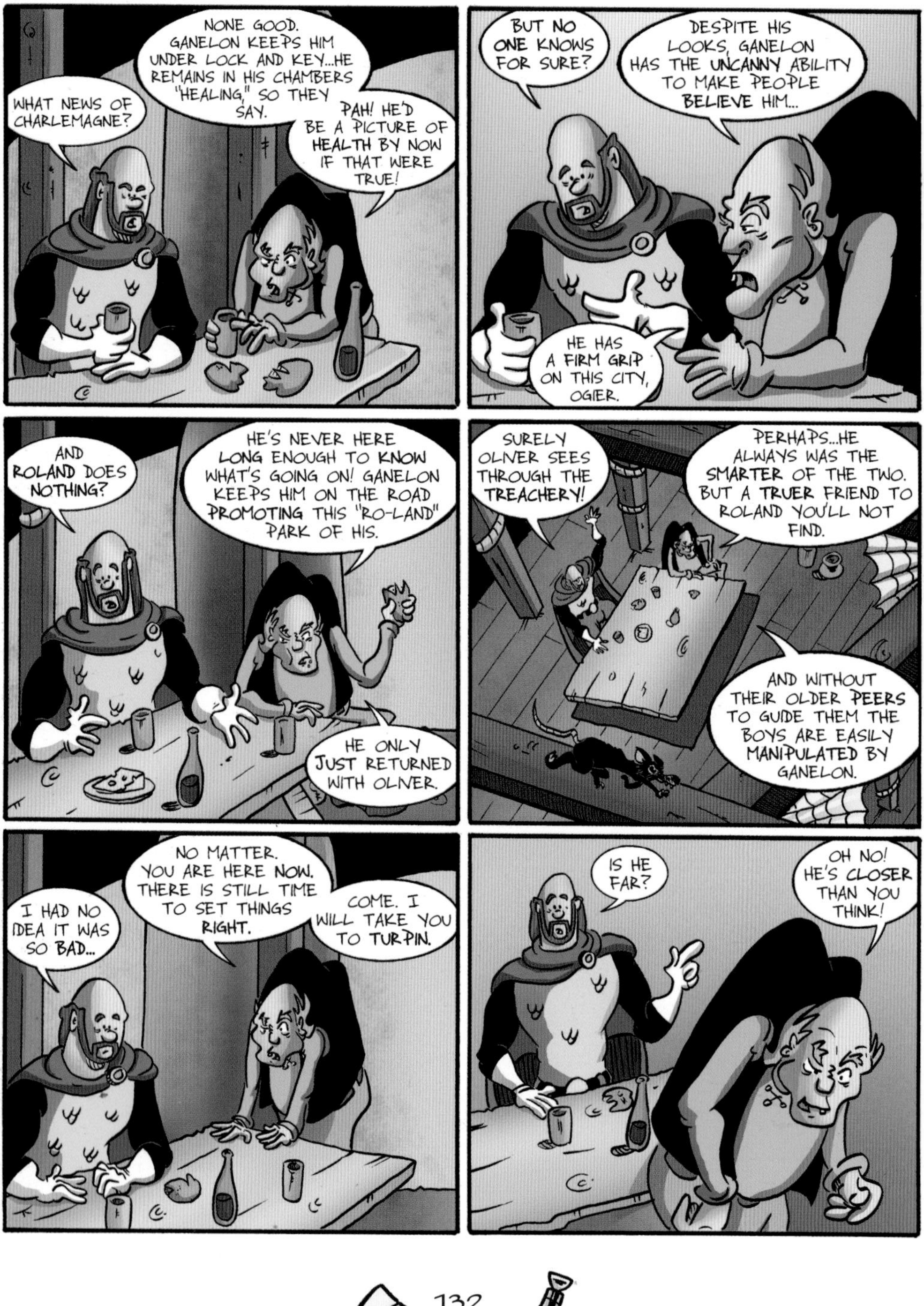
WHAT NEWS OF CHARLEMAGNE?
NONE GOOD. GANELON KEEPS HIM UNDER LOCK AND KEY...HE REMAINS IN HIS CHAMBERS "HEALING," SO THEY SAY.
PAH! HE'D BE A PICTURE OF HEALTH BY NOW IF THAT WERE TRUE!
BUT NO ONE KNOWS FOR SURE?
DESPITE HIS LOOKS, GANELON HAS THE UNCANNY ABILITY TO MAKE PEOPLE BELIEVE HIM...
HE HAS A FIRM GRIP ON THIS CITY, OGIER.
AND ROLAND DOES NOTHING?
HE'S NEVER HERE LONG ENOUGH TO KNOW WHAT'S GOING ON! GANELON KEEPS HIM ON THE ROAD PROMOTING THIS "RO-LAND" PARK OF HIS.
HE ONLY JUST RETURNED WITH OLIVER.
SURELY OLIVER SEES THROUGH THE TREACHERY!
PERHAPS...HE ALWAYS WAS THE SMARTER OF THE TWO. BUT A TRUER FRIEND TO ROLAND YOU'LL NOT FIND.
AND WITHOUT THEIR OLDER PEERS TO GUIDE THEM THE BOYS ARE EASILY MANIPULATED BY GANELON.
I HAD NO IDEA IT WAS SO BAD...
NO MATTER. YOU ARE HERE NOW. THERE IS STILL TIME TO SET THINGS RIGHT.
COME. I WILL TAKE YOU TO TURPIN.
IS HE FAR?
OH NO! HE'S CLOSER THAN YOU THINK!

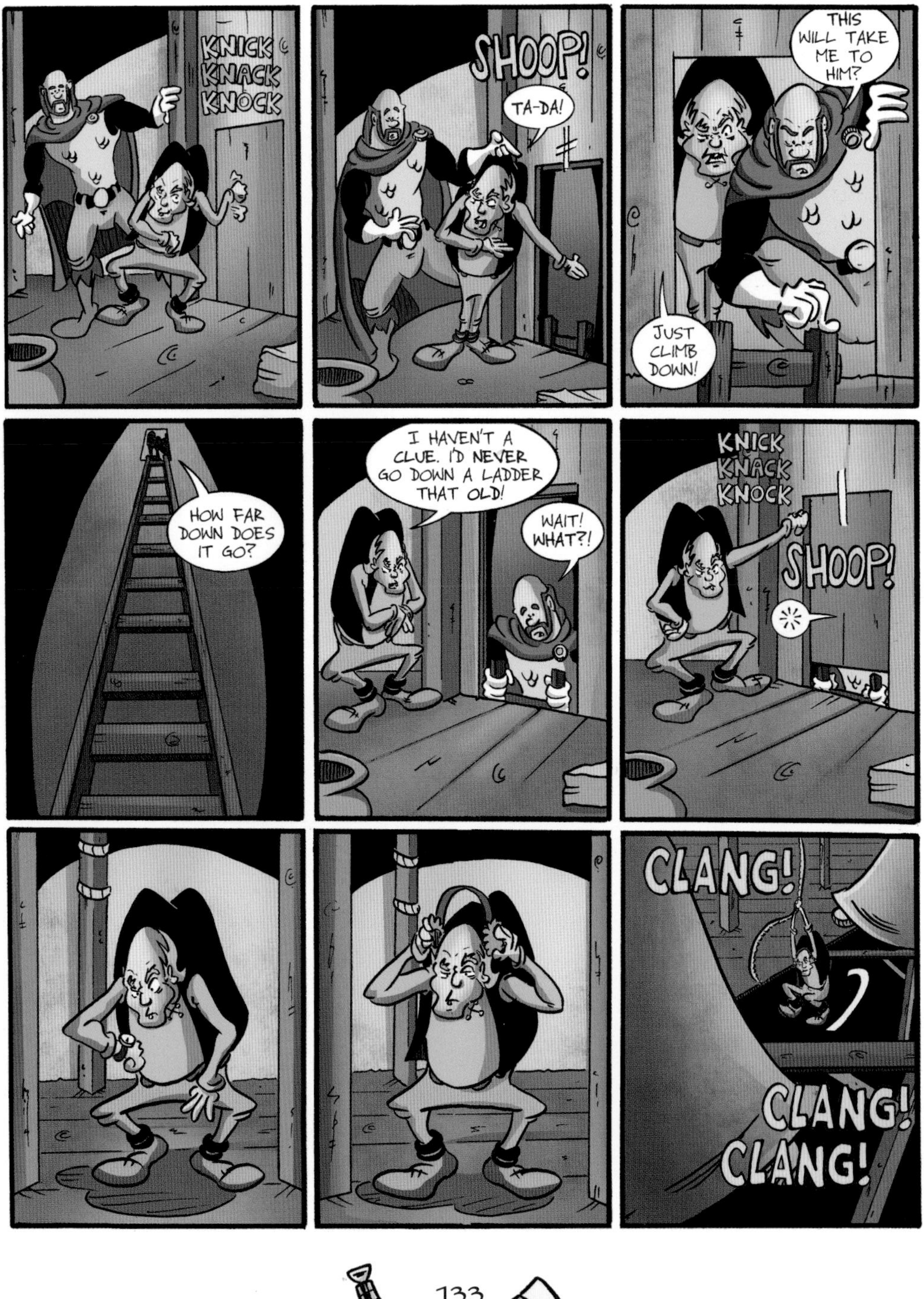
KNICK KNACK KNOCK
SHOOP!
TA-DA!
THIS WILL TAKE ME TO HIM?
JUST CLIMB DOWN!
HOW FAR DOWN DOES IT GO?
I HAVEN'T A CLUE. I'D NEVER GO DOWN A LADDER THAT OLD!
WAIT! WHAT?!
KNICK KNACK KNOCK
SHOOP!
CLANG!
CLANG! CLANG!

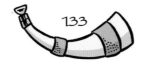

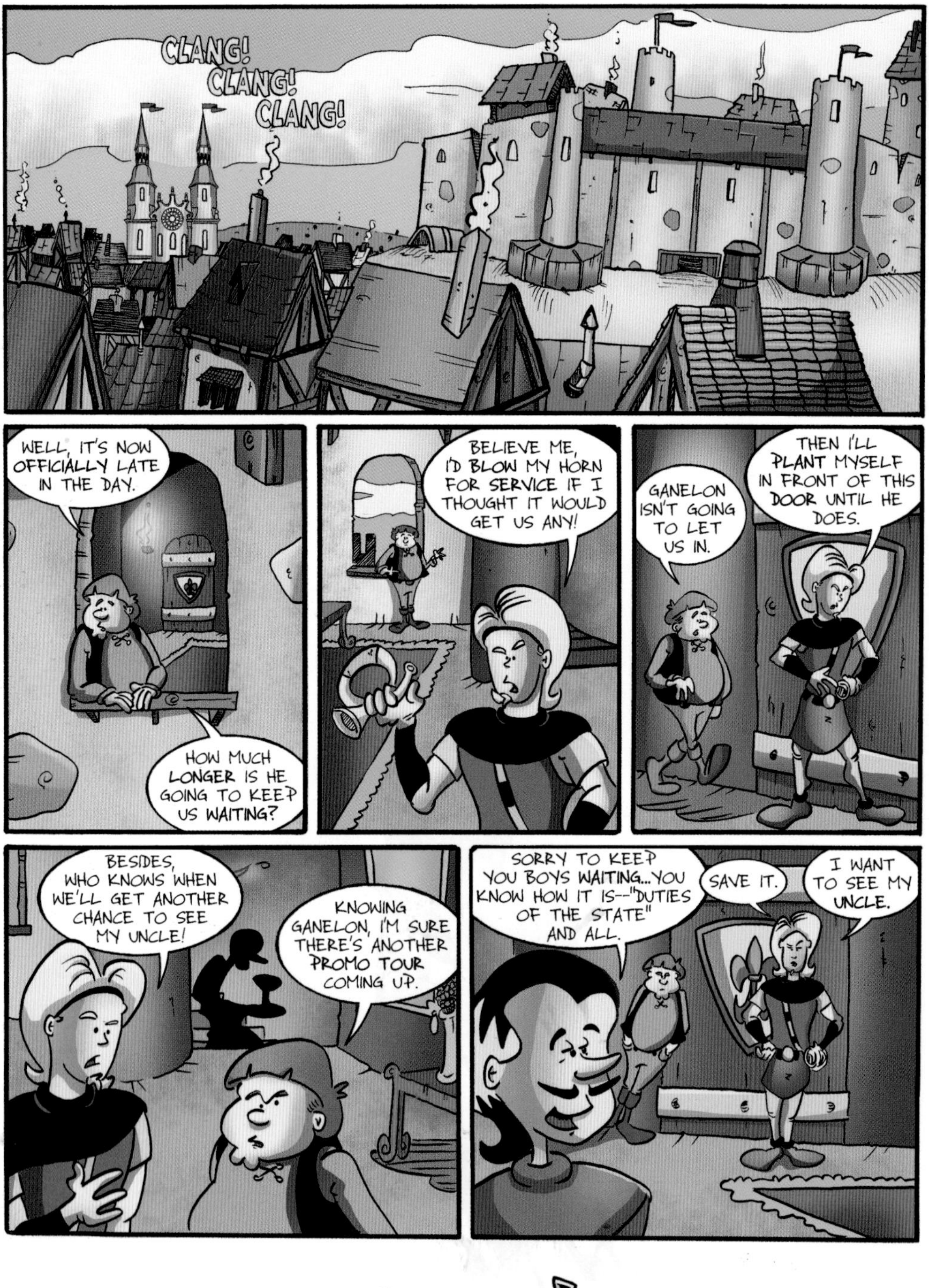
CLANG!
CLANG!
CLANG!
WELL, IT'S NOW OFFICIALLY LATE IN THE DAY.
HOW MUCH LONGER IS HE GOING TO KEEP US WAITING?
BELIEVE ME, I'D BLOW MY HORN FOR SERVICE IF I THOUGHT IT WOULD GET US ANY!
GANELON ISN'T GOING TO LET US IN.
THEN I'LL PLANT MYSELF IN FRONT OF THIS DOOR UNTIL HE DOES.
BESIDES, WHO KNOWS WHEN WE'LL GET ANOTHER CHANCE TO SEE MY UNCLE!
KNOWING GANELON, I'M SURE THERE'S ANOTHER PROMO TOUR COMING UP.
SORRY TO KEEP YOU BOYS WAITING...YOU KNOW HOW IT IS--"DUTIES OF THE STATE" AND ALL.
SAVE IT.
I WANT TO SEE MY UNCLE.

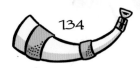

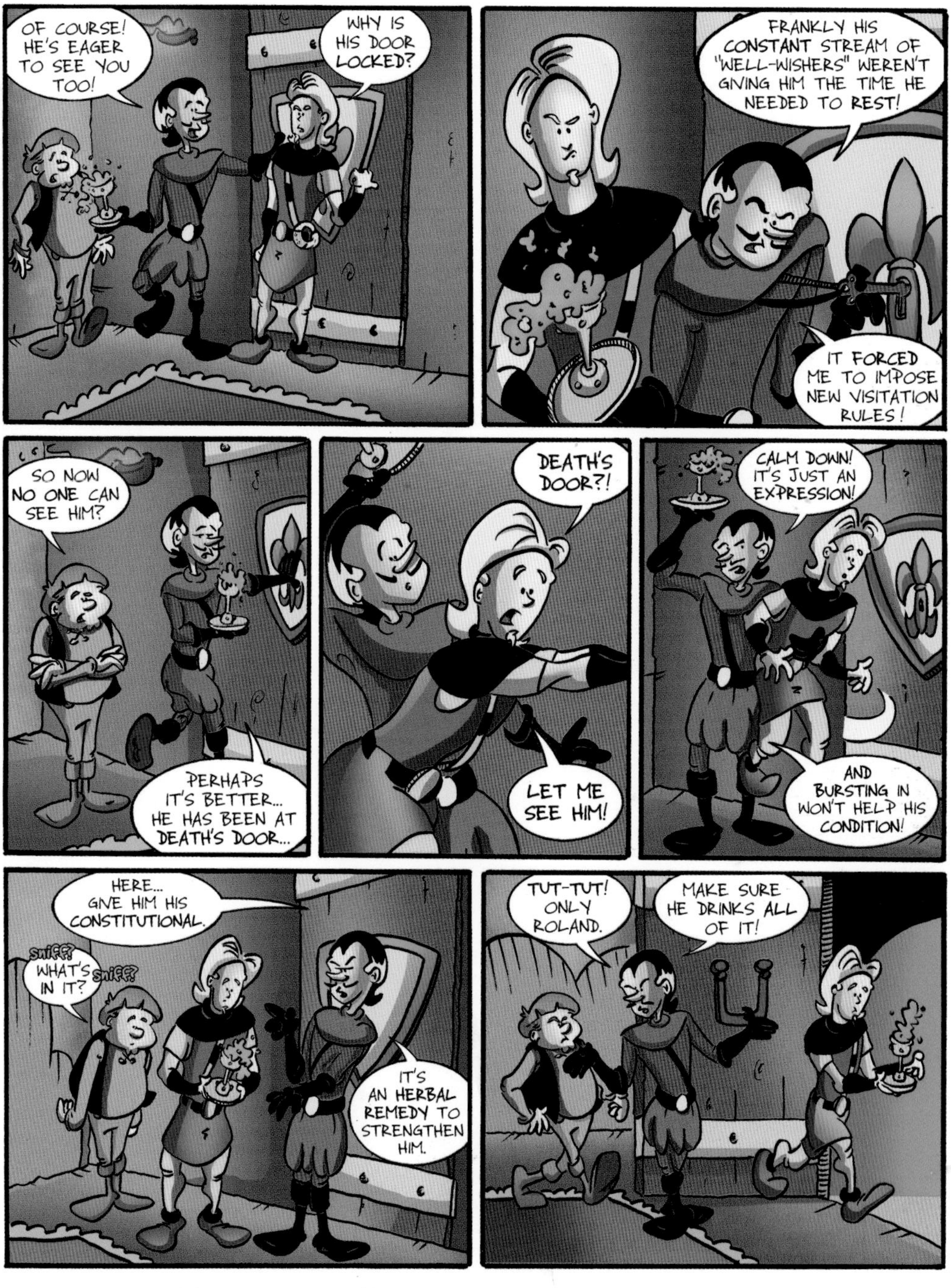
OF COURSE! HE'S EAGER TO SEE YOU TOO!
WHY IS HIS DOOR LOCKED?
FRANKLY HIS CONSTANT STREAM OF "WELL-WISHERS" WEREN'T GIVING HIM THE TIME HE NEEDED TO REST!
IT FORCED ME TO IMPOSE NEW VISITATION RULES!
SO NOW NO ONE CAN SEE HIM?
PERHAPS IT'S BETTER... HE HAS BEEN AT DEATH'S DOOR...
DEATH'S DOOR?!
LET ME SEE HIM!
CALM DOWN! IT'S JUST AN EXPRESSION!
AND BURSTING IN WON'T HELP HIS CONDITION!
HERE... GIVE HIM HIS CONSTITUTIONAL.
SNIFF?
WHAT'S IN IT?
SNIFF?
IT'S AN HERBAL REMEDY TO STRENGTHEN HIM.
TUT-TUT! ONLY ROLAND.
MAKE SURE HE DRINKS ALL OF IT!

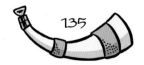

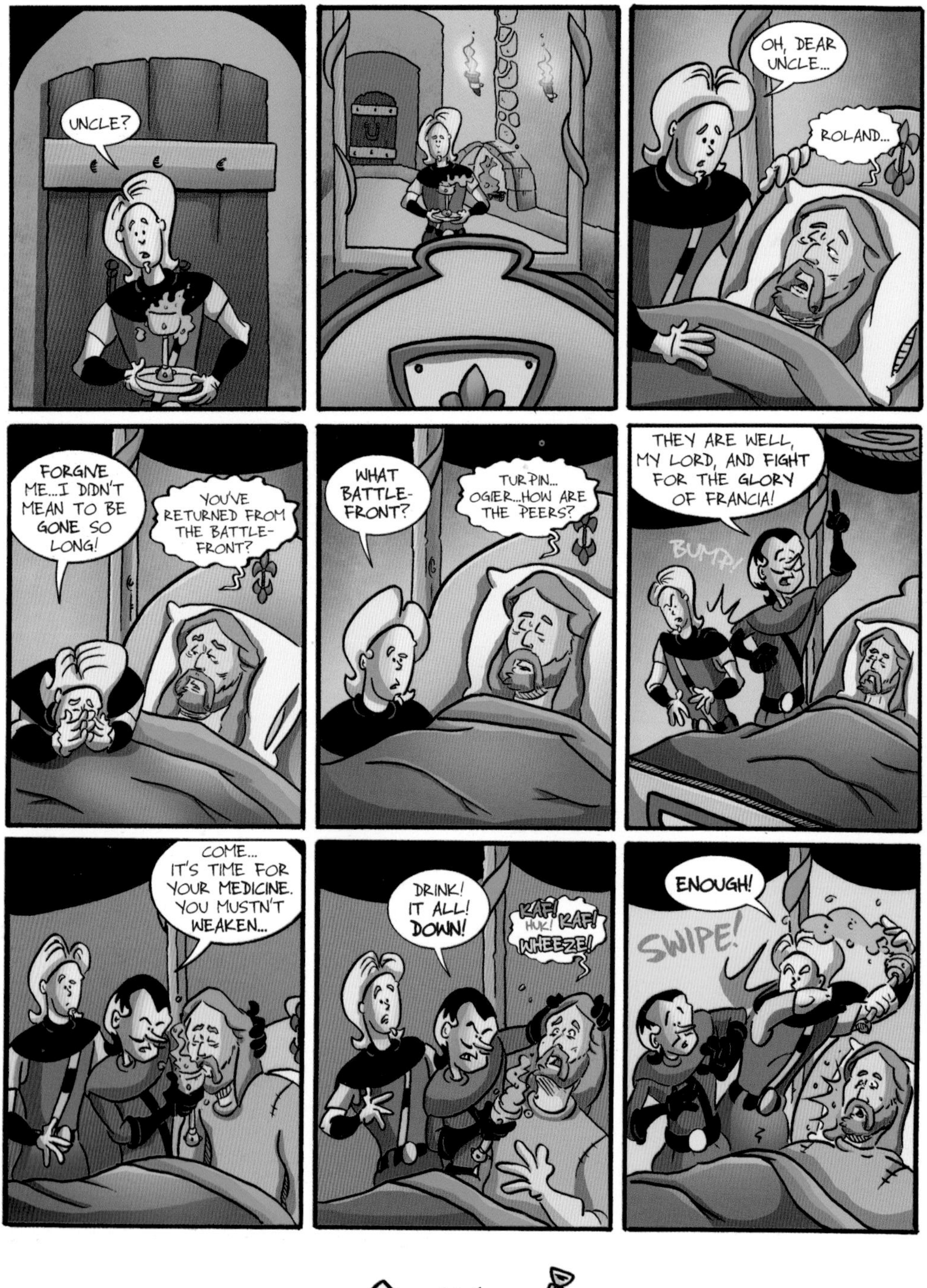
UNCLE?
OH, DEAR UNCLE...
ROLAND...
FORGIVE ME...I DIDN'T MEAN TO BE GONE SO LONG!
YOU'VE RETURNED FROM THE BATTLE-FRONT?
WHAT BATTLE-FRONT?
TURPIN... OGIER...HOW ARE THE PEERS?
THEY ARE WELL, MY LORD, AND FIGHT FOR THE GLORY OF FRANCIA!
BUMP!
COME... IT'S TIME FOR YOUR MEDICINE. YOU MUSTN'T WEAKEN...
DRINK! IT ALL! DOWN!
KAF! HUK! KAF! WHEEZE!
ENOUGH!
SWIPE!

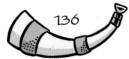

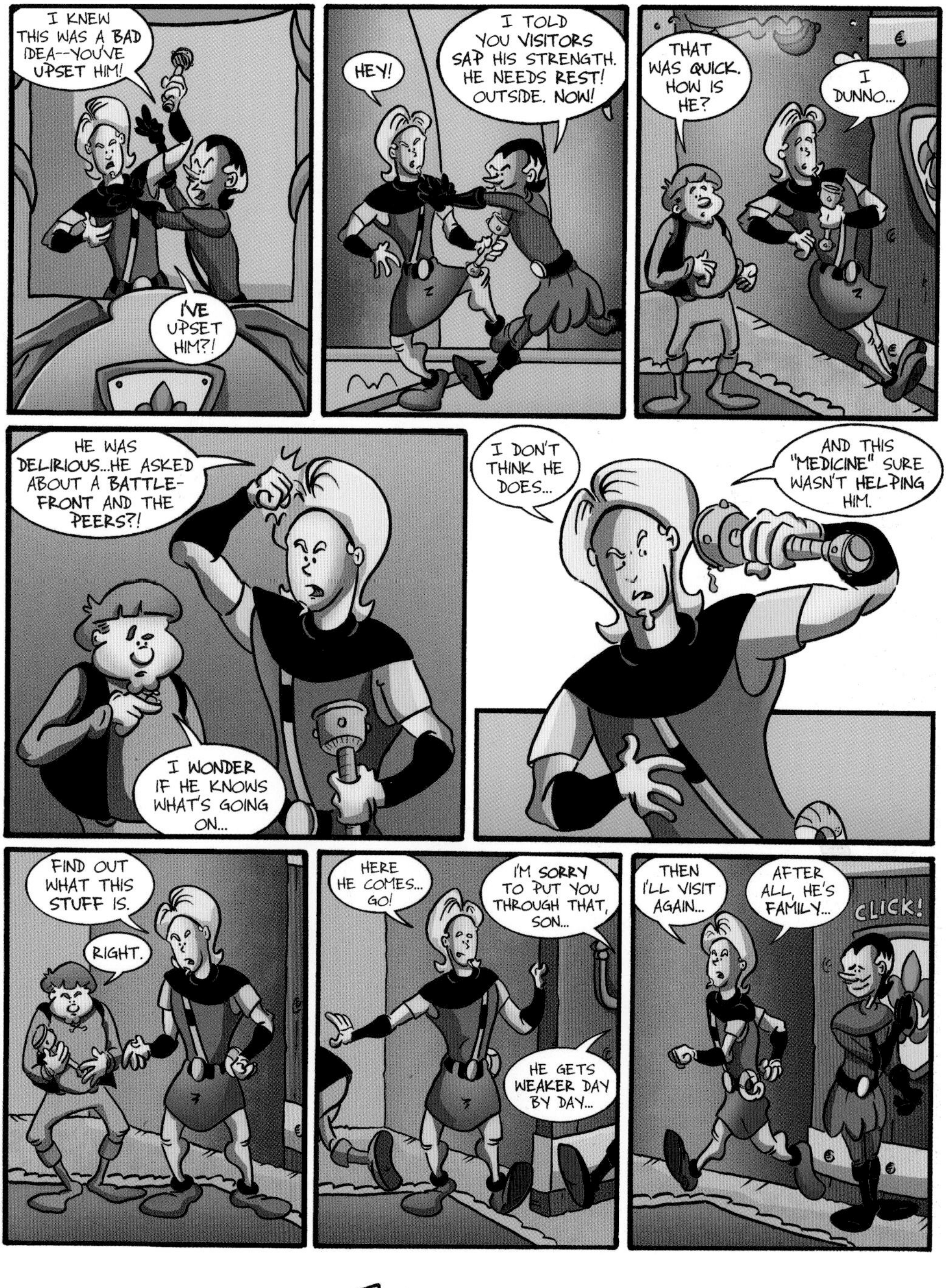
I KNEW THIS WAS A BAD IDEA--YOU'VE UPSET HIM!
I'VE UPSET HIM?!
HEY!
I TOLD YOU VISITORS SAP HIS STRENGTH. HE NEEDS REST! OUTSIDE. NOW!
THAT WAS QUICK. HOW IS HE?
I DUNNO...
HE WAS DELIRIOUS...HE ASKED ABOUT A BATTLE-FRONT AND THE PEERS?!
I WONDER IF HE KNOWS WHAT'S GOING ON...
I DON'T THINK HE DOES...
AND THIS "MEDICINE" SURE WASN'T HELPING HIM.
FIND OUT WHAT THIS STUFF IS.
RIGHT.
HERE HE COMES... GO!
I'M SORRY TO PUT YOU THROUGH THAT, SON...
HE GETS WEAKER DAY BY DAY...
THEN I'LL VISIT AGAIN...
AFTER ALL, HE'S FAMILY...
CLICK!

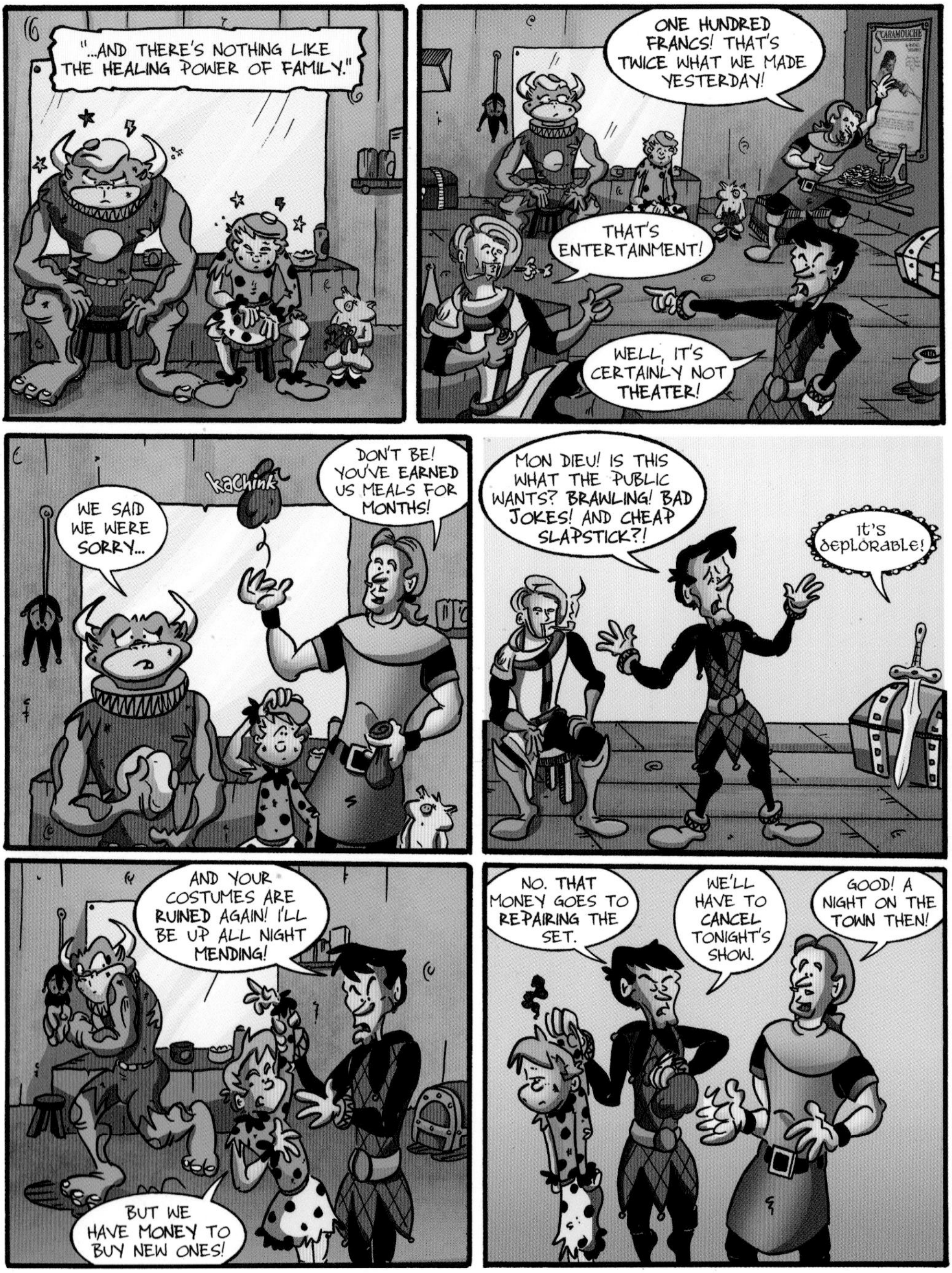
"...AND THERE'S NOTHING LIKE THE HEALING POWER OF FAMILY."
ONE HUNDRED FRANCS! THAT'S TWICE WHAT WE MADE YESTERDAY!
THAT'S ENTERTAINMENT!
WELL, IT'S CERTAINLY NOT THEATER!
WE SAID WE WERE SORRY...
KaChink
DON'T BE! YOU'VE EARNED US MEALS FOR MONTHS!
MON DIEU! IS THIS WHAT THE PUBLIC WANTS? BRAWLING! BAD JOKES! AND CHEAP SLAPSTICK?!
It's deplorable!
AND YOUR COSTUMES ARE RUINED AGAIN! I'LL BE UP ALL NIGHT MENDING!
BUT WE HAVE MONEY TO BUY NEW ONES!
NO. THAT MONEY GOES TO REPAIRING THE SET.
WE'LL HAVE TO CANCEL TONIGHT'S SHOW.
GOOD! A NIGHT ON THE TOWN THEN!

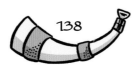

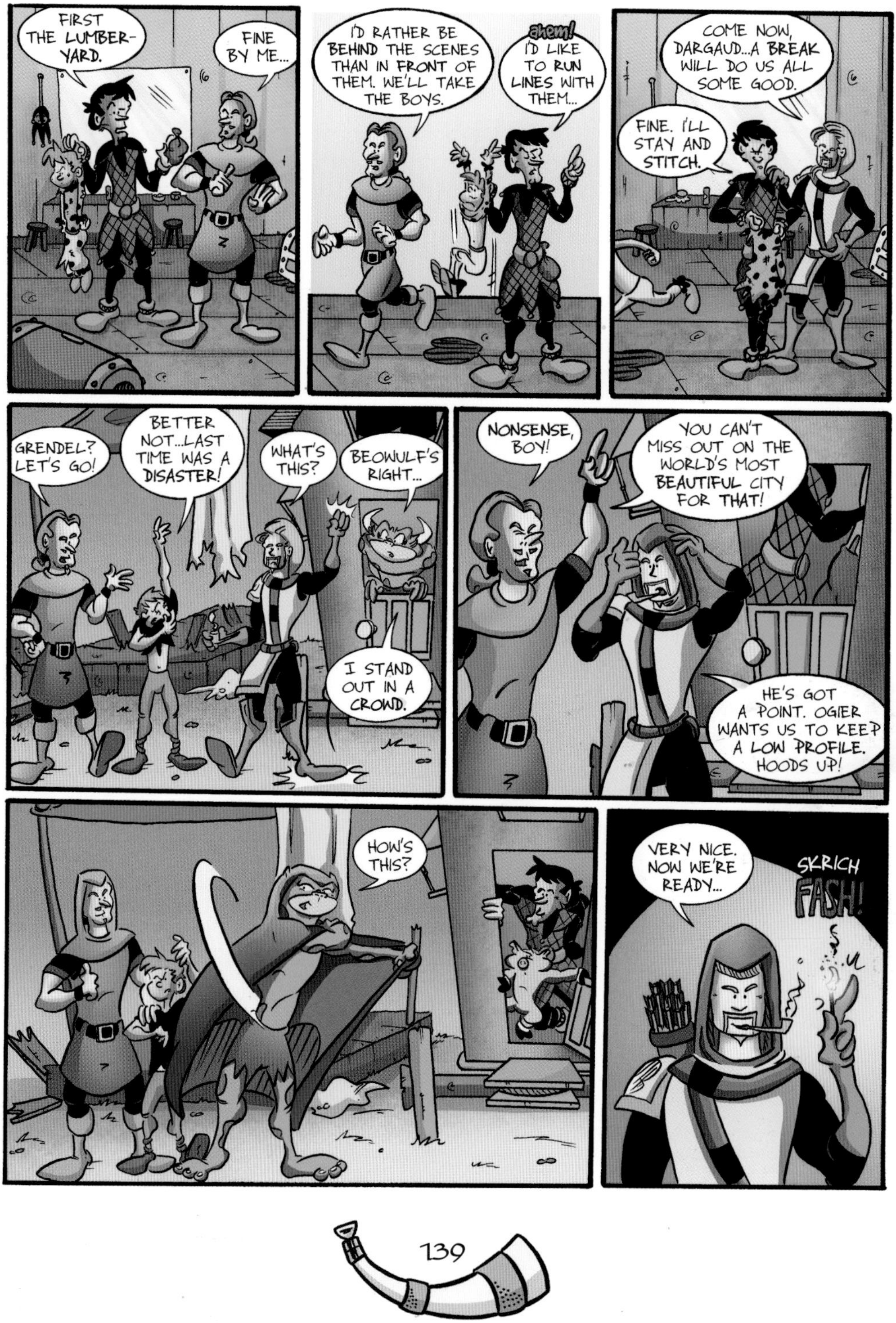
FIRST THE LUMBER-YARD.
FINE BY ME...
I'D RATHER BE BEHIND THE SCENES THAN IN FRONT OF THEM. WE'LL TAKE THE BOYS.
ahem! I'D LIKE TO RUN LINES WITH THEM...
COME NOW, DARGAUD...A BREAK WILL DO US ALL SOME GOOD.
FINE. I'LL STAY AND STITCH.
GRENDEL? LET'S GO!
BETTER NOT...LAST TIME WAS A DISASTER!
WHAT'S THIS?
BEOWULF'S RIGHT...
I STAND OUT IN A CROWD.
NONSENSE, BOY!
YOU CAN'T MISS OUT ON THE WORLD'S MOST BEAUTIFUL CITY FOR THAT!
HE'S GOT A POINT. OGIER WANTS US TO KEEP A LOW PROFILE. HOODS UP!
HOW'S THIS?
VERY NICE. NOW WE'RE READY...
SKRICH
FASH!

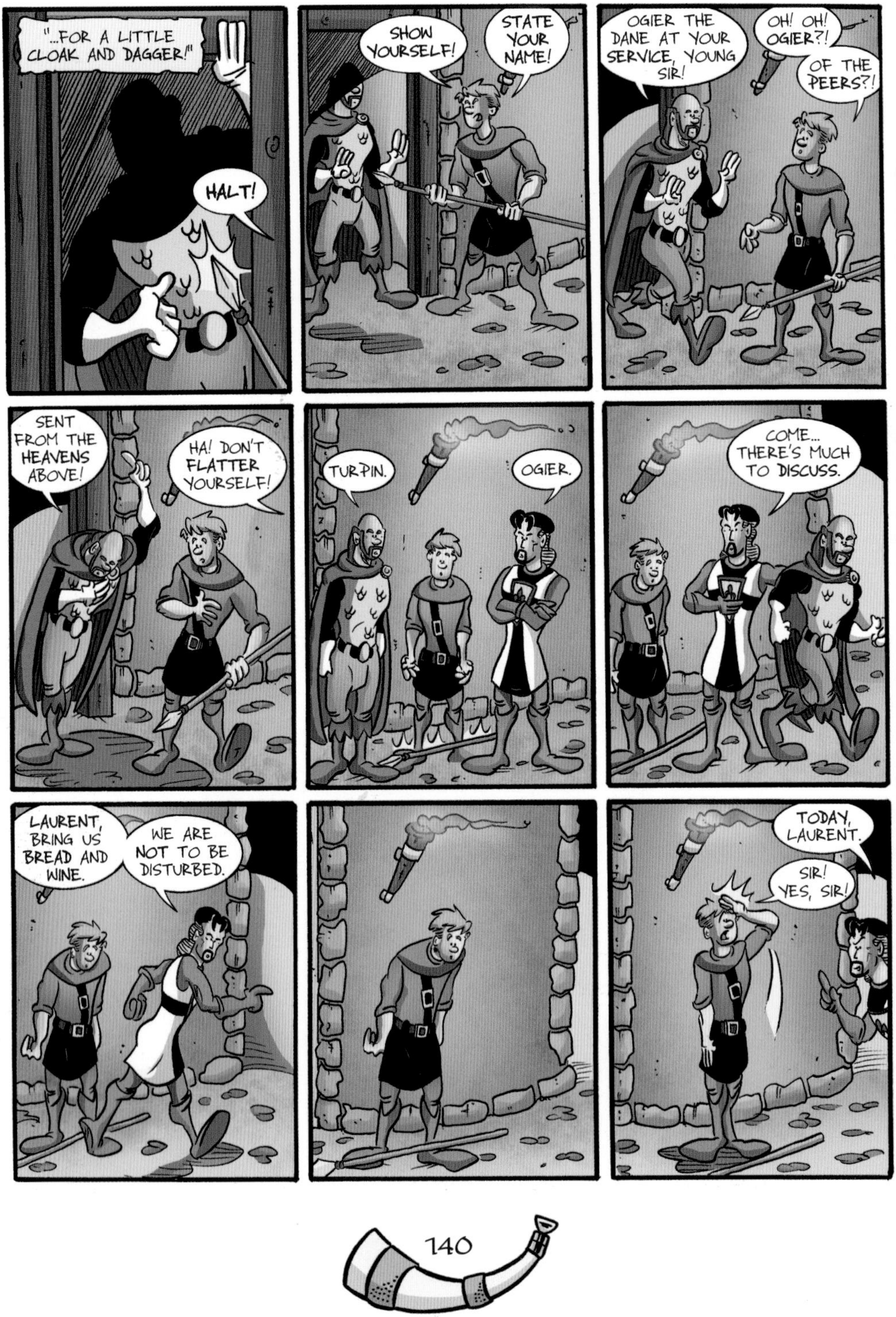
"...FOR A LITTLE CLOAK AND DAGGER!"
HALT!
SHOW YOURSELF!
STATE YOUR NAME!
OGIER THE DANE AT YOUR SERVICE, YOUNG SIR!
OH! OH! OGIER?!
OF THE PEERS?!
SENT FROM THE HEAVENS ABOVE!
HA! DON'T FLATTER YOURSELF!
TURPIN.
OGIER.
COME... THERE'S MUCH TO DISCUSS.
LAURENT, BRING US BREAD AND WINE.
WE ARE NOT TO BE DISTURBED.
TODAY, LAURENT.
SIR! YES, SIR!

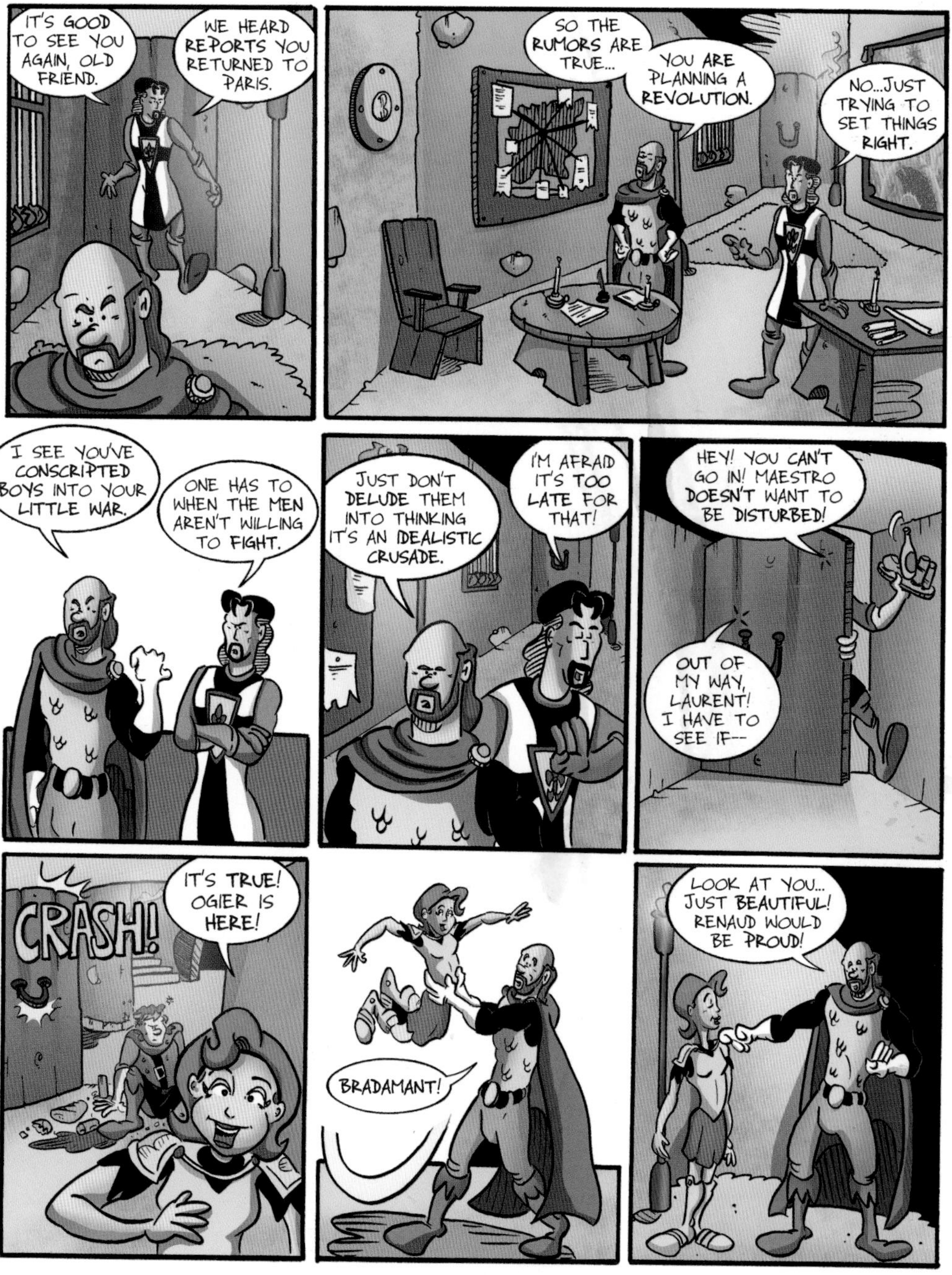
IT'S GOOD TO SEE YOU AGAIN, OLD FRIEND.
WE HEARD REPORTS YOU RETURNED TO PARIS.
SO THE RUMORS ARE TRUE...
YOU ARE PLANNING A REVOLUTION.
NO...JUST TRYING TO SET THINGS RIGHT.
I SEE YOU'VE CONSCRIPTED BOYS INTO YOUR LITTLE WAR.
ONE HAS TO WHEN THE MEN AREN'T WILLING TO FIGHT.
JUST DON'T DELUDE THEM INTO THINKING IT'S AN IDEALISTIC CRUSADE.
I'M AFRAID IT'S TOO LATE FOR THAT!
HEY! YOU CAN'T GO IN! MAESTRO DOESN'T WANT TO BE DISTURBED!
OUT OF MY WAY, LAURENT! I HAVE TO SEE IF--
CRASH!
IT'S TRUE! OGIER IS HERE!
BRADAMANT!
LOOK AT YOU... JUST BEAUTIFUL! RENAUD WOULD BE PROUD!

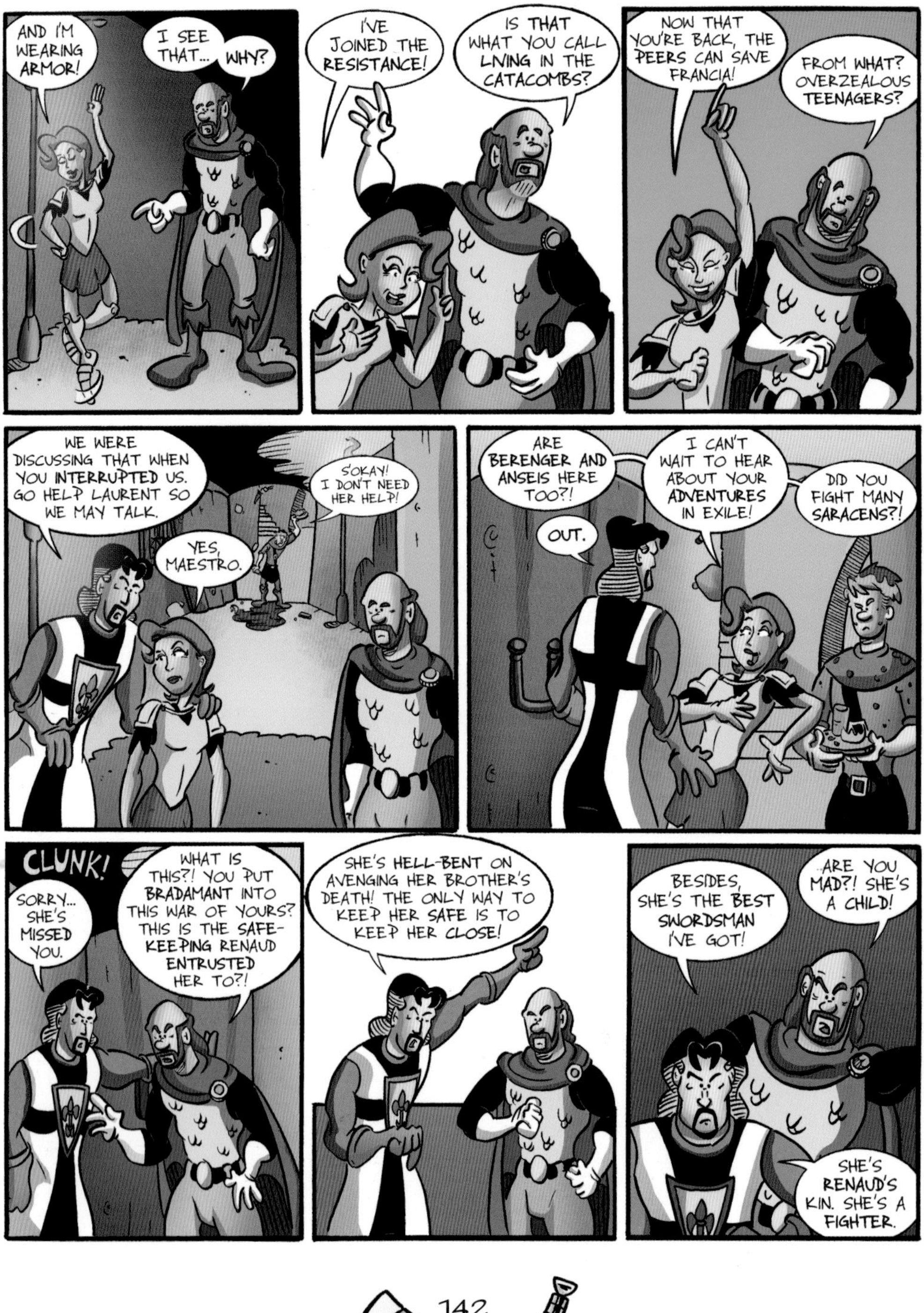
AND I'M WEARING ARMOR!
I SEE THAT...
WHY?
I'VE JOINED THE RESISTANCE!
IS THAT WHAT YOU CALL LIVING IN THE CATACOMBS?
NOW THAT YOU'RE BACK, THE PEERS CAN SAVE FRANCIA!
FROM WHAT? OVERZEALOUS TEENAGERS?
WE WERE DISCUSSING THAT WHEN YOU INTERRUPTED US. GO HELP LAURENT SO WE MAY TALK.
S'OKAY! I DON'T NEED HER HELP!
YES, MAESTRO.
ARE BERENGER AND ANSEIS HERE TOO?!
I CAN'T WAIT TO HEAR ABOUT YOUR ADVENTURES IN EXILE!
DID YOU FIGHT MANY SARACENS?!
OUT.
CLUNK!
SORRY... SHE'S MISSED YOU.
WHAT IS THIS?! YOU PUT BRADAMANT INTO THIS WAR OF YOURS? THIS IS THE SAFE-KEEPING RENAUD ENTRUSTED HER TO?!
SHE'S HELL-BENT ON AVENGING HER BROTHER'S DEATH! THE ONLY WAY TO KEEP HER SAFE IS TO KEEP HER CLOSE!
BESIDES, SHE'S THE BEST SWORDSMAN I'VE GOT!
ARE YOU MAD?! SHE'S A CHILD!
SHE'S RENAUD'S KIN. SHE'S A FIGHTER.

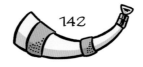

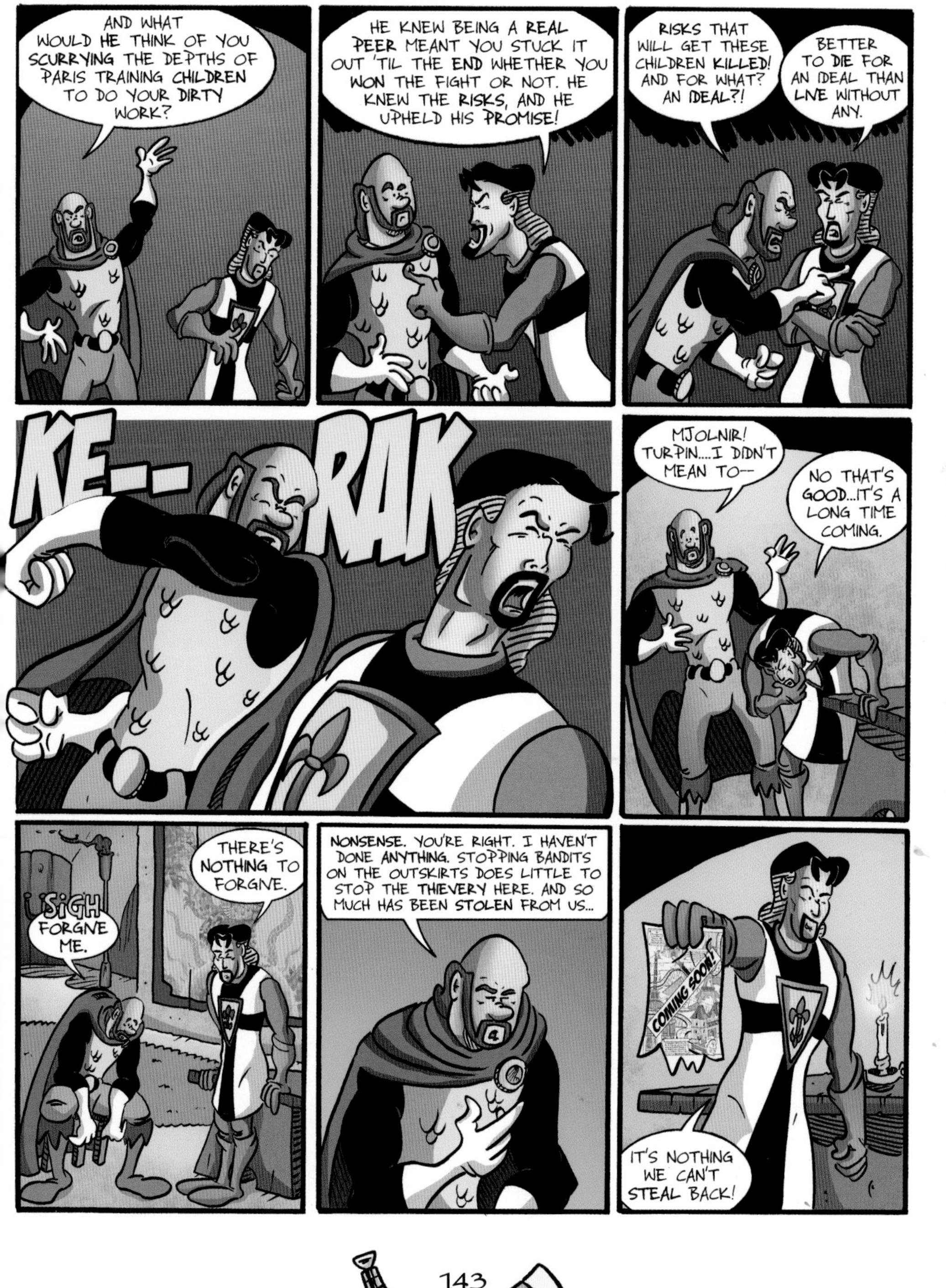
AND WHAT WOULD HE THINK OF YOU SCURRYING THE DEPTHS OF PARIS TRAINING CHILDREN TO DO YOUR DIRTY WORK?
HE KNEW BEING A REAL PEER MEANT YOU STUCK IT OUT 'TIL THE END WHETHER YOU WON THE FIGHT OR NOT. HE KNEW THE RISKS, AND HE UPHELD HIS PROMISE!
RISKS THAT WILL GET THESE CHILDREN KILLED! AND FOR WHAT? AN IDEAL?!
BETTER TO DIE FOR AN IDEAL THAN LIVE WITHOUT ANY.
KE...RAK
MJOLNIR! TURPIN....I DIDN'T MEAN TO--
NO THAT'S GOOD...IT'S A LONG TIME COMING.
SIGH
FORGIVE ME.
THERE'S NOTHING TO FORGIVE.
NONSENSE. YOU'RE RIGHT. I HAVEN'T DONE ANYTHING. STOPPING BANDITS ON THE OUTSKIRTS DOES LITTLE TO STOP THE THIEVERY HERE. AND SO MUCH HAS BEEN STOLEN FROM US...
COMING SOON!
IT'S NOTHING WE CAN'T STEAL BACK!

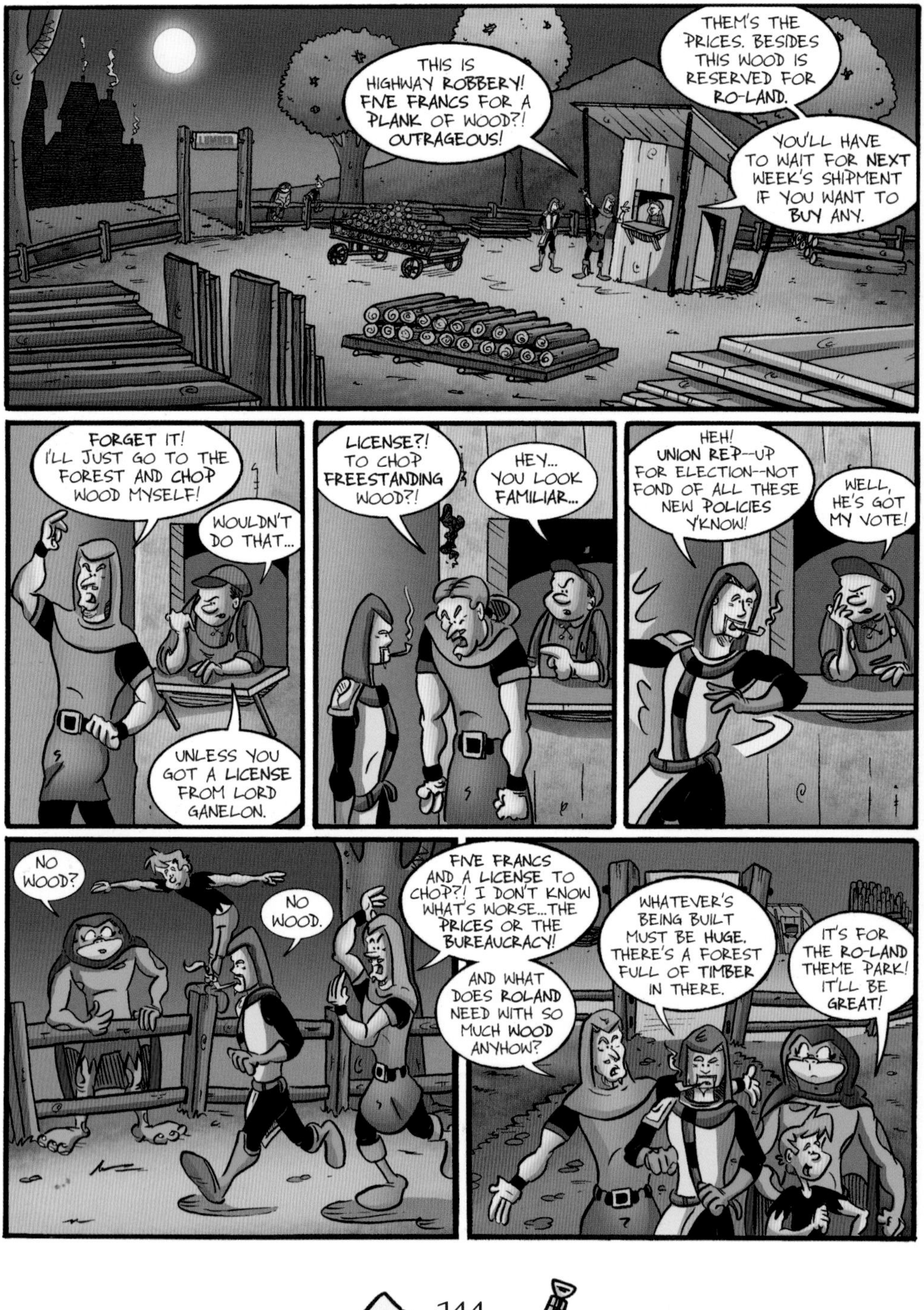
LUMBER
THIS IS HIGHWAY ROBBERY! FIVE FRANCS FOR A PLANK OF WOOD?! OUTRAGEOUS!
THEM'S THE PRICES. BESIDES THIS WOOD IS RESERVED FOR RO-LAND.
YOU'LL HAVE TO WAIT FOR NEXT WEEK'S SHIPMENT IF YOU WANT TO BUY ANY.
FORGET IT! I'LL JUST GO TO THE FOREST AND CHOP WOOD MYSELF!
WOULDN'T DO THAT...
UNLESS YOU GOT A LICENSE FROM LORD GANELON.
LICENSE?! TO CHOP FREESTANDING WOOD?!
HEY... YOU LOOK FAMILIAR...
HEH! UNION REP--UP FOR ELECTION--NOT FOND OF ALL THESE NEW POLICIES Y'KNOW!
WELL, HE'S GOT MY VOTE!
NO WOOD?
NO WOOD.
FIVE FRANCS AND A LICENSE TO CHOP?! I DON'T KNOW WHAT'S WORSE...THE PRICES OR THE BUREAUCRACY!
AND WHAT DOES ROLAND NEED WITH SO MUCH WOOD ANYHOW?
WHATEVER'S BEING BUILT MUST BE HUGE. THERE'S A FOREST FULL OF TIMBER IN THERE.
IT'S FOR THE RO-LAND THEME PARK! IT'LL BE GREAT!

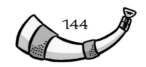

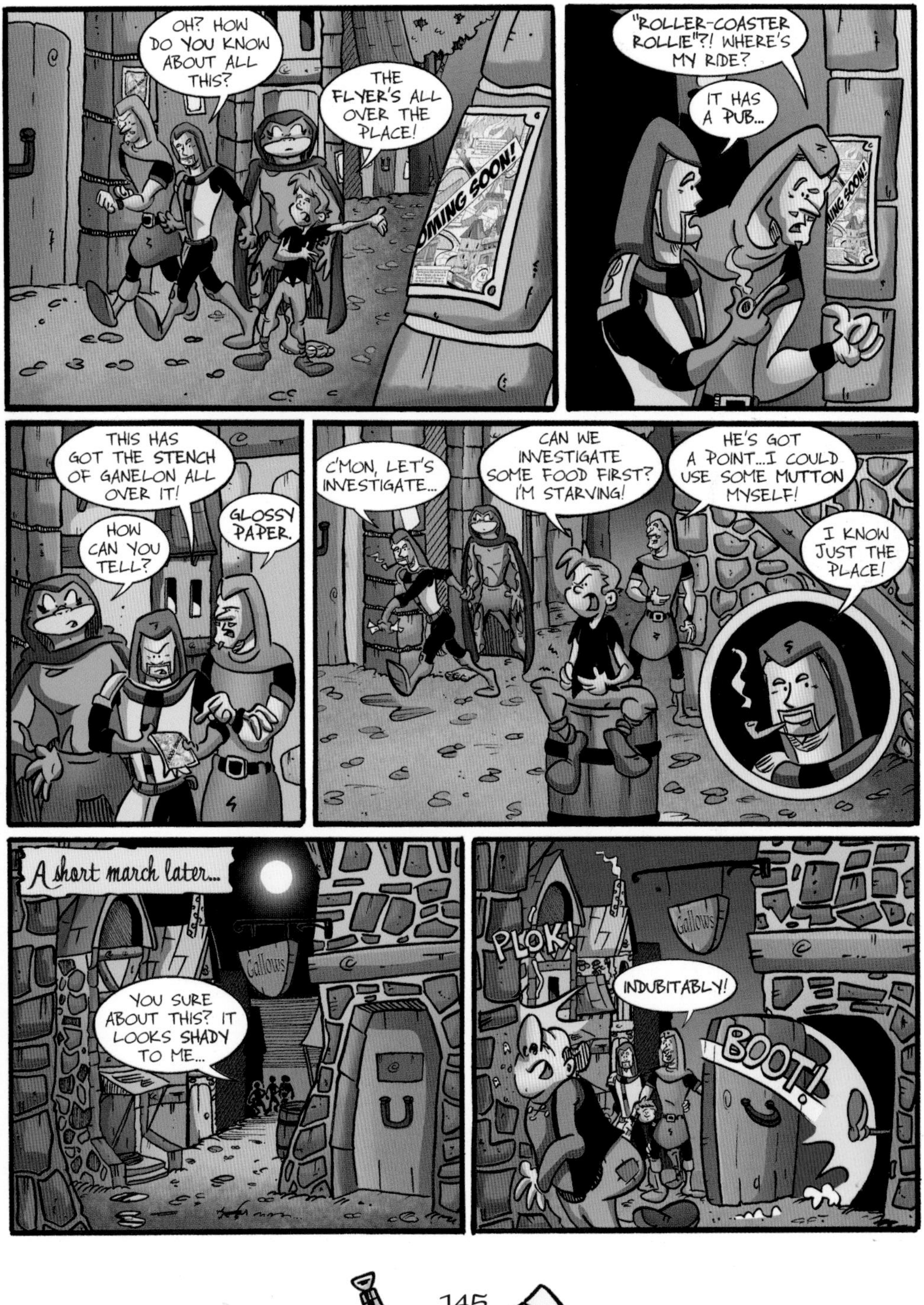
OH? HOW DO YOU KNOW ABOUT ALL THIS?
THE FLYER'S ALL OVER THE PLACE!
COMING SOON!
"ROLLER-COASTER ROLLIE"?! WHERE'S MY RIDE?
IT HAS A PUB...
THIS HAS GOT THE STENCH OF GANELON ALL OVER IT!
HOW CAN YOU TELL?
GLOSSY PAPER.
C'MON, LET'S INVESTIGATE...
CAN WE INVESTIGATE SOME FOOD FIRST? I'M STARVING!
HE'S GOT A POINT...I COULD USE SOME MUTTON MYSELF!
I KNOW JUST THE PLACE!
A short march later...
Gallows
YOU SURE ABOUT THIS? IT LOOKS SHADY TO ME...
Gallows
PLOK!
INDUBITABLY!
BOOT!

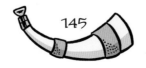

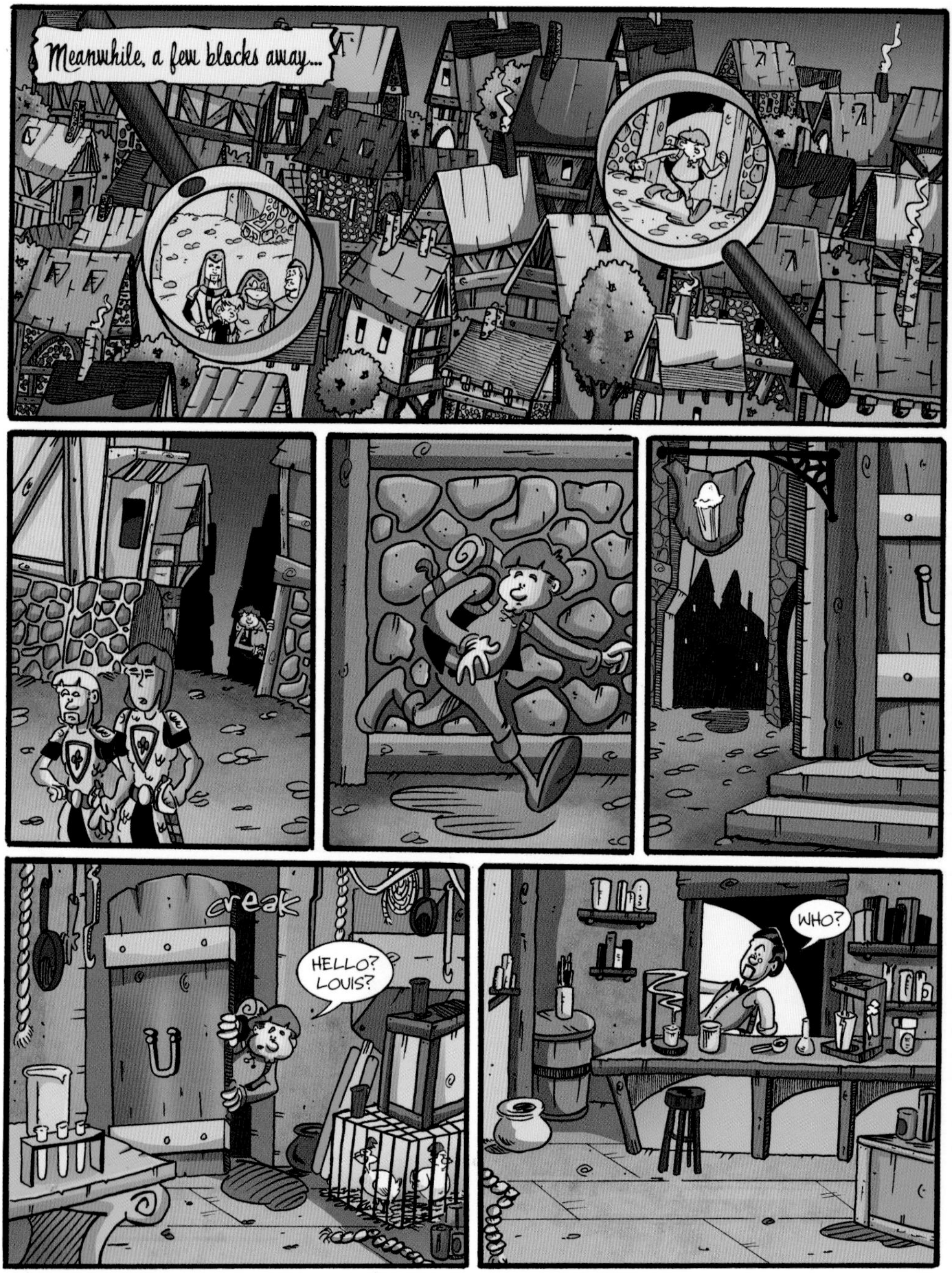
Meanwhile, a few blocks away...
creak
HELLO? LOUIS?
WHO?

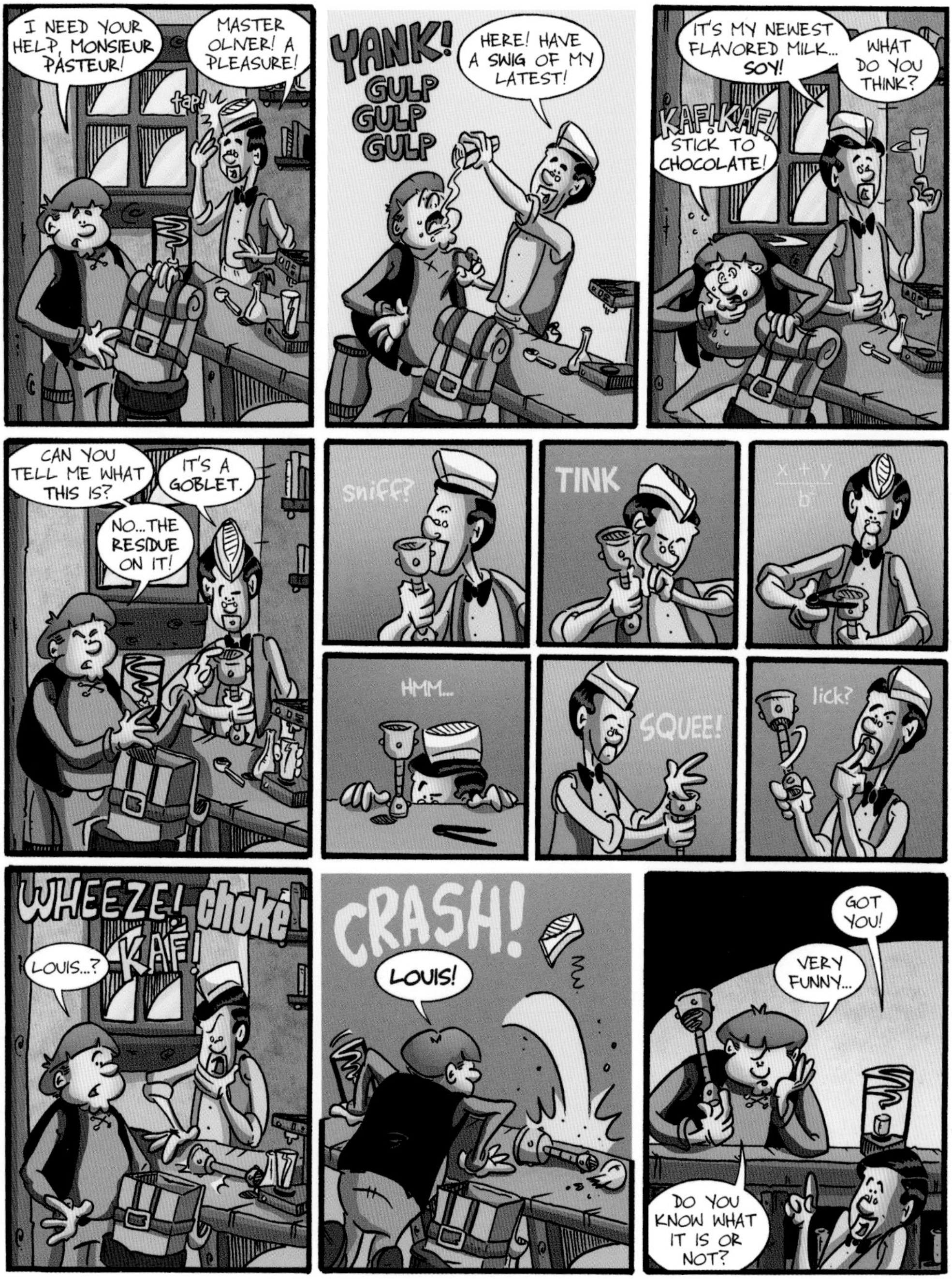
I NEED YOUR HELP, MONSIEUR PASTEUR!
MASTER OLIVER! A PLEASURE!
tap!
YANK!
GULP GULP GULP
HERE! HAVE A SWIG OF MY LATEST!
IT'S MY NEWEST FLAVORED MILK... SOY!
WHAT DO YOU THINK?
KAF! KAF!
STICK TO CHOCOLATE!
CAN YOU TELL ME WHAT THIS IS?
IT'S A GOBLET.
NO...THE RESIDUE ON IT!
sniff?
TINK
HMM...
SQUEE!
lick?
WHEEZE! choke
KAF!
LOUIS...?
CRASH!
LOUIS!
GOT YOU!
VERY FUNNY...
DO YOU KNOW WHAT IT IS OR NOT?

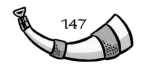

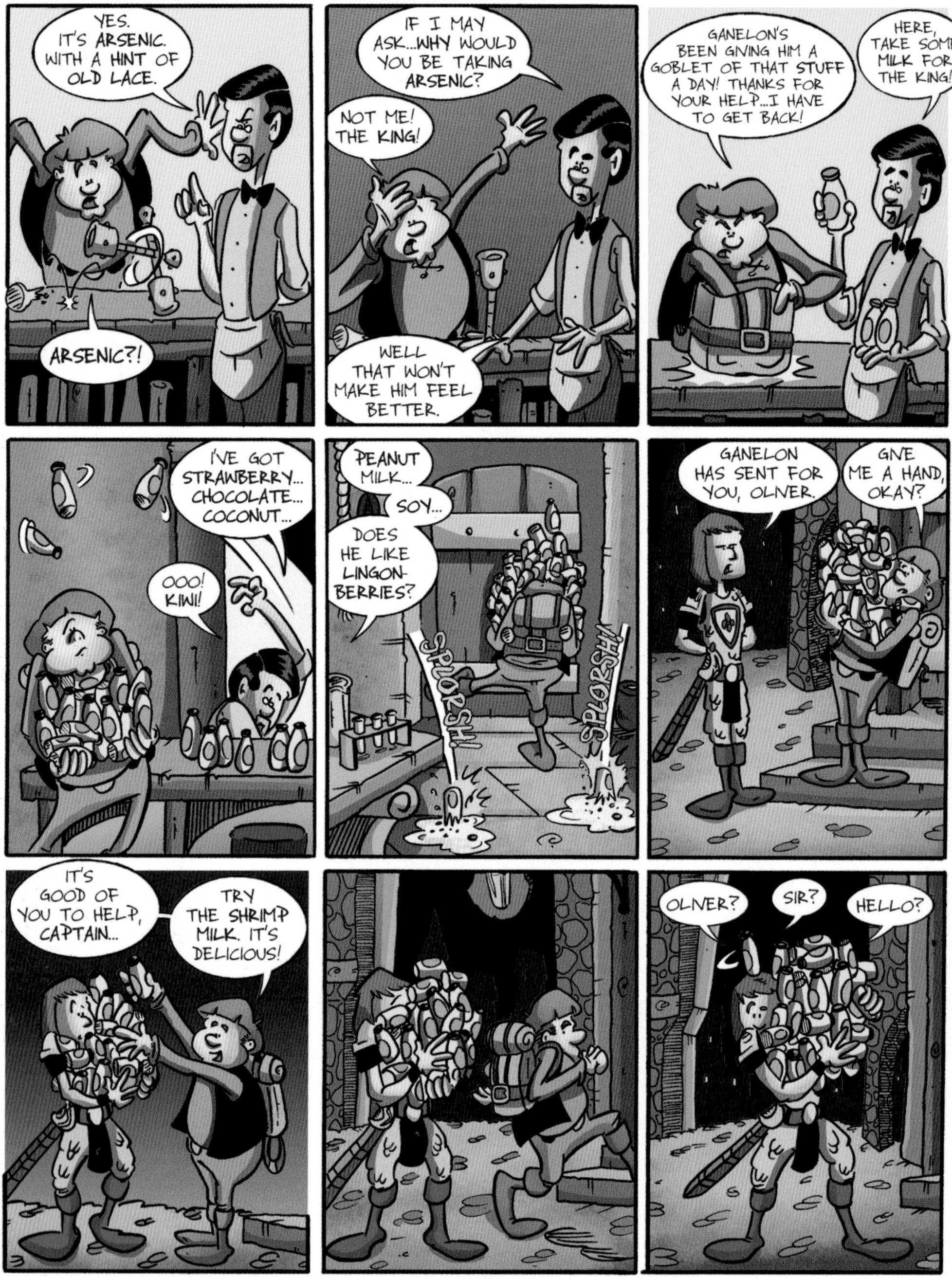
YES. IT'S ARSENIC. WITH A HINT OF OLD LACE.
ARSENIC?!
IF I MAY ASK...WHY WOULD YOU BE TAKING ARSENIC?
NOT ME! THE KING!
WELL THAT WON'T MAKE HIM FEEL BETTER.
GANELON'S BEEN GIVING HIM A GOBLET OF THAT STUFF A DAY! THANKS FOR YOUR HELP...I HAVE TO GET BACK!
HERE, TAKE SOME MILK FOR THE KING!
I'VE GOT STRAWBERRY... CHOCOLATE... COCONUT...
OOO! KIWI!
PEANUT MILK...
SOY...
DOES HE LIKE LINGON-BERRIES?
SPLORSH!
SPLORSH!
GANELON HAS SENT FOR YOU, OLIVER.
GIVE ME A HAND, OKAY?
IT'S GOOD OF YOU TO HELP, CAPTAIN...
TRY THE SHRIMP MILK. IT'S DELICIOUS!
OLIVER?
SIR?
HELLO?

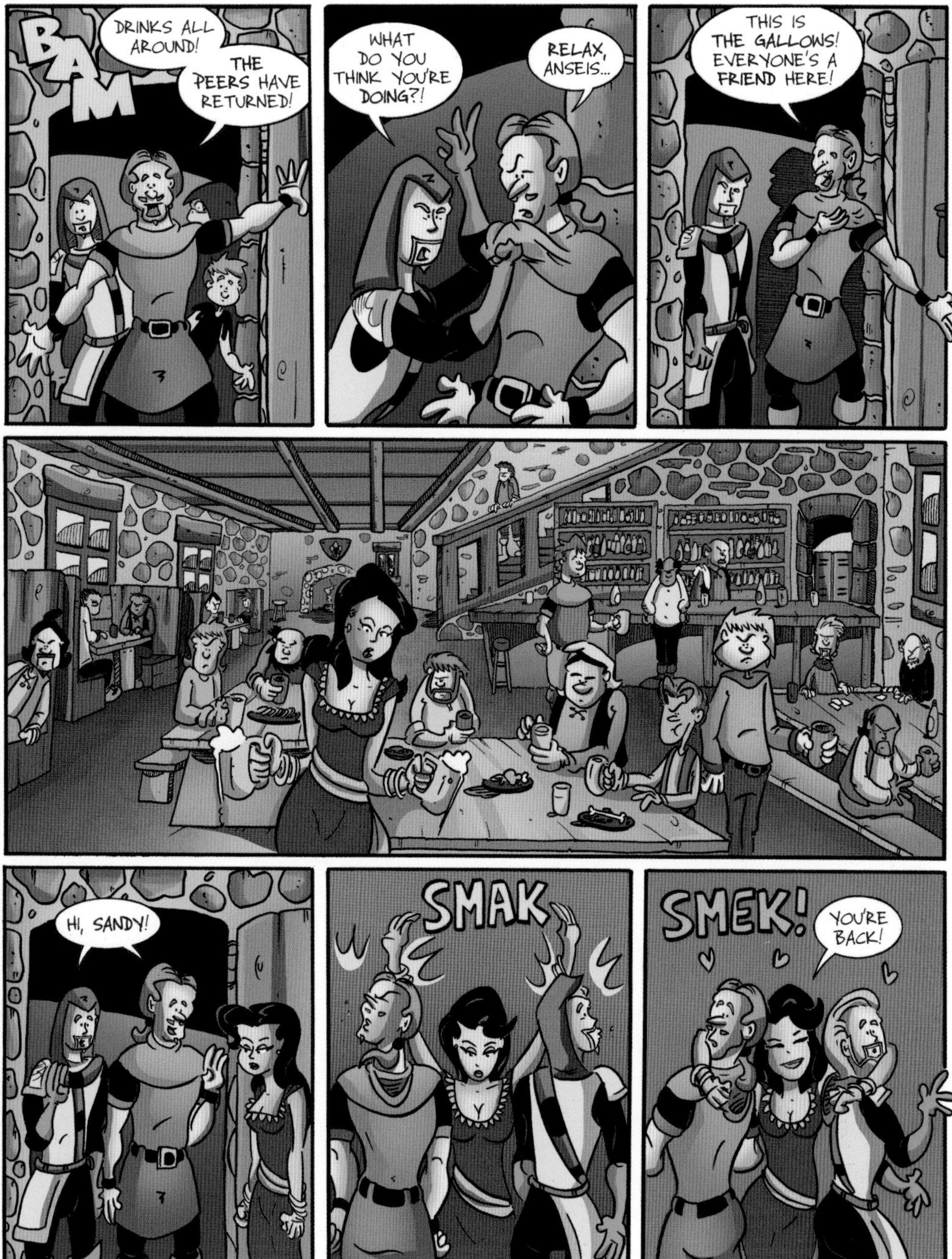
BAM
DRINKS ALL AROUND!
THE PEERS HAVE RETURNED!
WHAT DO YOU THINK YOU'RE DOING?!
RELAX, ANSEIS...
THIS IS THE GALLOWS! EVERYONE'S A FRIEND HERE!
HI, SANDY!
SMAK
SMEK!
YOU'RE BACK!

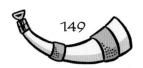

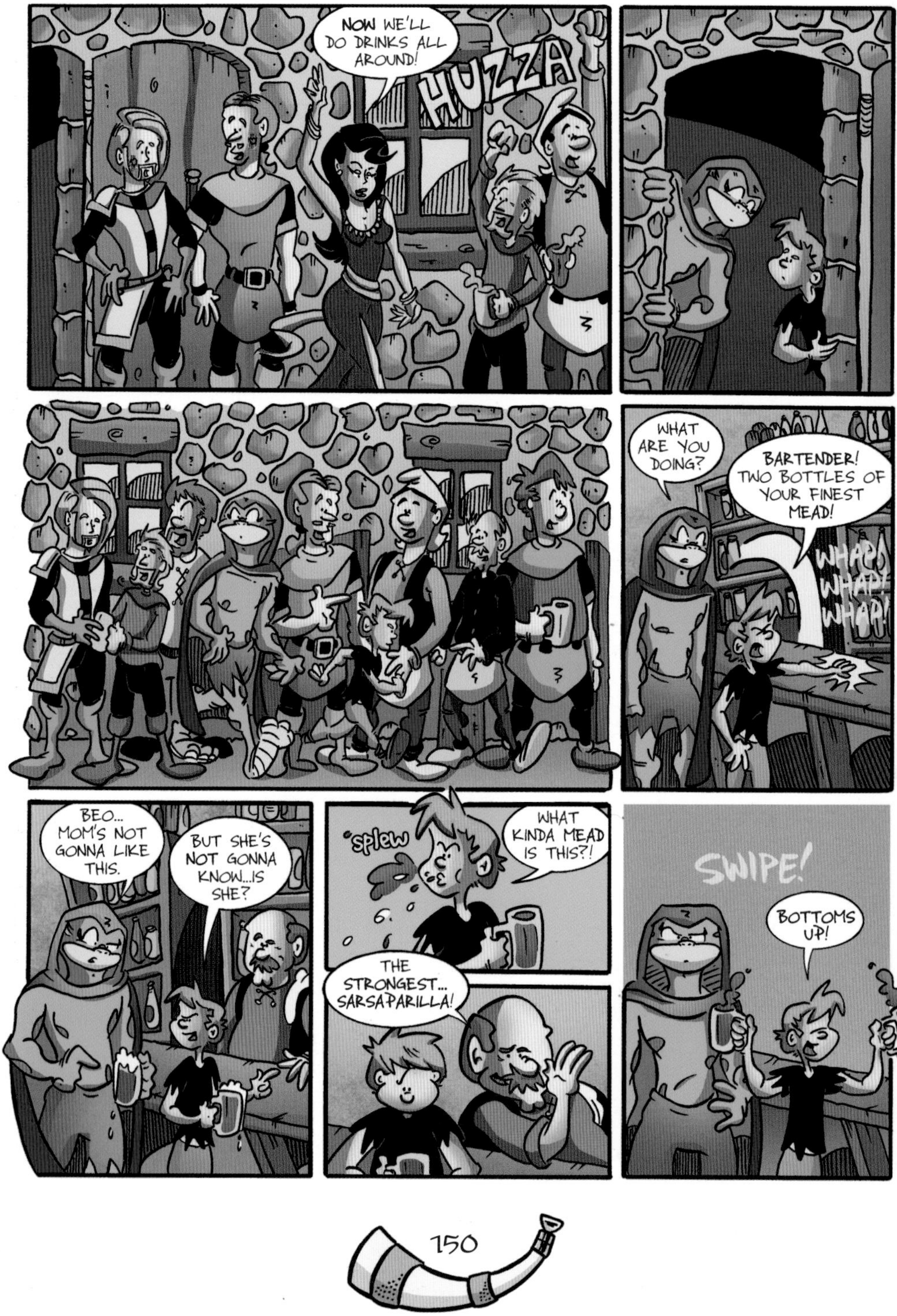
NOW WE'LL DO DRINKS ALL AROUND!
HUZZA
WHAT ARE YOU DOING?
BARTENDER! TWO BOTTLES OF YOUR FINEST MEAD!
WHAP! WHAP! WHAP!
BEO... MOM'S NOT GONNA LIKE THIS.
BUT SHE'S NOT GONNA KNOW...IS SHE?
splew
WHAT KINDA MEAD IS THIS?!
THE STRONGEST... SARSAPARILLA!
SWIPE!
BOTTOMS UP!

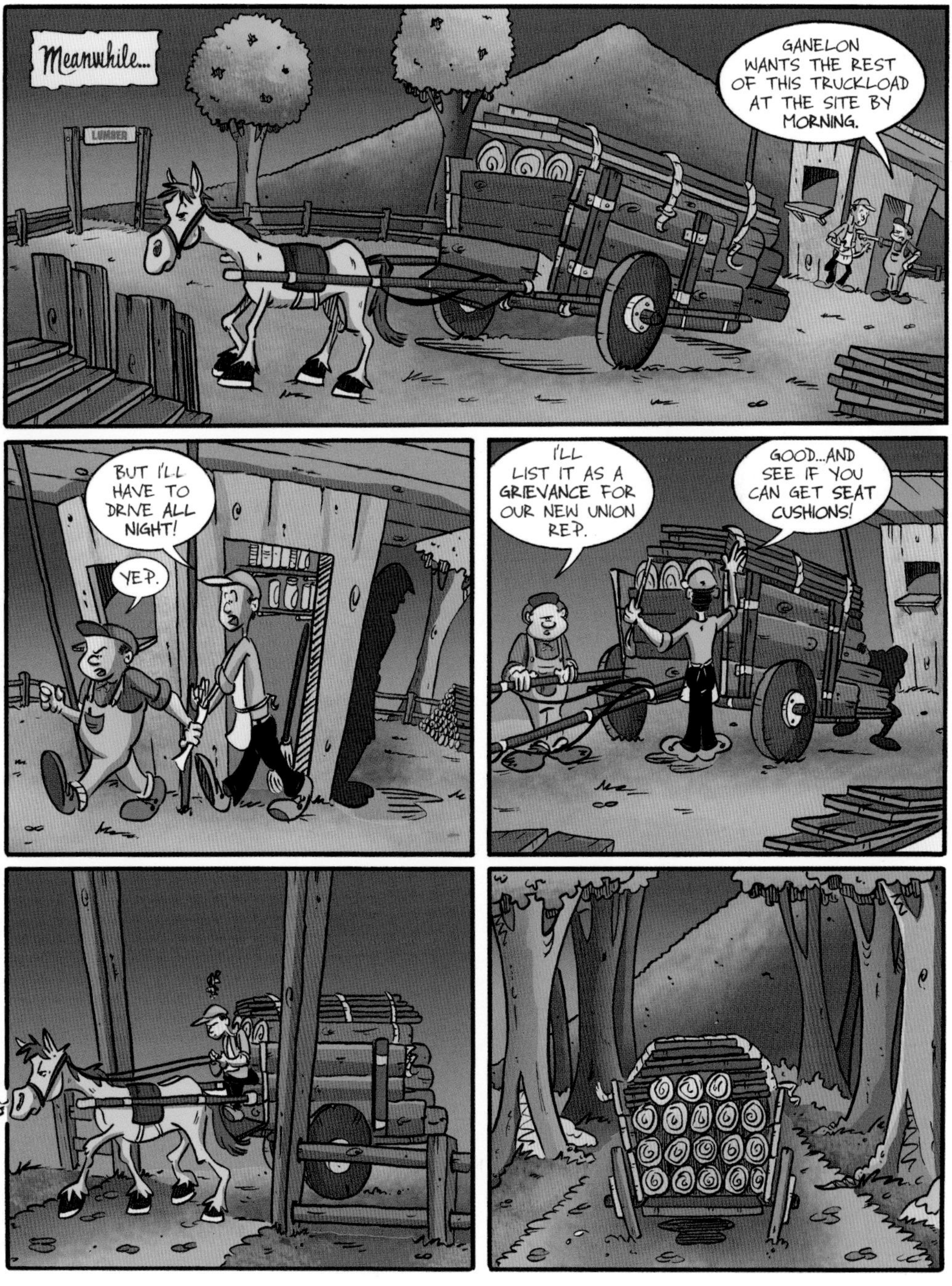
Meanwhile...
LUMBER
GANELON WANTS THE REST OF THIS TRUCKLOAD AT THE SITE BY MORNING.
BUT I'LL HAVE TO DRIVE ALL NIGHT!
YEP.
I'LL LIST IT AS A GRIEVANCE FOR OUR NEW UNION REP.
GOOD...AND SEE IF YOU CAN GET SEAT CUSHIONS!

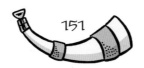

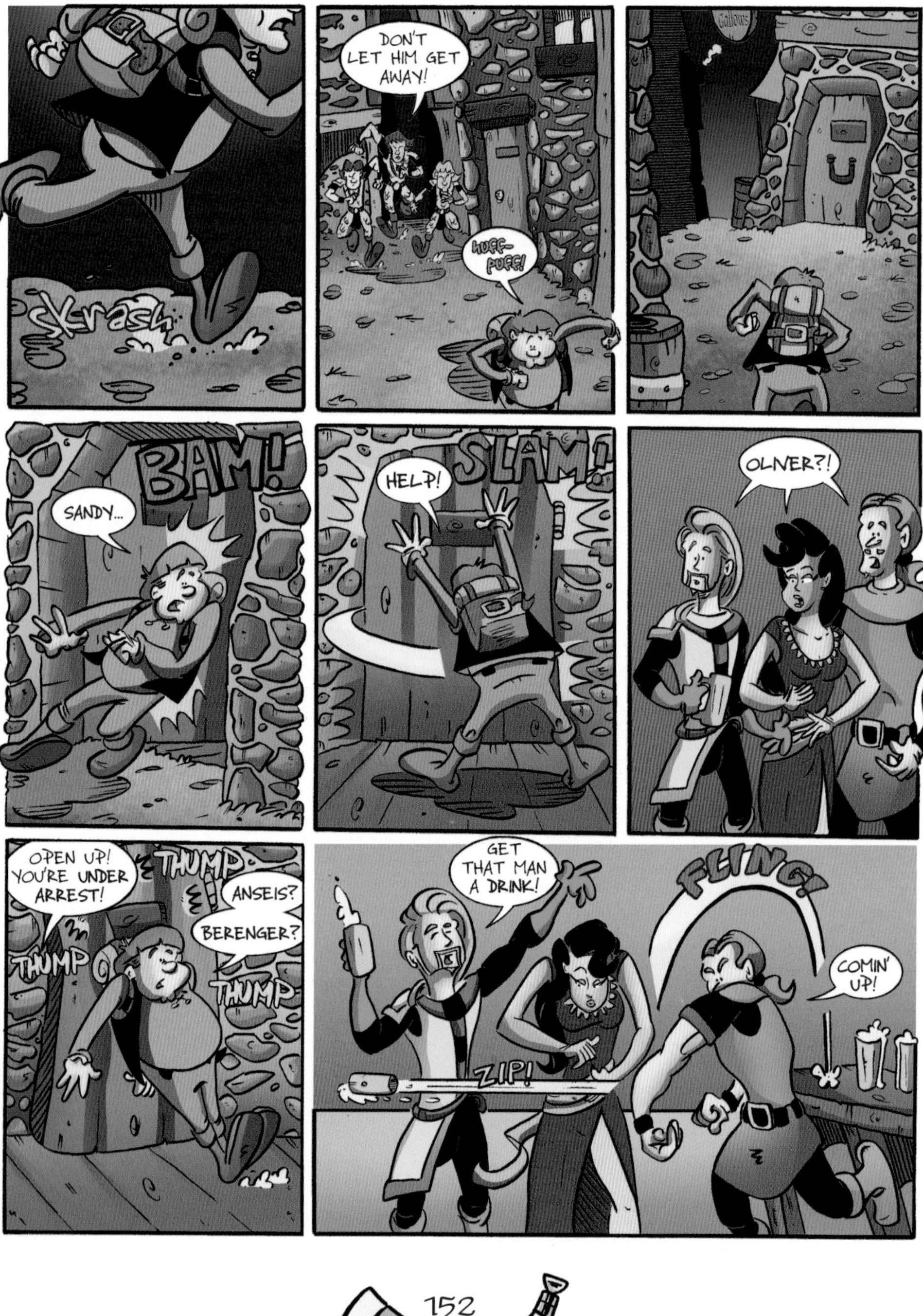
SKRASH
DON'T LET HIM GET AWAY!
HUFF-PUFF!
Gallows
BAM!
SANDY...
SLAM!
HELP!
OLIVER?!
OPEN UP! YOU'RE UNDER ARREST!
THUMP
ANSEIS?
BERENGER?
THUMP
THUMP
GET THAT MAN A DRINK!
FLING!
COMIN' UP!
ZIP!

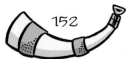

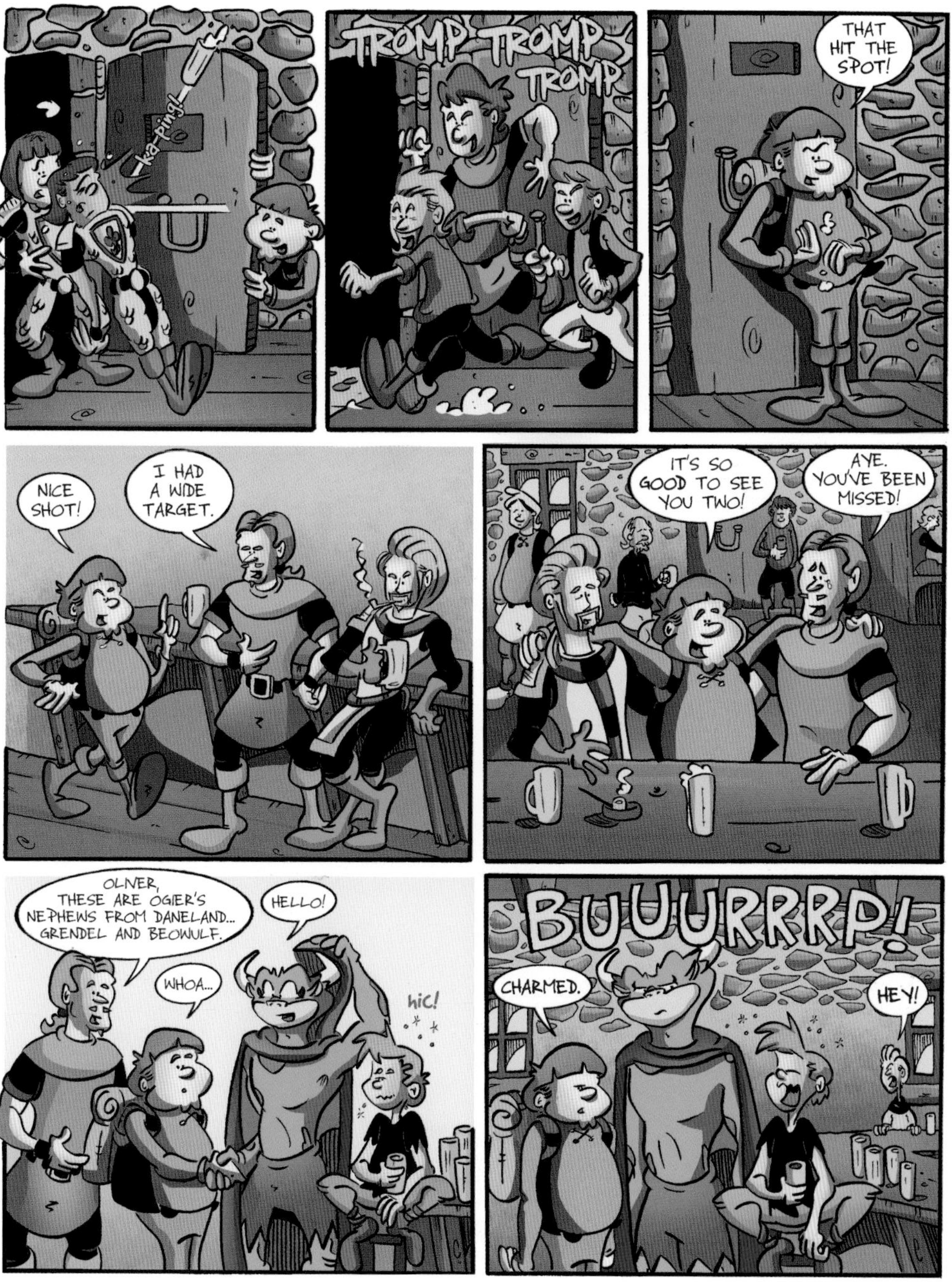
ka-ping!
TROMP TROMP TROMP
THAT HIT THE SPOT!
NICE SHOT!
I HAD A WIDE TARGET.
IT'S SO GOOD TO SEE YOU TWO!
AYE. YOU'VE BEEN MISSED!
OLIVER, THESE ARE OGIER'S NEPHEWS FROM DANELAND... GRENDEL AND BEOWULF.
HELLO!
WHOA...
hic!
BUUURRRP!
CHARMED.
HEY!

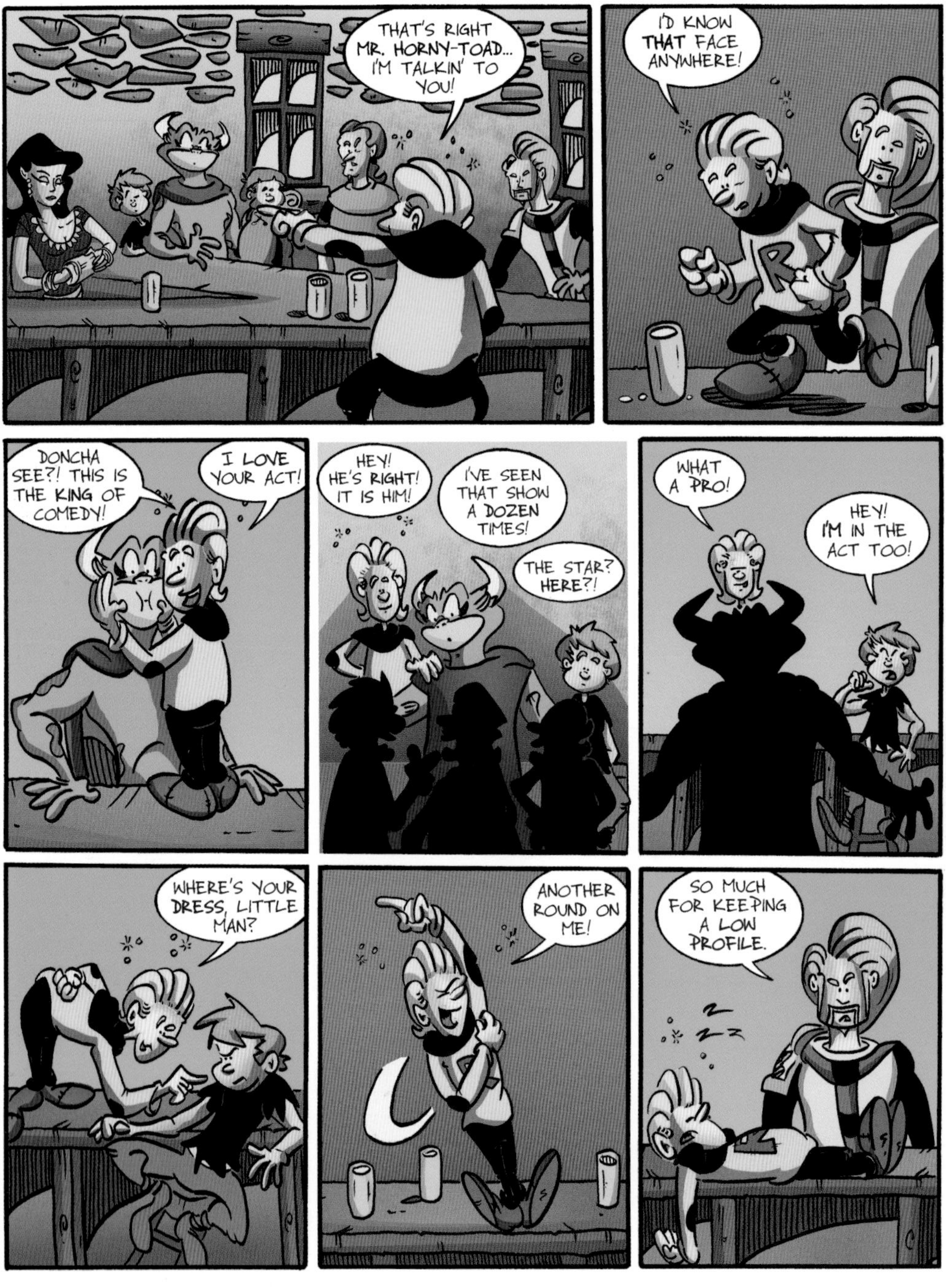
THAT'S RIGHT MR. HORNY-TOAD... I'M TALKIN' TO YOU!
I'D KNOW THAT FACE ANYWHERE!
DONCHA SEE?! THIS IS THE KING OF COMEDY!
I LOVE YOUR ACT!
HEY! HE'S RIGHT! IT IS HIM!
I'VE SEEN THAT SHOW A DOZEN TIMES!
THE STAR? HERE?!
WHAT A PRO!
HEY! I'M IN THE ACT TOO!
WHERE'S YOUR DRESS, LITTLE MAN?
ANOTHER ROUND ON ME!
SO MUCH FOR KEEPING A LOW PROFILE.
Z Z Z

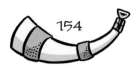

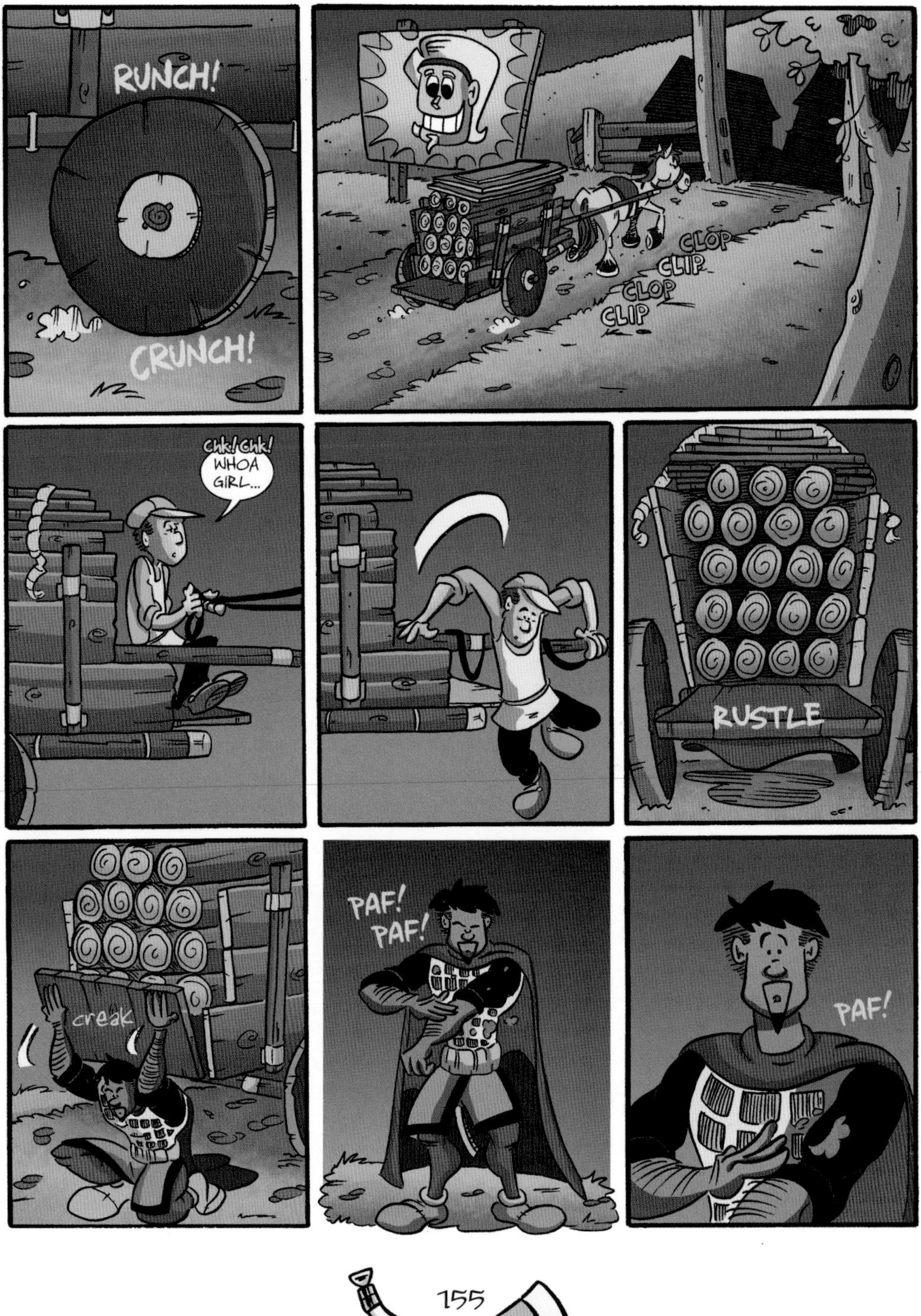
RUNCH!
CRUNCH!
CLIP
CLOP
CLIP
CLOP
Chk! Chk! WHOA GIRL...
RUSTLE
creak
PAF!
PAF!
PAF!

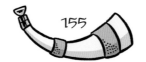

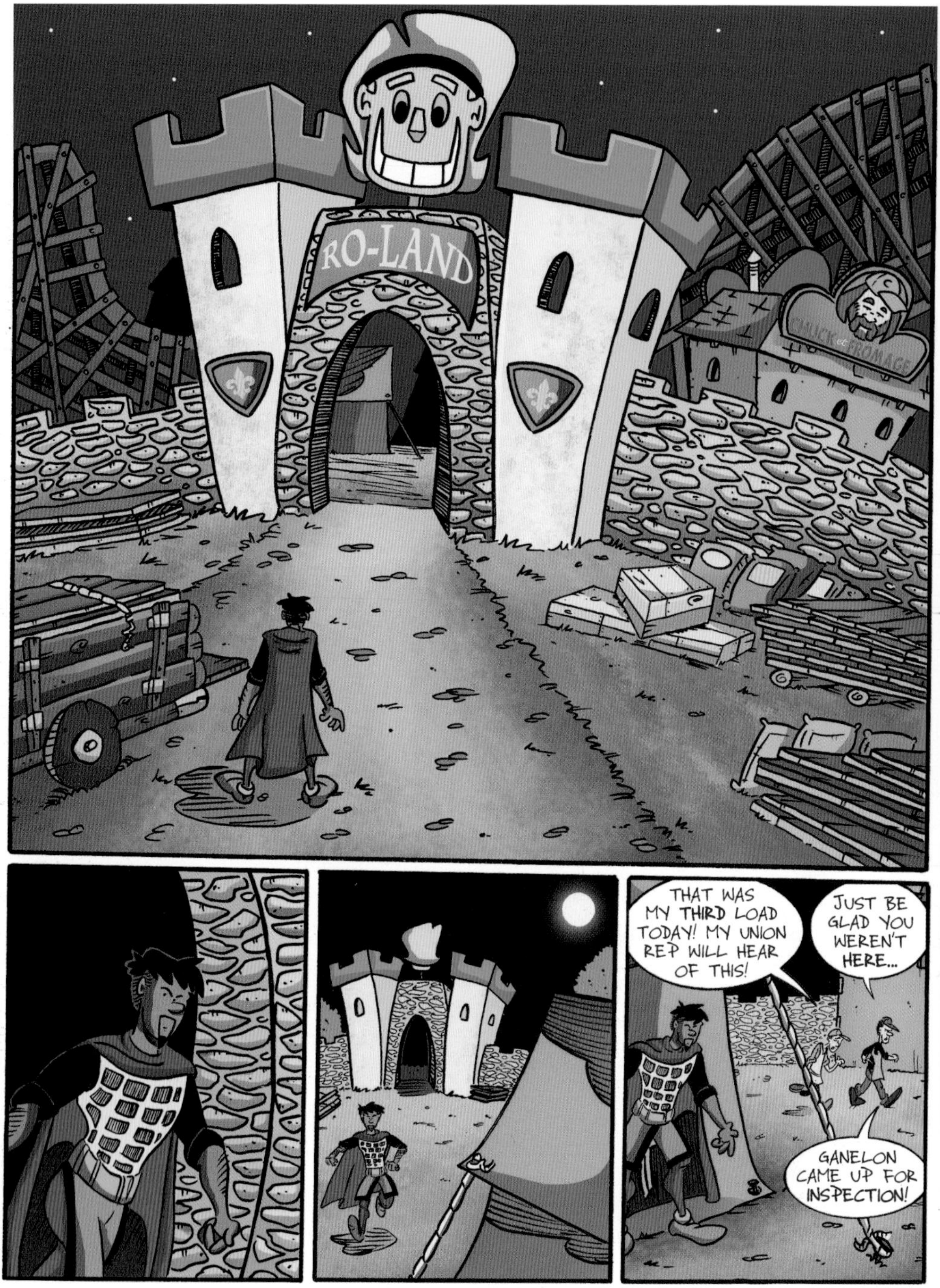
RO-LAND
CHUCK et FROMAGE
THAT WAS MY THIRD LOAD TODAY! MY UNION REP WILL HEAR OF THIS!
JUST BE GLAD YOU WEREN'T HERE...
GANELON CAME UP FOR INSPECTION!

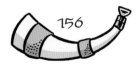

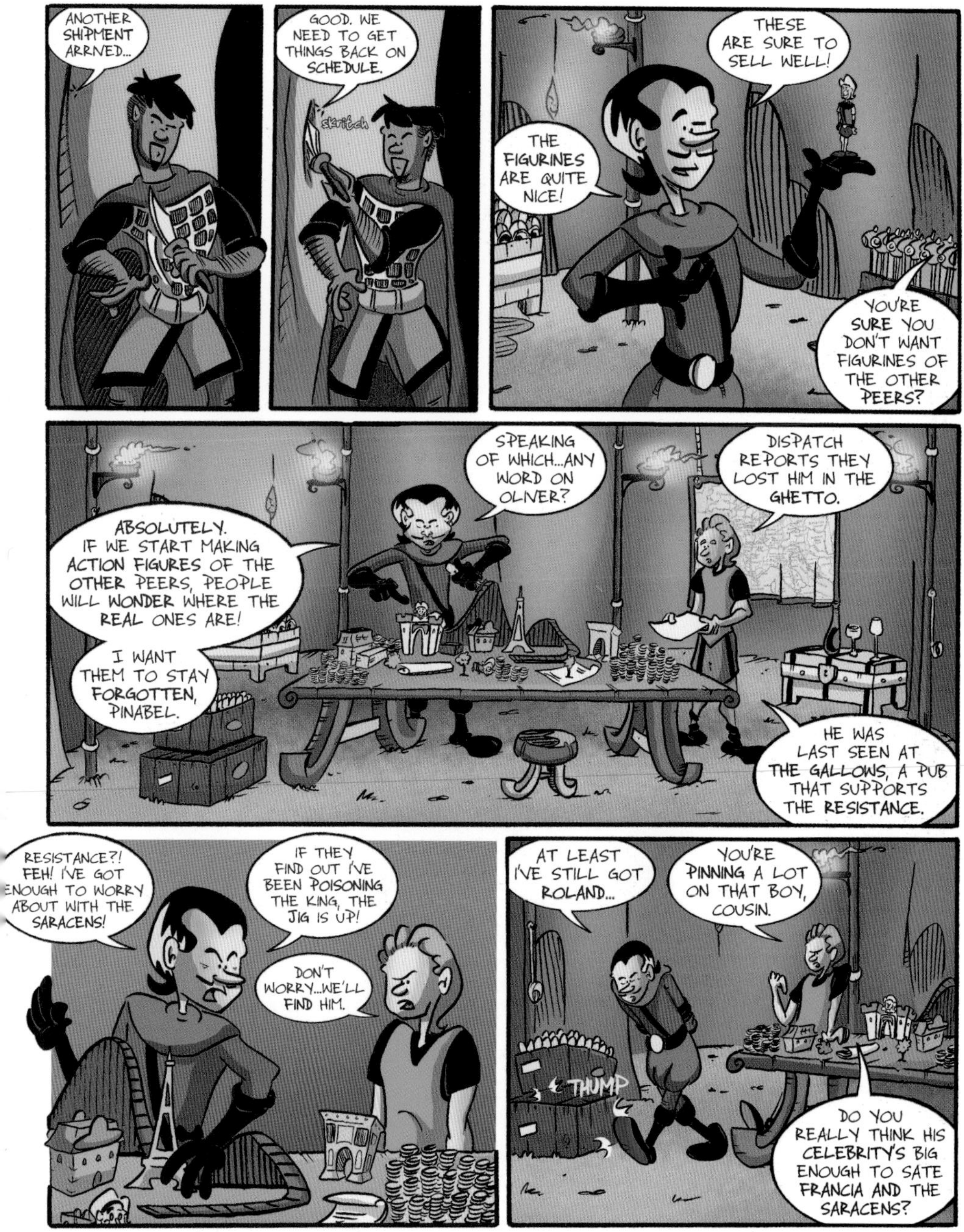
ANOTHER SHIPMENT ARRIVED...
GOOD. WE NEED TO GET THINGS BACK ON SCHEDULE.
skritch
THESE ARE SURE TO SELL WELL!
THE FIGURINES ARE QUITE NICE!
YOU'RE SURE YOU DON'T WANT FIGURINES OF THE OTHER PEERS?
ABSOLUTELY. IF WE START MAKING ACTION FIGURES OF THE OTHER PEERS, PEOPLE WILL WONDER WHERE THE REAL ONES ARE!
I WANT THEM TO STAY FORGOTTEN, PINABEL.
SPEAKING OF WHICH...ANY WORD ON OLIVER?
DISPATCH REPORTS THEY LOST HIM IN THE GHETTO.
HE WAS LAST SEEN AT THE GALLOWS, A PUB THAT SUPPORTS THE RESISTANCE.
RESISTANCE?! FEH! I'VE GOT ENOUGH TO WORRY ABOUT WITH THE SARACENS!
IF THEY FIND OUT I'VE BEEN POISONING THE KING, THE JIG IS UP!
DON'T WORRY...WE'LL FIND HIM.
AT LEAST I'VE STILL GOT ROLAND...
YOU'RE PINNING A LOT ON THAT BOY, COUSIN.
THUMP
DO YOU REALLY THINK HIS CELEBRITY'S BIG ENOUGH TO SATE FRANCIA AND THE SARACENS?

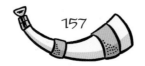

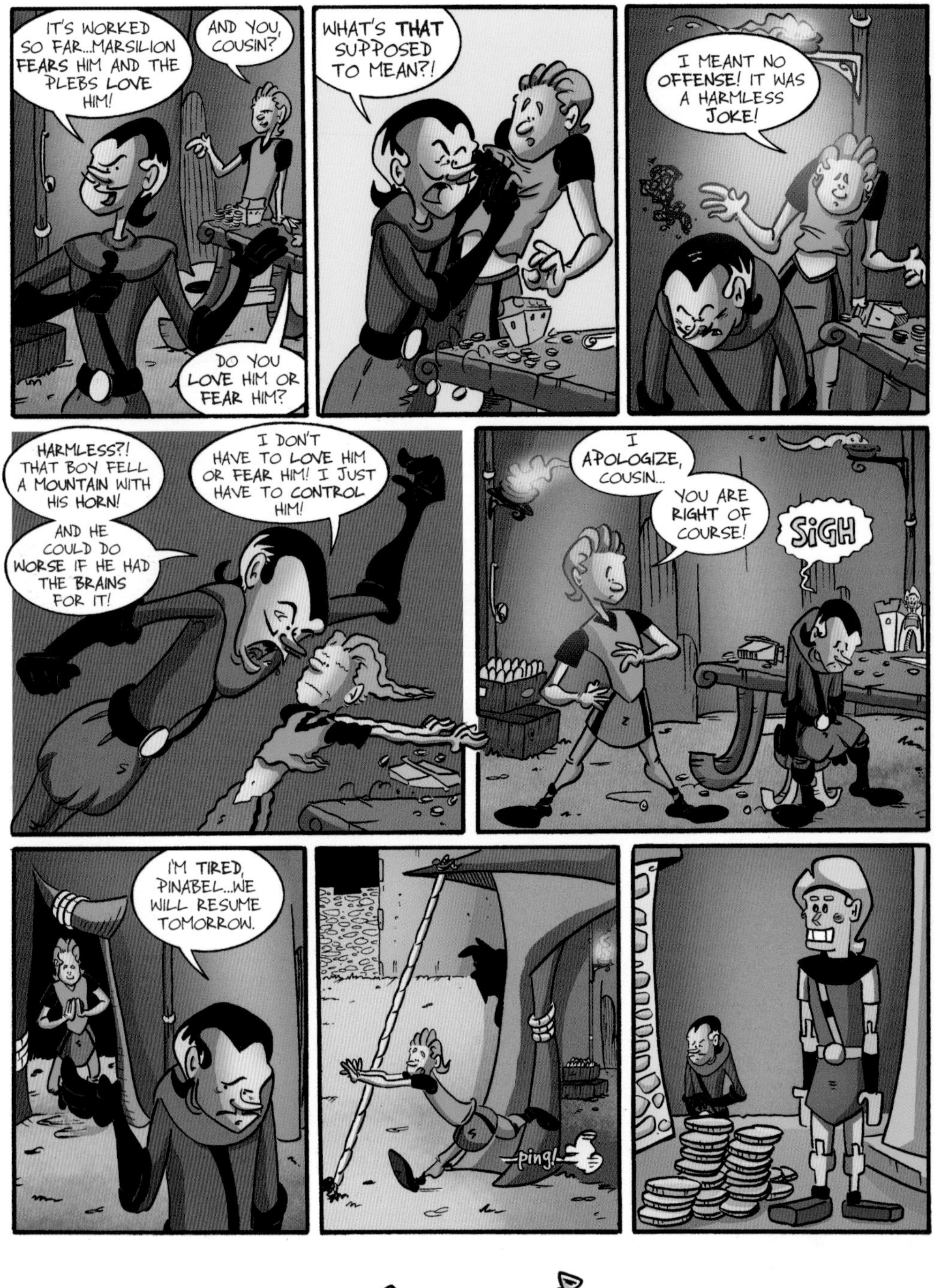
IT'S WORKED SO FAR...MARSILION FEARS HIM AND THE PLEBS LOVE HIM!
AND YOU, COUSIN?
DO YOU LOVE HIM OR FEAR HIM?
WHAT'S THAT SUPPOSED TO MEAN?!
I MEANT NO OFFENSE! IT WAS A HARMLESS JOKE!
HARMLESS?! THAT BOY FELL A MOUNTAIN WITH HIS HORN!
AND HE COULD DO WORSE IF HE HAD THE BRAINS FOR IT!
I DON'T HAVE TO LOVE HIM OR FEAR HIM! I JUST HAVE TO CONTROL HIM!
I APOLOGIZE, COUSIN...
YOU ARE RIGHT OF COURSE!
SIGH
I'M TIRED, PINABEL...WE WILL RESUME TOMORROW.
-ping!-

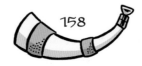

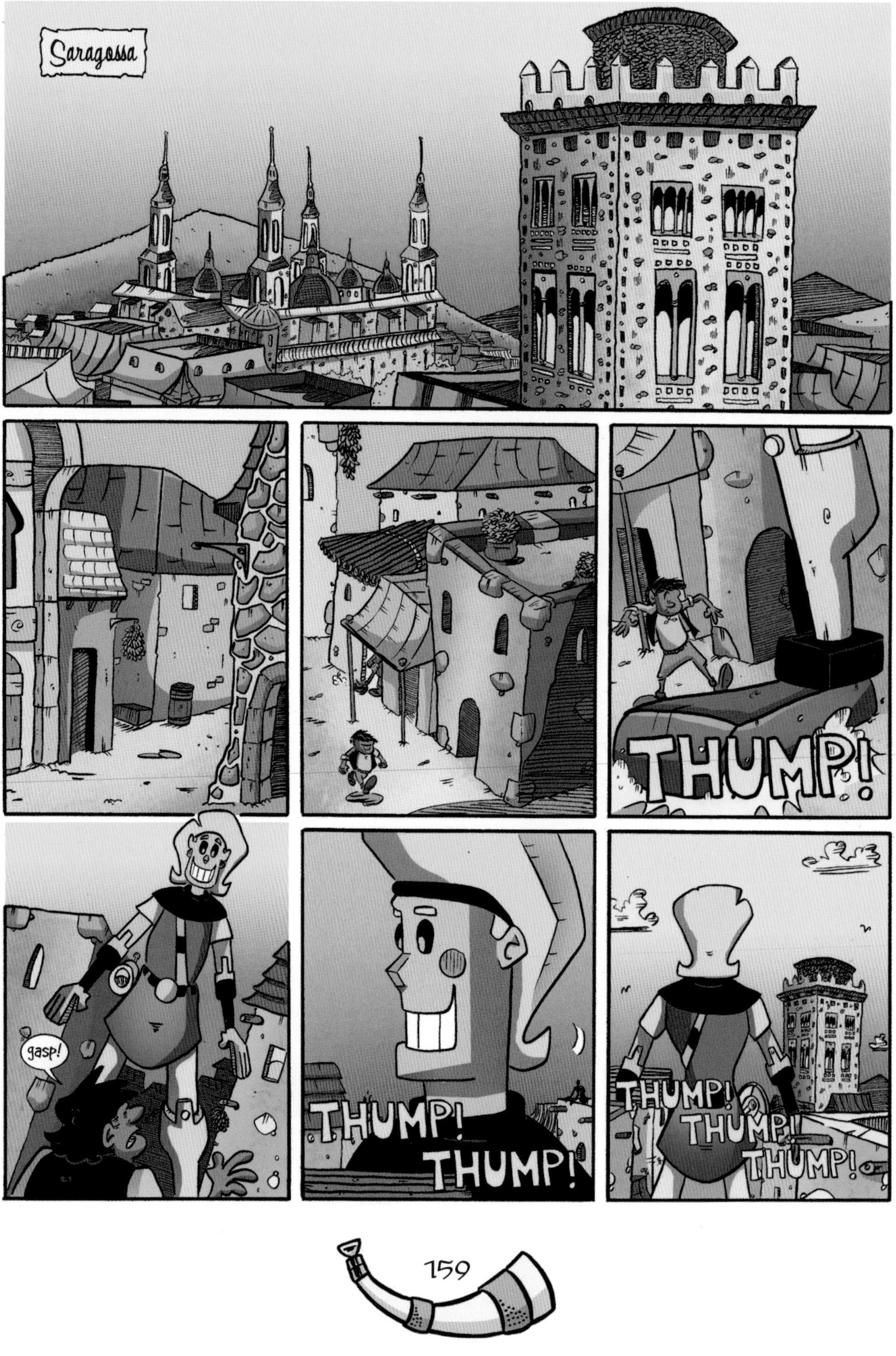
Saragossa
THUMP!
gasp!
THUMP!
THUMP!
THUMP!
THUMP!
THUMP!

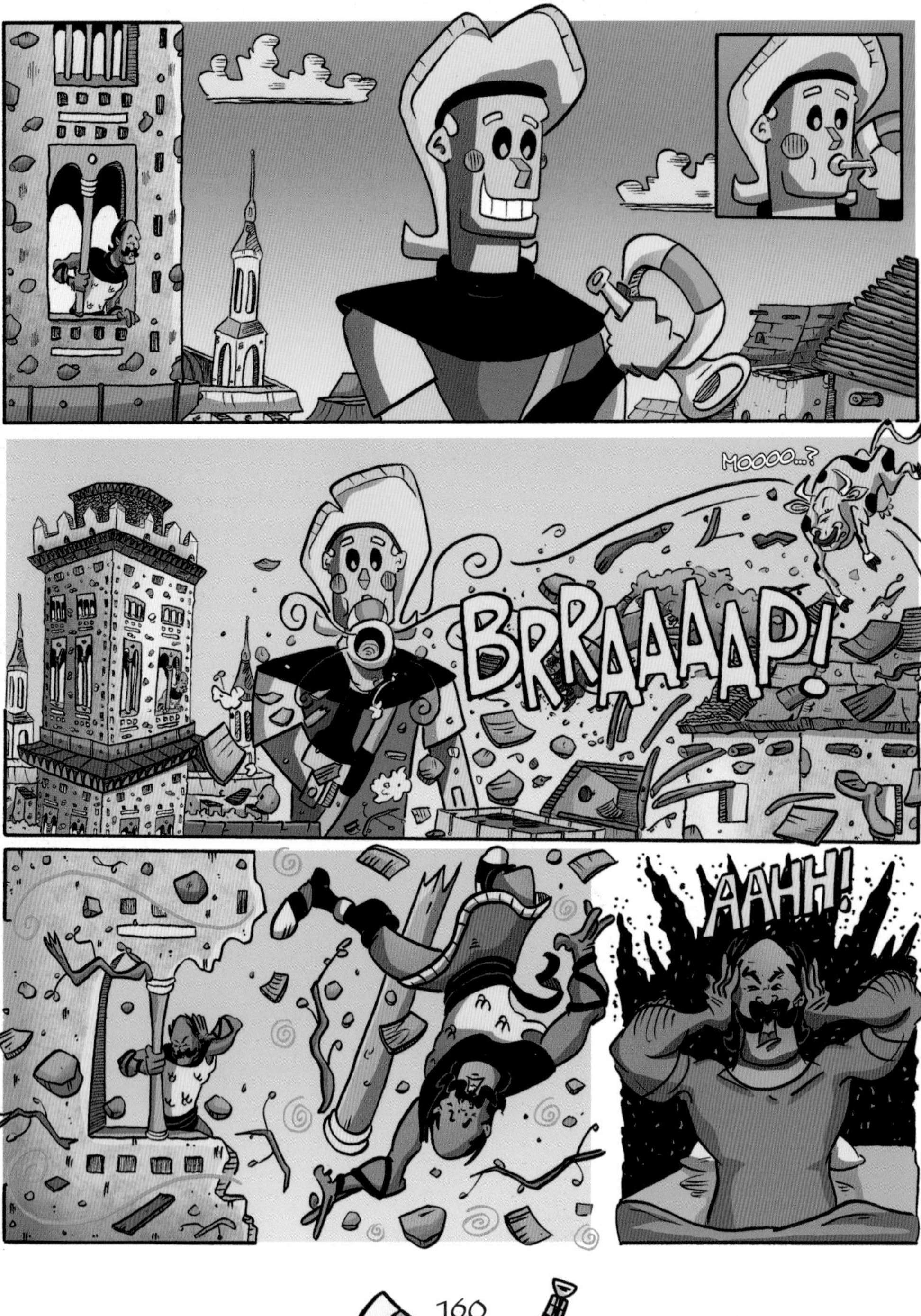
MOOOO...?
BRRAAAAP!
AAHH!

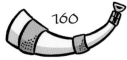

pant pant

ANOTHER NIGHTMARE?

ROLAND AGAIN...AND THAT BLASTED HORN! MY EARS ARE STILL RINGING!

HE CAN ONLY BE DEFEATED IN BATTLE. YOU KNOW THAT.

YOU WEREN'T THERE, BRAMIMONDE. THE BOY TOOK DOWN A MOUNTAIN!

AND YOU HAVE TAKEN DOWN EMPIRES!

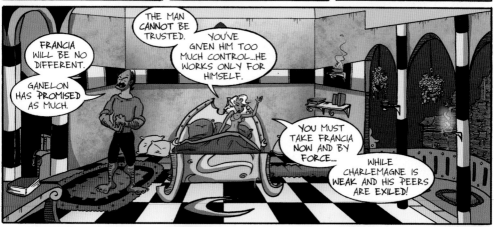

FRANCIA WILL BE NO DIFFERENT.

GANELON HAS PROMISED AS MUCH.

THE MAN CANNOT BE TRUSTED. YOU'VE GIVEN HIM TOO MUCH CONTROL...HE WORKS ONLY FOR HIMSELF.

YOU MUST TAKE FRANCIA NOW AND BY FORCE...

WHILE CHARLEMAGNE IS WEAK AND HIS PEERS ARE EXILED!

SO I ATTACK WHILE THEIR KING LIES HELPLESS? I FIGHT VILLAGERS INSTEAD OF KNIGHTS?

WHERE IS THE HONOR IN THAT? I AM A WARRIOR, NOT A BUTCHER.

YOU ARE GOD'S VASSAL. GOD WANTS FRANCIA.

TO THE END OF THE CROSS!

TO WHAT END?

WE LIT THE STREETS OF THIS BACKWATER COUNTRY. WE BROUGHT MUSIC TO ITS MOB.

GOD WANTS THE SAME FOR FRANCIA...

AND YOU WILL BRING IT. ROLAND OR NOT!

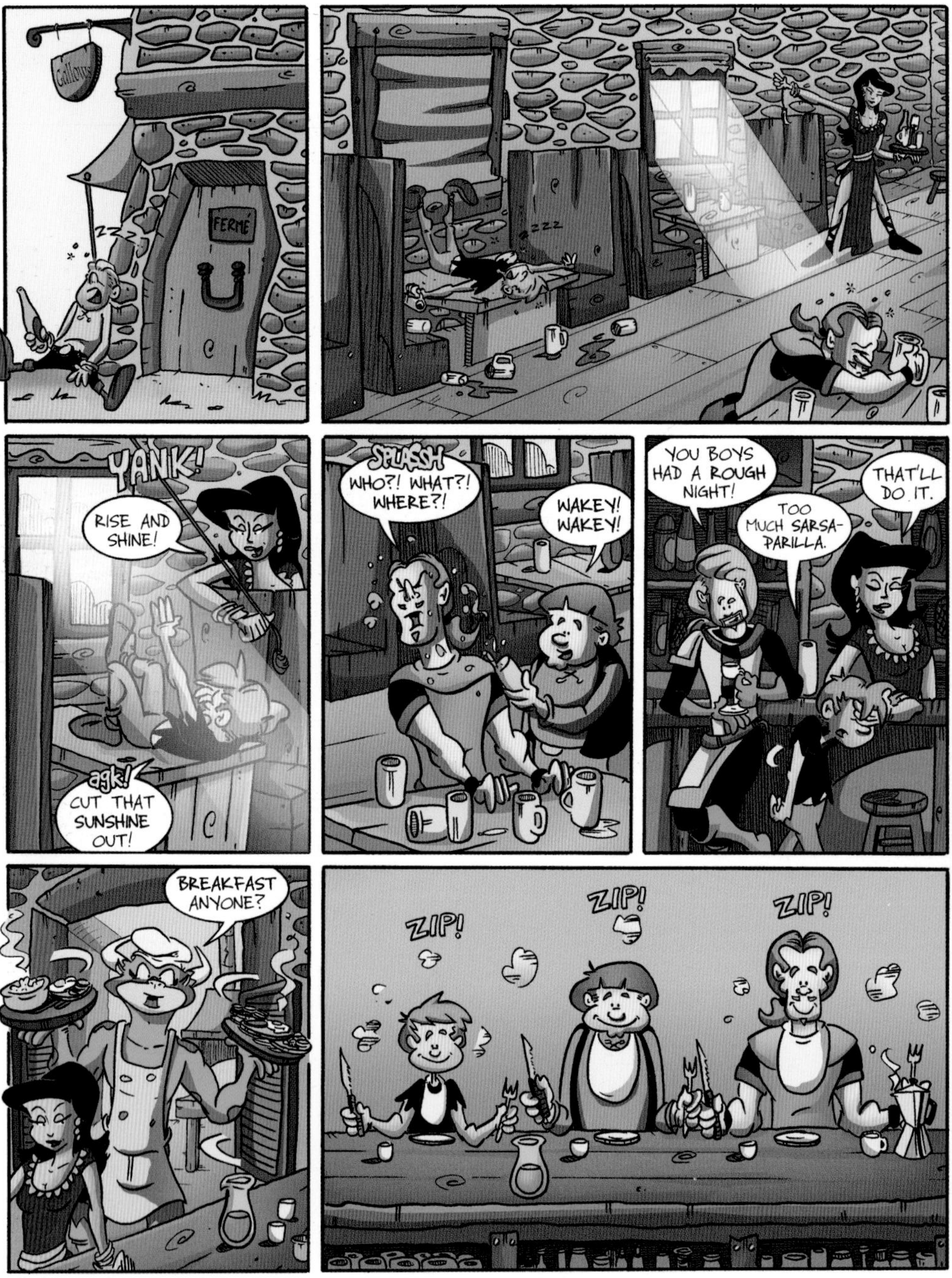
Gallows
FERMÉ
ZZZ
ZZZ
YANK!
RISE AND SHINE!
agk!
CUT THAT SUNSHINE OUT!
SPLASSH
WHO?! WHAT?! WHERE?!
WAKEY! WAKEY!
YOU BOYS HAD A ROUGH NIGHT!
TOO MUCH SARSA-PARILLA.
THAT'LL DO IT.
BREAKFAST ANYONE?
ZIP!
ZIP!
ZIP!

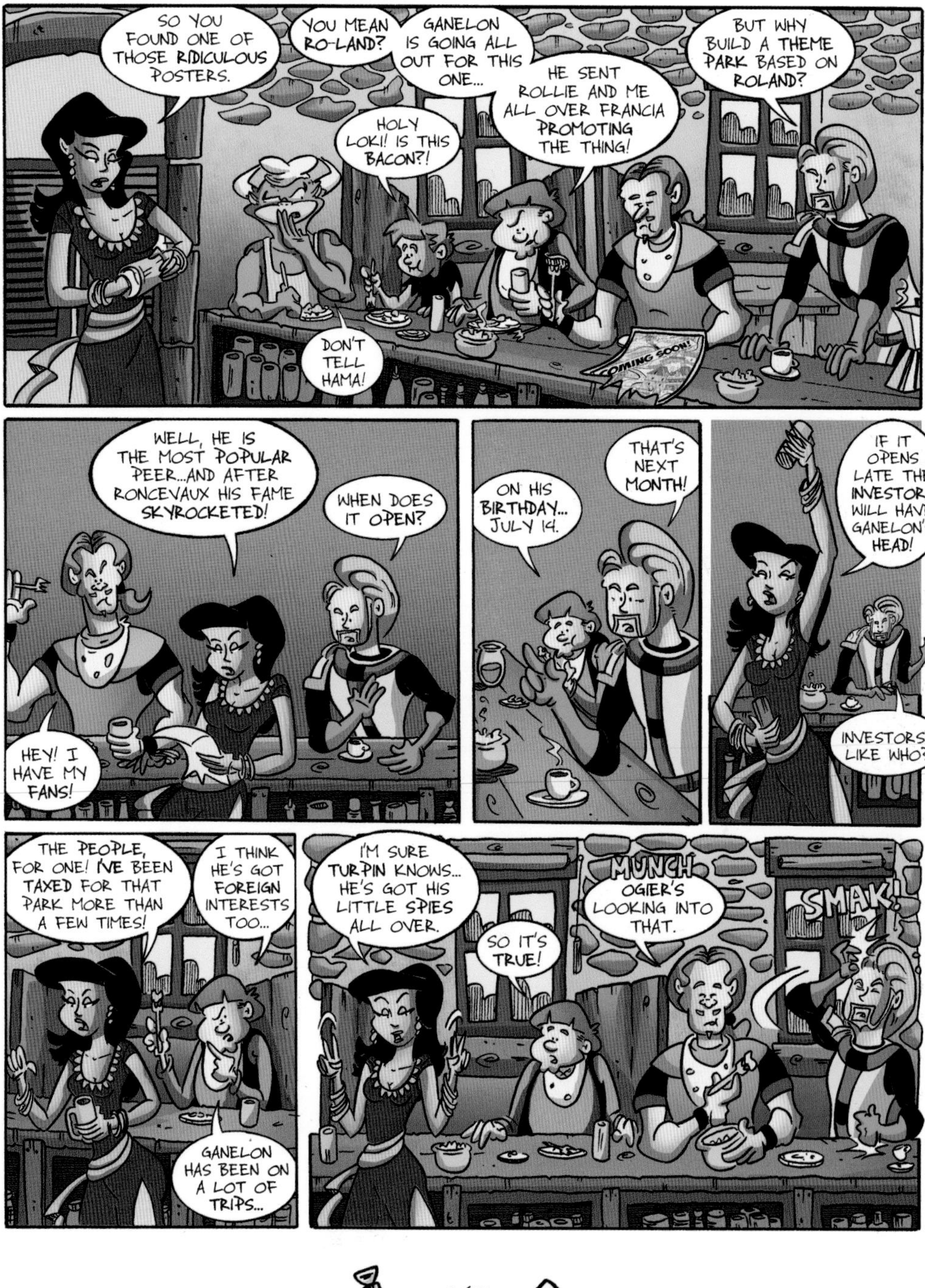
SO YOU FOUND ONE OF THOSE RIDICULOUS POSTERS.
YOU MEAN RO-LAND?
GANELON IS GOING ALL OUT FOR THIS ONE...
HOLY LOKI! IS THIS BACON?!
HE SENT ROLLIE AND ME ALL OVER FRANCIA PROMOTING THE THING!
BUT WHY BUILD A THEME PARK BASED ON ROLAND?
DON'T TELL HAMA!
COMING SOON!
WELL, HE IS THE MOST POPULAR PEER...AND AFTER RONCEVAUX HIS FAME SKYROCKETED!
HEY! I HAVE MY FANS!
WHEN DOES IT OPEN?
ON HIS BIRTHDAY... JULY 14.
THAT'S NEXT MONTH!
IF IT OPENS LATE THE INVESTORS WILL HAVE GANELON'S HEAD!
INVESTORS? LIKE WHO?
THE PEOPLE, FOR ONE! I'VE BEEN TAXED FOR THAT PARK MORE THAN A FEW TIMES!
I THINK HE'S GOT FOREIGN INTERESTS TOO...
GANELON HAS BEEN ON A LOT OF TRIPS...
I'M SURE TURPIN KNOWS... HE'S GOT HIS LITTLE SPIES ALL OVER.
SO IT'S TRUE!
MUNCH
OGIER'S LOOKING INTO THAT.
SMAK!

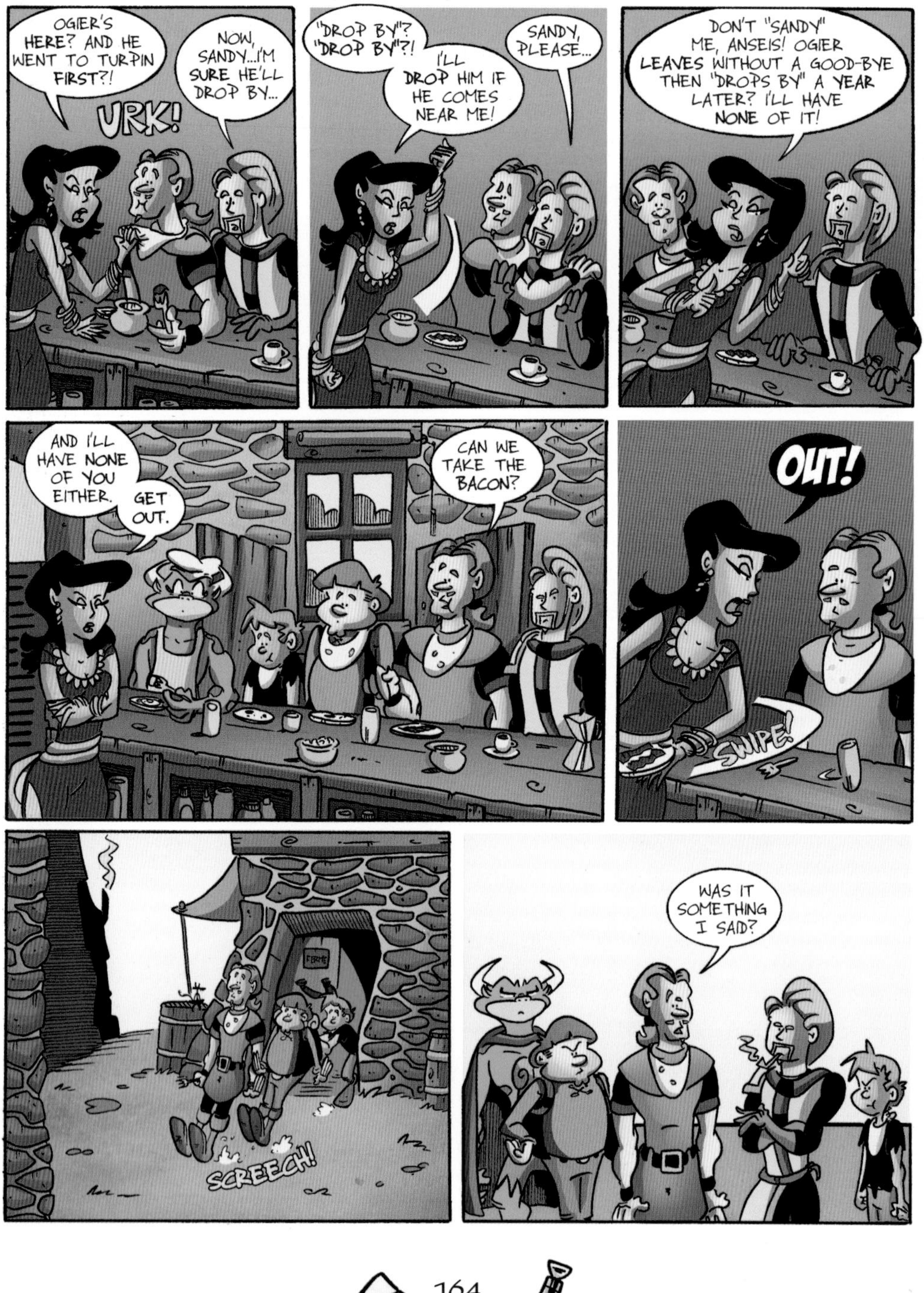
OGIER'S HERE? AND HE WENT TO TURPIN FIRST?!
NOW, SANDY...I'M SURE HE'LL DROP BY...
URK!
"DROP BY"? "DROP BY"?!
I'LL DROP HIM IF HE COMES NEAR ME!
SANDY, PLEASE...
DON'T "SANDY" ME, ANSEIS! OGIER LEAVES WITHOUT A GOOD-BYE THEN "DROPS BY" A YEAR LATER? I'LL HAVE NONE OF IT!
AND I'LL HAVE NONE OF YOU EITHER.
GET OUT.
CAN WE TAKE THE BACON?
OUT!
SWIPE!
FERMÉ
SCREECH!
WAS IT SOMETHING I SAID?

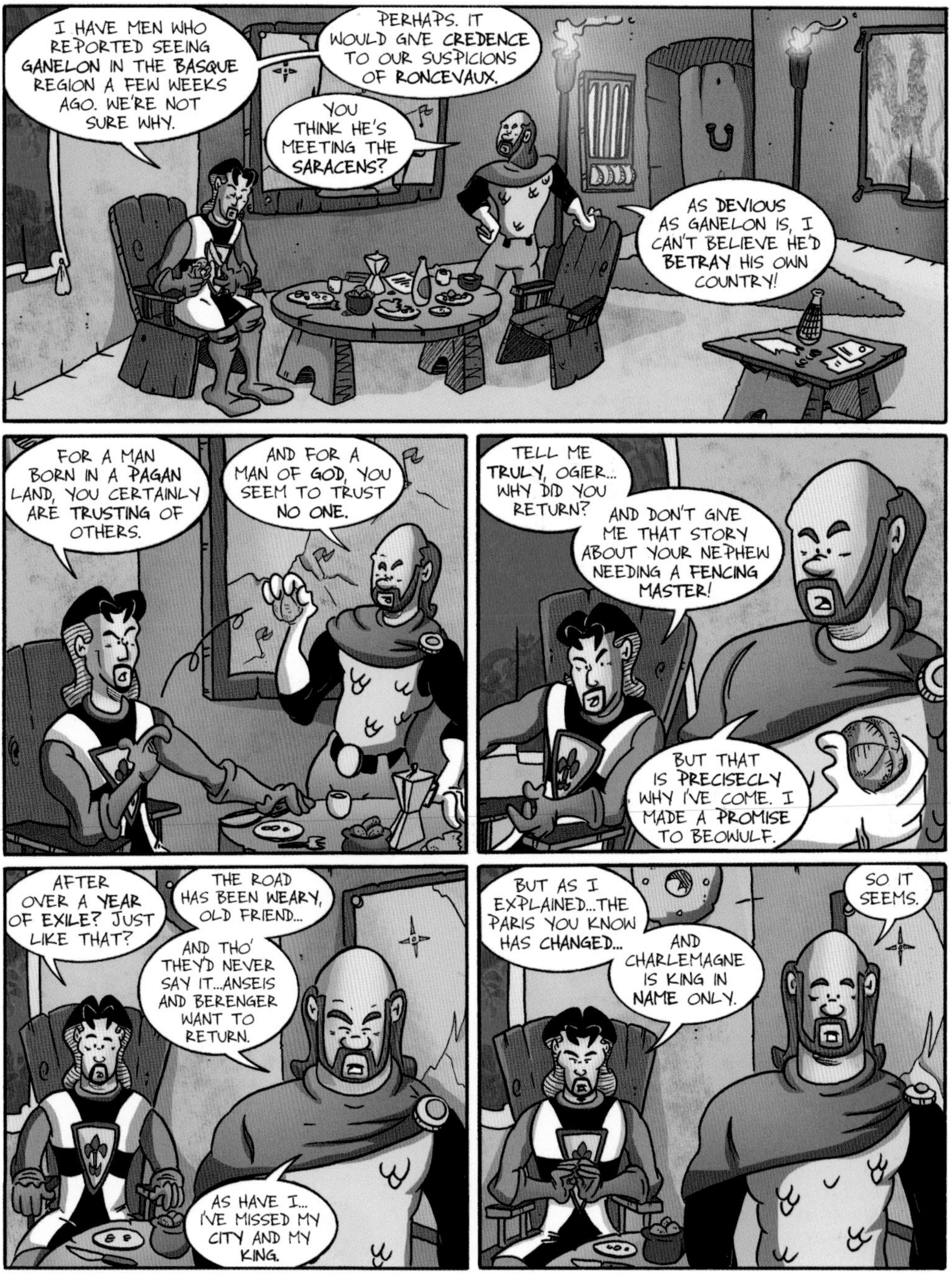
I HAVE MEN WHO REPORTED SEEING GANELON IN THE BASQUE REGION A FEW WEEKS AGO. WE'RE NOT SURE WHY.
PERHAPS. IT WOULD GIVE CREDENCE TO OUR SUSPICIONS OF RONCEVAUX.
YOU THINK HE'S MEETING THE SARACENS?
AS DEVIOUS AS GANELON IS, I CAN'T BELIEVE HE'D BETRAY HIS OWN COUNTRY!
FOR A MAN BORN IN A PAGAN LAND, YOU CERTAINLY ARE TRUSTING OF OTHERS.
AND FOR A MAN OF GOD, YOU SEEM TO TRUST NO ONE.
TELL ME TRULY, OGIER... WHY DID YOU RETURN?
AND DON'T GIVE ME THAT STORY ABOUT YOUR NEPHEW NEEDING A FENCING MASTER!
BUT THAT IS PRECISELY WHY I'VE COME. I MADE A PROMISE TO BEOWULF.
AFTER OVER A YEAR OF EXILE? JUST LIKE THAT?
THE ROAD HAS BEEN WEARY, OLD FRIEND...
AND THO' THEY'D NEVER SAY IT...ANSEIS AND BERENGER WANT TO RETURN.
AS HAVE I... I'VE MISSED MY CITY AND MY KING.
BUT AS I EXPLAINED...THE PARIS YOU KNOW HAS CHANGED...
AND CHARLEMAGNE IS KING IN NAME ONLY.
SO IT SEEMS.

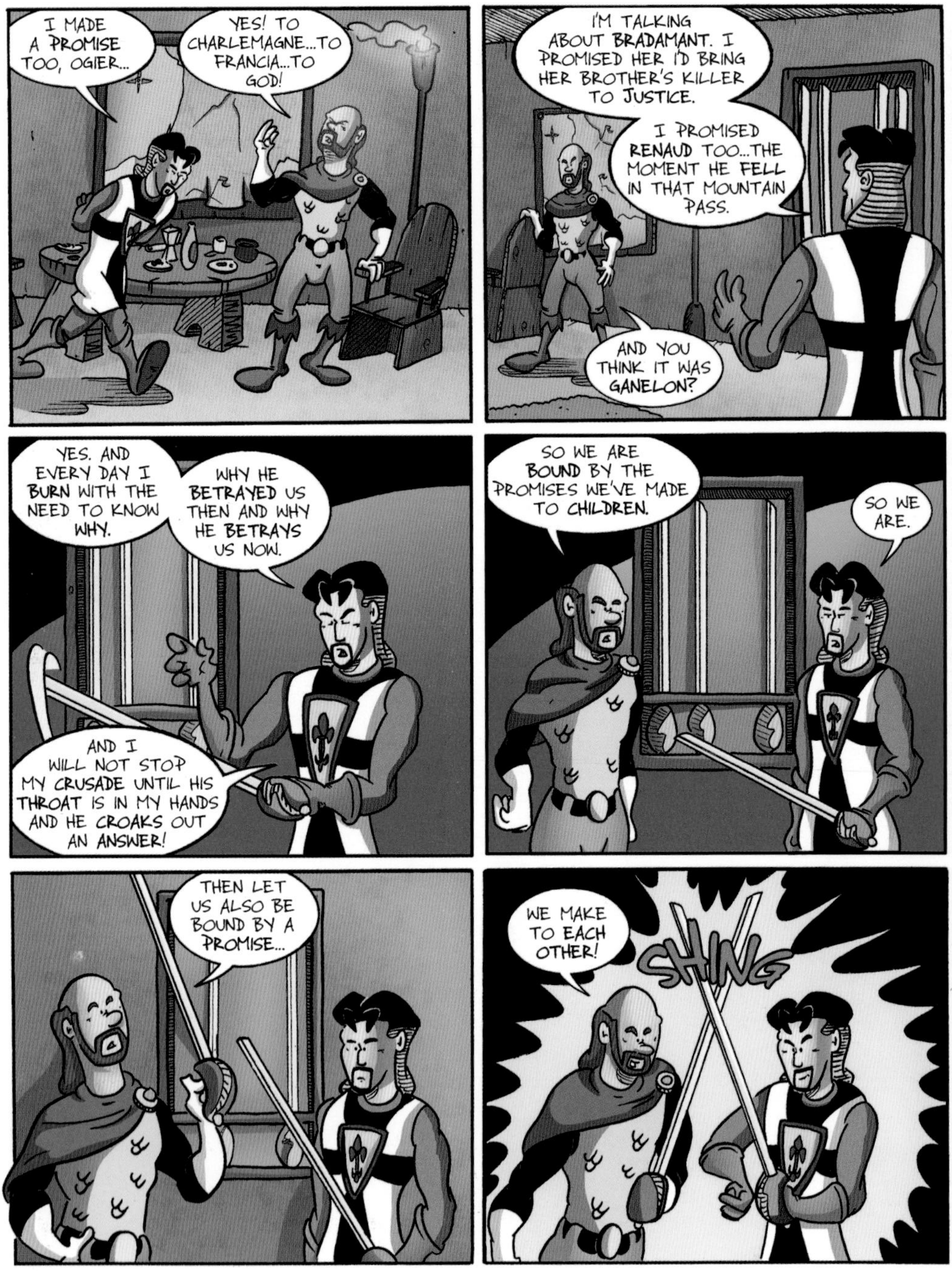
I MADE A PROMISE TOO, OGIER...
YES! TO CHARLEMAGNE...TO FRANCIA...TO GOD!
I'M TALKING ABOUT BRADAMANT. I PROMISED HER I'D BRING HER BROTHER'S KILLER TO JUSTICE.
I PROMISED RENAUD TOO...THE MOMENT HE FELL IN THAT MOUNTAIN PASS.
AND YOU THINK IT WAS GANELON?
YES. AND EVERY DAY I BURN WITH THE NEED TO KNOW WHY.
WHY HE BETRAYED US THEN AND WHY HE BETRAYS US NOW.
AND I WILL NOT STOP MY CRUSADE UNTIL HIS THROAT IS IN MY HANDS AND HE CROAKS OUT AN ANSWER!
SO WE ARE BOUND BY THE PROMISES WE'VE MADE TO CHILDREN.
SO WE ARE.
THEN LET US ALSO BE BOUND BY A PROMISE...
WE MAKE TO EACH OTHER!
SHING

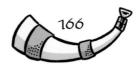

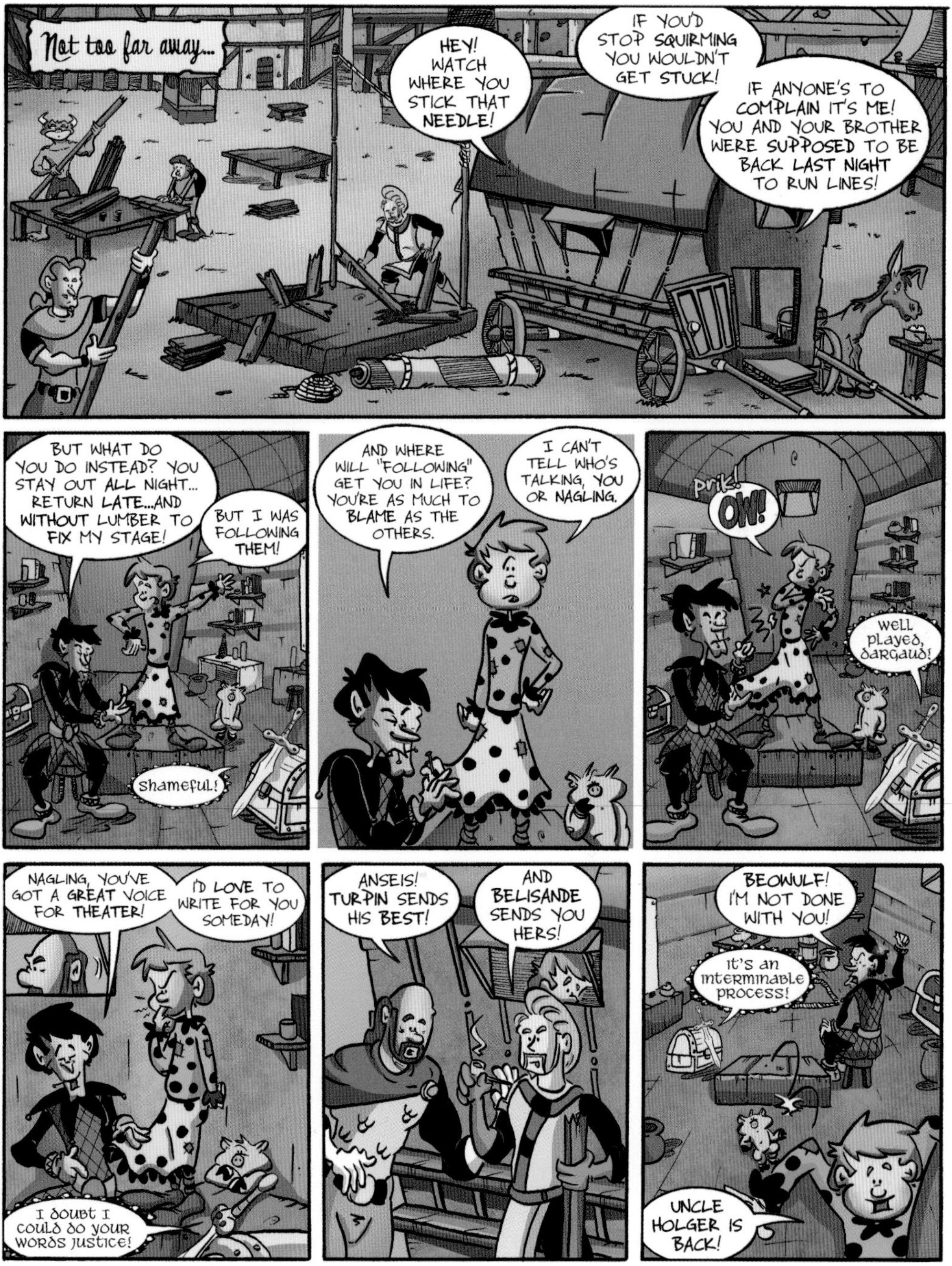
Not too far away...
HEY! WATCH WHERE YOU STICK THAT NEEDLE!
IF YOU'D STOP SQUIRMING YOU WOULDN'T GET STUCK!
IF ANYONE'S TO COMPLAIN IT'S ME! YOU AND YOUR BROTHER WERE SUPPOSED TO BE BACK LAST NIGHT TO RUN LINES!
BUT WHAT DO YOU DO INSTEAD? YOU STAY OUT ALL NIGHT... RETURN LATE...AND WITHOUT LUMBER TO FIX MY STAGE!
BUT I WAS FOLLOWING THEM!
shameful!
AND WHERE WILL "FOLLOWING" GET YOU IN LIFE? YOU'RE AS MUCH TO BLAME AS THE OTHERS.
I CAN'T TELL WHO'S TALKING, YOU OR NAGLING.
prik!
OW!
well played, dargaud!
NAGLING, YOU'VE GOT A GREAT VOICE FOR THEATER!
I'D LOVE TO WRITE FOR YOU SOMEDAY!
I doubt I could do your words justice!
ANSEIS! TURPIN SENDS HIS BEST!
AND BELISANDE SENDS YOU HERS!
BEOWULF! I'M NOT DONE WITH YOU!
it's an interminable process!
UNCLE HOLGER IS BACK!

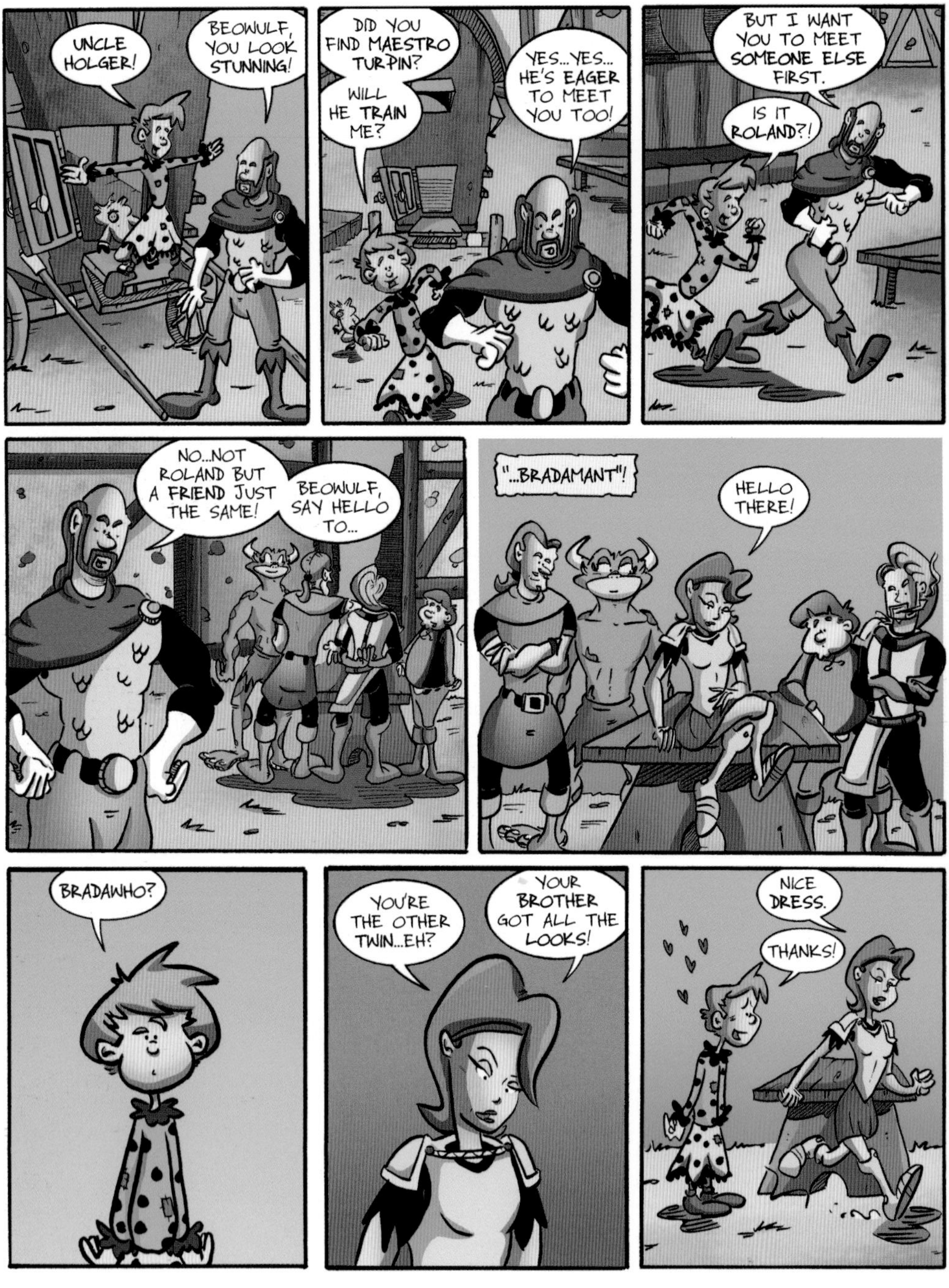
UNCLE HOLGER!
BEOWULF, YOU LOOK STUNNING!
DID YOU FIND MAESTRO TURPIN?
WILL HE TRAIN ME?
YES...YES... HE'S EAGER TO MEET YOU TOO!
BUT I WANT YOU TO MEET SOMEONE ELSE FIRST.
IS IT ROLAND?!
NO...NOT ROLAND BUT A FRIEND JUST THE SAME!
BEOWULF, SAY HELLO TO...
"...BRADAMANT"!
HELLO THERE!
BRADAWHO?
YOU'RE THE OTHER TWIN...EH?
YOUR BROTHER GOT ALL THE LOOKS!
NICE DRESS.
THANKS!

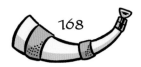

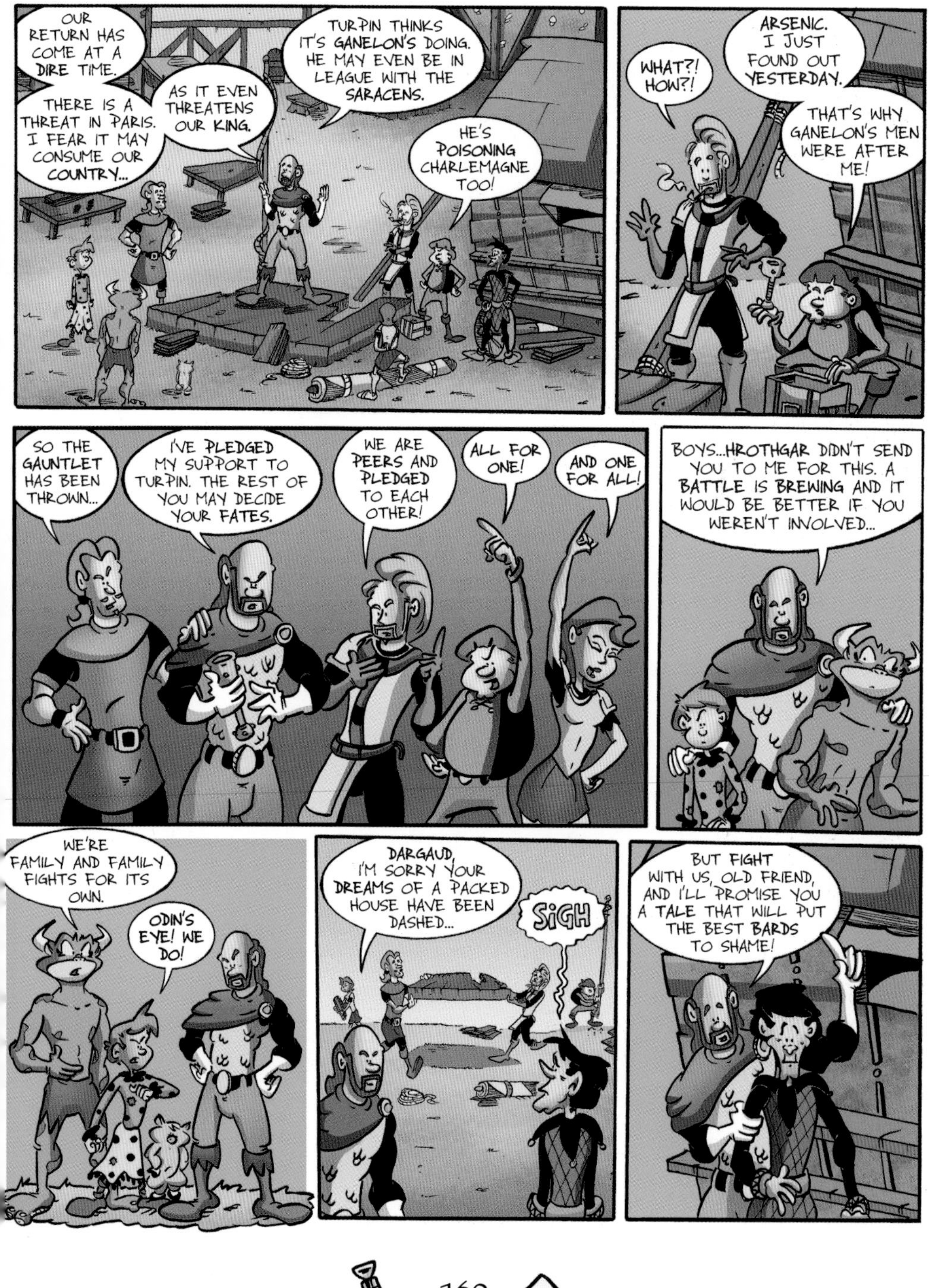

OUR RETURN HAS COME AT A DIRE TIME.
THERE IS A THREAT IN PARIS. I FEAR IT MAY CONSUME OUR COUNTRY...
AS IT EVEN THREATENS OUR KING.
TURPIN THINKS IT'S GANELON'S DOING. HE MAY EVEN BE IN LEAGUE WITH THE SARACENS.
HE'S POISONING CHARLEMAGNE TOO!
WHAT?! HOW?!
ARSENIC. I JUST FOUND OUT YESTERDAY.
THAT'S WHY GANELON'S MEN WERE AFTER ME!
SO THE GAUNTLET HAS BEEN THROWN...
I'VE PLEDGED MY SUPPORT TO TURPIN. THE REST OF YOU MAY DECIDE YOUR FATES.
WE ARE PEERS AND PLEDGED TO EACH OTHER!
ALL FOR ONE!
AND ONE FOR ALL!
BOYS...HROTHGAR DIDN'T SEND YOU TO ME FOR THIS. A BATTLE IS BREWING AND IT WOULD BE BETTER IF YOU WEREN'T INVOLVED...
WE'RE FAMILY AND FAMILY FIGHTS FOR ITS OWN.
ODIN'S EYE! WE DO!
DARGAUD, I'M SORRY YOUR DREAMS OF A PACKED HOUSE HAVE BEEN DASHED...
SIGH
BUT FIGHT WITH US, OLD FRIEND, AND I'LL PROMISE YOU A TALE THAT WILL PUT THE BEST BARDS TO SHAME!

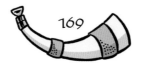

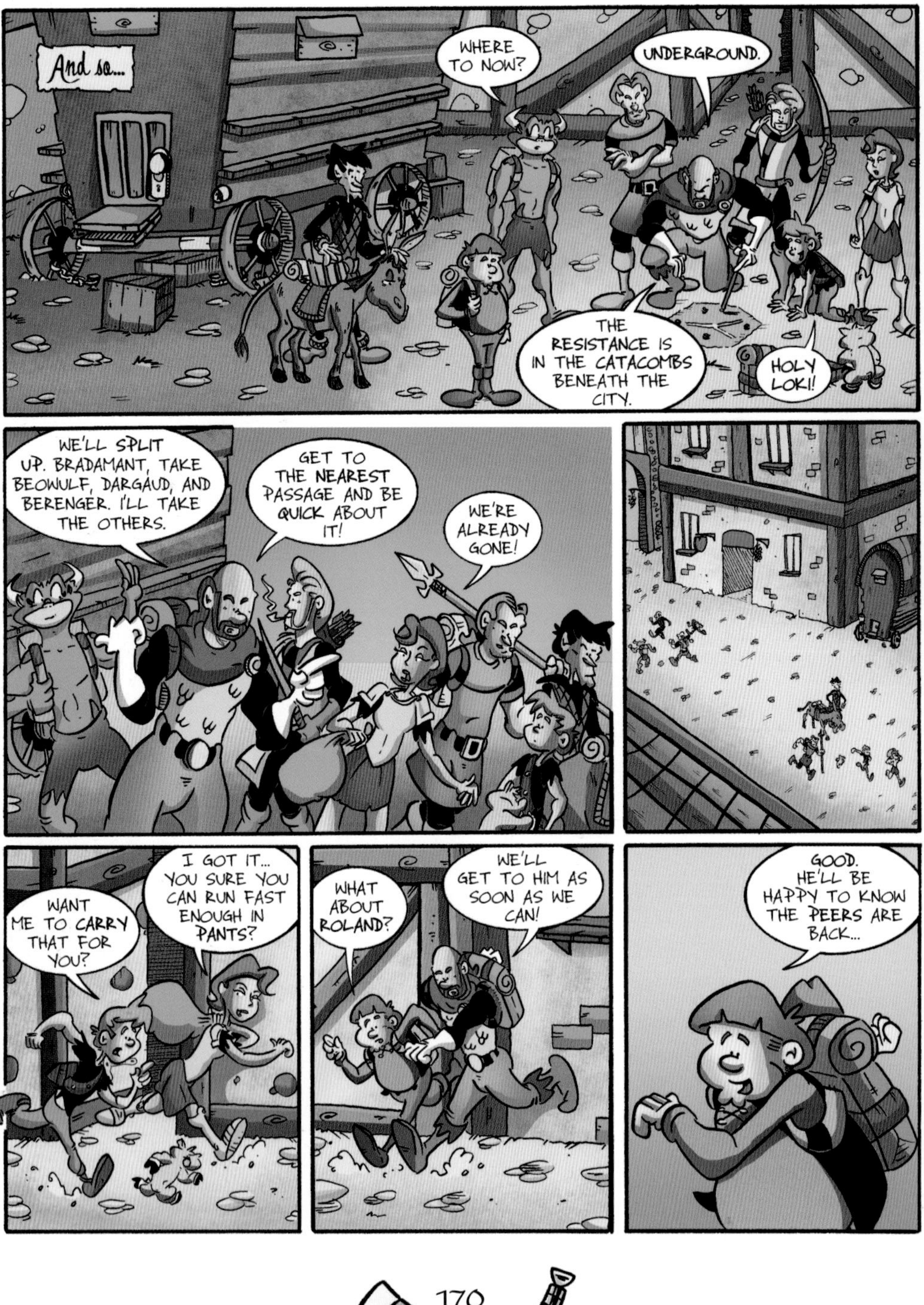
And so...
WHERE TO NOW?
UNDERGROUND.
THE RESISTANCE IS IN THE CATACOMBS BENEATH THE CITY.
HOLY LOKI!
WE'LL SPLIT UP. BRADAMANT, TAKE BEOWULF, DARGAUD, AND BERENGER. I'LL TAKE THE OTHERS.
GET TO THE NEAREST PASSAGE AND BE QUICK ABOUT IT!
WE'RE ALREADY GONE!
WANT ME TO CARRY THAT FOR YOU?
I GOT IT... YOU SURE YOU CAN RUN FAST ENOUGH IN PANTS?
WHAT ABOUT ROLAND?
WE'LL GET TO HIM AS SOON AS WE CAN!
GOOD. HE'LL BE HAPPY TO KNOW THE PEERS ARE BACK...

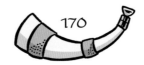

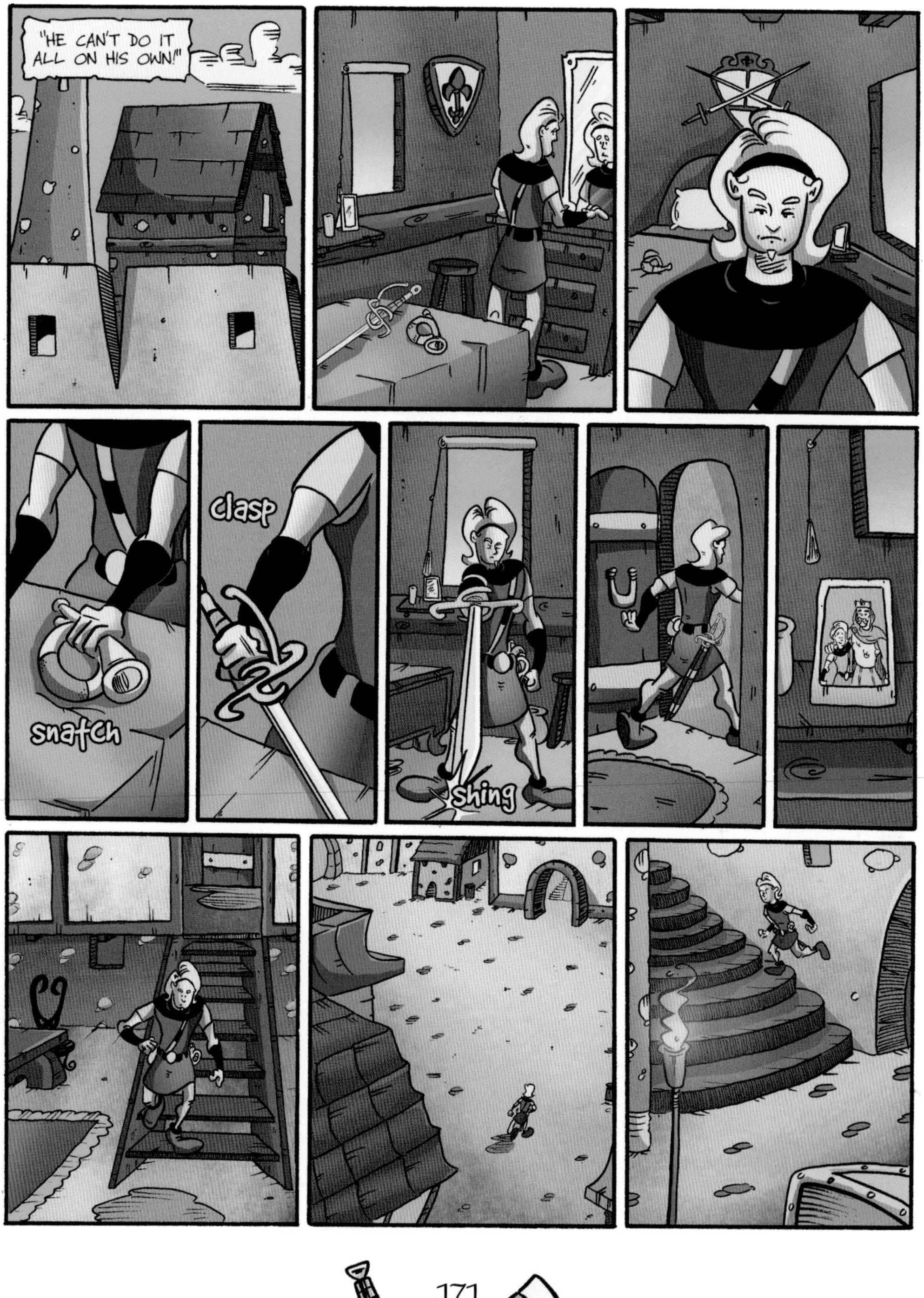
"HE CAN'T DO IT ALL ON HIS OWN!"
snatch
clasp
shing

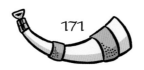

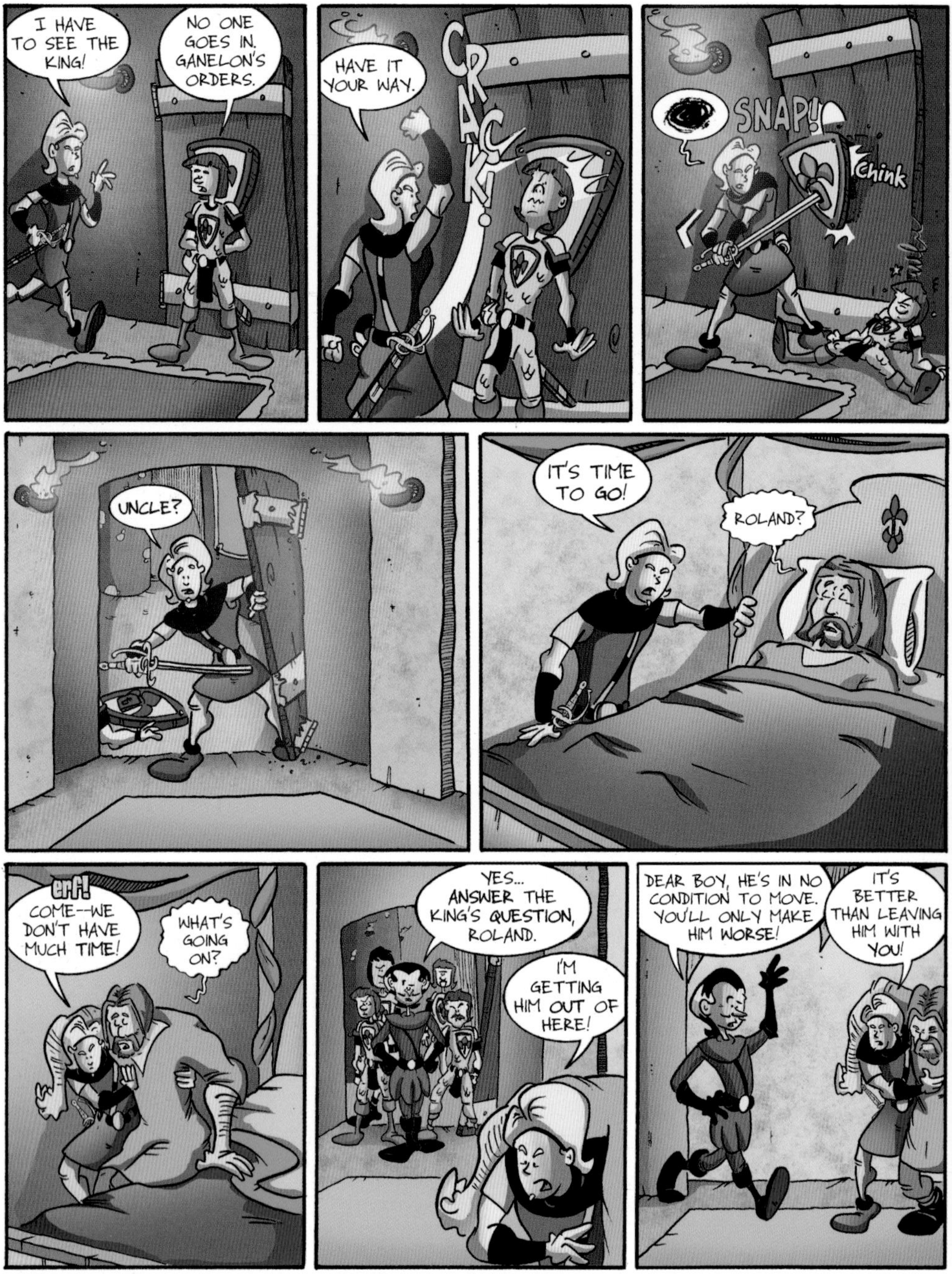
I HAVE TO SEE THE KING!
NO ONE GOES IN. GANELON'S ORDERS.
HAVE IT YOUR WAY.
CRACK
SNAP!
Chink
UNCLE?
IT'S TIME TO GO!
ROLAND?
erf!
COME--WE DON'T HAVE MUCH TIME!
WHAT'S GOING ON?
YES... ANSWER THE KING'S QUESTION, ROLAND.
I'M GETTING HIM OUT OF HERE!
DEAR BOY, HE'S IN NO CONDITION TO MOVE. YOU'LL ONLY MAKE HIM WORSE!
IT'S BETTER THAN LEAVING HIM WITH YOU!

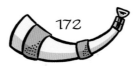

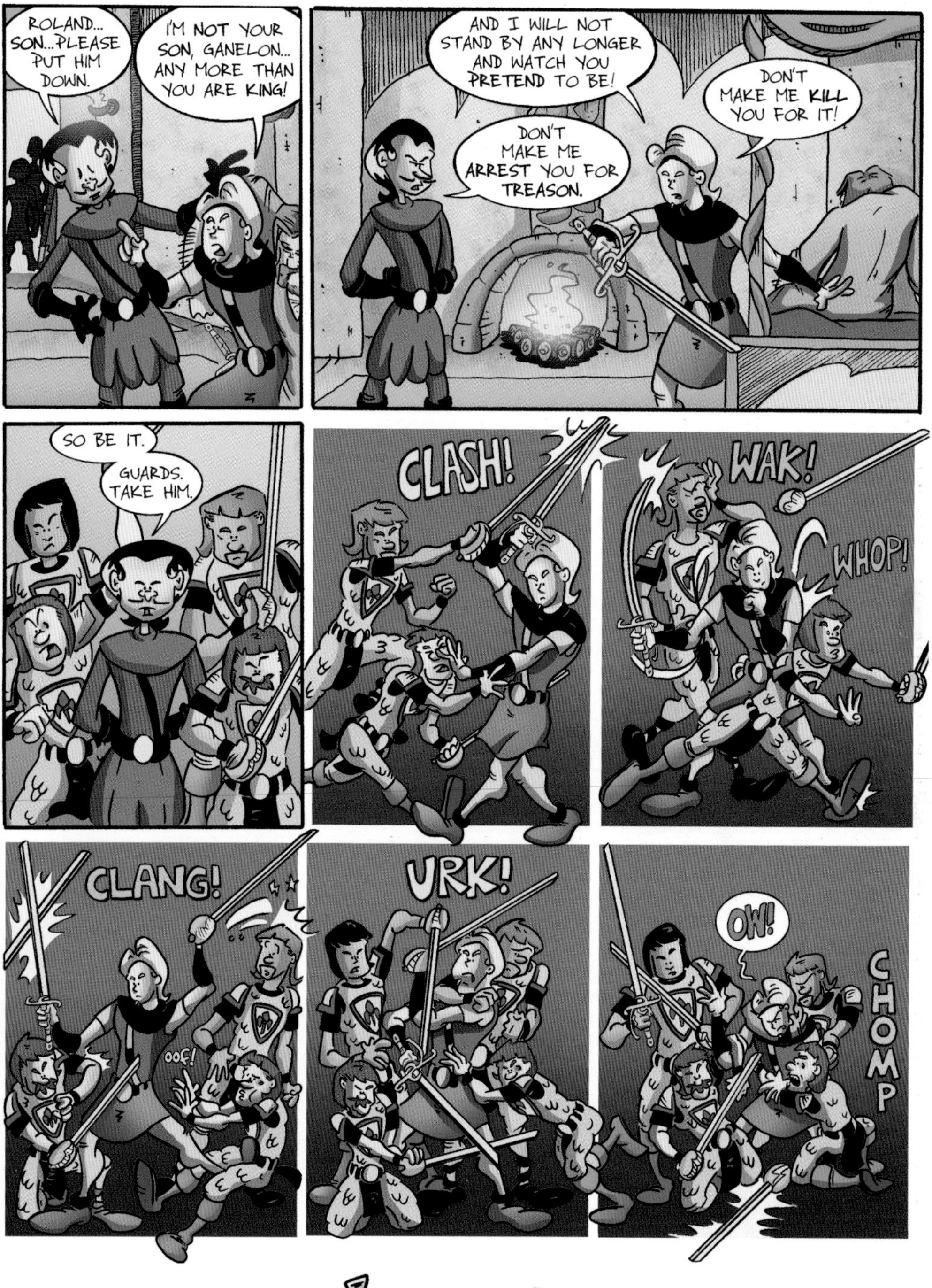
ROLAND... SON...PLEASE PUT HIM DOWN.
I'M NOT YOUR SON, GANELON... ANY MORE THAN YOU ARE KING!
AND I WILL NOT STAND BY ANY LONGER AND WATCH YOU PRETEND TO BE!
DON'T MAKE ME KILL YOU FOR IT!
DON'T MAKE ME ARREST YOU FOR TREASON.
SO BE IT.
GUARDS. TAKE HIM.
CLASH!
WAK!
WHOP!
CLANG!
OOF!
URK!
OW!
CHOMP

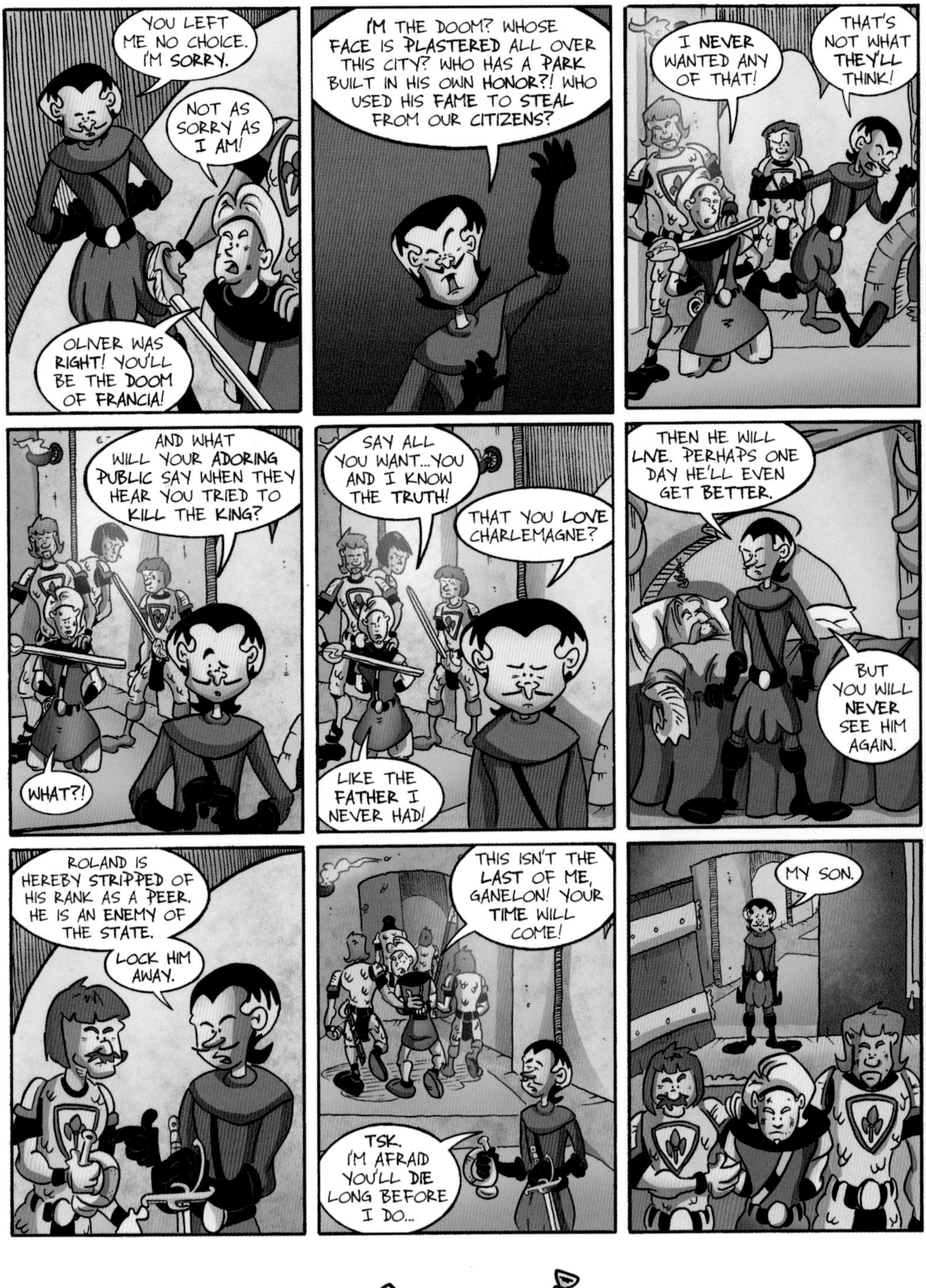
YOU LEFT ME NO CHOICE. I'M SORRY.
NOT AS SORRY AS I AM!
OLIVER WAS RIGHT! YOU'LL BE THE DOOM OF FRANCIA!
I'M THE DOOM? WHOSE FACE IS PLASTERED ALL OVER THIS CITY? WHO HAS A PARK BUILT IN HIS OWN HONOR?! WHO USED HIS FAME TO STEAL FROM OUR CITIZENS?
I NEVER WANTED ANY OF THAT!
THAT'S NOT WHAT THEY'LL THINK!
AND WHAT WILL YOUR ADORING PUBLIC SAY WHEN THEY HEAR YOU TRIED TO KILL THE KING?
WHAT?!
SAY ALL YOU WANT...YOU AND I KNOW THE TRUTH!
THAT YOU LOVE CHARLEMAGNE?
LIKE THE FATHER I NEVER HAD!
THEN HE WILL LIVE. PERHAPS ONE DAY HE'LL EVEN GET BETTER.
BUT YOU WILL NEVER SEE HIM AGAIN.
ROLAND IS HEREBY STRIPPED OF HIS RANK AS A PEER. HE IS AN ENEMY OF THE STATE.
LOCK HIM AWAY.
THIS ISN'T THE LAST OF ME, GANELON! YOUR TIME WILL COME!
TSK. I'M AFRAID YOU'LL DIE LONG BEFORE I DO...
MY SON.

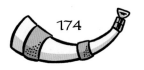

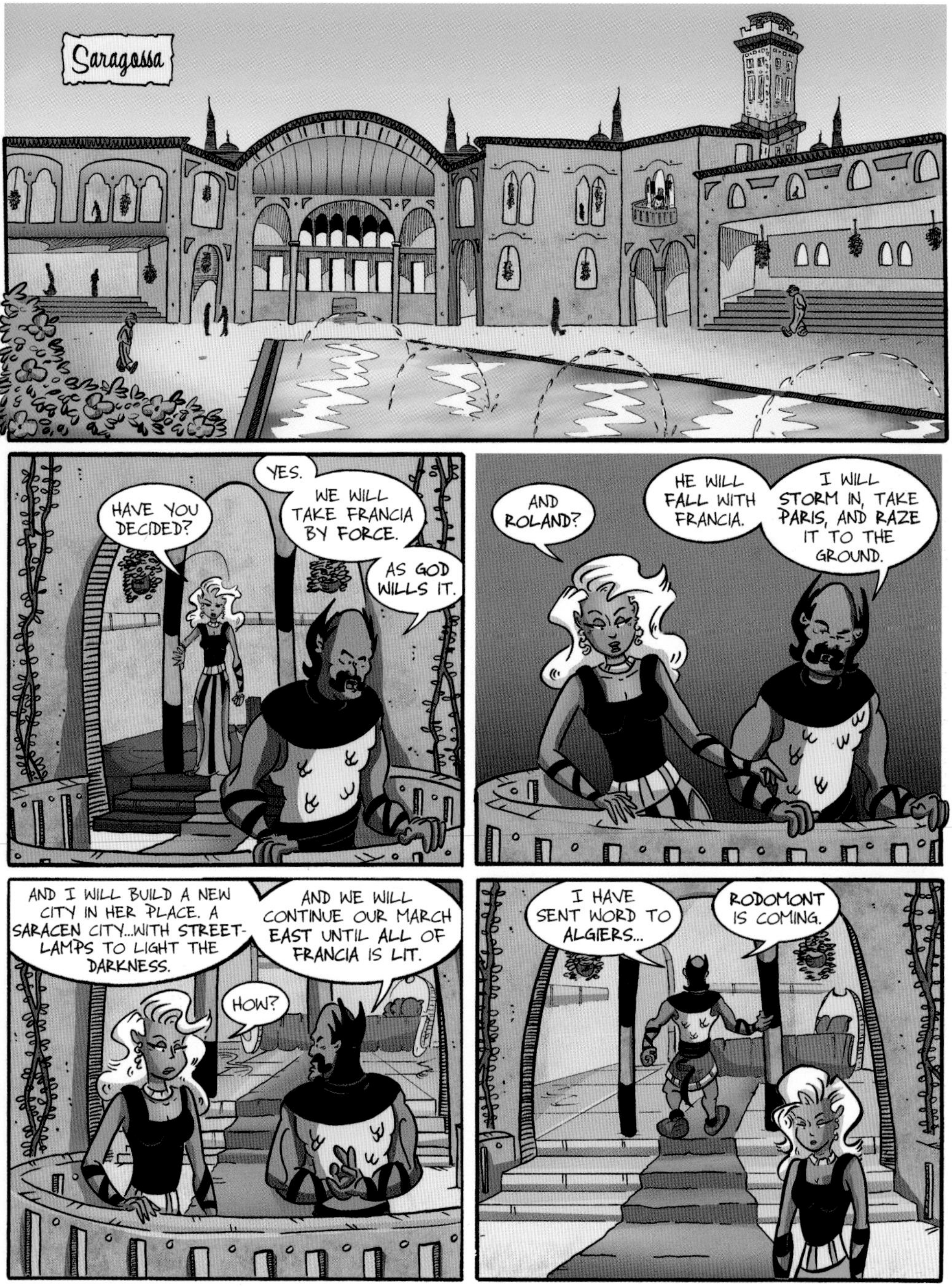
Saragossa
HAVE YOU DECIDED?
YES.
WE WILL TAKE FRANCIA BY FORCE.
AS GOD WILLS IT.
AND ROLAND?
HE WILL FALL WITH FRANCIA.
I WILL STORM IN, TAKE PARIS, AND RAZE IT TO THE GROUND.
AND I WILL BUILD A NEW CITY IN HER PLACE. A SARACEN CITY...WITH STREET-LAMPS TO LIGHT THE DARKNESS.
AND WE WILL CONTINUE OUR MARCH EAST UNTIL ALL OF FRANCIA IS LIT.
HOW?
I HAVE SENT WORD TO ALGIERS...
RODOMONT IS COMING.

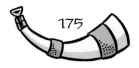

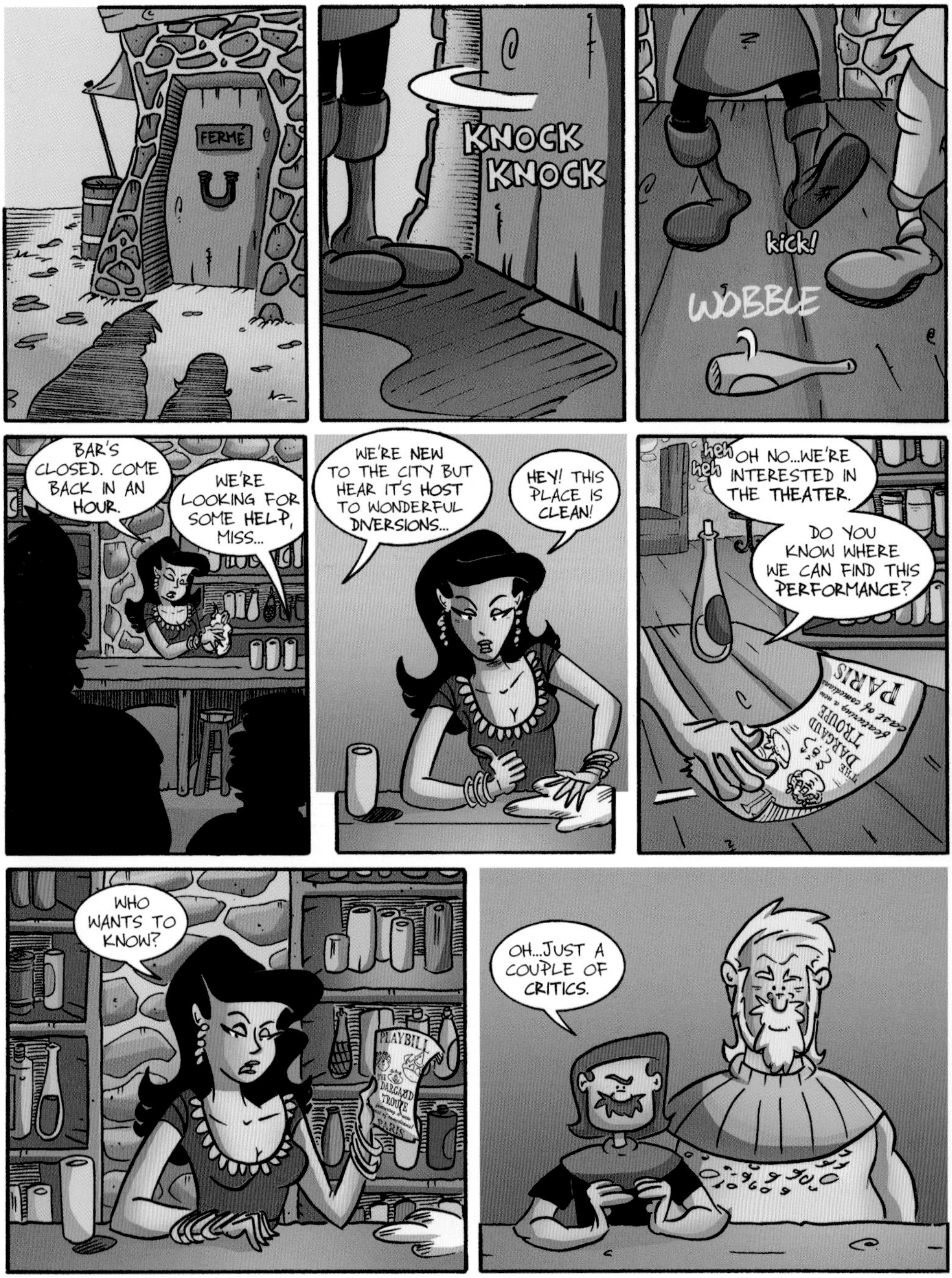
FERMÉ
KNOCK KNOCK
kick!
WOBBLE
BAR'S CLOSED. COME BACK IN AN HOUR.
WE'RE LOOKING FOR SOME HELP, MISS...
WE'RE NEW TO THE CITY BUT HEAR IT'S HOST TO WONDERFUL DIVERSIONS...
HEY! THIS PLACE IS CLEAN!
heh heh
OH NO...WE'RE INTERESTED IN THE THEATER.
DO YOU KNOW WHERE WE CAN FIND THIS PERFORMANCE?
THE DARGAUD TROUPE
PARIS
WHO WANTS TO KNOW?
PLAYBILL
OH...JUST A COUPLE OF CRITICS.

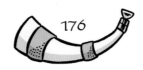

part four

for francia

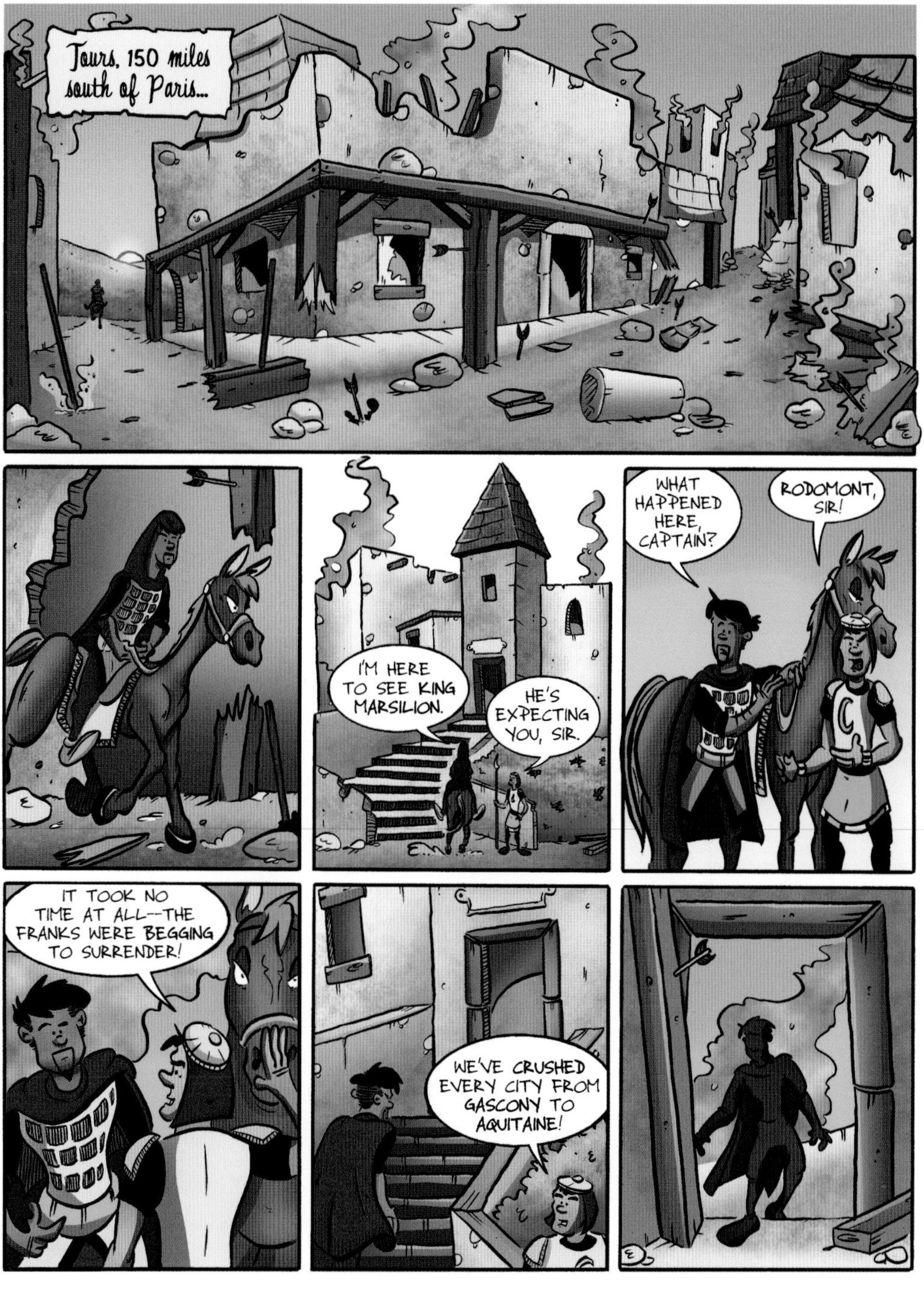

Tours, 150 miles south of Paris...
I'M HERE TO SEE KING MARSILION.
HE'S EXPECTING YOU, SIR.
WHAT HAPPENED HERE, CAPTAIN?
RODOMONT, SIR!
IT TOOK NO TIME AT ALL--THE FRANKS WERE BEGGING TO SURRENDER!
WE'VE CRUSHED EVERY CITY FROM GASCONY TO AQUITAINE!

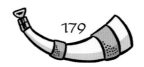

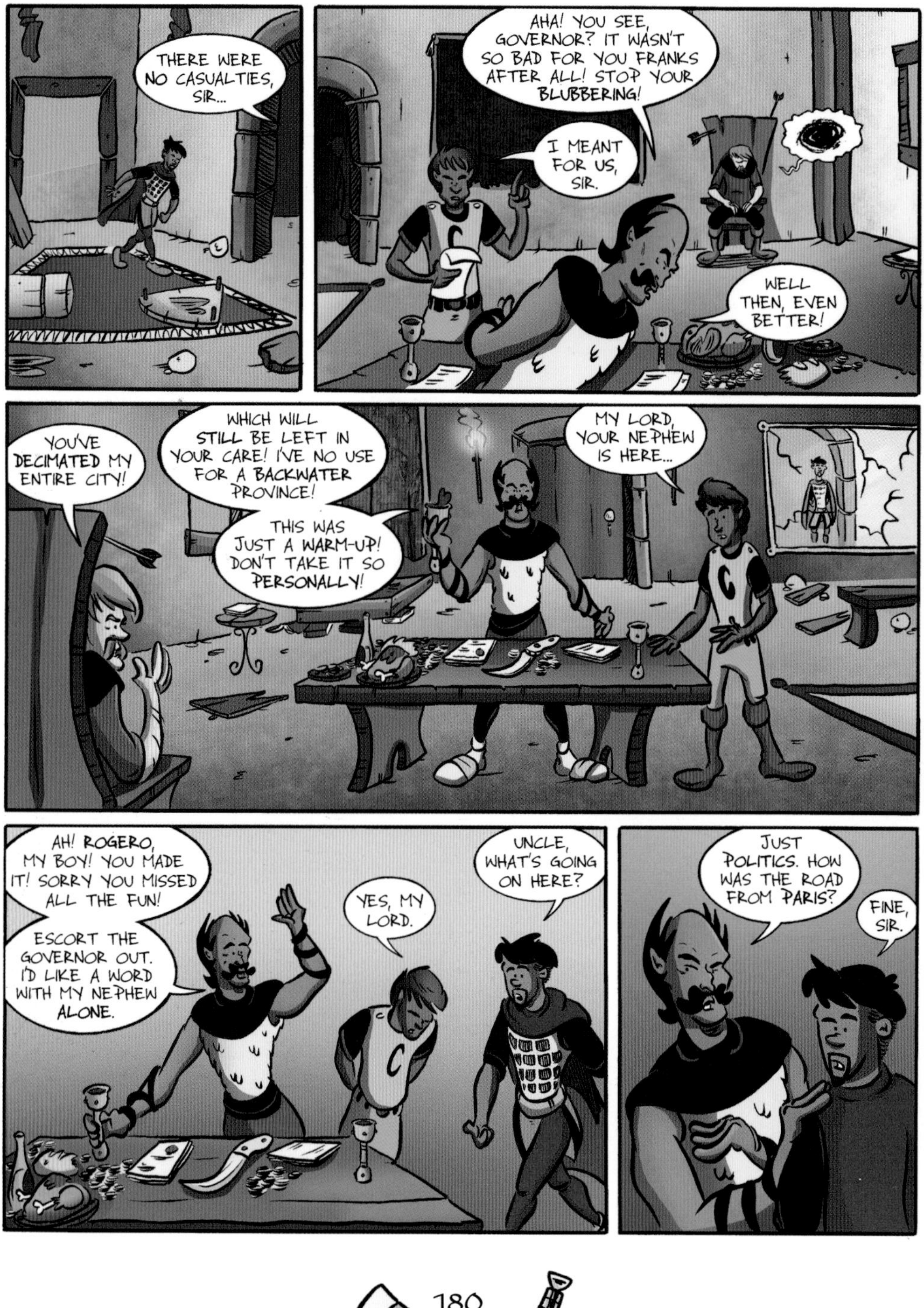
THERE WERE NO CASUALTIES, SIR...
AHA! YOU SEE, GOVERNOR? IT WASN'T SO BAD FOR YOU FRANKS AFTER ALL! STOP YOUR BLUBBERING!
I MEANT FOR US, SIR.
WELL THEN, EVEN BETTER!
YOU'VE DECIMATED MY ENTIRE CITY!
WHICH WILL STILL BE LEFT IN YOUR CARE! I'VE NO USE FOR A BACKWATER PROVINCE!
THIS WAS JUST A WARM-UP! DON'T TAKE IT SO PERSONALLY!
MY LORD, YOUR NEPHEW IS HERE...
AH! ROGERO, MY BOY! YOU MADE IT! SORRY YOU MISSED ALL THE FUN!
ESCORT THE GOVERNOR OUT. I'D LIKE A WORD WITH MY NEPHEW ALONE.
YES, MY LORD.
UNCLE, WHAT'S GOING ON HERE?
JUST POLITICS. HOW WAS THE ROAD FROM PARIS?
FINE, SIR.

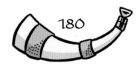

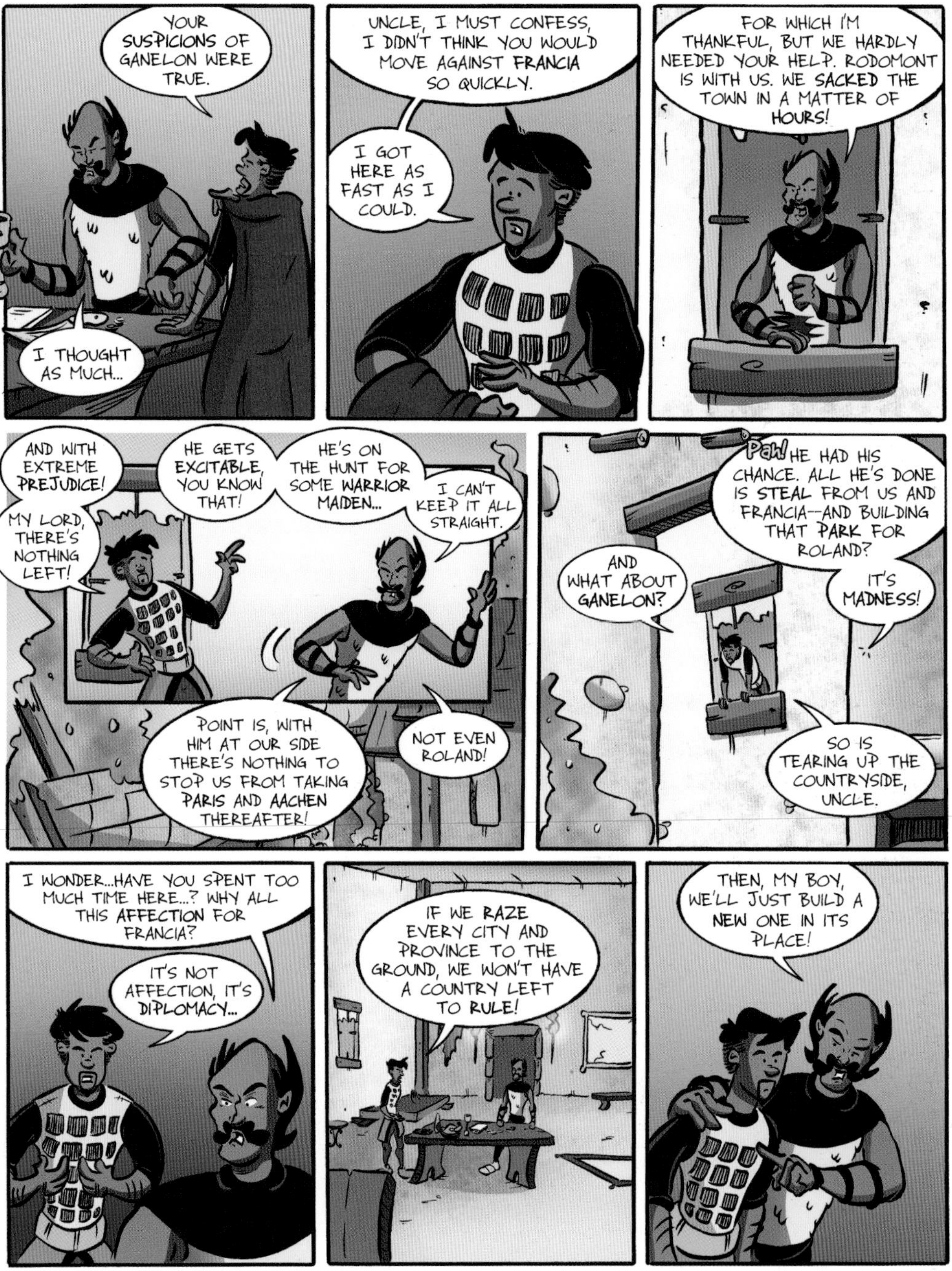
YOUR SUSPICIONS OF GANELON WERE TRUE.
I THOUGHT AS MUCH...
UNCLE, I MUST CONFESS, I DIDN'T THINK YOU WOULD MOVE AGAINST FRANCIA SO QUICKLY.
I GOT HERE AS FAST AS I COULD.
FOR WHICH I'M THANKFUL, BUT WE HARDLY NEEDED YOUR HELP. RODOMONT IS WITH US. WE SACKED THE TOWN IN A MATTER OF HOURS!
AND WITH EXTREME PREJUDICE!
MY LORD, THERE'S NOTHING LEFT!
HE GETS EXCITABLE, YOU KNOW THAT!
HE'S ON THE HUNT FOR SOME WARRIOR MAIDEN...
I CAN'T KEEP IT ALL STRAIGHT.
POINT IS, WITH HIM AT OUR SIDE THERE'S NOTHING TO STOP US FROM TAKING PARIS AND AACHEN THEREAFTER!
NOT EVEN ROLAND!
AND WHAT ABOUT GANELON?
PAH! HE HAD HIS CHANCE. ALL HE'S DONE IS STEAL FROM US AND FRANCIA--AND BUILDING THAT PARK FOR ROLAND?
IT'S MADNESS!
SO IS TEARING UP THE COUNTRYSIDE, UNCLE.
I WONDER...HAVE YOU SPENT TOO MUCH TIME HERE...? WHY ALL THIS AFFECTION FOR FRANCIA?
IT'S NOT AFFECTION, IT'S DIPLOMACY...
IF WE RAZE EVERY CITY AND PROVINCE TO THE GROUND, WE WON'T HAVE A COUNTRY LEFT TO RULE!
THEN, MY BOY, WE'LL JUST BUILD A NEW ONE IN ITS PLACE!

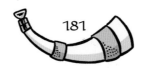

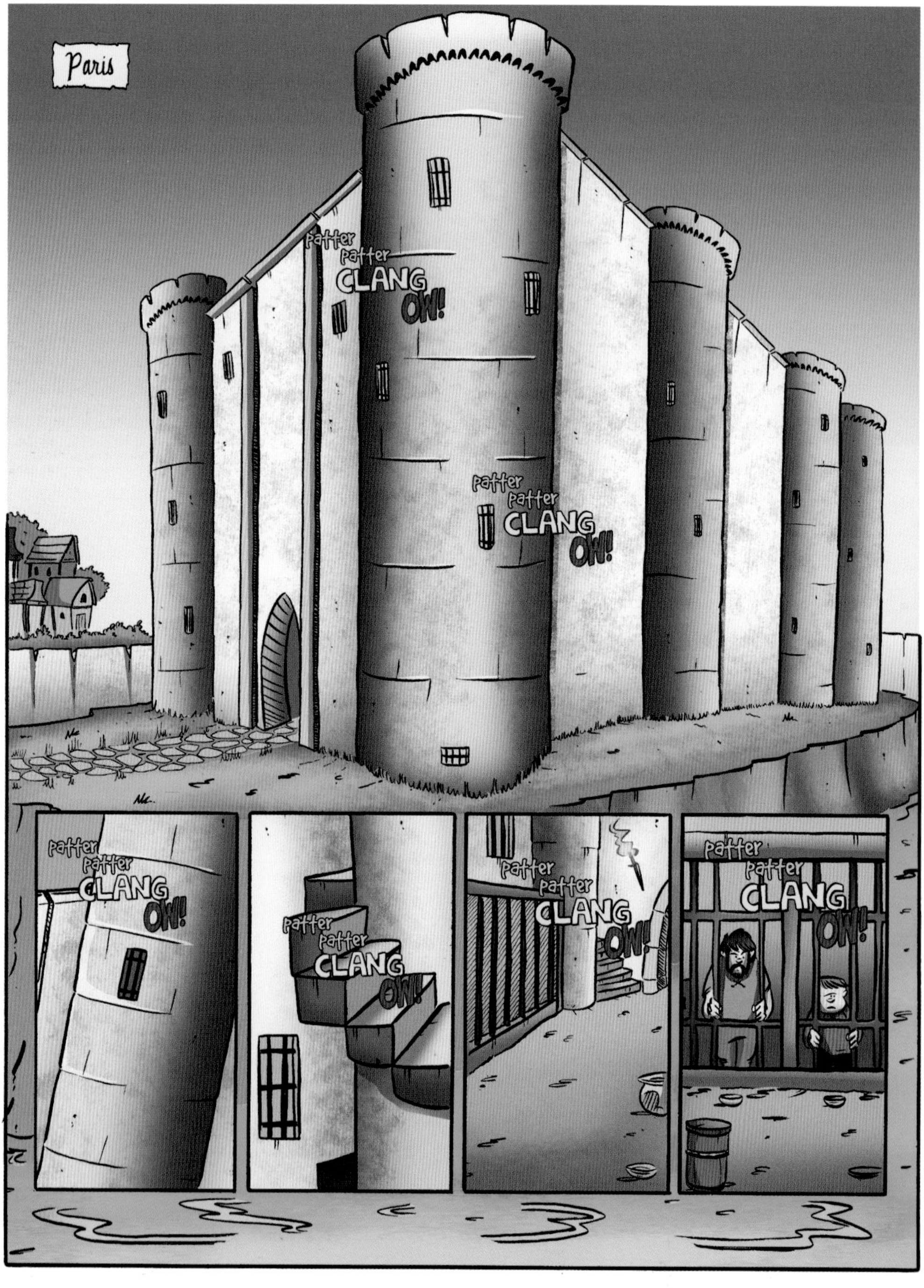
Paris
patter
patter
CLANG
OW!
patter
patter
CLANG
OW!
patter
patter
CLANG
OW!
patter
patter
CLANG
OW!
patter
patter
CLANG
OW!
patter
patter
CLANG
OW!

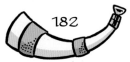

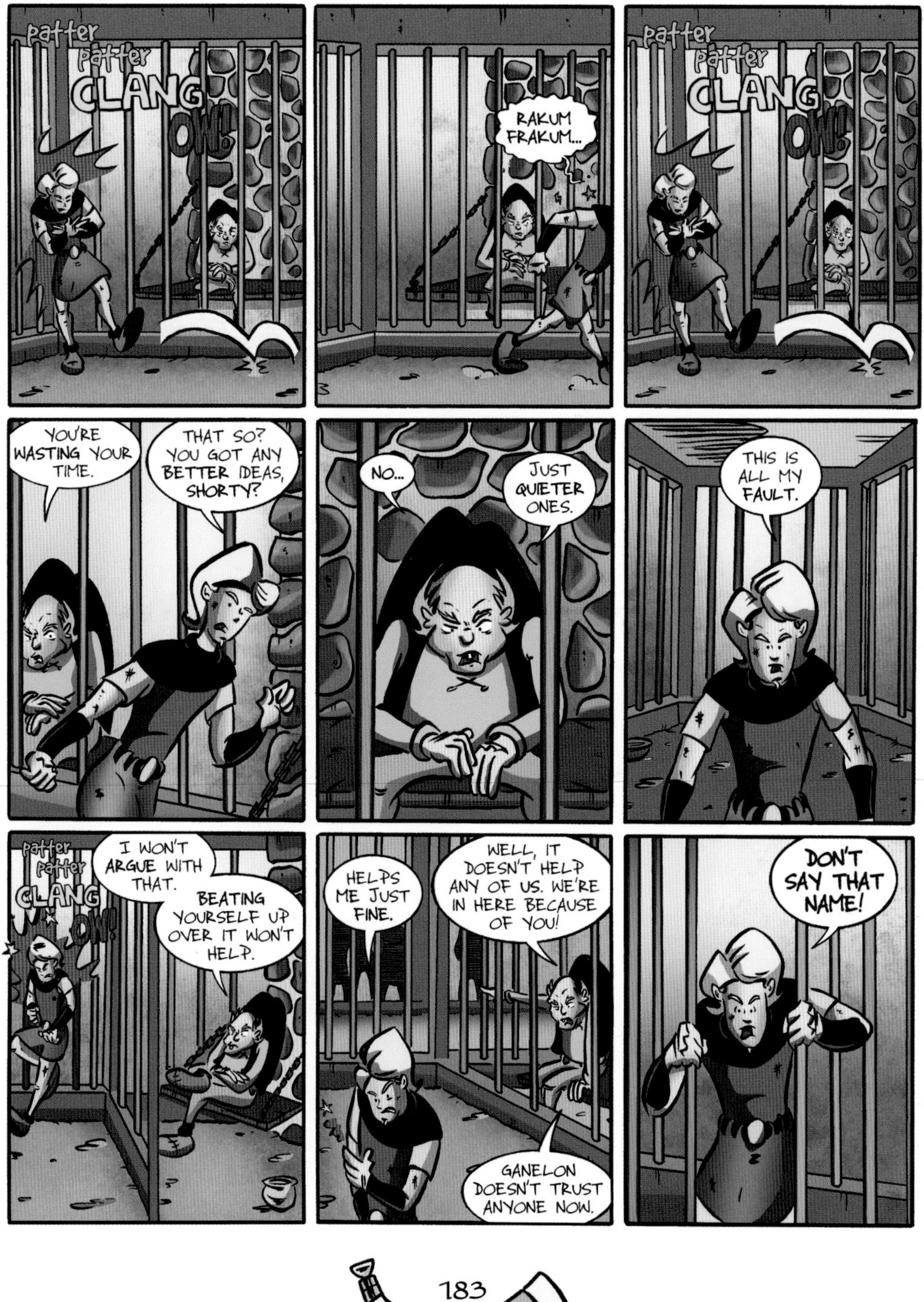
patter
patter
CLANG
OW!
RAKUM FRAKUM...
patter
patter
CLANG
OW!
YOU'RE WASTING YOUR TIME.
THAT SO? YOU GOT ANY BETTER IDEAS, SHORTY?
NO...
JUST QUIETER ONES.
THIS IS ALL MY FAULT.
patter
patter
CLANG
OW!
I WON'T ARGUE WITH THAT.
BEATING YOURSELF UP OVER IT WON'T HELP.
HELPS ME JUST FINE.
WELL, IT DOESN'T HELP ANY OF US. WE'RE IN HERE BECAUSE OF YOU!
GANELON DOESN'T TRUST ANYONE NOW.
DON'T SAY THAT NAME!

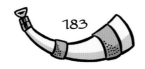

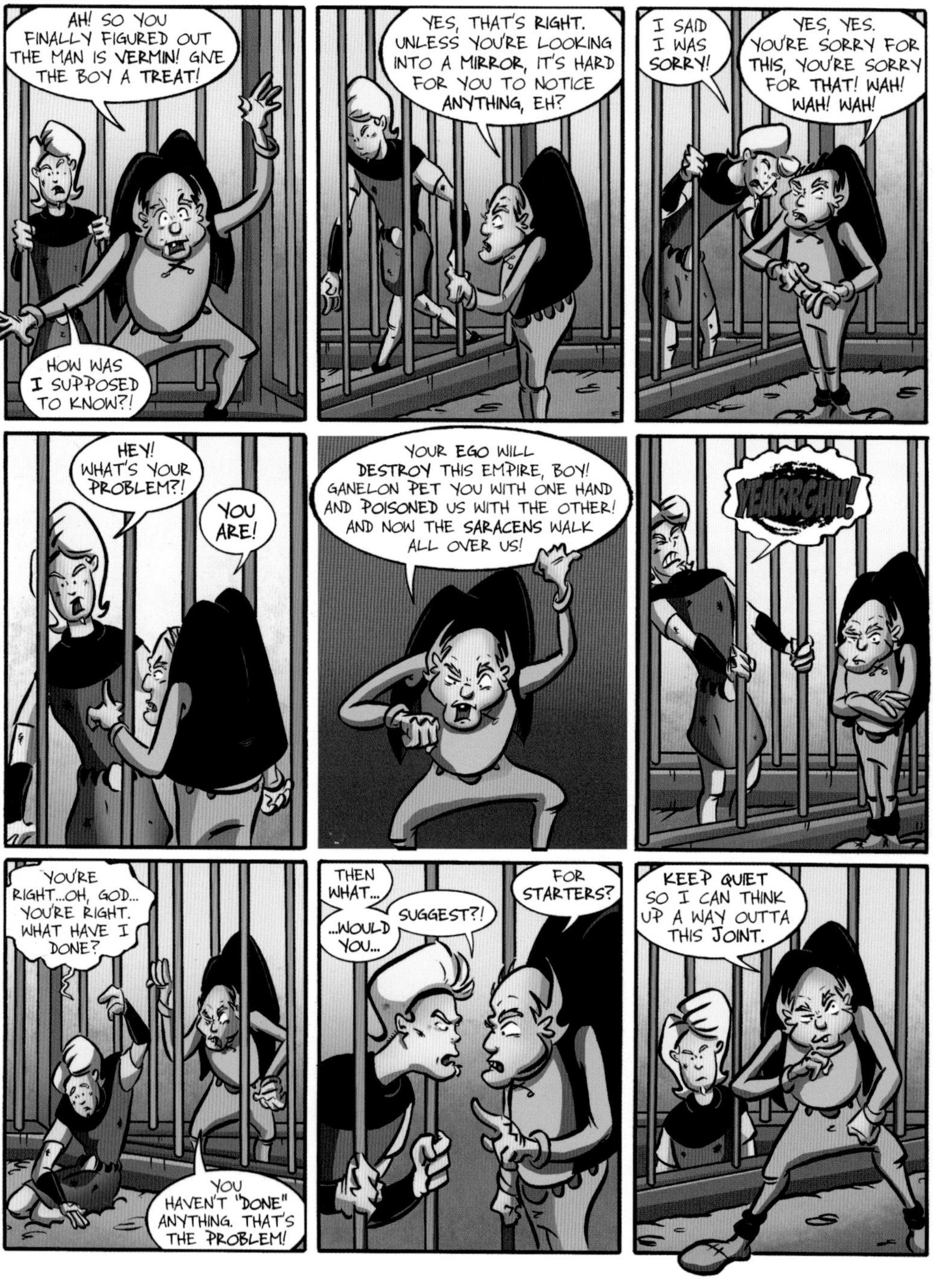
AH! SO YOU FINALLY FIGURED OUT THE MAN IS VERMIN! GIVE THE BOY A TREAT!
HOW WAS I SUPPOSED TO KNOW?!
YES, THAT'S RIGHT. UNLESS YOU'RE LOOKING INTO A MIRROR, IT'S HARD FOR YOU TO NOTICE ANYTHING, EH?
I SAID I WAS SORRY!
YES, YES. YOU'RE SORRY FOR THIS, YOU'RE SORRY FOR THAT! WAH! WAH! WAH!
HEY! WHAT'S YOUR PROBLEM?!
YOU ARE!
YOUR EGO WILL DESTROY THIS EMPIRE, BOY! GANELON PET YOU WITH ONE HAND AND POISONED US WITH THE OTHER! AND NOW THE SARACENS WALK ALL OVER US!
YEARRGHH!
YOU'RE RIGHT...OH, GOD... YOU'RE RIGHT. WHAT HAVE I DONE?
YOU HAVEN'T "DONE" ANYTHING. THAT'S THE PROBLEM!
THEN WHAT...
...WOULD YOU...
SUGGEST?!
FOR STARTERS?
KEEP QUIET SO I CAN THINK UP A WAY OUTTA THIS JOINT.

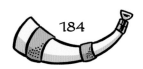

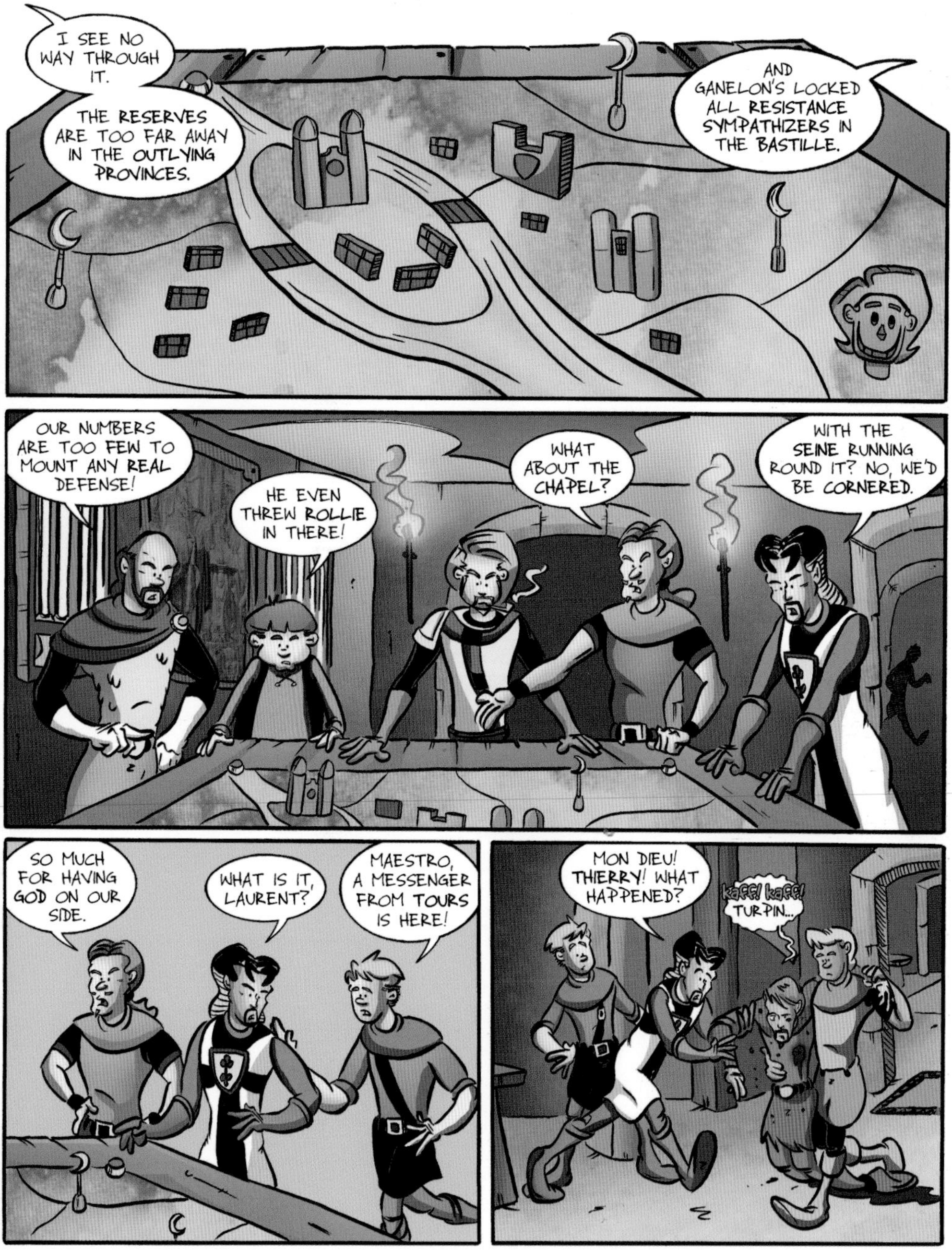
I SEE NO WAY THROUGH IT.
THE RESERVES ARE TOO FAR AWAY IN THE OUTLYING PROVINCES.
AND GANELON'S LOCKED ALL RESISTANCE SYMPATHIZERS IN THE BASTILLE.
OUR NUMBERS ARE TOO FEW TO MOUNT ANY REAL DEFENSE!
HE EVEN THREW ROLLIE IN THERE!
WHAT ABOUT THE CHAPEL?
WITH THE SEINE RUNNING ROUND IT? NO, WE'D BE CORNERED.
SO MUCH FOR HAVING GOD ON OUR SIDE.
WHAT IS IT, LAURENT?
MAESTRO, A MESSENGER FROM TOURS IS HERE!
MON DIEU! THIERRY! WHAT HAPPENED?
kaff! kaff!
TURPIN...

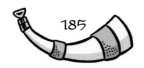

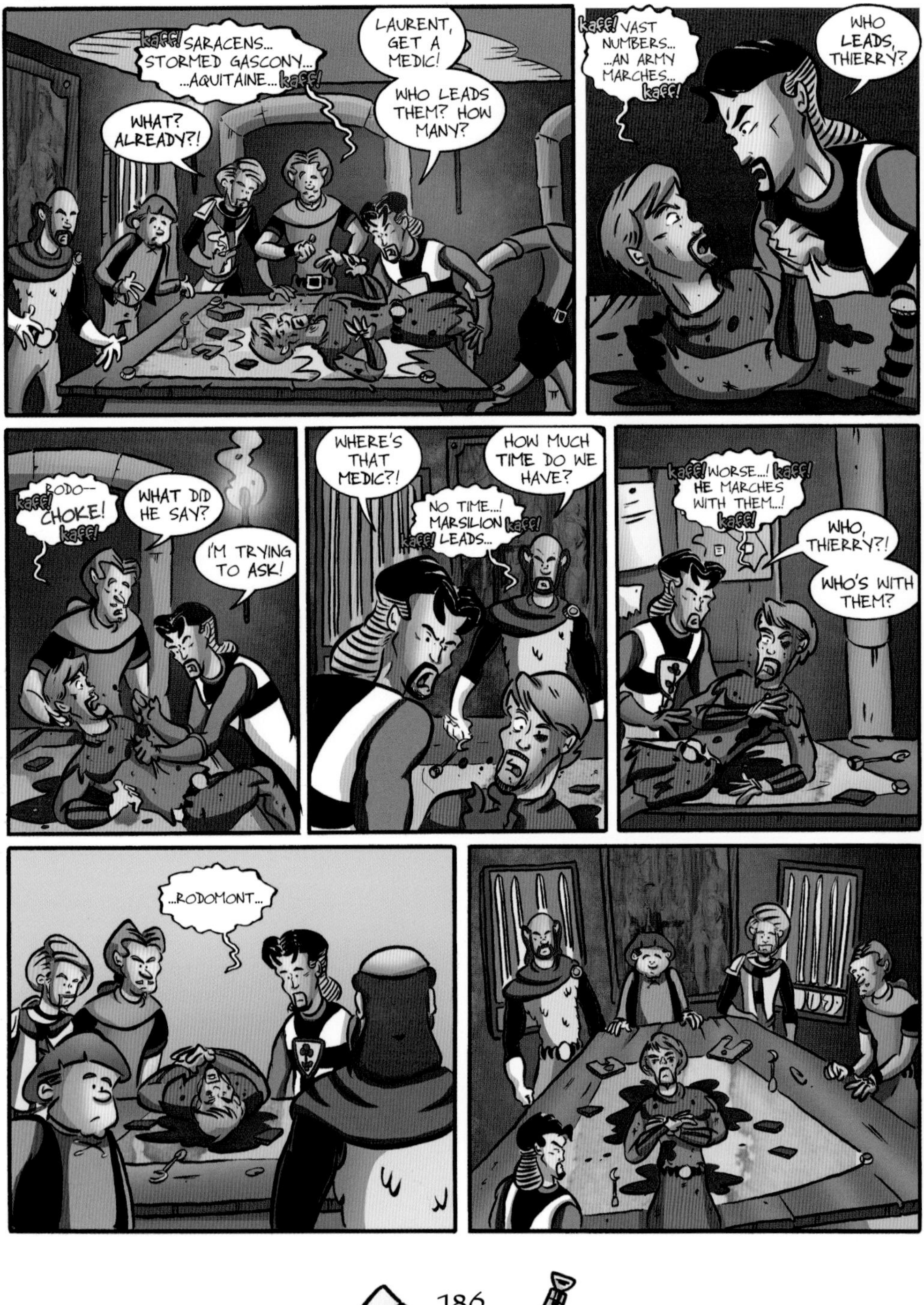
kaff! SARACENS... STORMED GASCONY... ...AQUITAINE... kaff!
LAURENT, GET A MEDIC!
WHAT? ALREADY?!
WHO LEADS THEM? HOW MANY?
kaff! VAST NUMBERS... ...AN ARMY MARCHES... kaff!
WHO LEADS, THIERRY?
RODO-- kaff! CHOKE! kaff!
WHAT DID HE SAY?
I'M TRYING TO ASK!
WHERE'S THAT MEDIC?!
HOW MUCH TIME DO WE HAVE?
NO TIME...! MARSILION kaff! kaff! LEADS...
kaff! WORSE...! kaff! HE MARCHES WITH THEM...! kaff!
WHO, THIERRY?!
WHO'S WITH THEM?
...RODOMONT...

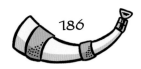

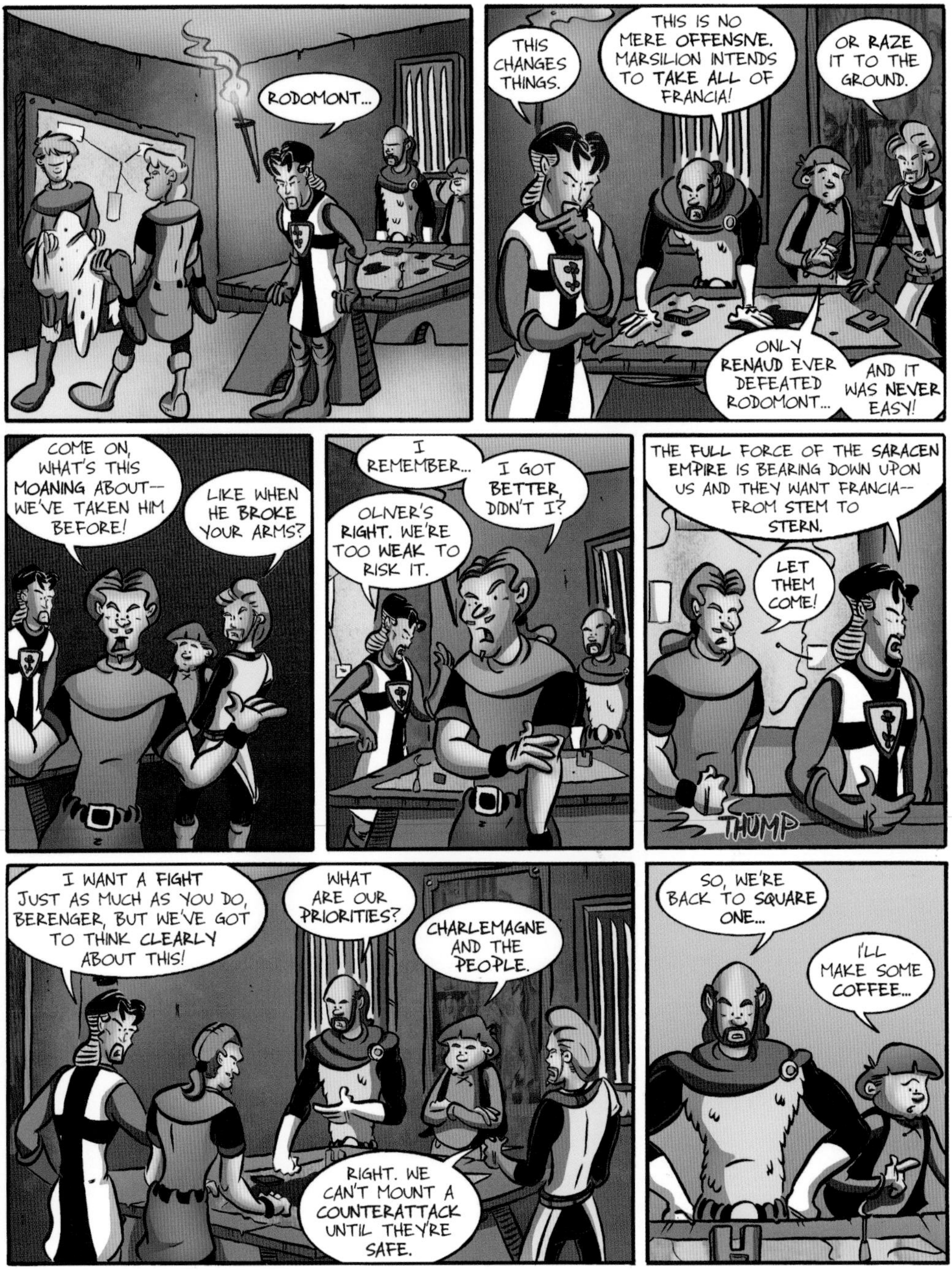
RODOMONT...
THIS CHANGES THINGS.
THIS IS NO MERE OFFENSIVE. MARSILION INTENDS TO TAKE ALL OF FRANCIA!
OR RAZE IT TO THE GROUND.
ONLY RENAUD EVER DEFEATED RODOMONT...
AND IT WAS NEVER EASY!
COME ON, WHAT'S THIS MOANING ABOUT-- WE'VE TAKEN HIM BEFORE!
LIKE WHEN HE BROKE YOUR ARMS?
I REMEMBER...
I GOT BETTER, DIDN'T I?
OLIVER'S RIGHT. WE'RE TOO WEAK TO RISK IT.
THE FULL FORCE OF THE SARACEN EMPIRE IS BEARING DOWN UPON US AND THEY WANT FRANCIA-- FROM STEM TO STERN.
LET THEM COME!
THUMP
I WANT A FIGHT JUST AS MUCH AS YOU DO, BERENGER, BUT WE'VE GOT TO THINK CLEARLY ABOUT THIS!
WHAT ARE OUR PRIORITIES?
CHARLEMAGNE AND THE PEOPLE.
RIGHT. WE CAN'T MOUNT A COUNTERATTACK UNTIL THEY'RE SAFE.
SO, WE'RE BACK TO SQUARE ONE...
I'LL MAKE SOME COFFEE...

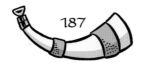

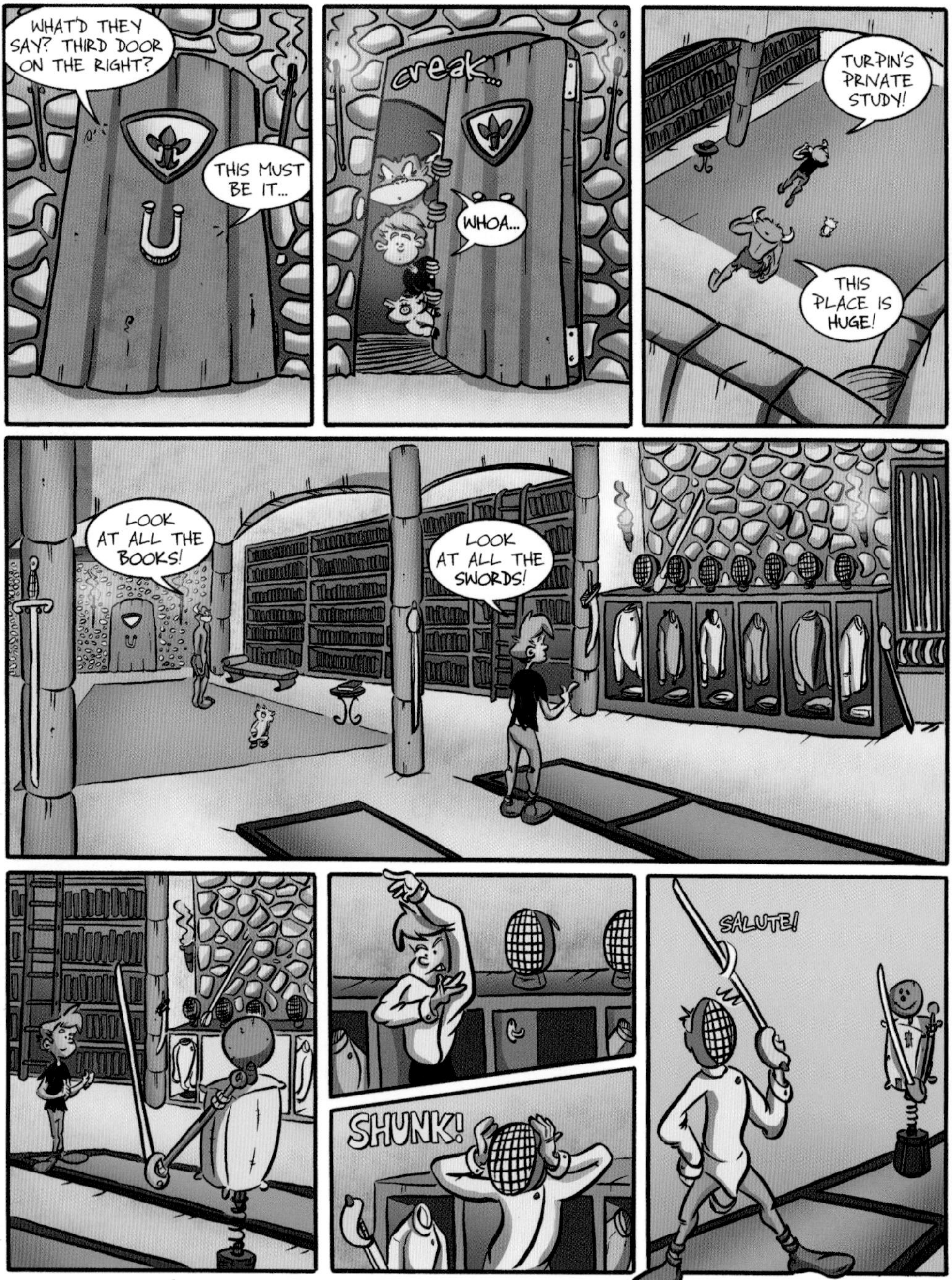
WHAT'D THEY SAY? THIRD DOOR ON THE RIGHT?
THIS MUST BE IT...
creak...
WHOA...
TURPIN'S PRIVATE STUDY!
THIS PLACE IS HUGE!
LOOK AT ALL THE BOOKS!
LOOK AT ALL THE SWORDS!
SHUNK!
SALUTE!

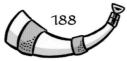

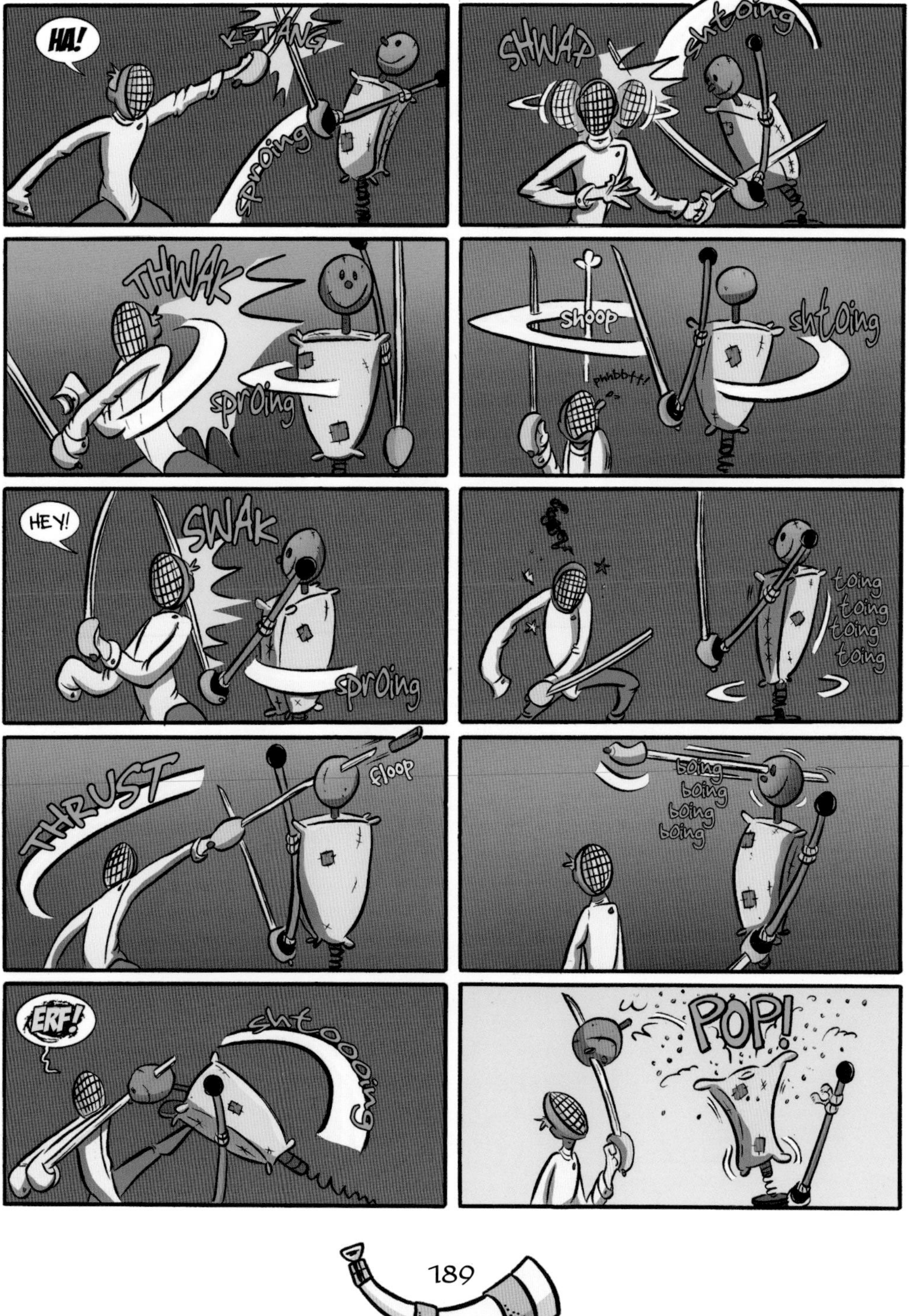
HA!
K-TANG
sproing
SHWAP
shtoing
THWAK
sprOing
shoop
shtOing
phhbbtt!
HEY!
SWAK
sprOing
toing
toing
toing
toing
THRUST
floop
boing
boing
boing
boing
ERF!
shtoooooing
POP!

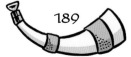

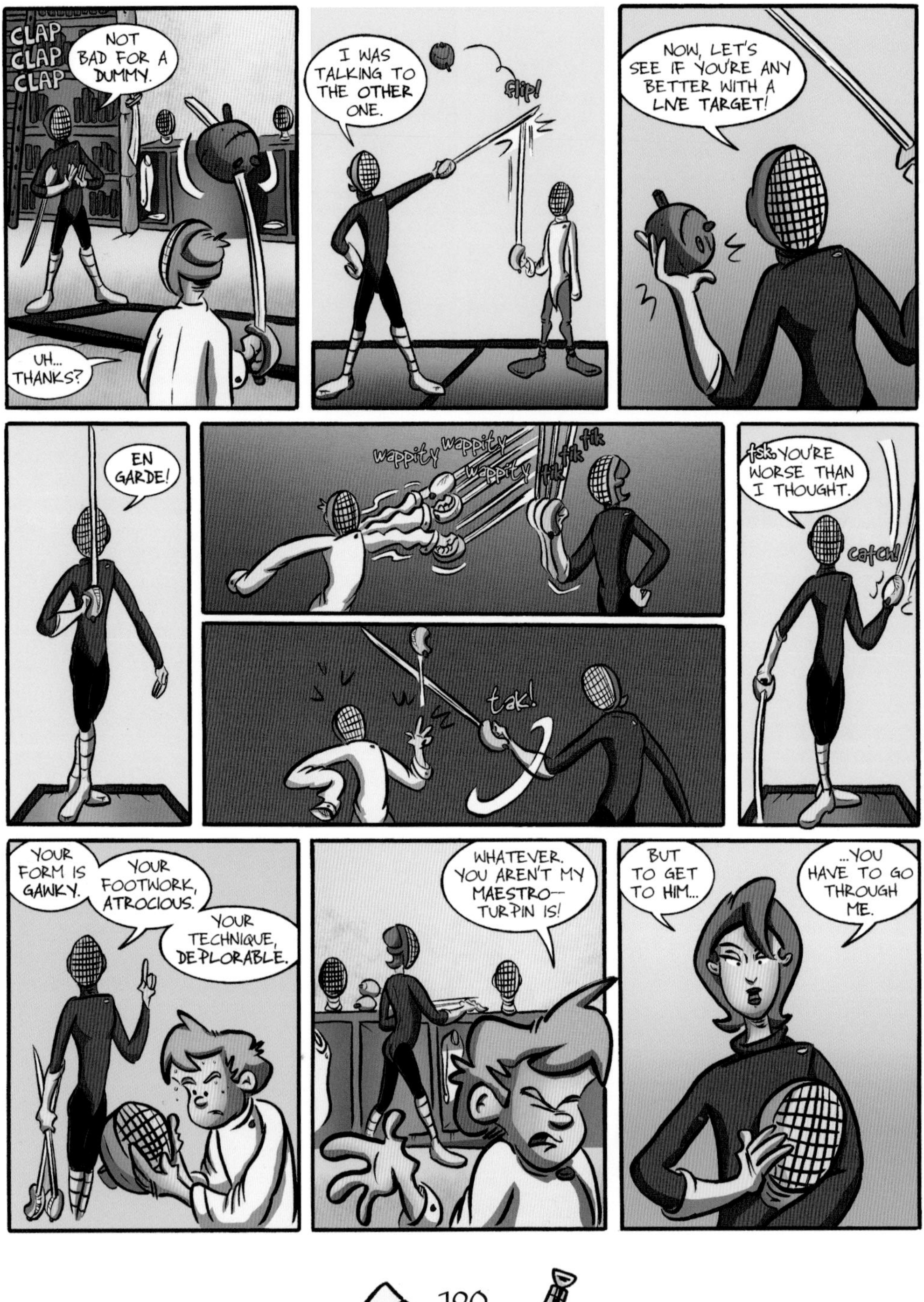
CLAP
CLAP
CLAP
NOT BAD FOR A DUMMY.
UH... THANKS?
I WAS TALKING TO THE OTHER ONE.
flip!
NOW, LET'S SEE IF YOU'RE ANY BETTER WITH A LIVE TARGET!
EN GARDE!
wappity wappity wappity
tik tik tik
tak!
fsk. YOU'RE WORSE THAN I THOUGHT.
catch!
YOUR FORM IS GAWKY.
YOUR FOOTWORK, ATROCIOUS.
YOUR TECHNIQUE, DEPLORABLE.
WHATEVER. YOU AREN'T MY MAESTRO-- TURPIN IS!
BUT TO GET TO HIM...
...YOU HAVE TO GO THROUGH ME.

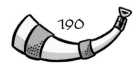

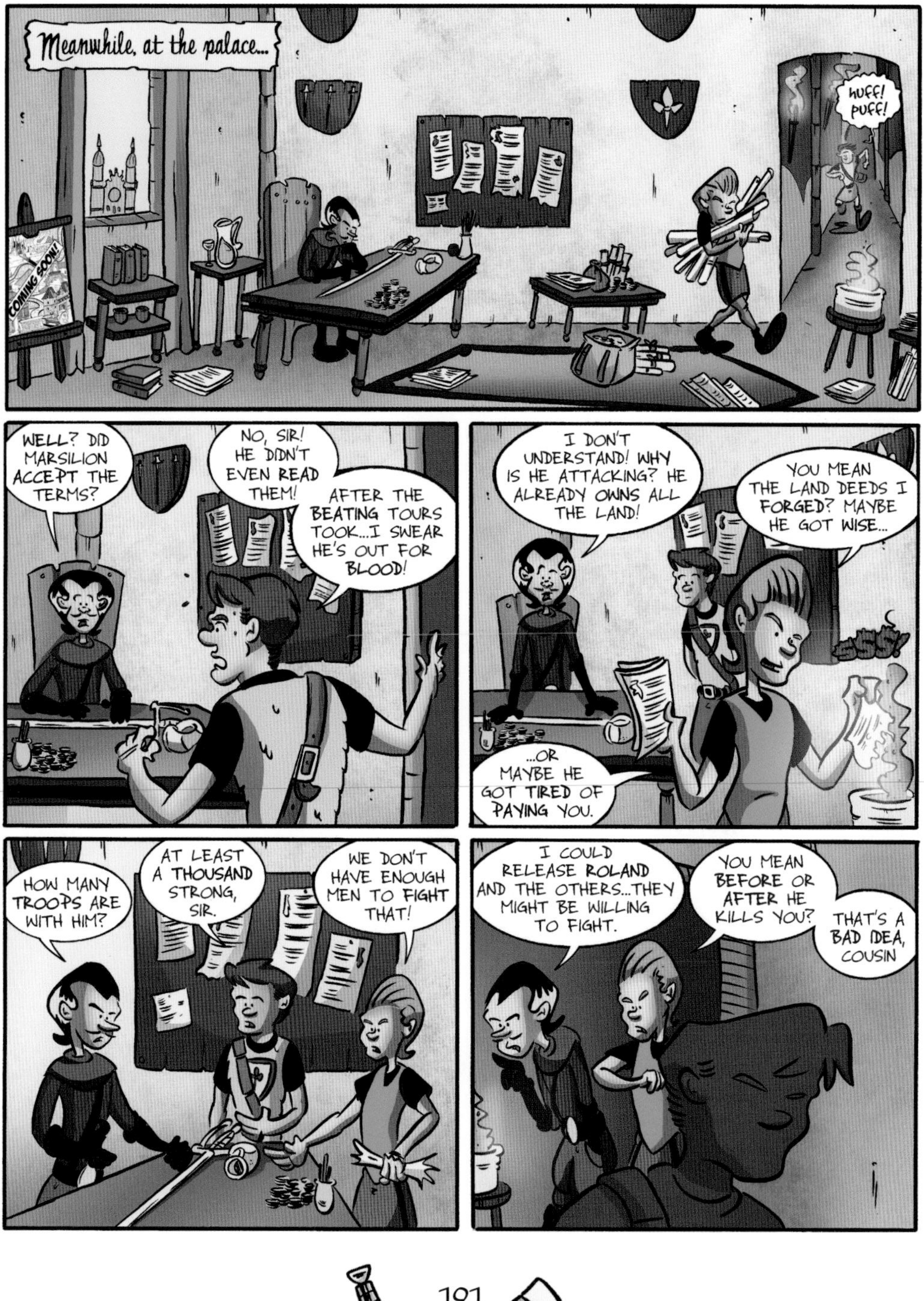
Meanwhile, at the palace...
COMING SOON!
HUFF! PUFF!
WELL? DID MARSILION ACCEPT THE TERMS?
NO, SIR! HE DIDN'T EVEN READ THEM!
AFTER THE BEATING TOURS TOOK...I SWEAR HE'S OUT FOR BLOOD!
I DON'T UNDERSTAND! WHY IS HE ATTACKING? HE ALREADY OWNS ALL THE LAND!
YOU MEAN THE LAND DEEDS I FORGED? MAYBE HE GOT WISE...
...OR MAYBE HE GOT TIRED OF PAYING YOU.
HOW MANY TROOPS ARE WITH HIM?
AT LEAST A THOUSAND STRONG, SIR.
WE DON'T HAVE ENOUGH MEN TO FIGHT THAT!
I COULD RELEASE ROLAND AND THE OTHERS...THEY MIGHT BE WILLING TO FIGHT.
YOU MEAN BEFORE OR AFTER HE KILLS YOU?
THAT'S A BAD IDEA, COUSIN

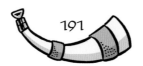

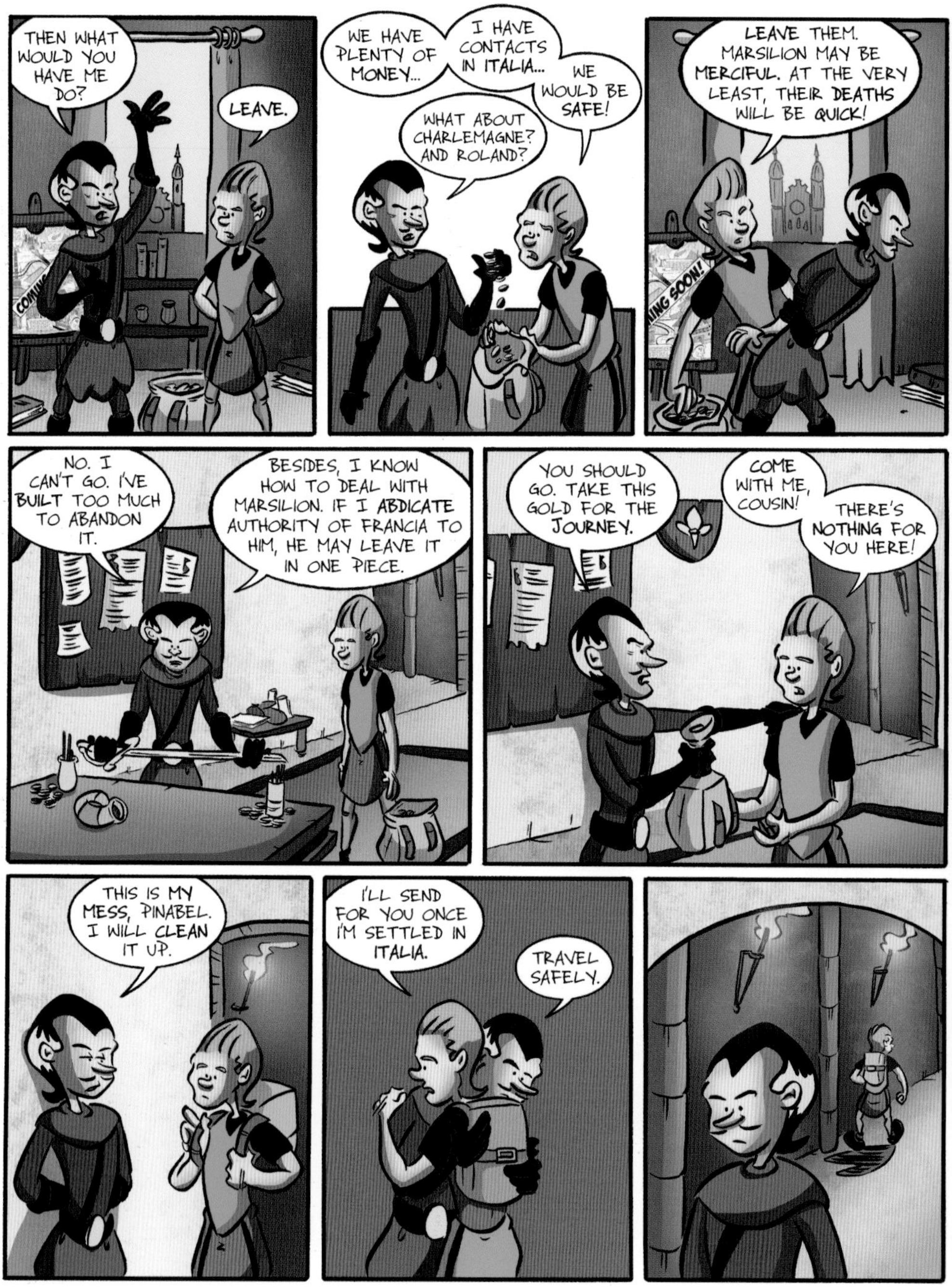
THEN WHAT WOULD YOU HAVE ME DO?
LEAVE.
COMING
WE HAVE PLENTY OF MONEY...
I HAVE CONTACTS IN ITALIA...
WE WOULD BE SAFE!
WHAT ABOUT CHARLEMAGNE? AND ROLAND?
LEAVE THEM. MARSILION MAY BE MERCIFUL. AT THE VERY LEAST, THEIR DEATHS WILL BE QUICK!
ING SOON!
NO. I CAN'T GO. I'VE BUILT TOO MUCH TO ABANDON IT.
BESIDES, I KNOW HOW TO DEAL WITH MARSILION. IF I ABDICATE AUTHORITY OF FRANCIA TO HIM, HE MAY LEAVE IT IN ONE PIECE.
YOU SHOULD GO. TAKE THIS GOLD FOR THE JOURNEY.
COME WITH ME, COUSIN!
THERE'S NOTHING FOR YOU HERE!
THIS IS MY MESS, PINABEL. I WILL CLEAN IT UP.
I'LL SEND FOR YOU ONCE I'M SETTLED IN ITALIA.
TRAVEL SAFELY.

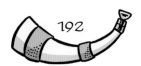

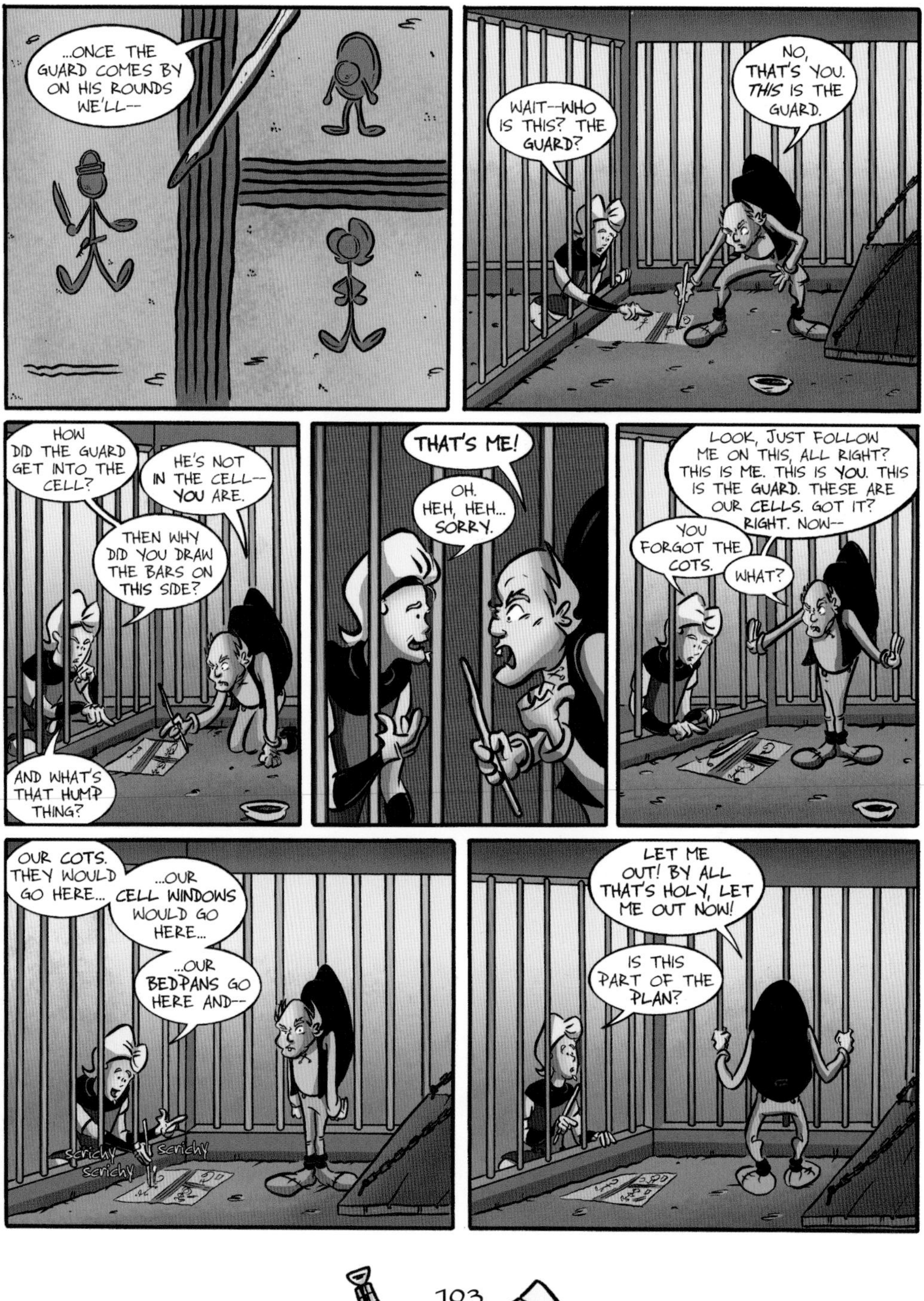
...ONCE THE GUARD COMES BY ON HIS ROUNDS WE'LL--
WAIT--WHO IS THIS? THE GUARD?
NO, THAT'S YOU. THIS IS THE GUARD.
HOW DID THE GUARD GET INTO THE CELL?
HE'S NOT IN THE CELL-- YOU ARE.
THEN WHY DID YOU DRAW THE BARS ON THIS SIDE?
AND WHAT'S THAT HUMP THING?
THAT'S ME!
OH. HEH, HEH... SORRY.
LOOK, JUST FOLLOW ME ON THIS, ALL RIGHT? THIS IS ME. THIS IS YOU. THIS IS THE GUARD. THESE ARE OUR CELLS. GOT IT? RIGHT. NOW--
YOU FORGOT THE COTS.
WHAT?
OUR COTS. THEY WOULD GO HERE...
...OUR CELL WINDOWS WOULD GO HERE...
...OUR BEDPANS GO HERE AND--
scrichy scrichy scrichy
LET ME OUT! BY ALL THAT'S HOLY, LET ME OUT NOW!
IS THIS PART OF THE PLAN?

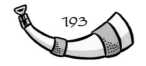

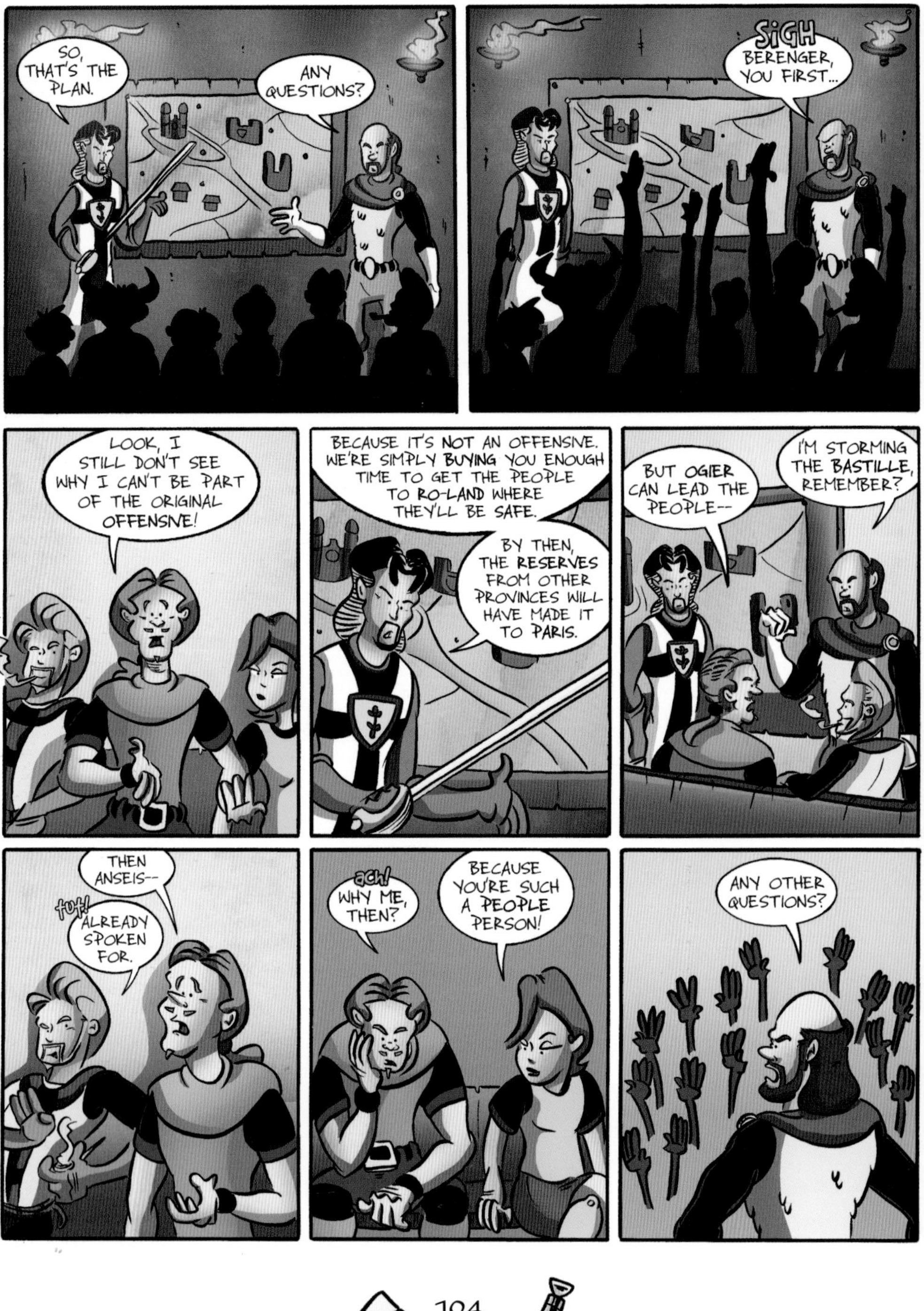
SO, THAT'S THE PLAN.
ANY QUESTIONS?
SIGH
BERENGER, YOU FIRST...
LOOK, I STILL DON'T SEE WHY I CAN'T BE PART OF THE ORIGINAL OFFENSIVE!
BECAUSE IT'S NOT AN OFFENSIVE. WE'RE SIMPLY BUYING YOU ENOUGH TIME TO GET THE PEOPLE TO RO-LAND WHERE THEY'LL BE SAFE.
BY THEN, THE RESERVES FROM OTHER PROVINCES WILL HAVE MADE IT TO PARIS.
BUT OGIER CAN LEAD THE PEOPLE--
I'M STORMING THE BASTILLE, REMEMBER?
THEN ANSEIS--
TUT!
ALREADY SPOKEN FOR.
ACH!
WHY ME, THEN?
BECAUSE YOU'RE SUCH A PEOPLE PERSON!
ANY OTHER QUESTIONS?

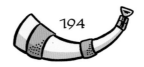

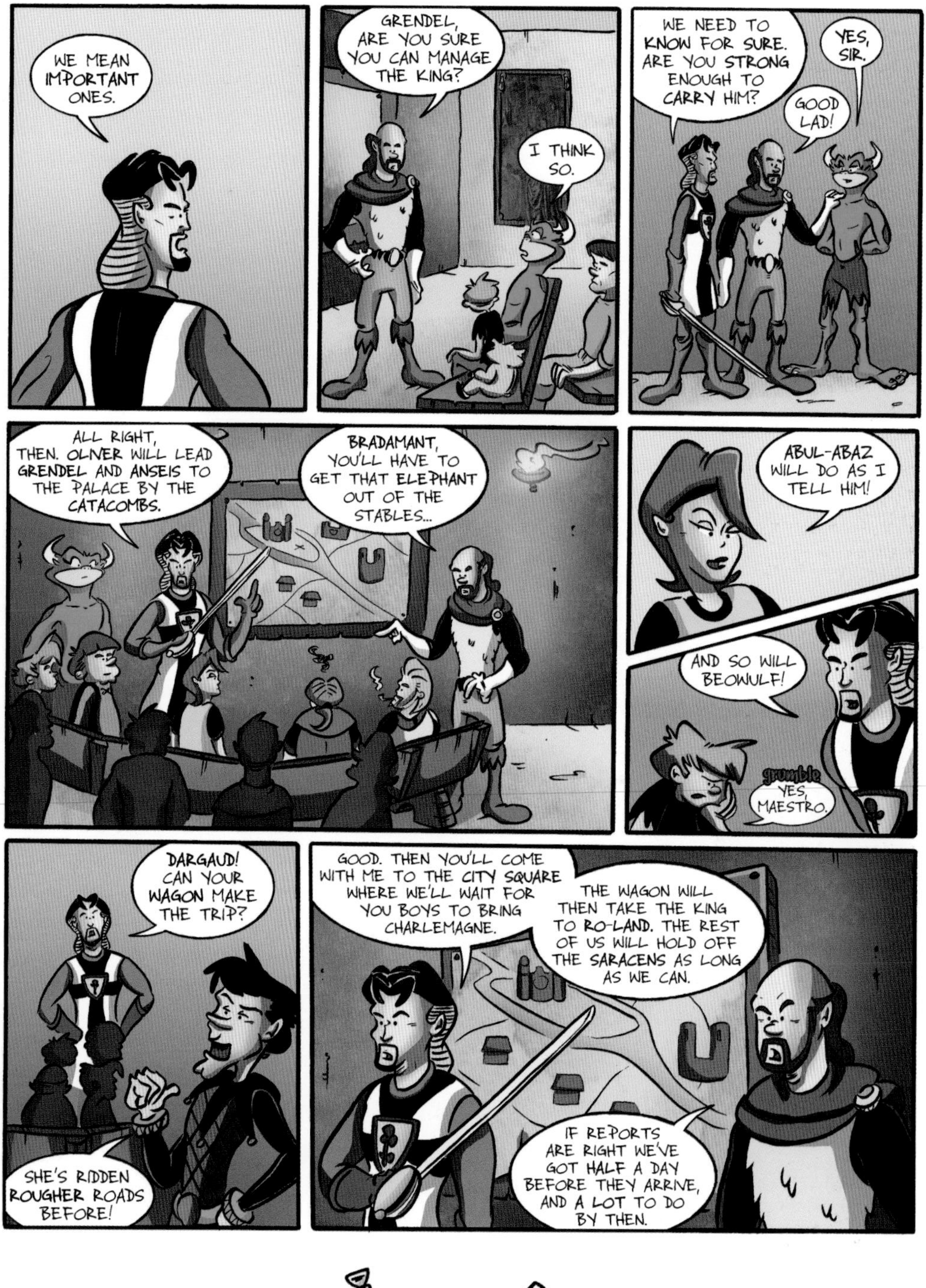
WE MEAN IMPORTANT ONES.
GRENDEL, ARE YOU SURE YOU CAN MANAGE THE KING?
I THINK SO.
WE NEED TO KNOW FOR SURE. ARE YOU STRONG ENOUGH TO CARRY HIM?
YES, SIR.
GOOD LAD!
ALL RIGHT, THEN. OLIVER WILL LEAD GRENDEL AND ANSEIS TO THE PALACE BY THE CATACOMBS.
BRADAMANT, YOU'LL HAVE TO GET THAT ELEPHANT OUT OF THE STABLES...
ABUL-ABAZ WILL DO AS I TELL HIM!
AND SO WILL BEOWULF!
grumble
YES, MAESTRO.
DARGAUD! CAN YOUR WAGON MAKE THE TRIP?
SHE'S RIDDEN ROUGHER ROADS BEFORE!
GOOD. THEN YOU'LL COME WITH ME TO THE CITY SQUARE WHERE WE'LL WAIT FOR YOU BOYS TO BRING CHARLEMAGNE.
THE WAGON WILL THEN TAKE THE KING TO RO-LAND. THE REST OF US WILL HOLD OFF THE SARACENS AS LONG AS WE CAN.
IF REPORTS ARE RIGHT WE'VE GOT HALF A DAY BEFORE THEY ARRIVE, AND A LOT TO DO BY THEN.

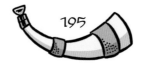

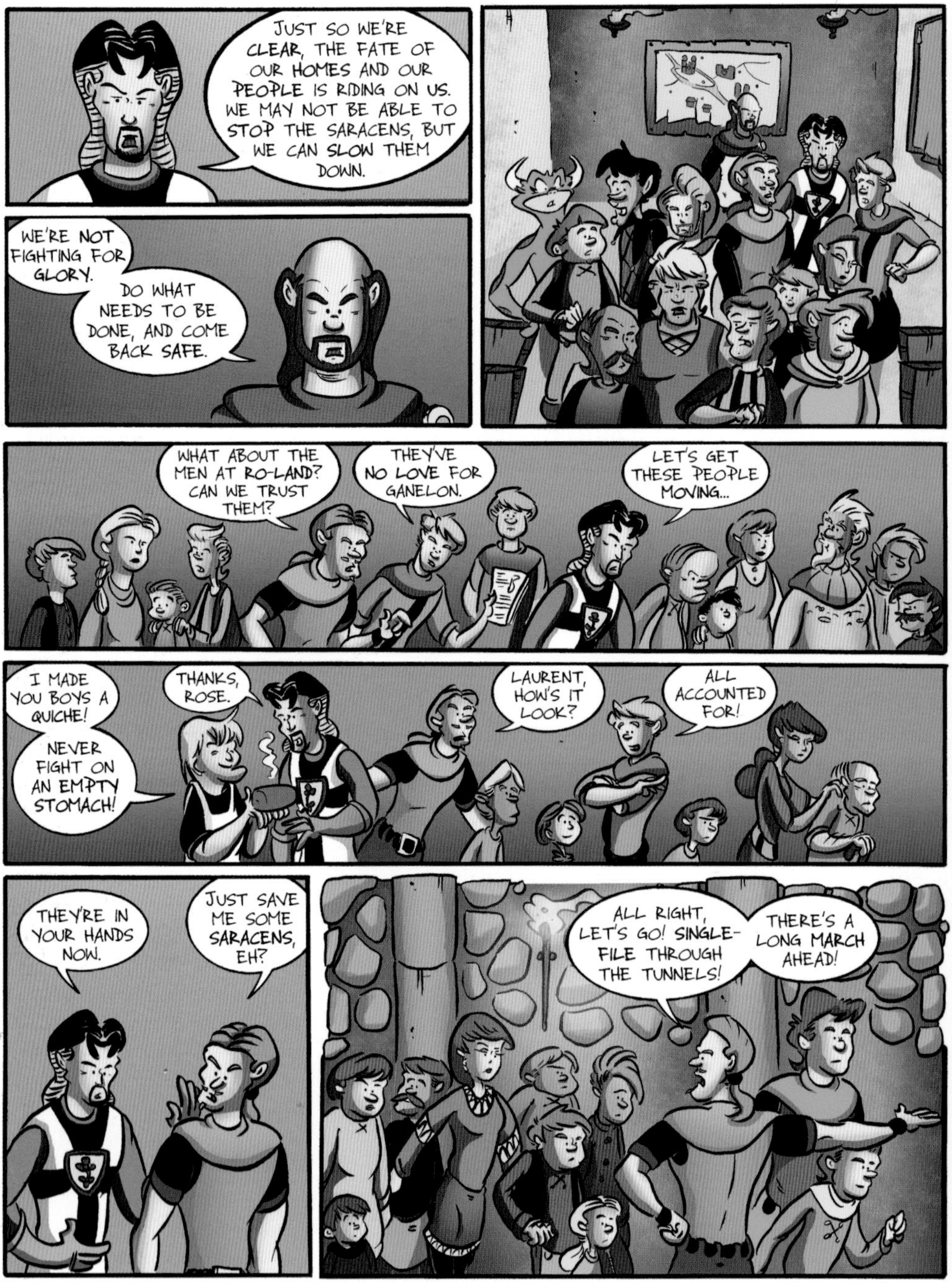
JUST SO WE'RE CLEAR, THE FATE OF OUR HOMES AND OUR PEOPLE IS RIDING ON US. WE MAY NOT BE ABLE TO STOP THE SARACENS, BUT WE CAN SLOW THEM DOWN.
WE'RE NOT FIGHTING FOR GLORY.
DO WHAT NEEDS TO BE DONE, AND COME BACK SAFE.
WHAT ABOUT THE MEN AT RO-LAND? CAN WE TRUST THEM?
THEY'VE NO LOVE FOR GANELON.
LET'S GET THESE PEOPLE MOVING...
I MADE YOU BOYS A QUICHE!
NEVER FIGHT ON AN EMPTY STOMACH!
THANKS, ROSE.
LAURENT, HOW'S IT LOOK?
ALL ACCOUNTED FOR!
THEY'RE IN YOUR HANDS NOW.
JUST SAVE ME SOME SARACENS, EH?
ALL RIGHT, LET'S GO! SINGLE-FILE THROUGH THE TUNNELS!
THERE'S A LONG MARCH AHEAD!

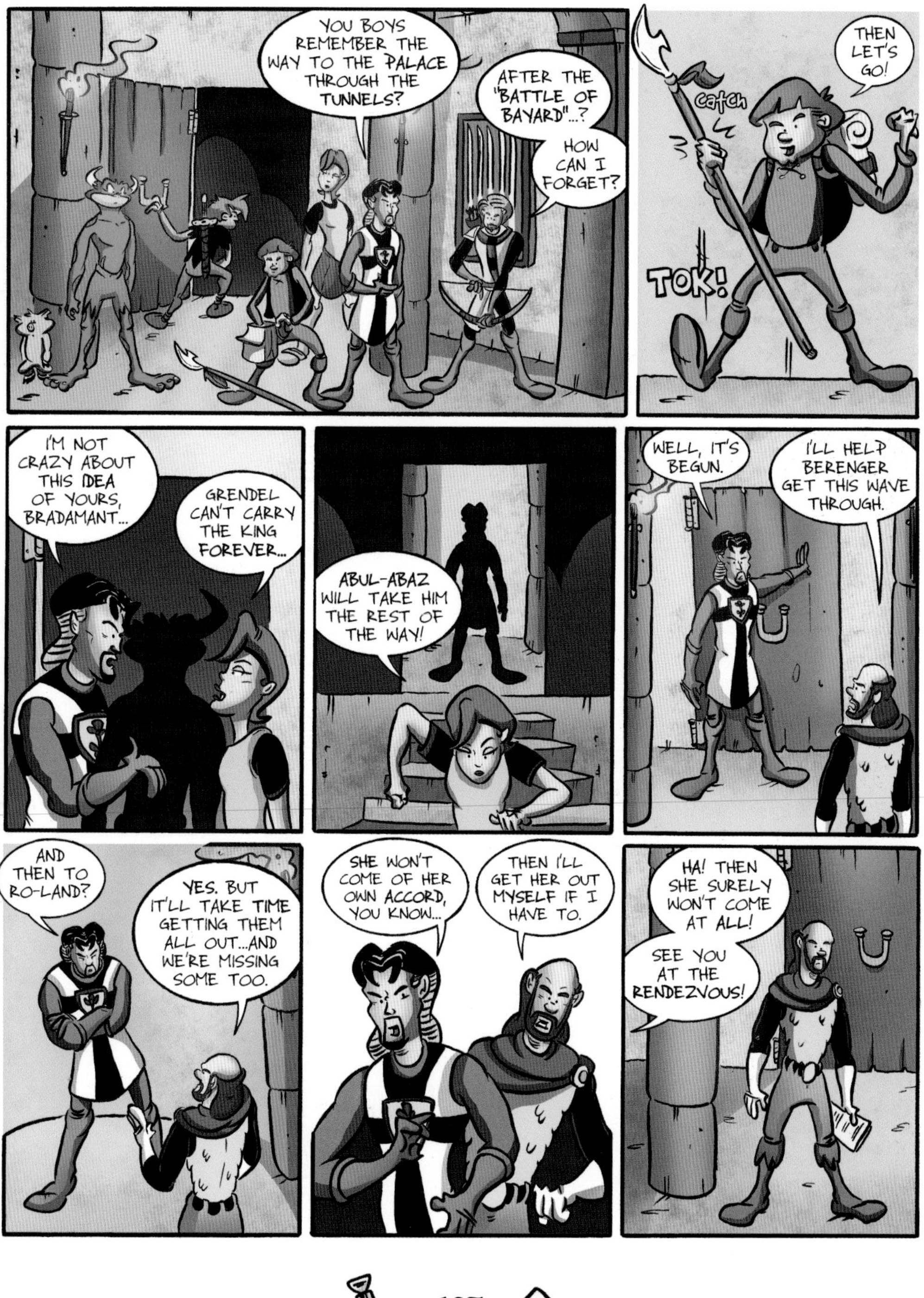
YOU BOYS REMEMBER THE WAY TO THE PALACE THROUGH THE TUNNELS?
AFTER THE "BATTLE OF BAYARD"...?
HOW CAN I FORGET?
THEN LET'S GO!
catch
TOK!
I'M NOT CRAZY ABOUT THIS IDEA OF YOURS, BRADAMANT...
GRENDEL CAN'T CARRY THE KING FOREVER...
ABUL-ABAZ WILL TAKE HIM THE REST OF THE WAY!
WELL, IT'S BEGUN.
I'LL HELP BERENGER GET THIS WAVE THROUGH.
AND THEN TO RO-LAND?
YES. BUT IT'LL TAKE TIME GETTING THEM ALL OUT...AND WE'RE MISSING SOME TOO.
SHE WON'T COME OF HER OWN ACCORD, YOU KNOW...
THEN I'LL GET HER OUT MYSELF IF I HAVE TO.
HA! THEN SHE SURELY WON'T COME AT ALL!
SEE YOU AT THE RENDEZVOUS!

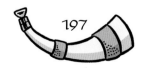

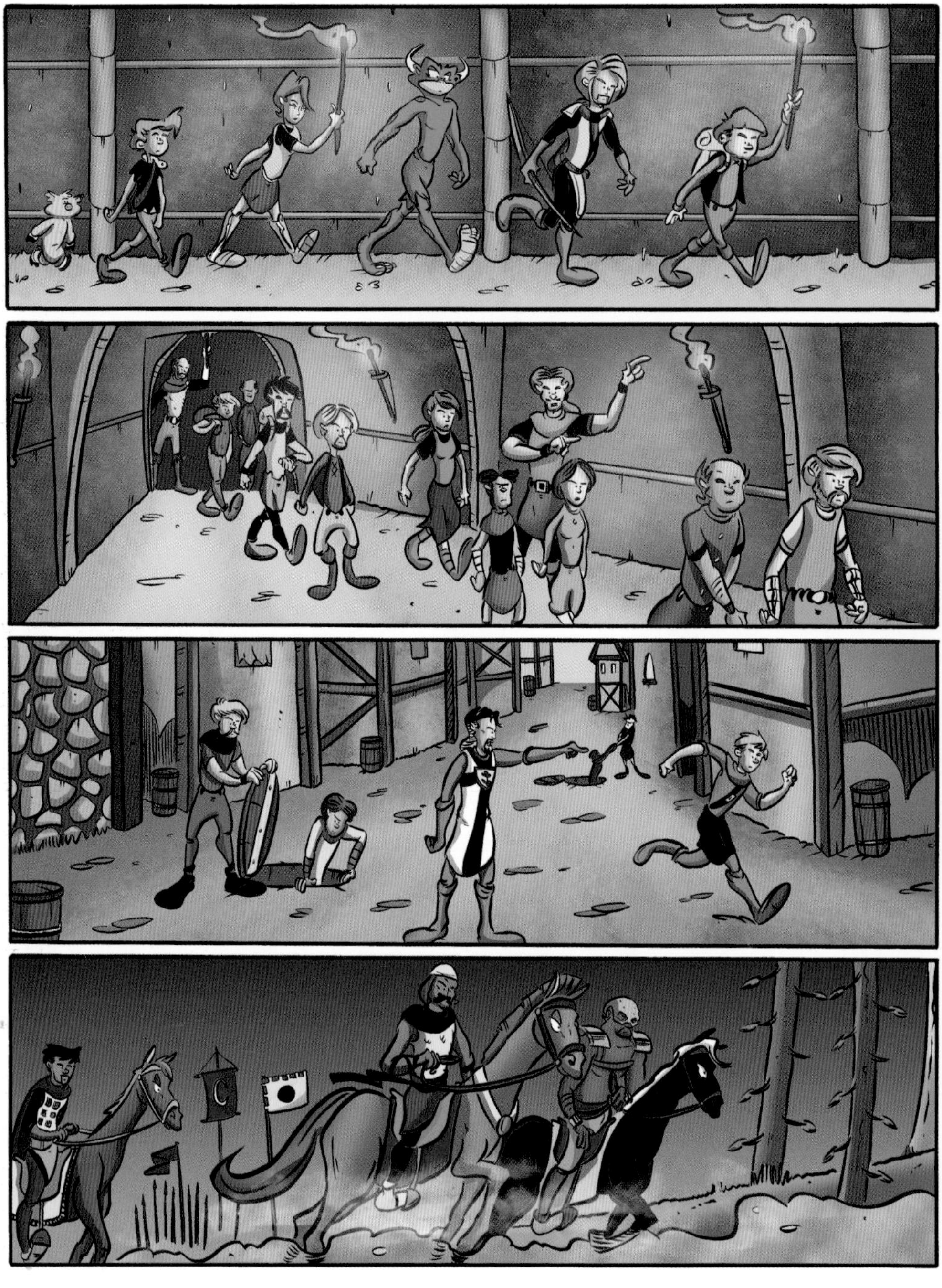
C

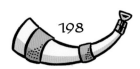

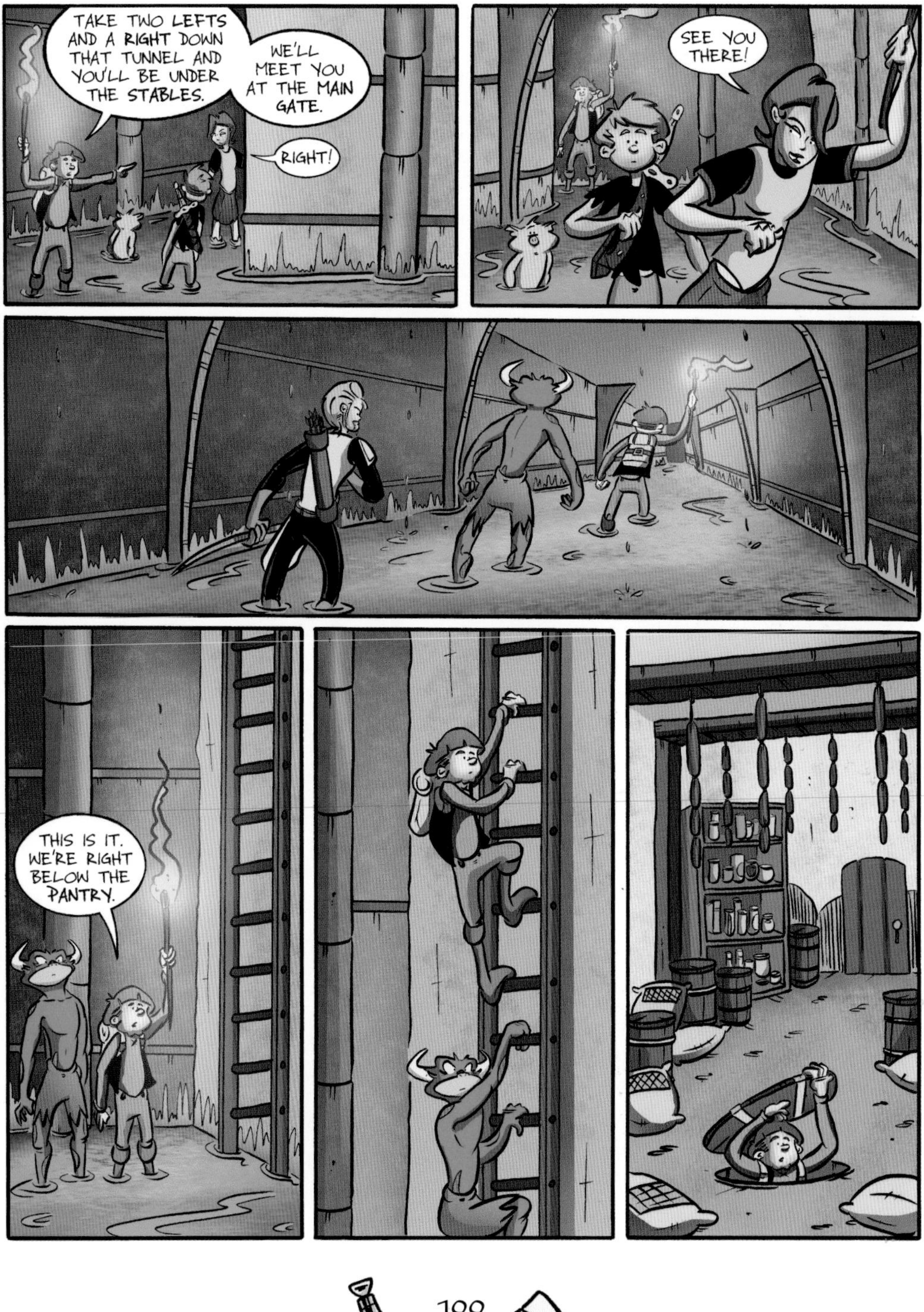
TAKE TWO LEFTS AND A RIGHT DOWN THAT TUNNEL AND YOU'LL BE UNDER THE STABLES.
WE'LL MEET YOU AT THE MAIN GATE.
RIGHT!
SEE YOU THERE!
THIS IS IT. WE'RE RIGHT BELOW THE PANTRY.

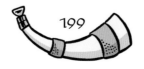

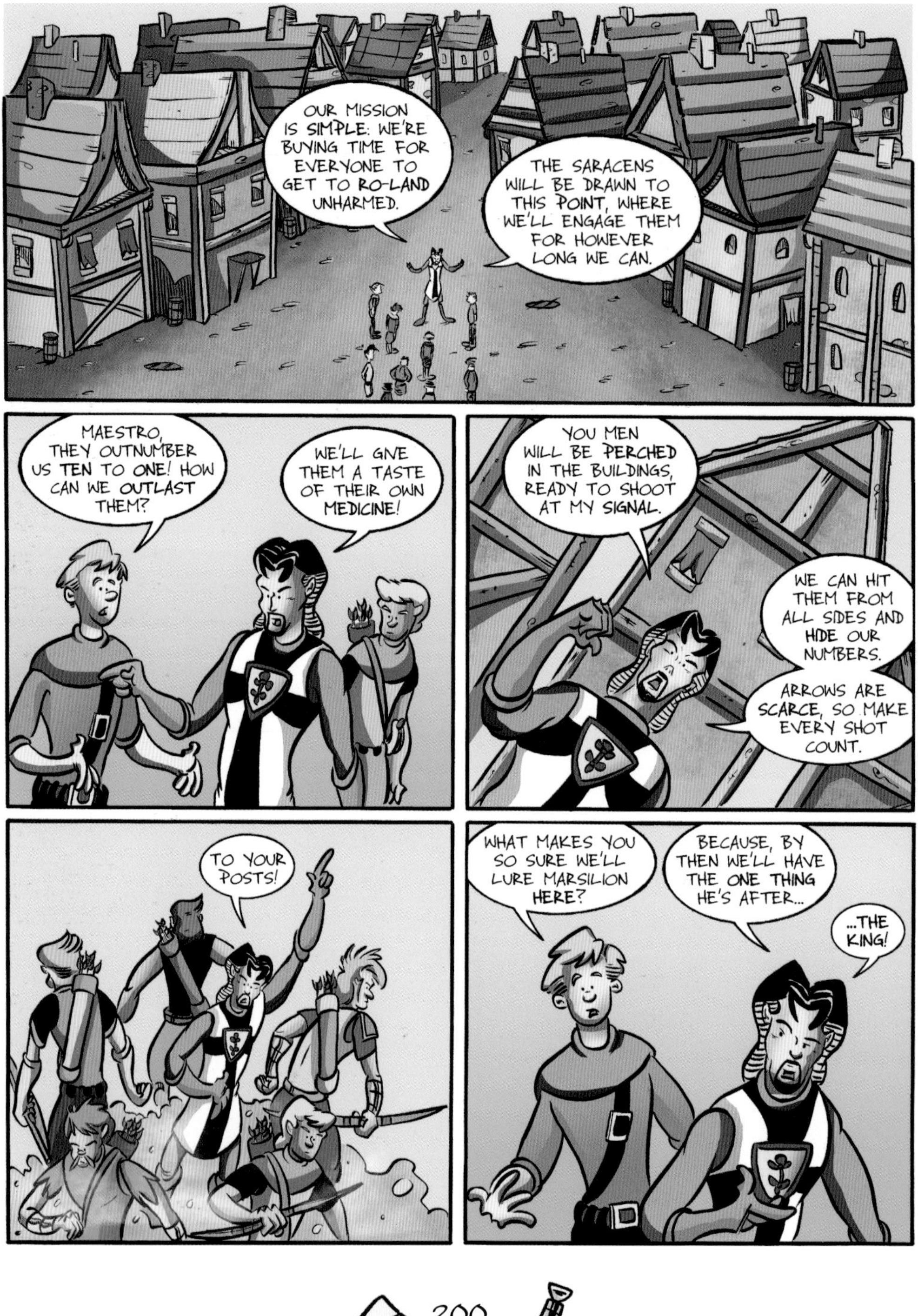
OUR MISSION IS SIMPLE: WE'RE BUYING TIME FOR EVERYONE TO GET TO RO-LAND UNHARMED.
THE SARACENS WILL BE DRAWN TO THIS POINT, WHERE WE'LL ENGAGE THEM FOR HOWEVER LONG WE CAN.
MAESTRO, THEY OUTNUMBER US TEN TO ONE! HOW CAN WE OUTLAST THEM?
WE'LL GIVE THEM A TASTE OF THEIR OWN MEDICINE!
YOU MEN WILL BE PERCHED IN THE BUILDINGS, READY TO SHOOT AT MY SIGNAL.
WE CAN HIT THEM FROM ALL SIDES AND HIDE OUR NUMBERS.
ARROWS ARE SCARCE, SO MAKE EVERY SHOT COUNT.
TO YOUR POSTS!
WHAT MAKES YOU SO SURE WE'LL LURE MARSILION HERE?
BECAUSE, BY THEN WE'LL HAVE THE ONE THING HE'S AFTER...
...THE KING!

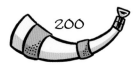

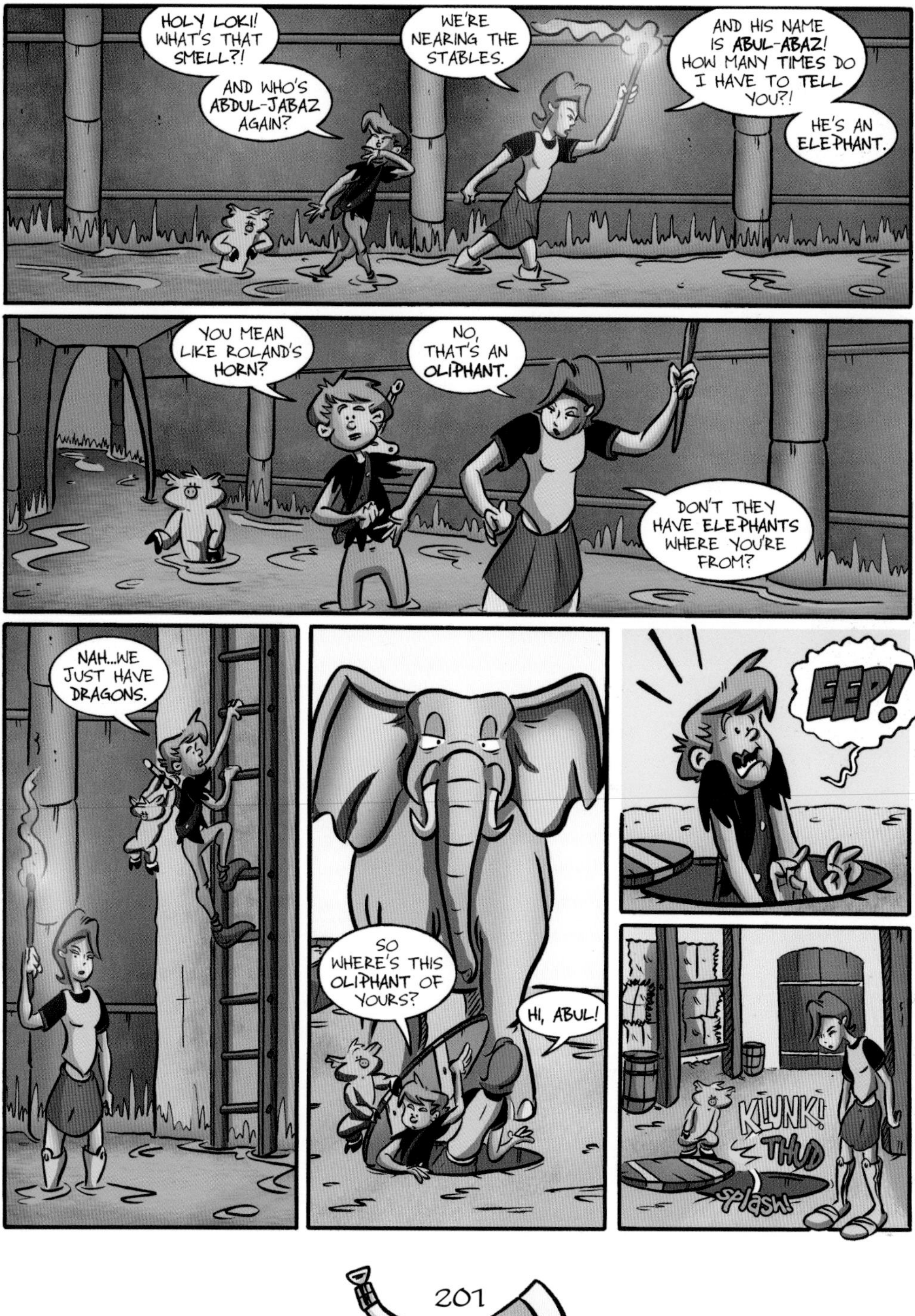
HOLY LOKI! WHAT'S THAT SMELL?!
AND WHO'S ABDUL-JABAZ AGAIN?
WE'RE NEARING THE STABLES.
AND HIS NAME IS ABUL-ABAZ! HOW MANY TIMES DO I HAVE TO TELL YOU?!
HE'S AN ELEPHANT.
YOU MEAN LIKE ROLAND'S HORN?
NO, THAT'S AN OLIPHANT.
DON'T THEY HAVE ELEPHANTS WHERE YOU'RE FROM?
NAH...WE JUST HAVE DRAGONS.
SO WHERE'S THIS OLIPHANT OF YOURS?
HI, ABUL!
EEP!
KLUNK!
THUD
SPLASH!

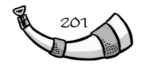

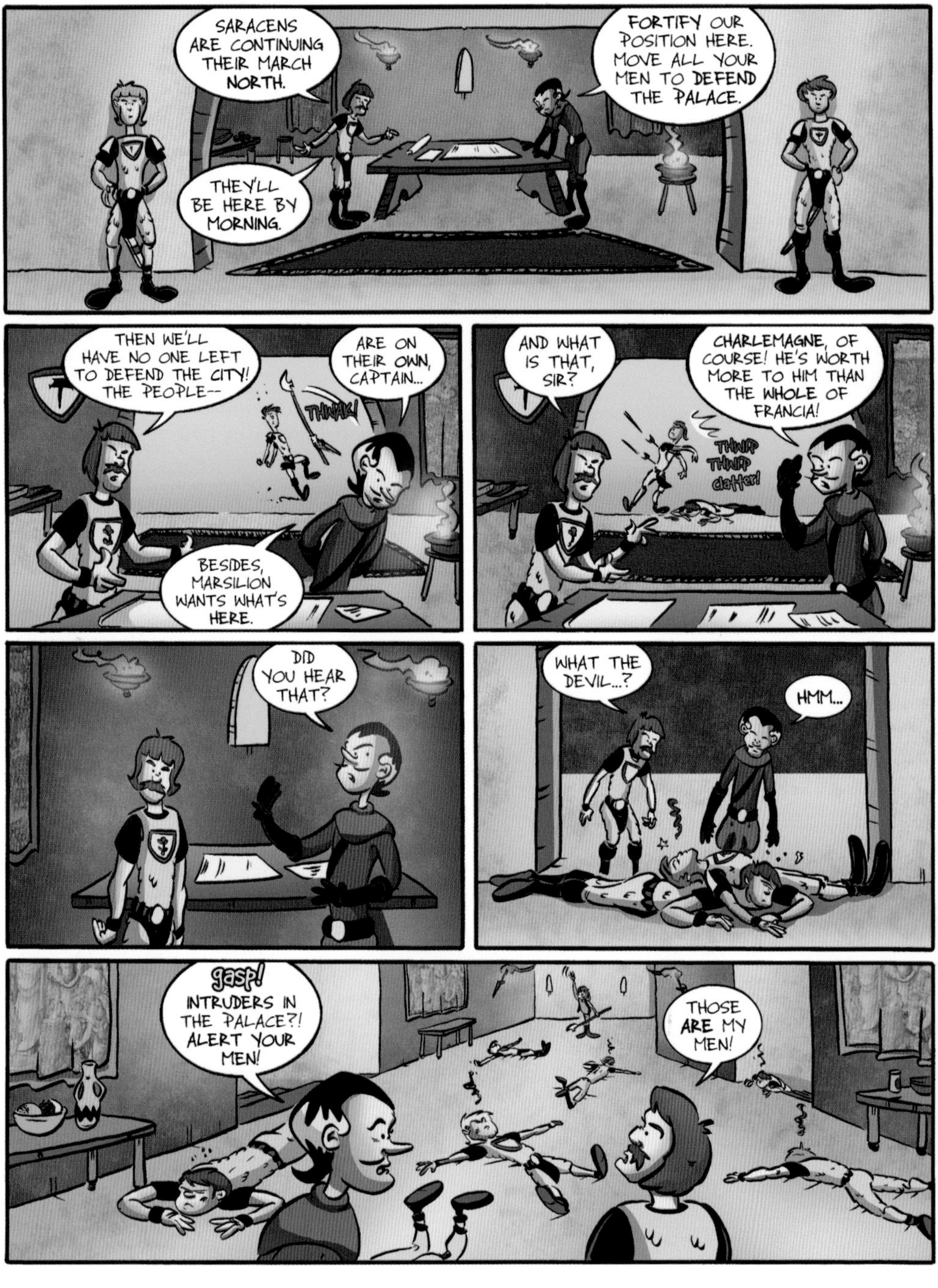
SARACENS ARE CONTINUING THEIR MARCH NORTH.
THEY'LL BE HERE BY MORNING.
FORTIFY OUR POSITION HERE. MOVE ALL YOUR MEN TO DEFEND THE PALACE.
THEN WE'LL HAVE NO ONE LEFT TO DEFEND THE CITY! THE PEOPLE--
ARE ON THEIR OWN, CAPTAIN...
THWAK!
BESIDES, MARSILION WANTS WHAT'S HERE.
AND WHAT IS THAT, SIR?
CHARLEMAGNE, OF COURSE! HE'S WORTH MORE TO HIM THAN THE WHOLE OF FRANCIA!
THWIP THWIP clatter!
DID YOU HEAR THAT?
WHAT THE DEVIL...?
HMM...
gasp! INTRUDERS IN THE PALACE?! ALERT YOUR MEN!
THOSE ARE MY MEN!

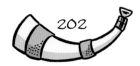

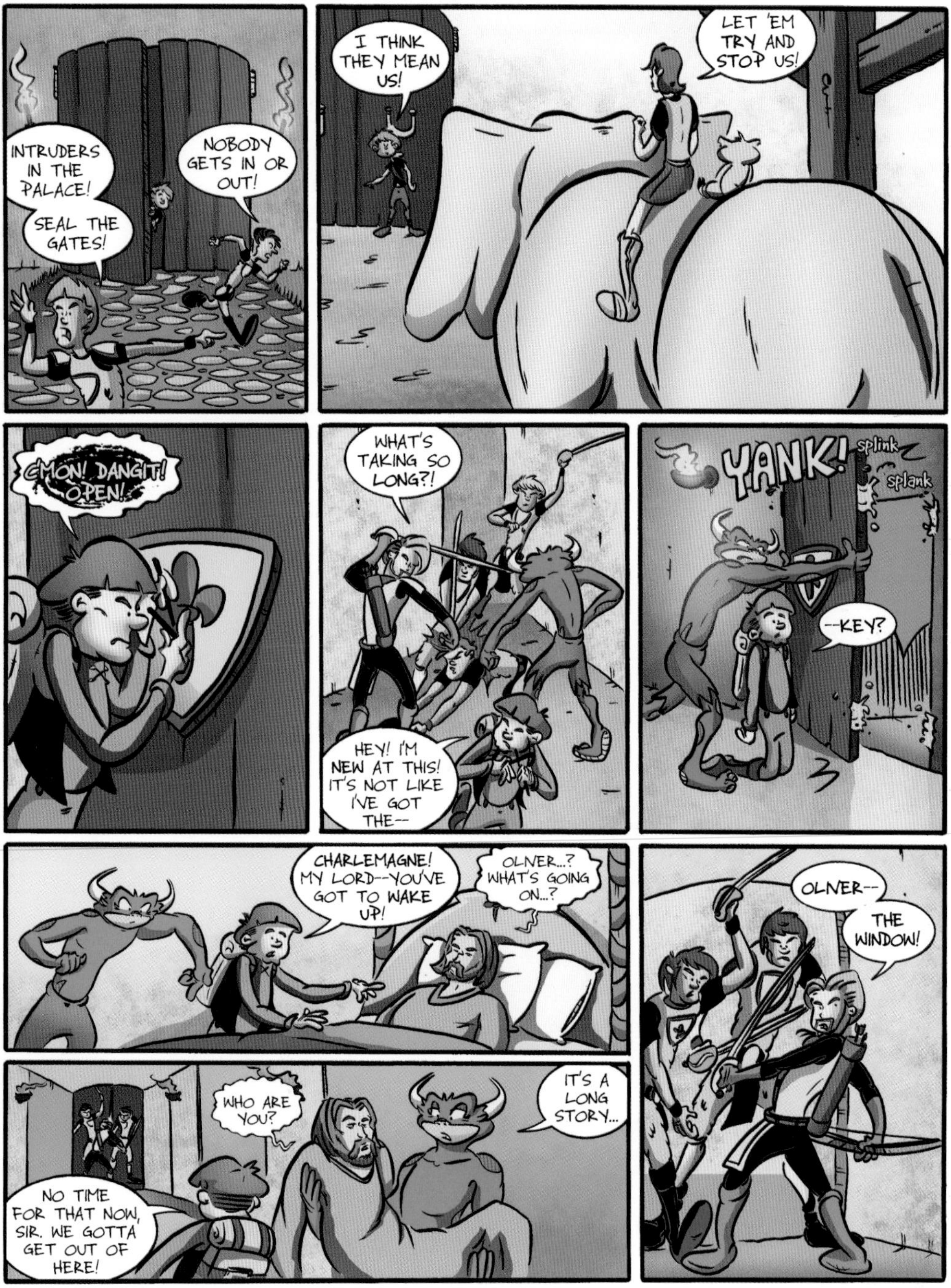
INTRUDERS IN THE PALACE!
SEAL THE GATES!
NOBODY GETS IN OR OUT!
I THINK THEY MEAN US!
LET 'EM TRY AND STOP US!
C'MON! DANGIT! OPEN!
WHAT'S TAKING SO LONG?!
HEY! I'M NEW AT THIS! IT'S NOT LIKE I'VE GOT THE--
YANK!
splink
splank
--KEY?
CHARLEMAGNE! MY LORD--YOU'VE GOT TO WAKE UP!
OLIVER...? WHAT'S GOING ON...?
OLIVER--
THE WINDOW!
WHO ARE YOU?
IT'S A LONG STORY...
NO TIME FOR THAT NOW, SIR. WE GOTTA GET OUT OF HERE!

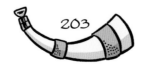

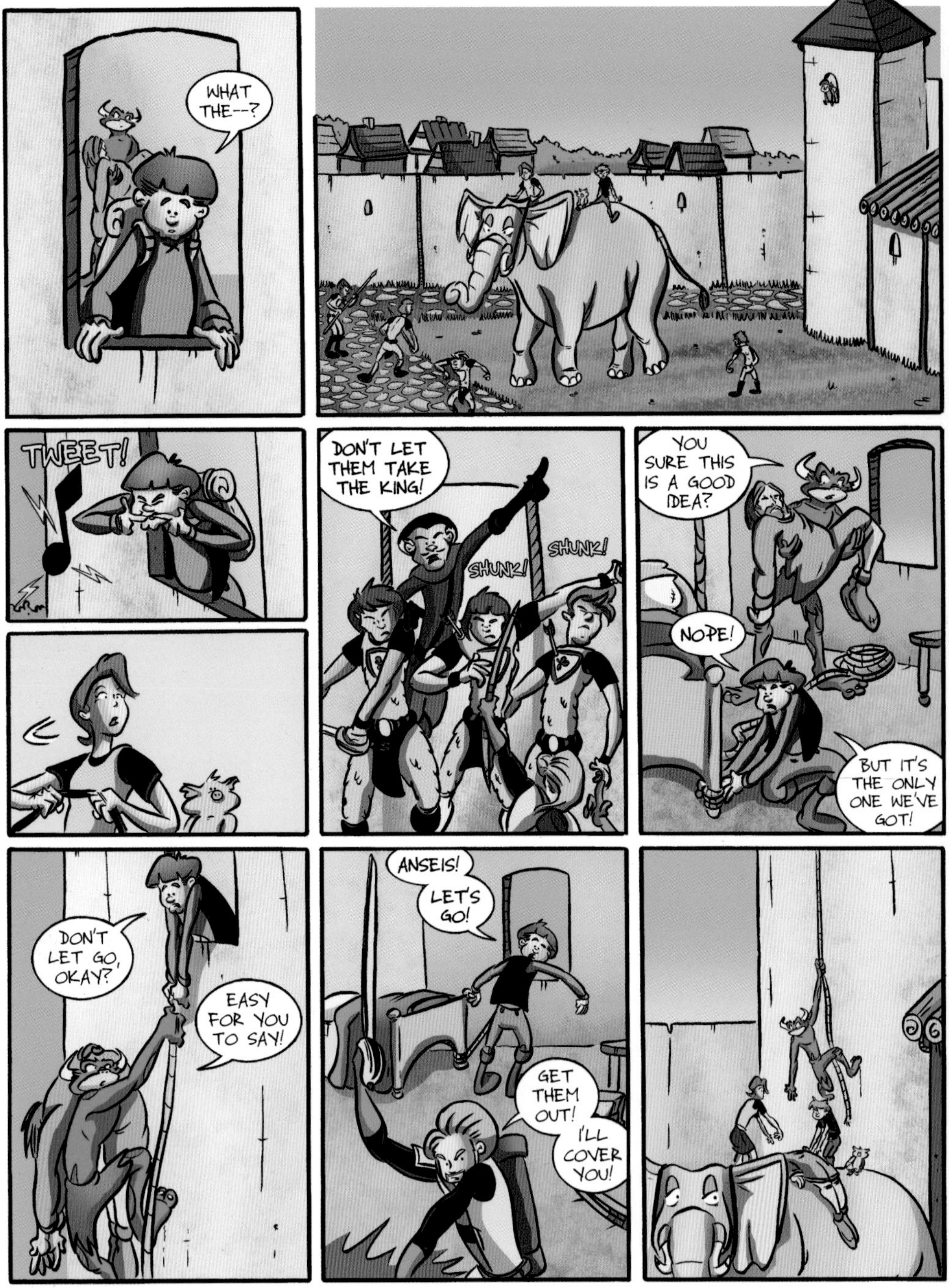
WHAT THE--?
TWEET!
DON'T LET THEM TAKE THE KING!
SHUNK!
SHUNK!
YOU SURE THIS IS A GOOD IDEA?
NOPE!
BUT IT'S THE ONLY ONE WE'VE GOT!
DON'T LET GO, OKAY?
EASY FOR YOU TO SAY!
ANSEIS!
LET'S GO!
GET THEM OUT!
I'LL COVER YOU!

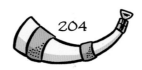

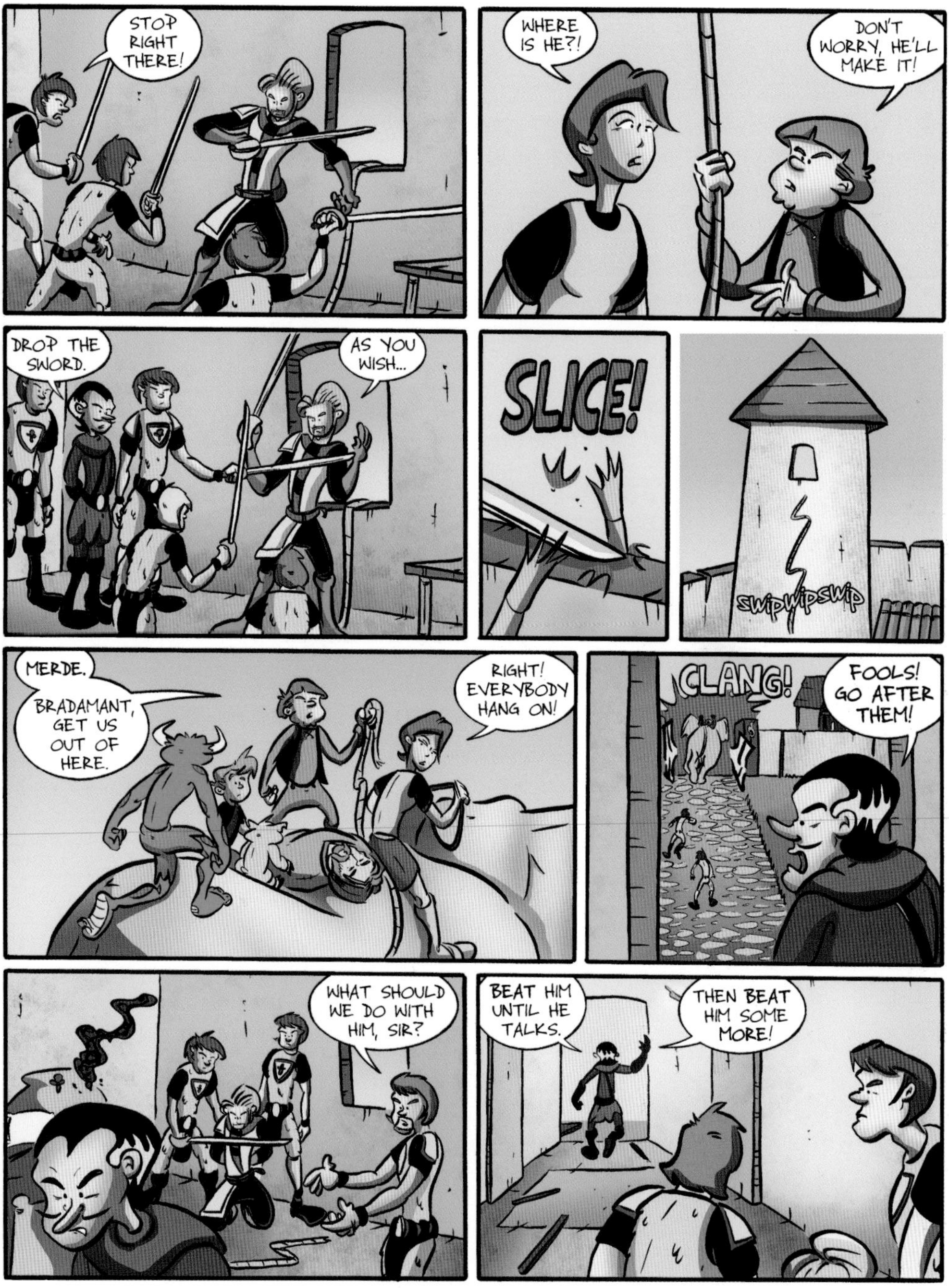
STOP RIGHT THERE!
WHERE IS HE?!
DON'T WORRY, HE'LL MAKE IT!
DROP THE SWORD.
AS YOU WISH...
SLICE!
swipwipswip
MERDE.
BRADAMANT, GET US OUT OF HERE.
RIGHT! EVERYBODY HANG ON!
CLANG!
FOOLS! GO AFTER THEM!
WHAT SHOULD WE DO WITH HIM, SIR?
BEAT HIM UNTIL HE TALKS.
THEN BEAT HIM SOME MORE!

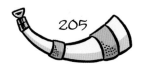

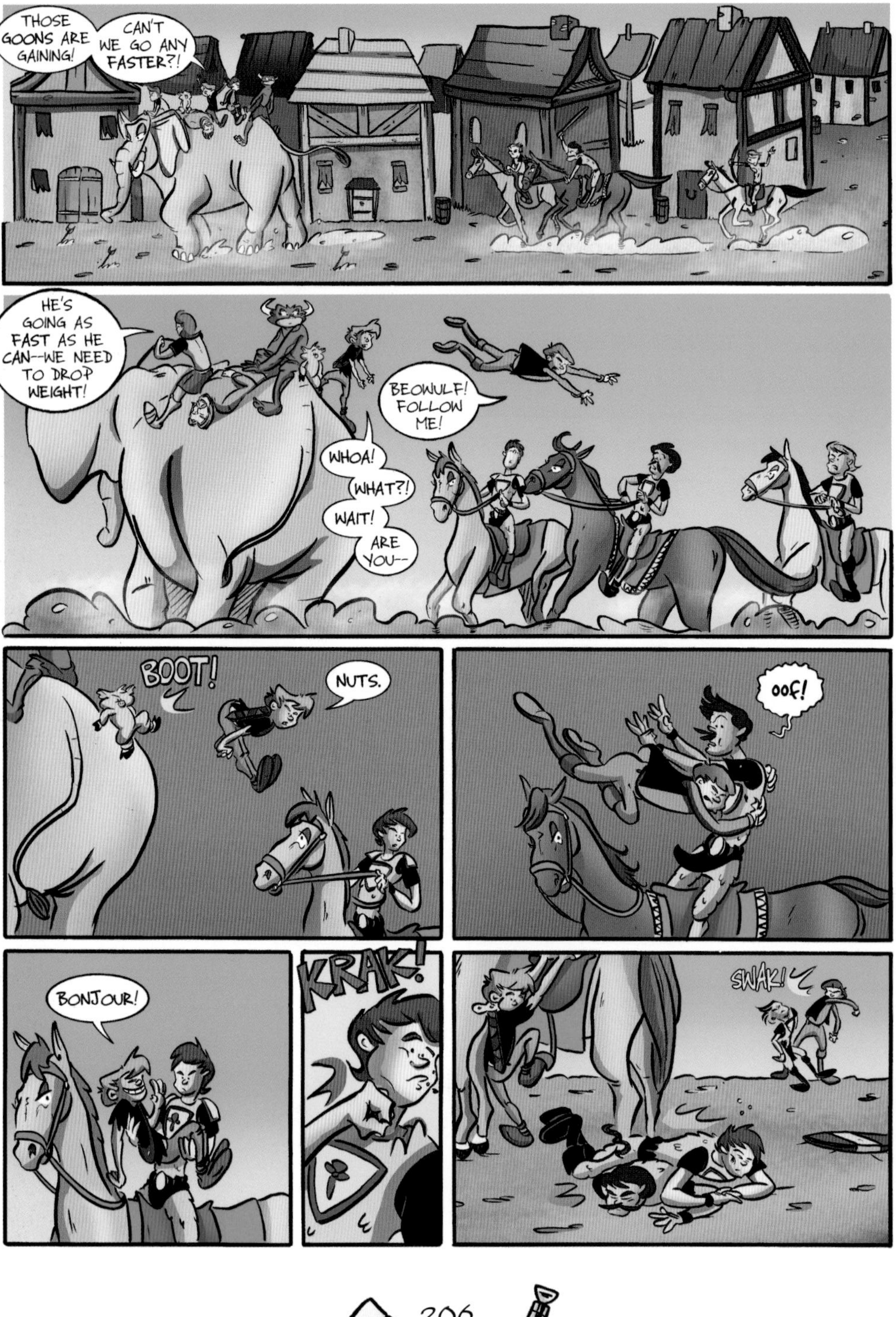
THOSE GOONS ARE GAINING!
CAN'T WE GO ANY FASTER?!
HE'S GOING AS FAST AS HE CAN--WE NEED TO DROP WEIGHT!
BEOWULF! FOLLOW ME!
WHOA!
WHAT?!
WAIT!
ARE YOU--
BOOT!
NUTS.
OOF!
BONJOUR!
KRAK!
SWAK!

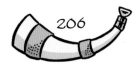

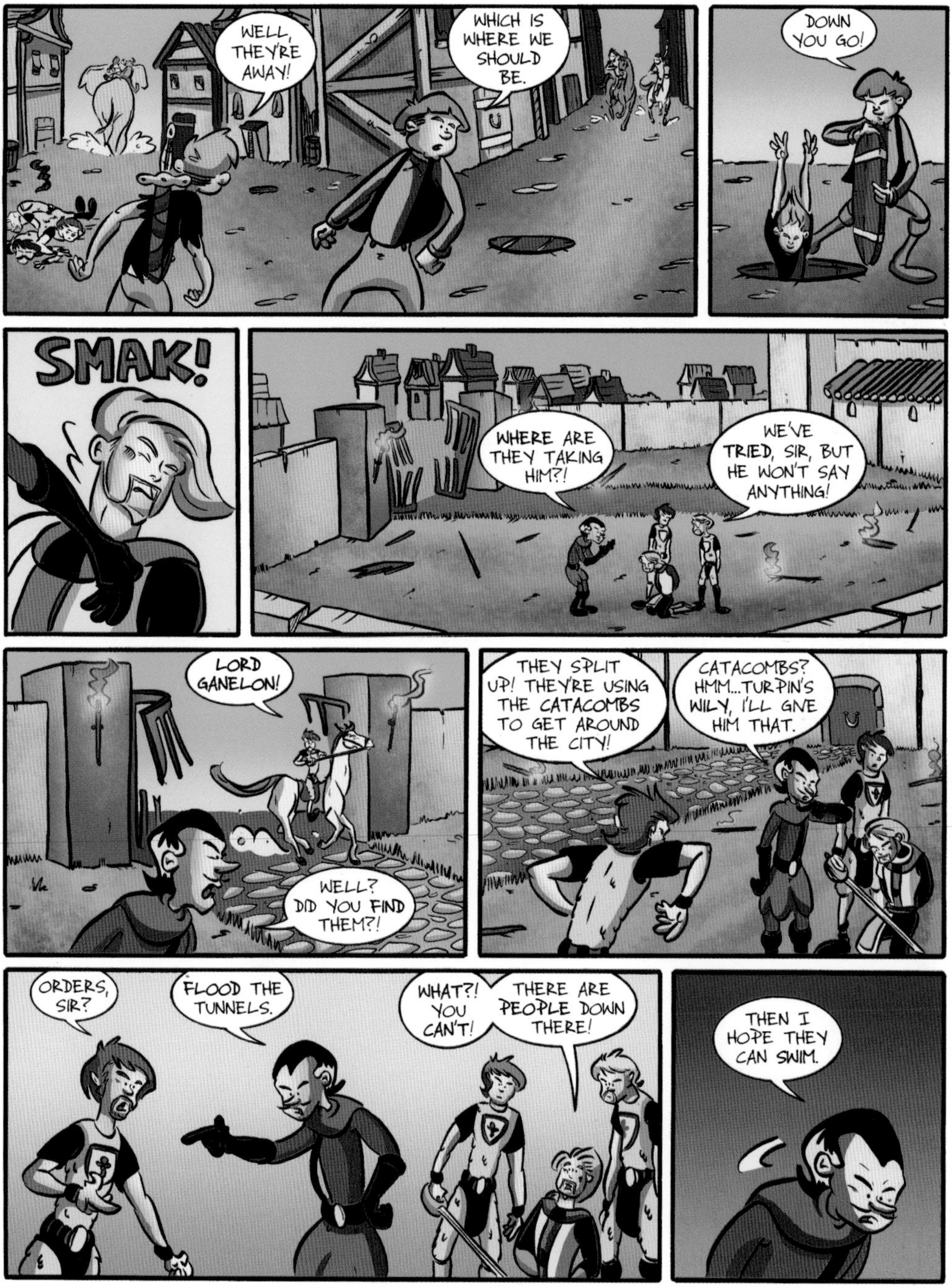
WELL, THEY'RE AWAY!
WHICH IS WHERE WE SHOULD BE.
DOWN YOU GO!
SMAK!
WHERE ARE THEY TAKING HIM?!
WE'VE TRIED, SIR, BUT HE WON'T SAY ANYTHING!
LORD GANELON!
WELL? DID YOU FIND THEM?!
THEY SPLIT UP! THEY'RE USING THE CATACOMBS TO GET AROUND THE CITY!
CATACOMBS? HMM...TURPIN'S WILY, I'LL GIVE HIM THAT.
ORDERS, SIR?
FLOOD THE TUNNELS.
WHAT?! YOU CAN'T!
THERE ARE PEOPLE DOWN THERE!
THEN I HOPE THEY CAN SWIM.

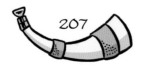

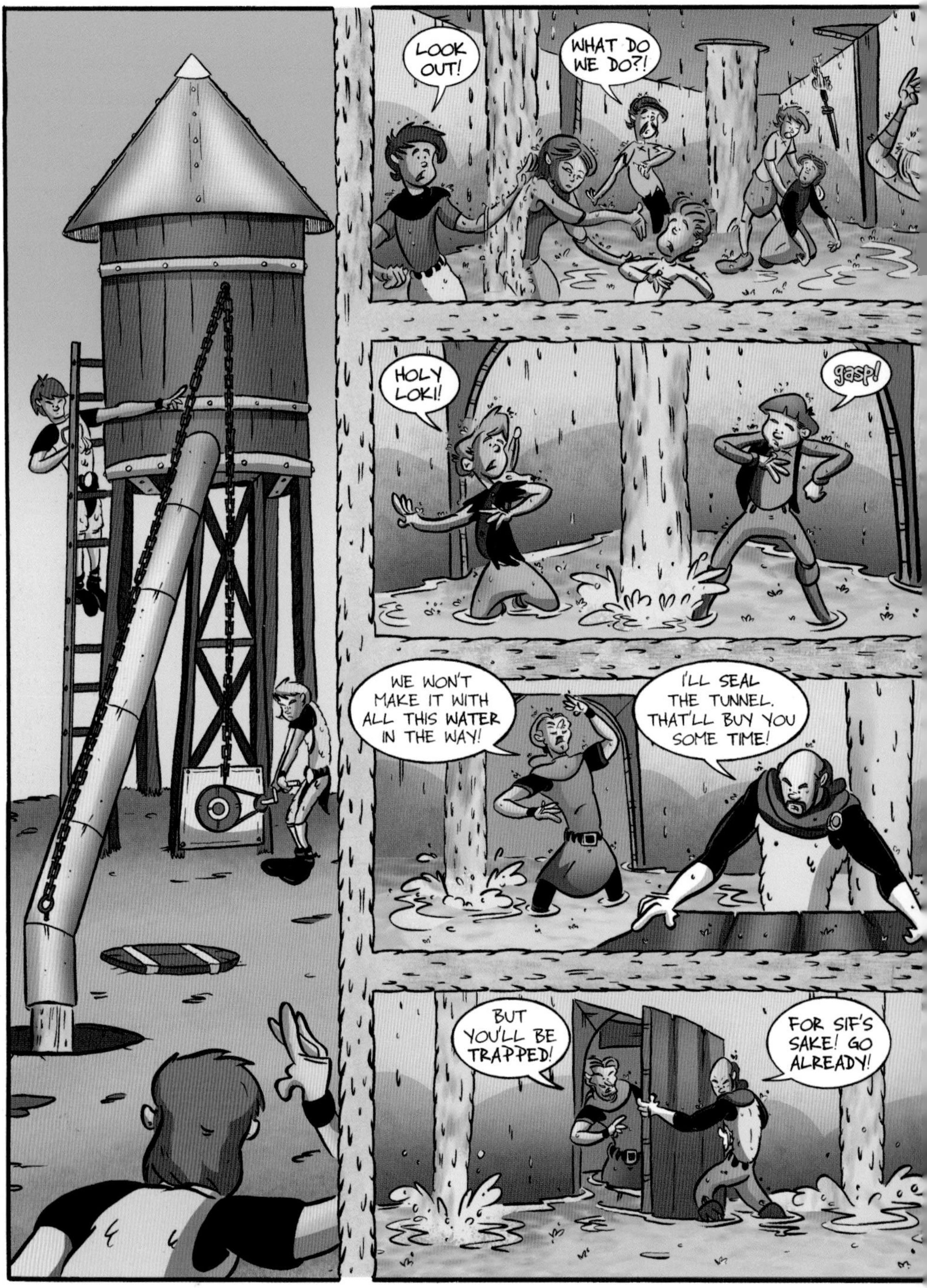
LOOK OUT!
WHAT DO WE DO?!
HOLY LOKI!
gasp!
WE WON'T MAKE IT WITH ALL THIS WATER IN THE WAY!
I'LL SEAL THE TUNNEL. THAT'LL BUY YOU SOME TIME!
BUT YOU'LL BE TRAPPED!
FOR SIF'S SAKE! GO ALREADY!

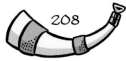

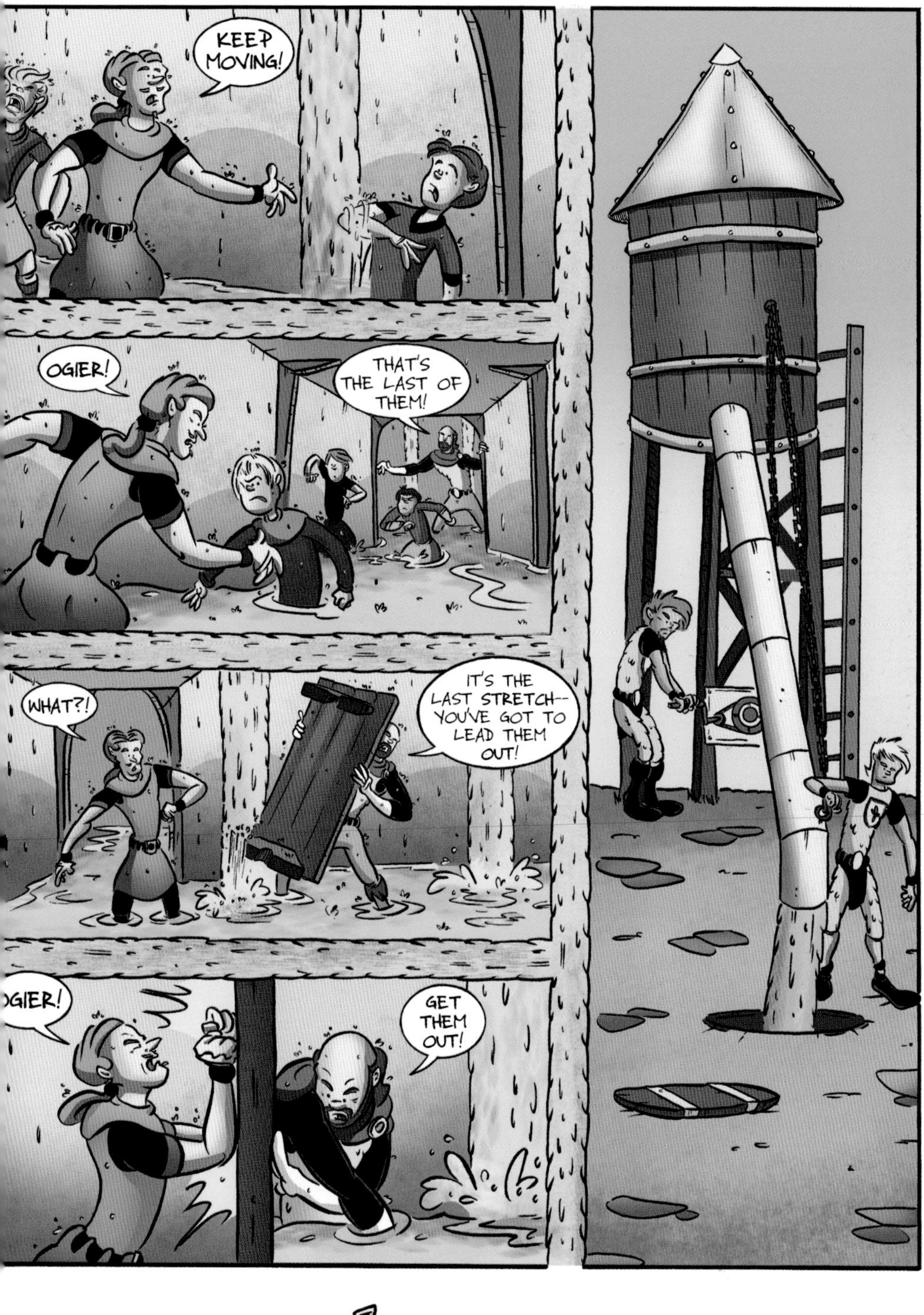
KEEP MOVING!
OGIER!
THAT'S THE LAST OF THEM!
WHAT?!
IT'S THE LAST STRETCH-- YOU'VE GOT TO LEAD THEM OUT!
OGIER!
GET THEM OUT!

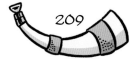

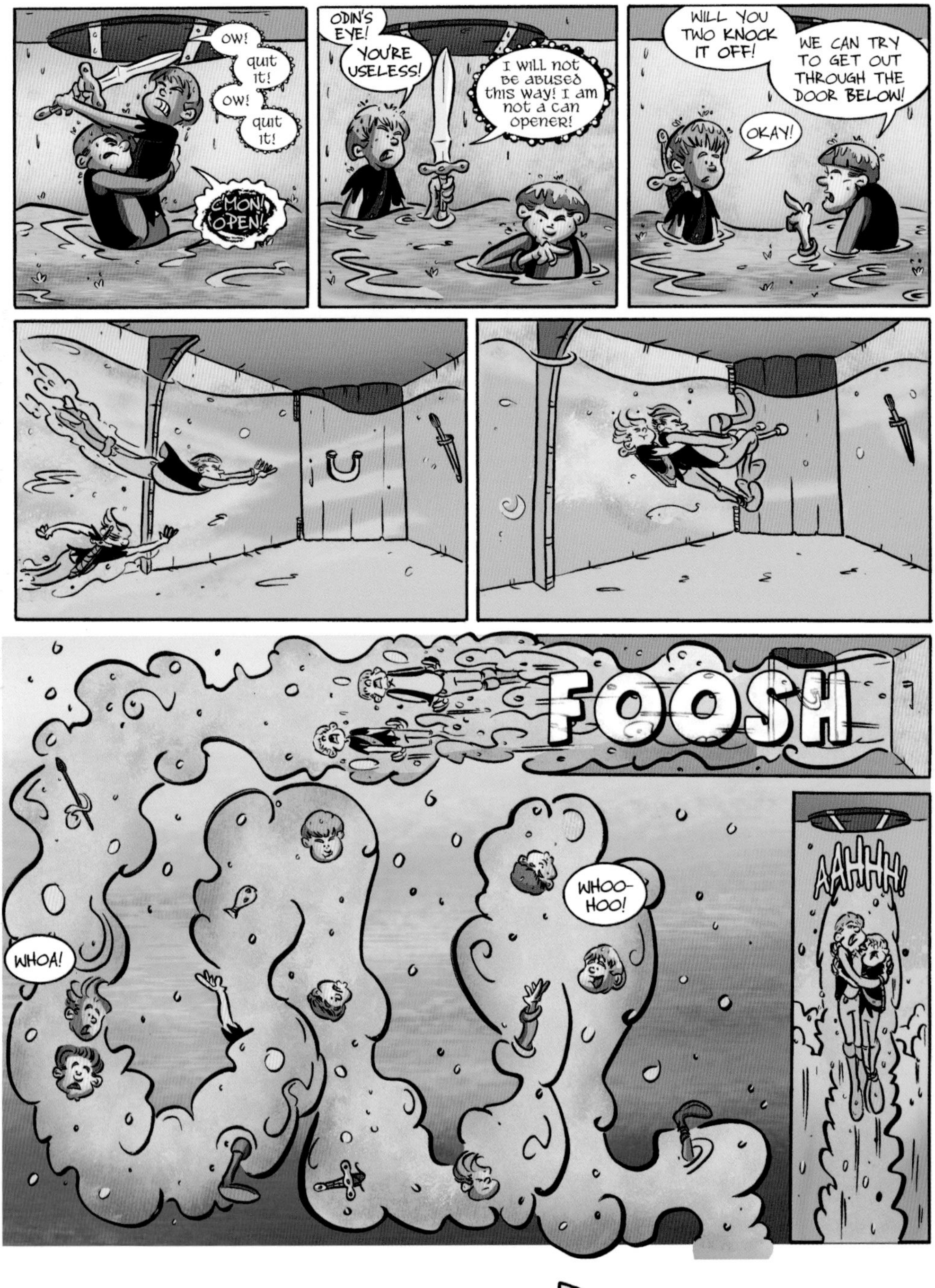
OW!
quit it!
OW!
quit it!
C'MON! OPEN!
ODIN'S EYE!
YOU'RE USELESS!
I WILL NOT BE ABUSED THIS WAY! I AM NOT A CAN OPENER!
WILL YOU TWO KNOCK IT OFF!
WE CAN TRY TO GET OUT THROUGH THE DOOR BELOW!
OKAY!
FOOSH
WHOA!
WHOO-HOO!
AAHHH!

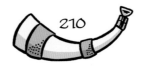

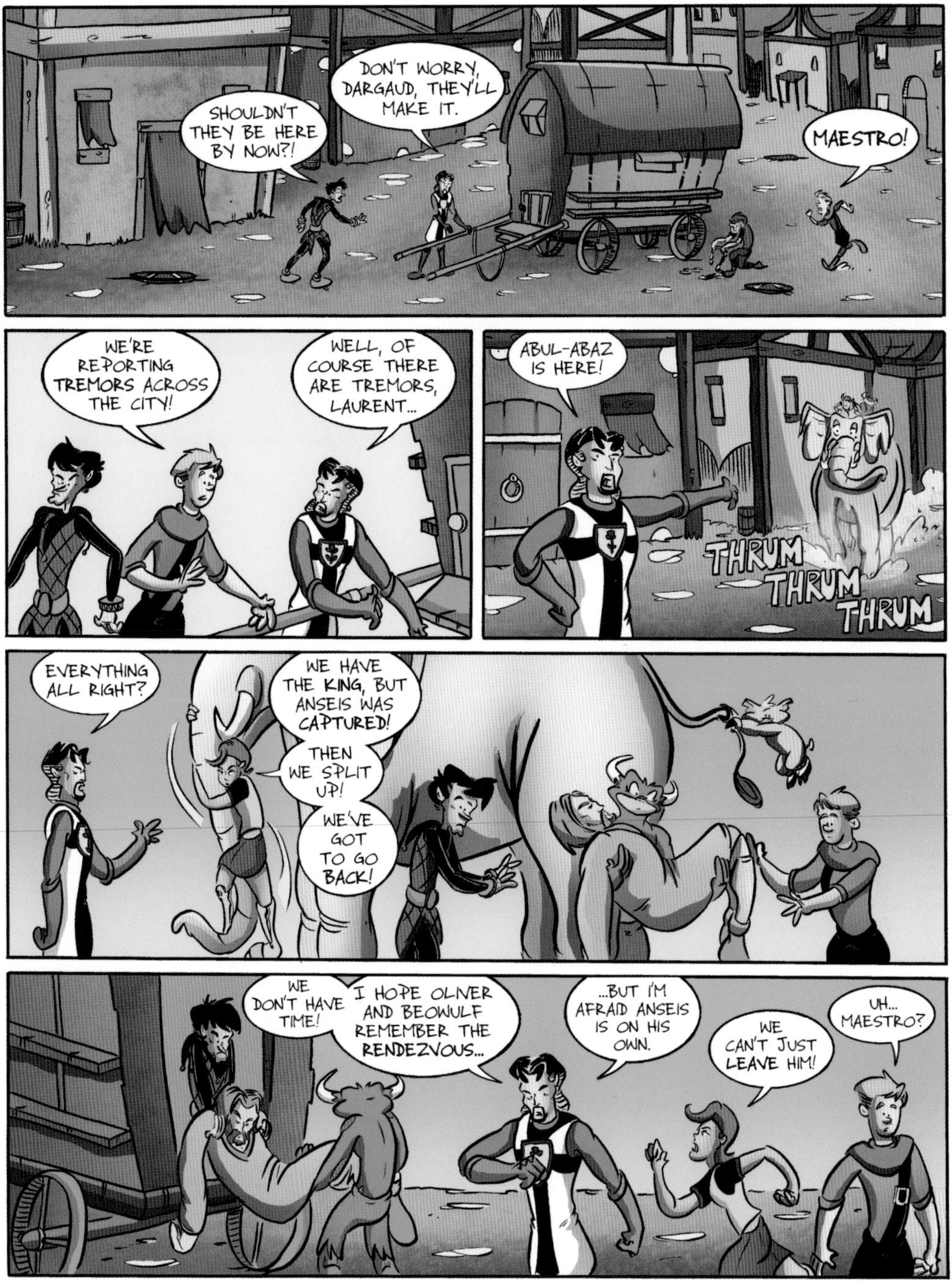
SHOULDN'T THEY BE HERE BY NOW?!
DON'T WORRY, DARGAUD, THEY'LL MAKE IT.
MAESTRO!
WE'RE REPORTING TREMORS ACROSS THE CITY!
WELL, OF COURSE THERE ARE TREMORS, LAURENT...
ABUL-ABAZ IS HERE!
THRUM THRUM THRUM
EVERYTHING ALL RIGHT?
WE HAVE THE KING, BUT ANSEIS WAS CAPTURED!
THEN WE SPLIT UP!
WE'VE GOT TO GO BACK!
WE DON'T HAVE TIME!
I HOPE OLIVER AND BEOWULF REMEMBER THE RENDEZVOUS...
...BUT I'M AFRAID ANSEIS IS ON HIS OWN.
WE CAN'T JUST LEAVE HIM!
UH... MAESTRO?

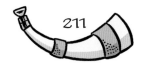

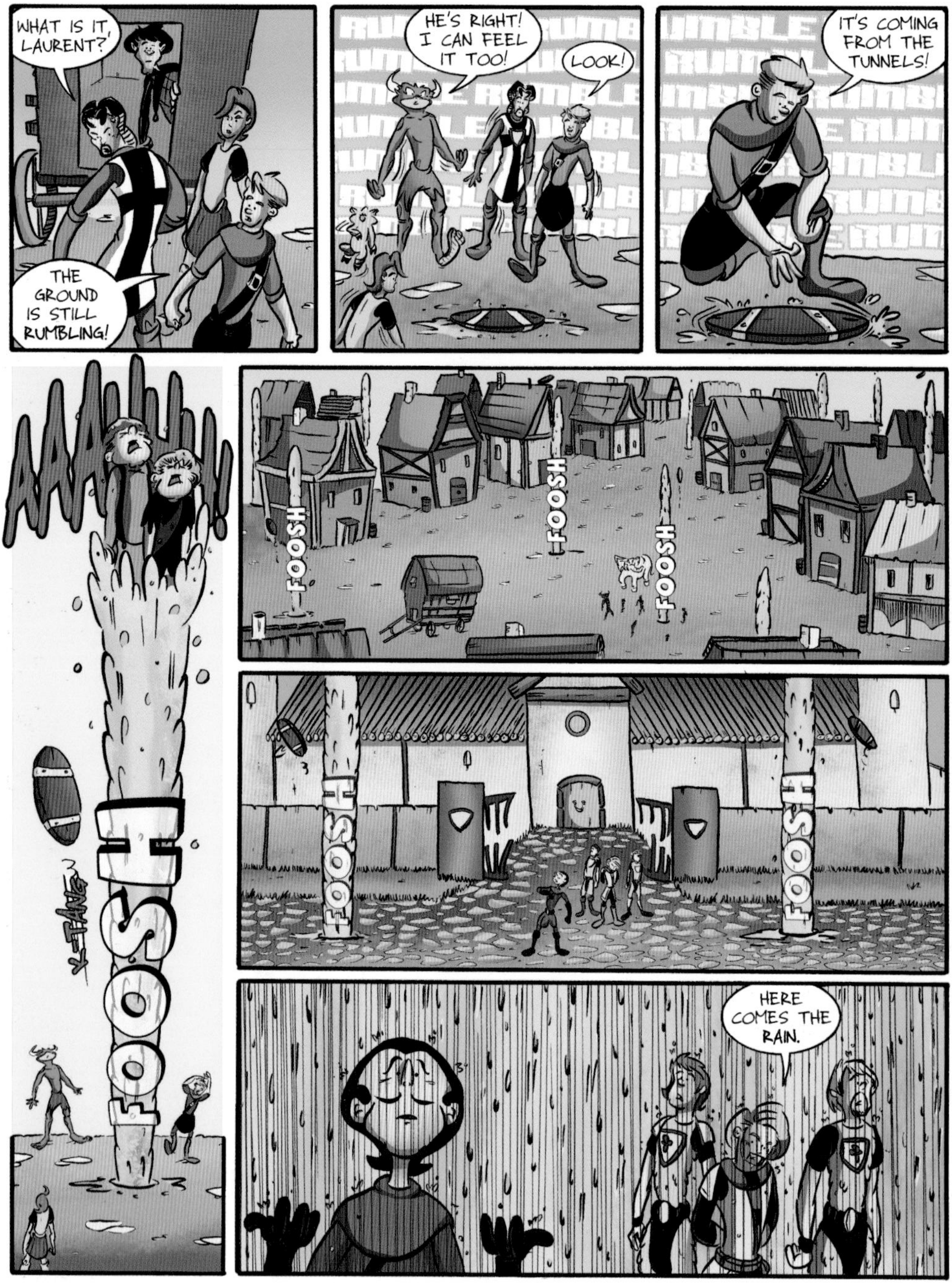
WHAT IS IT, LAURENT?
THE GROUND IS STILL RUMBLING!
RUMBLE RUMBLE RUMBLE
HE'S RIGHT! I CAN FEEL IT TOO!
LOOK!
IT'S COMING FROM THE TUNNELS!
AAAHHH!
FOOSH
FOOSH
FOOSH
FOOSH
FOOSH
FOOSH
HERE COMES THE RAIN.

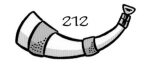

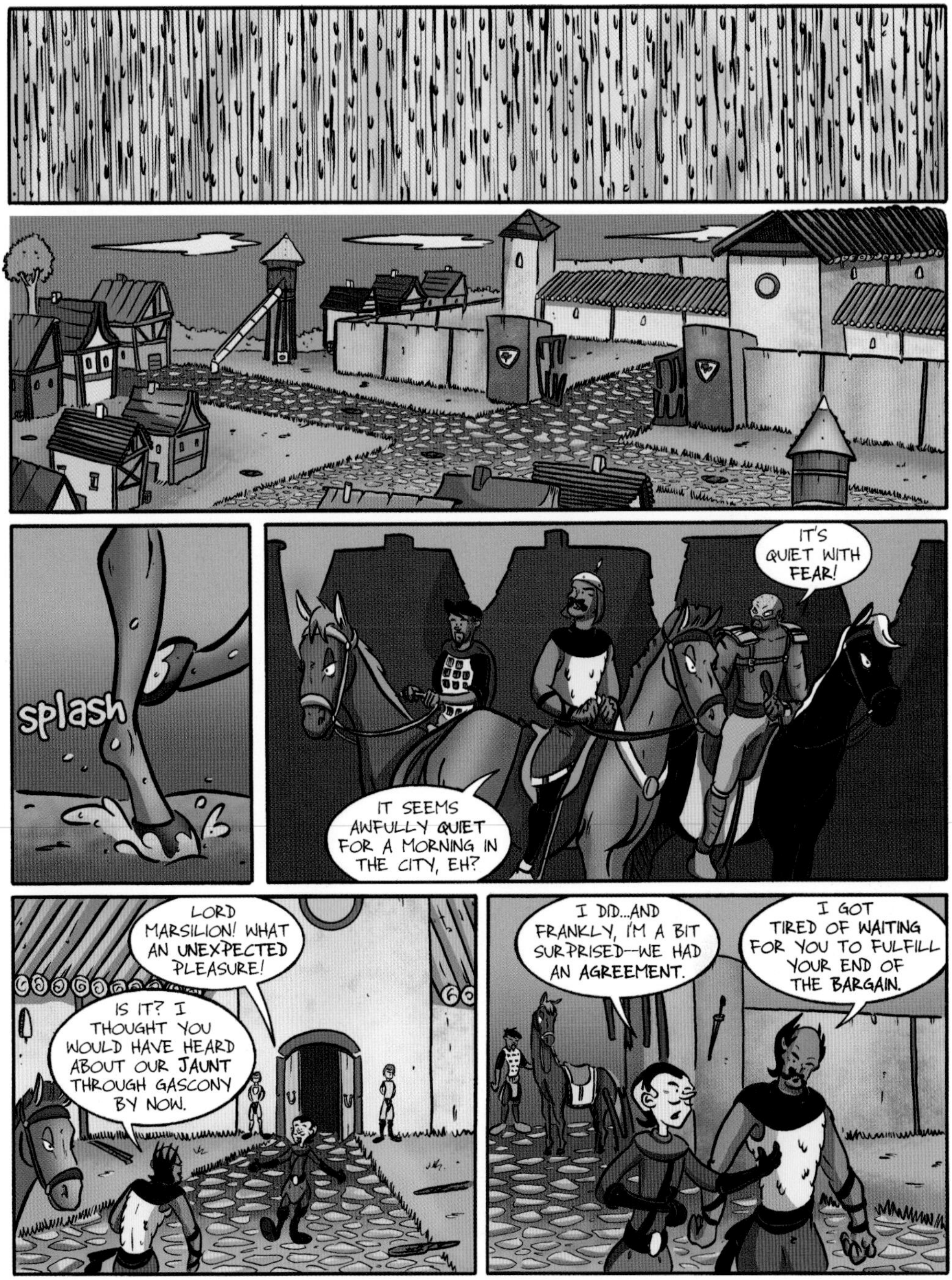
splash
IT SEEMS AWFULLY QUIET FOR A MORNING IN THE CITY, EH?
IT'S QUIET WITH FEAR!
LORD MARSILION! WHAT AN UNEXPECTED PLEASURE!
IS IT? I THOUGHT YOU WOULD HAVE HEARD ABOUT OUR JAUNT THROUGH GASCONY BY NOW.
I DID...AND FRANKLY, I'M A BIT SURPRISED--WE HAD AN AGREEMENT.
I GOT TIRED OF WAITING FOR YOU TO FULFILL YOUR END OF THE BARGAIN.

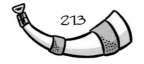

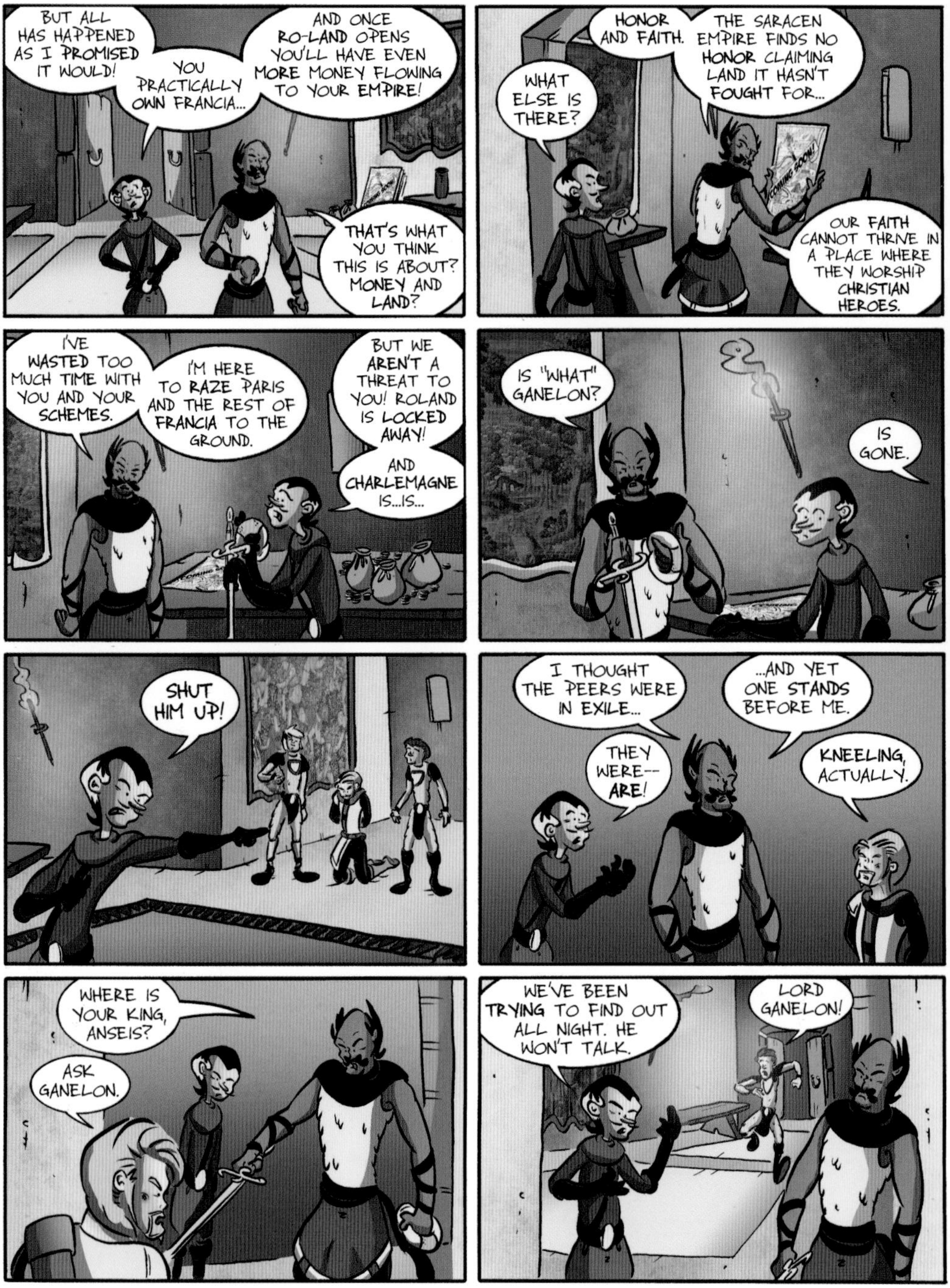
BUT ALL HAS HAPPENED AS I PROMISED IT WOULD!
YOU PRACTICALLY OWN FRANCIA...
AND ONCE RO-LAND OPENS YOU'LL HAVE EVEN MORE MONEY FLOWING TO YOUR EMPIRE!
THAT'S WHAT YOU THINK THIS IS ABOUT? MONEY AND LAND?
WHAT ELSE IS THERE?
HONOR AND FAITH.
THE SARACEN EMPIRE FINDS NO HONOR CLAIMING LAND IT HASN'T FOUGHT FOR...
COMING SOON!
OUR FAITH CANNOT THRIVE IN A PLACE WHERE THEY WORSHIP CHRISTIAN HEROES.
I'VE WASTED TOO MUCH TIME WITH YOU AND YOUR SCHEMES.
I'M HERE TO RAZE PARIS AND THE REST OF FRANCIA TO THE GROUND.
BUT WE AREN'T A THREAT TO YOU! ROLAND IS LOCKED AWAY!
AND CHARLEMAGNE IS...IS...
IS "WHAT" GANELON?
IS GONE.
SHUT HIM UP!
I THOUGHT THE PEERS WERE IN EXILE...
THEY WERE--ARE!
...AND YET ONE STANDS BEFORE ME.
KNEELING, ACTUALLY.
WHERE IS YOUR KING, ANSEIS?
ASK GANELON.
WE'VE BEEN TRYING TO FIND OUT ALL NIGHT. HE WON'T TALK.
LORD GANELON!

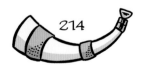

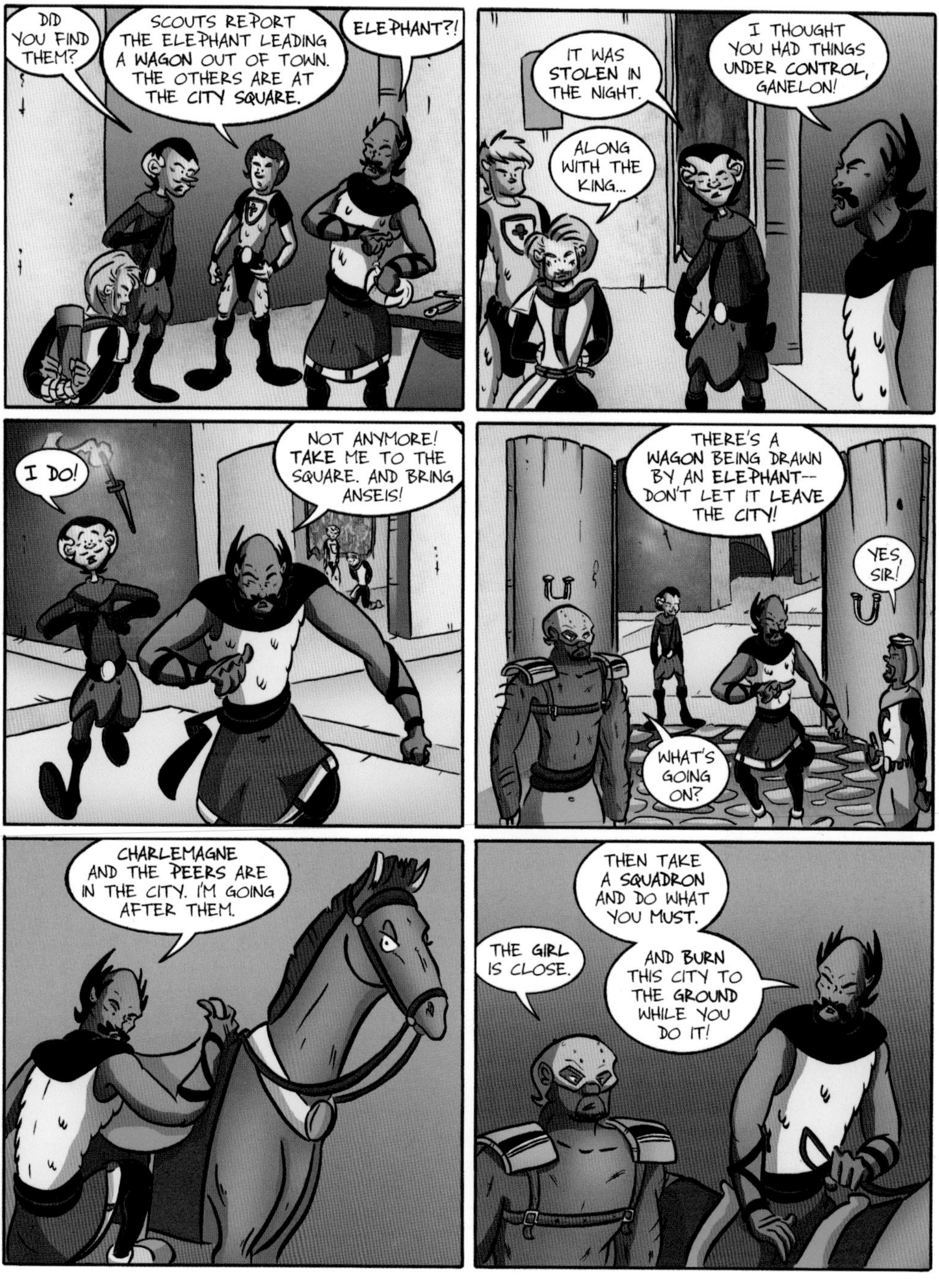
DID YOU FIND THEM?
SCOUTS REPORT THE ELEPHANT LEADING A WAGON OUT OF TOWN. THE OTHERS ARE AT THE CITY SQUARE.
ELEPHANT?!
IT WAS STOLEN IN THE NIGHT.
I THOUGHT YOU HAD THINGS UNDER CONTROL, GANELON!
ALONG WITH THE KING...
I DO!
NOT ANYMORE! TAKE ME TO THE SQUARE. AND BRING ANSEIS!
THERE'S A WAGON BEING DRAWN BY AN ELEPHANT-- DON'T LET IT LEAVE THE CITY!
YES, SIR!
WHAT'S GOING ON?
CHARLEMAGNE AND THE PEERS ARE IN THE CITY. I'M GOING AFTER THEM.
THEN TAKE A SQUADRON AND DO WHAT YOU MUST.
THE GIRL IS CLOSE.
AND BURN THIS CITY TO THE GROUND WHILE YOU DO IT!

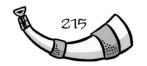

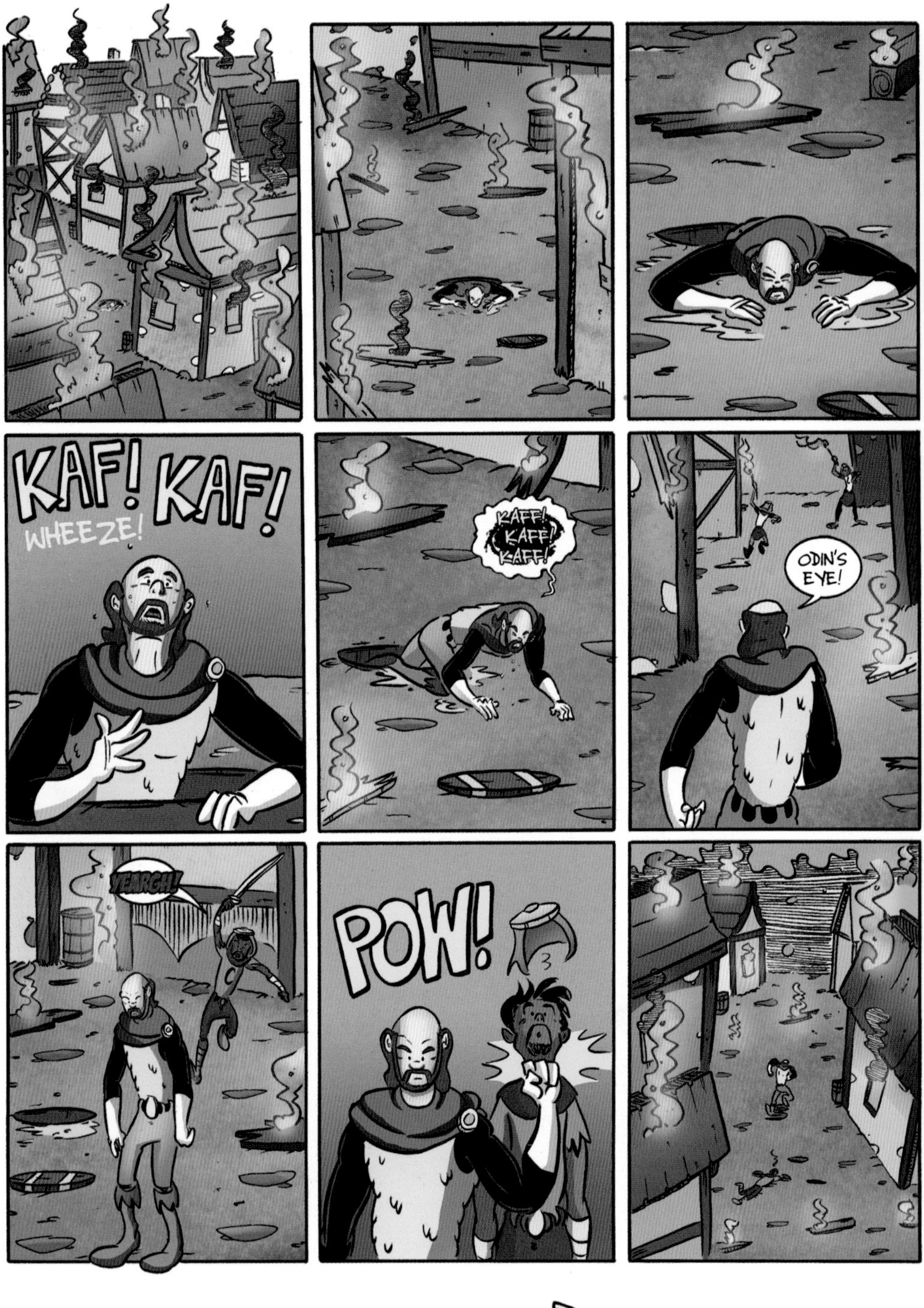
KAF! KAF!
WHEEZE!
KAFF! KAFF! KAFF!
ODIN'S EYE!
YEARGH!
POW!

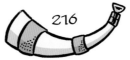

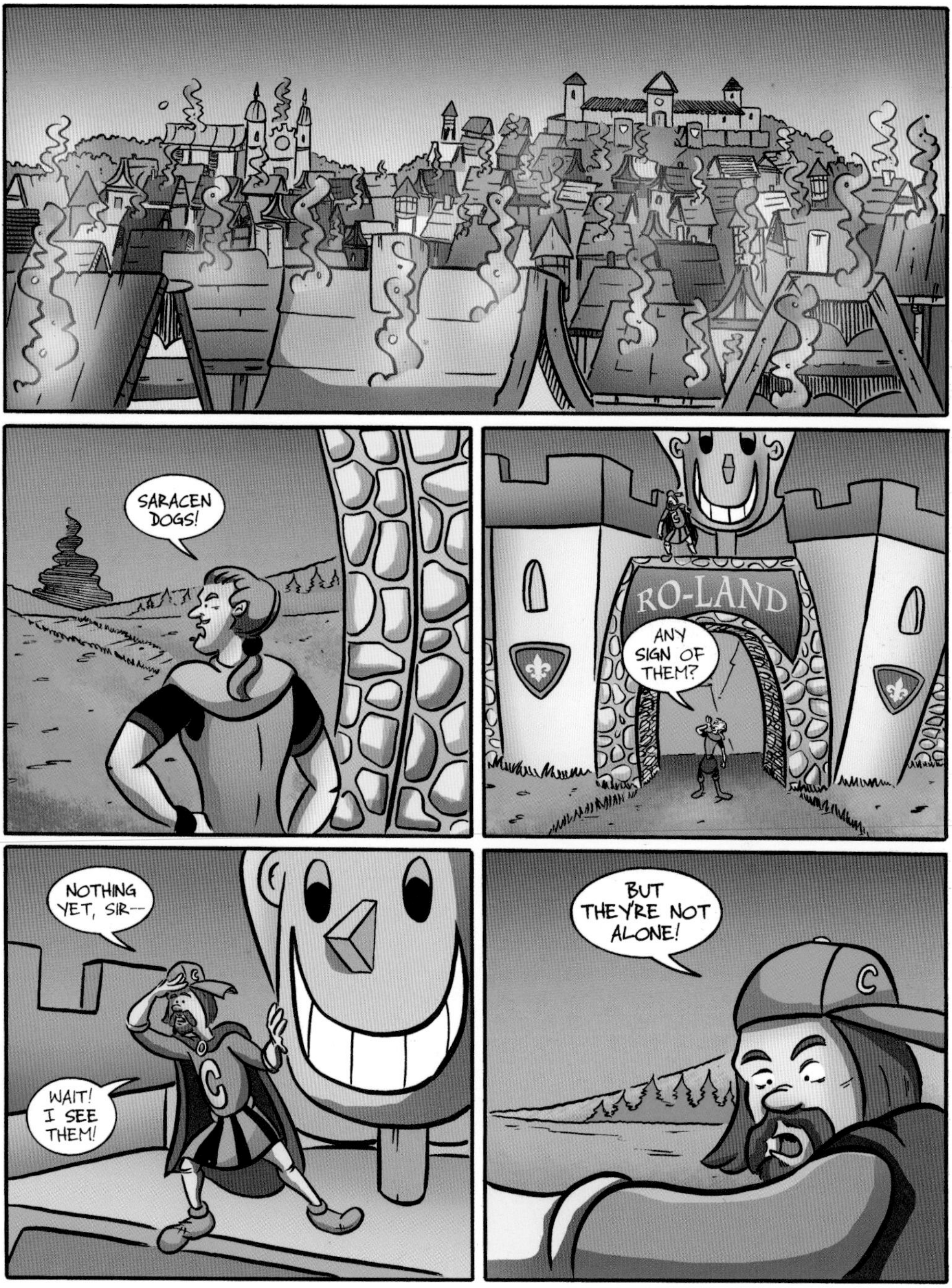
SARACEN DOGS!
RO-LAND
ANY SIGN OF THEM?
NOTHING YET, SIR--
WAIT! I SEE THEM!
BUT THEY'RE NOT ALONE!

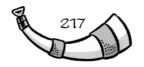

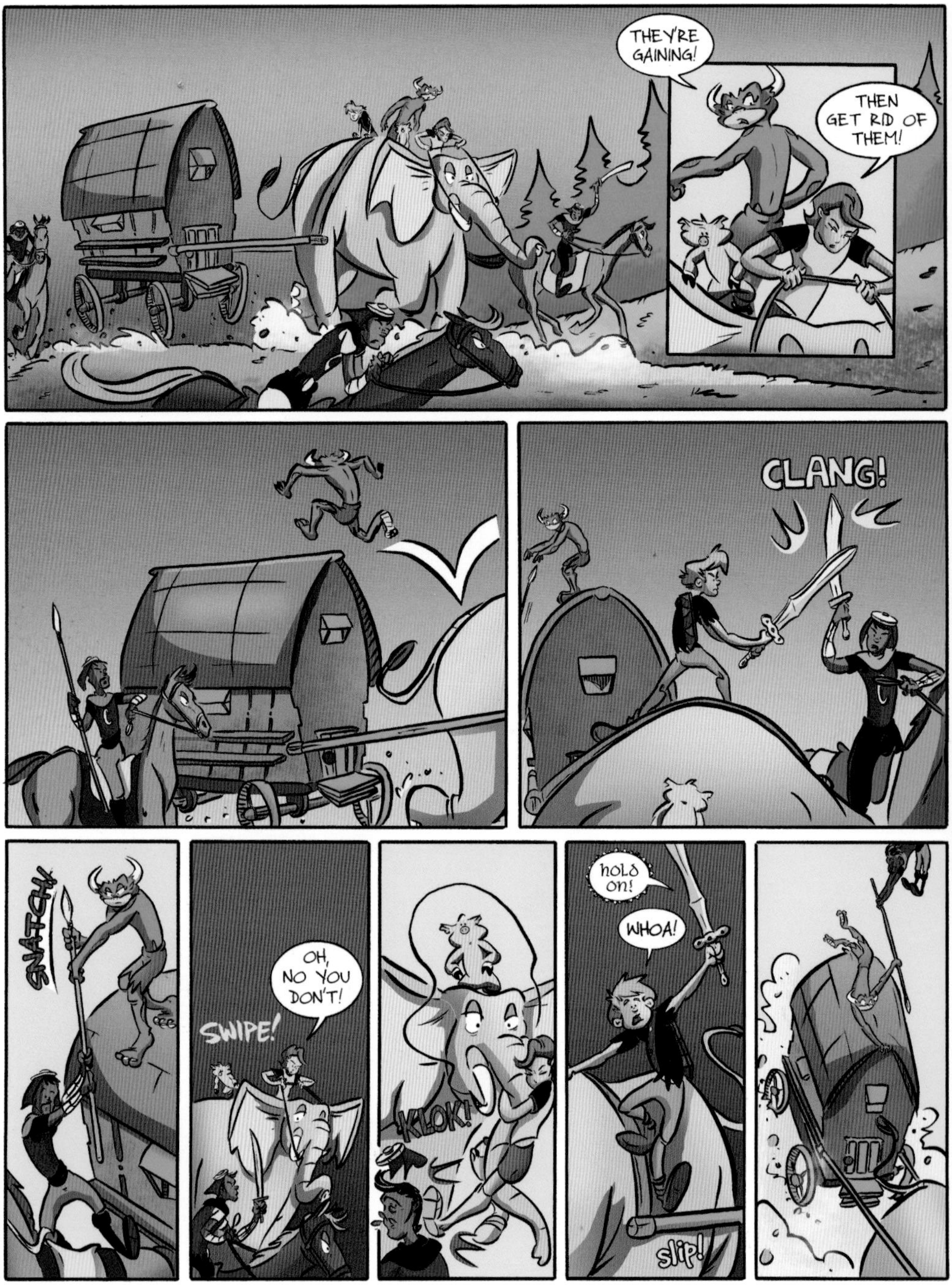
THEY'RE GAINING!
THEN GET RID OF THEM!
CLANG!
SNATCH!
OH, NO YOU DON'T!
SWIPE!
KLOK!
HOLD ON!
WHOA!
SLIP!

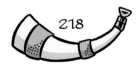

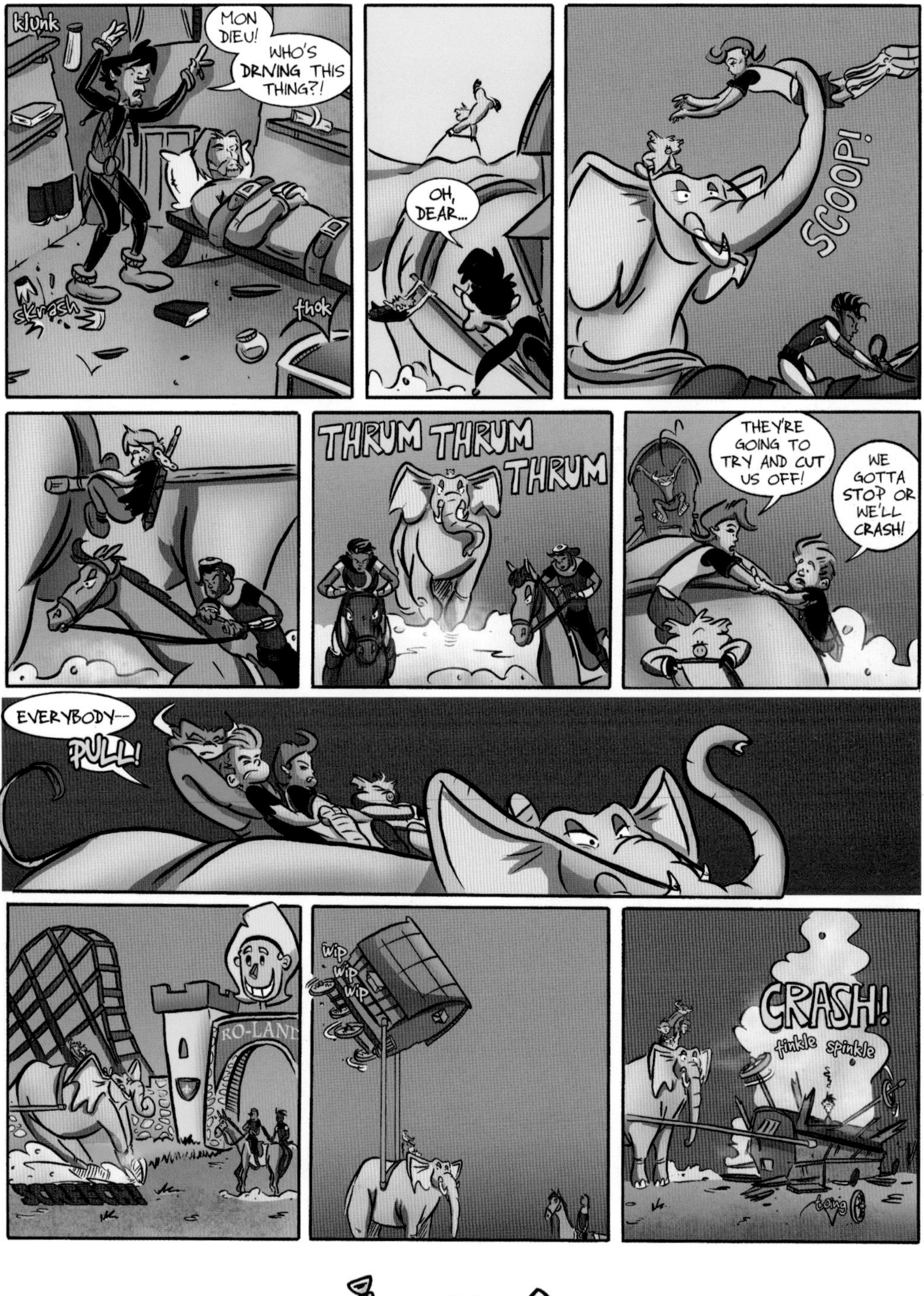
klunk
MON DIEU!
WHO'S DRIVING THIS THING?!
skrash
thok
OH, DEAR...
SCOOP!
THRUM THRUM THRUM
THEY'RE GOING TO TRY AND CUT US OFF!
WE GOTTA STOP OR WE'LL CRASH!
EVERYBODY--
PULL!
RO-LAND
wip wip wip
CRASH!
tinkle spinkle
toing

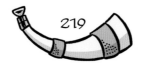

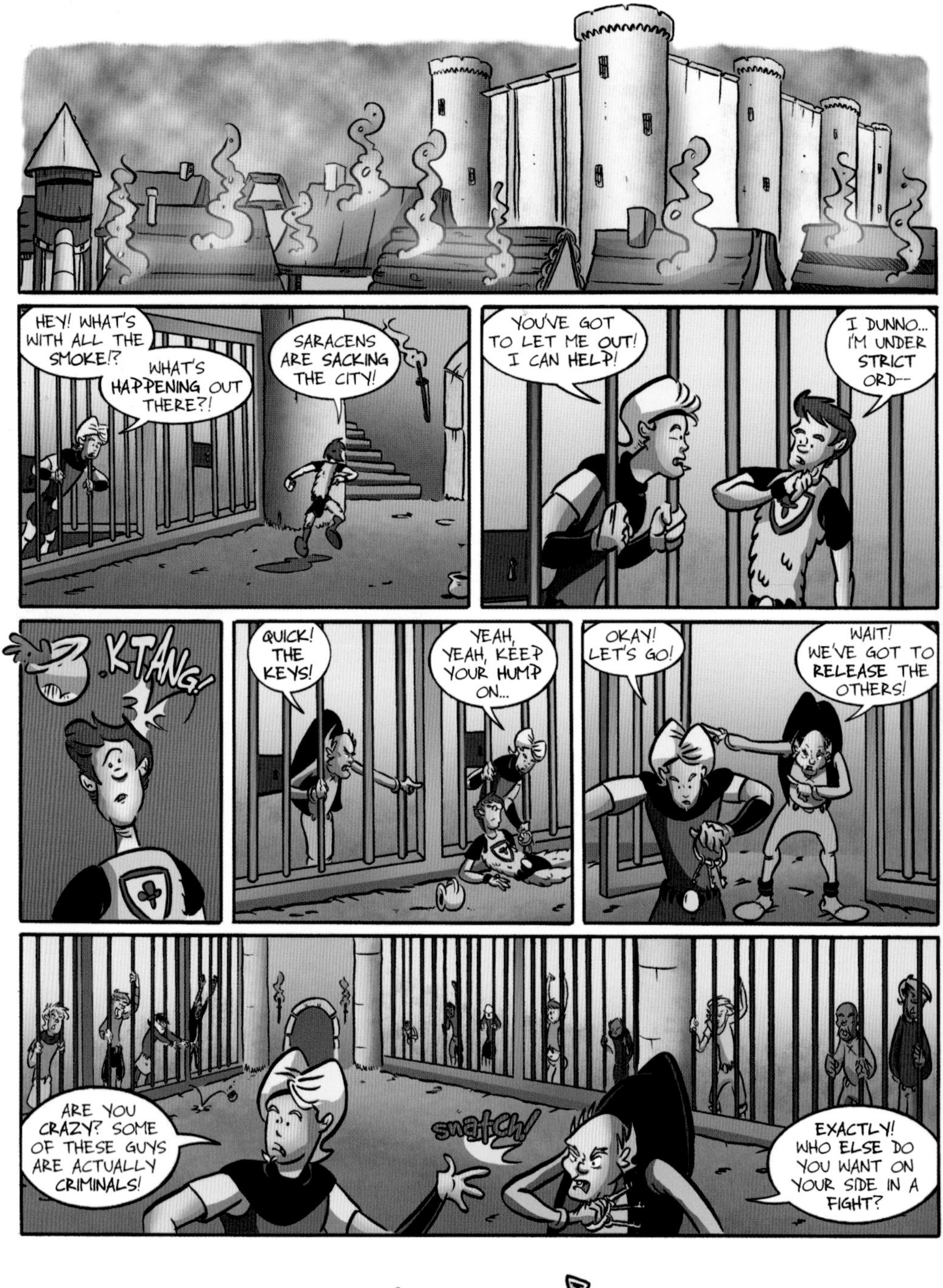
HEY! WHAT'S WITH ALL THE SMOKE!?
WHAT'S HAPPENING OUT THERE?!
SARACENS ARE SACKING THE CITY!
YOU'VE GOT TO LET ME OUT! I CAN HELP!
I DUNNO... I'M UNDER STRICT ORD--
KTANG!
QUICK! THE KEYS!
YEAH, YEAH, KEEP YOUR HUMP ON...
OKAY! LET'S GO!
WAIT! WE'VE GOT TO RELEASE THE OTHERS!
ARE YOU CRAZY? SOME OF THESE GUYS ARE ACTUALLY CRIMINALS!
snatch!
EXACTLY! WHO ELSE DO YOU WANT ON YOUR SIDE IN A FIGHT?

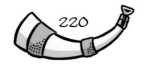

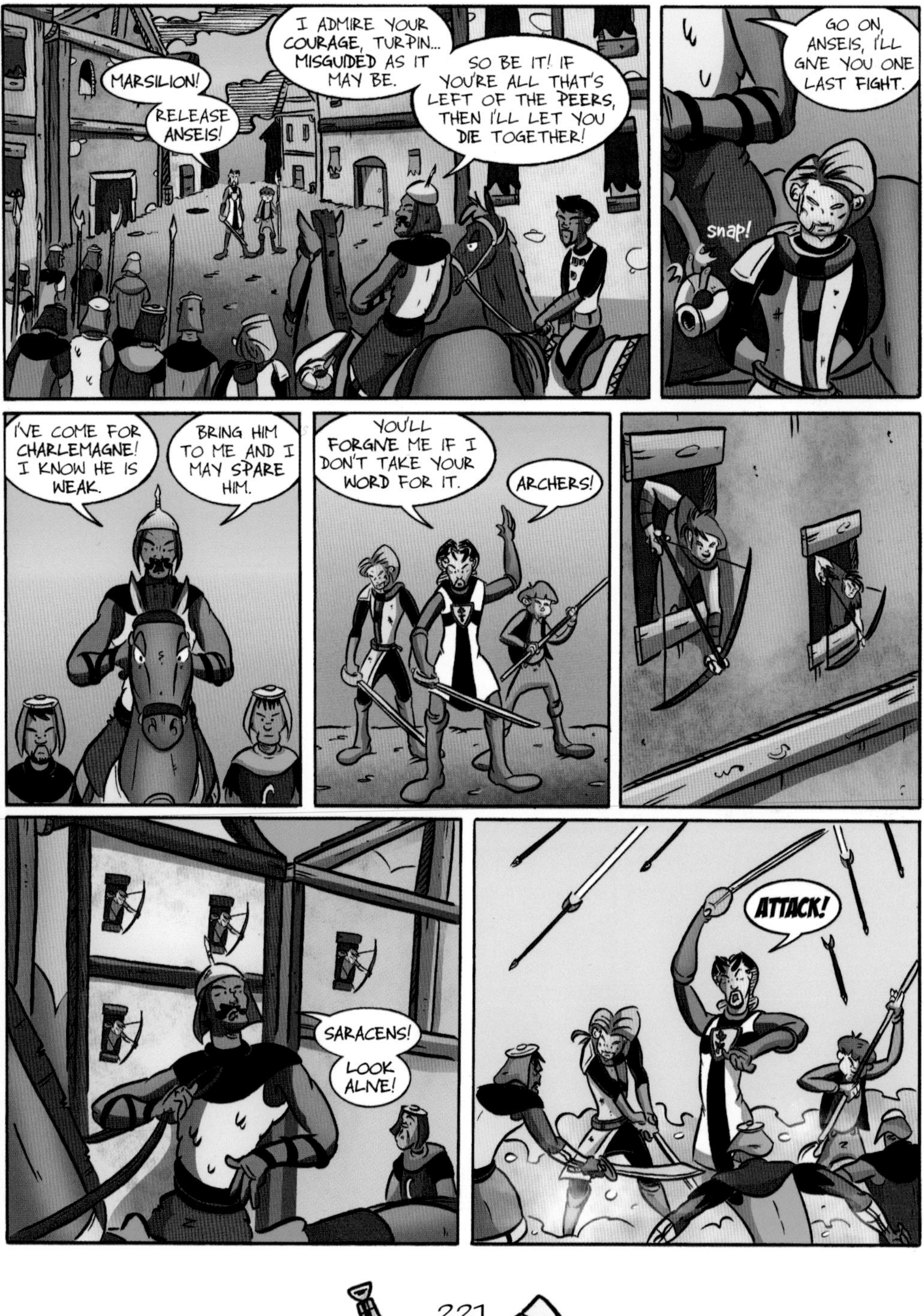
MARSILION!
RELEASE ANSEIS!
I ADMIRE YOUR COURAGE, TURPIN... MISGUIDED AS IT MAY BE.
SO BE IT! IF YOU'RE ALL THAT'S LEFT OF THE PEERS, THEN I'LL LET YOU DIE TOGETHER!
GO ON, ANSEIS, I'LL GIVE YOU ONE LAST FIGHT.
snap!
I'VE COME FOR CHARLEMAGNE! I KNOW HE IS WEAK.
BRING HIM TO ME AND I MAY SPARE HIM.
YOU'LL FORGIVE ME IF I DON'T TAKE YOUR WORD FOR IT.
ARCHERS!
SARACENS!
LOOK ALIVE!
ATTACK!

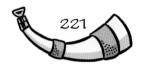

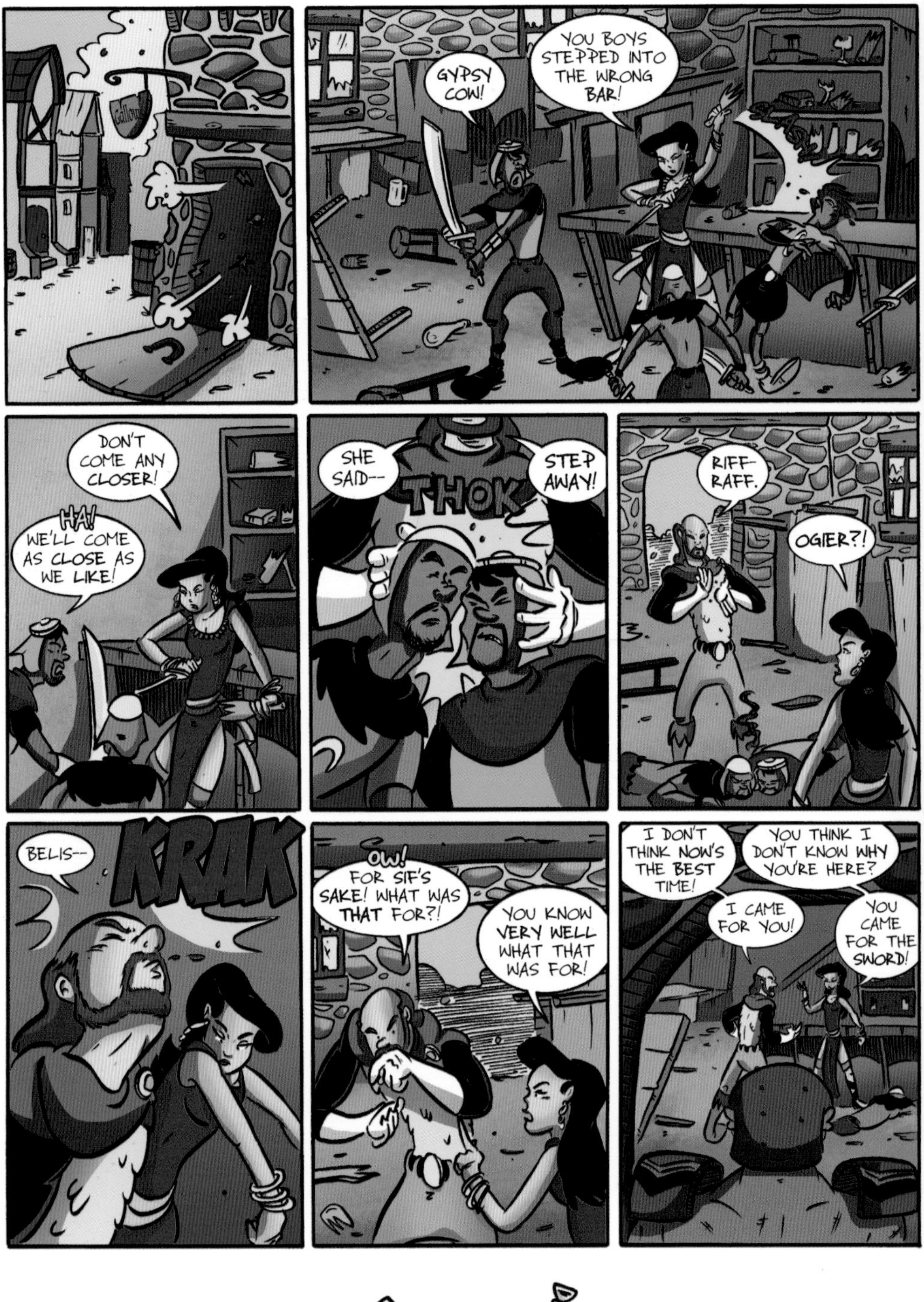
GYPSY COW!
YOU BOYS STEPPED INTO THE WRONG BAR!
DON'T COME ANY CLOSER!
HA! WE'LL COME AS CLOSE AS WE LIKE!
SHE SAID--
THOK
STEP AWAY!
RIFF-RAFF.
OGIER?!
BELIS--
KRAK
OW! FOR SIF'S SAKE! WHAT WAS THAT FOR?!
YOU KNOW VERY WELL WHAT THAT WAS FOR!
I DON'T THINK NOW'S THE BEST TIME!
YOU THINK I DON'T KNOW WHY YOU'RE HERE?
I CAME FOR YOU!
YOU CAME FOR THE SWORD!

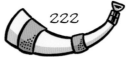

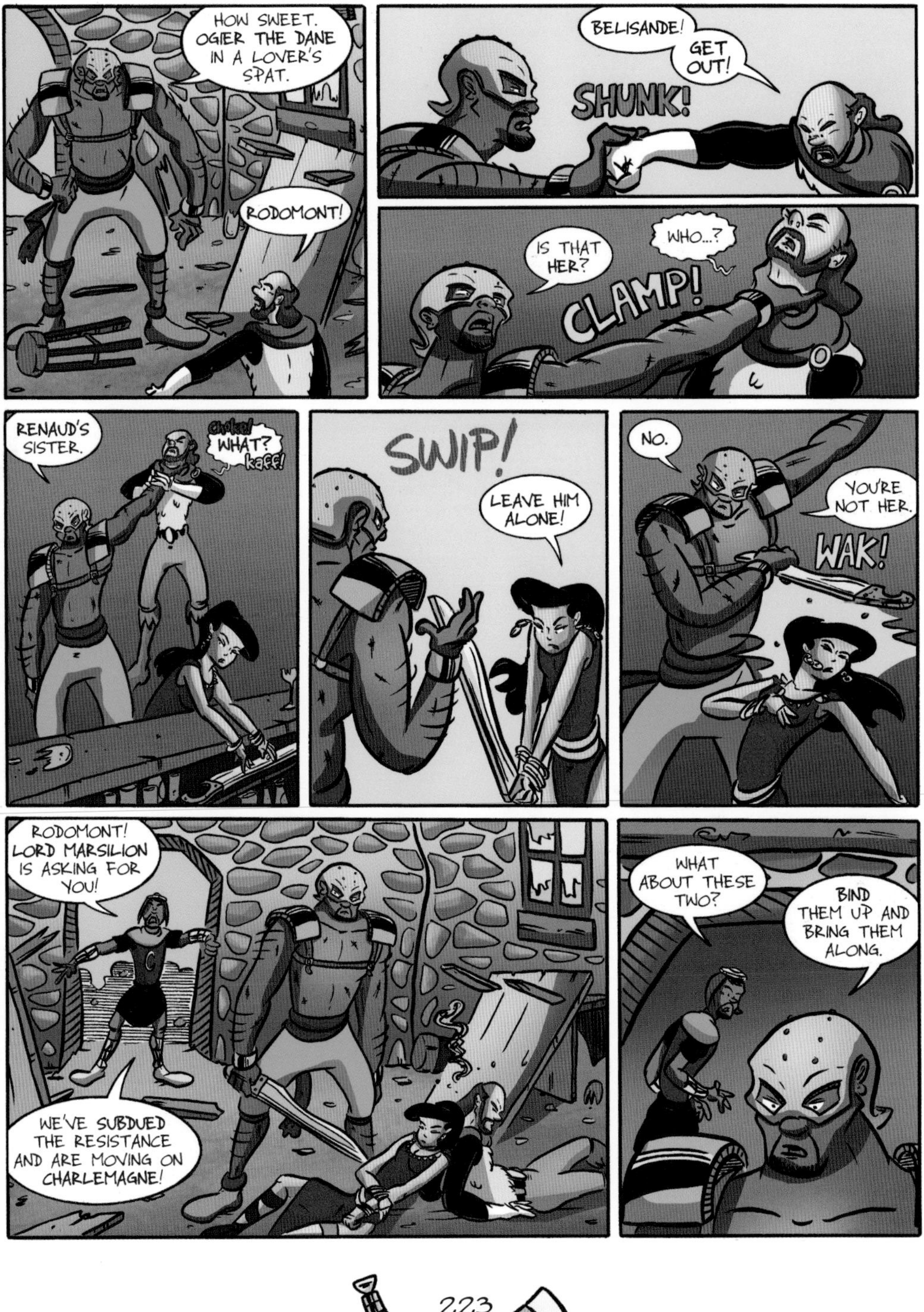

HOW SWEET. OGIER THE DANE IN A LOVER'S SPAT.
RODOMONT!
BELISANDE! GET OUT!
SHUNK!
IS THAT HER?
WHO...?
CLAMP!
RENAUD'S SISTER.
Choke! WHAT? kaff!
SWIP!
LEAVE HIM ALONE!
NO.
YOU'RE NOT HER.
WAK!
RODOMONT! LORD MARSILION IS ASKING FOR YOU!
WE'VE SUBDUED THE RESISTANCE AND ARE MOVING ON CHARLEMAGNE!
WHAT ABOUT THESE TWO?
BIND THEM UP AND BRING THEM ALONG.

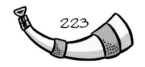

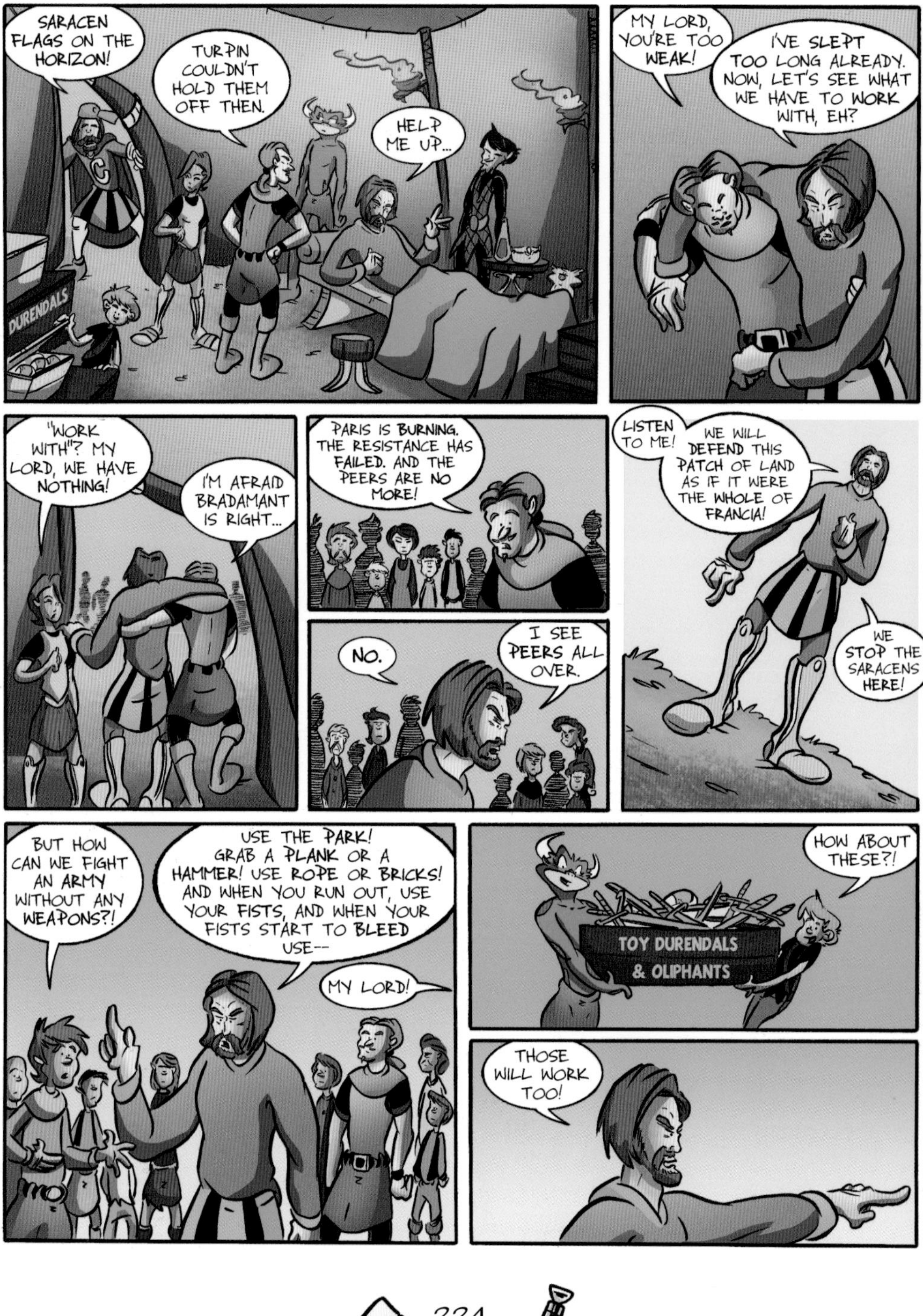
SARACEN FLAGS ON THE HORIZON!
TURPIN COULDN'T HOLD THEM OFF THEN.
HELP ME UP...
DURENDALS
MY LORD, YOU'RE TOO WEAK!
I'VE SLEPT TOO LONG ALREADY. NOW, LET'S SEE WHAT WE HAVE TO WORK WITH, EH?
"WORK WITH"? MY LORD, WE HAVE NOTHING!
I'M AFRAID BRADAMANT IS RIGHT...
PARIS IS BURNING. THE RESISTANCE HAS FAILED. AND THE PEERS ARE NO MORE!
NO.
I SEE PEERS ALL OVER.
LISTEN TO ME!
WE WILL DEFEND THIS PATCH OF LAND AS IF IT WERE THE WHOLE OF FRANCIA!
WE STOP THE SARACENS HERE!
BUT HOW CAN WE FIGHT AN ARMY WITHOUT ANY WEAPONS?!
USE THE PARK! GRAB A PLANK OR A HAMMER! USE ROPE OR BRICKS! AND WHEN YOU RUN OUT, USE YOUR FISTS, AND WHEN YOUR FISTS START TO BLEED USE--
MY LORD!
HOW ABOUT THESE?!
TOY DURENDALS & OLIPHANTS
THOSE WILL WORK TOO!

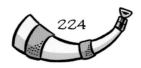

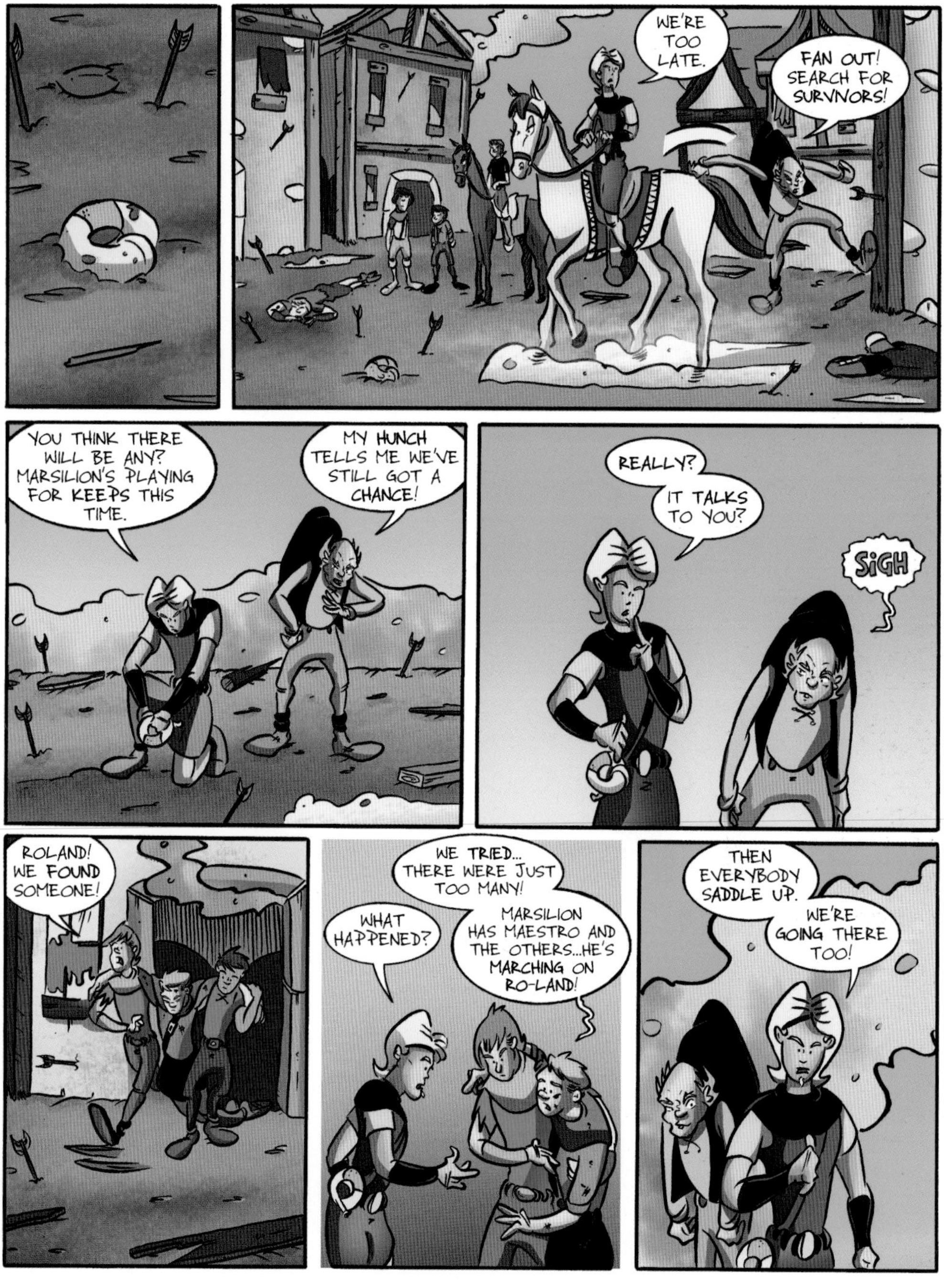
WE'RE TOO LATE.
FAN OUT! SEARCH FOR SURVIVORS!
YOU THINK THERE WILL BE ANY? MARSILION'S PLAYING FOR KEEPS THIS TIME.
MY HUNCH TELLS ME WE'VE STILL GOT A CHANCE!
REALLY?
IT TALKS TO YOU?
SIGH
ROLAND! WE FOUND SOMEONE!
WHAT HAPPENED?
WE TRIED... THERE WERE JUST TOO MANY!
MARSILION HAS MAESTRO AND THE OTHERS...HE'S MARCHING ON RO-LAND!
THEN EVERYBODY SADDLE UP.
WE'RE GOING THERE TOO!

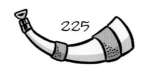

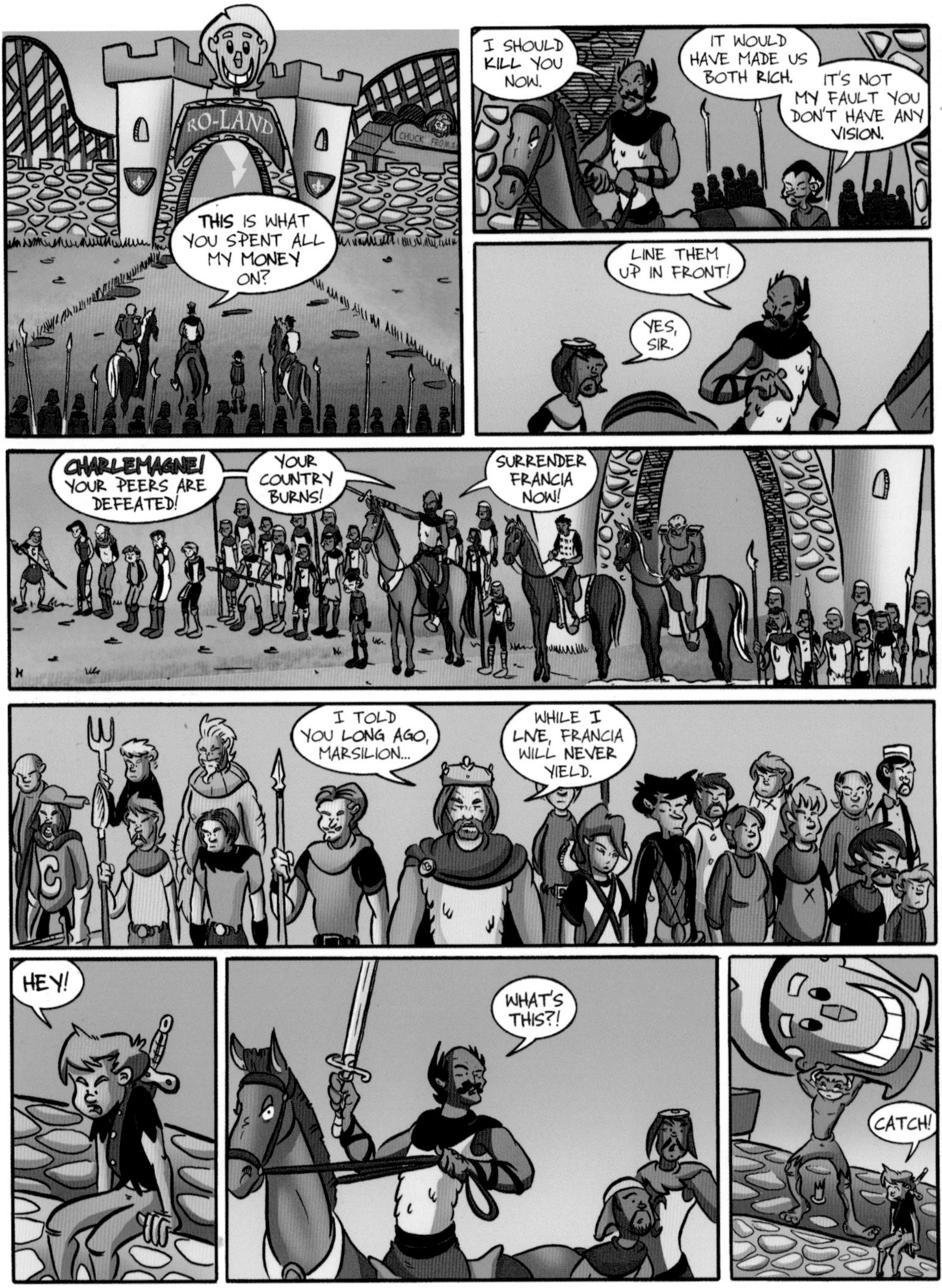
RO-LAND
CHUCK FROMA
THIS IS WHAT YOU SPENT ALL MY MONEY ON?
I SHOULD KILL YOU NOW.
IT WOULD HAVE MADE US BOTH RICH.
IT'S NOT MY FAULT YOU DON'T HAVE ANY VISION.
LINE THEM UP IN FRONT!
YES, SIR.
CHARLEMAGNE! YOUR PEERS ARE DEFEATED!
YOUR COUNTRY BURNS!
SURRENDER FRANCIA NOW!
I TOLD YOU LONG AGO, MARSILION...
WHILE I LIVE, FRANCIA WILL NEVER YIELD.
HEY!
WHAT'S THIS?!
CATCH!

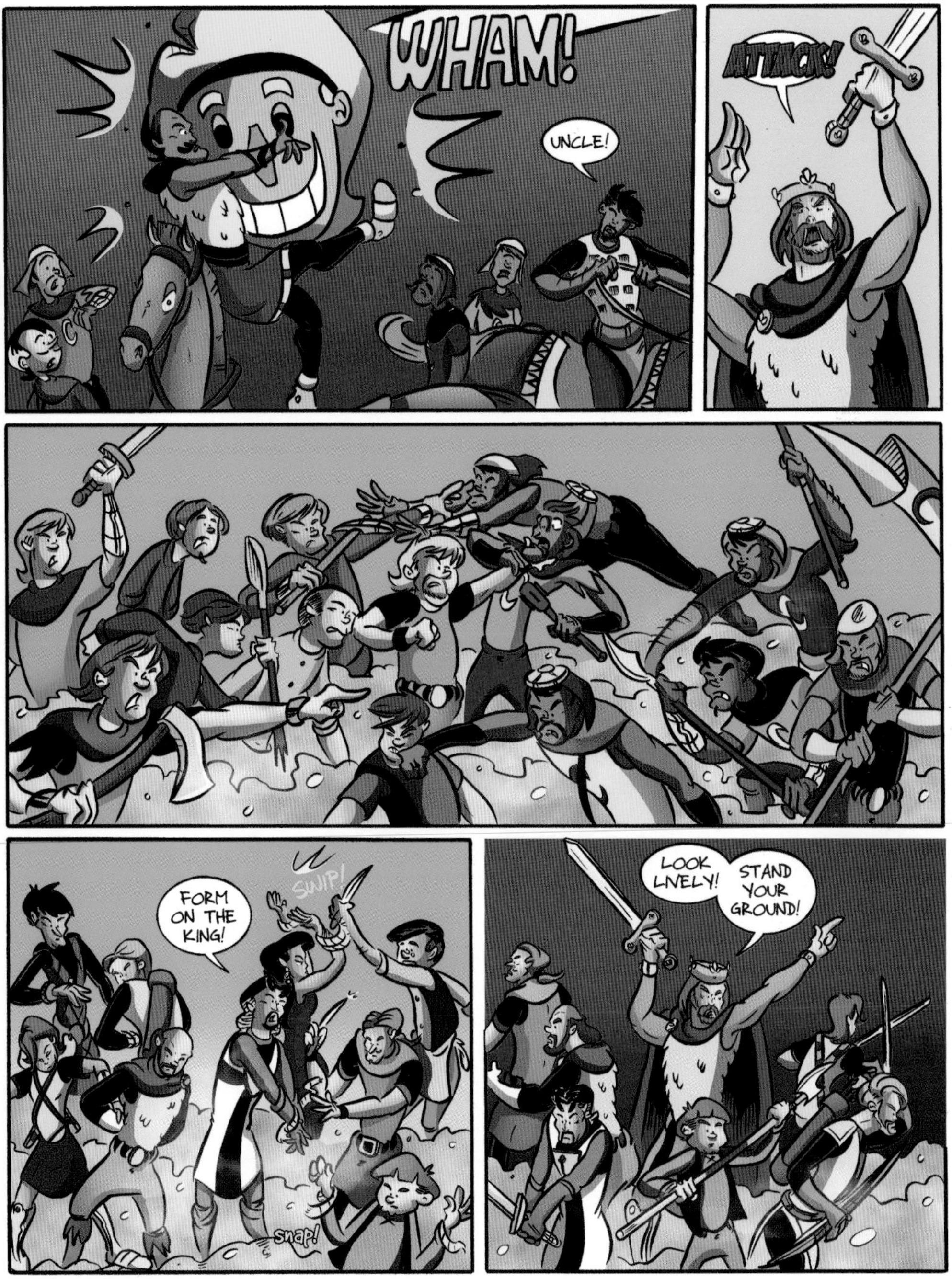
WHAM!
UNCLE!
ATTACK!
FORM ON THE KING!
SWIP!
SNAP!
LOOK LIVELY!
STAND YOUR GROUND!

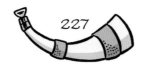

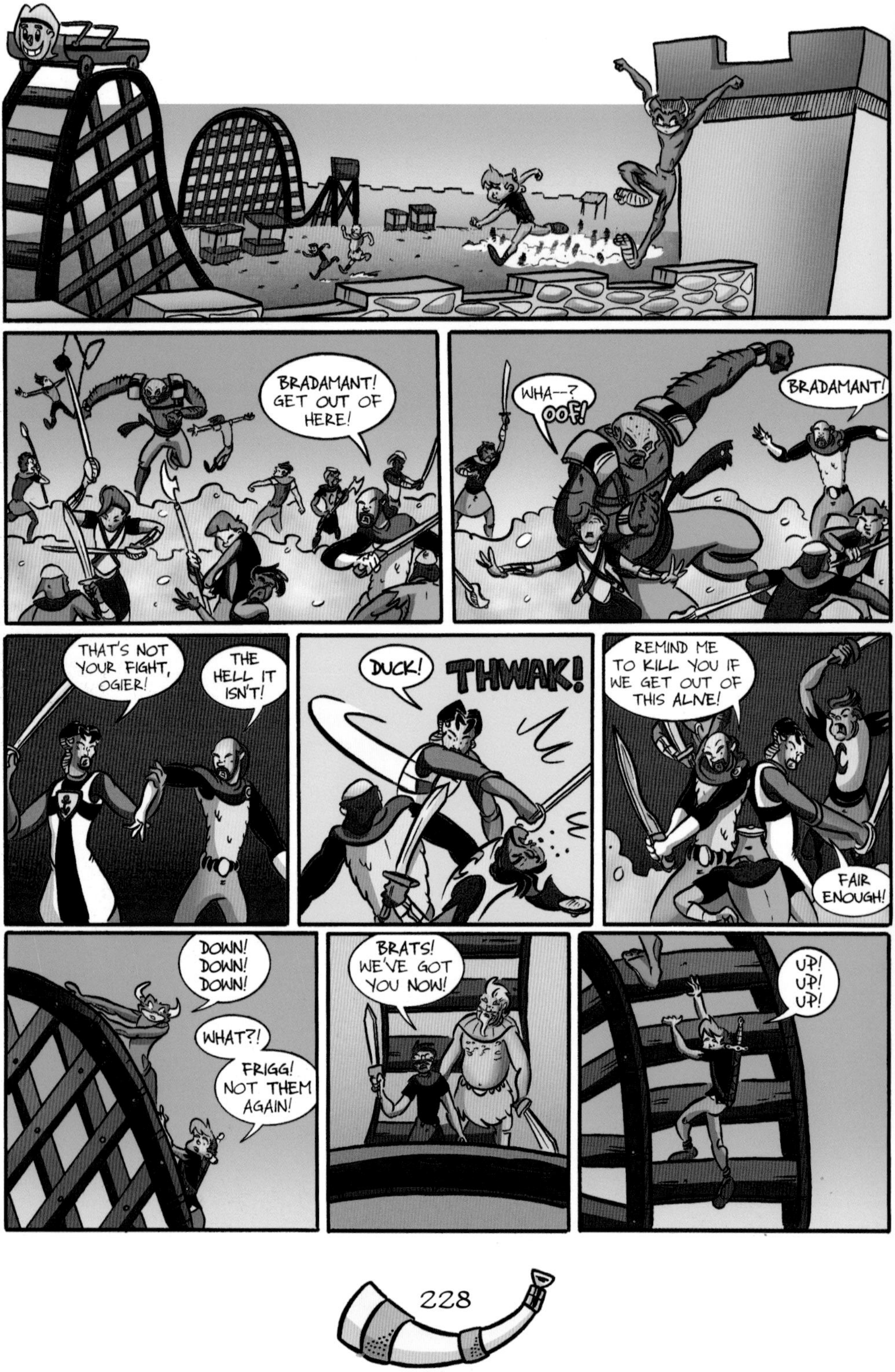
BRADAMANT! GET OUT OF HERE!
WHA--? OOF!
BRADAMANT!
THAT'S NOT YOUR FIGHT, OGIER!
THE HELL IT ISN'T!
DUCK!
THWAK!
REMIND ME TO KILL YOU IF WE GET OUT OF THIS ALIVE!
FAIR ENOUGH!
DOWN! DOWN! DOWN!
WHAT?!
FRIGG! NOT THEM AGAIN!
BRATS! WE'VE GOT YOU NOW!
UP! UP! UP!

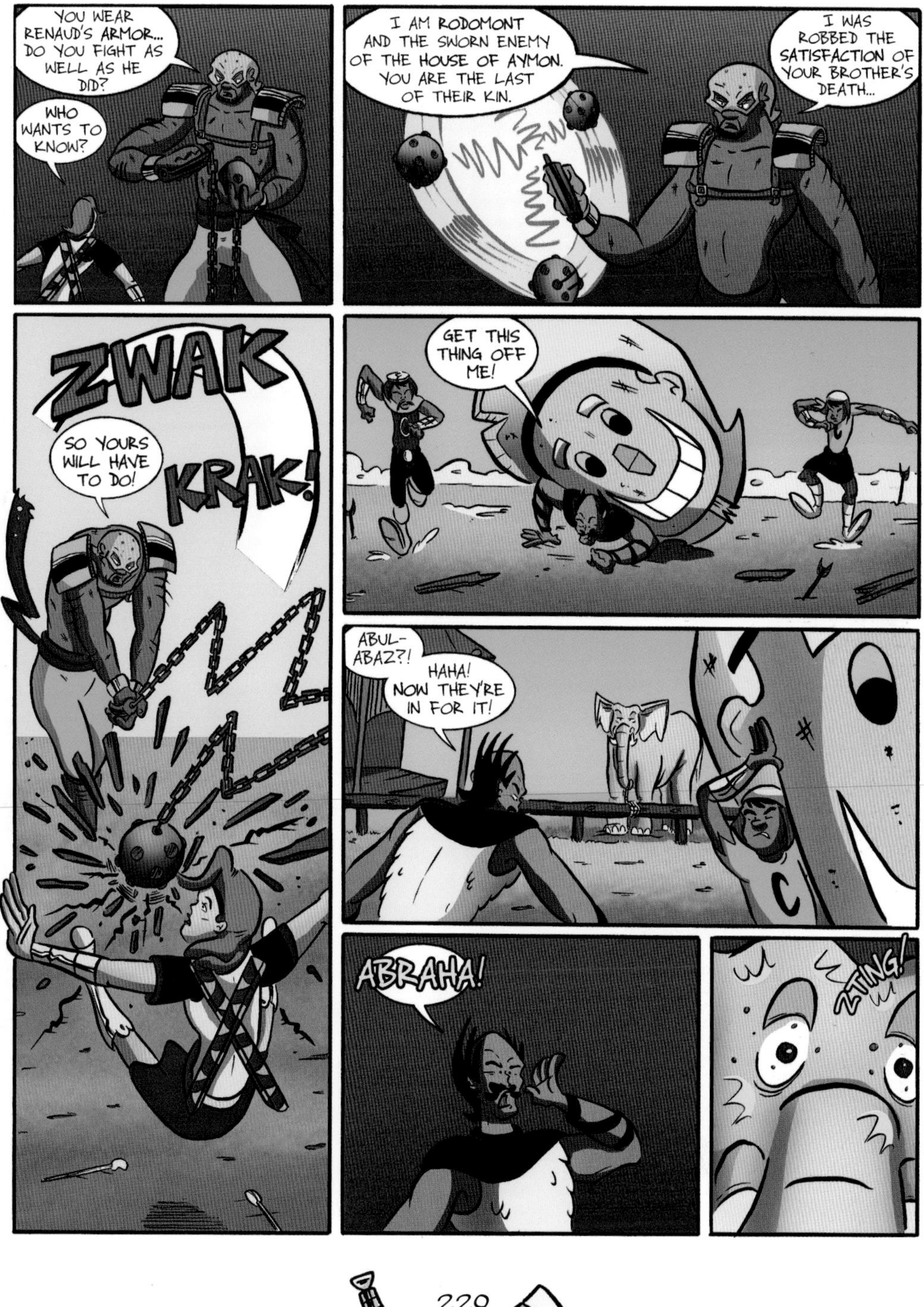
YOU WEAR RENAUD'S ARMOR... DO YOU FIGHT AS WELL AS HE DID?
WHO WANTS TO KNOW?
I AM RODOMONT AND THE SWORN ENEMY OF THE HOUSE OF AYMON. YOU ARE THE LAST OF THEIR KIN.
I WAS ROBBED THE SATISFACTION OF YOUR BROTHER'S DEATH...
ZWAK
SO YOURS WILL HAVE TO DO!
KRAK!
GET THIS THING OFF ME!
ABUL-ABAZ?!
HAHA! NOW THEY'RE IN FOR IT!
ABRAHA!
ZTING!

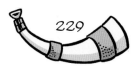

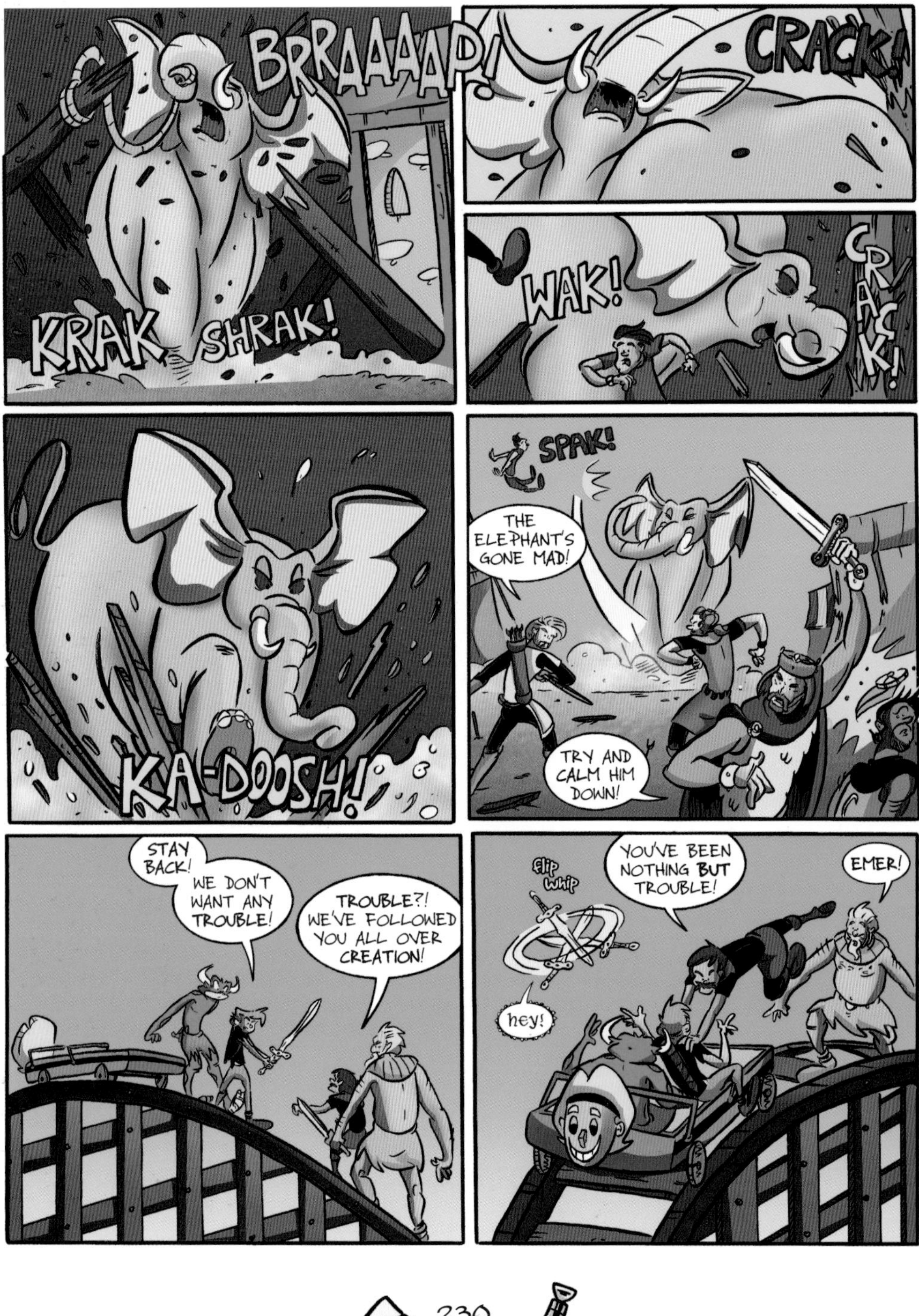
BRRAAAAP!
KRAK SHRAK!
CRACK!
WAK!
CRACK!
KA-DOOSH!
SPAK!
THE ELEPHANT'S GONE MAD!
TRY AND CALM HIM DOWN!
STAY BACK!
WE DON'T WANT ANY TROUBLE!
TROUBLE?! WE'VE FOLLOWED YOU ALL OVER CREATION!
flip whip
hey!
YOU'VE BEEN NOTHING BUT TROUBLE!
EMER!

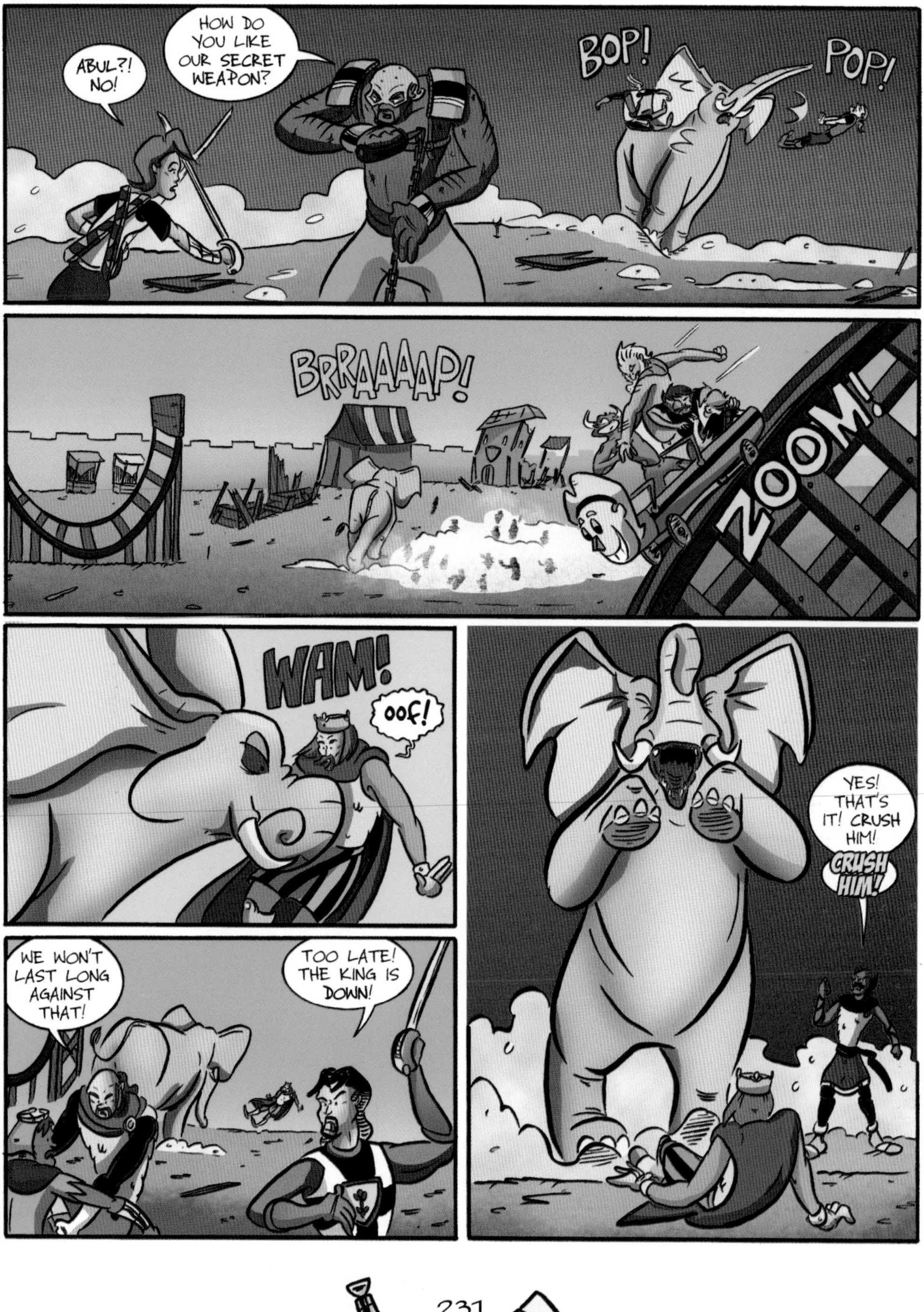
ABUL?! NO!
HOW DO YOU LIKE OUR SECRET WEAPON?
BOP!
POP!
BRRAAAAP!
ZOOM!
WAM!
OOF!
YES! THAT'S IT! CRUSH HIM!
CRUSH HIM!
WE WON'T LAST LONG AGAINST THAT!
TOO LATE! THE KING IS DOWN!

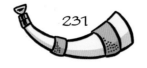

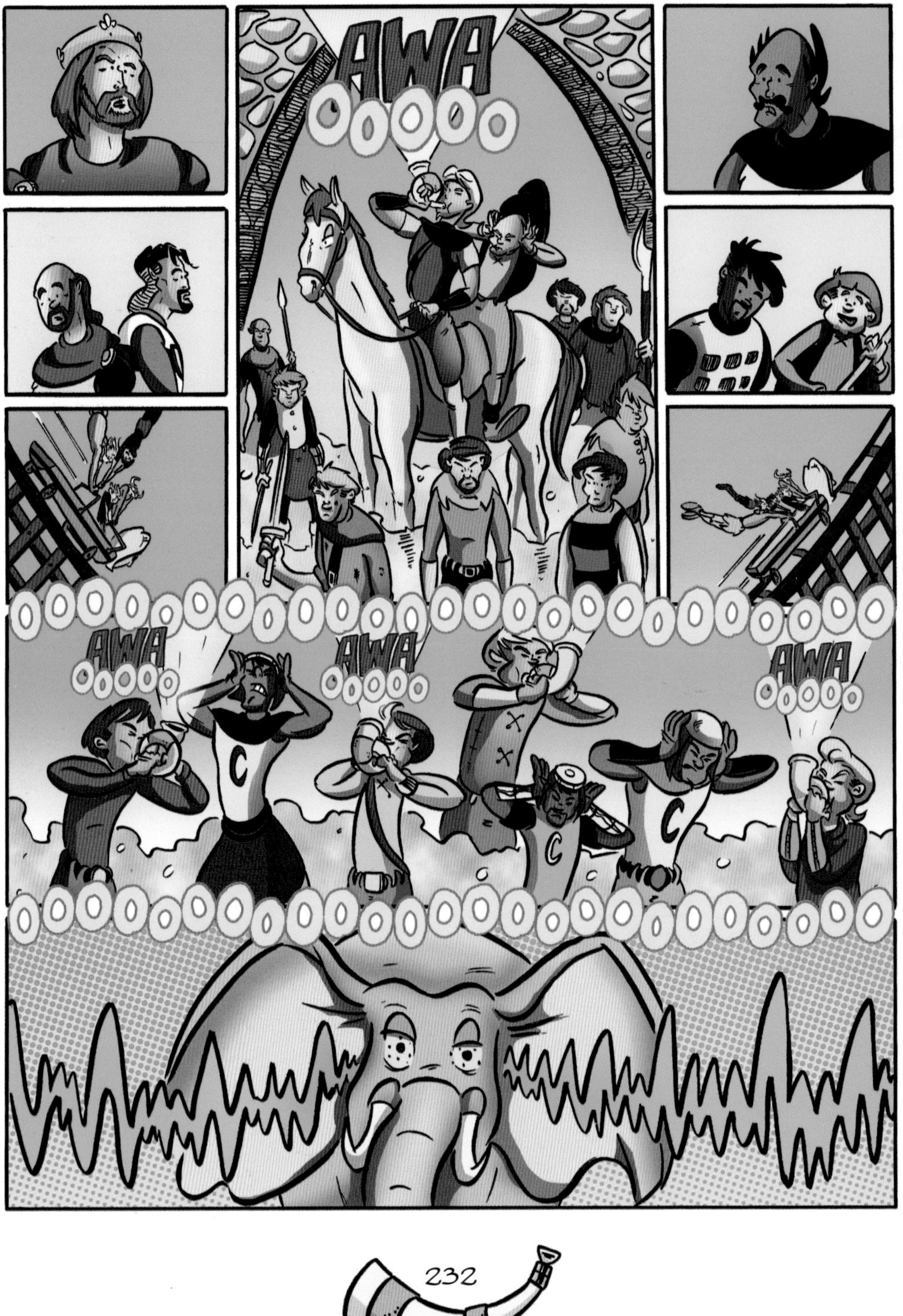
AWAOOOOOO
AWAOOOOOO
AWAOOOOOO
AWAOOOOOO

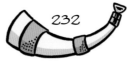

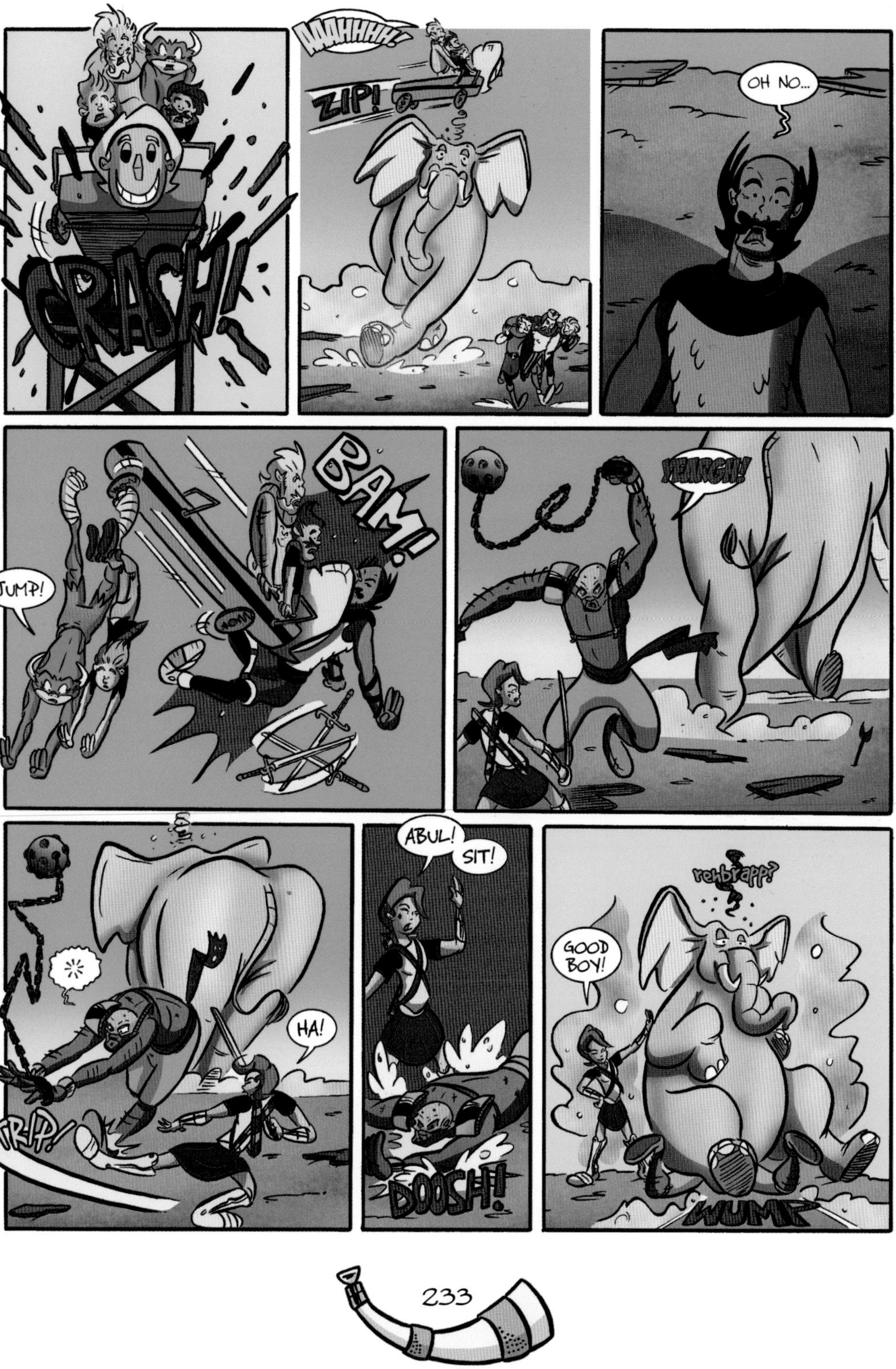
CRASH!
AAAHHHH!
ZIP!
OH NO...
BAM!
JUMP!
YEARGH!
TRIP!
HA!
ABUL!
SIT!
DOOSH!
rehbrapp?
GOOD BOY!
WUMP

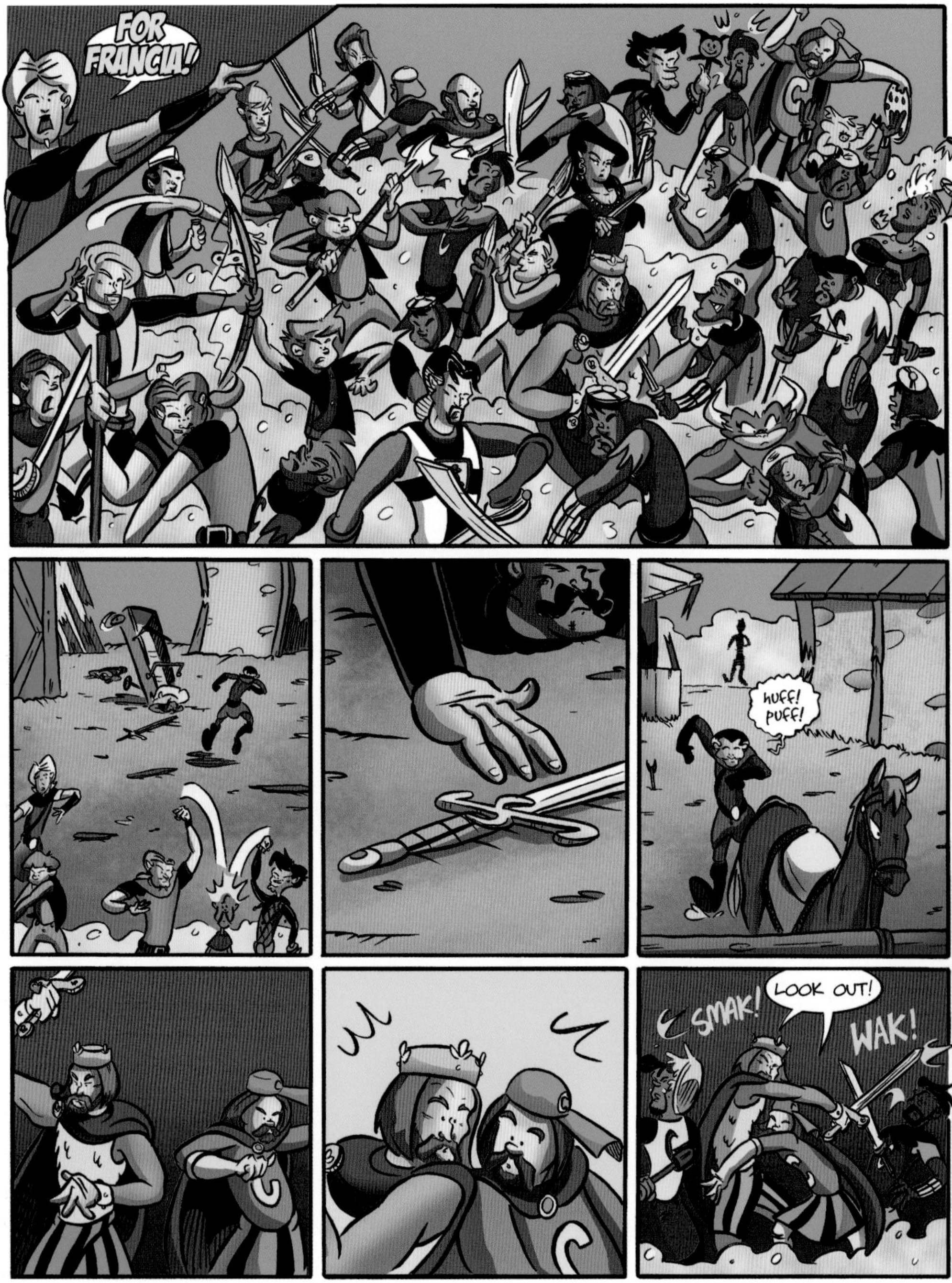
FOR FRANCIA!
huff! puff!
SMAK!
LOOK OUT!
WAK!

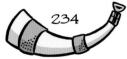

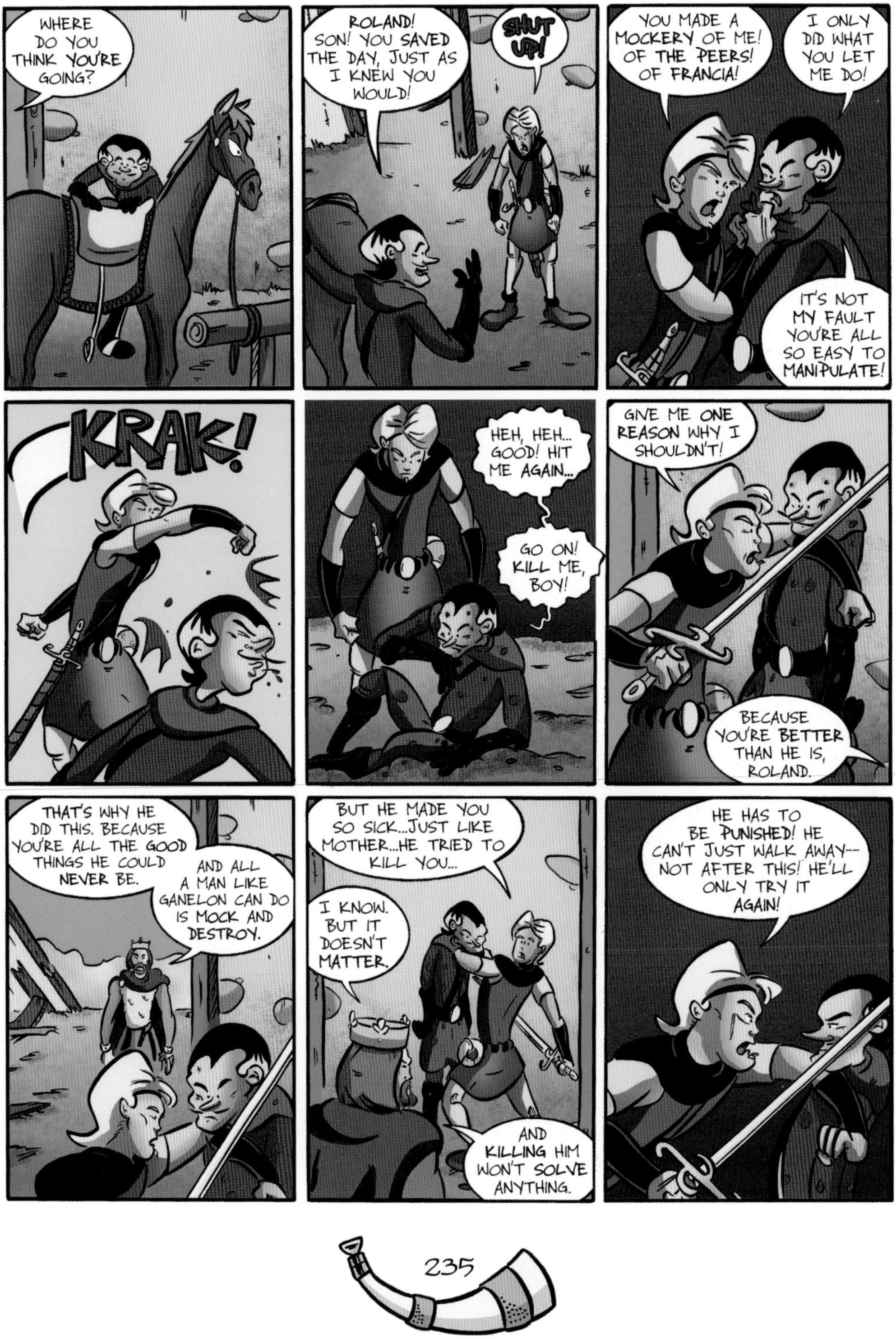
WHERE DO YOU THINK YOU'RE GOING?
ROLAND! SON! YOU SAVED THE DAY, JUST AS I KNEW YOU WOULD!
SHUT UP!
YOU MADE A MOCKERY OF ME! OF THE PEERS! OF FRANCIA!
I ONLY DID WHAT YOU LET ME DO!
IT'S NOT MY FAULT YOU'RE ALL SO EASY TO MANIPULATE!
KRAK!
HEH, HEH... GOOD! HIT ME AGAIN...
GO ON! KILL ME, BOY!
GIVE ME ONE REASON WHY I SHOULDN'T!
BECAUSE YOU'RE BETTER THAN HE IS, ROLAND.
THAT'S WHY HE DID THIS. BECAUSE YOU'RE ALL THE GOOD THINGS HE COULD NEVER BE.
AND ALL A MAN LIKE GANELON CAN DO IS MOCK AND DESTROY.
BUT HE MADE YOU SO SICK...JUST LIKE MOTHER...HE TRIED TO KILL YOU...
I KNOW. BUT IT DOESN'T MATTER.
AND KILLING HIM WON'T SOLVE ANYTHING.
HE HAS TO BE PUNISHED! HE CAN'T JUST WALK AWAY-- NOT AFTER THIS! HE'LL ONLY TRY IT AGAIN!

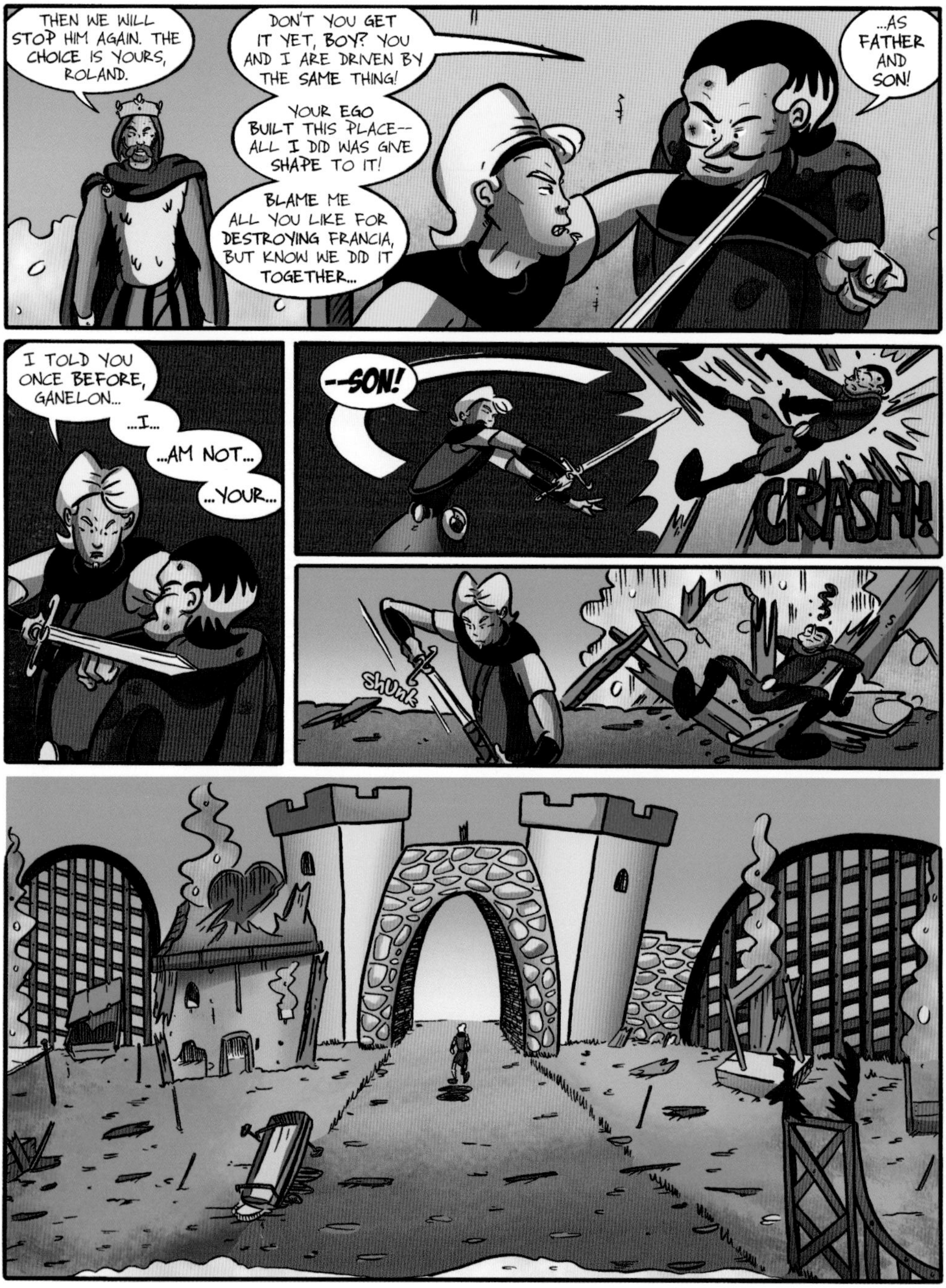
THEN WE WILL STOP HIM AGAIN. THE CHOICE IS YOURS, ROLAND.
DON'T YOU GET IT YET, BOY? YOU AND I ARE DRIVEN BY THE SAME THING!
YOUR EGO BUILT THIS PLACE-- ALL I DID WAS GIVE SHAPE TO IT!
BLAME ME ALL YOU LIKE FOR DESTROYING FRANCIA, BUT KNOW WE DID IT TOGETHER...
...AS FATHER AND SON!
I TOLD YOU ONCE BEFORE, GANELON...
...I...
...AM NOT...
...YOUR...
--SON!
CRASH!
SHUNK

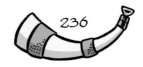

EPILOGUE

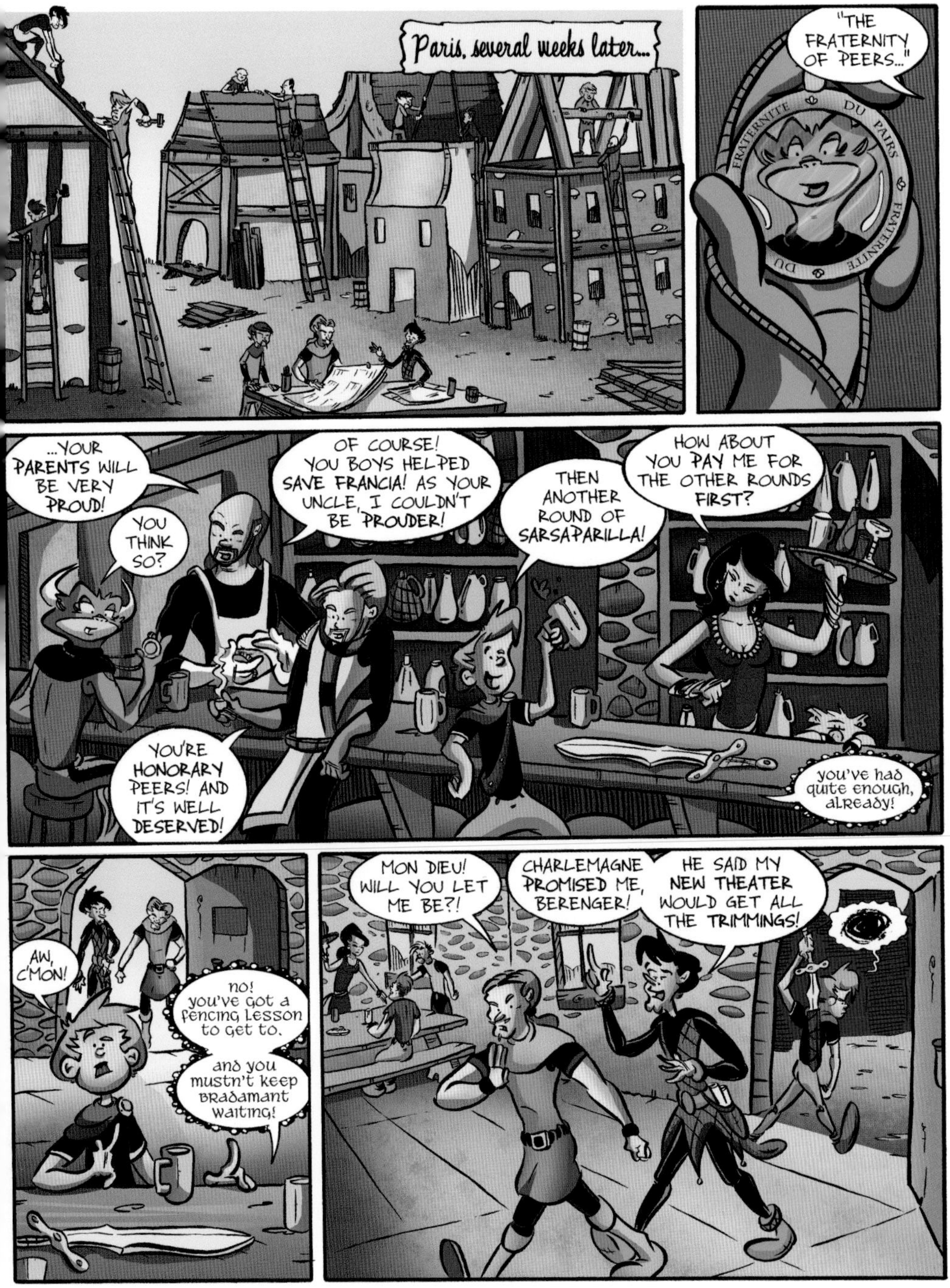
Paris, several weeks later...
"THE FRATERNITY OF PEERS..."
FRATERNITE DU PAIRS FRATERNITE DU
...YOUR PARENTS WILL BE VERY PROUD!
YOU THINK SO?
OF COURSE! YOU BOYS HELPED SAVE FRANCIA! AS YOUR UNCLE, I COULDN'T BE PROUDER!
THEN ANOTHER ROUND OF SARSAPARILLA!
HOW ABOUT YOU PAY ME FOR THE OTHER ROUNDS FIRST?
YOU'RE HONORARY PEERS! AND IT'S WELL DESERVED!
you've had quite enough, already!
AW, C'MON!
no! you've got a fencing lesson to get to.
and you mustn't keep Bradamant waiting!
MON DIEU! WILL YOU LET ME BE?!
CHARLEMAGNE PROMISED ME, BERENGER!
HE SAID MY NEW THEATER WOULD GET ALL THE TRIMMINGS!

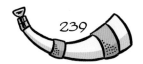

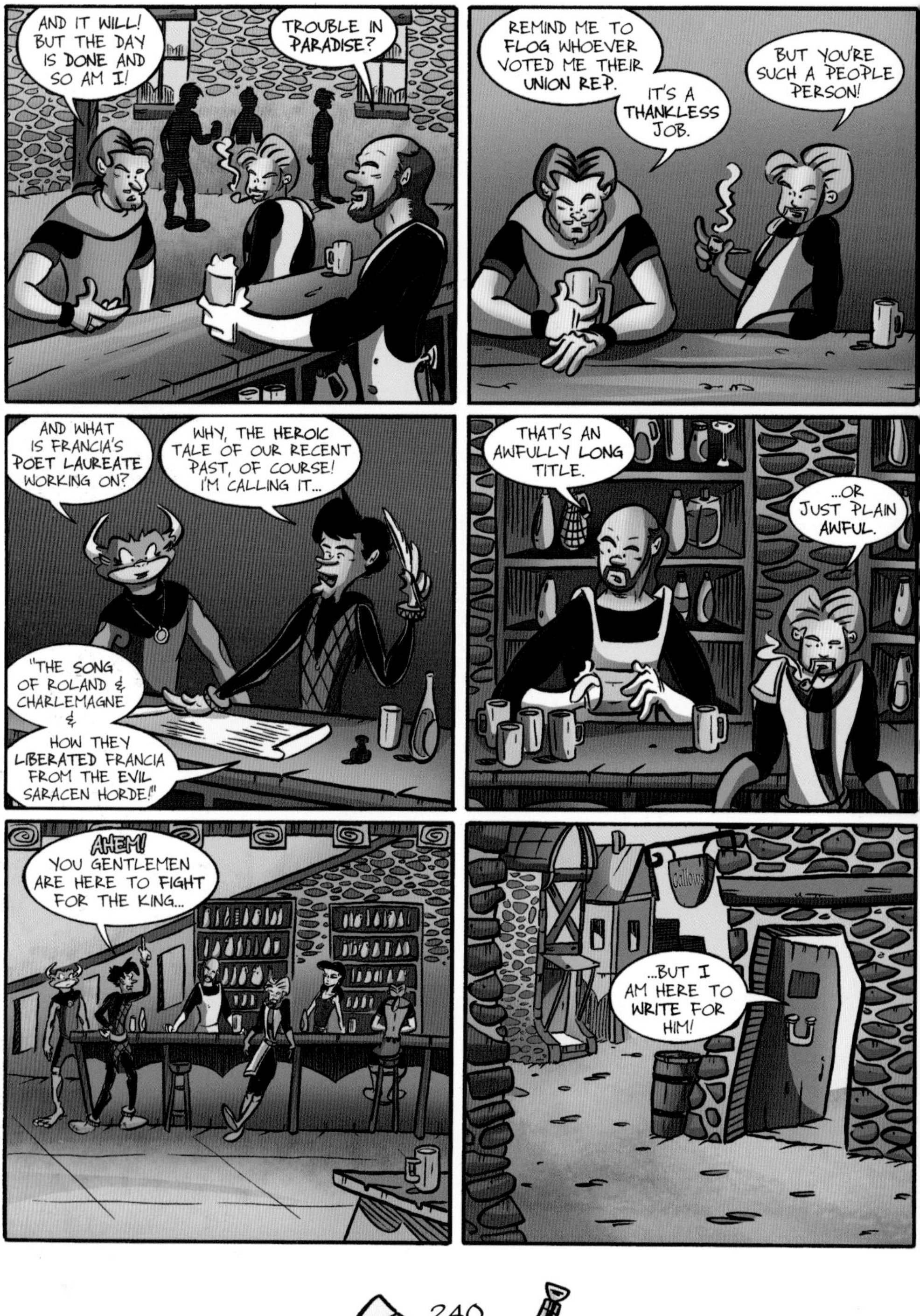
AND IT WILL! BUT THE DAY IS DONE AND SO AM I!
TROUBLE IN PARADISE?
REMIND ME TO FLOG WHOEVER VOTED ME THEIR UNION REP.
IT'S A THANKLESS JOB.
BUT YOU'RE SUCH A PEOPLE PERSON!
AND WHAT IS FRANCIA'S POET LAUREATE WORKING ON?
WHY, THE HEROIC TALE OF OUR RECENT PAST, OF COURSE! I'M CALLING IT...
"THE SONG OF ROLAND & CHARLEMAGNE &
HOW THEY LIBERATED FRANCIA FROM THE EVIL SARACEN HORDE!"
THAT'S AN AWFULLY LONG TITLE.
...OR JUST PLAIN AWFUL.
AHEM!
YOU GENTLEMEN ARE HERE TO FIGHT FOR THE KING...
Gallows
...BUT I AM HERE TO WRITE FOR HIM!

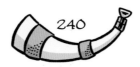

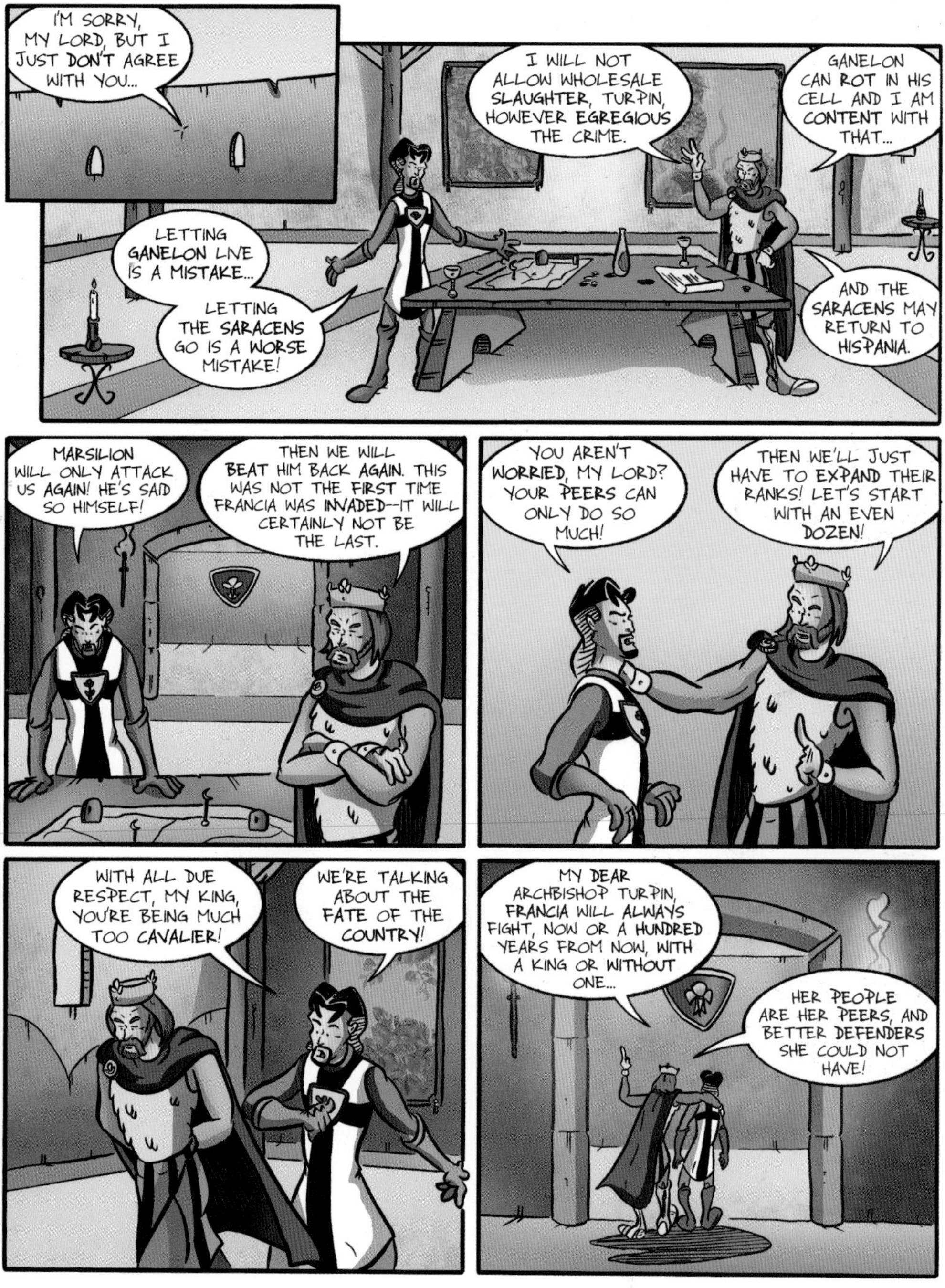
I'M SORRY, MY LORD, BUT I JUST DON'T AGREE WITH YOU...
LETTING GANELON LIVE IS A MISTAKE...
LETTING THE SARACENS GO IS A WORSE MISTAKE!
I WILL NOT ALLOW WHOLESALE SLAUGHTER, TURPIN, HOWEVER EGREGIOUS THE CRIME.
GANELON CAN ROT IN HIS CELL AND I AM CONTENT WITH THAT...
AND THE SARACENS MAY RETURN TO HISPANIA.
MARSILION WILL ONLY ATTACK US AGAIN! HE'S SAID SO HIMSELF!
THEN WE WILL BEAT HIM BACK AGAIN. THIS WAS NOT THE FIRST TIME FRANCIA WAS INVADED--IT WILL CERTAINLY NOT BE THE LAST.
YOU AREN'T WORRIED, MY LORD? YOUR PEERS CAN ONLY DO SO MUCH!
THEN WE'LL JUST HAVE TO EXPAND THEIR RANKS! LET'S START WITH AN EVEN DOZEN!
WITH ALL DUE RESPECT, MY KING, YOU'RE BEING MUCH TOO CAVALIER!
WE'RE TALKING ABOUT THE FATE OF THE COUNTRY!
MY DEAR ARCHBISHOP TURPIN, FRANCIA WILL ALWAYS FIGHT, NOW OR A HUNDRED YEARS FROM NOW, WITH A KING OR WITHOUT ONE...
HER PEOPLE ARE HER PEERS, AND BETTER DEFENDERS SHE COULD NOT HAVE!

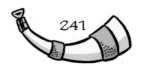

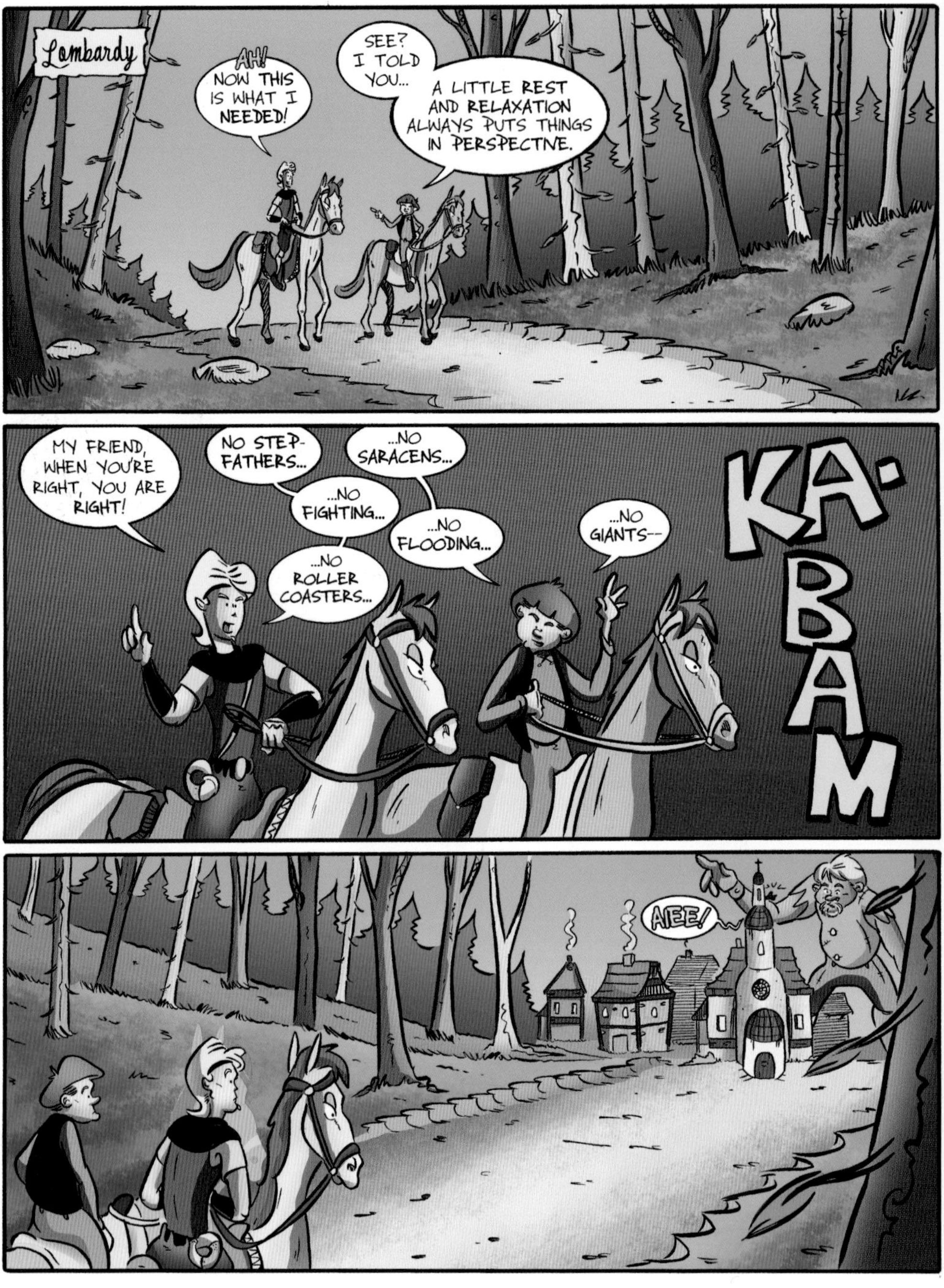
Lombardy
AH! NOW THIS IS WHAT I NEEDED!
SEE? I TOLD YOU...
A LITTLE REST AND RELAXATION ALWAYS PUTS THINGS IN PERSPECTIVE.
MY FRIEND, WHEN YOU'RE RIGHT, YOU ARE RIGHT!
NO STEP-FATHERS...
...NO FIGHTING...
...NO ROLLER COASTERS...
...NO SARACENS...
...NO FLOODING...
...NO GIANTS--
KA-BAM
AIEE!

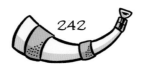

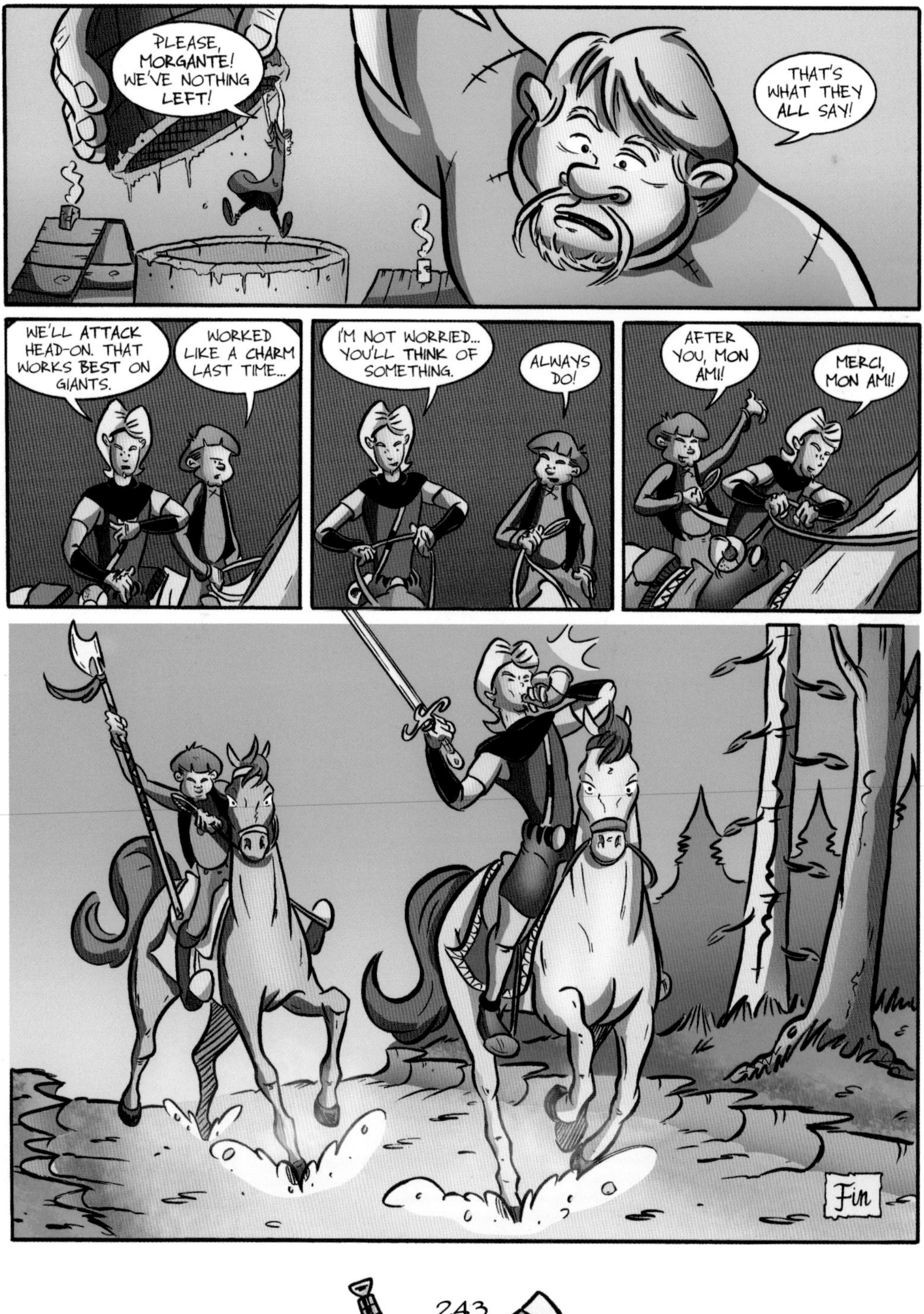
PLEASE, MORGANTE! WE'VE NOTHING LEFT!
THAT'S WHAT THEY ALL SAY!
WE'LL ATTACK HEAD-ON. THAT WORKS BEST ON GIANTS.
WORKED LIKE A CHARM LAST TIME...
I'M NOT WORRIED... YOU'LL THINK OF SOMETHING.
ALWAYS DO!
AFTER YOU, MON AMI!
MERCI, MON AMI!
Fin

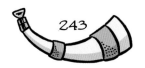

MORE TO EXPLORE!

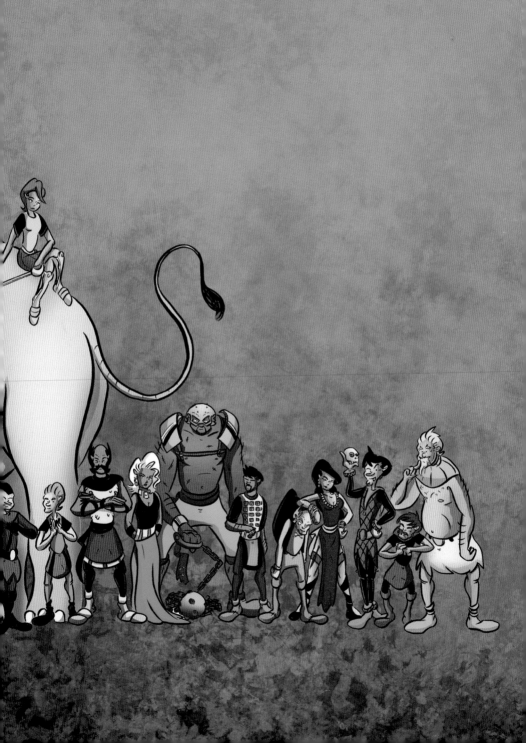

Francia Circa 750 A.D.

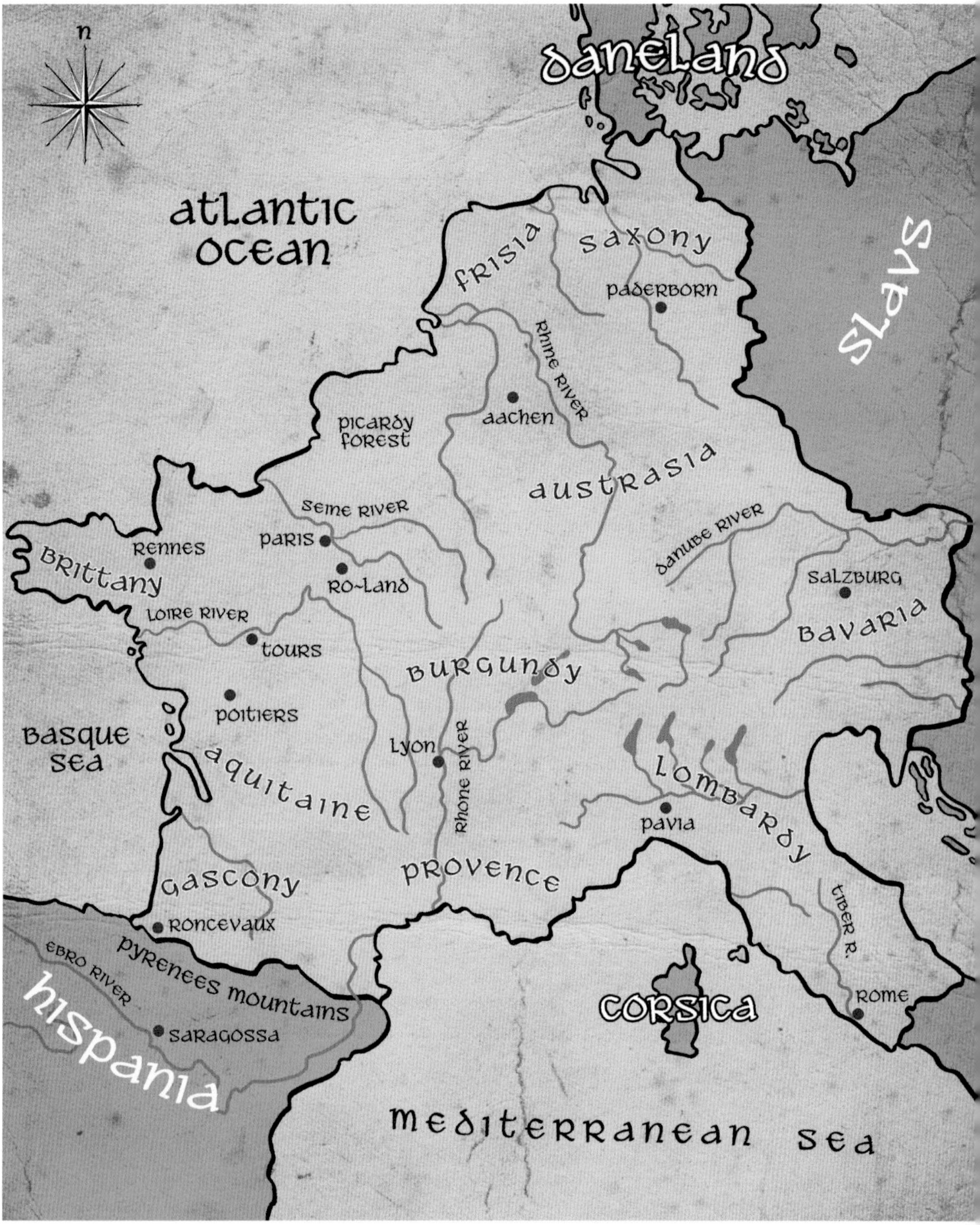
n
Daneland
Atlantic Ocean
Frisia
Saxony
Slavs
Paderborn
Rhine River
Aachen
Picardy Forest
Austrasia
Seine River
Paris
Rennes
Brittany
Ro-Land
Danube River
Salzburg
Loire River
Tours
Bavaria
Burgundy
Poitiers
Basque Sea
Aquitaine
Lyon
Rhone River
Lombardy
Pavia
Gascony
Provence
Roncevaux
Tiber R.
Pyrenees Mountains
Ebro River
Hispania
Saragossa
Corsica
Rome
Mediterranean Sea

Book two in the *Kid Beowulf* series takes place around 750 A.D. in Francia during the reign of King Charlemagne. Charlemagne was King of the Franks, and his lands extended into territories that today comprise France, Germany, and Italy—then called the Carolingian Empire. The Carolingian kings worked closely with the papacy in Rome, Christianizing the lands they conquered. Charlemagne reached the height of his power in the year 800 when he was crowned the Holy Roman Emperor by Pope Leo III on Christmas Day.

key terms

Chanson de Geste is Old French for "song of heroic deeds" and is a type of medieval narrative or epic poem that appears at the dawn of French literature and is typically connected to Charlemagne and his knights.

Cortana is the name of Ogier the Dane's sword. According to legend, the blade bears the inscription: "My name is Cortana, of the same steel and temper as Joyeuse and Durendal."

Durendal is the name of Roland's sword. In the epic *The Song of Roland*, the sword is said to contain in its golden hilt the tooth of Saint Peter, blood of Saint Basil, hair of Saint Denis, and a piece of the raiment of the Blessed Virgin Mary. It is known to be the sharpest sword in all existence. Other accounts claim the sword once belonged to Hector of Troy.

Franks are members of a Germanic-speaking people who invaded the western Roman Empire in the fifth century. Dominating present-day northern France, Belgium, and western Germany, the Franks established the most powerful Christian kingdom of early medieval western Europe. The name France (Francia) is derived from their name.

Joyeuse means "joyous" in French, and it is the name of Charlemagne's sword. It is said to have magical properties similar to Roland's sword, Durendal, and Ogier's sword, Cortana.

Oliphant is a type of horn made from an elephant's tusk and is the name of Roland's famous horn. In the epic *The Song of Roland*, the oliphant is what Roland uses to call for aid when the Franks are ambushed by the Saracens. The mighty blast from the horn is ultimately what kills Roland.

Peers (also known as the Paladins) are Charlemagne's elite knights. In the epic *The Song of Roland*, there are twelve Peers (to resemble Jesus Christ's twelve apostles). There are many stories surrounding the adventures of Charlemagne and his Peers, much like King Arthur and his Knights of the Round Table.

Roncevaux (pronounced "rhone-say-voe") is the name of the pass in the Pyrenees mountains on the border between France and Spain, and it is where Charlemagne's army was ambushed by the Saracen army. In the epic *The Song of Roland*, Roland and many of the other Peers died in battle at Roncevaux.

Saracen was a term to describe Muslims or Arabs during the time of the crusades. In the epic *The Song of Roland*, the Saracens rule Muslim Spain and are at war with the Christian Franks.

CHARACTER GLOSSARY

Abul-Abaz (ah-bool-ah-bahz) is an elephant given as a gift to Charlemagne by the Saracen King Marsilion. Abul-Abaz is more than just a curiosity, however. He is, in fact, a weapon of mass destruction, and when the trigger word "Abraha" is spoken, Abul-Abaz cannot be controlled.

Anseis (on-say-ees) is a Peer and is as sharp and quick-witted as the arrows he shoots. He is a reliable scout in the field and is able to discern the size and movement of an army from just a few tracks. Anseis often fights alongside Berenger, and the duo has had many adventures together battling Saracens, giants, and the occasional magician.

Belisande (bell-ee-zond) is bold, beautiful, and brazen. She owns The Gallows—the best bar in the worst part of town—where she serves all manner of bandit, outlaw, and Peer. She is a friend of the Peers and a Resistance sympathizer who was very much in love with Ogier long before he was exiled. While in exile, Ogier entrusted his sword, Cortana, to her, vowing he would return one day.

Beowulf (bay-oh-wolf) and **Grendel** (gren-del) are still pretty new to this "brother" thing. Even before they find their footing, they are thrust into a wild adventure in a far-off land. Hopefully they can help save Francia before they end up tearing each other apart!

Berenger (bear-ohn-jay) is a fierce and loyal Peer. He is not one to get mired in politics and prefers that others make the big decisions. Just tell him whom to fight and where. Berenger's gruff exterior belies a warmth underneath; he may be suspicious of you at first, but prove yourself in battle, and he will be your friend for life!

Bradamant (brah-da-mahn) is Renaud's younger sister and the last surviving member of the House of Aymon. She is sixteen and has grown up watching the Peers defend Francia. She yearns to someday be in their ranks. Bradamant has her brother's talent for fencing, and some say she is even better than Renaud. She is also the caretaker of the great elephant Abul-Abaz.

Bramimonde (brah-mim-onde) is the queen of Saragossa and Marsilion's wife. Though she spends her time in Hispania, she has been instrumental in orchestrating the downfall of Charlemagne and his Peers. She does not trust Ganelon, but she knows he is necessary to the Saracen Empire's ultimate goal of claiming Francia for itself.

Charlemagne (shar-la-mane) is the king and pride of Francia. As he goes, so goes the country. His large kingdom is at war with King Marsilion and his Saracen Empire. Thankfully, Charlemagne will always lead the charge, confident that his Peers will watch his back and Francia's.

Dargaud (dar-goh) is a playwright and a friend of the exiled Peers: Ogier, Anseis, and Berenger. He provided them aliases as actors in his troupe while they fought bandits and highwaymen during their exile. Dargaud has always dreamed of performing in Paris and bringing his work to a larger (and more appreciative) audience.

Emer (ee-mer) and **Ermlaf** (irm-laff) are Heathobards who are out to get Beowulf and Grendel. Ruled by their appetites, Emer and Ermlaf want gold, mead, and revenge, and not necessarily in that order. Thankfully, neither of them is much of a threat, and unless they grow another brain between them, Beowulf and Grendel are safe for now.

Ganelon (gahn-eh-lan) is Roland's stepfather and a truly devious fellow. He has no love for Roland, Charlemagne, or the Peers and has been secretly plotting with King Marsilion to destroy them all. Ganelon prides himself on being the smartest one in the room and enjoys defeating his enemies through nefarious, intricate, and long-term schemes, which he believes are the best ways to humiliate his enemies.

Marsilion (mar-see-lyon) is the King of Saragossa and the leader of the Saracen Empire. He is bound by his Islamic faith to pursue new lands for God and has set his sights on Francia, where he has been at war with Charlemagne and the Peers. Marsilion is driven by honor and faith, but he is also desperate, so he grudgingly turns to Ganelon for help.

Ogier (oh-jee-ay) is the alias for Holger, Beowulf and Grendel's great uncle from Daneland. Seeking redemption in a far-off land, Holger sets out for Francia, where he proves his worth in battle and saves Charlemagne. Knighted "Ogier the Dane," he becomes a Peer and finally finds the place where he belongs.

Oliver (all-i-ver) is Roland's best friend—and a better friend one could not have! Oliver is intelligent, resourceful, and always prepared. A good student, he loves to learn about everything, whether it is Latin, Danish, or chemistry. He has a penchant for cooking and believes that a good meal will turn the worst enemies into friends.

Pepin (pep-in) the hunchback is a curious fellow who spends his days keeping the hours of prayer at a local chapel in Paris. He is a longtime friend of the Peers and sympathizer with the French Resistance. He tries to stay out of the fray but will provide intelligence to those who seek it.

Renaud (ray-no) is a Peer who once had three brothers, but each was slain by the Saracen juggernaut Rodomont. Now, the last surviving "son of Aymon," Renaud must defeat Rodomont before the Saracen discovers there is one other Aymon alive: Renaud's younger sister, Bradamant.

Rodomont (roh-doh-mon) is a half-giant Saracen who possesses incredible strength and is virtually invulnerable. Rodomont is forever locked in battle with the House of Aymon and has defeated three of the four brothers from that noble family. Now there are only two descendants left for him to fight: Renaud and his little sister, Bradamant.

Rogero (roh-jer-oh) is King Marsilion's nephew and serves as his spy in Francia. Rogero has been keeping tabs on Ganelon and his odd money-making scheme, "Ro-Land." Rogero has also been watching the Peers and knows of the French Resistance; even though he is not sympathetic to their cause, he admires them all the same.

Roland (roe-land) is the nephew of Charlemagne, the stepson of Ganelon, and the best loved Peer in all of Francia. Even though he is much younger than the other Peers, his courage and fighting ability are unmatched, and with his weapons—the great sword, Durendal, and his horn, the oliphant—Roland is nearly invincible. For all his might, Roland is easily led astray by his naiveté and those who would do him ill.

Turpin (terr-pin) is Charlemagne's right-hand man and the field commander of the Peers. He is an expert fencer and has taught all the Peers the art of swordplay. Turpin expects the best from the Peers and his students and though he may press, it is all for a single goal: to defend the ideals of God, Charlemagne, and Francia.

Kid Beowulf
Character Map

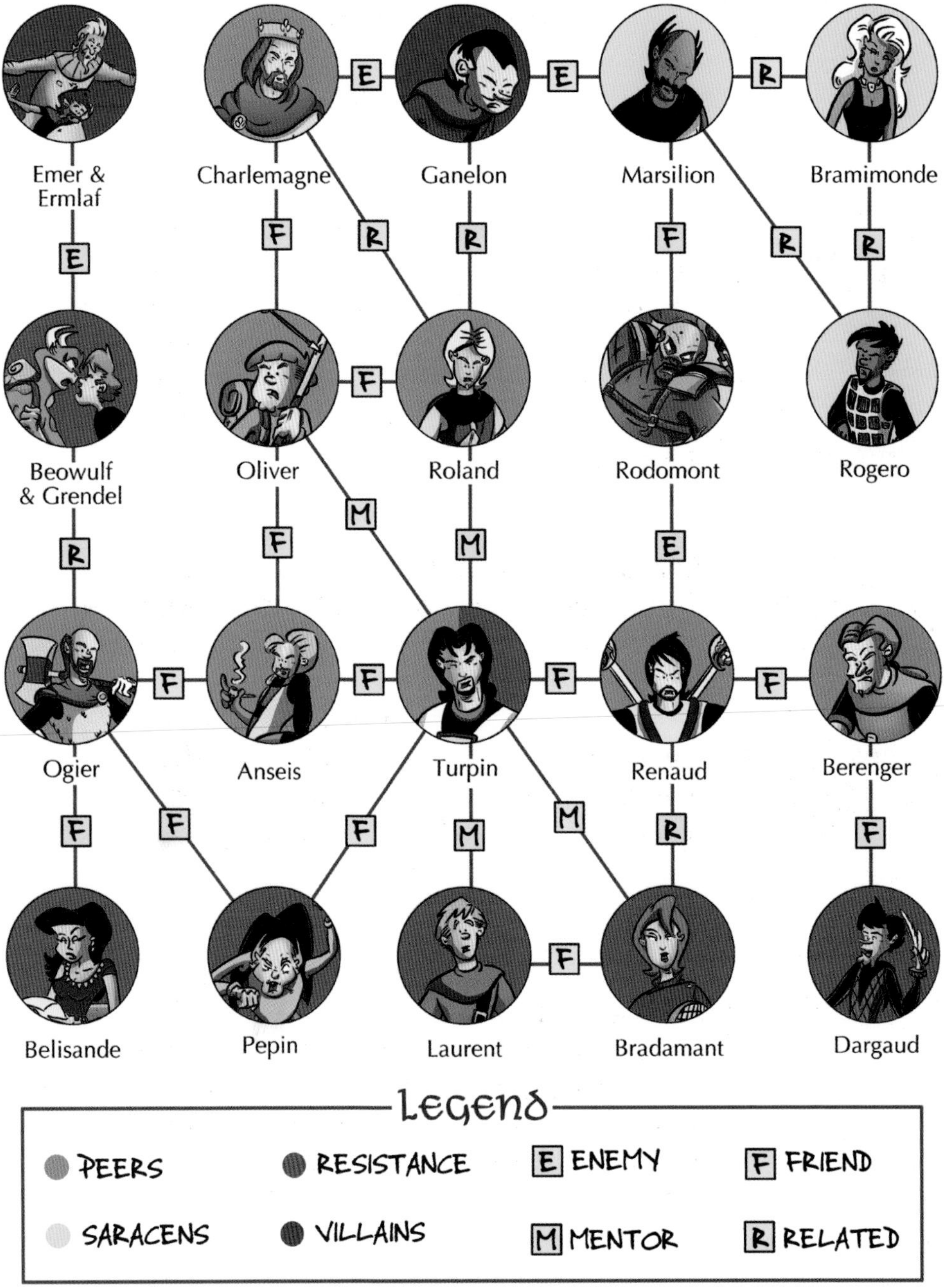

Emer & Ermlaf
Charlemagne
Ganelon
Marsilion
Bramimonde
Beowulf & Grendel
Oliver
Roland
Rodomont
Rogero
Ogier
Anseis
Turpin
Renaud
Berenger
Belisande
Pepin
Laurent
Bradamant
Dargaud
Legend
PEERS
RESISTANCE
E ENEMY
F FRIEND
SARACENS
VILLAINS
M MENTOR
R RELATED

the song of roland
origins of the epic poem

The Song of Roland is a French epic poem about the Battle of Roncevaux that took place in 778 and featured King Charlemagne, his Peers, and the most valiant knight among them, Roland. It is the oldest surviving major work of French literature and is comprised of 4,000 lines (or "laisses"). It was committed to paper in the eleventh century, possibly by a poet named Turold.

Unlike *Beowulf,* which is concerned with battles between men and monsters, *The Song of Roland* is about battles between men, specifically between Christian armies led by Charlemagne and the Saracen (or Muslim) factions of Spain.

At times the poem reads like a propaganda piece in which the Christians are holy warriors and the Saracens are dangerous pagans. Some suggest the story may have been used to incite the First Crusade in 1095.

The Song of Roland opens at the end of a long campaign in Spain. The King of France, Charlemagne, and the King of Saragossa, Marsilion, have made a deal: Spain will give France treasure and fealty if Charlemagne ends the war and returns to France. Charlemagne accepts the terms, but a messenger needs to inform King Marsilion. Roland nominates his stepfather, Ganelon, as messenger, and Ganelon sees this as a personal affront; he hates Roland and Charlemagne and decides to betray them to the Saracens.

On their return trip to France through the Pyrenees mountains, Ganelon plans an ambush of the French army. In a small pass called Roncevaux, the Saracens descend on the rear guard, which is led by Roland and the Peers (Charlemagne's elite knights), and a bloody battle ensues.

Roland and the knights are severely outnumbered, and Oliver, Roland's best friend, entreats Roland to blow his mighty horn to signal to Charlemagne (who is at the far front of the train) for back up. Roland, overwhelmed by hubris, refuses, and they continue to fight, but one by one, the Peers begin to fall, and Roland sees his folly. Finally Roland blows his oliphant and calls for Charlemagne and reinforcements, but it is too late: The Saracens have defeated them all. Roland rages back into battle as the last knight.

Roland is eventually slain, not by the Saracens but from blowing his horn so fiercely that it cracks his temple. After slaughtering the remaining Saracens, Roland drives his famous sword, Durendal, deep into the rock, faces the Spanish frontier, and dies.

Charlemagne arrives with the rest of his army and vows vengeance against Ganelon and the Saracens. The king marches back into Spain with a full force just as King Marsilion has called up his own reinforcements. It matters not to Charlemagne; he simply prays to "extend the day" so he may slaughter all the pagans who betrayed him.

Victorious, Charlemagne returns to France with the traitor Ganelon in tow. Ganelon is tried and found guilty, and his sentence is to be drawn and quartered. Charlemagne continues his kingship but is severely distraught over the loss of his Peers and particularly his nephew, Roland.

Though the events of *The Song of Roland* are tragic, Roland and Charlemagne's heroics became a source of great pride for the French, and the poem's themes of duty, faith, and honor still resonate today.

The epic poem sparked numerous adaptations, including the more fanciful Italian epics *Orlando Innamorato* and *Orlando Furioso,* the tales of chivalry in *Bulfinch's Mythology,* and more contemporary works like Poul Anderson's *Three Hearts and Three Lions* and Stephen King's *Dark Tower* series.

Carolingian Lore & Legends

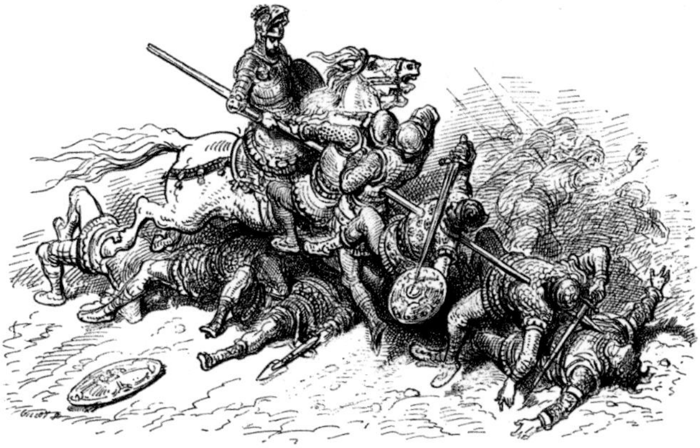

Orlando Furioso illustration by Gustave Doré

The story depicted in the *The Song of Roland* is part of a tradition of stories featuring knights on daring adventures called "chansons de geste" (Old French for "songs of heroic deeds"). Charlemagne and his Peers have a rich literary tradition just as grand and fantastic as King Arthur and his Knights of the Round Table. It is often referred to as the Carolingian Romances or the Matter of France.

In some of these stories the Peers fight giants, and in others they battle pagan armies and powerful wizards. Sometimes they fly hippogriffs, rescue the princess, and discover castles in the sky. For *Kid Beowulf: The Song of Roland,* I wanted to blend these tales together and introduce readers to a new set of heroes who are just as important as King Arthur and Sir Lancelot.

Roland & Oliver

One of Roland's origin stories features him growing up as a peasant on the streets of Italy where he's eventually discovered by his Uncle Charlemagne. Another story features a duel between Oliver and Roland: both in armor, neither one recognizes the other. The two fight for an entire day until at last they take off their helmets and see their opponent, at which point the two stop and embrace as friends. I combined these tales to create an origin story for Roland and Oliver.

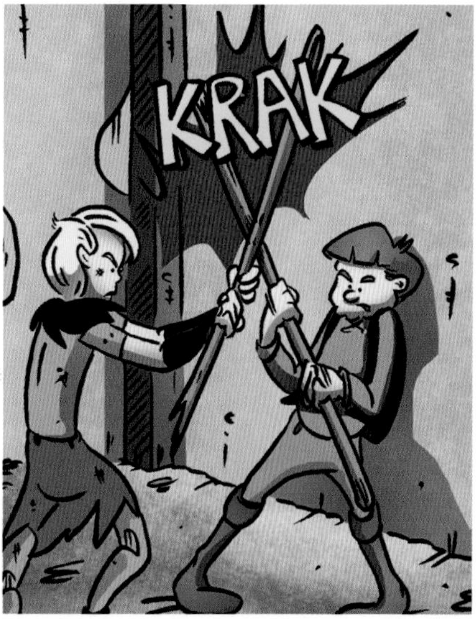
KRAK

FERRAGUS & ROLAND

The encounter with Ferragus and Roland is based on a similar story; however, in my version, I decided to add Oliver, who pries vital information out of the giant. This gave me a chance to show how Roland got his famous sword, Durendal, and his horn, the oliphant!

BRADAMANT & RODOMONT

In some stories Renaud and Bradamant are siblings; in others Renaud has four brothers ("the Sons of Aymon"), and they all ride the magical horse, Bayard. I combined some of these elements and tried to link the ongoing theme of "monsters and monster-slayers" by pitting Renaud and Bradamant against the Saracen colossus, Rodomont, who has a vendetta against the House of Aymon. Rodomont has sworn to defeat all the sons of Aymon but discovers he cannot defeat the daughter.

ABUL~ABAZ & CHARLEMAGNE

Abul-Abaz comes from the pages of history and was given as a gift to Charlemagne by the caliph of Baghdad, Harun al-Rashid. The word that sets Abul-Abaz off—"Abraha"—comes from Sura 105 of the Qur'an, which is called "The Elephant." It refers to an incident in which Abraha, a Christian prince of Ethiopia, tried to invade Mecca, but the Ethiopian war elephants knelt down before Mecca and refused to attack.

fun facts

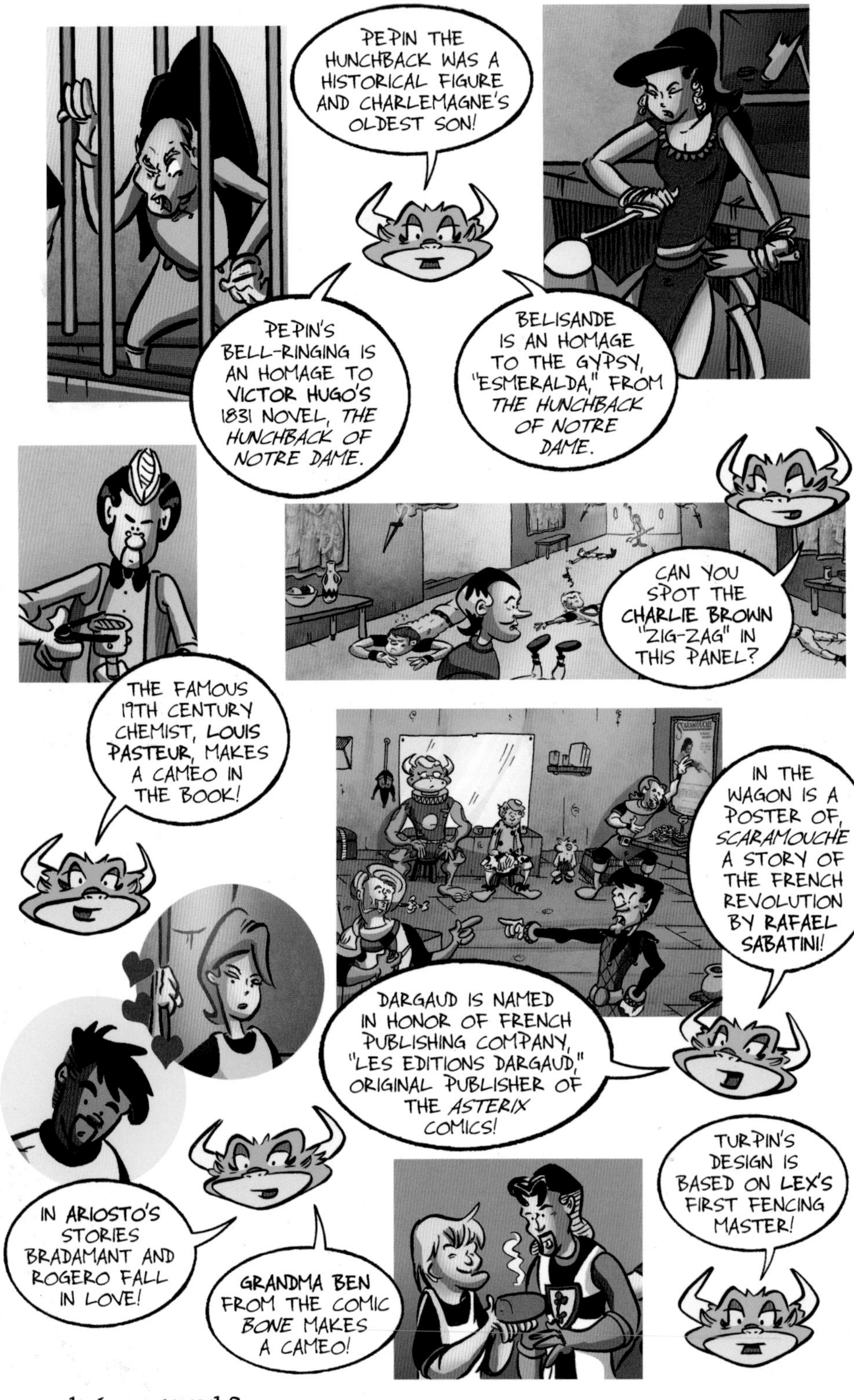
PEPIN THE HUNCHBACK WAS A HISTORICAL FIGURE AND CHARLEMAGNE'S OLDEST SON!
PEPIN'S BELL-RINGING IS AN HOMAGE TO VICTOR HUGO'S 1831 NOVEL, THE HUNCHBACK OF NOTRE DAME.
BELISANDE IS AN HOMAGE TO THE GYPSY, "ESMERALDA," FROM THE HUNCHBACK OF NOTRE DAME.
CAN YOU SPOT THE CHARLIE BROWN "ZIG-ZAG" IN THIS PANEL?
THE FAMOUS 19TH CENTURY CHEMIST, LOUIS PASTEUR, MAKES A CAMEO IN THE BOOK!
IN THE WAGON IS A POSTER OF, SCARAMOUCHE A STORY OF THE FRENCH REVOLUTION BY RAFAEL SABATINI!
DARGAUD IS NAMED IN HONOR OF FRENCH PUBLISHING COMPANY, "LES EDITIONS DARGAUD," ORIGINAL PUBLISHER OF THE ASTERIX COMICS!
TURPIN'S DESIGN IS BASED ON LEX'S FIRST FENCING MASTER!
IN ARIOSTO'S STORIES BRADAMANT AND ROGERO FALL IN LOVE!
GRANDMA BEN FROM THE COMIC BONE MAKES A CAMEO!

BIBLIOGRAPHY

The following books were used during the research and writing of this book. All come highly recommended!

PENGUIN CLASSICS
The Song of Roland

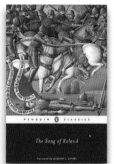

The epic poem comes in a variety of translations, and each one brings something new to the text. I read at least three different versions of *The Song of Roland,* including editions translated by Robert Harrison (Mentor), Dorothy L. Sayers (Penguin), and Frederick Goldin (Norton). The introductions for each edition are worth reading, too.

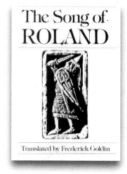

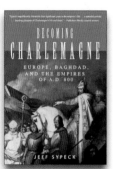

The Song of
ROLAND
Translated by Frederick Goldin

BECOMING
CHARLEMAGNE
EUROPE, BAGHDAD, AND THE EMPIRES OF A.D. 800
JEFF SYPECK

Becoming Charlemagne by Jeff Sypeck is a fast, enjoyable, and well-written account of Charlemagne's rise to power and the crucial world events surrounding the time period. *Two Lives of Charlemagne,* Einhard and Notker's biographies of Charlemagne, are also recommended and were written in the eighth century. (Einhard was part of Charlemagne's court!)

Penguin Classics
EINHARD AND NOTKER THE STAMMERER TWO LIVES OF CHARLEMAGNE

ORLANDO FURIOSO

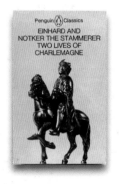

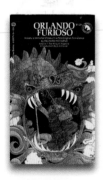

Orlando Furioso by the poet Ariosto and *Orlando Innamorato* by Boiardo are Italian epics that expand on the deeds of Roland (Orlando) and the Peers. The stories are much more fanciful than *The Song of Roland* and showcase exotic locales, mythological beasts, and the deeds of multiple heroes.

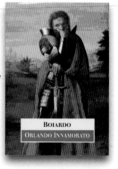

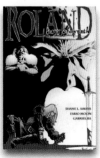

BOIARDO
ORLANDO INNAMORATO

ROLAND
days of wrath
SHANE L. AMAYA
FABIO MOON
GABRIEL BA

Roland, Days of Wrath by Shane Amaya, Fabio Moon, and Gabriel Ba is a graphic novel adaptation of *The Song of Roland.* It is a solid, "straight" retelling of the tale. *Quest of the Warrior Maiden* by Linda C. McCabe is a well-written and researched novelization of the adventures of the fierce female warrior, Bradamant.

LINDA C. MCCABE
QUEST of the WARRIOR MAIDEN

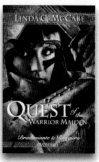

about the author

Alexis E. Fajardo is a student of the classics—whether Daffy Duck or Damocles—and has created a unique blend of the two with *Kid Beowulf*. When he's not drawing comics, Lex works for them at the Charles M. Schulz Studio in Santa Rosa, California. Lex hurt his back when he tried to lift this giant sword.

Discover more at *kidbeowulf.com*
Follow Lex on Twitter and Instagram *@lexkidb*
Become a fan on *facebook.com/kidbeowulf*
Download the game at iTunes & Google Play!

photo by Cathy Barrett

KID BEOWULF WILL RETURN

Andrews McMeel Publishing
a division of Andrews McMeel Universal
1130 Walnut Street, Kansas City, Missouri 64106

www.andrewsmcmeel.com

17 18 19 20 21 SDB 10 9 8 7 6 5 4 3 2 1

ISBN: 978-1-4494-7590-1

Library of Congress Control Number: 2016955274

Editor: Dorothy O'Brien
Designer: Brenna Thummler
Art Director: Tim Lynch
Production Editor: Maureen Sullivan
Production Manager: Chuck Harper

Made by: Shenzhen Donnelley Printing Company Ltd.
Address and location of manufacturer: No. 47, Wuhe Nan Road,
Bantian Ind. Zone, Shenzhen China, 518129
1st Printing - 12/5/16